Fight for Me

the complete collection

A.L. JACKSON

Show Me the Way

prologue

Alabama – Eleven Years Ago

Rain pelted from the angry sky, and heavy gusts of wind howled through the trees, which thrashed in the blackened night. In agony, I ran, sure my heart had to be beating as loud as the thunder that cracked through the heavens above.

I gasped when my foot slipped on the slick, muddy ground, and I stumbled forward, landing hard on my hands and knees. I cried out, unsure where the pain was coming from—my mind or my heart or my torn flesh.

Why would they do this to me?

I wept toward the ground, stricken with grief, with betrayal, before I heaved myself back onto my feet, trying to find traction. I staggered toward the house, which was lit up like warmth and light just off the road. Clutching the wooden railing, I propelled myself forward and then flung open the door and fumbled inside.

I whimpered in misery when I paused to look around the room. Loss hit me as hard as the storm that raged outside.

Why would they do this to me? How could they be so cruel?

It took about all I had, but I forced myself to move, knowing I couldn't stay. I had to leave. I had to get away. Choking back sobs, I clung to the banister and hauled myself upstairs and to my room. Knees caked in mud and blood, I dropped to the floor and dug out the suitcase from beneath the bed. I staggered to my feet and headed for the closet.

Tears clouding my vision, I tore clothes from their hangers and shoved them into the suitcase I'd tossed onto the bed, my movements becoming more frantic with each piece I ripped from its spot. The urge to escape only intensified when I moved to the dresser. Distraught, I ripped the drawers from their rails and tipped them upside down, dumping what would fit into the suitcase.

The whole time, I struggled to restrain the sobs bound in my throat. To keep them quiet. To pretend it hadn't happened. To pretend I didn't have to do *this*.

With shaking fingers, I tugged at the zipper.

"Rynna, what's going on?" The sleepy voice filled with concern hit me from behind.

Torment lashed like the crack of a whip. My eyes slammed closed, and the words trembled from my mouth. "I'm so sorry, Gramma, but I've got to go."

The floor creaked with my grandmother's footsteps. She sucked in a breath when she rounded me, shocked by my battered appearance. "Oh my lord, what happened to you?" Her voice quivered. "Who hurt you? Tell me, Rynna. Who hurt you? I won't stand for it."

Vigorously, I shook my head, finding the lie. "No one. I just . . . I can't stay in this stupid town for a second more. I'm going to find Mama."

I hated it. The way the mention of my mother contorted my gramma's face in agony.

"What are you sayin'?"

"I'm saying, I'm leaving."

A weathered hand reached out to grip my forearm. "But graduation is just next month. You've got to do your speech. Walk across the stage in your cap and gown. Never seen anyone so excited about somethin' in all my life. Now you're just gonna up and leave? If you can't trust me, then you can't trust anyone. Tell me what happened tonight. You left here just as happy as a bug in a rug, and now you aren't doing anything but runnin' scared."

Tears streaking down my dirty cheeks, I forced myself to look at the woman who meant everything to me. "You're the only person I can trust, Gramma. That's why I've got to go. Let's leave it at that."

Anguish creased my grandmother's aged face. "Rynna, I won't let you just walk out like this."

She reached out and brushed a tear from under my eye. Softly, she tilted her head to the side, that same tender smile she had watched me with at least a million times hinting at the corner of her mouth. "Don't you ever forget, *if you aren't laughing, you're crying.* Now, which would you rather be doin'?" She paused, and I couldn't bring myself to answer. "Wipe those tears, and let's figure something out. Just like we always do."

Sadness swelled like its own being in the tiny room. Loss. Regret. Like an echo of every breath of encouragement my grandmother had ever whispered in my ear. "I can't stay here, Gramma. Please don't ask me to."

With the plea, my grandmother winced. Quickly, I dipped down to place a lingering kiss to her cheek, breathing in the ever-present scent of vanilla and sugar, committing it to memory.

I tugged my suitcase from the bed and started for the door.

Gramma reached for me, fingertips brushing my arm, begging, "Rynna, don't go. Please, don't leave me like this. There's nothing that's so bad that I won't understand. That we can't fix."

I didn't slow. Didn't answer.

I ran.

And I didn't look back.

one

Rynna

Leafy shadows flashed across the windshield, interspersed by the blinding strikes of sunlight that burned from the sky as my car passed beneath the heavy canopy of trees where I traveled the winding two-lane road.

The closer I got, the harder my heart beat within the confines of my chest and the shallower my breaths grew. Cinching down on the steering wheel, I peered out at the worn sign on the side of the road.

Welcome to Gingham Lakes, Alabama, where the grass is actually greener and the people are sweeter.

Anxiety clawed through my nerves.

It'd been eleven years and what felt like a lifetime since I left the small city that could hardly be considered more than a town. I'd promised myself I'd never come back.

And there I was.

I just wished I had broken that promise sooner. Not when it already felt as if it were too late.

"Earth to Ryn."

I jumped when the voice boomed through the car speakers. I was losing it. It seemed fitting. I'd been questioning my sanity ever since I'd signed on that dotted line.

"Are you there, or have I already lost you to the Deep South?" Macy asked. I could almost see her raising a dark brow at me.

"You really are dead set on breaking my fragile heart, aren't you?" she continued. "You left me here to fend for myself. Not a soul to go out with on Friday nights and no one to make me miracle hangover breakfasts on Saturday mornings. That's a travesty. Don't you dare shred it more by pretending I don't even exist. BFFs, remember? Don't forget it, or I'll show up with the sole purpose of kicking your skinny ass. Oh, and to get back those black jeans I know you stole. I've been looking for them for the last two days. I bet you have them hidden at the bottom of one of those boxes."

"I wouldn't dare," I barely managed to tease through the thickness that lined my throat. "Where those jeans probably are is under your bed in that disaster of a room. You're worse than a twelve-year-old boy."

I was doing my best to inject a smile into my voice, but there was no disguising the hitch in my words as I rounded the bend and the town came into view in the valley below.

Gingham Lakes.

God, it was beautiful.

The valley was a vast expanse of green. Flush with abundant, flourishing trees. The massive lake tucked at the base of the opposite mountain range appeared little more than a glittering mirage in the far distance, the river so serene and calm where it ran through the middle of the city and segmented it into the two mirrored-halves.

This place was filled with the best and the worst of memories.

With the best of people and the worst of enemies.

There was only one person who ever could have persuaded me to return.

Leave it to Gramma to do it in the sneakiest of ways.

"Tell me you aren't having second thoughts now that you've driven all the way across the country? By yourself, mind you, since you refused to let me come. You act as if I'd be a nuisance instead of a help. I can lift like . . . a thousand pounds. Pretty sure I'm the best mover in all the history of movers."

"Says the girl who thought it was a good idea to let a box filled with glasses tumble down a flight of stairs rather than carrying it down."

Macy chuckled. "Don't be jealous. Just add creative to my list of skills."

"Creator of disasters, you mean."

She feigned a gasp. "I take full offense to that. I even made pizza and didn't catch the apartment on fire."

"No," I ribbed.

"Truth."

Quiet laughter rolled free as that heaviness throbbed. "I'm going to miss you, Mace."

Right then, San Francisco felt a million miles away. An alternate galaxy. Really, it was just a different reality than the one I was headed toward.

Somber silence filled the space, and Macy lowered her voice. "Are you sure this is really what you want? You left the city you love and an incredible apartment downtown. You resigned from a job any one of us would kill to have. Hell, you were halfway up the corporate ladder. Worst, you left *me*."

My heart clutched while I fought with the urge to turn around and head back to San Francisco. I wasn't that broken girl who'd run from Gingham Lakes eleven years ago. I was strong, and I sure as hell wasn't a quitter. "You know why I have to do this."

"I do, and I know how hard it has to be for you."

Grief pressed at my spirit. The perfect complement to the determination that lined me like steel. "It is, but I need to do this for her almost as much as I need to do it for myself."

"This city won't be the same without you, Ryn." In all the years I'd lived with Macy, I'd only seen her cry once. I knew she was trying to hold it back. Still, the soft sounds seeped through the line, touching me from across the miles.

I pressed a hand over my mouth and tried to keep the jumble of emotions that quivered and shook inside me at bay. "You'll come visit."

She released a soggy laugh. "Hell no. There are, like, alligators down there. One look at all my lush, curvy deliciousness, and they'll be inviting their friends over for a feast."

I wanted to tell her I was plenty *lush* when I'd run from this place. The alligators were the least of her worries. I bit it back, keeping all those old insecurities buried where they belonged.

"You don't think I'm worth the risk?" I asked instead.

She sniffled, and I swore I could see her grin. "Yeah, Ryn, you're totally worth it."

I cleared the emotion from my throat, wondering how I was going to do this when the road took another sharp curve and the speed limit dropped. "I better go. I'm getting into town."

"Good luck, babe. You've got this. I want you to know I'm proud of you, even though I'm going to miss the hell out of you."

"Thank you, Mace," I told her.

I was definitely going to need it.

two

Rex

My eyes went round, and I came to an abrupt stop in her doorway.

"Are you sure that's what you want to wear?" Sweeping a hand through the long pieces of my damp hair, I gave it my all to keep the panic out of my voice.

Honestly wasn't sure if I wanted to bust out laughing or drop to my knees and cry.

Such was my life.

We were already ten minutes late, and there she was on her bedroom floor, wearing a hot pink tutu over a bathing suit.

"Uh-huh. We gots to look so pretty for dance. Annie said all the best dancers wear leg warmies, and her mama bought her all the pretty colors. Like a rainbow," she rambled as she tugged on the black high-top Converse she'd talked me into at the mall last weekend.

Right over a pair of old tube socks she must have found in one of my drawers.

The hideous kind with the two blue stripes at the top that should have been burned years ago.

"So I gots these." She rocked her heels on the ground as she sat back and admired her handiwork.

She suddenly looked over at me with that smile that melted a crater right through the stone that was my heart. Her single tooth missing on the bottom row and her attempt at a bun that looked like she'd just walked out of a windstorm were about the damned cutest things I'd ever seen.

"I'm the best dancer, right, Daddy?"

"You're the best, prettiest dancer in the whole world, Sweet Pea Frankie

Leigh."

I just was betting that uptight bitch, Ms. Jezlyn, wouldn't agree. I'd already gotten one bullshit letter about "appropriate ballet attire," which was strictly a black leotard with *salmon* tights (what the fuck?) without any runs in them. Apparently, Frankie wasn't living up to those standards.

That was what I got for picking Frankie up late from Mom's and then coming home and telling her to get ready while I grabbed a quick shower. I'd been at the work site the entire day, had been drenched in sweat and grease and grime, and was trying to put my best foot forward.

Problem was, I was having a hard time figuring out how my best could ever be enough.

I pressed my palms together in some kind of twisted prayer. Then I dropped them and blew out a resigned breath. "All right, then. We need to get out of here before I get you in any more trouble."

Frankie hopped onto her feet and threw her hands in the air. "Ready!"

I chuckled beneath my breath, grabbed her dance bag from the pink bench right inside her room, slung it over my shoulder, and extended my hand. "Let's go, Tiny Dancer."

Giggling, she pranced over to me and let me take her miniature hand, so small and vulnerable in the massiveness of mine.

Following me out the door and down the hall, she skipped along at my side.

Innocently.

Joy lit up my insides. I swore all her sweetness held the power to blow back the thousand pounds of blackened bitterness built up around my heart. Like when this kid was around, it weighed nothing at all.

The day she was born, I'd sworn an oath to myself. I'd never allow her to be torn up by this vicious, cruel world. Refused to let it tarnish her the way it had me.

My entire life was protecting her from it.

I snagged my keys from the entryway table when I heard the sound of a door slamming somewhere outside. Frowning, I leaned back so I could get a glimpse out the window and across the street.

An older white Jeep Grand Cherokee was parked in the driveway of Mrs. Dayne's old house.

Guessed they had to finally be putting the place up for sale. Mrs. Dayne had lived there forever, long before we'd moved in across the street from her five years ago, but the place had been sitting empty for the last two months.

A fist tightened in my gut, grief I really shouldn't be allowing myself to feel. She'd just been so good to Frankie that it'd been impossible to keep her shut out. Hell, she'd barged right into our lives like she was supposed to be there, constantly bringing over dinner and those delicious pies from the diner-style restaurant she'd owned downtown.

Frankie rushed out the front door and onto the deck at the side of our house.

It was the way all the homes were situated in our neighborhood. The houses were elevated from the ground with the main doors located on the side rather than out front. Each had an open deck that extended out from the side of the house, giving a view of the street and neighbors' houses. The porch steps angled that direction and led down to the driveways that came up to the far side of the houses.

It probably would have looked strange if not for the big, leafy trees that outlined each of the lots.

They made everything feel cozy and secluded.

Just the way I liked it.

It was one of the main reasons I'd insisted on this place when I'd been looking for a fixer-upper to renovate.

Frankie released my hand and pointed across the street. "Hey, Daddy, look it. Someone's at Mrs. Dayne's house!"

Stepping out behind her, I closed the door before I attempted to tame a few pieces of hair that'd fallen from her bun and were now flying around her face in the hot breeze. I dropped a kiss to her forehead. "It's probably a realtor putting it up for sale, Frankie Leigh. Remember how we talked about that?"

With her head tipped back, she peered at me with confused but hopeful brown eyes. "She wents to heaven?"

"Yeah," I murmured softly.

The screen door at the side of Mrs. Dayne's house slammed, and I jerked my head up to find a woman crossing the small deck and jogging down the steps back toward the SUV.

Goddamn.

Maybe I was just caught off guard.

But just looking at her knocked the air from my lungs.

Let's just say I was unprepared for a woman that looked like that. Guess I'd been expecting someone dressed up. Older. And there was this girl, disheveled in a sexy, careless way. A massive mound of hair that was wilder than Frankie's was piled haphazardly on her head, wavy pieces falling out all around her. She wore a super tight white tank that disappeared beneath high-waisted jeans.

Those jeans should have made her look frumpy and unkempt, but instead, the whole package sent a skitter of lust racing through my veins and prodding at my dick.

She was the kind of woman who could make a grown man stumble on his feet.

Stunning.

Gorgeous.

Too sexy for her own damned good.

Or maybe mine.

I could call it a complication of abstaining for too long, but I was sure no woman had ever incited a reaction like this in me with just a glance.

She raked her arm over her sweat-drenched forehead as she headed straight for the cargo area of the SUV, which was crammed full of moving boxes. I wouldn't mind all that much if she were hauling stuff out of that house directly across the street, but it sure as shit looked like she was moving her things in.

Tell me this girl is not moving in next door.

I clenched my jaw and grabbed Frankie's hand, needing to get the hell out of there.

"Come on, Frankie Leigh, we've got to get a move on. You're already late."

But Frankie was already moving, bouncing down the stairs and along the walkway, waving her free hand in the air. The kid just adding to the stark sunshine that burned bright in the waning day. "Hi, hi, hi! I'm Frankie. Whose are you?" she shouted across the street.

Startled, the women's gaze darted our direction, and the determination in her step slowed when she caught sight of my daughter.

An amused smile grew on the rosy bud of her mouth when her gaze swept the ridiculous outfit Frankie was wearing. She seemed to hesitate for a second, eyes glancing around her like she was looking for something before she changed direction, heading our way. "Hey there, Frankie, I'm Corinne Dayne, but everyone calls me Rynna."

Rynna Dayne.

What the ever-lovin' hell?

Could damn near feel the bewildered excitement roll through my daughter while I stood there cursing the world that just fucking loved to curse me. "Your name's C'Rinne, too? That's Mrs. Dayne's name. She worked at the restaurant called Pepper's Pies and cooked all the pies, and my daddy ate them all, all, all the way gone. Sometimes we wents to go eat there, but mostly we ate at my house right here, but now she wents to heaven."

A bolt of sadness streaked through her expression, and fuck, if it didn't hit me, too. Still, the smile she wore only grew. "She made the best pies in the whole world, didn't she?"

Frankie's excitement only amplified. "Yes! You know Mrs. Dayne, too?"

She started to cross the narrow street, all chestnut hair and java eyes and a body that was built for temptation.

Awareness ridged my spine like a steely stake of lightning, and I stepped back, my jaw tightening at the same time I protectively took hold of my daughter's hand.

That was all that women were.

Temptation.

Trouble.

Forbidden fucking fruit.

Because all they did was condemn you in the end. So, I stayed away. Kept my distance. If I didn't step into the fire, then I wouldn't get burned.

Kneeling in front of my daughter, she stuck out her hand. "It's so nice to meet you, Frankie. It sounds like you were a good friend of my grandma's."

So yeah.

I'd already figured it out.

It didn't stop me from flinching.

Frankie had stars in her eyes as she enthusiastically shook her hand. She might as well have been meeting Taylor Swift. "She told me I was her favorite, favorite friend, and sometimes she even let me go to her house and make some pies."

"Is that so?" Rynna said with a tease in her voice.

"Yep."

Rynna leaned in, and I caught a whiff of something sweet. "Want to know a secret?" she whispered.

Frankie bounced on her toes. "Oh, yes, yes please, I love secrets. I won't tell nobody."

Soft laughter floated out from Rynna's mouth, a mouth that was getting harder and harder not to stare at, all plush and pink and perfectly pouty. "Well, this is a secret I hope you tell everyone, because guess what? I have some of the recipes for those pies."

Frankie's mouth dropped open, and damn it if my stomach didn't fucking growl.

"You gonna make me some?" she gushed.

"Definitely," Rynna said, taking that moment to look at me with the threat of a smile on her pretty face, the angle of her jaw sharp while everything else about her was soft.

That sweet scent was back. Billowing in the breeze. This warmth surrounding her. Hot cherry pie.

My teeth ground together, and the smile slid from her face when she saw what must have been my irritated expression, and I swore I heard the slight catch of her breath when she met my glare. Could see a slight quiver in her throat when she straightened and took a step back.

Still, she stood her ground.

There was something unwavering about her. Like she had something to prove. To herself or me, I wasn't sure.

"Hi. I'm Rynna Dayne. Was named after my grandmother," she managed, though the words were rough as she stuck her hand out toward me like she'd done to my daughter.

I just stood there staring at it like it held the venom of a viper bite. Finally,

I lifted my chin at her and gathered all the pleasantness I could summon. It wasn't much. "Rex Gunner. I'm sorry about your grandmother. And we're late . . . so if you could excuse us."

I gave Frankie a gentle tug of her hand. "Come on, Frankie Leigh. We've got to get you to dance."

Frankie trotted along at my side, looking back over her shoulder with what I knew had to be one of those adorable grins.

"What a jerk," I heard Rynna mumble behind my back when I turned and led my daughter to the passenger side of my truck.

Bitterness burned.

Yeah.

I was a jerk.

An asshole.

Whatever.

Better to burn bridges before anyone had a chance to cross them.

Shaking it off, I hoisted Frankie into the high cabin, making her squeal and pretend like she was flying. I strapped her in her car seat and jogged around to the front. I hopped into the driver's seat, wondering if it were possible for the roar of the engine to cover the hurt that sagged Rynna's shoulders as I took to the street.

Wondering why I felt like a complete piece of shit when I caught a glimpse of her in the rearview mirror. She just stood there in the twilight like she was caught in a dream.

Watching us go with disappointment on her face.

Befriending a sweet old lady was one thing.

Allowing a girl like Rynna Dayne into our lives—a girl that made my body react the way it did? Now that was pure stupidity.

three

Rynna

Why am I doing this?

Anxiety convulsed through my nerves as I waited for my computer to fire up. The truth was, I couldn't not know. I connected to my hotspot and logged on to Facebook. It felt like forever while I sat there, the screen churning, lighting up like a window to the past. I could almost feel it stretching its fingers out to touch me. To tease me with the control it'd held over me for so long.

For too long.

Fingers trembling, I managed to type the name into the search bar. A task I'd attempted at least twenty times before I'd set out on my journey back home. I had never found the courage to press enter.

Today, I did.

She was the third listing. A grainy picture. Almost indistinguishable. But I knew it was her.

Missouri.

She lived in Missouri.

I slammed the lid down.

That was all I needed to know.

As long as she wasn't here? I could totally manage staying in this town.

"Tell me you're miserable without me."

Laughing quietly, I flitted around the kitchen on my bare feet. My cell was pressed between my ear and shoulder as I slowly unpacked the few things I'd brought. I hadn't needed much since my grandmother had left everything she owned to me.

"Completely miserable," I told Macy, letting the tease wind into my tone as I hiked onto my toes to set my favorite Christmas mug on a high cupboard shelf.

"Huh. That's weird. I haven't even noticed you're gone," she deadpanned.

"Says the girl who's called me like ten times today," I ribbed.

She giggled. "Okay, okay, I might have kind of noticed." Her voice dropped to a whisper. "It's just that I think the apartment is haunted."

"The apartment is haunted? And this happened sometime in the last three days?" Skepticism rolled from my tongue.

"You know how these things work. Ghost girl has been stalking me, and the second she felt your absence, she slid right in to take your place."

"You know you're absolutely ridiculous, right?"

"Which is precisely why you love me."

Affection pulsed. How was I ever going to live without seeing her every day?

"Honestly, though, Ryn. How are you doing there by yourself? It must be weird to be alone in that old house. God knows it's weird around here without you."

I paused to look around at my dated surroundings—the floors linoleum, the cupboards hailing from the early eighties, the beige Formica countertops dingy and faded to a dreary yellow. The décor was mainly all the trinkets my grandmother had collected over the years, and the same two floral placemats I remembered from my childhood were still on the small round table.

It was as if she'd been waiting for me to return all this time. Next to nothing had changed since I left eleven years ago.

The house needed a full renovation. That was when, or if, I ever had the money to do it. Honestly, I still didn't know how I was going to manage to hold on to all these frayed threads, if I could come back here and take over where my grandmother had left off. If I had what it would take to breathe life back into everything she had built.

But when I inhaled? I could almost smell the lingering memory of sugar browning in the oven. When I focused hard enough, I could almost taste the tart cherries and sweet crust melting on my tongue. When I listened intently enough, I could almost hear the steadfast belief in her voice echoing from the walls.

"Honestly?"

"Yeah," she said.

An old warmth surrounded me, all mixed up with the reservations and fear that had kept me away for so many years. "It feels like home. Like I never left. Like I could walk through the door and my grandmother would be standing right in this kitchen, pulling a pot pie from the oven for dinner." I swallowed over the lump that grew heavy at the base of my throat, the loss that echoed back her presence. "I just wish I would have come back earlier. Before it was too late."

My heart clutched at the memory of the phone call I'd received two months before. A social worker had been on the other end of the line telling me my grandmother had suffered a massive heart attack while behind the wheel of her car, that though the responders had tried, there had been nothing they could do. She was pronounced dead upon arrival at the hospital.

Macy's voice dipped in sincerity. "You can't blame yourself, Ryn. Even if she didn't know the reason you left, I think she at least understood why."

"Then why does it feel like such a pathetic excuse now?"

"Maybe I was never lucky enough to meet your grandma in person, but in all the time we lived together, I don't remember a day that passed without you talking to her. So maybe the circumstances sucked. But I promise you that she knew how much you loved her. And you want to know why it feels pathetic now? Because you've moved beyond it. Above it. You're not even close to being that timid, insecure girl who answered my ad for a roommate eleven years ago. You've grown, changed. Your grandma got it. That was one smart woman."

I exhaled slowly. "I know. I just . . . I wish I would have come back before it was too late."

Wished she had let me know she was in trouble. I wished we had more time.

But I guessed us Dayne women were stubborn that way.

"I'm betting your grandma didn't see it that way, which is the very reason you're back there now."

I gulped around the emotion, voice hushed. "Thanks, Mace. I needed to hear that."

She tsked softly. "Of course you did. This is why you have me."

From the other end of the line, I heard rustling, could feel her mood changing course as she settled back in the plush couch in the den. I could almost see the glass of red wine in her hand. "So, how is it being back in Gingham Lakes so far? Have you run into anyone you know?"

Her voice turned wry. "Tell me you found out bitch-face took a deep dive into the lake and never came back up for air. Or maybe she took a sharp curve driving a little too fast? Which would you prefer?"

A low chuckle rumbled free. "You're horrible, Mace."

"Psh. Don't tell me you haven't imagined it a thousand times."

"Okay, okay, maybe I imagined her demise a time or two."

Like every time I'd closed my eyes for two years after it happened. Wondering what it might have been like if I could have turned the tables on her and wishing all the same she could just take it back.

What had I ever done to warrant that level of cruelty? Could she possibly have known just how badly what she'd done had hurt?

Old memories twisted my stomach into knots. Traces of that evil, depraved laughter touched my ears, visions of her standing there like it'd meant nothing at all while she'd destroyed my entire world. It was as if crushing me had been nothing but entertainment.

"And no. I looked her up. She moved to Missouri."

"You looked her up?" Surprise coated Macy's tone.

"I just . . . had to."

Silence filled the space between us. "I get it," she finally said.

Bending down, I pulled my coffee pot from the box, puffing out a breath as I did. "To answer your question, no, I haven't seen anyone I know. My Gramma was right, the city has really grown since I left. It's not filled with the familiar faces like it used to be. I stopped by the grocery store this afternoon and didn't recognize a soul."

"Is that a good thing or a bad thing?"

I sighed. "I don't know . . . both, I guess. I used to love that I knew everyone. That I'd go into the restaurant and knew at least half the people there. It made it feel safe. But after everything? The rumors?" My lips pursed. "It's nice to be somewhere I love and have a clean slate. It feels like a second chance."

I just prayed it remained that way.

"Well, if there aren't any familiar faces, tell me there are at least some panty-melting ones you've run across. You know, some yummy to my tummy hotties hanging around, waiting to steal your heart? Knowing you're getting some will at least ease some of my worry for you."

A scoff scraped my throat. Leave it to Macy. "Oh, there's a hottie, all right, but he definitely isn't hanging around waiting to steal my heart."

It was that moment when I heard the low rumble of a powerful engine approaching in the distance.

Of course.

Gramma had always told me all you needed was to speak of the devil and he'd appear.

There'd been something about our encounter this morning that had left me unsettled. Something about that gorgeous stranger that had left me restless and curious.

Interest piqued.

The man was a paradox.

Hard and brittle and cold.

Yet so incredibly gentle with the little girl, who'd clung to his hand as if he were the center of her world.

There seemed to be nothing I could do but edge toward the window, stealing to the side to remain out of sight.

I pulled back the edge of the curtain and peeked out.

Headlights cut into the night, and my stupid heart kicked an erratic beat. That intrigue increased my pulse to a thunder. I was riddled with that same fierce attraction I'd felt when I'd looked up earlier today to find him towering over me, the way my stomach had twisted and the nervousness that had followed me back to Gingham Lakes took a new form.

The headlights grew brighter, illuminating the space between our houses before the monstrous truck slowed and turned into the driveway across the street.

"Oh, oh, oh, tell me all about it. Someone sounds pouty . . . and turned on."

"You know how my luck goes when it comes to men." The scales were always tipped to bad. "You shouldn't be surprised that my neighbor is like . . . gorgeous."

Macy squealed. "How gorgeous?"

I watched as Rex hopped out of his truck and went straight for the backseat.

All six feet three inches of mouthwatering deliciousness lit up by the moonlight.

"Like Greek God with a sledgehammer gorgeous."

I could hear her kicking her feet. "And how is this a bad thing?"

"I was pretty sure he would have preferred to drag me to the lake and drown me rather than tolerate my living across the street from them."

"Them?"

"I met his daughter, too. At least she was super excited to meet me."

I suppressed laughter as I thought of her rushing out of their house. The little girl had been a perfect kind of disaster in that hot pink tutu and those atrocious socks she had to have stolen from her dad.

She was a bluster of energy and innocence.

It was almost worry that entered Macy's playful tone. "Oh God, tell me you're not actually crushing on the married guy next door? That's just poor form, Ryn."

Through the milky, opalescent night, I watched as he pulled a sleeping Frankie from the backseat and shifted her so her head rested high up on his shoulder. He ran a hand over the back of her head and set a kiss to her temple.

The image was so at odds with the hostility he'd met me with earlier.

That intrigued attraction flared, my mouth dry as I watched him start up his walkway.

Maybe what struck me most was there was something sad about him, too. Something helpless and scared beneath all the harsh, hard dominance he wore so well. Something bitter and broken.

I found myself whispering when I came to the realization. "I'm thinking there's no wife."

"No wife . . . so . . . he's like . . . a single dad?"

"Maybe," I uttered so quietly as I peered through the night, drinking in the way his long legs took the steps, and then the way he angled through his front door with his sleeping little dancer girl. "I think so. I'm not sure."

Why did I want to know so desperately?

"Why are you whispering?" Macy whispered back.

I bit down on my bottom lip while guilty silence spun around the room.

Macy busted up laughing. "Oh my God, you are spying on him right now, aren't you?"

"Shut up," I told her, quick to let the curtain drop. I got straight back to work unpacking.

"Someone has a crush," she sing-songed.

"Stop it."

I was so not spying, and I so didn't have a crush.

I'd just met them, and the worst thing I could do was get mixed up with the angry guy across the street with his sweet, adorable little girl, who was a big fan of my grandmother. Apparently, she had really good taste.

But her dad? He obviously had some ginormous chip on his shoulder, and I had enough to worry about without giving thought to the flecks of sadness scored in the depths of his eyes.

Eyes the color of sage. Rimmed in the darkest gray.

No, I wasn't thinking about those soft, full lips barely hidden by the sexy scruff on his strong jaw. And I definitely hadn't noticed his big hands or the strength in his deeply tanned, muscled arms.

Nope.

Not at all.

A guy like that had heartache written all over him.

And I'd had enough of that to last me a lifetime.

The sound of a whisk clanging against metal echoed through the kitchen. With the bowl tucked under one arm, I cut butter into the flour in the other, giving myself over to the sense of deep peace that had taken me over.

The late night was like a warm blanket wrapped around the old house, holding me safe and secure, the vast silence a comfort as I slowly swayed in the kitchen.

I had the crumpled letter smoothed out on the counter beside me where I worked. Every so often, I would peek over at it, relishing in her presence. I had to have read it close to a million times since it'd slipped out with the file the attorney had given me two months ago. But I kept going back to it, wondering, why now?

Why hadn't she asked this of me before?

When you left, you told me I was the only one you could trust. Your broken heart had mine breaking that night. Isn't it funny how things come around? Because no matter how many years have passed, in the end, you are the only one I trust with this.

I know right now you're scared and questioning my intentions. But I'm asking you to trust me one last time. I made a life within those walls, gave it my whole heart. Maybe you never realized it, but all along, I was working so one day, I could give it to you. Now, it's yours. Give it life, Corinne Paisley. I'll be with you every step of the way.

My chest tightened as a wave of grief and love slammed into me.

I could feel the weight of her spirit dance around me. Soft, soft encouragement. The same as she'd always given me.

Belief. It was right there. Shining with all the questions that still remained.

"I am scared, Gramma. I'm not sure how I can do this without you. But I promise you that I'm going to try. I'm going to do whatever it takes to make you proud."

I jumped when the oven dinged, letting me know the temperature had reached three hundred and seventy-five degrees.

Maybe I really was letting this old house get to me.

I set the bowl aside and dug into the paper sack to find the almond extract.

Almond extract I was certain I'd purchased this afternoon at the store.

Almond extract that wasn't there.

With a frown, I sank back onto my heels. Frustration leaked into my veins. Damn it.

My first pie, and I was already failing. It was one of those ingredients I could probably get away with not using, but it just wouldn't be the same. Looking around, my attention landed on the pantry.

"Let's see what you've got, Gramma," I mumbled, opening the pantry door and rummaging through the few items that hadn't already been discarded.

"Aha." It was a cry of victory as I held the bottle of almond extract in the air.

Victory that was short-lived. It'd expired three years ago.

"Damn it," I muttered again. I tossed it into the garbage bin right before my eye caught on a white envelope tucked on a shelf at the side of the pantry wall. Like a forgotten partner to all the expired spices and extracts. A token of the past.

Apprehension swelled, anxious and uneasy, and I slowly moved forward.

It felt as if it were some kind of secret.

As if I were on some kind of forbidden mission.

Silly, I knew, but my fingers trembled when I reached in and tugged it free, the paper tacked to something sticky on the pantry wall.

That anxiousness thickened like molasses, my throat full and bobbing, my stomach twisted in a vice.

My name was written across the front, the familiar handwriting scratchy from an unsteady hand.

"Oh God." Grief came swooping back in, but I smiled through the tears that were suddenly clouding my eyes as I ripped into the letter.

There was so much comfort in knowing she felt confident that one day I would find what she'd left for me.

I tugged it out and quickly scanned the card.

All moments matter. We just rarely know how important they are until the chance to act on them has already passed.

My spirit flooded with love, and I clung tight to the reminder of this amazing woman who'd always viewed the world as if it were right on the cusp of something magical. The tough times nothing but a stepping-stone to propel us to where we were supposed to be.

I took a fumbling step back when I sensed the change outside my kitchen window. A light had flickered on across the street. Drawn, I inched across the creaking floor, again keeping myself hidden as I crept toward the window. I pulled back the edge of the lacy drape and peered that direction, not sure if I felt guilty for doing it or if it was somehow my duty.

Because this time there was no question I was spying.

Unable to look away.

Somehow knowing I didn't want to.

The bulk of him took up the entirety of his kitchen window, his hair, which was a dark, golden blond and a little long on top, was in complete disarray and stuck up in all directions. As if he'd spent the night tossing in bed, waging a war I didn't understand. I couldn't make out his expression with the way he had his head dropped between his shoulders, his hands most likely propped on the counter to hold himself up. But that didn't mean I couldn't clearly see him fighting with whatever demons plagued him.

"Shit," I whispered, clutching the letter in my hand, waging my own war. The battles I'd once fought in this town had been lost. The memories of them stalled me with trepidation, the strength I'd found through the years away coming against them and instilling me with courage.

I glanced at the letter again.

And I chose to take a chance.

Before I could think better of it, I moved through the arch and out into the dated living room. I slipped on my sandals I'd left by the door.

Then I let myself out into the muggy, Alabama night, the air heady with wafts of honeysuckle and fresh-cut grass.

Moon, huge and high, cast the slumbering houses and trees in a silvery glow, and the steady trill of cicadas danced all around.

It felt like stepping straight back into my childhood. The memories of the nights I'd spent on the porch with my grandmother staring up at the stars seemed so close it felt as if I only had to reach out to go back to that time.

Inhaling the vestiges, I kept my footsteps as light as possible. Even still, they crunched against the gravel driveway, and I sucked in an emboldened breath when I stole through the night and across the street, silently making my way up his walkway.

Carefully, I climbed his steps, hand on the railing as if it offered moral support, and crossed his freshly stained deck. I stopped at his door, my heart the thunder that incited a storm within my chest.

What was I doing?

This was insane.

This guy hated me for no apparent reason at all.

Still, I found myself lifting my hand, my fist quietly knocking at his door.

I was shaking all over by the time the latch turned and the door flew open, and I was again met with the same unwarranted fury from earlier. Although this time it was harder.

All of it.

His scowl and his glare and every gloriously defined ridge of his body.

Oh. My. God.

There was nothing I could do to keep my eyes from dropping to explore the wide expanse of exposed flesh. His shirt was missing, and he was wearing nothing but boxer briefs.

I gulped. That foolish attraction drenched me through, wet and hot and sticky. Flaming free and leaving me weak in the knees.

My gaze latched on the tattoo that ran the entirety of his left upper arm. It was a landscape of a jagged cliff with a waterfall pouring over the side. The splashes rising up from the seething pool of water were bright, colorful feathers that floated and twisted as if blown by the breeze.

Sorrow and hope.

They were so clearly impressed into the depiction.

"What are you doing here?"

The severity in his voice cut through the night, impaling my stupor, jerking my attention up to his face.

Of course, it had to be equally as striking as the rest of him.

Powerful and dominant.

I shook as I took a fumbled step back.

Oh, wow, was this stupid. So damned stupid.

Still, I lifted my chin. "I was just . . ." I fumbled for an excuse to be standing at his door at one in the morning. "Wondering if you had any almond extract?"

His head cocked, and if it were possible, his eyes narrowed even more. "Do I look like I have almond extract?"

"Ummm . . ." I stammered.

Great.

I was a blubbering fool.

This man set me totally off balance. He was so different from the men I was used to back in San Francisco.

Rougher.

Unpolished and raw.

More dangerously beautiful than any man had the right to be.

Maybe it was because he reminded me a tiny bit of Aaron. The asshole back in high school who'd had a hand in the breaking of my heart.

But this was more.

Different.

Everything about Rex Gunner was unique.

Blinding in his darkness.

Warm in his coldness.

"I just—" I gestured back to my house across the street. "I was making my gramma's cherry pie and was missing almond extract when I saw a light on over here. I thought I would take a chance."

All moments matter. We just rarely know how important they are until the chance to act on them has already passed.

Was this one of those moments that mattered?

And why did I feel like I had to take this chance?

Rex

Lust sieged my body as I stared at her standing in the moonlight like some kind of vision.

Like some kind of wicked enchantress with the face of an angel.

Baking my fucking favorite pie, nonetheless.

Her scent was all around me. Cherries and sugar.

My mouth watered, and I clenched my fists in an effort to keep myself from reaching out and taking a taste for myself.

Maybe I was still back in bed and this was just a new element of the nightmares that haunted me night after night.

If this were a dream, I'd be inviting her in and sinking into that tight body. Fucking her hard and wild. Just the way I liked it. That would be right before she grew fangs and ripped me apart. Hell, with the way she was looking at me, it was clear she was already poised to tear me to shreds.

"Some chances aren't worth taking," I said, voice rough with warning. She needed to know she was crossing into territory where she wasn't welcome. Banging on my door in the middle of the night was completely off-limits. How could this girl possibly think this was okay?

I set my forearm high on the jamb, knowing every inch of me was bristling with the challenge.

All except for my dick. Apparently, that was the only part of me that didn't seem pissed off at the intrusion.

Her strong chin lifted in her own challenge. "No? Haven't you ever heard you never know if you don't try?"

"And how many doors have gotten slammed in your face because of that philosophy?"

"More than I could count. And why do I get the feeling you're about to add another to that number?"

A disbelieving chuckle rumbled in my chest. This girl was all kinds of grit and determination. "I'm easy to read, I guess."

A tiny snort huffed from her nose. "Hardly."

She angled her head, and those warm eyes turned almost pleading. "Listen, I'm going to be living right across the street . . ."

Just the thought of it left me antsy and agitated.

Her voice softened. "I don't know anyone around here anymore, and it'd be nice to have a friend. I thought maybe you and Frankie could use one, too."

Laughter ripped up my throat.

Cruel and low.

"Sorry, but I have all the friends I need, and I'd appreciate it if you stayed away from my daughter. She doesn't need anyone else making her promises they have no intention of keeping."

Before I could do something stupid, I slammed the door shut in her face. Exactly the way she'd been expecting me to do. I leaned my back against the wood, trying to catch my breath, to slow the raging in my spirit, that part of me that hated being such an asshole.

All the while trying to remind myself why it was necessary.

There was something about her that set me on edge. Left me feeling off-balance.

Self-control was not normally something I lacked, and fuck, it wasn't like she was out there offering herself up like a warm slice of pie.

But just looking at her had me itching for a taste.

I could feel her on the other side, her presence that swept the air unsettled and thick. Like I'd caused her physical pain with the rejection and she was projecting it right back to me.

Maybe she really was just trying to be nice.

Maybe she didn't have ulterior motives.

But that was a *chance* I just couldn't take.

Fear tumbled through his veins and clanged in the hollow of his chest. Frantic, he stumbled through the brushy undergrowth, the world buried by soaring trees. Branches lashed at the exposed skin of his arms and thorns latched onto the fabric of his shirt in an attempt to hold him back.

It propelled him harder.

Faster.

He screamed her name. "Sydney."

Sydney. Sydney. Sydney.

The howl of wind answered back.

Sydney.

I shot upright, chest heaving as I struggled to catch my breath. To orient myself to the movement that jostled me awake and pulled me from the dream.

"Daddy, Daddy, Daddy! Wakey, wakey, wakey. I made you breakfast."

Frankie was grinning at me as she jumped on my bed. Brown hair wild and free, just as wild and free as the way she looked at the world. At the way she loved. Wholly and without reservation.

I scrubbed both palms over my face, dropped them just as fast. It was not all that hard to return her grin.

Her expression alone was enough to chase away the exhaustion that constantly weighed me down. The few hours of sleep I managed were restless. Plagued with the curse that darkened my life.

I swallowed back the fear. The terror that one day it might steal her from me, too.

"You made me breakfast?" I asked, voice groggy, my touch tender as I brushed her too-long bangs back from her innocent face. "That's awful nice of you, thinking of your daddy first thing in the morning."

She giggled. "Of course I thinks about you, Daddy. And I made a whole big bowl, 'cause Grammy says you could eat a whole cow."

"Oh, she did, huh?"

She nodded emphatically, her eyes going wide when I hopped up and tossed her over my shoulder. Frankie roared with laughter, the kid dressed in shorts and a tee with that same damned hot pink tutu around her waist.

So fuckin' cute.

"That Grammy is going to be in big, big trouble when I see her today," I teased my daughter, who was bouncing on my shoulder as I started running with her down the hall.

She squealed, kicking her feet and holding on to me for dear life. "Oh, no, don't tell Grammy! It's our secret."

"I thought you said you were good at keeping secrets?"

Damn it.

The last thing I needed to do was bring up the conversation she'd had with Rynna yesterday. Just the mention of that woman had fantasies slamming me from all sides. Her face and her hair and that body.

Sweet, mouthwatering sugar.

I'd thought maybe the morning would have scraped the idea of her from my consciousness.

No such luck.

I shoved off the thoughts, refusing to give them voice. That was right when I came to an abrupt stop when I entered the kitchen I'd just finished remodeling.

Frankie scrambled upright, pushing those unruly locks from her face with both hands, a hopeful smile plastered on her face. "I mights have spilled a little milk, Daddy. Is that okay? I'm gonna clean it all gone, but I didn't want your cereal to get all gross and swoggy. Bleh."

Her nose scrunched, and her lips turned down as if she'd tasted something sour.

I frowned when I saw a "little" milk was actually the entire gallon minus what she'd managed to pour into the cereal bowl. A pool of white swam between the small table set for two and the refrigerator against the far wall, the emptied plastic container floating in the middle of it.

Her shoulders went to her ears, her voice quieting. "Is you mad?"

Hugging her close, I pecked a kiss to her chubby cheek. "Of course, I'm not mad. We're just gonna have to get you to the gym with me so we can start building up these muscles." I lightly squeezed her tiny bicep. "How's that sound? You ready to start pumping some iron? Before you know it, you'll be as strong as The Hulk."

She giggled like it was the funniest thing she'd ever heard. "The Incwedible Hulk? You're crazy, Daddy. I'm gonna be Wonder Woman. Don't you know I'm a girl?"

She threw both her arms in the air before she started shimmying down my body, getting free of my hold, and heading straight for the drawer where we kept the dishtowels. She climbed up the step stool so she could reach it, that smile lighting up the whole room when she looked over at me. "Right, Daddy? Can I be the best dancer in the whole world and Wonder Woman?"

I crossed the kitchen to help her clean up the mess. "Yeah, Tiny Dancer, you can be whatever you want to be."

I'd make sure of it.

Because she was the single wonder of my life.

I'd do whatever it took to keep her that way.

five

Rynna

Sunlight poured in through the long row of dark tinted windows that overlooked the bustling street. It struck the murky space like a blazing orb of fire against the quiet darkness that held fast to the silenced space, the light still muted in the far reaches of the restaurant.

It left the space filled with a dim hue of warmth, the atmosphere an intricate dance of peace and regret and the remnants of my lingering fear.

Lovingly, I dragged my fingertips through the layer of dust that had gathered on the bar, exposing the shiny white counter hiding underneath.

Buried, but not forgotten.

Yearning pulsed through my being, my spirit full and my heart heavy, that lump at the base of my throat prominent as I slowly wandered through the old diner-style restaurant that for so long had been the center of my life.

How many days had I spent at this counter? A little girl coloring and painting who turned into a teenager studying for the SAT?

How many mornings had I been there before dawn, standing on the step stool so I could see over the counter back in the kitchen? I'd watch in awe as my grandmother would mix the ingredients, helping her pour them into the bowl, my arm straining as I'd followed her instructions and pressed the dough into pie crusts. The whole time I would quietly listen to her chatting about life, the woman so easily relating everything to the pies she made.

How much life had buzzed in the bustling diner, the families that had gathered in the booths and the old men who'd sat at the bar with their tall tales to tell?

That life had been silenced, but it wasn't gone. I could feel it. Bated, but simmering. Trembling all around where it was restrained, pressing and vying to be freed.

Waiting for someone to believe in it again.

For someone to breathe that life back into its walls.

And Gramma had somehow put her faith in me that I would be the one to do it.

Even after I'd run like a coward.

I just prayed I could live up to her belief.

I jumped when the old bell jingled above the door and someone called, "Knock, knock."

Heart leaping to my throat, I spun around. I did my best to beat down the jolt of fear that had taken hold. My eyes narrowed as I tried to make out the two figures in the doorway.

They stepped forward, coming into view in the dimmed light of the diner.

Two women.

Their faces unfamiliar, but both had to be around my age, maybe twenty-eight or thirty. One was dressed in something like I would have worn to the office back in San Francisco. A perfectly fitted pencil skirt, blouse, and heels, her black hair done up in an intricate twist. The other was more casually dressed in trendy jeans and a flowy tee, her hair cropped and messy.

Dusting off my hands on my jeans, I walked their direction. "Can I help you?"

"You must be Corrine Dayne's granddaughter."

I gave a slight nod.

"We heard you were coming into town," she said. "I hope we're not intruding, but we wanted to introduce ourselves. I'm Lillith Redd." The woman in heels stepped forward with a welcoming smile and pushed her hand out in front of her.

I rounded the corner and shook her hand. "It's nice to meet you, Lillith. I'm Rynna."

The other woman laughed. "Ah, forget that 'Lillith' nonsense." She hooked her thumb in her friend's direction. "This one right here goes by Lily Pad. Don't fall for that suit-wearing, straightlaced attorney vibe she's rockin'. She's actually kind of a wild child when you get to know her. And we finally get to meet *the* Rynna Dayne, not to be confused with Grandma Corinne. I pretty much feel like we're already best friends since your grandma never stopped talking about you. I'm Nikki Walters."

There was a kind, playful confidence about her, no hesitation when she reached out to take my hand.

Confidence.

Right then, I scrambled within myself to find it. To remember who I'd become in the years I'd been away. The strength and boldness I'd found. It was crazy how coming back to this town incited the instinct to cower and hide. "It's really nice to meet you, Nikki."

I glanced between the two of them. "So, you two knew my grandmother?"

It actually felt nice to find someone other than Frankie and her dad who remembered my grandmother. The fact I was there by myself and facing this alone was beginning to set in. That loneliness growing bigger with each second that passed.

It didn't help Rex Gunner had quite literally slammed a door in my face last night.

Standing on his porch like a fool as I'd offered myself up, only to have him so callously reject me, had stung. I wanted to hate him. To think him nothing but a jerk. But I couldn't.

Maybe it was the way my grandmother had raised me. To slow down and look deeper. Beyond the surface and the shallow to what was concealed underneath.

God knew I'd been judged enough as a child. I might as well have been on trial for my appearance alone, a thousand convictions made with each passing, sneering glance. And I had looked deeper at Rex. What I saw was pain and fear and a rickety defense lurking right under the hostility that seeped from his pores like poison. There was something so ferociously protective behind the shield of venom and animosity.

It filled me with the urge to break through it. To chip it away, piece by piece. To dig deeper until I'd discovered everything that was hiding underneath.

It didn't help that one look at him made my stomach shiver and shake.

I had no idea what it was about this guy, but every time I saw him, I was struck with an overpowering shock of attraction. The kind that spun my head and left my knees weak with the impulse to run my fingers over the hard planes of his body.

Which was crazy. I didn't know him. But I couldn't scrape the idea from my consciousness that I was supposed to.

Nikki's eyes widened as if my question had been absurd. "Of course we knew your grandma." With a moan, her eyes rolled back in her head as she tipped her face toward the ceiling. "She made the freaking best pies. Like, to die for."

Wistful laughter tumbled free. "Yeah, they kind of had that effect on people, didn't they? Now that woman could bake."

Her pot pies were almost as legendary as her sweet pies.

"Tell me you're actually reopening this place and you have all her secret recipes," Nikki pleaded as if my answer might save her life.

I glanced around the diner that had been shut down for the last two months, but with the poor shape it was in, you'd think it had been vacant for years. The entire place was covered in an inch of dust, the red pleather booths cracked, some torn. More concerning was the equipment in the kitchen that was old and in far worse shape.

Resolve set into my bones. "I'm going to try."

Lillith laughed a tinkling sound. "Oh, if you're anything like your grandma made you out to be, I think you'll fair just fine."

A sad smile emerged at just the edge of my mouth. "I think there's a chance my grandmother might have played me up to be something I'm not."

"Psh." Nikki waved a flippant hand. "As long as you have those recipes, you're golden."

"Well, following her recipes is the easy part. It's the two hundred thousand dollar loan I need to whip this place back into shape that I'm worried about," I returned, trying to make it a joke and not let the reality of it bring me down.

All the while, I wondered why these two set me so at ease that I felt comfortable sharing such personal details with them.

But I did.

Concern flitted across Lillith's face, her expression knowing. "I heard there was a tax lien?"

I sighed, but there was satisfaction behind it. "There was, but I was able to sell off some of my things back in California to pay the lien, as well as the back payments due on the house. That left me with the keys to both." A wry chuckle rumbled out. "And you know, about five dollars to my name." I wasn't quite that destitute, but it was close.

"Hey, a strong woman can work magic with five dollars," Nikki said, her grin wry.

"I just might need a little magic to come into play if I'm going to make this happen."

Sympathy lined Lillith's face. "I'm so sorry your return is under these circumstances. I hope you know your grandmother was a huge asset to this community and an even better friend. She is greatly missed. If there's anything we can do, don't hesitate to ask. I'm an attorney, and I'll do whatever I can to help you get this place reopened, whether you need me to file anything or need legal advice or even if you just need a friend to talk to."

Her words were carefully phrased, but there was a genuineness that seeped out with them.

"That's really nice of you. Thank you. I may need to take you up on that offer," I told her.

She smiled. "The entire town is really excited by the prospect of the diner reopening, especially with the hotel going in across the street. The whole intention of the Fairview Street Restoration Project is to mesh the old with the new. A cohesive fusion of the past and present, and I'd personally love to see this diner become a part of that."

Pride lifted in her expression when she looked over her shoulder and out the window at the construction taking place directly on the other side of the street.

Nikki almost rolled her eyes. She dropped her voice as if she were whispering conspiratorially, though not low enough that Lillith couldn't hear. "You'll have to excuse her. Her fiancé's company has the hotel going in, and this one right here is kind of pathetically in love."

Lillith swatted at her. "Shut it." She looked at me, grinning. "Nikki is the one who pretty much insisted I give him a chance, and now that we're together, she won't stop giving me crap about it. I think she might be jealous."

"Hey, don't act like you don't want to kiss my feet for bringing the two of you together. That was nothing but pure matchmaking skill. Think of all the orgasms I earned you."

"Nikki, what is wrong with you?" Lillith smacked her again.

Nikki set her hand over her heart. "I'm just a speaker of the truth. And yes, for the record, I am very, very jealous of all the orgasms. I mean, not that I want Broderick to be the one giving them to me. That would be kind of gross and wrong."

Nikki sent me a wink. "You know, considering we're best friends and all. I'm just envious of the sheer number of them."

She feigned a sad shake of her head. "It's a little greedy if you ask me. No one person needs that many orgasms."

"Oh, believe me, I need them all." Lillith was both fighting a grin and the redness on her cheeks when she said it, once again looking behind her to the construction site.

It was a large section of land cordoned off by a chain-link fence, the frame of a massive building just starting to take form.

I smiled at her dreamy look. It was impossible not to like them. They seemed polar opposites; yet, I was unable to imagine one without the other.

Lillith turned back to me almost reluctantly. "We'd better get out of your way so you can get back to work, but we wanted to stop in and introduce ourselves. Honestly, if you need anything, let us know."

"I'm glad you did, and I definitely will."

"Oh." Nikki's eyes lit up. "It's Friday!"

My brow rose in question.

She looked at me as if it should be obvious. "Um . . . hello? Friday Funday? That means you totally have to come out with us tonight."

"Really?"

Okay, maybe I was a little overenthusiastic. But I missed Macy like crazy and the truth was, I needed that—companionship and friendship. The true kind. The feeling of belonging when the last couple of days had made me feel as if I'd stepped out of bounds, directly into a place I knew so intimately but still so far removed.

Lillith nodded. "Oh, good idea."

"Of course it's a good idea," Nikki shot back.

Lillith widened her eyes at me. "For the record, if you say no, chances are Nikki will just come drag you out anyway. It's best to just concede and go along for the ride. God knows, I do." It was all soft, playful affection.

"At least you know what is good for you," Nikki tossed at her before she grabbed me by the wrist and shook my arm around. "Come with us. Please! I already feel like I know you, and . . . well, I think that you might be the missing *three* in our amigo. You complete us."

With both index fingers, she drew a heart in the air.

"See?" Lillith asked. "Just go with the crazy."

I grinned. I was totally going with the crazy. Forget the fears. It'd been eleven years. Who would even recognize me? And if they did, why would they even still care?

A shiver trembled through me.

What if they did?

Shaking it off, I smiled. I could do this. I *wanted* to do this. "That sounds like fun. Where should I meet you and at what time?"

Nikki slung her arm around my shoulder, and I walked with them toward the entrance. "Eight at Olive's. It's on the corner of Macaber and 5th."

"Why do I get the feeling you know this place well?"

Lillith widened telling eyes. "That's because Ollie owns it. This one can't stay away."

Nikki sighed dramatically. "Ollie. Hottest man in all the land. Friend-zoner extraordinaire. But one day, I will make him see what he's missing."

"Ah, things are beginning to make sense now," I said.

Nikki feigned sadness with the grim shake of her head. "No, Rynna, men make absolutely no sense whatsoever. There is no sense to be found."

I laughed. God, I really liked them.

"Isn't that the truth?" I said.

Lillith pushed open the glass door. It was smudged with its own layer of greasy dust, and the white logo on the front claiming Pepper's Pies was barely visible. Still, I could read it as if I'd drawn it myself. It was a shaker tipped on its side, flecks of pepper pouring over a tumble of pot pies and sweet pies and pizzas.

Gramma's offerings had always been unique and perfectly peculiar.

Just like the woman behind it.

I was washed with another wave of warmth, and I couldn't help but think I was supposed to return. That no matter what the past held, this was where I had always belonged.

We stepped out into the hot Alabama summer day, and I blinked against the sudden glare of sunlight and the rush of sticky humidity.

Clouds threatened in the distance, building in the sultry heat.

Lillith hummed with a near imperceptible bounce on her toes. Her attention locked on the small group of men across the street, who'd gathered in a circle just inside the chain-link fence.

Most of them were in work clothes: jeans and long-sleeved shirts and boots. Though a single man with his back to us wore a black suit and a yellow hard hat.

Nikki leaned in and mock-whispered in my ear, "Suit-guy would be the fiancé, Broderick Wolfe. You know, the one who constantly has this one's panties on fire. Look at her . . . she can hardly contain herself."

I bit back laughter, my whisper just as faked. "How long until she goes running over there?"

"Oh, I'd say about two point five seconds."

Lillith swatted at *my* arm, and God, for the first time since I'd returned, I felt truly, completely as if I were home.

"Stop it, you two. Like I don't hear you over there."

We both laughed. Nikki dropped her arm and moved to face me, pulling her cell phone from where it was tucked in her back pocket. "What's your number in case you get lost?" she said with a grin hugging her mouth as she dipped her head to look down. Her fingers were poised to input my number.

I almost got the entire thing out before my mouth went dry and the numbers came to a sluggish, sticky halt, my tongue unable to form a sound.

The man standing next to Broderick had turned around and was looking in our direction.

The smile slid right off his gorgeous face when he saw me staring at him. But somehow, the transformation into the hard scowl was just as mesmerizing.

Just as hypnotic.

Maybe more so.

Because I felt weightless beneath his glare.

Fluttery and uneasy.

Mesmerized.

Those sage eyes were so hard and intense. Capturing me. Holding me hostage. So dark they should have held the power to conceal the fire that raged in the depths, scored like markers in his spirit.

But I saw it. Felt it where it stuck in the heated, stagnant air.

The pain buried underneath.

Nikki lifted her head in question, her fingers ready for the last two numbers. "Hello?"

Snapping out of it, I cleared my throat. "Oh . . . um, sorry, six-two."

"Got it," she said before she gave me a salute and backed away. "Eight o'clock, my friend. Don't make me hunt you down. You know I will."

I tore my attention from the man pinning me to the spot from the other side of the street. His hold was just as heavy as if he were right in front of me, physically restraining me with those massive hands.

"I'll be there," I told her.

"You'd better be." She winked.

Lillith squeezed my hand gently before she backed away to cross the street. "It was great to finally meet you, Rynna. This is going to be good. I can just feel it. I'm so glad we took the chance and stopped in."

She said it without realizing the impact her words had on me. The way they flooded me with warmth and hope. The way they nudged the aspirations at the root of who I was, freeing them from where they'd been trapped deep inside.

My gaze roamed, drawn back to the man who hadn't moved an inch. Hostility rippled off him like heat waves.

I had no idea why I felt it. Compelled. Driven toward a man that seemed so rigid, so dangerous to my sanity.

But I felt it. He needed someone to revive his faith just as desperately as I did.

Because looking at him?

I suddenly knew he had none of it. That something had gone dim inside him.

That was the thing about chances.

We didn't know their outcomes.

If we'd succeed or if we'd fail.

It didn't matter.

I had to take a chance on him.

Six

Rex

"You sure you want to be here tonight?" I asked Ollie. Guilt was threatening to consume me. Suck me down. Take me under.

I fought it, trying to be strong, because it wasn't fucking right for me to be the one falling apart.

Ollie, Kale, and I were in the back office at Olive's where it was quiet. Private. The elevated voices from the throng of people out front were dulled, barely seeping through the walls, the evidence of the live band little more than a throb that vibrated the floors.

Ollie roughed a tattooed hand over his mouth like that single act might hold the power to erase the burden. A low, humorless chuckle rumbled from his chest. "Doesn't make much of a difference where we're at, now, does it? Fuckin' day will follow us, anyway."

"Yeah," I mumbled. Doubted there was a statement I agreed with more. This fucking date haunted us no matter where we went. No matter how much time had passed. There was no outrunning it.

Kale rocked back in the office chair where he sat at Ollie's desk. He had spun the chair around so he could face us, his long legs stretched out in front of him and his fingers threaded at the back of his head. "Twelve years. Twelve years, and it doesn't get any easier, does it?"

Ollie dropped his head back on the wall he rested against and squeezed his eyes closed. "Twelve years." Ollie's voice was nothing but a moan, close to tears. "Shut my eyes and, I swear to God, it feels like yesterday."

Ollie was a big, burly asshole, who was covered in tats, and if you didn't know him, he was intimidating as fuck. I'd seen grown men cross the street when he was heading their direction.

He'd bought Olive's back when it was little more than a dive, when the place was in shambles and going under. I'd come along beside him, doing the physical labor to restore the interior. But it was his vision that made it the most popular bar in Gingham Lakes.

"And a fucking century at the same damned time," I said, shifting on the file cabinet I was leaning on.

"I just . . ." Kale trailed off, unable to say the things every single one of us were thinking.

That it was too late.

That there was no chance.

There was no hope.

Even when it felt impossible to give it up.

Kale had always been the one who carried us through. He was an ER doctor over at the local hospital. He worked his ass off and usually did it with a smile on his face.

He was the kind of guy who would walk through hot coals for a friend. Hell, he'd stand right in the middle of the flames if it meant he could help a man out. Make your load lighter. The guy carried around the weight of the world, thinking it was his duty to offer relief.

Kale, Ollie, and I? We'd been through hell together. Each of us were so different, sometimes I wondered if we would have grown apart if it hadn't happened. Had to wonder if that fateful day had forged something indestructible between us. A bond and a burden that never should have been shaped.

A blessing given just the same as the curse.

Ollie groaned then fiercely shook his head, like he was shaking off the memories, the horror, before he strode across the small area and grabbed the bottle of whiskey. He poured it across the shot glasses and passed one to me and Kale.

He lifted his in the air. "To Sydney. We'll never forget."

I lifted mine, Kale did the same, the three glasses clinking in the middle. "We'll never forget."

I tossed back my shot, the burn of it sliding down my throat and filling my stomach with flames.

No.

There was no chance I would ever forget.

Ten minutes later, Kale and I had moved out into the front of the bar. I grabbed our regular table, which was tucked in the back, while Kale went to grab us drinks.

A blur of voices echoed off the red brick walls of the bottom floor. Olive's was all the rage in Gingham Lakes. Trendy and popular and packed.

A place I probably wouldn't step foot in if it weren't for the fact Ollie was the owner.

The din was a mind-numbing thrum that dulled the senses in the same way the dimmed, muted lights hanging from the ceiling somehow slowed the atmosphere, the band playing tonight super mellow and adding to the laid-back vibe.

Made me feel like I was right in the middle of everything without setting foot in the throng, this impression that the night might go on forever and it was all gonna end in the blink of an eye.

Raucous laughter and shouting seeped down from the upstairs area that housed a bunch of pool tables and led to the huge balcony that overlooked the river.

Tonight was no different than most nights at Olive's. The bar was packed, crawling with people out seeking a good time. A few minutes to cast aside their worries and cares.

I fought the urge brimming in my gut to pack it up and head home.

Truth was, I hated the idea of that, too. I knew my daughter was undoubtedly curled up on the couch next to my mom, who was all too happy to have her spend the night. Frankie Fridays, as she liked to call them, were their standing sleepover date.

If I showed up, Mom would shove me right back out her door. The woman was constantly nagging me to get out more. Insisting I needed time to "find myself" and figure out just how it was I was going to live my life.

She just had no clue I didn't need this bullshit. I had zero interest in the women who were watching the men who crawled the bar like hawks and the men who were watching them like prey.

That fucking game they always liked to play.

So, week after week, I sat back and pretended like I wasn't even there. Oblivious to it all.

I'd managed it for years. Until tonight. All that self-control fled the second the door swung open.

Twilight billowed in and the goddamned air was sucked from the room.

For fuck's sake.

Was she stalking me?

There had to be no other explanation. The woman kept popping up everywhere. Invading my space. Conjuring thoughts I couldn't entertain.

But there she was.

Again.

She walked right through the door of Olive's. Her presence stampeded out in front of her. Consuming everything.

Agitation lit me up, singeing my skin.

Tonight, she looked like she'd just stepped off the runway with those long, long legs encased in a tight pair of black pants and super high heels. Chestnut hair, which was normally all mussed and heaped on her head, swished around her like the silky calm of a midnight river.

Fuck. Me.

I didn't know if I liked her better like this or the total mess she normally was, the way she'd been earlier this afternoon when she'd stopped me in my tracks when I was in the middle of giving my crew instruction in front of Broderick Wolfe. No doubt, I looked like some kind of blundering idiot who couldn't find words.

Tongue-tied.

That was because I was too busy letting my dick do the talking, the traitor perking up at the sight of her standing outside her grandma's run-down, closed-up diner that had seen far better days.

Had taken Broderick calling me on it, all while wearing a knowing smirk on his face, before I'd snapped out of my stupor and had gotten back to the meeting.

Guessed I should have expected trouble the second I'd seen her outside Pepper's Pies with Nikki and Lillith.

I would have been right.

Her face split into a grin when her sight landed on the two of them. They were sitting at the bar, drinking their frilly drinks and chatting like they did just about every Friday night.

From behind me, a hand suddenly clamped down on my shoulder.

I jumped like some kind of pussy.

Just fucking awesome.

Kale laughed. "Dude, why so jumpy?" He set a fresh beer in front of me and pulled out a chair. By the time he sat, he was all grins and amusement.

That was just Kale's way. He had the ability to find the good in the moment, something light and easy and fun, even on a day like today.

"Did you start shit with one of those big fuckers and now you're scared?" He wasn't so discrete when he pointed at a couple of guys who looked like they'd probably rolled up on bikes and had rap sheets a few miles long. "Don't tell me I'm going to have to step in and protect you."

Leave it to Kale.

But that sure as hell wasn't what had me on edge.

I shifted a bit so Rynna was off to my side and not directly in front of me, situating myself in a way that let me pretend she wasn't there.

Pretended I couldn't feel the heat radiating from that tight body.

Pretended that feeling didn't exist. The one that left me restless.

Edgy.

Hungry for something I couldn't quite put my finger on.

I shot him a glare. "You wish, asshole. If anyone needs protecting, it's you, standing around looking like a pretty boy. You're just begging to get your ass kicked."

He cracked up.

"Hey, someone wants to kick my ass? It's only because they wish they were me. All the ladies love me."

He smirked, slinging back a gulp of the dark liquid dancing in the rocks glass he clutched in his hand. Kale was the cockiest asshole around. It was a total mindfuck he still managed to have the biggest heart of them all.

Sitting there, people had to think he'd stumbled to the wrong table. There I was, looking like I belonged with the guys he was just referring to while he was all sharp angles and crisp lines, clean-shaven, his blond hair slicked back, and his button-up and pants perfectly pressed.

"Take it you're not on call this weekend?"

He rocked back with a big, satisfied sigh. "Nope. I've got the whole weekend off. Don't have to be back until Sunday night. It's like a goddamned Christmas miracle right smack dab in the middle of summer." He hefted a shoulder. "Besides, figured Ollie might need me, too, so I asked for it off. Somehow it was approved."

I nodded, understanding, trying not to let myself get dragged right back into the somber mood from back in the office, knowing neither Ollie nor Kale needed that shit. Dwelling wasn't going to change a goddamned thing.

"So, how's my Frankie-girl?" Kale asked, quick to change the subject.

The smile on my face was instant. "Good. Started taking ballet. Cutest damned thing I've ever seen."

"No shit?" He shook his head. "She's getting so big. Time flies, doesn't it? Seems like only yesterday she was learning to walk."

I roughed a hand through my hair. "Yeah. Goes by too damned fast. Blows my mind she only has another year before she starts kindergarten."

He pointed at me with the same hand wrapped around his rocks glass, laughter falling out around his words. "School . . . dude . . . you are so fucked. If I think you're overprotective now . . ."

I wiped the sweat that was suddenly beading on my brow. Honestly wasn't sure how I was going to handle that. Someone else being responsible for her care. The fact that I might not know exactly where she was at all times and who she was with.

I stomped down those thoughts, refusing to give them voice, and started to tell him about her bitch of an instructor, figuring he'd get a kick out of it.

That was right when I felt the air thicken.

I rubbed at the back of my neck, fighting it.

The shock of awareness that sliced through the darkened bar.

Tense and tight and hot.

It was a bitch knowing its origin and not being able to do a goddamned thing about it.

I barely cut my gaze to the side and peered through the dimmed lights. A smoky glow hugged the room, and my eyes climbed right back to the spot they shouldn't. I was nothing but a glutton for punishment, because there I was, desperate for a glimpse.

Still, I was unprepared. Unprepared for the way my skin itched when I caught her stealing a glance at me at the same time I was stealing one of her.

Quick and furtive.

Like she'd just realized I was there.

"Kid really is so damned adorable, don't know how you stand it." Kale was rambling, musing about the sweetness of my daughter and how my life had turned out totally different from what I'd ever expected it to. I sat there, shifting uneasily in my seat like a fool, letting myself feel something that had no reason to be there.

Lust for a woman I didn't even know.

Kale was bringing his glass to his lips when he suddenly let it drop a fraction, studying me from over the top. "What the hell is going on with you, man?"

"Nothin'."

"You seem . . . anxious." One quirk of a knowing brow. That was the pitfalls of having friends for life. Sometimes they knew you better than you wanted them to.

Because this was obviously not about the anniversary.

Still, I shrugged. "Nothing at all."

Doubt billowed through his expression, and another rush of disquiet had me shifting again. His eyes flicked off to my side before he looked back at me like he'd hit a bull's-eye. "Nothing, huh? Then why do you keep glaring at Lillith and Nikki like they've all of a sudden grown horns? I mean, it's no secret you've up and decided women are the devil, but those two you at least seem to tolerate. What happened?"

I pasted what I hoped appeared to be a look of indifference on my face. "Don't know what you're talking about. Nothing happened."

His brow drew tight, and he peered in their direction again, studying what had changed. Then he was cocking his head to the side with a knowing grin. "Who's the hot new chic? Doesn't look like she's from around here."

Another shrug. "Dunno."

Apparently, that shrug was the indicator of a lie, because Kale laughed. Far too loud and at my expense. "Oh, I see what's happening here. Seems someone actually is still in the possession of his dick."

"Don't." The warning came out hard. Nothing playful about it.

He knew better.

He shook his head. "That bitch sure as hell did a number on you, didn't she? You think it's a good thing for Frankie to grow up with you hating every woman who crosses your path? That shit's not healthy, man. You need to figure out your issues before you mess up your daughter's head with that chip you love to wear on your shoulder."

Yeah. That stung. My hand clenched around my beer bottle. "You're really going to sit over there and tell me I'm raising my kid wrong?"

He scowled. "Isn't that what friends are for? To call you out when you aren't seeing straight? Because it's time you realized your vision is completely skewed. It's been three years. And fuck, man, you know you're a great dad, but don't sit over there and act like there's not something missing."

He rocked back in his chair, arms going across his chest, like he was offering up a dare. "When's the last time you got laid?"

Ollie took that opportune time to show up at our table with a fresh round of drinks. He placed the rocks glass down in front of Kale before he slid an icy bottle my direction.

Ollie forced a smile, dude wearing his own special kind of veneer, shoving all the bullshit down, locked up and contained. "Pretty sure this one's cock has shriveled up and died. It's a sad, sad state of affairs."

My brow rose. "Thanks, man," I said, totally dry.

"Hey, just keeping it real," he said, giving me a clap to the back.

Taking a swig of my beer, I shook my head. "Why don't you keep it 'real' with someone else?"

A smirk pulled beneath his beard. "Now, what would be the fun in that?"

Kale leaned forward. "Seriously, man. Think about what you're doing. The vibe you're feeding and how that affects not just Frankie but you, too. You can sit there and pretend all you want, but I know you're lonely."

I swallowed around the lump, doing my best not to look Rynna's direction.

Call me a failure.

Because my gaze was slanting that way, drinking her in.

Fuck, I was a fool.

The way I welcomed the bolt of need that slammed me.

It was so goddamned wrong. But this unwanted feeling bubbled up inside me, latching on to the sight of her laughing from across the room. The way her chin lifted and her mouth curved. Something so free.

A quality that didn't belong to me.

In discomfort, I looked back at Kale. "Believe me. Frankie's the only girl I need."

My everything.

The one I lived for.

The one I'd gladly die for.

And I'd never give anyone the chance to threaten that.

Seven

Rynna

"Who do you keep looking at?" Nikki swiveled on her stool, straining to look behind her. Muted light cast a shimmery drape of warmth over the bar, tossing it with shadows and mystery.

But one man stood out amid it all. And he was looking right back at us.

I smacked her leg, my voice a panicked whisper. "What are you doing?"

She had no shame.

She looked at me as if I were crazy. "Um . . . trying to figure out which lucky bastard has already snagged my new friend's eye. That's my job, you know. I'm head matchmaker, right, Lily Pad?"

She smirked in Lillith's direction.

Lillith just wagged her ring finger adorned with the huge rock as proof while she took a sip of her wine.

"No one's caught my eye," I said.

Honestly, it was a useless defense. Not with the way I couldn't stop from stealing another glance at the man who was beginning to consume my every thought. I wasn't one prone to obsessions. Or stalking. Or spying.

But there was something about him that wouldn't let me go.

Something that fascinated and enthralled.

Maybe it was his adorable daughter.

It had to be. It was the only explanation.

Nikki followed my gaze. She froze for a beat before her head whipped back in my direction. Her mouth hung open in blatant shock. "Oh my God! Tell me Rex Gunner isn't the one who has you all spun up over there?"

Before I could give her another futile excuse, awareness dawned on her face. "Holy shit. He lives right across from you." She rapidly snapped her fingers in front of my face as if she were on to something. "Oh, and his company has the contract for the hotel that's on Fairview . . . right across from Pepper's Pies."

My shoulder lifted as if I didn't care at all. As if he didn't actually have me so spun up I could feel the knots lining my stomach. "I went over and introduced myself to him the other day. That's it."

I conveniently left out the part where he'd slammed his door in my face. I figured guilt was found in the small details.

The ironic laughter dripping from Lillith's tongue sounded like a warning. "You should probably leave it at that. The only women Rex Gunner likes are his daughter and his momma. Otherwise, watch out. That boy is as cynical as they come."

I glanced his way again, snared by the way his throat was exposed when he tipped back his beer, the way the thick muscles rolled as he swallowed, that short, trimmed beard little more than a five o'clock shadow.

God, he was gorgeous in an earth-shattering way. As if I could feel the vibrations coming from him rippling under my feet.

I edged forward, my voice quieted to a whisper, way too eager for my own good. "What happened to him?"

Lillith and Nikki shared a look.

Nikki leaned forward, dropping her tone to match mine. "His wife just . . . disappeared. No one knows for sure what happened to her."

Was it fear that flashed through my blood? The man screamed danger and peril and risk. But my heart told me for an entirely different reason than the flicker of morbid intrigue that tickled my consciousness. Still, my eyes were round as I leaned even closer to her. "Like . . . do people think she's . . . dead?"

Nikki howled with laughter and sat back, smacking her knee, obviously thrilled I'd followed her into that trap. "Ha! He probably wishes she was. My guess is she's just a selfish bitch who walked out when taking care of a baby became too much. Not that anyone knows since he doesn't talk about her, but I was never a fan."

She shrugged and took a sip of her cosmo.

Case closed.

"Not about her or about anything really," Lillith added, back to waving a caution flag. "I've known him since we were kids. We went to school together on the other side of town with Ollie and Kale. The three of them have had some horrible stuff happen in their lives. It affected them, shaped who they became. But Rex? He changed after his wife left. Don't get me wrong, he's a great guy. Honest. An incredibly hard worker. He grew his small construction company into the most successful contractor in the area. Loyal to the bone, and there's no doubt he loves that little girl. But I'm pretty sure his bitterness has seeped all the way to the marrow."

That sense I'd been feeling grew stronger. The need to look deeper inside the man who'd built a fortress around himself. Needing to protect himself from the pain so clearly etched in his eyes.

Mournful eyes I could feel continually flashing my direction.

Scorching me deeper with each hidden pass.

Nikki laughed. "You should see your face right now. Girl, you're in so much trouble. It looks to me like you're taking that warning as some kind of invitation. I told you I was the queen matchmaker, but I don't think even I'm that good."

Lillith almost rolled her eyes. "This from the girl who's been trying to get Ollie to look her way for the last five years."

"Hey! Sometimes these things take time. I'm a patient woman."

Her attention jerked toward a man who came out from the back of the bar.

"He's back. Look, there he is. That's who I was telling you about. That's my Ollie," Nikki raved not so quietly as she slapped my thigh a bunch of times to get my attention.

With the way she shivered at the sight of him, I would say her patience was wearing thin. I understood her fascination.

Ollie was rough and hard and incredibly good-looking. As good-looking as the other straightlaced guy who sat on the other side of the table from Rex.

There had to be something in the water, because both of them were almost as beautiful as the man who'd taken my thoughts hostage.

Almost.

But there was something about Rex that completely set him apart. Something that made him shine in all his surly darkness. Something that twisted my belly into a mess of anxiousness, attraction, and intrigue.

This prodding force that insisted I get to know someone who seemed desperate to remain unseen.

Nikki sighed when Ollie grabbed a couple drinks from behind the bar and carried them to Rex's table. "God, I love him."

With a sip of her wine, Lillith shook her head. "I'm beginning to think you're just infatuated with what you can't have."

Nikki blinked at her. "Isn't that the same thing?"

A tumble of laughter rolled from Lillith. "Not even close."

Nikki's gaze trailed back after Ollie. Not even trying to hide her stare when he rounded back behind the bar to help the other bartender. "For real . . . love or not, I would eat up that man."

I giggled quietly. On the drive over, I'd worried I had made the wrong choice. Worried I'd be continually looking over my shoulder. Wondering who might recognize me. If there would be rumbles and whispers and rumors.

But I hadn't felt it. Not for a second. I loved that these two had invited me out. That they were happy to make me feel a part of their tight-knit world.

That they seemed to have no qualms about welcoming me into it.

I startled when a tall figure suddenly cast a shadow over us. I looked up to find a man towering at my side, his brown eyes raking me up and down, a grin riding his full lips.

I would have shrank away if I hadn't been one-hundred percent sure I'd never seen him before.

Apparently, there really was something in the water.

He was ridiculously attractive. Clearly, he'd discarded the jacket of his dark gray suit, the sleeves of his button-down rolled up his forearms. His stance was so casual and confident as he looked expectantly at me.

"I just noticed you sitting over here, and I thought I could buy you a drink," he said, his attention fully trained on me. "Name's Tim."

Nikki cleared her throat, the words ripe with mock offense. "I do hope that drink buying includes the rest of us."

He glanced at her. "If that's what it takes."

Tim was a little cocky for my taste.

And he wasn't Rex Gunner.

I lifted my margarita toward him, the green yummy goodness swishing in the salt-rimmed bowl. "I think I'm just fine. But thank you."

"You sure about that? You look awful lonely over here by yourself."

Irritation bristled beneath my skin. I was sitting there with my friends. How the hell could I appear lonely? But I was used to these kinds of pick-up lines in San Francisco when Macy dragged me out with her.

So I pasted on a fake smile and said, "I'm sure."

The guy shrugged. "Whatever. Your loss."

He turned on his heel and sauntered away.

"What an asshole," I mumbled under my breath, my eyes trailing him with a special kind of disgust.

Nikki jerked my attention back to her by swatting me on the knee and lifting her spent glass. "Speak for yourself, Ryn-Ryn. I totally could have used another drink."

I laughed. "At what expense?"

She widened her blue eyes. "Oh, come on. Take one for the team."

Giggling, I dabbed at the trickle of margarita clinging to the edge of my lip. "He might not be bad to look at, but he was kind of a jerk. No thank you."

Nikki nudged Lillith with her elbow. "Yet, she likes Rex Gunner."

Lillith grinned before her expression shifted, swelling with soft affection. "I guess we like what we like. Broderick was definitely an asshole of the worst kind when I first met him."

I made the mistake of letting my attention wander back to Rex. Ollie was back at his table, and he and the other guy were engaged in their own conversation.

Rex seemed totally removed from it.

Just sitting there.

Glaring at me.

Unabashedly with intense, heated hatred.

"Maybe there's hope for everyone," I mumbled.

Tearing my gaze from him, I pushed to my feet, cleared my throat, and pasted a smile on my face. "I need to use the restroom."

Lillith gestured toward the hall to the right of the stairs. "Down the hall and on the left."

"Thanks."

I wound through the crowds huddled around the high-top tables. Voices were lifted to be heard above the hum of the band, laughter loud as people let go of the stresses of the week, embracing the chance they had to unwind.

I took the hall and ducked into the restroom, used it, and then washed my hands. I let a small smile lift the corner of my mouth.

Being there felt so right, even if Rex Gunner was messing with my head.

I dried my hands, swung open the door, and stepped out into the haze of the dimly lit hall. I gasped when the same guy who'd approached me at the bar stepped out in front of me, stopping me in my tracks.

"Hey," I said uneasily, peering behind him at the people loitering at the far end of the hall. The noise level had escalated to a dull roar, the mood becoming rowdy, increasing with every second that passed.

I shifted anxiously on my feet, wondering if anyone would even hear me if I called for help.

Okay.

So maybe I was getting ahead of myself.

But getting backed into a corner by a guy I didn't know wasn't high on my list of safest situations. Not when a shiver of apprehension skated down my spine. A cold warning.

"Finally got you alone," he said.

I took a single step back and to the side, trying to put space between us. "If you'll excuse me, I was actually headed back to my friends."

He reached out, running the tip of his index finger down the side of my cheek. "You should ditch them and spend a little time with me."

Nausea turned my stomach. "I'm really not interested."

He inched forward. "No?"

"No." The word shot from my mouth.

I was so absolutely not interested. But this guy didn't seem to be able to take a hint.

"I think you're lying. I think you're really interested and you just don't want to look like a slut in front of your friends. Let's get out of here. I won't tell anyone."

What the fuck?

This guy was ridiculous. I took it all back. Any appeal he had was obliterated by his foul, offensive character.

I scoffed out a laugh. "And I think you're a total prick who can't seem to comprehend the fact I'd rather gouge my eye out with a fork than spend the night with you."

Anger flashed across his face, and he jolted forward, making me stumble back.

So maybe that was the wrong thing to do. Inciting this jerk. It was a risk. Some guys needed someone to knock them over the head before they got it and there were some who never understood the meaning of no. Apparently, he was the latter.

"Ah. Playing hard to get. I like it."

"I'm not playing, Tim." This time, the words trembled with a tiny spurt of fear. "I mean it. Just . . . leave me alone."

He slipped forward another inch, backing me the rest of the way into the wall. "See? You even remembered my name. Stop playing coy."

"She said she wasn't interested." The voice that rumbled in the hallway was rough. Low and dangerous.

My skin shivered for entirely different reasons.

Tim swung around to look over his shoulder, still keeping his body angled so I was backed against the wall but allowing me to see farther down the hall.

Rex was there. Fists clenched. Jaw rigid. Anger radiated from him in shocking waves. Those sage eyes glinted with hate as his lean, sinewy muscles twitched with restraint.

I just didn't know which of us he hated most.

It didn't matter.

I sucked in a breath of relief, succumbing to a feeling of safety so staggering it weakened my knees.

Tim clung to that sleazy cockiness. "Think you should turn around and mind your own fucking business."

"And I'd suggest you back the fuck away before you don't have the chance to walk out of here." It was nothing less than a growl.

Aggression ricocheted between the two of them. Growing and spinning and spiking.

Finally, Tim cracked a flippant, arrogant grin. Though, I could have sworn I saw his quake of fear. The realization that he didn't have a fighting chance.

Rex Gunner would beat him bloody.

He stepped away from me. "Whatever, man. You want her, have her. She's not worth the effort."

I sagged forward, dragging a bunch of cleansing breaths into my too-tight lungs.

Rex glowered at him, never breaking his menacing stare when Tim angled his shoulders to the side to slip past him, his pace increasing the second he was on the other side of Rex's raging hostility.

He disappeared at the end of the hall, and I pushed my bangs back from my forehead, which was sweaty and slick with the adrenaline.

"You okay?" Rex asked, voice still shaky and rough.

I nodded. "Yeah . . . he was . . ." I trailed off, forcing myself to stand straight. "Rex. Thank you. I—"

He cut me off with harsh, cold words. "You should go home before you get yourself into any more trouble."

Then he turned around and stalked away.

I stood there, staring after him, wondering what in the hell had just happened. Finally, I shook myself out of it, feet prodding down the hall. At the end of it, I searched the crowded room until my gaze latched on to the back of the man as he wound through the throng toward the bar.

For a beat, I contemplated, wondering if it was even worth it. Putting myself out there when he seemed to shut me down at every turn.

It didn't take long to come to the conclusion.

I followed the same path, angling through the bodies that seemed to grow thicker with each moment that passed.

I came to a stop behind him. He had gone straight for the bar, arms rested on top of it, gesturing with his chin to Ollie. Ollie only gestured back, as if they spoke some sort of secret language, a fresh beer gliding across the shiny dark mahogany and landing in Rex's grip.

He brought it to his lips and took a deep pull, that strong throat bobbing again. But there was a new kind of agitation that radiated from the movement.

As if he were upset.

I swallowed down my reservations and sidled up to him, wondering what had possessed me. What made it impossible to turn away from this man I barely even knew.

That intrigue grew greater and greater with each glimpse that took me a little deeper.

He exhaled heavily when he realized I was there, taking another sip without looking my way.

"I said thank you," I reiterated just loud enough to be heard over the din.

He sighed, rubbed his fingertips over those plush lips, and barely cut an eye my direction.

"You're welcome." It was gruff. Reluctant.

"Am I?" I challenged.

He coughed out a laugh with a quick shake of his head before he looked at me for a moment. Seriously. Genuinely. "Yeah, you are. Would have preferred to take the fucker out, honestly."

"Then why are you so pissed at me?"

He sighed again, this time as he scrubbed a hand over his face as he looked straight ahead. "It's just . . . let's just say today's not the best of days."

"What happened?"

He flinched, and his trembling hand ran over his short beard. "Some things are better left unsaid, Rynna Dayne. Only thing dragging history out into the open does is remind you just how fucking bad it sucks that there's not a damned thing in the world you can do to change it."

I studied him, trying to make sense of what he said, realizing it was a locked door I had no chance of getting through. Instead, I hiked myself up onto the stool.

Ollie's eyes went wide when he approached, his attention flicking between the two of us as if he were shocked Rex might actually be talking to me.

"What can I get you?" Ollie asked.

"A margarita would be nice."

Rex and I sat in silence for a few moments, saying nothing while Ollie mixed my drink and placed it in front of me. "Thank you," I said, taking a sip before I chanced a peek at Rex.

At his profile.

At his nose and his lips and his jaw.

Shivers rolled and those butterflies swarmed.

"Your daughter is adorable."

A smile flickered on his lush mouth. "Yeah . . . she's a handful."

His words were pure adoration, and for the first time, Rex dropped his shield.

As if just the mention of her had the power to send it tumbling down.

So maybe I melted a little.

"I'd venture that kind of handful is the best kind."

His chuckle was slow. "Sometimes I wonder how I handle that little hurricane. Barely can keep up most days." Even though it came out playful, there was an undercurrent of sadness. A suggestion of fear.

I nodded before we both turned away, facing forward and sipping from our drinks. It was as if we both needed a breather, a moment to sort through whatever was happening between us.

It felt like maybe in the silence, we were calling a truce.

The band playing at the small stage behind us at the other end of the bar moved into another song. I'd barely been paying attention to them all night, the songs only a backdrop to the vibe, the band members just as trendy as the bar itself.

But this . . .

This was a song I knew so well.

They were singing a haunting cover of "Awake My Soul" by Mumford & Sons.

Slower and quieter than the original.

The lyrics were full of longing and heartache.

Mournful and somehow hopeful.

I sipped my drink, getting lost in the feel. In the comfort of the soft, scratchy voice of the singer, in the startling warmth that radiated from Rex.

My grandmother's face flitted through my eyes, her belief a whisper in my ear.

My teeth caught on my bottom lip when I turned to find him watching me.

Intently.

Something fervent rose between us. Alive and potent. It sent my nerves spiraling free.

He took a slow pull of his beer, his words measured. Careful. "I'm really sorry about your grandmother, Rynna. She was a really good woman." Sadness flashed through his expression. "Don't know of anything worse than losing someone you love."

Emotion thickened my throat, stunned by his sudden care and swimming in the stark loss. "I feel like I lost her a long time ago."

The admission was strangled, ripped from my chest as if I couldn't keep it in for a second longer.

That stunning gaze searched my face through the shadows. "Had it been a long time since you saw her?"

There was no accusation behind it. Just honest curiosity.

"Yeah."

"Why'd you stay away so long?"

I choked out an uncertain laugh. "Because I wasn't brave enough."

He frowned. "You seem awful brave to me."

My head shook. "No. I'm not brave. Or maybe I just wasn't brave soon enough."

The lyrics lifted in the atmosphere, words about life and death and the impermanency of our bodies. I swore I saw Rex's spine go rigid.

I touched his arm, unable to stop myself. My skin lit up at the contact. He stared at it before he jerked away and pushed from the bar.

Shocked, I spun around.

His chest heaved and he looked . . . panicked.

"Rex—"

He roughed a hand over his face, cutting off whatever connection we'd shared. "I've got to get out of here."

Then he turned, stalked through the crowd, shoved open the door, and disappeared into the night.

Leaving me sitting there staring at the vacancy he'd left behind, wondering exactly what I'd done wrong.

Rex

was agitated.

Pissed and confused.

A disorder trembling me to the bone.

As hard as I tried, there was no corralling it. No shaking the bristling anger that had followed me through all of last night and into this morning.

It was a blinding fury that had taken to my veins when I'd found her backed into a corner by that piece of shit.

Hell. It'd been ignited the second I'd looked up from the table and saw him talking to her.

I didn't even know her, and she sure as hell wasn't mine, but I couldn't stomach the idea of her leaving with him. Of her going back to his place or maybe him going to hers.

The vision of him following her up her stairs had made me want to claw my eyes out. Two of them falling into her bed.

It was no surprise he turned out to be a pussy-bitch pretty boy who had the misconception he had the right to reach out and take whatever he wanted whether someone wanted to give it or not.

Would have relished in teaching him the lesson.

Enlightening the fucker on what it meant to show a little respect.

But that was the problem when someone affected you. The problem when someone got under your skin. When someone made you start entertaining all kinds of foolish ideas. Ideas of stepping up and getting involved in matters that were none of your concern.

Treading a line you had no business walking.

That fact had never been as striking as when she'd reached out and touched me at the bar. She was making me want things I couldn't want.

Things I had no fucking right to take.

But it didn't matter.

They'd been there, and I knew I had to get the fuck away before I did something I couldn't take back.

Before I crossed a line I couldn't cross.

I had one priority.

One focus.

A single reason to keep on the straight and narrow.

And that reason was currently hurtling down the walkway.

Brown hair flying and spirit soaring. Grin wide. As bright as the sun that blazed as it climbed the sky behind her.

The second I'd pulled my truck to the curb, she'd bolted out my mom's front door, arms lifted over her head and that sweet voice riding the wind.

"Daddy!"

I hopped out of my truck and went straight for her, scooped her up, and tossed her into the air.

Let her laughter rain down around me. A drenching reminder of what I was living for. I caught her, hugging her close while she tightened her chubby arms around my neck in a death grip. "Daddy! Guess what?"

I pulled back a fraction so I could see her face. "What?"

"Grammy gots me paints, and I painted a tree and a mountain and a squirrel, and now I'm gonna be an artist and take paintin' lessons and be the best dancer in the whole world and Wonder Woman when I goes to the gym with you."

It was then that I spotted the thick smear of white paint across her cheek and the rainbow of splatters on her shirt.

I glanced at my mother, who was grinning like the Cheshire where she leaned against the doorjamb with her arms crossed over her chest.

"Now you're going to be an artist, too, huh?"

"Uh-huh. Grammy said my picture was so, so pretty. You think I could sell it and get so much money and then I can buy a dog? Oh, Daddy, please, I wants a puppy so bad."

I chuckled under my breath because it was the only thing I could do.

"I don't think a puppy is a good idea right now, Frankie Leigh."

"Oh, but, Daddy!" She stuck out her bottom lip before she grinned. "You wants to see my picture?"

I laughed. "Nothing I'd like better than to see that picture."

Wasn't lying last night. The child was a handful. A whirlwind that spun from one idea to the next without giving me time to process the first.

Sweet to the brim.

Most likely because all those dreams and ideas were gushing out from the inside.

I arched a brow at my mom as we approached. "So, we're painting again?"

Taking the single step up to the door, I dropped a kiss to Mom's cheek.

Her smile grew. "Oh, yes. We are definitely painting again. We had a blast, didn't we, Frankie Leigh?"

"So, so, SO much fun. Can I spend the night here every night?"

I feigned offense. "And you're going to leave your daddy all by his lonesome every night."

Frankie's horror was real. "Oh, no, Daddy. You can spends the night here, too. Right, Grammy?"

"Oh, Sweet Pea Frankie Leigh, I think your daddy might be too old for sleepovers. Unless he finally decides to start participating in the right kind. You know, of the *adult* variety."

The last she mumbled under her breath, and the woman had the nerve to shoot me a wink.

Mom had just turned fifty-two and was about as pretty as they came. The years had been good to her, and her spirit was as free as Frankie's.

"Sly, Ma. Real sly."

She laughed. "Oh, everyone needs a little push in the right direction every now and again. Speaking of, how was last night?"

I shrugged. "Uneventful."

That felt like a bold-faced lie.

But the last thing I needed to do was mention Rynna moving in across the street. Mom would hop on that so fast that I'd never hear the end of it.

I set Frankie back on her feet, scooting her in the direction of her room. "Go get your stuff, Sweet Pea."

She took off down the hall, and I straightened and looked at my mom. Obviously, she was dying for any juicy details she could get.

"Met Ollie and Kale for a couple of drinks then called it a night," I told her.

A long, restless night.

A pucker formed on Mom's lips. "You're no fun. Here I am, nice enough to have your daughter over for the entire night, and you don't even do me the service of having a wild night on the town. You know I'll be having one tonight."

Amusement shook my head. "You really are a terrible influence. I think I'm going to have to rethink these sleepovers."

She pressed a hand over her heart. "You wouldn't dare."

"Don't test me." It was purely a tease.

Everything about her softened. "How are my boys?"

A smile ticked up at the corner of my mouth. "Good. Kale has the weekend off, so I'm sure he's off making up for any fun I'm not having. Ollie is . . . it was twelve years yesterday."

A soft puff of air blew from her mouth. "Oh . . . I didn't even realize.

How is he doing?"

"As well as can be expected, I guess."

Or maybe worse than could be expected. I didn't fucking know.

God knew that it still ate me alive.

A beat of silence hovered in the atmosphere, that same sadness that was always there, lurking in the background, before Frankie broke it. She came bursting back into the living room with her backpack bouncing on her shoulders, a poster board in one hand and her doll clutched to her chest with the other.

"Look it, Daddy."

Proudly, Frankie lifted her painting that was nothing but thick swashes of color.

"That's beautiful, Sweet Pea."

"What are we gonna do today?" she dove right in. "You wants to go swimming?"

I swung her into my arms. "Is that what you want to do? Go to the lake?"

She grinned that grin. The one that knocked all the foolishness free and the sense back into me. My heart heavy and full.

Devoted.

"Yes!"

I ruffled a hand through her rebellious hair. "Then, it sounds like we're going to the lake."

My headlights cut through the emerging night.

Twilight was at its deepest, the entire earth cast in that shadowy blue that stifled the air in the moments just before the night fully took hold of the day.

Frankie and I had spent the entire day at the lake, playing in the water, hiking, building a fire, and grilling the burgers I'd picked up before we'd taken the twenty-minute drive out to our favorite spot. The lake calm, the beach secluded, the sky cloudless.

It'd been the perfect kind of afternoon.

That same twenty-minute drive home had rocked Frankie to sleep in the back of the truck, her little head bobbing to one side where she dozed in her car seat.

I pulled my truck into the driveway at the side of the house and killed the engine before going directly for Frankie, unbuckling her and then lifting her into my arms.

She felt so small and light like this, when all that energy had finally drained and she was just the tiny little thing that had been given into my care. The one who needed me to protect and shield her. Her shelter and her harbor.

I angled her to the side so I could slide the key into the lock and let us into the stillness of the small house that I did my very best to make a home. Half the time it felt like I didn't have a single clue what the fuck I was doing, but I got up every single morning and did it anyway.

Frankie barely stirred when I laid her on her twin bed and tugged the flip-flops from her feet, changed her into her pajamas, and tucked her under the cool sheet. Her head was on her pillow, those wild, tangled locks all around her. I brushed them back from her face, gazing down at her and wondering how something so good could come out of a situation that was so utterly fucked.

Wondering if she was my blessing.

My reprieve.

Or if the insane worry that constantly roiled inside me was another element of the curse that would haunt me for the rest of my days.

Pushing it down in the depths of my spirit, I leaned down and pressed a gentle kiss to her forehead, silently promising her it didn't make a difference either way.

That it didn't change my devotion to her.

This mad kind of love that took up every cell in my body. It came into existence the first time I'd held her in my arms.

Sparked to life that cold winter night.

A permanent flame.

One I'd thought had been forever dimmed.

On a sigh, I pushed to my feet and shuffled from her room, leaving the door open a crack and a light on in the hall in case she needed me. I headed into the kitchen, pulled a cold beer from the fridge, and popped the cap.

I took a swig as I peered out the kitchen window. It was the exact same picture that'd been there since the day I'd moved in. Though, I doubted I could ever consider the view the same.

nine

Rynna

The oven buzzed.

My nerves went haywire, shooting into overdrive as I grabbed the mitts and pulled the pie from the oven. The sweet, decadent scent spilled into the kitchen and basked it in a homey warmth.

"Perfect," I murmured beneath my breath, my chest filling with pride and something wistful as I took in the way the crust, which I had made from scratch, had baked to a golden brown. The sugar I'd sprinkled on top had caramelized to perfection, and piping hot cherries bubbled up through the hole in the middle.

I had the fleeting thought that this was the easy part. Baking something to perfection. It was the changing of minds that was difficult. Drawing people to what you had to offer and convincing them it was exactly what they needed.

So help me God, Rex Gunner was going to be my first customer.

And we weren't talking dollars and cents.

We were talking trust and camaraderie.

Friendship.

If I were being honest, I would admit I might envision more. Admit there was something about him and his little girl that called to me. Awakening that place in me that I'd shored away, a place that had always wanted the simple things in life.

Simple is better.

How many times had my grandmother told me that very thing as she worked her recipes that always related so easily to life?

At the very least, I was seeking a truce in this cold war Rex seemed intent to wage against me when I'd committed no offense or crime.

I let the pie cool for a few minutes before I gathered my courage and slipped on my shoes. I stepped out into the breaking night. Once again, I was struck with the overpowering sense of comfort.

The scent of the fragrant honeysuckle. The sound of the bugs that trilled in the bushes. The towering trees blowing in the whispering breeze.

Home.

That same small window that gave a direct view into Rex's house was lit. I could see him sitting by himself at a small table somewhere to the back of the kitchen area, continually raking a hand through his hair as he nursed at a beer.

He appeared so utterly alone even though I'd seen him return home with his daughter about forty-five minutes ago.

My spying no longer gave me the sense of violating his privacy.

It felt like a mission.

That it held a purpose for his greater good. Or maybe his little girl's. I didn't know.

I just knew there was absolutely nothing I could do but stand at his door with a peace offering.

A thank you.

Balancing the gooey pie in both hands, I nudged at the door with my elbow. My heart sped when I heard the scraping of chair legs against the floor and the rustling within the house, my blood becoming a thunder that rushed through my veins.

Then I sensed the pause. The presence that was so clearly right on the other side of the door, that severity hot as it blazed through the wood.

There might as well have been no separation between us.

Because I could feel him. The conflict and reluctance.

God, why did he have this kind of effect on me?

It only grew when I felt the resignation, heard the slow slide of metal and the creak of hinges as he barely cracked open the door, only a single wary eye visible. "What are you doing here, Rynna?"

I lifted my hands so he could see what I was holding. "I baked you a pie."

Exasperation bled into his tone as he opened the door a bit wider. "Why did you do that?"

"Because it's a neighborly thing to do." It almost came across as irritated. But then I was taken back to the way he'd stepped into the line of fire for me. The way he'd talked to me at the bar. Openly. As if he wanted to let me in but he didn't know how or if he could. The way he'd taken off as if I had suddenly become a danger to him.

My voice deepened with sincerity. "You saved me last night, Rex, I wanted to properly thank you."

"It's not necessary," he said, words gruff. If it weren't for that flash in the depths of those eyes, I would have bought the act.

"I just—"

"Please . . . leave us alone, Rynna." It was a plea.

He started to shut the door in my face again, but he winced, freezing when the sweet, excited voice broke through the aversion. "Ms. Dayne? What'cha doin' here?"

She rubbed her tiny fists in her bleary eyes. The little girl took the definition of bedhead to a whole new level.

Rex cringed, his lips pursing and that throat that kept making me lose my train of thought bobbing heavily. An edge of defensiveness threaded into his words. "We were at the lake all day . . . she didn't get her bath before she fell asleep."

"I not tired anymore, Daddy," she said, shaking her head as if she were shaking off even the idea of going back to bed.

"It's late, Frankie Leigh."

She totally ignored her dad, her smile so wide when she shot forward and wrapped her tiny arms around his thigh before gazing up at me. "What do you gots? Is that a Pepper Pie? Oh, yummy." She jumped in place and tugged at her dad's shirt. "Daddy, she gots a Pepper Pie! Is that for me?"

At least someone appreciated my efforts.

I smiled down at her. "It is for you. But it's super hot right now, so you'll have to wait until tomorrow to have a piece so you don't burn yourself. That's if your daddy says it's okay. And be sure to save a piece for him in case he wants one. Deal?"

"Deal!" She blinked at me. "I want a puppy!"

I subtly shifted the brunt of the weight of the pie from one hand to the other, the scalding temperature making its way into the mitts. "You do?"

"Uh-huh. But Daddy said it's not a good idea rights now. Do you gots any good ideas?"

"Um . . . I'm not sure." Light laughter slipped free, her sweetness tugging at my chest. Maybe there was such a thing as too adorable. Because right then, I'd probably give her anything she asked me for.

I shifted the mitts again, and Rex sighed.

"Is that hot?" His teeth gritted when he asked it. As if he were dreading my answer. As if he didn't want to be concerned but couldn't stop himself.

I shifted it again. "A little bit."

He looked to the ground, issuing a soft curse beneath his breath, the word only ringing in my ear because I was able to read it on the movement of his soft, full lips. On a resigned sigh, he stepped back and widened the door the rest of the way. "Come in . . . set it on the kitchen counter."

With the way he cringed, I'd have thought the invitation caused him physical pain.

I whispered, "Thank you," and slipped inside, my body grazing his when I passed.

A tiny gasped breached my lips. The heat on my hands was nothing compared to the heat that scorched my skin.

Attraction swept me head to toe.

It was possibly the most foolish emotion I'd ever felt.

Because it was unfathomable.

Overwhelming.

Too much.

Sucking in a breath, I forced myself to step the rest of the way inside.

My jaw dropped in awe. "Wow."

The interior of their house was totally not what I'd expected. I'd expected something closer to my grandmother's house. A quaint, comfortable home that could use a fresh coat of paint among a million other things.

Shabby and totally missing the chic.

Rex's place had been entirely renovated. The floors were a gorgeous, shiny wood, and the white crown molding lining the ceilings matched the mantel and hearth of the fireplace, which was the focal point of the living room. A big television hung on the wall above, and a brown leather sectional sat in the middle of the room.

And the kitchen.

Good God.

The kitchen.

It was a dream with its butcher block island, huge oven, and farm-style sink. That small table that was my vantage through the window was nestled in the middle of the two rooms.

"This is unbelievable."

Suddenly, I was remembering Lillith telling me how he'd grown a small construction company into the biggest contractor in the area.

I spun around. "You did this?"

Discomfort rippled across his gorgeous face, something humble and vulnerable showing through the rigid veneer. "It's kind of what I do."

"You definitely do a good job of it." I didn't mean to whisper it, didn't mean to get locked in his stare, didn't mean for my mouth to go dry, or my belly to tumble and twist and flip with the most foolish kind of butterflies.

Because his jaw clenched, and his spine went rigid with my compliment.

Swallowing down the lump in my throat, I forced myself to turn away and take a breath. To get myself together. I set the pie on the counter and turned back around. "I'm sorry to barge in the way I did. I just wanted to say thank you. I really hope you enjoy the pie. I know my grandma would have wanted you to have it."

I started to make my escape, when Frankie snagged my pinky finger in her tiny fist, her voice just as excited as ever. "You wants to see my room?"

My eyes darted to Rex.

That same anger from the first day, the anger I couldn't make sense of, the anger that seemed barely contained, flamed in his eyes. Glints of fire beneath the ornate pendant lights.

I could barely force out the words. "I'm not sure that's a good idea right now. I think it's past your bedtime."

"Oh, oh, I know. You can reads me my bedtime story. How's that sound? You wanna read with me? Can she, Daddy?" She was grinning at her dad, one hundred percent oblivious to the sudden rage I could see crawl just beneath the surface of his tanned skin, the muscles ticking as he stared me down.

"I—"

"Oh, please, please, please."

I looked at Rex for help, already knowing I was so far out of bounds. My mission taking me too deep into enemy territory, and I'd tripped a bomb.

But somehow, he softened when he looked down at her. As if the little hurricane was his calm. "Five minutes, Frankie Leigh, then lights out."

"All right, Daddy. Five minutes," she promised with a resolute nod. She turned and hauled me toward the hall that opened right between the living room and kitchen, just on the other side of the table.

I stumbled along behind her, chancing a glance over my shoulder to look at her father.

Fear.

It was so blatant beneath that hard, rigid, beautiful exterior that it clamped down on my chest, a fist on my heart.

The terror in his expression tore through me like a storm.

Whipping and rending.

I pried my gaze away and followed Frankie into her room, wondering what on earth I'd actually hoped I'd achieve when I'd decided to bake him a pie.

What I knew for sure was this wasn't it. Not that it mattered. That fist on my heart squeezed with soft affection when Frankie turned around and lifted her arms out to her sides.

Pure pride as she offered me all the pink.

"You likes it? My daddy let me helps him paint all the walls, and he took me to the store and let me picks my blankies and my drawers and ever'fing! Did you knows I been painting, and I'm gonna be a painter? My grammy says so."

My gaze traced the walls. Walls that were pink. More than pink. Wisped with the hints of fairy tales and happily ever afters, the faintest outlines of rainbows and unicorns and princesses lost in the strokes of color.

Delicately.

Carefully.

Beautifully.

At the bottom of one wall was a mess of color, choppy strokes and splotches so clearly added by a tiny hand.

Oh my God. Who was this man?

Frankie dropped to her knees in front of a bookcase and pulled free a thin, worn book, waving it in the air. "This one's my favorite."

"*Stellaluna?*" I asked, a small smile ticking up at the corner of my mouth when I saw the adorable bat on the cover, the story totally unfamiliar.

"Uh-huh."

She scrambled onto her bed. "You reads it."

I knelt by the edge of her bed. "Okay."

I opened it and began to read, that lump in my throat growing as I read each page. There was something about the way Frankie listened, quieted and subdued, glued to the words that tumbled from my tongue as I read about a baby bat that'd lost its mother and was raised by a mother bird, only to be reunited with its mother at the end, remaining friends with the birds who'd welcomed it to their nest.

Why did I feel like I might cry when I finished the last page? It was a happy ending, after all. But it was still there, heavy in the air when I looked back at Frankie. She had her sheet pulled up to her chin and was clutching the material. "Did you know I lost my mommy, too?"

She whispered it like a secret.

Like trust.

I guessed that was what I'd come seeking, but I was wholly unprepared for this kind of offering. My hand was trembling when I reached out and lovingly ran my knuckles down the side of her face. "I'm so sorry, Frankie. I lost my mommy when I was little, too."

Her eyes went wide. "You did?"

"Yeah."

Her voice dipped even lower. "Did you finds her?"

"No. I tried to, but I don't think she wanted to be found. But guess what? My grandma loved me so, so much, and she took such good care of me so I didn't have to be sad."

She smiled the sweetest smile, and that fist on my heart squeezed. Squeezed and squeezed so hard it made it difficult to breathe. "My daddy takes good care of me and loves me so, so much."

"He seems like a good daddy."

Vigorously, she nodded.

Leaning forward, I set a soft kiss on her forehead, knowing I had to get out of there before I lost myself any further. "I better go. Five minutes are up, and you need to get to sleep."

"Okay," she whispered, staring up at me, our noses two inches apart.

I smiled, getting drawn deeper into the heart of this little girl before I forced myself to stand. My footsteps slowed as I walked across her room. I flipped off the light and went to pull her door closed, but at the last second, I left it open a crack. Almost instinctively.

Quietly, I edged down the hall, slowed by the turbulent silence bound to the atmosphere.

I pressed my hands to my tremoring belly when I saw Rex standing in the middle of the kitchen. The expression he wore promised he'd overheard the conversation Frankie and I had shared.

Broken, splintered fury.

It poured from him in a torrent of agony.

"I'll just go," I mumbled.

Dropping my head, I started for the door, unsure if I was cowering or if I was just staggered by what I'd unwittingly forced my way into. I felt like a fool. Naïve and reckless. Because I'd come seeking something I hadn't understood.

And I'd just stumbled into the awareness that their lives were pieced together precariously.

Fragilely.

A tender, loving, imperfect balance.

It would only take one misstep to send everything toppling over.

I reached for the latch when I felt the flurry of intensity slide up behind me, the tension suffocating, the movement stealing the air from the room.

I spun around, my back plastered to the door as he approached.

Coming closer and closer.

He wasn't touching me.

But he might as well have been.

He rested a hand on the door above my head, his face dipping toward mine, his words a breathy grunt at my ear. "What the fuck do you think you're doing to me, Rynna?"

Lust and confusion trembled through my bones, this man pushing me away and then drawing me closer.

I thought maybe neither of us could ignore it.

The overpowering attraction.

Because the fever in my veins ignited a fire in my belly.

Torrid.

Blistering.

No words would form on my tongue.

"Tell me, Rynna. What do you want with us?" he murmured, low and rough. "Because I don't have anything to offer you, and I won't let you take anything else from us."

I attempted to process what he said, what he meant.

But I couldn't focus. Couldn't see. Could feel nothing but the heat radiating between us.

Wave after blinding wave.

I gasped a breath, and he inched closer, a single knee wedging between my legs. He planted both hands on the door above my head.

Caging me in.

I felt it when he gave, the strangled sound that left him on a groan when he pressed against me.

The man was so hard.

So big.

So overwhelming.

That bottled heat reached a boiling point. Desire throbbed, lighting up between my thighs.

"Oh . . . God." I whimpered when he rubbed his cock against my hip.

A desperate sound rumbled through the strength of his chest.

A hand was suddenly on my jaw, thumb under my chin, tipping my face up to meet the ferocity in his gaze.

Rage and restraint and desire. I couldn't decipher what was happening. The push and the pull. The hatred and the need.

I could barely speak. "I . . . I thought maybe you could use a friend."

"Told you I already have all the friends I need."

Frustration bled free, my words a quieted plea. "Fine, Rex. You don't need any more friends, but maybe I do. And maybe, just maybe, I don't want to ignore this."

My hand curled in his shirt. The beat of his heart was wild beneath my hold, the energy severe.

A brilliant, neon tether that burned between us.

A live wire.

Electric.

His jaw clenched, and he rocked against my thigh. His fingers sank into my sides, as if he didn't know whether to pull me closer or force me away. "This is wrong, Rynna. You can't do this to me."

"Do what?" I whispered.

"Make me want you."

"Why?"

Pain wrenched his face.

I struggled for the words, finally forcing them into the dense air. "The last thing I want to do is hurt you. You think I don't see it? That you've been hurt enough?"

His thick throat bobbed. "You don't know me, Rynna."

"And that's why I'm here. Because I want to."

Regret seized his expression, and he peeled himself away, putting space between us. "I can't."

My spirit coiled in rejection, and those old insecurities flared. Vying for dominance. I drove them back, refusing their chains. "Because you're afraid or because you don't want me?"

Releasing a jolt of bitter laughter, he raked both hands over his face. "It's a little more complicated than that."

"You can tell me, Rex."

He shook his head. "You should go home. It's getting late."

Disappointment gusted through me. Heavy and oppressive. "Maybe you're just a coward."

He flinched, and I turned away and pulled open the door. I started to step out when his voice hit me from behind.

"You know what it feels like to be left behind, Rynna?" There was a plea behind it.

I slowly turned back to look at him.

His hands were in his jean pockets, surrender on his face, begging me to grasp something he wouldn't allow me to see.

I swallowed down everything I wanted to say and instead gave a slow nod of understanding.

Then I stepped out and quietly latched the door shut behind me.

The second I stepped outside, I was swamped with the clear memories of it. Because all too well, I knew the feeling of being left behind.

Rynna – Five Years Old

Cold gusts of wind whipped through the playground. Laughter floated on its wings from where groups of children ran through the fields, playing in their heavy winter coats.

My head was drooped between my shoulders, my hands close to freezing where I had then wrapped around the metal chains. The tips of my toes barely touched the scooped out dirt, and I dug them in, slowly rocking myself on the swing.

I glanced up as a group of girls raced by.

Laughing.

Giggling.

My chest felt funny and my tummy hurt.

I looked up when a shadow suddenly blocked the sun.

A smile wanted to climb to my mouth, but I didn't know how to make it shine.

"Corinne Paisley," my grandmother said so softly. She knelt down in front of me and covered my freezing hands.

"Gramma."

"Why aren't you playin', child?"

"They don't like me."

She frowned. "What do you mean, they don't like you? You got the invitation. That means the birthday girl wanted you here."

I quieted my voice. "They said I'm too slow."

My grandmother huffed. "Too slow? You're the fastest thing I've ever seen."

I shook my head and clung tighter to the chains. "No, Gramma."

My grandmother brushed her knuckles down my cheek, hooked her index finger under my chin, and forced me to look in her knowing eyes. "Why do you say that?"

That feeling in my tummy was back. It hurt and made me feel like I might throw up.

"I couldn't catch her, Gramma. I couldn't catch Mama. I ran so fast . . . but I couldn't catch her."

My grandmother stood and stretched out her hand. "Come on, child. Let's go home."

ten

Rex

I jerked up to sitting. Darkness played against the walls, my bedroom lit with the faintest hue of the moon streaming in through the crack in the curtains. I blinked away the edge of sleep I'd been riding, shaking off the nightmare that drenched my skin with sweat, glancing at the clock that told me it was just passed three a.m. on Monday morning.

This time . . . this time, it wasn't the dream that'd pulled me from sleep.

I tilted my head and focused on the faint sound that seeped into my room. Crying.

That was all it took for me to throw back my covers and jump to my feet. I flew out my door and through Frankie's, skidding to a stop at the side of her bed.

She wasn't fully awake, just tossing and whimpering in her shallow sleep.

"Shh . . . what's wrong, Sweet Pea?" I urged, voice a whisper as I was reaching for her, brushing back the hair matted to her forehead.

A flash of terror jolted up my spine.

She was hot.

I pressed my palm against her forehead.

Her skin was sticky with sweat.

Shit. She was burning up.

She blinked, her eyes searching for me in the shadows. "I don't feels good, Daddy."

I scooped her into my arms, pressing a bunch of kisses to her temple like the action alone had the power to soothe away any discomfort she might feel. Fighting the panic that churned within me, I carried her into my room, flipped on the light switch, and headed straight for the attached bathroom, flipping that light on, too.

Frankie blinked against the brightness.

"Sorry, Sweet Pea," I muttered, setting her on the counter but keeping one hand on her while I rifled through the medicine cabinet to find the thermometer. "What hurts?" I asked as I fumbled to get the plastic guard on the earpiece.

"Ev'ryfing."

My hands were shaking, and it took me for fucking ever to get the damned thing snapped in place. I forced myself to slow, to be careful as I slipped it into her ear, my heart thundering in my chest as I waited the five seconds for it to beep.

104.3

Fuck.

That panic surged.

That is bad, right?

Truth was, Frankie's health wasn't a gamble I'd ever take.

I gave her a dose of Tylenol then grabbed a washcloth from the linen closet, ran it under cool water, and pressed it to her forehead. I held it there as I picked her back up and carried her out to my bed, laying her on it. "Hang on one sec, Frankie. Daddy's going to make sure you get all better."

She just gave me a trusting nod and curled up on her side, clinging a little tighter to the doll she was always dragging around. I slipped into a tee, jeans, and a pair of shoes, before I had her back in my arms, grabbing my keys and wallet from the entryway table, and rushing her out into the night.

The hour was deep, moon hanging midway on the horizon, peeking out from behind a streak of wispy clouds stretched in front of it. I wrenched open the back door of my truck and got her into her booster seat, buckled her quickly, and jogged around to the front. I slid the key into the ignition and turned it.

The engine cranked but didn't turn over.

"Shit," I muttered under my breath. I pumped the accelerator and tried the ignition again.

A slow dread sank in with the realization.

Fuck.

The cabin lights hadn't illuminated when I'd opened the doors. I glanced up. The overhead light switch was still set to on.

Fuck.

Frankie had asked for the light so she could look at a book when we were driving back from the lake on Saturday night, and I'd forgotten to switch it off. Leave it to my old-as-shit truck. Or just to me.

The battery was dead.

"Shit." I drummed my thumbs on the wheel, calculating just how long it would take me to get the battery charger out of the shed to juice this thing up, when my attention snagged in the rearview mirror.

The sleeping house behind us was bathed in a shallow pool of moonlight, the windows darkened and encased in silence.

The woman probably hated me.

At least she should.

I still couldn't believe the dick move I'd pulled two nights ago, the way I couldn't stop from pressing myself against her, taking a little bit of what I couldn't have.

I knew better.

But I couldn't stop after I had heard what'd gone down in Frankie's room. That quiet understanding that had poured from Rynna, like she might actually have the ability to get what me and Frankie had been through. Like maybe she'd been through some of the same bullshit, too.

Goal had been nothing more than thanking her. But I'd gone and gotten stupid. Had gotten too close. Had touched her because I couldn't stop myself.

Not when I was engulfed with her presence. Cherries and sugar. So goddamned sweet.

None of that mattered right then. The only thing that mattered was Frankie, who was moaning in the backseat, her head bobbing all over the place. Worst was I couldn't tell if she was nodding off to sleep or truly coming in and out of consciousness.

Any loyalty I had didn't come close to touching that.

I hopped out of the truck, wrenched open Frankie's door, and had her back in my arms in the next second. With one arm holding her against me, I grabbed her booster seat and then strode across the vacant street.

There was no hesitation when I bounded up the steps and pounded on Rynna's door.

I stood there, shifting my feet anxiously while I waited, that unease growing tenfold when I saw a light flicker on through an upstairs window. Thirty seconds later, footsteps were shuffling across the floor. I could almost feel her confusion when I sensed her peering out the peephole at us.

But the second she did, there was no delay, and she was tearing open the door.

Concern was written all over that face.

That goddamned striking face that made something inside me light up at the sight of her.

"Oh my God, Frankie Leigh." It was whispered panic pouring from her pretty mouth. "What happened?"

Those java eyes darted to my face.

Worry.

Fear.

I forced down every convoluted feeling I had about her. "She woke up with a fever. My battery's dead in my truck. Need to borrow your car so I can take her to the ER."

"I'll drive you," she said instead of agreeing. The girl was already sliding on a pair of flip-flops that had been sitting by the door.

"That's not—"

She held up a hand, cutting me off the way I had continually done to her. "She's sick, and you're obviously upset." Her tone softened. "I'll drive you. It's not a problem."

The part of me that always needed to prove that I could raise my daughter alone wanted to rear its head and fight her. I bit it back. Focused on the feeling of my daughter in my arms.

Frankie's well-being was my only concern.

"Thank you."

I should absolutely not be accepting this woman's generosity.

Every fucking one of the reasons why surged to the forefront of my mind. Screaming at me why this was wrong. To watch the line I was toeing.

Somehow, I couldn't bring myself to care.

Rynna grabbed her purse and stepped out, still wearing what she'd obviously gone to bed in—a pair of thin cotton striped pants and a black tank.

I dropped my gaze. At least I managed to find the self-control not to watch the sweet sway of her luscious ass.

Guessed it was the little wins.

I followed her to her SUV, situated Frankie into her booster seat in the backseat, and climbed in beside my daughter.

I pretended I couldn't feel the weight of Rynna's worry when she kept glancing through the rearview mirror at us, pretended her concern wasn't there, palpable in the air.

Pretended it didn't mean more to me than it should.

I brushed back Frankie's hair and pressed a kiss to her forehead, feeling the heat radiating off her, praying she was fine. I told myself every kid got sick. It was a part of life. But that didn't mean my guts weren't twisted. It didn't mean the fear wasn't there. It didn't mean that every day of my life I wouldn't be terrified of losing her, too.

eleven

Rynna

The big double doors Rex and Frankie had walked through three hours before swung open for what had to be the millionth time that night. I shot to my feet when this time it was finally Rex carrying out a sleeping Frankie in his arms.

The same blond-haired guy who'd been sitting with Rex at the bar on Friday night followed close behind them, and I had to do a double take when I saw he was wearing a pair of blue scrubs and a stethoscope around his neck.

Even though he still exuded that same uptight, rigid stance, Rex seemed relieved. The bounding tension that had orbited his being seemed to have dissipated.

And that relieved . . . me.

It was true.

Gone was the weight that had crushed like a pile of rubble and stone while I'd sat there alone, waiting for word. For anyone or anything to confirm that sweet little girl was fine. My rationale told me it was just a virus or a bug. Yet, this other part of me—the one that had panicked when I'd found the two of them standing outside my door in the middle of the night—had worried and fretted the entire time they'd been in the back.

God, it'd taken a matter of days for me to get in over my head.

But I'd barely been able to focus on anything else since I'd left Rex Gunner staring after me on Saturday night after I'd read Frankie that story. More confused than I'd ever been. His touch lingering on my skin and his words rambling through my head.

Honestly, I'd been shocked when he came to me for help.

But any reservations I'd wanted to hold had been wiped away by the sheer terror he'd attempted to keep veiled in the vast abyss of those stormy eyes. Eradicated by the fierce protectiveness that had radiated from him.

Most of all was this helplessness he couldn't seem to keep contained. It was in the way his chin had quivered as he'd stood on my porch with his daughter held in the safety of his arms.

"How is she?" I whispered, even though the waiting room was loud and bright. I couldn't do anything but reach out and thread my fingers through her brown hair. She was absolutely peaceful in his hold, and that simple touch sent a wave of affection bounding through my veins.

I sucked in a breath, surprised by the sudden, all-encompassing emotion.

Quickly, I turned my attention to search Rex's face.

His stunning, hard, brutal face.

Obviously, it was a more dangerous place to avert my attention. Because the emotion grew.

"It's just a virus." That rough, scruffy jaw was held tight, though there was a heavy solace that flooded out with the words.

The man who'd followed him out elbowed Rex in the ribs. "Rex here takes overprotectiveness to a whole new level. If he had let that Tylenol kick in, he would have known she was just fine."

Rex grunted. "Not a chance I was willing to take."

I wondered just what chances Rex was ever willing to take.

Though, I had to agree with him on this one. "It was good you brought her," I told him, hoping to encourage him. Hoping he'd get that I saw the kind of father he was.

The man next to him laughed a disbelieving sound, as if he took some kind of satisfaction in the situation. He shoved his hand toward me. "Dr. Kale Bryant, at your service."

I returned his shake. "Rynna Dayne."

A smug smile took to his handsome face, his eyes darting between Rex and me, his voice fueled by an undercurrent of laughter. "Oh, you have no idea just how nice it is to meet you, Ms. Dayne."

Rex almost rolled his eyes. "*Dr.* Kale Bryant. I remember the days when I used to let you cheat off my math tests, asshole. Take it down a notch."

Kale clapped him on the back. "Hey, don't go knocking that whole doctor bit. Your ass would still be sitting out here waiting to have your daughter seen if it weren't for me."

"I'm not knocking anything. You know I owe you."

Maybe I was surprised to hear the sincerity behind his admission. I guessed I shouldn't have been. Not with the way he clutched Frankie to him.

Guarding her.

Protecting her.

"We should get her home," I offered. Again, I glanced at his precious child. Her chubby cheek was pressed so perfectly to his chest and her fist was wound in the fabric of his shirt, as if the steady beat of his heart had lulled her into peace.

Rex lifted his chin to Kale. "Thanks, man. Honestly . . . don't think you know how much I appreciate you being there for her like this."

Waving him off, Kale let his gaze slide to the sweet child. "Anything for Sweet Pea Frankie Leigh. That's my godbaby, you know."

He looked at me when he said the last, and a smile was pulling through the exhaustion that threatened to drag me under. "No way."

Kale was all dimples as he raised his arms to the sides. "Don't let all these awesome good looks fool you. I'm totally capable of raising a kid." He threw a playful punch into Rex's shoulder. "Almost as good as this guy."

My smile grew as my eyes volleyed between the two of them, totally taken aback by the closeness Rex shared with Kale. But in a pleasant way. Maybe he didn't need any more friends, after all.

I looked back at him, and my stomach twisted.

But that didn't mean he didn't need something.

Someone to fill that glaring void that was so obviously radiating within him.

And with every layer that was exposed, more and more I wanted to be that person.

"I've got her," he grumbled barely above his breath when I attempted to help him get her out of the backseat of my car.

A calm stillness held fast to the cool air, daybreak just a hint of a blaze that lifted from the horizon. Glittering rays chased away the night and lit the sky in pinks and oranges and a welcoming blue.

The day brand new.

Bursting with possibilities.

"At least let me get the door open for you." I said it with zero frustration when I wrenched free the keys he had clutched in his hand and quietly climbed the porch steps.

Somehow, I'd come to understand this man felt he needed to do things on his own.

Or maybe he'd just been forced into that role, and he knew nothing else.

Behind me, I could feel them, this buzz of energy that emanated from their skin. It made me feel as if I stood at the very edge of something magnificent, a stranger peering in to witness something pure and absolute. Alive and profound. A thriving force that threatened to suck me into its depths.

Sliding the key into the lock, I turned the lever and opened the door, standing aside as he headed straight through, his long legs eating up the floor as he disappeared down the hallway.

I wavered there, my mind flashing back to two nights ago when he'd had me pinned just inside. The memory spun around me, that fury that had been so blatantly evident.

Almost as acute as the brokenness that had seeped from his flesh and poured into mine.

Nearly as intense as the desire that had lashed between us.

I didn't even know him, and the man was so mesmerizingly conflicted that he had me overwhelmed with the need to step closer. To dip my fingers in to explore and discover.

But it was more than that. There was something about him that made me ache. Something that made my chest and my spirit and my stomach revolt at the thought of walking away.

Sucking in a breath, I came to a quick decision. Stepping inside, I closed the door behind me and crept down the hall, unable or maybe unwilling to stop myself from peering through the doorway into Frankie's room.

My insides trembled as I watched them.

Rex carefully laid her in her bed. Gently, he brushed the chaotic tangle of hair from her forehead. His gaze was so tender when he stared down at her trusting face, his spirit so soft when he edged forward and brushed a kiss to one of her rosy, plump cheeks.

My throat thickened, and I clung to the jamb.

Enthralled and transfixed.

God.

This. Man.

He was undoing something inside me.

Uncovering something I'd never even realized I wanted.

Slowly, he stood. His body seemed so big in the emerging day, the raw strength of him wrapping me in chains. When he shifted, those eyes locked on me, his shadowy figure moving my direction.

I struggled to find air. Reason.

I fumbled a step back into the hallway, fortifying myself, never sure where his anger might take us or where this attraction might lead us.

He stopped in the doorway. His breaths short and heavy.

That same awareness flickered to life. Only this time, it seemed as if it'd gained power from the rising sun.

"Thank you." The words landed on me like a rough caress.

"Of course. When I told you I thought you might need a friend, I meant it. That means if you need me . . . I'm here."

He nodded, though it seemed reluctant. As if he were crossing an invisible line by agreeing. "Okay."

I nodded back, shocked that he'd yielded. "Okay. I'll . . . talk to you later. Just"—I fisted a hand over my heart—"please let me know if you or Frankie need anything at all. I'd really like to know how she's doing. I know I'll be thinking about her all day."

With that, I turned and headed for the door. I needed to get out of there.

Clear my head of the foolish ideas that had begun to spin. This foolish impulse to jump into torrid waters when I couldn't see the bottom. To sate the churning need that prodded at my consciousness.

Most of all, I wanted to respect him. The space he so clearly needed.

But I had no idea how that was going to work when it was starting to hurt when I walked away.

twelve

Rex

watched her escaping down the hallway.

At least, that was what it felt like. Like she was fleeing. Putting as much space between us as possible.

She should.

Maybe she was smart enough to run from whatever steadily built in the atmosphere whenever we shared the same space.

Ominous and powerful and unrelenting.

Her footsteps were swift, that silky mound of chestnut a complete disaster where she had it twisted high on top of her head. It left the creamy, delicate flesh of her neck exposed.

I itched, fighting against every single emotion I couldn't allow myself to feel.

Fuck.

I needed her out.

Gone.

Away.

Where she couldn't confuse, corrupt, and confound.

Where she couldn't riddle my mind and tempt my hand.

Where she didn't hold the power to squeeze between the cracks she continually chipped and etched into my spirit, like the exterior I'd built didn't even exist. The girl eased into those spaces that were meant to remain closed off and shut down.

Not that it seemed to matter.

The tension only amplified the farther she got. Her footsteps grew fainter, but the space between them ignited a new kind of gravity.

Everything grew taught and tight and rigid. The air. My chest. My thoughts.

Drawing me in a direction I knew I shouldn't go.

But standing there? I had no power. Because her scent still lingered around me, clouding my senses.

My mouth watered. Cherry and sugar. So goddamned sweet.

I was suddenly inundated with the way she'd felt against me two nights ago.

Her warmth and her comfort and that fucking insane body that made me lose my mind.

It'd been in that foolish moment when I'd given in to temptation when I should have been chasing her away. A single brush of her body had heated every inch of me. My cock harder than it'd ever been, desperate for a different kind of taste from the one she'd been offering. Fuck. How badly had I wanted to get lost in the slick heat of her tight body?

Every perfect curve seduction.

Every defined inch sin.

But it was the way she'd looked at Frankie when we'd rushed through the emergency room doors that had tipped me to uneven ground.

The floor crumbling from under me.

Logic shot. My feet were moving without my brain ever giving me time to calculate the consequences.

But right then?

I didn't fucking care.

Didn't care what this would cost.

I stalked down the hall and through the living room.

The air sparked with every determined step.

She was already down the porch steps by the time I caught her by the wrist, and she gasped one of those throaty, sexy sounds that shot straight to my dick.

Fuck it all, if that simple contact point didn't ignite to an all-out boil. Heat streaked through my veins, eclipsing everything. Reason and sanity and judgment.

I whirled her around. In a second flat, I had her back pressed against the front of my truck where no one could see us. My fingers tangled in that mess of unruly hair, our faces a breadth apart. My heart stuttered when those innocent eyes latched on to mine, so wide and confused when she realized I had her pinned.

Just like me.

I crushed my mouth to hers, because I had no fuckin' time for hesitation. I just needed to feel something different from the constant turmoil that raged inside. For just a moment, touch on something that felt like hope.

Even when I knew it was so fucking wrong.

On a sigh, she opened for me. Her lips so damned soft when they began to move with mine.

Sweetly.

Tentatively.

I coaxed and prodded, needing more. My lips tugged and nipped at the soft plumpness, my mouth growing hungrier with each desperate pass. Begging for the kind of reprieve I was terrified only she could give.

She gave. Her breaths turned ragged when I swept my tongue into the well of her mouth for a taste.

God. I was right.

So damned sweet.

I deepened the kiss. Taking more with each lick of my tongue. Or maybe it was Rynna who was stealing bits of me with each nip and tug of those full, full lips.

Lust.

It consumed me.

Blinding.

Constricting my cells and straining my muscles.

I pressed every rigid, hard line of my body into all her soft curves. Overwhelmed. Aching in a way I hadn't in years. Like maybe if I got close enough things might not hurt so bad.

"Rex." It was all a whimper when she sank her fingers into my shoulders, and her touch became just as desperate as mine.

Her kiss just as mad.

Her hands coasted from my shoulders down my arms, hitting my biceps where we were skin on skin. The contact burned in the most blissful kind of way, and I sucked in a shattered breath when she was pushing up under the sleeves of my T-shirt, fingertips tracing across the tattoo etched on my arm.

I groaned.

In pleasure.

In agony.

I didn't know.

"Rynna," I grated at her mouth. I cupped that bewitching face in my hands before I glided my palms down her neck and tipped back her head. "I don't even fucking know you. How is it possible you have this kind of hold on me?"

The words were a jumble of incoherency. I moved my mouth down over her jaw. I was sure I was getting drunk on her breaths, getting lost in the crash of her heart that hammered with the thready beat of mine.

My hands trailed down that body. That body that had taunted me since the moment I'd seen her come barreling out of her grandmother's door. I traced her shoulders, moving across the hollow of her throat, trailing down her chest.

Maybe I'd known it then. That this girl would wreck me. Because I could feel myself coming apart. Piece by piece.

She sighed a barely audible, "Yes."

Fuck.

What was I doing?

But my dick was so on board, and all the reasons this was the damned worst idea I'd had in years went galloping into the distance.

I palmed one of those gorgeous tits, her nipple firm beneath the thin fabric of her tank.

She gasped and pushed harder into my touch.

"Shit," I muttered. Maybe it was that very second that insanity took me over, because I didn't care that we were outside. That someone might hear us.

Instead, I edged back to look at her where she writhed against the grill of my truck, her chest arching with her need for me, her lips swollen and sweet.

Everything shook around me.

An earthquake.

Trembling and cracking and crumbling.

I yanked down the collar of her tank and exposed her.

She was braless. Her tits just shy of a handful, skin so smooth, nipples a dusky pink and pebbled tight.

"Gorgeous," I rumbled before I ducked down to lap at the peak, drawing her rosy nipple between my teeth.

She drove her fingers in my hair. Pulling. Begging. "Rex. Oh my God . . . please."

I growled, my mouth moving upward through the valley of her chest, my nose nudging beneath her chin to grant me access to the snowy skin of her neck.

Her pulse beat an erratic, unsteady thrum.

I latched on to it. Sucking her flesh into my mouth as I slipped my hand down her side, over her hip, and down to her knee. I hooked her leg around my waist, all too quick to press my eager dick to the overwhelming heat that blazed from her pussy.

Barely a hint of her through her sleep pants and underwear, but I nearly came right there.

It'd been so long. So fuckin' long, and I was losing my grip, sanity just slipping out of my reach.

I kept rocking my cock covered by my jeans against her clit, loving the way she moaned and whimpered my name, the girl struggling to stay quiet so her moans weren't carried on the wind.

Shit.

It was so sexy, the girl in the spotlight of the breaking day.

I wanted to tear every scrap of clothes from our bodies and sink all the way in.

Disappear in that tight heat of her body.

I bit down on her collarbone as I thrust against her like some teenaged kid who'd never gotten his dick wet.

But that was what it felt like.

Like I was coming up on something great.

Something bigger than I understood.

Every muscle in Rynna went tight, and she sucked a sharp breath into her lungs before she started quaking all around me.

She did her best to stifle a deep moan while she came right there against my truck.

Her knees went weak while I continued to work myself against her hot body, wondering just how far I was going to let this madness go.

It only took the weak cry floating from Frankie's room for me to find that answer.

For me to come tumbling back down to reality.

To the truth of who I was. To my responsibilities.

I edged back, fighting the dread that spiked like barbs at the base of my throat.

"Shit." I shook my head, trying to orient myself. To rip myself from her body. I stepped back, my body still raging, barely able to look at her after the shit I'd just pulled.

Rynna reached for me with a trembling hand. "Rex . . ."

How was it possible that I saw understanding flash through her expression?

"I'm so fucking sorry, Rynna. God, I don't know what the fuck I'm doing."

Rynna resituated her clothing, stepping back out onto the walkway, all lit up in the new day laying siege to the summer sky. For a moment, she just stared back at me. That energy flickered in the air. The softest smile rimmed her mouth. "You don't have to be."

Then she turned and crossed the street while I stood there like a fool, staring at the spot she'd just left vacant.

I guessed maybe that was what I'd always been.

A fool.

Shaking myself off, I rushed back up the steps and inside.

"Daddy." The tiny cry filtered down the hall, and I reined in all the emotions and locked them there where they belonged.

Because just like I'd told Kale, I only needed one girl in my life.

And right then?

My girl needed me.

The doorbell rang. The words to the book I'd been reading Frankie trailed off. Instantly, my breaths turned shallow, my heart skyrocketing with a boom.

God. I really had lost it, my mind and body still reeling from whatever the fuck it was I'd thought I was doing earlier this morning when I'd had Rynna up against my truck.

I'd resisted for years.

And it was the girl next door who'd become irresistible.

Guilt welled in the deepest parts of me. In those sacred places I'd just desecrated.

I shifted where I was propped up on the headboard of Frankie's bed with the book lifted out in front of us. My daughter was sprawled halfway across my chest, her head twisted to the side so she could see the pictures.

I'd basically been there all day, alternating between reading her stories, checking her temperature, and watching her sleep.

"Who's that?" she whispered. Those brown eyes lit with a flash of excitement, promising me whatever sickness she'd been suffering from had finally begun to run its course.

"Not sure. You expecting a party or something?" I teased, tapping my index finger against her button nose, trying to pretend like the mere idea of Rynna standing on the other side of the door didn't have me in knots.

She scrunched that nose with the cutest grin. "People aren't suppose to gets a party just for feelin' better, silly."

"No?" I feigned ignorance.

"No way! Only prize people gets for feelin' better is having to go backs to work."

Laughter shot from my mouth in the same second affection stabbed me in the chest, so deep I thought it might cut me in two. But that was the thing about loving Frankie Leigh.

I loved her so much it physically hurt.

I ruffled a playful hand through her hair. "Sounds to me like you've been spending too much time with your grammy."

Shock had her mouth dropping open. "There's no such thing as too much Grammy times, Daddy. Don't you knows that?"

I laughed again, almost deciding to ignore the door, but then Frankie hopped off the bed. She wrapped both her tiny hands around one of my wrists, yanking with all her might. Of course, the only nudge she gave was the one that shot through my heart. "Come on, Daddy. There's someone ats the door. We gots to see who it is."

"Okay, okay," I said, relenting, hating the way my nerves buzzed through my body when I did. The way those defenses wanted to go up.

All the while, I was wishing there was a way I could throw rescue ropes over the side.

That I could climb out of the bullshit mess I'd made of my life and jump into one where taking a girl like Rynna Dayne would be okay.

With Frankie's hand wrapped around my index finger, I stumbled along behind her. The kid was far too chipper as she bee-lined for the door. Maybe I had overreacted.

She popped up on her toes to peer out the side window and out on to the porch. She huffed when she dropped back onto her heels. "I finks we were too late. Nobody's there." I set a hand on her shoulder, guiding her behind me, that kick of protectiveness always at the ready to take hold. I twisted the lock so I could open the door and peer outside.

She was right.

No one was there.

But someone had been.

To my right, someone had left a tray on the short wooden table between the two rocking chairs. I'd made them what seemed a million years ago, back when I'd been nothing but a fool. We'd just been moving into this place, and I'd been thinking maybe I'd finally outrun that shadow.

The scar that forever eclipsed the true joy of my life.

I should've known better.

A large lidded bowl rested on the tray, and a tented card was propped to the side of it.

Squealing, Frankie flew out from behind me. "Oh, look it, Daddy. It gots my name on it. It *is* a present for me."

My gaze darted across the street. The old house sat silent and unmoving, just the branches of the big trees that fronted her yard waving their welcome.

Emotion slammed me. Unstoppable. Too much. Overwhelming.

Pushing out a sigh, I forced myself to walk all the way out.

My senses were punched again when I reached down and grabbed the handles of the tray. Only this time, it was the amazing aroma that lifted from the bowl, striking me like comfort and warmth.

Comfort and warmth that was intended for my daughter.

Thoughtful in a way I couldn't allow the woman to be.

My sweet girl trotted along beside me while I carried the offering inside and set in on the small dining table.

"What's it, Daddy?"

She peered up at me with that trusting grin, her fingers threaded together where she leaned against her elbows on the table to get a better look. She looked like she was already issuing up a prayer for the food she'd been given.

"Careful," I warned, lifting the lid.

It was a chicken pot pie. The kind Corinne Dayne had been famous for.

Homemade.

Handmade.

The aroma of it so overpowering, my mouth watered.

My damned hand was shaking when I reached down and snatched the note. Frankie's name was written across the front in the prettiest handwriting I'd ever seen.

I lifted the flap to find what was written inside.

Dear Frankie Leigh,

Remember when I told you I had some of the recipes to my grandma's pies? I have a special secret just for you—I have the recipe for the pot pie she used to make me whenever I felt sick, too. It was always my favorite, and sometimes, I didn't even mind getting sick, because I knew she would make it and soon everything would be better. I remember being a little girl, just like you, eating this same pie at our kitchen table right across the street. With every bite I took, I knew that my grandma had to love me more than the whole wide world.

Last night, I wished with all of me that I could have taken your sickness away. But maybe there's a chance this pie might make you feel better the way it always did me. I sure hope so.

All my love,
Rynna

Damn her.

Damn her straight to hell for teasing me this way.

Damn her for weaseling her way in and making herself a place in a spot where she knew she would never stay.

Fuck me for wanting it.

"Read it to me! Oh, read it to me, Daddy! Wha's it say?"

"It's from Rynna next door," I told her, trying to keep the thick emotion from clotting my voice. "She said her grandma used to make her this same pot pie when she wasn't feeling well. She thought it might help you feel better, too, so she made you some."

Those big brown eyes went wide with hope, and her voice dropped like it might be a secret. "Do you think it mights be as good as cherry pie?"

My attention darted to the sweet pie still sitting on the countertop. The pie I'd dipped my finger into the second I'd gotten a chance this afternoon. Because shit. That little taste of her outside this morning had not been close to being enough.

"How about we test it out? You get some of this food into your belly, and I'll heat you up a small piece of cherry pie. How's that sound?"

"It sounds like you're the best daddy in the whole wide world . . . just like Rynna's grammy."

If only that were the truth.

thirteen

Rynna

I stepped out of my grandmother's diner and was smacked in the face by the Alabama heat. A sticky sheen of sweat slicked my skin, and my arm still burned from the exertion of scrubbing on at least thirty years of built-up lard and oils splattered on every surface in the old kitchen. I figured it wouldn't hurt to work on what little could be salvaged inside. It at least gave me something to keep my hands busy while I waited for my appointment with the bank so I could officially put in my application for a loan.

It was painful waiting. Not knowing. Wondering if I was going to have what it took to bring this dusty diner back to life. If anyone would believe in me. If they'd give me a chance to make this old dream a reality.

After today, I was bone tired. But there was an eager hum that whirred through my blood. A satisfaction that had been lacking in all the years I'd been away. While in San Francisco, I'd attempted to convince myself a life outside of Gingham Lakes was what I wanted.

Some part of me had always known it'd been a lie.

I could almost hear my grandmother whispering in my ear, *"Do what makes you happy, child. In my experience, joy is a choice. Life is rough. Don't expect it not to be. But if we aren't laughin', we're cryin'. Choose to laugh. Choose what brings you joy. And when you choose your path, it might not always be the easiest one, but it'll always be the right one."*

I lifted my face to the blue sky, squeezed my eyes closed, and silently murmured, "I chose this path, Gramma. Even if it's not the easiest one, I know it's where my joy is waiting for me."

My eyes opened, my gaze landing on the construction site across the street. It was deserted, work done for the day, but that didn't stop my mind from wandering to Rex.

After I'd left his house yesterday morning, I'd gone home and crawled straight into bed. With being awake at the emergency room for most of the night, I'd anticipated I'd immediately fall asleep, but I'd tossed.

Exhausted but wired.

Drained but restored.

As if I'd been left spinning somewhere in limbo.

Lost in a blissful kind of purgatory where I'd stumbled upon a man with the skill to bring me to orgasm with a few mind-rending strokes of his body. But there had been so much pained remorse in his expression afterward that it'd sent me crashing to the ground.

No question, he'd needed to run to Frankie. It was exactly what he should do. His child should always be his first priority.

But what hurt was it was clear his regret went so much deeper than the simple fact we'd let ourselves lose control where we'd been hidden by his massive truck. Deeper than the fact he needed to pull away to return to her.

And with Rex?

I felt out of control.

Spinning from a thread and barely hanging on.

He knocked the ground out from under my feet.

Shaking myself out of it, I pushed from the door and locked up before stepping out onto the sidewalk.

The scene in front of me made me wonder how I'd ever left this place. The old buildings built up on each side, massive shade trees grown up through the planters and shading the store fronts that still boasted some of the old shops my grandmother had gone to when she'd been my age.

You'd think the restoration in progress would have stolen from the charm.

It didn't.

It only amplified.

The renovated buildings bore crisp new awnings and eaves, and the new brick structures climbed up between them to give the exact cohesive feel Lillith had been so proud of the day I'd first met her.

One day soon, Pepper's Pies would be a part of this rebirth.

I inhaled a satisfied breath and started for my SUV, glancing down to fiddle with my key ring to grab the right one.

Then I smacked right into a firm body.

"Oh goodness, I'm sorry, excuse me," I mumbled through my surprise.

Hands came out to steady me by the shoulders.

"Whoa, slow down." The man chuckled, and my attention shot up. My eyes grew round, and my mouth went dry, my heart bottoming out in my stomach.

He smiled at me.

Confused by my reaction.

His head angled to the side, tone filled with an easy chuckle. "Tiny thing like you should slow down before you fall and mess up that pretty face."

I took a staggering step backward. Still unable to say anything. Still unable to respond.

I couldn't breathe, my heart locked in the center of my chest.

A rush of dizziness swept through my head, my balance lost.

He didn't even recognize me.

The bastard didn't even recognize me.

I pressed a hand over my mouth, trying to keep back the cry that clamored up my throat, just standing there, staring at him.

Unable to move.

Paralyzed.

Frozen by shock.

By fear.

By hatred.

"You okay, beautiful?" he asked as if he had the capacity to care.

I wished with all of me I had the strength to slap him across the face. Or maybe spit in it. Scream at him to go to hell, right where he belonged.

Instead, I stood there staring at him in terrified disbelief.

He started to reach for me, and I finally snapped out of my stupor. I frantically smacked his hand away as I stumbled back. Fighting tears, I broke away and rushed for my Cherokee. I fumbled with the key, hands shaking so badly I could barely get it into the lock. Another rush of dizziness swept through me, a violent storm, taking me under.

I could barely haul myself into the driver's seat.

Nausea whirled.

I slammed the door and locked it, hands squeezing on the steering wheel. I fought the urge to shift my truck into drive, tuck tail, and run.

He was there.

He is here.

Bile climbed my throat when Aaron looked back over his shoulder at me. He shook his head as if I were insane then turned and continued down the sidewalk as if it meant nothing at all, as my mind was jerked back to the days I'd do anything to forget.

Rynna - Twelve Years Old

I grinned eagerly, excitement blazing through my nerves. I couldn't believe I'd been invited.

Something about this felt special. As if things were finally gonna change. I hated being left out. Gramma said it was just because I was too shy, but I wasn't so sure.

I threaded my fingers together and set them on my lap where I sat with my legs crisscrossed on Janel's bedroom floor.

We'd made a circle.

The circle.

My eyes made a pass over the faces: Kimberly, Sarah, Ben, Kerry, Janel, and Aaron.

Aaron.

Butterflies stormed my belly and sweat slicked my palms.

Aaron.

I kept glancing at him, wishing I was sitting right next to him, but I was too nervous to make the move.

But at least I was there. That was all that mattered.

A dim light glowed from a bedside lamp, but otherwise, the lights were off.

Janel set the bottle in the middle of the circle.

Kerry giggled. "This game is so stupid." But she was peeking at Ben when she said it, and I wondered if she was as nervous as I was. If everyone was.

Janel cleared her throat, and I thought no. Janel was never scared.

"Okay, these are the rules," Janel said. "When you spin the bottle, whoever it lands on, you have to kiss them for three seconds." Her voice dropped with the scandalous challenge. "On the lips."

"Even if it's a girl?" Kimberly asked.

Janel huffed. "Isn't that what I said?"

"Ewww." Sarah kicked her feet and violently shook her head.

"Stop being a baby," Janel said, eyeing her hard. "You said you wanted to come, so you have to play by my rules."

Janel was the leader. She'd always been. Me and Janel had known each other forever. Janel's momma worked at the diner with my gramma, so we were together a lot. Of course, that didn't mean I got invited to things like this.

Janel spun the bottle first. It landed on Sarah. Janel crawled over and kissed her on the lips. Everyone counted to three. Janel sat back. "See, that wasn't so bad, was it?"

Sarah pressed her hand over her mouth. "I don't think I want to kiss anyone."

Janel glanced at Kimberly with a roll of her eyes. "I told you she wasn't cool enough."

Janel set her gaze on me. "How about you?"

The nod of my head was emphatic, my nerves abuzz.

"Good. You're next."

Was it possible my belly could move all the way to my throat? Clumsily, I spun the bottle. It landed on Kimberly. I squeezed my eyes closed when I leaned across the circle and kissed her, a peck to the lips. It wasn't so bad. But that wasn't who I wanted to kiss.

And I felt so shaky, my heart fluttery and funny while we spun and spun, continually taking turns.

Aaron spun the bottle again. The bottle spun and wobbled until the top of the neck finally pointed at me. Those butterflies smacked their wings, my stomach wild.

Aaron started to lean across the circle. Janel set her arm out in front of him. "I think you two should do this in private. In the closet."

My eyes grew wide. "But—"

"My house, my rules, remember?"

I climbed to my feet, suddenly feeling sweaty as I glanced down at my body then at Aaron's when he reluctantly stood. Janel hopped to her feet. "This way."

I followed her across her room to the closet. Janel opened the door. "Get in."

It was dark inside, and for a second, I hesitated. Everything felt wrong and funny, the warnings my gramma had always given me about being smart and if something felt off, it probably was. To trust my gut.

I ignored it. I had finally been invited and I wasn't going to mess this up. I stepped inside, waiting for Aaron to step in with me, but then Janel laughed so loud a shudder rolled through me just as the door slammed shut in my face.

Laughter roared from the other side. Panic welled. I jerked at the handle, but it didn't budge. "Come on, Janel, it's not funny. Let me out."

More laughter. "Did you really think Aaron would want to kiss a fat cow? You're so stupid, Rynna Dayne. Like he would ever like you. Like any of us would like you."

Tears burned in my eyes. "Please."

"Twenty minutes time out for the cow," Janel sing-songed. Their laughter rang through the thin door, and I sank to the floor of the closet, hugging my knees to my chest, wondering if I would ever stop feeling so alone.

fourteen

Rex

"Open wide and say ah."

From her spot on the edge of the exam table, Frankie did as she was told, opening her mouth so wide I didn't know how he wasn't looking at the inside of her stomach. She gurgled an elongated *ahhhhh* that was mixed with a giggle and did her best not to fall into a fit of laughter when Kale put a depressor against her tongue and shined a light on her throat.

"Oh, no." If Kale weren't acting a fool, exaggerating his worry, I would have been on him in a flash, demanding to know which of the bajillion horrible illnesses could be the actual culprit for her symptoms.

So yeah.

I'd tumbled down the rabbit hole of internet searches on my phone while I'd been watching her sleep her fever away this last weekend.

Apparently, Google was the number you were actually supposed to multiply your worry by.

Because that shit was scary.

But Kale was being Kale.

Tossing out teases at Frankie like they were candy.

Frankie's eyes went wide. "What's it, Uncle Kale?"

He dropped his voice to a secretive whisper. "Don't tell anyone, but I think there are monsters living in your throat."

Frankie giggled harder and lifted her shoulders to her chubby cheeks. "Nu-uh. There no monsters livin' in my throat."

Kale huffed dramatically. "And how do you know that? I'm the doctor here."

"My daddy told me there's no such fing as monsters."

"And your daddy is smarter than I am?" With the way Kale cut me an evil eye, I wondered how much of his offense was feigned.

"Course he's smarter than you. He's the smartest daddy in the whole, whole, whole wide world." Her arms pumped up higher every time she repeated the word. She glanced over at me. "Right, Daddy?"

I shrugged from where I was leaned against the wall with my arms crossed over my chest. "My daughter is the smartest kid around. She knows her stuff."

He quirked a brow. "And that *stuff* is that you're actually smarter than I am?"

My lips twitched. "Guess so."

This time Frankie threw her arms all the way in the air. "I know all the stuffs."

"Is that so?" He poked her belly. Instantly, she was howling, grabbing at his hand.

"It's so! It's so! It's so, so, so." She kept chanting as he jumped into a full-fledged tickle attack, and my chest was doing that crazy thing where it felt too full and too proud and too content, which happened just about every damned time I looked my daughter's way.

I was telling no lies.

She was my light.

The life inside me.

She sobered about as quickly as she'd collapsed into laughter. "Am I alls better, Uncle Kale?"

He touched her chin with his knuckle. "All better, pumpkin pie."

Her face scrunched. "I don't likes punkin' pie, Uncle. I likes cherry pie."

Of course she did.

Incredulous, his brow lifted. "You want me to call you cherry pie?"

He was holding back laughter, looking over at me like he was just waiting for me to bust up.

"Uh . . . can we not?" I said, pushing from the wall, irritated because I knew exactly where Kale's mind had gone traipsing. Right to that damned Warrant video Ollie had made us watch on repeat for the entire summer between third and fourth grade. Apparently, fourth grade was right about the time when Ollie had decided girls weren't exactly *gross*.

Or maybe I was irritated simply because the mention of cherry pie had my mind traipsing straight to thoughts of Rynna.

Neither of us could seem to resist whatever the fuck that insanity was that burned between us. No question, she was just as much a prisoner to the ruthless energy that thrived between us as I was. This violent need. Growing stronger every time it forced us together.

Irresistible.

Stupid.

Reckless.

God knew that was what touching her had been.

Reckless. Just because you knew something that didn't make you wise.

And I swore that touching her had scored the very depth of me.

It'd been too much. Too good. Too right when I knew every second of it was so goddamned wrong.

Most terrifying part was I wasn't sure I'd ever wanted a girl the way I wanted her.

Not in all my life.

Watching her walk away with all that understanding on her face? That had been a kick to the gut. Hurting her when it was the last thing I wanted to do. But the only thing I had to offer her was the fucking mess I'd made.

I shook myself from the thoughts. "Everything look okay?"

"All's good, my friend."

From under the arms, Kale lifted Frankie, hoisting her into the air and making her squeal and flap her arms like she was flying, before he set her on her feet. He patted the top of her head. "Good as new, right, Frankie Leigh, Cherry Pie?"

He winked at me, and I elbowed him in the side. "Don't even, man."

Gasping through a laugh, he clutched his ribs. "Dude, not cool. Not cool. I'm just messing with you. Why so serious all the time?"

Frankie started skipping around the small examination room. "Rynna makes the bestest cherry pies ever, ever. Daddy even said they mights be better than her grammy's."

Kale looked down at her before looking at me with something gleaming in his eye. "Rynna, huh?"

"Yep," Frankie answered, not having a clue that Kale's question was actually directed at me. "She bringed me one when I had the sicks and her pots pie made me all better. Oh, Uncle Kale, it was soes good!"

"This Rynna sounds really nice," Kale said. Again, eyeing me like the bastard he was.

"Mm-huh! She's so, so nice. She even wrotes me a letter." Frankie rambled off all the details I sure as hell didn't want Kale to have as he opened the door. She kept at it as she capered down the hall, alternating between skipping and twirling and leaping, which she'd learned at ballet yesterday.

When we hit the waiting room, she darted for the children's play area set up in the corner. The small space was packed with a ton of kids, their parents, most of them their moms, sitting around in the bright plastic chairs waiting for their names to be called.

I turned to Kale. "Thanks for doing this, man. Know it's not standard for you to do follow-ups in here like this."

Blowing out a long breath, he glanced over at Frankie, who had already struck a conversation with a little boy about her age. Swore the kid didn't have a shy bone in her body. Always making friends wherever she went. Social in a way that made me itch. I always had to watch her like a hawk. Not that I wouldn't anyway.

"I was happy to, Rex." He shifted back to look at me, the amusement he'd been wearing since the moment we'd stepped through the clinic doors replaced by his worry. "It's time you stop thinking you have to go this alone all the time. I'm here for her, too. I love that kid. You have to get that."

On a sigh, I roughed a hand through my hair, my attention moving back to my daughter, who had climbed the steps to the short plastic slide and was propelling herself down. "I know, man. It's just—"

"It's just that you think you're supposed to," he cut in, his arms going across his chest. "You think if you give up even a second of the responsibility, a second of the worry, you're betraying your daughter in some way."

"That's not true."

"Isn't it? Hell, I'm surprised you even let your mom take care of her in the afternoons when she gets out of preschool."

I let a smirk climb to my mouth. "I'm kind of questioning that, actually. She'd look pretty dammed cute with a hard hat on the job, don't you think?"

His eyes narrowed. "I'd be laughing right now if I didn't think you might actually be serious."

I chuckled, head shaking with a bit of amusement before I dropped my gaze toward my booted feet. "Nah, man. I . . ."

Kale set his hand on my shoulder. "You're a disaster, man. Know you don't want to hear it, but you have issues, and I'm worried about you."

"It's just . . . it's so goddamned hard to let her out of my sight. Feel like I'm always scrambling to stay in front of everything, trying to stay one step ahead to make sure she's safe."

His voice softened. "You know that's not always going to be possible."

Dread curled in my stomach. That same old misery that stalked me in the day and hunted me in the night. The helplessness and fear and agony that had scraped and scraped at my spirit.

Perpetual torture.

I wondered how there was anything left of me.

"You've got to understand, Kale."

"Of course, I understand. I was there, man. I went through it, too. But you can't spend the rest of your life a prisoner to that time."

How the fuck were we supposed to move on from it when that time was unending?

"I'm trying."

"Are you? Then why don't you come clean about what's going on with this Rynna girl? The smoking hot chick who just so happened to be at the emergency room—at two-thirty in the morning—with the guy who refuses to accept help from anyone other than me, Ollie, and his mom, and barely even then."

Unease stirred through me. That same feeling that had been nagging at me for days. The dread and the need and confusion. "Battery was dead in the truck."

"Hmm."

"Hmm, what?"

"You're an awful handy dude for having to ask a woman for help in the middle of the night."

"Frankie was sick. Didn't have time to spare."

"You needed someone, and you went to her."

Fuck.

He was right.

I needed someone. And I went to her.

I went to her.

Agitation had me shifting on my feet.

He squeezed my shoulder a little tighter. "Tell me what's going on with you two."

My attention was locked on Frankie as I rubbed a hand over my mouth, trying not to think about the way I'd felt pressed against Rynna. The way her heart had beaten and mine had come alive for the first time in years. "Only thing that's going on is shit that can't be."

"And why's that?"

My chest tightened, and I looked to the ground, voice dropping so low I wasn't sure he could hear my confession. "It feels like cheating."

I could feel Kale's sympathy all mixed with a bolt of exasperation. "And who exactly are you cheating on? Because that bitch left you and Sydney is gone. They are both gone, man, and they aren't coming back."

My entire being flinched. Anguish and this blinding guilt that ate me up from the inside.

Kale's voice dropped to match mine. "You need to tell Ollie, Rex. Fucking get this off your chest once and for all so you can finally move on."

"I'm not sure how to do that."

Question was, did I really want to?

Rynna's face spun through my mind. I swore I could feel that place that had ached forever transform. Grasping for something different. Something better.

And that scared the shit out of me.

I glanced over at Kale. When I caught his expression, my irritation came back full force. "Why the fuck are you grinning?"

"Oh, you know . . . because it's super entertaining to watch you realize you just might want something but the thought of it makes you want to crawl right out of your skin."

"Always such an asshole," I mumbled.

"Who doesn't hesitate to say it straight. Admit it. You like her."

"I don't like her. I don't even know her."

"But you want to." The jackass had the audacity to sing it as he twirled his finger in a circle in front of my face.

I smacked it away.

He was worse than a thirteen-year-old girl.

"Come on, man. Admit it. You want to." He flashed me one of those ridiculous smiles that had every girl in town dying to lock that shit down. All fucking dimples and bright white teeth. "Tell me about that pie." He waggled his brows, keeping right on with the ribbing, having no idea the knives he was driving into raw flesh. "Tell me how badly you want her to eat yours."

My throat bobbed, that guilt rising around me like jagged cliffs. Guilt for giving in. I had already made more mistakes with her than I could make excuses for. Had already gotten deep enough that I wasn't sure I was ever going to climb out.

"Oh shit," Kale muttered under his breath. "You lucky bastard, you already did. And you're over there pouting about it."

I shifted away, not needing to pretend I was keeping a close eye on Frankie. "Not like that . . . we just . . ."

Visions assaulted me. The ecstasy on her face when she'd come with the sun shining on her gorgeous face. How good she'd tasted. How right she'd felt in my arms.

"Just what?" he pressed.

I blew out a frustrated breath, voice barely a gritted whisper. "It was just a kiss."

Kale laughed. "Just a kiss, huh? Considering you haven't touched a girl in years, I'd bet the pink slip to my car, which you know is my baby, that it meant a whole lot more to you than it just being a kiss. You have some kind of superhuman strength or balls of steal or some shit, because those fuckers should be so blue they'd have fallen off by now." The guy knew me better than anyone, and he didn't hesitate to pull punches.

"You think you regret whatever you're feeling now? Just wait to see how much regret you feel when you don't do anything about it." He sighed. "It doesn't have to be a big thing, Rex. Test it out. Hang out with her as a friend. See how it goes. It's not like you're asking her to marry you."

I flinched with that, and he snorted, shaking his head before he spun all the way around and waltzed over to the reception desk. Two nurses behind it immediately tuned in to whatever the flirty bastard had to say as he rested his forearms on the counter and leaned toward them.

And I wondered how he'd done it.

Managed it.

Overcome it.

Or maybe I was the one who'd really been at fault all along.

Rex

Hand rubbing over the tense muscles at the back of my neck, I paced, boots crunching on the gravel in front of her house.

Back and forth.

Back and forth.

Shit.

Shit. Shit. Shit. Get it together, man.

Friends.

That was what Kale had said.

I could do that.

I forced my feet to carry me up the steps and across her porch, and I gave a good pound to her front door. It took all of thirty seconds and what felt like an eternity for the door to crack open. I almost backed the fuck out because all I saw was hesitation in her movements before something like relief took to her features.

"Rex," she whispered, opening the door wider.

"Hey."

A small smile graced that gorgeous mouth. "How is Frankie?"

Something about that calmed the erratic racing of my heart, and I felt myself smiling in return. "As good as new. It might have had something to do with a pot pie that mysteriously showed up at our door."

A flush touched her cheeks, and she bit her bottom lip, everything about her completely genuine. "I hope she liked it."

"Oh, there's no question of that."

That redness deepened. "I'm so glad she's feeling better."

"Me, too. Can't thank you enough for helping me out that night."

"I meant it, Rex. I'm here."

I nodded, rushed my fingers through my hair, the air growing thick around us. A swirl of that potency.

"So . . ." I trailed off like the pathetic fucker I was.

"So . . ." she prodded, those dark eyes going warm and soft.

I sucked in a breath, fingers going back to nervously thread through my hair. "There's this thing Broderick Wolfe invited me to tomorrow night at Olive's. Just a small party to celebrate the progress that's been made on the Fairmont Hotel. I know Lillith and Nikki will be there. Thought it'd be cool if you came. You know, as friends," I added way too quickly.

Smooth.

So goddamned smooth.

I had to stop from rolling my eyes at myself.

"Friends?" she asked, a brow lifting, the word nothing but a doubtful tease. Couldn't blame her, especially considering the last time I'd seen her, she was coming against my truck.

"Yeah," I said, shoving my hands into my pockets. My tone turned deep with honesty. "Not sure I have a whole lot more to offer right now, Rynna."

Silence pulsed around us. Thick with implication. With our reservations and all the things I didn't know how to say.

She blinked back at me then finally spoke. "That sounds great. I'd love to go."

I breathed out in relief. "Good." I backed away, letting a huge smile climb to my face. "That's really good. I'll pick you up at eight."

She smiled the softest smile with another short nod then closed the door.

And I felt good. Really fucking good. I could do this.

sixteen

Rynna

Rex held open the door. "Ladies first," he said with a tiny smirk lifting on the corner of his sexy mouth.

Nerves tumbled through my body, and my teeth caught on my bottom lip. "Thank you," I murmured, ducking my head and stepping inside the packed bar.

A warm dimness held fast to the trendy space, the dull roar of voices an easy drone in the air. Edison bulbs hung from the ceilings and flickered against the red brick walls like flames.

People were everywhere, vying to get a stool at the bar or snag one of the high-top tables situated throughout, totally lost in their own worlds as they cast their troubles aside and stepped into the carelessness of the weekend.

That didn't change the fact I felt as if I were in a spotlight.

I didn't know if it were the fact I stood beside who had to be the most beautiful man I'd ever seen. Or maybe it was because I was still reeling from running into Aaron outside Pepper's Pies four days ago.

When Rex had asked me to come to this party, my first instinct had been to tell him no.

Both because just looking at the man had me fearing for my heart and because the impact of him merely standing at my door leapt to my throat and spread beneath my skin like a slow burn.

The other had been nothing but straight fear.

Pure, petrified fear.

But I refused to allow history to chase me away. Not from the place I loved. Not from where I belonged. Not ever again.

So, I'd stepped out of my comfort zone and said yes. This man was worth the risk I knew I was taking.

He lifted his chin, and I followed his line of sight to the bar. Ollie was behind it, giving him the same gesture of welcome. Turning that potent attention on me, Rex angled his head to the side. "This way."

He ushered me ahead of him and toward the stairs. A sign was set up beside it stating the second level was closed for a private party.

Warily, I glanced over at him. "I thought you said this was a small party."

He released a low chuckle. "Broderick Wolfe doesn't exactly do anything small. Big seems to be his middle name."

My brow arched with the tease. "Ah, I see how it is. You actually invited me along to protect you."

His gaze flicked down my body.

Hot.

Needy.

Those magnetic eyes skated across my bare shoulders and dipped to the valley between my breasts. I released a shaky breath as his gaze drifted over the soft peach dress I wore. The thin straps were satin and crisscrossed over the open back, and the front of the fitted bodice dipped into a shallow V. The skirt was flowy and soft and landed just above my knees.

Those eyes slowly trailed up to meet mine. "I think it's safe to say there won't be a soul looking at me. Not with you looking like that."

A shiver raced down my spine.

Friends. Friends. Friends.

I chanted his defense in my head, as if I might hold the power to claim it and make it real when standing next to Rex Gunner felt nothing like being friends.

It felt like sex and need and desperate hearts.

It felt like hope and healing.

There was no question we'd both been hurt. Beaten down and broken in life's own cruel ways.

I wanted to reach out and discover his wounds. Maybe let him discover mine.

"You aren't looking so bad yourself," I managed, choking over the words like a fool. Uttering them aloud seemed foolish. Not when he was dressed in fitted jeans and a light pink button-up, the sleeves rolled up his forearms. High enough to reveal a few of the colorful feathers inked on the top of his forearm.

I'd nearly stumbled over myself when I'd opened my door to find him that way. So ridiculously sexy, his scruff trimmed, his hair that perfectly imperfect mess.

The tension on the ride over in his truck had nearly been more than I could bear. I'd been hyper-aware of every movement, from the flex of his lean muscles as he'd shifted into gear to the clench of that chiseled, stoic jaw.

He'd seemed to have to hold himself rigid in restraint, barely offering a word because one more stimulus might have been the one to tip us over the edge. The detonator to a bomb. The one to shatter our shaky, flimsy ground.

He seemed to war with what to say before he shook his head and pasted on a thin grin. "Come on, let's get up there before Brody thinks I bailed on him."

I started up the steps. Rex placed his hand at the small of my back. I bit back a gasp. It was almost impossible. Not with the way electricity raced through me like a shot of adrenaline.

He groaned the smallest sound. But I felt it, the rumble he emitted. I wasn't alone in this.

We managed to make the climb to the top, and I was sucking in another breath when we stepped out onto the second floor. It was magnificent.

Just . . . jaw-dropping beauty.

The interior matched downstairs, the walls red brick and warm with age. Rows of pool tables lined the far back of the massive room and another elegant bar ran the adjoining wall. Linens, floral arrangements, and formal place settings adorned the tables set up in the middle of the room, all of it obviously brought in exclusively for tonight's party.

What really captured my attention was what faced out front. An accordion wall of glass and rustic wood had been completely opened to the balcony. Planters filled with trees were strategically placed around the area, and strands of Edison bulbs that matched downstairs were strung up between them, covering the outdoor space like a sparkly, glittering ceiling.

It was hard to tell where one space ended and the other began.

But it was the view of the river winding through the city I loved that sent a tumble of nostalgia battering my senses.

"It's beautiful, isn't it?"

I jerked with the rough voice beside me.

I shook myself out of the stupor and offered Rex a small smile. "I almost forgot how beautiful Gingham Lakes is."

A frown pulled at his brows, and he searched my face. "Is that what you wanted? To forget?"

My laughter was tremulous. "It's easier that way, isn't it? Forgetting? Forgetting means things don't hurt so bad."

Pain gusted through his striking features. "And sometimes pain is better than forgetting."

My stomach twisted, and I fumbled for something to say, wanting to reach in and discover exactly what it was he was clinging to. He stopped me by speaking first with an easy diversion. "I'm going to head to the bar. What can I get you to drink?"

"Chardonnay would be nice."

He dipped his head before he headed that direction, winding through the small groups of people who were gathered around. Their conversations were quiet, and the band playing on a small elevated stage in the corner were hardly more than an accent to the vibe.

"Oh my God!"

I spun on my heel at the screech that came from behind me. Nikki was coming right for me, dressed in a flaming red dress, eyes wide with excitement. She hugged me as if she hadn't seen me in years. "Oh my God," she said again, holding me by the outside of my upper arms. "What are you doing here?" Her eyes looked me up and down. "And holy shit, you look fabulous. Are you trying to make us all look bad?"

I felt the heat rush to my face. "Thank you."

Compliments from friends used to be difficult for me to take. Macy had thought it her God-given duty to wipe that idea from my existence, and she'd done a good job of it. She'd nearly scraped all the old insecurities away, and I refused to let them settle back into my skin.

I took her by both hands, squeezing as I smiled. "And are you serious right now? You look like a freaking goddess."

She hiked a shoulder. "What can I say? If given the opportunity to dress up for my Ollie, I'd be a fool not to take it."

I chuckled. God, I really loved her. "Well, he'd be a fool not to notice."

It was almost hurt that flashed in her eyes, but she shook it off. "So, what are you doing here? Did Lillith invite you?"

Again, she was looking around. It was right when Rex broke the crowd, the man so ridiculously gorgeous my breaths turned shallow and my heart took off at a sprint as he strode our way. All lean strength and powerful presence.

"Oh wow." Nikki whipped her attention back to me, mouth dropping open in disbelief.

"It's nothing," I whispered. "We're just friends."

"Really?" Her voice was a wry, scandalous accusation.

"Really," I promised, even though it somehow felt like a lie.

"Nikki," Rex said a little hard with a slight dip of his head.

"Rex," she returned, laughter in her voice.

He handed me the glass of wine. "Here you go."

"Thank you."

I took a sip when I caught sight of Lillith moving our direction. Her hand was wrapped up in the man I knew to be her fiancé.

Broderick Wolfe.

He was tall and wide and impeccably dressed in a suit that had clearly been tailored to perfectly fit his muscular body.

"Rynna. You're here. I love it. All my favorite people in one room." Lillith walked up to me and hugged me before she stepped back and angled her head. "Rex, how are you? It's so nice to see you."

There was a bit of worry in her voice when she asked it. As if she might be protective of me.

"Good," he said in that rough voice. He turned and shook Broderick's hand. "Thanks for the invitation. The place looks great."

Broderick shook his head. "I'm glad you're here. None of this could happen without RG Construction. You're company is the backbone of the operation."

Wow.

That was some kind of praise.

I glanced at Rex. His expression was rimmed with satisfaction as he returned Broderick's handshake. "My men are incredibly skilled. I couldn't be prouder of them."

Broderick laughed, this loud, boisterous laugh as he set a hand on Rex's shoulder. "Always so humble." Broderick looked around the group. "This man right here is the driving force behind an incredible team. He literally has saved my ass at least a thousand times during this project."

He returned his attention to Rex. "You didn't earn your reputation for nothing. I sought you out because *you* are the best. In three short years, you brought RG Construction back from what could have been its demise. That is no easy feat."

Rex flinched.

It was subtle.

But I saw it. Felt it.

His voice was hoarser when he spoke. "If we're looking for someone to give credit to, let's give it to my mother. She was the one who taught me there is nothing hard work won't achieve."

God, this man was an enigma. Hard and soft. Modest and proud. Layers and threads and dimensions of mystery.

Broderick just shook his head as if he couldn't believe Rex, either, before he turned a charismatic smile on me. "And who do we have here?" He reached for me, taking my hand between both of his.

Lillith had her hand tucked under his arm, her smile so free. "This is my friend Rynna I was telling you about. She's the one who inherited Pepper's Pies across the street from the new hotel."

Broderick's face lit. "It's so nice to finally meet you. I was hoping you would choose to reopen rather than selling. Pepper's Pies has an important history in Gingham Lakes, and I know it'll remain the same in the future. If there's anything you need to help with the process, please, don't hesitate to let me know." Even though his words could have been used in a boardroom to sell his next biggest idea, there was a distinct tone of sincerity woven into them.

"It's nice to meet you, as well. And I will definitely keep that in mind. Thank you for the offer."

Broderick looked around the room. "I'm a firm believer Gingham Lakes's revitalization belongs to all of us. We're all responsible for coming together to make it a better place for all residents."

Lillith pushed her cheek into his arm, as if she were overcome by her love for him, and he pressed the softest kiss to the top of her head.

My heart throbbed, and I couldn't help but glance at Rex, drawn to this man who stood stoically at my side.

Broderick gestured to the room. "Dinner should be served in a few minutes. Why don't we all find a place to sit so we can enjoy ourselves?"

As he led us over to a large round table where we all took seats together, Broderick worked the room, welcoming the rest of his guests and inviting them to take a seat. Dinner was served, and we ate and drank and laughed. Lillith and Nikki made it easy to fit in, and it even seemed as if Rex might. Even though there was some part of him that remained reserved.

Afterward, Broderick stood and asked if he could have a word with Rex.

"Excuse me for a minute?" he asked.

"Of course," I told him.

Lillith was in deep conversation with a couple at the next table, and Nikki made an excuse to head downstairs, undoubtedly to find Ollie.

I went to the bar and ordered another glass of wine then wandered out onto the balcony, drawn to the view.

It was quiet, the air still warm, though it'd cooled with the night, and a slight breeze added to the peace in the air. A blanket of stars opened up the vast canopy that stretched on forever above, and I inhaled the scents of the city, the honeysuckle and the river and old buildings.

Home.

I got lost in it, in the soft music that fell on my ears and the peace that radiated back from the city I'd tried to forget I loved.

I jumped when the breath landed on my bare shoulder. "I'm sorry I ditched you."

A small smile tugged at my mouth, and I glanced over my shoulder at the gorgeous man standing right behind me. "I understand. It's a work party."

"I'd rather be hanging out with you."

Butterflies.

Was that normal? It didn't matter. They were there, fluttering at my insides, whipping and stirring and inciting. I slowly turned to face him. "I'd rather be hanging out with you, too."

A soft gust of wind blew through, soft lashes at the longer pieces of his hair, those hypnotizing eyes filled with so much turmoil and questions. He reached up and touched my cheek. "Rynna."

Chills skated my spine.

The band had shifted songs, and strains of an acoustic guitar filled the air. The scruffy voice of the same singer who'd played the last time I was there rode on the breeze. He was singing "Collide" by Howie Day. The lyrics grazed across my skin, eliciting a rash of goose bumps, the same as the callused fingertips that trailed down my arm.

The words spun around us, and slowly, Rex edged forward. His arm slid around my waist and pulled me against him.

His palm went to the small of my back, his thumb just brushing against the bare skin exposed by my dress, the other hand landing on my neck.

My entire world shook.

Slowly, we began to rock in the slowest kind of dance. Both mesmerized by the song and the feel and the overwhelming vibe, his heart thrumming in sync with mine. We were caught up in it, as if time had stopped, the two of us giving ourselves over to the moments that passed. I would have been content for it to go on forever.

He drew me closer, his nose running along the back of my ear. "You are so beautiful, Rynna," he murmured. "So beautiful it fucking hurts to look at you."

"Rex," I whispered, my fingers curling in the fabric of his shirt.

He suddenly stepped back, leaving me gasping as he roughed a frustrated hand over his face. "Think we should get out of here."

Slowly, I nodded and followed him back inside.

seventeen

Rex

What the fuck was I thinking? Inviting her there? Thinking I could handle this?

Friends.

I bit back bitter laughter and led her inside, trying to keep some distance between us when the only thing I wanted was to strip her from that dress and sink inside. We said our goodbyes, thanking Broderick. Lillith gave me a look that promised she would cut off my dick if I did wrong by her friend.

But that was the fucking problem.

I didn't know how to do her right.

Had no idea how to give her what was so clearly building up between us.

A savage storm.

Brutal.

We stepped outside and into the night. Our footsteps echoed on the sidewalk. All the things we wanted to say roiled in the silence between us. I unlocked my truck and helped her into the front seat. My entire body went rigid when I was struck with another wave of that sweetness, the girl inundating me with every tempting, delicious part of her.

Sugar and spice.

Cherry fucking pie.

She was goddamned stunning.

I rounded the front of my trunk and hopped into the front seat. But I didn't start the engine. I just held onto the steering wheel, peering out front and letting her confused silence impale me.

"I'm sorry," I finally said.

She smiled a tentative smile, graced with all that understanding. "For what?"

I scoffed out a laugh as I shifted into gear and pulled onto the road. "For always being such a dick."

She laughed the faintest sound. "You're not always a dick, Rex. I know there's more to you."

"How's that?" I asked. The words flinging between us were almost playful.

"There's no mistaking it when you're with your daughter."

Gruff affection rumbled in my chest. "That's 'cause she's the best part of me."

"She's amazing," Rynna mused, staring out the windshield, her striking face filling up my periphery.

"Yeah. She's all I've got."

I could feel her gaze land on me. Hot and heavy. Demanding in her stare. "Is that the way you want it?"

Unease itched beneath my skin. "That's just the way life goes for me, Rynna. It feels like most days I'm barely hanging on. Barely getting by. She's my life. My heart. Don't think I have room for anything else."

"Because you lost the other half of it?"

Pain lanced through me, cutting me in two. "Lost myself a long fucking time ago. Not sure I'm ever going to get it back."

Her gaze returned out front, her voice growing so soft as she murmured her confession. "You know . . . when I came back here, I was terrified of what might be waiting for me." I could feel her turmoil, the grief this gorgeous girl had kept inside. "Terrified of what had chased me away in the first place. But I knew that what I'd left behind, what was waiting for me, was worth the risk. I didn't want to be afraid anymore."

A frown pulled at my brow. "What were you running from?"

Her laughter was hollow. "Shame. Embarrassment. When I look back, I think maybe I was running from myself." Her chuckle seemed to be completely at her own expense, and her attention dropped to her fingers, which she wrung on her lap. Locks of that chestnut cascaded around her delicate neck. "When I was younger, I was the chubby girl. Awkward. Uncomfortable in my skin."

My eyes lifted, dragging down her body in a sweeping pass. She was lush and curved and fucking perfect, and I hated the idea that she'd once felt anything less.

Her voice softened in wonder. "It feels so ridiculous now, the way I'd let the teasing affect me. I don't know if it was really my size or if I just was insecure and everyone knew it and they took advantage of it. When my momma left, she left a vacancy I didn't understand at the time. I was so lonely, and I think the lonelier I got, the hungrier I got for interaction, but I seemed to always get excluded. I think somehow the kids fed on that. It got worse as I got older."

She glanced at me. Helplessness struck on her features. "It got to the point where I couldn't take it anymore, so I ran."

A shot of rage tumbled through my veins. For her as a little girl. Couldn't imagine it. What if someone treated Frankie like that? "I'm so sorry, Rynna."

She shrugged. "Maybe it made me stronger. For years, I was too afraid to return. But after my grandmother passed, it finally set in. I lost all those years with her, and I didn't want to run anymore. I was tired of running from who I am. Even if I still find myself looking over my shoulder, I won't allow anyone to chase me from my home."

"You belong here," I managed.

I could feel her eyes flicker over to me. "I don't think it's any mistake you and Frankie were the first people I met."

Hesitation brimmed around me. I knew what she was saying. What she was asking for. Never had I felt more at war with what I wanted and what I knew was right. I turned right onto our street, the words grating from my tongue. "My life's a train wreck. One that just seems to go on forever. Every fucking time I think I'm doing something right, it goes to shit."

"What happened with your company three years ago?" she suddenly asked. Peering over at me, she fiddled with the silky strap on that lust-inducing dress. Like she knew asking it was crossing a line. Pushing me further and willing to do it, anyway. "What Broderick mentioned?"

"Just another time life stabbed me in the back. This time it was my business partner. Asshole nearly destroyed me. He made me look like I was a part of his shady practices, stealing from clients, falsifying documents. I very well might have ended up in jail like he did. I managed to prove I had no clue what kind of bullshit he was pulling back at the office while I was out working my fingers to the bone with the crew. Still nearly lost the company because of it, but somehow I managed to hold it together."

Hatred pulsed through my veins. Still couldn't believe the bastard had pulled that shit. It'd nearly knocked me on my ass. The blow was almost as harsh as coming home and finding my wife had left me.

"That's horrible."

Nodding, I pulled into her drive. "It was. Pisses me off the fucker just got released. Takes about all I have not to hunt him down."

She laughed this incredulous sound, honesty gliding onto her face. "You want to hunt yours down and the weak part of me wants to run the other direction."

"Don't ever let anyone chase you from what belongs to you, Rynna Dayne."

eighteen

Rynna

Tension roiled between us. That tether pulled taut. Drawing us closer. I swallowed around it and reached for the latch. He was quick to open his door, jumping out and rounding to my side before I had time to step out of his massive truck. He helped me down, and his hand scorched where he aided me by holding on to my elbow.

"Let me walk you to the door. Last thing I need to be worried about is you here by yourself and some asshole taking advantage of you."

He quirked this belly-flopping grin that pierced me like an arrow. "Unless of course that asshole is me."

He barely angled his head to the side. There was something so endearing and self-deprecating about it. Everything about him right then was at odds with the surly, bear of a man I'd met weeks ago, the man exposing himself, layer by layer.

I lifted my chin, both in strength and vulnerability, tossing all the uncertainties and questions out into the open. "Should I be afraid?"

"Yeah, you should be." His response was hard, but there was no missing the fact his irritation was aimed at himself. He set his palm on the small of my back, helping me through the gravel drive in my heels, an inch behind as we ascended the porch steps.

We crossed the planks. That tension wound higher with each step until we were nothing but needy pants at my door. Slowly, I turned around to face him.

His presence sent a ripple of energy vibrating across the floorboards, the overwhelming sight of him the owner of my breath.

He stood beneath the faint glow of the hurricane lamp that hung outside the door. A sculpture of sinewy muscle and raw strength, forged through years of obvious physical labor. Every inch of him was rugged, from those roughened, callused hands to the crinkles set deep at the edges of his eyes.

The man was a carving of pure, daunting beauty.

"What exactly am I supposed to be afraid of, Rex?" My brow twisted, and my voice quieted with the admission. "Because when I'm around you, the last thing I feel is afraid."

"I fuck everything up, Rynna, and the only thing I've got to offer you is my mess. I *can't* do this."

Restraint rumbled in his chest, the sound so deep I felt it shake the ground beneath my feet.

I gently cupped one side of his rugged face. "I'm not afraid."

It was a promise.

An appeal.

"You should be," he grated. "Warned you, my shit doesn't ever end well."

"Maybe that's a chance I'm willing to take."

He groaned and he planted his hands high above my head. The man panted above me, torn, desperate, his nose just brushing mine. "God damn it, Rynna. God damn it."

I felt the moment he broke. When the thread pulled too tight and this mesmerizing man snapped. His mouth descended on mine.

Overpowering.

Overwhelming.

Dizzying.

Lips and tongue and nips of teeth.

And those hands. They were on my face. My neck. My waist. Somehow, I managed to hold on to him and spin away as I fumbled with the lock. He pressed against my backside, his cock against my bottom, and his mouth leaving a trail of fire at the side of my neck. We stumbled into the darkness of my house, breaking apart as I turned to face him.

The only light trickled down from the lamp I'd left on upstairs.

Slowly, he clicked the door shut behind him. We stood there, two feet away from each other, staring.

Chests heaving.

Before we collided.

A tangle of tongues and bodies.

The man frantic, trying to touch me everywhere.

"What am I doing? Fuck, what am I doing?" he muttered incoherently, kissing me deeper. Madder. Wilder.

I pushed up on my toes and tore my mouth from his so I could kiss down the strong column of his throat. His head thudded back against the door, his entire body pressing against it as if he needed it to keep him standing.

He grated my name, and I kept kissing at his throat while I worked free the button on his jeans, hands shaking.

Every reservation spun out of control.

Out of reach.

It was only spurred further when the defined muscles of his abdomen jumped and twitched beneath my touch, when he mumbled, "You're killing me, Rynna. Fucking killing me."

Desire rippled from him in heady waves.

And I felt so brave and bold, my kisses brazen as I nipped at the hollow of his throat, my fingers sure as I inched down his zipper.

Before I could consider it—the ramifications and the repercussions and the distinct threat to my heart—I dropped to my knees and pulled his jeans and underwear down to the middle of his thighs.

I refused to think of anything but setting him free.

Hoping he'd find a little of that freedom in me.

Even if it was only for a few stolen moments.

But God, I was unprepared. Just an unsuspecting, naïve fool when his thick cock bobbed out in front of me, level with my eyes.

Engorged and hard.

As big and ruggedly beautiful as the rest of him, the fat head already dripping with his need.

A flood of desire rushed me, and my stomach twisted into a thousand knots. It incited an ache in the deepest part of me. My core was a ball of fire. Heat spreading fast and throbbing between my thighs.

I pressed them together as if it might offer relief, my mouth dry, my heart thrashing against its boundaries.

Racing ahead of me as if it already knew our destination.

Those big hands were suddenly on the sides of my head. He forced me to look up at him. Hunger glinted in his eyes, a dangerous cocktail of sorrow and need and restraint.

That mesmerizing sage deepened to steel. It was when I knew he'd taken another turn.

All needy, dominant man.

"Is this what you really want? You want me to fuck that sweet mouth?"

I shivered with the promise of his words. Again caught off guard by this man who'd left me on unstable ground.

"I just want to make you feel good," I whispered.

He was so hard. Every inch of him. From the clench of his jaw to the ripple of his stomach to his length that protruded and dipped and bounced in front of me.

The tip barely grazed my lips. My tongue flicked out and swept across the velvet flesh.

Rex hissed. "Fuck . . . Rynna. I can't fucking do this. This is wrong. So fucking wrong."

But instead of pushing me away, he tugged me closer. A raw groan escaped him when I wrapped both my hands around him at the base and sucked his crown into my mouth.

He rasped a curse and rocked forward. Control slipping. Control I somehow knew he used as a defense. As a way to keep everyone at arm's length.

My tongue pressed at the underside of his cock, and I pulled him deeper.

Drawing him in.

Slowly.

Just as slowly as I began to work him with my hands.

And maybe I should have known I was in trouble when I began to shake. When the entire room spun at the feel of him. At the impact of him.

At the way I completely succumbed when he muttered, "That mouth," as he hooked his fingertips below my jaw, drawing my eyes up to meet his.

His thumbs brushed the curve of my cheeks before he moved them to the edge of my lips. His eyes flashed with something tender. Soft and gentle.

Before something else entirely took them over. Something raw. Possessive. Intense.

His hips began to snap, jutting forward. He pressed himself deeper into my mouth. Filling me so full I struggled not to gag. So turned on I writhed where I knelt on the floor. The man so powerful I had to surrender.

"God . . . Ryn . . . Ryn . . . feels so good. Fuck . . . so good. That mouth."

A flood of words poured from his mouth as he fucked mine.

Wildly.

Madly.

Greedily.

And God. I liked it. I liked it that he'd taken control. Liked that he stood over me, taking what I wanted to give. Liked that I held the power to make him moan.

I liked *him*.

I liked him so much. More than I should. In a way that was getting messy. In a way that was soft and fragile, breakable, as it spun the most complex web inside me. Strands of want and ribbons of need.

"Rynna . . ." He grunted my name, a deep, reverberating utterance that echoed the walls. I swallowed around him, taking him as deep as I possibly could. Every part of me ached. My jaw and my heart and that needy throb at begged at the juncture of my thighs.

His thrusts turned rough. Hard and demanding. "Harder . . . please . . . take it."

I pumped him savagely, just as ruthlessly as he took my mouth, my hands picking up the same frantic rhythm as his assault.

And I could feel it. His balls tighten and lift. The ripple of his abdomen, those powerful thighs straining.

That electricity licked and lapped.

Striking.

"God damn it, Rynna. God damn it."

His hips snapped twice more.

Frantic and frenzied.

Before every glorious inch of him went rigid. A tightly keening bow.

He pulsed with his orgasm, and his head kicked back on a guttural roar as he let himself go.

It was exactly what I'd wanted.

To see this man undone.

To get a glimpse of him with his walls toppled.

And the sight of it . . . the sight of it was magnificent.

His cock throbbed and jerked as he spilled into my mouth, and I gulped him down as I stared up at the ecstasy on his face.

Slowly he opened his eyes, but the same frenzy remained in them. Fire. He quickly lifted me from the floor. Before I could make sense of it, my bottom was balanced on the back of the sofa, my dress around my waist, his fingers spreading me.

Filling me.

His eyes were desperate as he stroked me deep. I moaned as he fucked me with his fingers, his thumb bringing me to ecstasy.

So fast.

So fast I was shocked by the bliss that exploded in my body. A flashflood that came out of nowhere.

Laying me to waste.

My fingers dug into his shoulders as I came. Wave after wave.

He slowed, panting, eyes wild. He stepped back as if he couldn't make sense of what had just happened between us, slowly lowering my feet to the ground.

"God damn it." His words cracked.

I sagged, holding onto the back of the couch for support. Spent. Drained. Confused.

He was quick to tuck himself back into his jeans. Looking everywhere but at me, he roughed agitated hands through his hair. "God damn it. *God damn it.* Friends. Friends. What bullshit."

He started to frantically pace.

"Rex," I whispered, trying to break through whatever freak out he was having.

"I can't . . . I can't believe I just—fuck!" he shouted and threw an aimless punch into the air. "I can't do this."

My knees were shaky, and my heart was erratic. I stretched a hand out toward him. "Why can't you? Why can't you do this?"

I'd never been a beggar. I'd never chased a man except for the one who'd broken my heart the day I'd turned eighteen. I was a quick learner. If a man didn't want what I had to offer, then he didn't deserve me.

Yet, there was something about Rex Gunner that made me want to shout and plead and pound on his chest. Demand he open up. Show me everything he kept shored up inside.

That same something told me he *needed* what I had to give. That whatever I'd been lacking, he'd found in me, too.

"I have to get out of here," he said, stalking for the door.

Shocked and confused, I watched, hurt bubbling up and coating my tongue with disbelief.

He was just going to leave? After what we'd just done?

I pressed my lips together, my chin trembling as I fought tears. Tears bred of hope and frustration. "I told you I'm not afraid. Why are you? All I'm asking is that you take a chance on me. Life's not worth living without taking them."

He froze at the door, and he laughed this horrible, cutting sound. He shifted to look at me from over his shoulder. "You want to know why I'm afraid, Rynna?"

His head angled to the side, and his eyes brimmed with a kind of hatred I knew wasn't directed at me. "I'm afraid because I fuck everything up. I'm afraid because everything I touch? Everything I love? Eventually, I taint it. Ruin it. And then there's nothing left but misery and suffering and fear. And my daughter . . . my Frankie? She's all I've got left. She's the one good thing that remains unblemished. And the few bits remaining of me? They belong to her, because I've already given everything else. I told you, I don't have anything to offer you. I'm sorry. I'm so fucking sorry, but I refuse to do anything selfish or stupid that would put her happiness at risk."

He opened the door, but he paused, wavering before he peered back at me again. Surrender carved into every line on his gorgeous face. "I don't have any chances left to take, Rynna Dayne. I've already used up all the ones I've been given, and if I take anything else? I'd be nothing but a thief."

Without another word, he strode out, letting the door drop closed behind him.

It was that moment when the man officially twisted me in two.

Because when he walked out that door? He took a part of me I had no chance of ever getting back.

nineteen

Rynna

I was going to be late.

Shit.

I was going to be really, really late.

And I couldn't be late.

Everything was riding on this meeting.

In one heel and wearing a fitted skirt, I stumbled out of the walk-in closet, which was filled with a bunch of boxes my grandmother had left behind.

I stumbled, my hand darting out to the wall for support, and paused for a beat in an attempt to shimmy on the other heel. Once I was at least the same height on both sides, I tried again.

Two steps away from the small dressing table on the far side of the room, my ankle rolled.

All the way to the side.

Pain splintered up the outside of my leg.

"Shit," I yelped as I tried to rebound and stop my fall. The only thing I managed to do was to propel myself forward. Falling fast. My hands shot out, and my fingertips just snagged the edge of the stool a split second before my face slammed against the floor.

My knees weren't so lucky.

They dug into the worn carpet, pantyhose shredded.

Awesome.

My head dropped between my shoulders, and I fought the sting of tears that rushed to my eyes.

Tears of frustration. Tears of worry. Tears of this heartache that had grown every day since Rex Gunner had walked out my door two weeks ago without another word.

I'd told myself I was just being stupid. Foolish. Chasing a man who obviously wanted nothing to do with me. Just because I told myself those things didn't mean I could so easily convince myself of them. Not when they felt like a lie.

God. Why did life have to be so complicated? I had enough to worry about without the gorgeous man and his adorable daughter who lived across the street. And somehow, they had become the center of every thought.

Laughter jutted from my mouth.

The maniacal kind.

The kind that could have been sobbing. It all depended on how you heard it. Or maybe on the way you looked at it.

If you aren't laughing, you're crying. Now, which would you rather be doing?

My grandmother's soft encouragement prodded at my consciousness, and I could almost feel the pad of her thumb brushing across my cheek.

I drew in a deep breath, hoping it might give me clarity, guidance, the words a chorus of convoluted whispers that tumbled from my tongue. "I don't know if I know the difference anymore, Gramma. Things are getting complicated. So complicated, and I don't know how to handle them all. I don't know if I can do this. It feels like I'm going to fail."

God. What if I failed?

The thought made that gulp of air in my lungs throb and threaten to burst. It was a complete rejection of the idea.

Needing to pull myself together, I lifted my head and started to climb to my feet. A frown pulled across my brow when my sight latched on an envelope I'd never noticed before. It was tucked in a small cubby on the dressing table.

"Oh, Gramma."

I sat up on my knees, fingers trembling with affection and grief. I reached out and pulled the envelope free. I was quick to turn it over, rip open the flap, and tear out the card.

I devoured the words.

Obstacles are everywhere. They often feel insurmountable. Impossible. Sometimes they are nothing but stepping-stones. Other times, they are a diversion. A distraction. More often than not, they are there with the simple purpose of showing you that you *can*.

But every now and again, they are a redirection. A deviation. A repurposing. And this detour? It will guide you to a destination you never imagined you'd go but where you belonged the whole time.

"What are you trying to tell me, Gramma?" I whispered into the nothingness. That nothingness echoed back. Crushing me with affection.

With loss. With the memories of her voice and her reason and everything she'd given up for me.

I clutched the letter to my chest. Cherishing her words. It didn't matter that I couldn't decipher them. All that mattered was that they were meant for me. Given in a moment I needed them most.

My grandmother always had that way about her. Insight. The uncanny ability to know when I needed a kind word or a soft prod.

Resolved, I pushed to my feet, tore off the ruined pantyhose, and shoved my feet back into the shoes. I dusted a little powder on my nose and ran some shimmery nude gloss across my lips.

I looked at myself in the mirror. "You can do this, Rynna Dayne. You wanted this. Now, go and get it."

I rushed downstairs and through the living room, grabbing my leather bag and the portfolio I'd prepared that waited inside. Silently, I went through the details in my head. The things I would say, employing some of the strategy tools I'd learned back in San Francisco.

Maybe I was supposed to have gone there. Maybe that experience had been preparing me for this day all along.

I didn't mean to falter a step when I strode outside and into the morning light.

But I did.

Because Rex Gunner was there, just backing out of the backseat of his truck where I knew he had just gotten done strapping his daughter into her booster seat. His care for her was nearly as breathtaking as his presence.

Regretful eyes moved my direction. I thought maybe he didn't have the power to stop them. Just the same way as I couldn't stop my own. My gaze drank him in as if he were forbidden fruit. Something—*someone*—I wanted so desperately I was willing to try to pluck him free from all the thorny barbs and spindly spines that kept him bound.

That *destination* perilous.

Hazardous to my health.

Sucking in a stealing breath, I shook off the reaction and forced myself to walk down the steps and to my SUV, barely glancing back when I pulled out of my drive and headed down the road.

But in that barest glimpse I saw him.

I saw his pain. I saw his fear. I saw his regret. And I swore I saw him standing there, held back by that gnarl of branches, wishing I could reach him, too.

But sometimes we have to admit when those obstacles just run too deep.

Spine stiff and straight, I shifted anxiously in the hard plastic chair. My legs were perfectly pressed together, from my thighs to my knees to my ankles, the portfolio neatly placed on my lap as I waited.

Each second that passed was excruciating, my heart thundering so loud I kept expecting someone to lean my direction and shush me. To tell me to rein in the riot of nerves that stampeded out ahead of me, only to do laps around the small waiting room of the bank.

My gaze darted everywhere, to the tellers, then to the few clerks who were opening and managing accounts in the grouping of cubicle offices that took up the right front side of the bank.

Who would these people be rooting for in this race?

For me?

For my grandmother?

For the vacant, deserted diner that sat only three miles away, begging for someone to take mercy on its desolation?

Scrubbing away the grime would only get me so far.

If I were going to get any farther, I needed money. God knew that *five dollars* I'd had left to work magic with hadn't gotten me very far.

A woman appeared at the end of a hall. "Ms. Dayne?"

"Yes?"

She cast me a generous smile. "Mr. Roth will see you now. Right this way."

Trembling, I stood, fingers shaking as I straightened my skirt. "Thank you."

I attempted to gather my wits, to put on a brave face, to wear resolve and confidence. I knew I would be riding the fine line of approval since my loan was high risk, and I could only hope my belief in the business would throw it over the edge in my favor.

I followed her down the short hall to where the private loan offices were located. My heels clicked on the tile floor, in tune with the hammer of my heart. It drummed harder and harder with each step.

She gestured with her arm into an office, murmuring, "Good luck," as she turned to walk back the direction we'd come.

Swallowing hard, I lifted my chin, painting on that firm confidence and forcing myself to wear a smile as I turned the corner of the doorway and stepped into the office.

I faltered to a standstill.

My breath gone.

Stolen.

Stopped by an obstacle I wasn't sure I could overcome.

Timothy Roth.

Tim.

Handsy asshole from the bar.

Doesn't understand the word no.

He cracked an arrogant smile. "Well, well, well, if it isn't the lovely . . ." He paused to inspect the name on the application that sat open on his desk. The pre-approval application I'd dropped off three days ago before my scheduled appointment with the head loan officer.

Timothy Roth.

"Corinne Dayne." He rocked back in his big leather office chair, looking as if he'd just won the lottery. Or more like he was just holding hostage the numbers to my winning lottery ticket.

That sounded about right.

Dread slithered up my throat, like the slow, slimy slide of a snake. Constricting from the outside. Suffocating from the inside.

"Mr. Roth." It was a breath of uncertainty. Of indecision and doubt.

Why? First Aaron, and then this asshole? What was I going to do?

He gestured a little too eagerly to the chair that sat across from his desk. "Please, shut the door and take a seat."

My body quaked, but I did what I was told, the door snapping shut behind me, my feet unsteady as I took the three steps to stand in front of his desk. In discomfort, I eased down onto the chair.

Get it together, Rynna. This is too important for you to mess up now. Don't let either of these jerks hold you back.

I wasn't fool enough to think all things didn't come at a cost. And sometimes that cost was your pride.

"Thank you for meeting with me," I managed.

He had his elbow propped on the armrest of his chair, his index finger at his temple and his thumb under his jaw. Blatantly, he looked me up and down. His eager smile curved into a smirk. "The pleasure's all mine."

I ignored the lump that thickened in my throat. "I hope you've had the chance to look at my application."

"Yes, I have, and we appreciate you looking to our establishment for your needs."

Okay. This was good. We could totally ignore our previous awkward situation.

I nodded, continued. "As you read, I inherited Pepper's Pies from my grandmother when she passed away several months ago." God, I hated the way it came out, as if she were nothing but a distant memory. Not when her loss was a fresh wound that ached inside of me. I forced a small smile. "The location is on Fairview, a prime location, especially with all the renovations currently happening in the area."

He thumbed through the paperwork. I eased a little, my rigid spine softening when he turned his attention from me and to the reason I was here.

"And you're asking for two-hundred-thousand dollars?" he asked, still perusing the sheets. "How did you come to this number?"

"Yes. I had an estimator come in before I took over holdings on the building. It should be sufficient to get us up and running again."

He nodded. "That's good."

Hope blazed to life.

I shifted to the edge of the chair. "You can see we have the profit and loss estimates on page thirteen. With the reputation of the diner, I was told I could expect profits to exceed the loss within a year. It will give me plenty for the upkeep of the diner, a modest salary for myself, and the ability to pay the loan each month."

Okay, maybe it was a bit of a stretch. I'd be riding a fine line. But I was willing to put in the extra work.

Studying that page, he rubbed his chin. "Estimates are estimates, Ms. Dayne. There's no guarantee customers will be rushing back to the diner."

That hope fizzled a little, but I pulled it together, prepared for this type of resistance. "I wouldn't consider my situation atypical. Most small businesses begin with a loan, just the same as I'm seeking from this bank. And most start-ups don't already have a name behind them. We have a built-in customer base, and with the hotel going in across the street, there will be hundreds of hungry people in front of my restaurant every single day."

A smile twitched at the corner of his mouth, and I smiled back eagerly. He flipped the folder closed and rocked back in his seat, threading his fingers together. "I'll tell you what . . ."

"Yes?" I edged forward more just as he leaned over his desk, unable to stop myself from mimicking his posture, those dreams I'd once held now dangling right out in front of me like a carrot.

His voice lowered as he leaned even closer. "We discuss this over dinner and you can show me just how badly you want this loan."

Something sinister had infiltrated those words.

Something dark and vulgar.

The hairs at my nape prickled in a sickening kind of awareness.

"Excuse me?" I asked, barely able to speak.

"You look like a smart woman, Ms. Dayne. I think you're playing coy again."

Every sleazy memory of him came rushing back, the arrogant man who didn't know how to take no for an answer and thought women should bow at his feet. But this was his job. Was he really going there?

"I think you need to *demonstrate* just how good you are." Every word was packed with innuendo. "Show me why I should recommend this loan for approval."

He cocked his head. The man with all the power. My dreams held hostage in his filthy paws.

Nausea turned my insides.

"So you're saying I have to go out with you in order for you to recommend my application be approved?"

He glanced over my shoulder toward the closed door before his seedy gaze returned to me. "Call it a business exchange."

"You can't . . . that isn't legal." I was floundering, looking behind me to the closed door. Praying by some miracle someone was standing there and could vouch for this insanity.

Because he was out of his mind.

"I'm merely asking for a meeting, Ms. Dayne." His intentions were so much more than a meeting.

And I wondered how many *meetings* this vile man had held over his client's heads. No doubt, I wasn't the first.

Stunned, I climbed to my feet. Memories of Aaron ripped through my head. The manipulation. I would never allow it again. "You are unbelievable. I would rather work every hour for the rest of my life to save the money to reopen my grandmother's restaurant than degrade myself with you."

He rocked back in that massive chair that was almost as big as his head. "All I asked for was proof of how much you wanted this loan, Ms. Dayne. I have no idea what you're insinuating."

I sneered. "And you are nothing but a liar. For the record, I want that loan more than anything. I'd just rather die than let you touch me."

Wrenching open the door, I flew out into the hall. Fury rose to the top of the tangle of emotions he had me in, my instincts kicking in.

Timothy Roth had messed with the wrong girl.

I was going right around this obstacle. Deviating course. Going straight to the top and reporting him.

I would see to it that Timothy Roth would never manipulate another woman sitting in his office again.

It was late Friday afternoon when there was a knock at my door. A shiver of nerves rocked through me, but I forced them down, refusing the insecurities that kept trying to creep back into my consciousness.

I crossed the living room and peered into the peephole, frowning when I could only make out the arm of a man wearing a dress shirt.

Warily, I unlocked the door and cracked it open, a crest of unease washing over me.

Unease that hadn't been in vain.

I should have listened to my gut.

Just like my gramma had always told me.

I tried to slam the door shut when I saw the angry, twisted features of the man looming on the other side.

It was the same second I hit a wall of fear.

Or maybe I toppled headfirst into a vat of it.

Because it swallowed me. Saturating every inch. Every cell. Every fiber.

Screaming, I turned my back to the door and planted my feet against the floor. I pushed back as hard as I could.

"I already called the police. They're on their way."

Lies. Lies I prayed would break through his derangement. Because I'd been right. Timothy Roth was insane. Just in an entirely different way than I'd ever imagined.

Blood sloshed in my ears and terror slogged through my veins.

A steady *thwump, thwump, thwump.*

Liquid metal.

Heavy.

Too much.

Panic and fear.

No. No. No.

The threat did nothing to deter him. The door banged open an inch before I was bearing down again. With all my might. With all the fight I had in me. The latch so close to catching.

His voice seeped like venom through the crack he made. "You fucking bitch. You fucking bitch whore. I'll kill you for what you did. I know it was you. You ruined my life, you stupid bitch, and you are going to pay."

Fingers were in the frame, forcing it open.

Adrenaline and anguish. I screamed with them as I shifted a fraction. I rammed into the door with my shoulder.

I gave it everything I had.

The pain of it nearly split me in two.

But sometimes wills and physical strength were two different things.

Because he kicked the door, sending it crashing against the interior wall.

I flew to the floor.

Tim pushed his way inside, a menace that cast a shadow on my grandmother's house as he stepped toward me. I slid back across the floor, the bare skin of my thigh chaffing against the carpet.

Sobbing.

Hating that I couldn't stop the terror from taking hold.

Hating the words that fumbled from my mouth.

That I pled

That I begged.

"Please. No. Oh, God, please, I'll do anything."

Anything.

Because it was the brutal truth of the horrible matter.

I *wouldn't* rather die than let Timothy Roth touch me.

twenty

Rex

I was going to lose my fuckin' head. I stormed through my kitchen, raking my fingers through my hair like it might stand the chance of calming me down.

Frankie was having her usual Friday night sleepover at my mom's, and I was supposed to be heading out to meet up with Kale to grab a bite to eat, after which no doubt we'd end up at the bar so we could hang out with Ollie for a few hours.

But there I was.

Fuming.

I had no claim. No right to think of that girl as mine. That didn't mean my heart and body and mind weren't screaming it when the piece of shit who'd been giving her a hard time at Olive's a few weeks back pulled into her driveway. When he stumbled out of his shiny silver Mercedes and staggered up the inclined bank toward the deck steps.

What the hell was she thinking? Messing around with that scumbag?

My brain spun with a shit-ton of possibilities I didn't want to entertain.

Had she gone back to the bar on a night I hadn't been there and run into this douche and decided to give it a go? Had she given him her number that night? Had something been going on all along?

No. I knew better than that. There was no chance she'd been fucking around with him before I'd been a complete bastard and pushed her away.

My thoughts headed south.

Right to that mouth.

That fucking mouth that had been wrapped around me two weeks ago.

Warm and wet and sucking me deep, the girl on her knees like some kind of offering.

A sacrifice.

Somehow, I'd gotten that was what it'd been. That she'd been cutting herself wide open. Letting me take and use and exploit.

And I'd wanted it. Wanted it so badly. Wanted *her* so badly. But how the fuck could I do that to her? Not when I still couldn't make sense of the disaster zone that was my heart. Not when I was locked up in bullshit chains that she didn't need to be tied to. The last two weeks had been torture, pretending she wasn't right there, across the street. That I didn't care when there was a fucking uproar demolishing my insides.

I made another pass through my kitchen, peering out the window like some deranged ex-boyfriend.

Did I actually think that asshat was any worse than I was?

Shit.

Maybe I did. Because I was back to glaring out my kitchen window with my fingertips digging into the granite countertop. Hoping they might sink in and permanently embed themselves. Anchor me so I couldn't do something supremely stupid.

Like run out the door and start making demands I had no right to make.

Why the hell was the fool hesitating at the base of her steps? Why were his shoulders and back heaving, hands in fists?

This guy . . . it was like . . .

Like he was pissed.

Not pissed.

Enraged.

My heart did something funny when he finally snapped into action. It was a slow, unfurling of awareness that pushed around the periphery of my consciousness as I watched him climb the steps. An overwhelming sense that slicked like ice down my spine, forcing me to stand and take note.

My eyes narrowed, scrutinizing his every move.

I didn't have a direct view of the door since it was on the side of the house, only the deck where the douchebag stood fully in my line of sight. He pounded on her door with the back of his fist.

There was movement. I couldn't actually see her door, but somehow, I knew she'd cracked it open. It was a shift in the atmosphere. I *knew* she opened it just as assuredly as I knew that she tried to force it closed.

Then the piece of shit was trying to shove it open. He reeled back, lifted a foot, and kicked it in.

Rynna.

Rynna.

Every fear I'd ever had tumbled free and lit my veins.

Gasoline and flames.

My soul screamed.

I wouldn't fucking let this happen.

Not again. I flew out my door, down the steps, and across the street before I was barreling up hers.

My heart was in my fucking throat, stomach twisted in a single knot of dread. Dread that raged. A steely demand that I protect her.

Save her. Defend her. Keep her. It chanted through that hollow space.

Would have run out to protect anyone. I knew I would. Still, there was no questioning the driving force was completely different when I came up behind the bastard and saw Rynna sobbing on the ground.

Fear consumed her, her expression full of horror and pleas as she scooted back across the floor.

He loomed over her, encroaching, filled with that rage I'd sworn I'd witnessed from the window. He was spewing a verbal attack I knew was mere seconds from becoming physical. "You fucking bitch. You ruined my life."

He was so consumed with debasing her that he hadn't noticed I was there. That I was inching forward, trying to quiet my breaths that were jolting from my lungs in spastic quakes.

A chill climbed to the air. Freezing. Clotting the tension. Every second stretched out. Dense and dark and deep.

A whimper from the ground, and my heart nearly fucking left my chest when those java eyes flashed my direction.

It only lasted for one of those extended seconds, but there was more communication in that brief exchange than in any conversation I'd ever had in my life.

Relief.

Deliverance.

Trust.

She poured it into me. Filling me full.

And this girl . . . this girl looked right back at him, continuing to beg like I wasn't even there.

So fucking smart and aware.

It would make taking out this piece of shit a whole ton easier than it would have been if he knew I was coming.

He didn't.

I rushed, and from behind, I hooked my arm around his neck. I cinched down against his throat, my other hand held around my wrist to keep my hold locked tight, my mouth at his ear. "Hey, fucker, remember me? Warned you last time if you didn't leave the girl alone, you wouldn't be able to walk away. You think I was joking?"

For a blink, he went slack, a huge breath sucked into his lungs at his surprise, his own awareness seeping through his rage and into his consciousness. That was all it took for every muscle in his body to tighten before the bastard started fighting back. His fingers sank into the flesh of my forearm, nails digging in like a bitch, the pussy battling to break free.

I tightened my hold, teeth gritted as I struggled to keep him restrained. "Rynna, call the police so we can send this dick where he belongs."

She was already on her knees, pushing to stand, her limbs shaking uncontrollably as she tried to find balance. Her eyes darted to the spot behind me where I remembered she'd stowed her purse the night I'd shown up here with Frankie.

No doubt, that was where her cell phone was.

I met those eyes again, not needing to say a word.

Go. I've got you. I won't let anything happen to you.

She bolted that direction.

The bastard thrashed, throwing an elbow into my ribs at the same time as he threw back his head. His skull cracking against my nose almost sent me to my knees. Pain exploded across my face. Blinding. Splitting. Enough that I momentarily lost my hold.

It gave him enough time to kick out a leg, tripping Rynna as she was rushing around us to make it to her purse.

She flew forward, slamming her head against the corner of the entryway table that was set against the wall next to the door as she fell face-first to the ground.

Rage.

This time it was my own.

"You asshole. You think I'm gonna stand here and let you hurt her?"

Never.

Fuck.

Never.

Once again, he was going her direction. I lunged for him, plowing into his side and catching him off guard. He stumbled and lost his footing. The two of us toppled to the floor where we were a tangle of limbs and punches and splattering blood.

His.

Mine.

I straddled his chest. Pounding my fist into his face. Blow after blow.

But the fucker fought. Fought and fought and fought.

Clipping me on the chin, he sent me sailing back, and he scrambled to get on top of me. He was on me, pinning me down. He smashed his elbow into my cheek.

"You piece of shit . . . is that all you got? Only way you can get a woman is by forcing her? Huh? Is that how the game is played by pussies with nonexistent dicks? Or is it just so small no one knows it's there?"

I knew I was taunting him. Enraging him more. Inciting him to keep pounding on me.

But that was just fine.

Only thing I was doing was buying time.

Because the girl had already dialed 9-1-1, shouted out her address, had given the vile piece of shit's name.

She'd be safe.

That was all that fucking mattered.

I tried not to wince when I saw him cock back his fist, his knuckles going straight for my temple. This shit was gonna hurt. Probably knock me out flat.

She was worth it. She was worth it. She was worth it.

Sirens whirled in the distance, coming closer and closer.

She would be safe. She would be safe.

But that fist never met its mark. The asshole howled in agony. He flew off me, catching air, tumbling across the floor before he was bent over on his knees, clutching the side of his head. Blood poured out from between his fingers and dripped to the carpet.

I squinted, wondering if I was having some kind of hallucination. The perfect kind. The one where the most gorgeous girl I'd ever seen was standing above me. That chestnut hair matted, mangled with blood. Chest heaving. A huge glass vase gripped in both her hands, an enormous crack zigzagging down the middle of it, and a river of fractures splintering out.

Outside, engines roared. By the sound of it, at least three cruisers came to a screeching stop in front of Rynna's house. Feet pounded and voices shouted.

Seconds later, they were piling into her house, shouting for everyone to freeze.

Rynna dropped the vase. It finally gave up its fight with the impact, shattering into a thousand pieces when it hit the floor. Just as Rynna was doing the same. Dropping to her knees and hitting the floor.

Sobs wracked her body when she realized it was over.

That she was safe.

Right then? It was the absolute only thing that mattered.

twenty-one

Rynna

"Thanks again, man," Rex said to Seth, the last officer at my house. He was a guy Rex had apparently known since high school, someone Rex considered a friend.

"Just, stay safe," Seth said, glancing between the two of us before he ambled down my porch steps and slipped into the driver's seat of his Ford sedan and pulled away.

Timothy Roth had been fired this afternoon. Apparently, my complaint of sexual harassment hadn't been the first he'd received. Apparently, when his wife found out the reason for his termination, she'd kicked him out.

His wife.

I trembled at the thought of it, at the arrogance and stupidity of the man and how much worse it could have been.

The taillights of Seth's patrol car splashed another dose of red into the blaze of reds and oranges and purpled blues that twisted into the sunset as he accelerated down the narrow neighborhood road.

Then it was as if the dial had been turned up on the silence.

So loud it was profound.

As loud as Rex Gunner's presence that eclipsed all.

A thunder.

A thriving, living being.

His gruff voice cut into the tension. "Don't like that you refused treatment. You sure you don't want me to give Kale a call?"

I chanced looking over at him where he stood behind me on the far side of the deck.

My savage savior.

Streaks of blood were dried on his face, and a small gash oozed from the corner of his eye. His clothes were tattered, soiled with sweat and blood, his hair a mess, body still bristling with remnants of pent-up rage.

My lungs inflated at the mesmerizing sight of him. Every part of me expanded. Reaching toward him.

"You're worried about me?" I managed. "You're the one who came to my rescue. The one who put himself on the line. Again. I can't . . . what if . . ."

His head angled and his shoulders rolled back, and the man took a powerful step forward.

The energy spiked.

"You think I'm not worried about you?" It almost sounded like an accusation. He took another step forward, the man a raging tower of protection. "You think I wouldn't do it all over again? You think I would have let him hurt you?"

He was suddenly in front of me. My breath gone when he stood over me.

An imposing, conquering shadow.

Eclipsing the fear that had taken me hostage. If it weren't for Rex, today would have ended in an entirely different way.

He lifted his fingers and brushed back a chunk of hair stuck to my cheek. His words rumbled like a threat. "I wanted to kill him, Rynna. He was going to hurt you, and I wanted to kill him. I would have. Second I saw you were in trouble, my heart was screaming out to protect you. To protect what *belonged* to me. To shelter what was *mine*."

Mine.

The word trembled around us.

"Thank you," I whispered. A tear slipped free, and my body began to shake with the aftermath. With the reality of it all.

A gasp ripped from my chest when I was suddenly swept off my feet and into the strength and security of Rex's arms. He had one arm under my back and the other beneath my knees, my body held possessively against the strength of his chest.

"Won't let anyone hurt you," he murmured against my forehead. Carrying me, he angled through the door. "I'm gonna take care of you."

"Rex." It was a whimper.

"Shh. I know, baby. I know."

I clung to his neck as he carried me upstairs. At the landing, he took a left and headed into my bedroom, pushing right past my unmade bed and through the cutout arch that led to the bathroom.

As if this man already knew the way.

He set me on unsteady feet and turned me to face the counter. My eyes met his in the mirror. A low growl climbed his throat, and he leaned around me to turn on the faucet.

The air constricted.

Charged.

I swore, our slowed, measured movements attracted every molecule within five miles. He wrapped his arms around me from behind, taking my hands in his and placing them beneath the fall of warm water. He gently rubbed our hands together, the basin filling with pink-tinged water as he scrubbed the blood free from our dirtied hands.

"Two weeks, Rynna. Two weeks I've been dying, hating the way I left things between us. Hating that I hurt you."

His words brushed my cheek, and his presence filled my senses.

Overwhelming.

He squirted soap onto our hands, continuing to wash away this afternoon, as if he wanted to erase the possibility of what could have happened.

Carefully.

Meticulously.

His voice was a soft scrape at the shell of my ear, sending shivers down my neck, turning my heart into a thundering orb at the center of my chest. "All that time, I was wishing with every part of me I could change my circumstances. That I could be right for you. Then *this*, Rynna. Then this happened and I don't fucking care, anymore. Don't fucking care that this is wrong."

His eyes captured mine through the mirror. They flashed with a warning. An omen. A prediction.

"I'm not afraid," I whispered, my promise striking the throbbing air. He gathered my hair in his hand, shifting it all to one side, exposing my neck. He pressed his lips there in the barest kiss. "That's funny, because I'm fucking terrified of you." His nose ran up to the back of my ear. "Terrified of this."

A shiver rolled down my spine, and Rex eased back a fraction, taking the hem of my shirt and drawing it slowly up my body.

That shiver shifted. An avalanche of chills. He peeled it over my head before he did the same to his own, scrubbing at his face before he tossed his shirt to his feet.

My gaze traced him through the mirror, and I swallowed around the emotion that grew thick at the base of my throat.

This complicated, amazing man drove me crazy with desire. Crazy with need. Crazy with this want that had become its own entity inside of me.

He reached up and let his fingertips flutter across my exposed shoulder and down my arm. Tingles spread in a slow slide. All the fear I'd felt earlier transformed into this emotion I wasn't sure I'd ever felt before.

Something so real it staggered my senses.

He reached back and unfastened my bra, drawing the straps down my arms.

My nipples pebbled as my breasts were exposed, and his chest heaved with a grunt. "So beautiful. So goddamned beautiful," he murmured.

His fingers pressed under the waistband of my shorts.

"You want this, Rynna? You want me?" There was a tremor in his words. That same warning that flamed in his eyes. "Because I'm done running from you."

"I want you so badly it hurts."

He heaved a breath before he dipped down and kissed a path down my spine as he dragged my shorts and underwear down my legs.

"Oh God," I whimpered, hit by an onslaught of sensations.

Need and want and desire.

But it was that emotion that pulsed in the depths of me that nearly sent me to my knees. Wave after wave. Seeping and saturating. Trembling in my throat and tightening in my stomach.

"Rynna." It was a groan as he kissed down the cleft of my bottom and unwound my clothing from my feet, the sound so guttural it rumbled against the walls.

Then I was back in his arms and he was carrying me to my bed, lying me in the middle.

He stood with his chest heaving. So much stunning strength. The man so gorgeous and darkly appealing my mouth went dry.

Every thought and reservation fled from my mind. Every pep talk I'd given myself over the last two weeks about forgetting him and moving on scattered in the wind.

Because when it was just him and me?

There was nothing but the beat of our hearts.

Nothing but the call of our spirits. It was something louder than all the questions. Something bigger than his past. Something higher than our obstacles.

Something fierce rippled as he looked down at me completely naked on my bed.

"Are you sure?" he grated.

My hands fisted in my sheets, my body arching toward him. Needing him in a way I'd never needed anyone before. "I already told you I'm not afraid. You, Rex Gunner, are a chance I'm willing to take."

"You shouldn't be real." It was rough. Just like the man.

I bit my bottom lip, loving when he let me glimpse under all that hardness. "Yet, here I am."

"And what happens when you're gone?" There was something so sorrowful in it, a stab right to the center of my chest.

Slowly, I climbed up onto my knees and stretched out my hand. I brushed my fingertips down the side of his rugged face. "And what happens if I stay?"

For a beat, his eyes dropped closed, and he leaned into my touch before he snatched me by the wrist and pressed my palm to his mouth. "And what if I don't let you leave?"

God, this man. He pushed and pulled. Taunted and tugged.

Slowly he edged back, eying me with those mesmerizing eyes as he kicked off his boots. Without freeing me of his gaze, he unfastened his belt. His abdomen flexed and bowed as he tugged on his fly and lowered the zipper.

Desire swept through my body.

A battering storm.

Anticipation and need.

He nudged the jeans down his legs and took his underwear with them.

He stood there in the shadows that fell into my room.

Completely naked.

Bare.

So beautiful a downpour of desire soaked me through.

I hadn't been lying to Macy. This man was what gods were made of. Sleek and defined. Carved in hard, indestructible perfection.

All except for the broken pieces I knew he tried to keep concealed, buried deep inside. I saw them so clearly. Held in the depths of those eyes. Those eyes that were looking at me as if maybe I should run if I didn't want to be devoured.

But I did.

I so desperately did.

He edged forward an inch, big hand splayed across my chest, nudging me down onto the mattress. I was spread across its width, the man towering over me from the side.

I writhed, hips jutting into the air, not caring for a second that I was desperate.

That I needed him.

His touch and his body and that spirit that had already taken me whole. He ran a fingertip down the inside of my thigh. "Last two times I touched you nearly ruined me. Seeing you like this? Don't think I'm ever going to be the same. Stealing my sleep. Stealing my breath. Stealing my sanity. Little thief."

Chills flew. A chaos of sensation.

His hands were on my knees, pulling them apart.

I'd never felt so exposed, and I gasped out a shocked breath when he leaned down and gave one long lick up my slit.

He pulled back, and it was almost a smirk that was riding his sexy mouth as he stared down at me, as if he were looking at the sunrise for the very first time. Shifting his attention to my face, he grazed just the tips of his fingers through my folds. "Stunning. Fucking stunning. Feel like I'm in a dream when I'm touching you this way. Like I'm lost in some kind of fantasy and I don't ever want to wake up."

Redness flushed across the surface of my skin

"And you . . . you make me feel like I've finally found my reality. Like I finally figured out exactly where I'm supposed to be." A million emotions flashed across his mesmerizing face. Regret and lust and this consuming affection he couldn't keep contained.

He crawled over me.

Slowly.

Carefully.

I sucked in a staggered breath when the man was suddenly caging me, hands planted on either side of my head, those powerful thighs wedged between mine.

His cock bobbed against my belly, and a shudder ripped through my body.

He sank down onto his elbows, hot hands framing my face. "I don't understand this, Rynna. The hold you have on me. But when I look at you? Get this feeling that I'm looking at everything right."

"Rex." His name was a tremor.

A plea.

He leaned down and kissed me.

He kissed me carefully.

Gently.

Tenderly.

That energy lapped through the air. A slow, steady built. A current stoked by each pass of his tongue, by the heat that sizzled across our flesh, by our hands that explored. I ran my palms across his chest and over his wide shoulders, down the sinewy muscle of his back to his narrow hips.

I wrapped my hand around him, stroking him slow from the base of him to the tip.

He pulled his mouth away from mine. Head tilting back, he released a long groan. "Rynna . . . fuck . . . Rynna."

He pressed back up onto one hand, touching my face, a hand on my cheek before he edged back even more. He grasped me by the back of my knee and spread me wide. Jagged pants ripped from his lungs as he took himself in his hand and rubbed just the head of his cock through my center.

Flames.

I swore that single touch set me on fire.

"Rynna . . . fuck . . . you are gonna destroy me."

I whimpered, "Please."

Jaw clenched, he began to work himself inside me, tiny thrusts as he spread me, as he stole my breaths and seared himself into my body.

He was so big, so big that my nails sank into his shoulders. I knew he was holding himself back, forcing himself to remain in control.

He slowly worked himself farther.

Deeper.

Until he was seated fully.

Owning me.

His cock throbbed in the tight clutch of my walls.

The hand that had been on my thigh skimmed over my hip and up my side, cupping my breast, gliding to my jaw. "Fuck, Rynna . . . you feel so right. So fucking right."

"We are right," I murmured toward his face.

He groaned again before he pulled almost all the way out and paused, that mesmerizing stare held fast on my face. As if he held the power to see straight inside me.

Or maybe he was just begging me to look to the depths of him.

In that moment, everything went electric, that current lashing and zapping in the air.

Then he consumed me with one dominating thrust.

A thrust that shocked the air from my lungs and sent it scattering somewhere in the vicinity of my heart. My heart I could feel shattering. Shattering with emotion.

With need and affection and this feeling that was rising to obliterate all else.

The same annihilated heart that struggled to keep up with the battering crash of his.

He went back to holding me behind the knee.

He watched down on me while he dominated my body.

Eyes raking my flesh. My face. My breasts. Where we were joined.

Again and again.

As if he couldn't get enough. As if he never wanted it to end.

His body glistened with sweat as he worked over me. Muscles bowing.

His fucks deep.

Passionate.

Whole.

Pleasure glowed. Bright white flames.

He was looking at me as if I weren't real.

As if I were a fantasy.

Something he could never deserve or hold or keep.

When he'd already won every part of me.

Body and mind and quivering soul.

He shuddered through a frantic swallow, barely hanging on. "Fuck . . . baby . . . Ryn. Baby. You are a fucking miracle. No woman should feel this good. Fuck . . . I don't know if I can hold back."

"Then don't."

"Shit. You are so fuckin' sweet. So goddamned sweet." And I loved the grin that quirked at the side of that mouth. That mouth that was descending on mine, his hand on my neck. He kissed me until my head spun then he edged all the way back onto his knees and grabbed me by the waist.

He lifted my hips in the air.

My body arched.

All spread out.

My hands fisted in the sheets. I held on while Rex Gunner let go.

His control gone. The man driving to the depths of me. Where bliss spun and tightened and burned.

Gasps shocked from my mouth.

His fucks so desperate they were almost sweet.

He hissed through the wild rocks of his hips. "You are a miracle. Look at you. So damned sexy. So gorgeous and you don't even know."

He drove harder.

Faster.

His frenzied pants lifted into the air.

He tightened his hold with one hand, the other grazing over my trembling belly, and his thumb found my clit.

"Oh God," I cried out.

And I could feel my own reality slipping away. The burn of pleasure he incited with every thrust of his cock.

The man fucked like a barbarian that had perfected his art. Rough and grueling and driving me mad.

Higher and higher toward where day and night spun.

"Rex—"

Everything burst.

Strobes of light that flashed behind my eyes and the pleasure that exploded in my body.

Fracturing.

Scattering wide. Bliss.

It rode every nerve and obliterated every cell.

A sound tore from my throat, given voice where it came to life from somewhere in my spirit.

Because just like Rex had said, this shouldn't have been real.

It was too good. Too much. Too overwhelming.

Pleasure rushed.

A landslide.

So intense I thought it might go on forever.

Rex drove deeper and harder and wilder. His fingers sank into my hips, and he jerked my body to meet each dominating thrust. The man coming unhinged. Every breath a grunt. He gripped me as if he were clinging to safety, afraid he would be swept away, too. His head kicked back, and he roared toward the ceiling.

And I floated on his ecstasy. My walls clutching him tight. My heart holding on tighter.

For a few moments, we remained there, his shoulders and chest heaving as he panted for air. He slowly lowered my hips to the bed, wincing as he pulled out before he slumped down on top of me.

Threading his fingers through my hair, he rolled us to our sides. He stared at me, blinking in wonder as he brushed his thumb over the curve of my cheek. "That was . . ."

"Incredible," I whispered, almost shy.

"Incredible might be an insult. Feeling this way should be impossible, Rynna Dayne. Not sure how I'm going to walk out of this house and ever be the same."

"What if I don't want you to walk out of here ever feeling the same?"

"Don't think there's any worry about that." He studied me, hesitating, before he spoke, his admission scratchy. "I haven't been with anyone since Frankie's mom."

Shock burned through my mind and jolted my spirit, questions tumbling through my head, this man who was such a mystery.

I shifted onto my elbow, causing Rex to roll onto his back. I searched him in the shadows. "What? Why now? Why me?"

"Because you change everything, Rynna. You walk in a room, it's better. And when you walk away, everything grows dimmer. Colder. And I'm tired of living in the dark." He brushed back the hair that fell against my cheek. "But that doesn't mean I'm not terrified. That I'm not scared I'm doing something wrong. Making bad choices, the way I have all along. Last thing I want to do is hurt you."

I dipped down and placed a soft kiss to his chin, rising back up to meet the intensity of his stare. "The only thing that would hurt me is you walking away."

"My daughter . . ." I watched the heavy bob of this thick throat, the fierce protectiveness seeping through his pores.

I pressed my palm over the erratic thunder of his heart. "I know. Your daughter . . . your beautiful Frankie. I promise you I would rather die than hurt her, just like I know you'd rather die than see her hurt."

His heart pounded harder, and a dent pulled between his eyes. "How's it you just get it?"

"There are some things that just aren't that hard to understand. Like loving a child. It's complete. Absolute. There's no middle ground. So yeah, I get it."

"She's gonna fall for you, Rynna."

A soft smile pulled at my mouth, and I scratched my fingertips through the scruff on his jaw. "That's good, because I'm already falling for her."

Falling for you.

I didn't say it. Because I had my own fears. That he might not be ready. That the words might push him away. I figured when he looked at me, it was blatant, anyway.

Tentatively, I reached down to run my fingers through the soft locks of his hair. "What happened with Frankie's mom?"

He flinched. "I don't fucking know, Rynna. I came home one day, and she was . . . driving away. She didn't even stop when she saw me pass her on the road." His eyes squeezed shut. "Thought everything was fine. Left for work that morning, and then boom . . . gone. Some bullshit letter left behind about me working too much and she couldn't take it anymore."

Nikki was right. What a selfish bitch.

"What was she like?"

Emotion flashed through his eyes. Hurt and hatred.

"Last thing I want to be talking about is her when I'm lying here with you. Because right here? With you? That's where I want to be, and the last thing I need is her here in the middle of it."

"You don't need to tell me anything, Rex," I whispered, just as softly as my fingers that trailed across his jaw. "But when you want to? When you're ready? I'll be right here, ready to listen. I promise you there isn't anything you could say that would turn me off or send me in the other direction. Because this is where I want to be, too."

He nodded, his hand on my neck. "You know . . . your grandma . . . she was there with Frankie when I got home that night. Watching over her. Caring for her. She helped to get me through that time."

At the thought of my grandmother with Frankie, warmth spread beneath my skin. She truly had been a part of their lives. I guessed I'd only related it to the pies. But she'd meant something to them.

Without a doubt, they'd meant something to her.

"I'm so glad she was there for you."

"She was amazing."

"Yeah," I whispered.

Contentment rolled through my being as a slow, slow caress, and I snuggled closer, laying my head on his chest, my ear against the steady thrum of his heart.

"Can't believe what nearly went down this afternoon," he muttered, lightly gliding his fingertips along my bare back.

Fear flickered in my spirit. "Me, either. But it's over. I don't want to dwell on what might have been or could have happened. I just want to be thankful for what did."

"But the loan you were after that set that bastard off? What now?"

I kept drawing patterns on the rippling muscles of his pecs, words subdued. "I wait, I guess. Pray that they approve it and this whole mess doesn't affect it in any way."

"You mind me asking how much you were asking for?"

"No, I don't mind. Two hundred thousand. When I found out my grandmother left everything to me, the attorney had an estimator go in to give me and idea of what repairs would be needed to reopen. He wanted to give me the option to cut my losses and sell it off for what it was worth."

"And that's what you wanted? To come back here and take all that on?"

Soft affection slipped from my mouth. "When I was growing up, running that restaurant was the only thing I wanted. I couldn't imagine anything but being there at my grandmother's side."

"Why'd you leave, Rynna?"

Sadness wove into the fibers of my being and I tilted my face so I could see him. "Because I thought I was in love and it turned out it was nothing but a joke. I couldn't be the joke anymore, Rex. It hurt too bad."

"Fuck . . . I hate him."

"It wasn't just him. It was everything. Everyone. The school. This town. I knew if I stayed, everyone would be laughing at me."

I could still see Janel, that evil, depraved laugh, no care as she crushed my soul and destroyed my world.

"I was humiliated. Betrayed. At the time, I saw no other option than running, thinking I couldn't stay here and face the people I thought cared about me. I was so young. Looking back now? It seems ridiculous that I let them affect me so much."

He tightened his hold. "It's amazing how much power the ones we care about most hold. Especially when they're hurting us."

"Yeah," I whispered. "I just wish I hadn't stayed away so long. I wish had come back when she was still alive. She wanted so badly for me to come home, even though she paid for my college, encouraged me to find what I loved. What made me happy. And I was fine in San Francisco, satisfied on some level, but it never brought me the true kind of joy I knew she wanted for me. And then . . . she was gone . . . and I was too late."

He shifted a fraction, staring at me intently, almost cautiously. "Did you come back for her, or for you?"

"At first? I—" I blinked, wandering through the emotions I'd felt at the news.

Agony.

Grief.

Guilt.

The fear that had stumbled my feet and the hope that had pushed me forward.

"I was terrified to come back, but I did it because there was a part of me that had never let this place go. It didn't take more than my walking through the doors of that restaurant for me to realize this was where I belonged. All the years I spent working in a corporate office and, it turns out, I just want my fingers buried in dough."

Warm laughter floated out. "And here you are . . . home . . . right where you're supposed to be."

"Yeah."

"Making pies." A tease slipped into his tone.

A grin pulled at the corner of my mouth, and I edged back onto both hands, grinning down at him. "Oh, you like those pies, huh?"

He leaned up, kissing the tip of my nose, the caress of his lips chained to my heart. "Mm-hmm . . . I definitely like those pies."

I could feel the heat flush my body, my voice growing quiet when I asked, "Did you eat the one I made you?"

He rumbled a greedy sound. "Every single bit. All except for the piece Frankie had to have. And fuck me, if I didn't want that piece, too."

"Stingy."

"You can't blame a man who knows what is his." He was all smirks, this easy cockiness where he lay in the middle of my bed.

God. He was beautiful and I still couldn't believe he was there. That this was real.

A rush of joy took me over. This happiness that spread far and fast. I fell into his playfulness, the ease I had no idea this man could show. "Is that what won you over? My pies?"

"Maybe . . . a little."

I swatted his chest. "No more pies for you."

A shock of surprise jutted from my lungs when he suddenly flipped me, straddling me from above. His fingers dove into my sides, this hard, callused man, laughing as he tickled me. "Those are just wicked words, woman. Don't you dare tease me like that."

"Oh my God . . . Rex, stop! Stop! I'm so ticklish," I squealed, struggling to break free and never wanting to go anywhere.

"Not until you make me all the pies."

I tried to catch my breath and fight him off and hold him all at the same time. "No. No more pies for you."

"Tell me, Little Thief. Tell me you're going to make me all the pies." He kept on with his sweet, sublime attack until we were a laughing mess of prodding, tingling fingers, hysterical, shrieking laughter, and wild, pounding hearts.

It tapered off when he pinned my hands to the bed above me, those piercing sage eyes holding me firmer than the hold he had on my wrists.

That awareness spun. Fierce and intense.

"You belong here, Rynna. You'll make it work. I have faith in you."

And then he was kissing me as if he didn't ever want to stop.

twenty-two

Rex

Fear tumbled through his veins and clanged in the hollow of his chest. Frantic, he stumbled through the brushy undergrowth, the world buried by soaring trees. Branches lashed at the exposed skin of his arms and thorns latched onto the fabric of his shirt in an attempt to hold him back.

It propelled him harder.

Faster.

He screamed her name. "Sydney."

Sydney. Sydney. Sydney.

The howl of wind answered back.

Sydney.

I panted and thrashed. My head spun, fumbling through my thoughts to make sense of where I was. Warmth surged through my body when hands smoothed across my face, the softest voice cutting through the darkness. "Shh . . . I'm right here, Rex. I'm right here."

Relief gushed out on a shattered breath, and I grabbed her and pulled her against my body.

I buried my face in her hair.

"Are you okay?" she whispered.

"I am now," I told her. Because it was the truth.

Rynna.

Fucking Rynna.

Little Thief.

She was making me pie.

Fuck, she was making me pie.

She fluttered around her kitchen, this amazing girl spinning me up more with every swish and sway of her hips.

She had pulled on a pair of lace underwear and had slipped on a long-sleeved, red-and-black plaid button down that she'd rolled up her forearms. The bottom hem of the shirt just barely covered that glorious, round ass, and those sexy legs were bare. Long and sleek and driving me wild.

Obviously, she was right when she said this was exactly where she belonged.

I wasn't talking some bullshit chauvinist crap like that fucker who'd thought he could take whatever he wanted from her, either. Her body. His vengeance.

I was talking about her ease and grace. The joy that was so apparent in her eyes, and the pride that poured from her every time she glanced at the recipe she'd clearly memorized. But still, she kept peeking at it with an outpouring of love. Like she felt her grandma right there with every step.

I shifted on the wooden chair, trying to rein it in. Ideas barreled out ahead of me. Everything I was so fucking stupid for wanting calling out for me like it just might be within my grasp. Of course, all the reasons I couldn't have them taunted me just in the periphery. Threatening to reach in and pluck me straight out of this moment.

Problem was, that asshole piece of shit who had shown up at her door earlier this evening had stolen something from me, too.

My damned sanity. After what went down, there wasn't a whole lot of it left anymore.

Proof of it? I was sitting at the small table beneath the kitchen window that faced my house.

At two in the morning.

After I'd woken from that same fucked-up nightmare. After I'd let this amazing girl see that part of me.

She'd comforted me, whispered her belief when she had no idea where my panic was bred. When she had no clue there was a part of me that was screaming out in grief. Terrified. Feeling guilty for letting her soothe me when that part of me was condemned to agony for all my life.

I'd rolled over her, taken her, soft and slow while she'd gazed up at me through the shadows of the night.

We'd showered and then fallen back into her bed where we'd slept for a few hours. I woke to her sweet body wrapped around me, and we were right back at it again.

It seemed once we got started, neither of us could get enough. Afterward, she'd tugged at my hand and hauled me downstairs. There was a knowing grin on her stunning face, turning me inside out when she'd plopped me right here and told me to stay.

Like I was going anywhere.

I'd already had her three times tonight. It shouldn't have been possible, but there it was.

Lust. Curling in my guts. My dick way too eager for another round as I watched her light footsteps as she crossed the floor, the way her hair fell across the silky skin of her neck as she leaned over to pull the piping hot cherry pie from the oven.

A pie that smelled like its own kind of miracle.

Night pressed against the drawn drapes, and the simple globe light on the ceiling cast a pool of golden warmth over her. While she'd worked for the last forty minutes, we'd been chatting

About anything and everything.

Two of us completely at ease. I'd asked her about her time in San Francisco and what it was like to work for a corporate accountant. She'd told me all about her best friend, Macy, that sweet softness in her expression when she'd talked about the girl who'd helped her out of her shell.

Of course, she'd been all too eager to know how Kale, Ollie, and I had first met, the girl laughing as I told her about the trouble we'd constantly gotten into as kids.

I'd wanted to tell her. Just lay it all out. But how could I expect to rein her with something that was so complicated when I still couldn't figure out how I was feeling myself? When I still didn't know how much I could give her when there was this antsy part of me that wanted to give her everything?

"Just a couple more minutes," she told me with a smile from over her shoulder.

"You really are trying to ruin me, aren't you, woman?"

She giggled. Fuck, that was cute, too. "How's that?"

"I think you know exactly what you're doing."

"And what would that be?" Playing along, each of her words dripped with the sexy tease.

"Charming me with those pies and bewitching me with that body."

"If that's all it takes," she said, tossing me a grin as she cut into the pie.

"You got more ammunition in your arsenal? Because you come at me any harder, I'm done for."

She laughed, shaking her head as she slipped an angled spatula into the pie and pulled out a steaming sliver, quick to set it on a plate. She padded over to the freezer, grabbed a gallon of vanilla ice cream, and scooped a heaping pile of that on, too.

I could see it almost sizzle when it hit the pie, melting fast. My stomach growled in anticipation.

"Since you're so impatient, this is still super hot, so it's going to be more like cobbler."

I grunted. "You can't expect me to wait with something that smells that good."

Redness heated her cheeks, this humble sweetness taking hold.

Damn, I really liked that. I liked that she was proud and brave and didn't hesitate to say what was on her mind. Her pride came with this modesty that made me want to wrap her up and sing her every praise that could ever fall from my lips.

I was starting to believe she deserved every single one of them.

She was still smiling when she moved my direction. My mouth watered. Wasn't sure if it was because I wanted to devour that pie or sink my teeth into those hips that swished back and forth.

Hypnotizing.

Stirring.

Inciting.

Fuck. This woman.

I leaned back in the chair when she came to stop at my side. Setting the plate down in front of me, she leaned close to my ear, her voice soft. "At least somebody appreciates my pie."

My hand went out, palming one of those hips, voice turning sincere. "I won't be the last. I promise you that. People are gonna flock to that diner in droves as soon as the word gets out."

She cupped the side of my face, and my heart was doing that crazy thing again, speeding and knocking and thrumming.

"How do you make me feel like I can do anything?" she whispered.

"Know you can." The words were gruff as my hand slid from her hip to her waist.

She let out a little yelp when I hoisted her onto the edge of the table, then she was giggling as she grabbed the fork and scooped up a bite, holding it up in front of my mouth. "What, you need me to feed you, too?"

For an answer, I cinched down on the outside of her thigh and tugged her closer. "Apparently, I'll take whatever you're willing to give me."

"How about this?" She waved the fork in front of my face, teasing me, taunting me. I reached out and grabbed her by the wrist, opening wide and pulling it inside.

On all things holy.

It melted on my tongue, an explosion of tart and sweet.

"Good?" she asked. A sudden dash of insecurity threaded its way into her tone.

My approval rumbled around the fork as she slowly pulled it free. I chewed and swallowed, watching her face the whole time, her expression nervous as she waited for my reaction. "It's perfect, Rynna. Perfect like I'm starting to believe you might be."

Her delicate throat bobbed, her expression wistful when she glanced at the pie. "I'm not close to being perfect, Rex. I just want to do it justice. Make my gramma proud and find joy in it at the same time."

A soft puff of laughter jetted from her lungs. "And sometimes it seems silly . . . how badly I want it. How much it means to me."

I brushed my thumb across the top of her thigh, hand still clinging to the side of her, needing that connection. "You want all the good things, Rynna. There isn't any shame in that."

I took the fork from her and scooped some onto it. "Here. Taste."

Nearly died when she moaned around the fork, the way her eyelids drifted closed.

Savoring.

"See. You've got nothing to worry about, baby."

Her eyes fluttered open, and her lips parted. A fleck of sugar was stuck to the corner of her bottom lip. Edging forward, I licked it clean.

"Delicious," I murmured at her mouth, and she was moaning again, her fingers locking themselves in the skin of my shoulders. I kissed her a little deeper, and that sweet tongue slid against mine. Slowly this time. Like she was savoring me just the same as she was savoring the pie.

Pulling back, I dug the fork back into the pie and slipped another bite into her mouth.

She chewed slowly, watching me.

The air shifted between us.

Charged.

That current coming alive.

I swore that this girl emitted her own kind of gravity.

I dove back in.

Tasting her mouth.

Her tongue.

Her lips.

Relishing.

Wondering how a single moment could feel this good.

She took a fistful of my hair, nudging me back so she could take the fork and feed me another bite. She watched me chewing while my fingers tapped across the top of her thigh and to the inside. I brushed my fingertips along the edge of the lace that covered her.

A whimper, and she was feeding me more, just as I was pushing those panties aside, exposing her pussy, which was just as delicious as the rest of her. Wet and throbbing. I slicked my fingers through her slit, circling them around her engorged clit, my eyes never leaving her face while I rolled that pie around on my tongue.

"Rex."

"Yeah?" I rumbled, not minding a bit when she was feeding me another bite. With my free hand, I gripped her knee and hooked her heel on the edge of the table, teasing her the whole time, before two of my fingers were pressing inside the warm well of her body. Her walls clamped down, throbbing and needy. I began to drive them in and out, the girl all spread out on the table, as delectable as her dessert.

She cried out when I pulled my fingers free, and then I watched her eyes glaze over when I dipped those fingers in the pie and lifted it to her mouth.

"Oh . . . God . . . what . . ." It was all a strangle of words as I pressed my fingers between those lush, full lips.

The girl sucked them clean.

"A little dirty and a whole lot sweet. Just the way I thought you'd be," I said, gruff and hard.

She moaned. The sound vibrated around my fingers, and I ripped them free. In the same second, I was grasping the back of her neck and jerking her forward. I kissed her mad while my fingers went back to work, sliding deep and sure, because shit, I wasn't leaving this house without driving this girl just as wild as she was driving me.

She gasped when I suddenly had her by the outside of both thighs, spreading her wide. I licked her up and down. Her clit. Her ass. Everywhere in between.

Hands fisted in my hair, and I couldn't help but smile. She was guiding me to her clit. "Please. I can't . . . I need you."

I lapped and sucked as she continued to whisper incoherent words.

Her own kind of praise.

The girl nothing but the tease of perfection that I held in the grasp of my hands.

I pulsed my fingers into her, letting my other hand wander along the crease of her ass, the girl releasing all these shocked sounds of pleasure into the air.

Feeding that gravity.

Making it feel like it just might be impossible for either of us to walk away. She came with a cry. With her fingers curling in my hair. With her heart manic and her breaths harsh.

And mine. Mine ached and wished this chance were one I should actually take.

She slumped forward.

Shaking.

Boneless.

Standing, I slid an arm under her legs and the other under her back, and carried her back upstairs to her room.

The whole way, I prayed I wasn't making the biggest fucking mistake I'd ever made.

twenty-three

Rynna

Shooting upright, I clutched the sheet to my bare chest and struggled to pull in a breath. A deep sense of dread echoed from my bedroom walls. This unsettled feeling that something was off. I squinted through the play of shadows outside my window where daylight slowly breached the sky.

It took me all of two seconds to realize what was amiss.

I was alone.

After what had happened between Rex and I last night, I'd hoped to wake up in the safety of his arms, praying he'd found some of that same security in mine, too. I wasn't sure I'd ever felt so helpless than when I'd woken to find him flailing and jerking in my bed, lost to some kind of torment I couldn't understand.

I'd wanted to.

To understand it.

To understand him.

I hungered for him to embrace the feelings that grew between us.

Steadily.

Greedily.

I'd seen it last night, emerging through the storm in his eyes, scaling those fortress walls he built around himself and tumbling free to the other side.

He kept allowing me deeper and deeper, below those layers that fought to remain concealed. Just the same as I allowed him into mine, giving him bits of the horror that had sent me running.

Sliding from my bed, I stood. My attention caught on the small piece of folded paper that had dropped to the floor. It must have been tangled in the sheet. For a moment, I blinked at it, both terrified and eager to read what it might say, before I reached down and tentatively picked it up.

Slowly, I unfolded it, my eyes quick to scan the choppy scratch of handwriting dented on the page.

You are more beautiful than the sun breaking the day. Believe me. This morning, I had the privilege of watching them both, and I didn't want to stop. Little Thief, what am I going to do with you?

My heavy heart gave, fluttering and flapping, so insanely light. I pressed the letter over the manic thrum, not even attempting to hold back the grin that took hold of my face.

Rynna - Sixteen Years Old

"What are you doing?" Worried confusion streaked through my mind when I entered the back office to clock out. Pepper's Pies was getting ready to close. The day had been busy, and I was tired and hungry. I'd spent the last six hours rushing around the dining room, taking care of customers, along with Janel and her mother, while Gramma had been in the back with the cook baking.

The aroma of chicken pot pie still wafted through the diner, the flaky crust and seasoned vegetables and savory chicken teasing my nose with the thought of finally sitting down to eat.

But it was the sight in front of me the clenched my chest.

Janel was lingering at the far wall where we hung our personal items, tucking a stack of cash held together by a money wrapper into her apron pocket. Shock had widened her eyes when she whipped around to face me where I stood in the doorway.

She wouldn't.

Janel's surprise shifted into a smirk. "Don't be jealous I got great tips today and you made next to nothing. If you didn't spend so much time eating the pies, you might actually make some money around here."

Her jibes sank into me like darts, making me bow back, hit with physical pain. "I had more tables than you," I said, forcing off the hurt, because that was just Janel's way. I had learned to live with it. It was the only way I could remain friends with her, if that's what I even wanted to call it.

Janel swept a long lock of blonde hair over her shoulder. "Well, tips have more to do with how you look and make a customer feel that putting their stupid food in front of them so they can stuff their faces. But I know you can't relate to that."

Anger slithered beneath my skin. I stilled when I heard my grandmother grumbling from out front. "What on earth . . . till is short a full hundred dollars."

My mouth dropped open again, my head slowly shaking when I looked back at Janel. Guilt flashed through her pale blue eyes, and she rushed across the tiny room and grabbed my arm by both hands. "Rynna, please don't say nothin'. My momma has been real short this month. Don't think we're gonna make rent. I'm so sorry. I just . . . I'm so ashamed. I didn't want you to know."

My head shook again, torn, my voice dropping to match Janel's. "Why didn't you just tell Gramma? You know she'd understand. Front you the money."

"You know Momma's pride," she begged.

I swallowed around the jagged rock that cut up the base of my throat. This felt all wrong. So wrong.

I hesitated, and Janel squeezed my arm. "Please."

I barely nodded and shifted to call down the hall, "Oh, Gramma, I'm so sorry I forgot to tell you. I needed it for new gym shoes."

Gramma rounded the corner. "Corinne Paisley, you need to remember these things. Here I was, getting all worked up over nothing."

"It slipped my mind. I'm really sorry," I promised, glancing over my shoulder at Janel who'd turned away and was changing her shirt.

"Just glad it's accounted for. Why don't you get yourself some dinner, and I'll sit down with you in a minute."

"That sounds great."

"How about you, Janel? You and your momma want to sit with us?"

Janel grabbed her purse from the hook. "Have plans, Mrs. Dayne. But thank you."

Janel blew by both of us, and I headed out to the kitchen to grab a plate, hating the way regret had gathered in the pit of my stomach. The way everything felt wrong. Off. Like I was an accomplice of something I didn't want partner to.

Filling a plate with dinner, I wound out front, stopping at the soda machine to grab a Coke. Laughter rang out behind me, and I swiveled to peek at one of the few tables still occupied in the diner.

It was filled by four boys.

Boys who were getting close to being men.

Aaron was at the window, his brown hair buzzed, so handsome that achy spot inside me flared.

I startled when I heard the giggle behind me. Janel was shaking her head as if she felt sorry for me. "Oh, Rynna, don't do that to yourself. You know he's so far out of your league. That crush you've had for all these years just makes you look pathetic."

Discomfort climbed my throat, a sticky hurt that slicked my skin. I wanted to tell her to shut her stupid mouth. That I was so tired of her mind games. Of her manipulating every situation.

It wasn't the first time I'd covered for Janel.

Not by far.

But I didn't say anything. I just dropped my head and walked to the other side of the diner and sat down in the booth I always shared with my grandmother.

twenty-four

Rex

"Daddy!" Frankie came barreling out my mom's door, brown hair a disaster and flying all around her. The kid was sporting that smile that melted me into a puddle of goo. Nothing but sticky sap right at her feet.

She had on a tank top and shorts. Since it was Frankie Leigh, she wasn't about to stop there. She was also wearing an old pair of suspenders, which she'd gotten God knows where, and sky-high heels she'd pilfered from my mom's closet that were ten sizes too big.

And surprise, surprise, that damned hot pink tutu.

Couldn't help but grin.

Guess I really was a sucker for all that Frankie flare.

"There's my girl." The second she reached me, I swooped her into my arms and tossed her into the air. Exactly the way I knew she liked. My heart gave an extra boom at the sound of her laughter that rang through the morning. That sound alone had to be my single greatest joy.

I caught her, hugging her to my chest, pushing my nose into her hair, breathing in my little girl.

"I missed you," I whispered into the mess of hair on her head. I held her to me a little closer, and Frankie wrapped those tiny arms around my neck, the force of her smile touching me even when I couldn't see her face.

"I misses you, too, Daddy! But mes and Grammy had so much fun. She lets me do my very own *skupture*, right, Grammy?" She wiggled out of my tight hold, shifting in my arms to look back at my mom, who was standing at her usual place in the threshold and grinning back at us.

"A sculpture?" I clarified as I carried Frankie up the sidewalk.

"Uh-huh."

"And what did you sculpt?" I asked.

Those brown eyes widened like I was clueless. "A puppy, silly. I told you I wants a puppy so, so bad. Oh, Daddy, can I? Can I have a puppy? I'll be the best puppy mommy ever!"

A pang hit me hard.

Cutting me deep.

I fought against it, the memories threatening just at the cusp of my consciousness. Since Rynna had come into my life, it felt like everything was right there, trembling beneath my nose, begging to be exposed.

The thought of Missy still killed me, finding my girl dead at the side of the road on the same damned day my wife had left me. I'd had that dog since before I'd lost Sydney, and she'd been my solace, a reason to live when I hadn't wanted to go on.

But life was brutal that way.

Threatening to take everything in one fell swoop.

If what happened with Sydney hadn't been enough to make me ridiculously overprotective of Frankie, desperate to keep her safe, the cruelty of that day had solidified it.

I shoved the thoughts down and softened my voice. "Still don't think that's the best idea right now, Frankie."

"When's a good time?"

"Now we're sculpting?" I asked when I got within a couple feet of my mom, praying it'd distract Frankie from demanding an answer to that question.

"We dabble in all the art forms, don't we, Sweet Pea Frankie Leigh? Call us multitalented. Just like your daddy." Mom ruffled her fingers through my daughter's hair. There was so much affection in her gaze when she looked at us both, I couldn't help the surge of love that went crashing through my senses. It was like something inside me had been unlocked, and every sort of emotion I'd tried to keep repressed billowed out without my permission.

The love.

The longing.

The fear.

The regret.

Rynna's face glided through my consciousness, her touch a faint whisper across my skin, breathing all that beauty and life.

Stirrings of hope shook through me like tremors of warning. Like quivers that staked deeper, demanding more. The ground shifted between the two extremes. Tossing me back and forth with no idea which was going to send me stumbling straight into a free fall.

Guilt throbbed, urging me to take heed of that distorted sense of loyalty. Thing was, I was having a harder and harder time remembering just what I was supposed to be loyal to.

Mom's head tilted as she studied my face. Saw the second she came to a conclusion, because her brow lifted in a slow, knowing arch. "You have a good time last night?"

I tried to form a quick lie, but it wouldn't come fast enough. Not before my mom latched on to something in my expression that sent her mouth curling into satisfaction.

"Ahh, I see," she said. "Looks like you had a *really* good time last night."

How the woman still had the power to send a rush of embarrassment flooding my face, I didn't know. But there I stood like a twelve-year-old kid who was trying to come up with an excuse for his mom finding his dirty magazine stash under his bed.

"Ma," I said with a huff of a breath as I set my daughter on her feet. The kid wobbled in those ridiculous shoes.

Shit. I felt guilty for even holding her when I was suddenly belted with a thousand memories from last night.

Rynna.

Fucking Rynna.

Little Thief.

Guessed the woman conquering my body wasn't all that unexpected. But it was the way she'd taken hostage of my mind that was close to sending me into a tailspin. The way she'd stolen a place for herself inside me. A place I didn't think it was possible for her to keep.

For years, I'd never been tempted. Had never given in, because I knew what I was living for. The reason for every beat of my heart. My gaze dipped to that reason. To the tiny thing that swayed clumsily in her tutu and those heels, her hands over her head as she attempted a spin she wasn't even close to being capable of pulling off.

My perfect Tiny Dancer.

"Go get your stuff, Sweet Pea." My voice was quieted, muted to the point where the only sound was my devotion flooding the room.

"'kay." Frankie scooted across the room, heels catching on the carpet, the little thing disappearing at the head of the hallway.

I jerked with the soft hand that suddenly landed on my forearm. "Hey," Mom said. Her voice was the same gentle command as the one she'd raised me with. All the innuendo she'd been teasing me with had vanished. "What's going on with you, Rex?"

Looking at my boots, I roughed a palm over my mouth, like it might have the power to seal in all the things I was itching to confess. "Nothin'," I said.

"Don't *nothin'* me. You think I don't know you? My boy? My son? My kid, who's worn that same expression since he was seventeen? You think I don't know when you're terrified? And that's something that just about never leaves those eyes, Rex. But today? It's different, and I know you know it, just as well as I do."

I forced myself to meet her knowing gaze.

"When are you going to realize you deserve to be happy?" she prodded.

My head shook. "I'm trying, Ma. But I'm terrified of doing something stupid. Making a wrong choice, the way I always do. Of doing something that jeopardizes Frankie."

"And you finding happiness again threatens that? That just sounds foolish to me. The way I look at it? The happier you are, the happier she's gonna be."

Guilt flamed all around me, worry closing my throat. "You think she's unhappy?"

Her brow creased into the few lines that showed her age. "God, no. Not at all. That's not what I'm saying. What I'm saying is that child adores you. Thinks you walk on water. Thinks you can do no wrong. But there's gonna come a day when she's old enough to see the shadows in your eyes. The ones that are chased away just by looking at her. She's your life, Rex. We all know that. Finding happiness again won't mean that you love her any less."

She moved to stand closer to me. She set her hand over my heart. "This? It's missing something. It's been for a long, long time. Long before that bitch ever up and left you two. Maybe it's time you find it. You can't move forward without moving on."

Emotion ran my throat. Stinging and burning. I attempted to swallow it down, but the words were scratchy when I released them. "But what if being with her is wrong? What if I fuck up again and chase her away? What if Frankie falls for her?"

What if I do?

Couldn't even bring myself to state the last because I already knew I was well on my way.

Glee flashed in Mom's eyes, her grin victorious. "So you're saying there is a girl?"

"Ma." Affectionate frustration. She knew exactly how to goad me.

She softened again, her smile going gentle, understanding brimming in the warmth of her eyes. "There are no certainties in this life, Rex. We fail, we win, and we straight up lose. You know that first hand. But what you haven't accepted is that the only security we have is how we use the moments we're given. We waste them or embrace them. We cherish them or we let fear taint them. And yeah, some chances are higher risk. Of course they are, and I'm not saying to run out and be reckless. You don't have to rush in or make any big decisions. You can protect your daughter while you test the waters. But you aren't ever gonna know unless you *try*. You just have to decide if this girl's worth giving her that chance."

Chances.

I almost smirked. Almost wanted to tell her she sounded just like Rynna.

Rynna.

Fucking beautiful Rynna.

"I don't even know where to start," I admitted through a sigh. "Been keeping people at arm's length for so long, don't have the first clue about how to get back in the dating game."

But there was something about me and Rynna that felt like we'd already surpassed all of that. Our connection went deeper than testing the waters. Bigger than dating or seeing how it went.

Something strong blazed between us. A connection that shackled us together.

Unavoidable.

Irresistible.

Truth was that last night I'd felt closer to her than I'd felt to anyone in so damned long, and I wasn't talking Frankie or my mom or the guys.

This was about being united with someone. Bonded. Tied.

That connection had lit into a frenzy when I'd sat in the darkness of her room and watched her sleep.

Fuck.

She was gorgeous.

The kind of gorgeous that wasn't just skin deep, even though that body made me crazy with need.

I was talking about the goodness that poured from her.

Sunshine and sweet.

I'd watched her until the sun started to show, like it was drawn to her the same as I was to this girl. Finally, I'd forced myself from her bed so I could clear my head.

Thing was, the confusion had only grown the more distance I put between us. That gravity calling me back to her while all my resolutions and dedications had warned I was making mistake after mistake.

"You could start by doing something nice for her," Mom said.

"Nice?"

She laughed. "Don't tell me you're so far gone you don't know what nice is? There's gotta be something you could do for this girl to let her know you care. That you're interested. Doesn't have to be extravagant. Just show her you aren't the uptight, grumpy pants this whole town thinks you are." A smile slipped into the words.

My brow rose. "Grumpy pants?"

Frankie was suddenly right at my side, dancing around, singing, "Grumpy pants, grumpy pants, my daddy is a grumpy pants," over and over again.

Maybe Frankie could see it better than I'd thought.

And maybe it was fucking time I did something about it.

twenty-five

Rynna

𝒫anic had me sailing out from the back of the kitchen and rushing through the dining room of Pepper's Pies.

But this was a different kind of panic.

Not the kind incited by Timothy Roth.

This was a huge banging on the other side of the wall, the floors shaking and the fixtures trembling, so fierce I was terrified my grandmother's restaurant was about to come crumbling down.

Confusion jolting me back, I skidded to a stop at the end of the hall that led to the restrooms.

My eyes narrowed as I attempted to make sense of the scene.

"What in the world are you doing?" I finally managed. Dust billowed in the enclosed area, and three strange men were in the midst of it, tearing out the plasterboard of the wall that blocked off the restrooms.

One stocky guy barely grunted an answer. "It's demo day."

Demo day?

"What are you talking about?" Exasperated, it tumbled out as I took a lurching step forward.

Another guy, dressed in a paint-stained tee, jeans, and work boots, tossed the piece of plywood he'd pried free into a small pile, which was growing quickly. "Boss sent us over. Told us this needed to get done and fast."

"Boss?"

"Gunner," the other guy huffed as he ripped free a huge piece of plywood that sent another plume of white dust billowing in the air.

Gunner.

Gunner. Gunner. Gunner.

The name spun through that haze before realization broke through the fog.

Oh God, what did he do?

I stepped back, trembling, the emotions tumbling through me too convoluted they were too much to fully understand. So, I latched on to one. That one that was frustrated and shocked, unable to process the actions of this unexpected man.

I rushed back into the kitchen and grabbed my purse and keys before flying out the door and hitting the road, my destination clear.

RG Construction.

I haphazardly parked and then flew through the entrance of the building. The interior space small enough that I didn't need to do anything but round the secretary, who jumped to his feet.

"Excuse me, ma'am."

I didn't slow, I just thrust open Rex's office door. I barged right in, the door banging against the inner wall when I did. I was flustered and angered and awed all at the same time. "You'd better have a good explanation."

Surprised, his attention jerked up from the papers he was pouring over. "Rynna."

God. He knocked the breath right out of me. I stood in the doorway, trying to brace myself, to remember why I was upset in the first place. Oh, yeah. "Why are there three men at my restaurant tearing it apart?"

Slowly, he stood, stealing a little more of the air. The man so powerful . . . so beautiful that I couldn't think.

"You needed a job done, and I had the resources to do it," he said.

Shaking myself out of the stupor, my eyes narrowed. "So, you just . . . sent them over? Without consulting with me? I . . . I . . . I . . ."

I had absolutely no idea what to say to him. When I finally figured it out, it came rushing on a screech of frustration. "I don't have any money to pay you."

"You don't need to pay me."

"What?" Another screech. This time with a foot stomp. He was insane. We'd spent one night together. Okay. The most extraordinary kind of night. One that had altered my world. That and about two magical hours making out on his porch like teenagers in the middle of the night last night—but that was totally beside the point.

"I care about this community, Rynna." There was almost a smirk hiding behind the staunch somberness of his expression and ridiculousness of his words.

"Are you kidding me?"

"Gingham Lakes is flourishing, and re-opening Pepper's Pies is only going to be an asset to it." I saw him rubbing his thumb and forefinger together. As if he'd been practicing the speech and he was making sure he was keeping time.

"You can't just—" I threw my hands in the air. "You can't just go into my restaurant and have your way with it. I have plans. I want . . . I *need* to do this. To figure it out myself. Not have some guy come in and do the job for me because I'm not capable."

Pricks of tears burned at my eyes. Maybe I was revealing too much. Getting to the heart of the matter that came flooding out without my permission. The fear I didn't have what it took to make it. That I was going to fail before I even had the chance to get started.

But shock dammed them when Rex flew around his desk and backed me against the wall. "Some guy?" he demanded.

All the aloofness he'd attempted to wear was gone. In its place was the same compelling, confusing man who'd pushed and pulled and taunted me since the day I'd met him. "That's all I am to you? Some guy?"

I stared up at him, trying to decipher what was in his eyes.

Hurt.

It was hurt and fear and there was so much of it that it made my heart wobble. Thrown off. The man always managed to catch me off guard. "You know what I meant," I said softly.

He blinked at me, his words nothing but honest. "No, I don't."

I reached up and touched the thunder at his chest. With trembling fingers, I let them tap across the vibrating strength. "What I meant is it's not fair for you to come in and take over for me. Not when you didn't even ask me. That's my grandmother's restaurant. She gave it to me. Trusted me with it. And for you to go in and take over without consulting me? It makes me feel as if you think I can't do this. As if you think you need to rescue me. You're not just some guy, Rex. You mean so much to me. More than you know."

My voice dipped at the confession, and he sighed this strained sound, both hands planting above my head. He inched closer, pinning me to the wall. It spun my mind, the heat of him trembling all the way to my soul. God. He was too much. Devastating and overwhelming and irresistible.

When he spoke, his voice was raw. "And what if you're doing a little of that rescuing yourself? You think I don't believe in you? Fuck, Rynna . . . I'm doing it because I believe in you so much, I want to be a part of making it happen. I just . . . wanted to surprise you."

Shivers tumbled down my spine, landing in a pool of emotion that just kept getting deeper and deeper. Pretty soon, this man was going to drown me. Take me all the way under.

Emotion clotted my throat, and I forced the shaky words out around it, fiddling with his shirt and barely peeking up at him when I spoke. "Rex, I am so grateful. *So grateful.* But this is one of those things you should have asked me about. It's a big deal, and it's a lot of money, and if you do believe in me? Then you need to respect me enough to talk to me about something that is going to affect my life this much. I can't take that kind of money from you. I can't because it's not right. I want to work for this. Earn it. Breathe life back into Pepper's Pies because *I can*."

"I just wanted to do something nice for you."

I laughed softly, letting my touch glide up against the hot flesh of his neck. "Nice? Your idea of nice is a little extravagant, don't you think?"

A light chuckle rumbled in his chest. "Maybe. I warned you I'm not so good at this."

He edged back and set a hand on my cheek, stark sincerity climbing into his expression, that sincerity a revelation of his fear. "I told you I didn't have anything left to give you. And now, I want to give you everything."

Every part of me softened. "Rex . . ."

And, God, I wanted it, everything he was willing to give.

"Too much, too fast?" he asked, a self-deprecating grin rimming his mouth, so sexy and sweet.

"I'm not sure there's ever going to be too much when it comes to you. I'm just asking you to talk to me."

His thumb brushed the angle of my cheekbone, and my mouth dropped open a fraction, relishing in the feel of his simple touch. "Warned you I have no goddamned clue what I'm doing. That I always manage to fuck up."

"You're not fucking up. We're just . . . learning each other."

He pressed against me, his voice growing rough. "Like all the ways I'm learning you."

I clung to his shirt, flooded by warmth.

He edged back. "How about I make you a deal?"

"What kind of deal?" Cautious. Careful.

"You need a loan."

"Rex," I warned, already knowing what he was getting ready to say.

"Just hear me out." He paused, waiting for me to give him a tiny nod before he continued. "You figure out how to get all the equipment for the restaurant, but we do all the installation and renovation."

"Rex—"

He pushed a finger against my lips. "And you pay me back. Consider it a loan for something I believe in."

My heart thundered, and my breaths became shallow. He pressed the gentlest kiss to my forehead, the word a vibration against my skin. "Please."

Setting my hands on his waist, I chewed at my bottom lip as I shifted to look up at him. "What does this mean?"

What do we mean?

I wanted to ask him, but the tensing of his body cut me off. As if he didn't want me to say it. To bring it out into the open. The fact that neither of us seemed to truly know where we stood. If we were coming or if we were going.

He pulled me against him. "I need to figure out some shit in my life, Rynna. I warned you, it's a mess. But I'm going to fucking try. There's a lot I can't make sense of, but it's time I do. Figure out who I am and who I'm supposed to be. Take care of some shit I should have a long time ago. But the one thing I do know? The one thing I know is I want you in my life. And if I can at least give you this? Then please . . . let me. Let me take this chance."

Rex

Rain battered the roof and lightning lit up against the darkened windows. Thunder a constant rumble in the toiling sky.

I was already rushing for the door after I'd heard the bell ring.

My jaw dropped a bit when I flung it open and found her standing there. Drenched. Chestnut darkened to mahogany.

Standing there in the rain looking like a second chance. A better day.

Four soaked paper bags were wrapped in her arms, precariously clutched to her chest like she could keep them from ripping apart and sending all the items contained inside from toppling to the ground.

"Rynna," I finally managed when I processed she was really there, standing on my stoop. I widened the door. "Come inside before you get struck by lightning."

She ducked past me, filling my senses with all that sweet, intensified with the soak of the rain.

Fuck. She was undoing me. Minute by minute. I let the door fall shut behind her. "Here, let me help you with that." I took two bags from her.

"Thank you."

"What are you doing here?" I finally asked, feeling the satisfied grin slide to my face, because I sure as shit wasn't gonna complain.

She cast me a cautious smile. One that slammed me right in the center of the chest. Kind of the way Frankie annihilated me every time she looked at me a certain way. Though, this was different. Obviously. This was lust and want and confusion and every-fucking-thing I wanted more and more.

She hefted a shoulder. "I just thought I would do something nice for you."

Nice.

My chuckle rumbled like a partner to the sky. "Nice, huh?"

She bit her bottom lip with a nod. "Yeah. It seems my neighbor is a little on the *thoughtful* side. I figured I'd return the favor. How does dinner sound? Of course, I might owe you dinner for the rest of my life."

I dipped my head her direction, whispered at her ear, "Why's that sound like the best damned payback I've ever been offered?"

She giggled and headed for my kitchen. "I see how it is. You want me when I'm baking for you."

A growl slipped free, my eyes honing in on the slow sway of her delicious ass as I followed her. Voice lowered to keep my next words from little ears. "Oh, believe me, baby, I want you all the time. But you don't actually think I'm going to refuse you cooking for me, do you? Especially considering I was just about to take out a frozen pizza to toss into the oven."

Setting the bags on the counter, she looked back at me with a feigned gasp. "Blasphemy."

I set the bags I was carrying beside them. "A man's got to do what a man's got to do."

Her expression went tender, and she reached up, cupping my cheek in one of those soft, soft hands. "And you should know I would consider it an honor that I get to help with that now."

She peeked in the direction of the hall where we could hear Frankie playing, talking and squealing, living in her own blissful little world. "Is this okay? That I'm here? I don't want to confuse her or rush you. I just . . . I wanted to spend the evening with you. With her," she added quickly, like it might scare me away.

And fuck. Yeah. It scared me, just not the way she was probably thinking. I wanted it, I was just too scared to hope for it. But it didn't matter, that anticipation was right there, strumming an escalating beat inside of me.

Savage and fierce. As fierce as the storm that rattled the windowpanes and drummed on the roof.

I threaded my fingers through hers, brought her knuckles to my lips. "What do you say we take it slow in front of her? Get her used to the two of us. She's gonna have questions, and when she does, we answer them."

She worried her lip, peeking up at me. "And what's the right answer, Rex?"

Releasing her hand, I let my fingers glide into those silky locks of damp hair. That was all the contact I needed for my chest to tighten, for the things held within to go haywire. A disorder that was shifting into something new. I pulled her closer and set a kiss to her forehead, murmured against it, "We tell her we care about each other. Simple as that."

Did she know that's how I was feeling? Did she know every time I looked at her, another piece crumbled out from under me, my footing no longer my own?

I leaned down, my mouth barely brushing the edge of hers. "I want you here." I inched even closer, the heat of her body lighting me up. "Really fucking want you here. In the end, I think that's all that matters."

I moved to grip her by the waist, and her breath caught as my fingers cinched around her, everything growing thick when I let my nose trace up the column of her neck.

That overpowering scent was back. Radiating from her skin. Sweet, sweet bliss. Cherry pie.

I groaned, and she exhaled, then we both froze when we heard the pound of little feet thunder down the hall.

I stepped back, putting space between us, and a rush of redness bloomed on Rynna's neck.

Like she'd been caught.

It was so fucking cute.

Frankie skidded to a stop at the end of the hall when she saw Rynna in the kitchen. "Rynna! What's you doin' here?"

My daughter kicked right back into action, flying across the floor, jumping around in front of Rynna to grab her attention.

As if she didn't already have it. Because Rynna smiled when she saw my kid. Smiled like it meant something.

A bolt of old fear struck somewhere deep in my chest. A warning that I'd crossed a line when I'd let Rynna into our lives. That I'd been begging for trouble. Taunting me with a reminder of that penalty I'd forever serve. Punishment for what I'd done. Did I think I was exempt?

Rynna knelt in front of my daughter, her expression soft, almost as soft as the way she brushed her fingers through Frankie's wild mane of hair.

"I thought maybe you could help me make dinner. What do you think about that?"

Frankie's eyes went wide with excitement. "Really? I gets to make dinner? Oh yes! Are we gonna make a Pepper Pie?" She threaded those tiny fists together, pressing her hands up under her chin in a plea. "Oh, please, let's make a Pepper Pie!"

Light laughter fluttered from between Rynna's lips. Those goddamned lust-inciting lips. I tried not to think about them wrapped around me when she tugged one of Frankie's hands free and hooked her pinkie finger with Frankie's tiny one. A team. "Did you think we'd make anything else? How about a shepherd's pie and then a cherry pie?"

With that, Rynna peeked up at me. Searching for my reaction. My reaction that felt like I'd just had a fucking metal arrow speared straight in to my heart. It attached to something unseen, something buried, once thought dead, and plucked it out.

"That sounds like the best deal in the whole wide world!"

"Come on, let's get your hands washed. We have a lot of work to do."

Rynna sent me a wink when she picked Frankie up from under the arms, turning her attention fully on my daughter when she did. Carefully, Rynna squirted Frankie's hands with soap and held them under warm water, rubbing and rinsing her hands together, two of them giggling at something silly Frankie said.

"Here we go . . . you sit right there." Rynna hoisted her so she was sitting on the edge of the counter, steadying her with a hand against the belly. "Be careful, okay?"

"'kay," Frankie promised, and Rynna went to work, pulling ingredients from the bags, talking to Frankie the whole time. "My grandma used to sit me right up on the counter when I was a little girl like you. Right up close where I could see and help."

"Dids you like cookin' with C'rinne?"

"I loved cooking with Corinne." Something wistful seeped into Rynna's tone. "I miss it so much. But it makes me happy that I get to teach you the same as she did me."

"I likes you teachin' me. Did you know I'm gonna be a painter? My grammy says I'm such a super good painter, like my daddy."

Rynna glanced at me with a small smile. No doubt, my daughter was getting ready to spin into one of those conversations that jumped from topic to topic faster than a person could keep up.

"Is that so?"

"Oh yes! And I'm gonna get a puppy. I wants a puppy so bad."

This time Rynna's glance back at me was curious, searching, before she slowly turned back to the green beans she was running under the faucet. "You want a puppy, huh?"

"Oh yes. Oh yes, yes, yes."

I sighed, trying not to show any frustration that was focused solely on myself. "Told you it's not a good idea right now, Frankie Leigh."

She started to pout, and Rynna was quick to hand her a bottle of cream and a measuring cup. "Do you think you could fill that up to that line for me?" she asked, running her finger along the one-cup indicator. She purposely redirected my kid like a pro.

"There you go," she encouraged as Frankie carefully poured the cream into the bowl, and Rynna placed the bowl on Frankie's lap. She took her hand and showed her how to whip up the mixture before she was back to rinsing something else. It was kind of amazing how the girl juggled three different recipes at the same time. Second nature. Right back to that graceful ease she'd shown me back at her place five nights ago.

I leaned against the far counter with my arms crossed over my chest.

Watching them.

Trying to keep that feeling reined. Trying not to get too far ahead of myself.

But I could feel it. Everything barreling that direction when I listened to the way Rynna spoke softly with my daughter. She gave her instructions, let her help, laughed as Frankie made mess after mess. The entire time, she was completely patient with a child I was well aware required a lot of patience. Rynna's tolerance never slipped, and I swore, it wasn't faked.

Swore she wasn't putting on a show.

Swore this wasn't some kind of pretense.

And fuck, it was terrifying.

As terrifying as it was perfect.

Because I wanted it.

I wanted her.

An hour later, the three of us were sitting around the table, sharing dinner, the best fucking shepherd's pie I'd ever eaten.

I told both of them, too.

Frankie grinned, gave Rynna a high five.

"We dids it, Rynna," she said, my kid so damned happy.

Maybe as happy as I was.

Maybe, just maybe, this was where we were meant to be.

That for once in my life, I'd been granted reprieve.

She slipped out the door with a peck and a reluctant goodbye.

I couldn't stop myself, I bolted right after her, snatching her around the wrist, unable to let her go. My kiss a demand as I pushed her against the outside wall. She whimpered, hands on my face, mine on her hips.

"I really should go," she whispered.

"I know . . . but I don't know how to let you." I hoisted her up, those legs around my waist. She rubbed against my jeans, her pussy a tease. My dick pressed at the fabric, desperate for release. "Fuck, Rynna. What are you doing to me? Making me lose my mind. Have no control when you get in the room."

She nipped at my mouth, kissing me, rocking against my cock. "The only thing I know is how desperately I want you. How desperately I want *this*."

"What is it you want?" I barely managed. Groaning deep, I strained harder against her, wondering just how horrible of a parent I'd be if I stripped her right there and fucked her against the wall.

"This. You. Us. Frankie."

At her confession, I froze, my heart going stone in the center of my chest before it started thudding. Thudding with possibility.

I pulled back to search her eyes through the darkness. The air was bogged down with humidity, the residual of the storm a wet mist coating our heated skin.

She stared back.

No reservations.

No fear.

Just blatant, unblemished hope. A beacon calling me out of the storm.

"I . . ." All the bullshit that still haunted my life stalled my words, the promise I wanted to give her freezing on my tongue. Because the last thing I wanted was to do her wrong.

Hurt flashed through her expression before it filled with soft understanding. Because that was just the way this girl was—flush with grace. Too good to be real. She edged back a fraction to search my face. Reluctantly, I released her, helping her slide down onto her feet.

I stood there, a shadow blocking all that light.

She tilted her head, her hand on the side of my face. "Do you still love her?"

My chest grew so damned tight I was sure it was going to explode.

"Your ex-wife?" she pressed.

That was the problem. Her hunch was off base. Thrown in the wrong direction. But when it came down to it, Frankie's mother was the problem. That stupid fucking loyalty I'd clung to for far too long.

It lashed at me, a scourge of regret.

"Fuck, Rynna," I whispered harshly, the ground swept right out from under me. "I—" I averted my gaze to the wooden planks, struggling to find the correct answer to her question. Because she deserved to know, and still, I didn't know how to tell her.

Warily, I shifted my attention back to her and plucked out the only honesty I could find. "When it comes to Frankie's mom? The only emotion I can process is hate." I blinked, swallowing hard. My insides burned. Flames. Unrelenting hell. "But then I wonder if I have the right to hate her. Not when I was the one who drove her away."

"She left you. She left Frankie. I don't know the circumstances. But for that alone? I hate her. I hate her for the simple fact that she could possibly walk away from you two. If I had been given a gift like that, I wouldn't ever have let it go."

A soft puff of air escaped my throat, and I wound an arm around her waist and pulled her against me. I pressed a kiss to the top of her head. "Rynna."

Rynna.

Fucking Rynna.

Little Thief.

Trying to steal my heart.

Frankie squealed, clapping her hands as she dropped to her knees on our front porch. The tiny puppy scuttled toward her, jumping up on her chest, licking her face. "Daddy! Daddy! It's a puppy. Look. It's a puppy. It's the cutest puppy in the whole wide world."

She hugged the wiggling body against her probably a little too tightly, but the little ball of fur just went wilder, clawing up her chest to get closer to her face so he could lick her like he'd found his long lost best friend.

Unfortunately, Frankie was under the impression she'd found hers.

Shrieks of laughter rang in the air. "Daddy! He's kissin' me. He's kissin' me. I fink he loves me."

The sight of it sent a rock sinking straight to the pit of my stomach.

My gaze cut to Rynna, who was standing there watching the two of them with an affected smile on her face. Her eyes were full of an emotion I wasn't sure I was ready to recognize.

A lump formed in my throat. Heavy. As heavy as that rock that sat in the pit of my stomach. It only grew when Rynna edged forward and knelt in front of Frankie. Then she reached out and gently ran her hand over the puppy's head, her gaze growing even softer as she looked at my daughter.

"He's a golden retriever. What do you think we should name him?" she asked.

"How's about Milo? Milo's my friend at school who's a boy and he's so nice and this puppy is a boy so I finks we should name him Milo because he's nice, too."

Rynna didn't even skip a beat at the ramble that fell from Frankie's mouth. She just let her smile grow, glancing down at the puppy. He was currently on his hind legs thinking he could jump his way onto Rynna's lap. "He is a nice boy, isn't he?" she cooed, letting the puppy lick her face. "Milo it is, then."

"Milo! I love Milo! I love Milo. Can I take him for a walk? Do you gots a leash?"

And the two of them? They disappeared, trotted alongside the road, Frankie screeching her joy, Rynna right there in case the puppy tugged hard enough to get loose.

Thirty minutes later, I watched as Frankie ran with the puppy nipping along at her heels through Rynna's front door. Rynna stood on the same deck that had changed everything, hugging her arms across her chest and biting at her lip as she watched the two of them bound inside.

I'd held back, standing against the railing, unable to process what was going on inside me.

I edged up behind her. I could feel it. The chill that skated her spine, the way she shook as I released a breath against her ear. A few strands of chestnut rustled with the air and tickled my lips. "A dog, huh?" I whispered.

There was a swift intake of breath before she cautiously turned around to face me. "I . . ." She glanced back at the house. "I'm living here alone, and I thought I could use a friend. It gets lonely at night."

She turned around to face me fully. Bewilderment twitched along her brow. "Do you not like dogs?"

A vice of grief wrenched up my insides. I was right. Ever since Rynna Dayne had come into my life, every old wound had been unbound, released from its confines, spinning and taunting me where they danced right under my nose.

"Of course I like dogs." Could barely force it out through the hardness that ridged my lips.

Longing twisted through her features when she glanced back at the door, looking back at me like she was begging for me to understand. "I know you and I are new. But Frankie . . . I saw that puppy and the only thing I could think about was her. About how excited she would be. I . . . I wanted to give her something she didn't have." Rapidly she blinked, and tears threatened at her eyes. "I wanted her to love something that's a part of me. Are you mad?"

I couldn't hold back anymore. I jerked her against me. "Fuck, Rynna. Of course I'm not mad."

I hugged her tight. Kissed the crown of her head. Wishing I could explain how it brought back memories I didn't know how to deal with.

I was numb as I stood by the side of the road, staring blankly as the taillights disappeared in the distance. I tried to blink through the squiggle of red, neon lines that lit up against my bleary vision. It was like looking at the sun and then closing your eyes. Or maybe I just wished they were closed. But they were open wide, my gaze sucked down.

Down.

Down.

Missy dead at my feet.

I gulped around the vision, bile in my throat, agony in my chest.

Mrs. Dayne was there, her hand on my forearm. "Don't worry. I've got her. You do what you've got to do."

She picked up Frankie where she was laying on the gravel, face-down, barely able to process what was happening through the daze that clouded my mind. My daughter's cries. Taillights.

What had I done?

What had I done?

A shovel.

Dirt.

Sweat on my nape.

I struggled for a breath, that numbness fracturing when I picked Missy up and carried her to the hole. I laid her in it.

I squinted, trying to see through the haze.

A shovelful of dirt.

Another.

A mound of nothing.
My girl. My wife. Gone.
They always were.

"You wants to be my bestest friend?" Frankie's small voice slipped through the thin wall, muted just the same as the light. Rynna's echoed back, so goddamned soft it penetrated to the depths of me.

"You want me to be your best friend?"

There was no answer, but my mind was conjuring a clear picture of Frankie vigorously nodding her head against her pillow. Could picture Rynna where she knelt on the ground beside her bed where she'd been reading my daughter her bedtime story.

Of course, because Frankie had again insisted.

"I'd like that," Rynna murmured, and there was shuffling, what I knew was a tender kiss.

My heart fisted. There was a special kind of terror when things felt too right. Too good. That lulling calm before your life was demolished by a devastating storm.

"Good night, Sweet Pea," Rynna said.

My ear was tuned to the movement in Frankie's room as Rynna stood and flipped off the light. Her presence grew denser with each step. Could feel it swallow me from behind when she emerged at the end of the hall.

An avalanche of need.

A landslide of desire.

She edged around the couch. Since Frankie was safely tucked away in bed, Rynna curled up at my side. We were still being careful, easing Frankie into the idea of Rynna and me.

I wound an arm around her, pressed a kiss to her temple.

Milo yipped, and Rynna cooed, pulling him into her arms. She settled back into my chest and released a contented breath.

A breath that filtered through me like peace.

Like warmth and light.

Milo nudged my hand, and a restless sigh pressed between my lips when I looked down to find those huge brown puppy eyes staring up at me. He whimpered again, his snout damp, prodding at me. Relenting, I ran my hand over the soft, soft fur of his head.

My chest tightened and I felt another piece of me break.

God damn it.

Rynna snuggled closer. God damn it straight to hell.

Rynna.

Fucking Rynna.

Little Thief.

twenty-seven

Rynna

"No." Nikki sat forward as if the tiny bit of information I'd let slip was the most scandalous thing she'd ever heard.

I glanced around the quaint city sidewalk where Nikki, Lillith, and I sat out front of a small café under an umbrella sipping our coffees. People meandered, peering into the large storefront windows, enjoying their Saturday morning. Lush trees grew up from planters, strategically placed along the walk, their bright green leaves and thick branches shade for the old two- and three-story buildings that had been renovated as part of a restoration project over the last ten years.

Macaber Street was much like what was happening on Fairview where the diner was located and the new hotel was going up. I could only pray Pepper's Pies would see this same kind of revitalization. That it would flourish and mobs of people would move in and out of its doors. It was the life I was looking for right there. Within my reach.

Which was what had Nikki in a stir.

I lifted a shoulder and took a sip of my ice-cold Frappuccino. "What?"

She gave me a look that told me I was insane. "Um . . . you did just say RG Construction had taken over the renovation on Pepper's?"

"So?"

She laughed and glanced at Lillith, who was burying her smile in the plastic lid of her coffee. Disbelief filled Nikki's tone when she aimed her inquisition back on me. "RG. As in Rex Gunner. Asshole extraordinaire, who just so happens to be your neighbor and you have so clearly been crushing on since the day we met you."

I would have bristled at the insinuation of Rex being an asshole if it weren't for the heat that rushed to my cheeks, beating any other emotion to the punch. There was no stopping it. Not when I was immediately assaulted with the memories of last night.

Frankie had been at her grandma's, which meant Rex had me all night. Again and again. The man hard and commanding and rough. Demanding my pleasure just as sure as he'd demanded his. My body his claim. I'd never had sex like that. Not in all my life.

I shifted in the metal chair.

Nikki's mouth dropped open. "Oh. My. God."

My eyes widened in as much feigned innocence as I could muster. "What are you talking about?"

Yeah. I was brilliant when I was put on the spot. I wasn't much of a player of games. But I honestly didn't think Rex would appreciate me gossiping about how freaking fantastic he was in bed to my friends.

"Don't you 'what' me, young lady. I know there's a story behind all of that." She circled her finger around my face, as if in my expression was a written confession. "And a good one, too. Fess up. There's no way you two are just doing *business* together." She air-quoted the business part.

Lillith swatted Nikki's arm. "If she doesn't want to talk about it, don't force her." Lillith looked back at me with an apologetic grin. "I swear that she chases all the good ones away because she thinks she needs to know every detail about everything."

"That's what friends are for. The details. I want all the details." She looked to the sky as if she were casting up a petition. Her attention dropped right back to me with a plea on her face. "Come on, Rynna. Tell me. I can't stand it. I want to know how you convinced Rex to work for you. I mean, not that you're not all kinds of gorgeous, because we all know you are, and I'm pretty sure you could enchant just about any man with your sexual wiles, but we're talking Rex Gunner here. "

Leaning forward, I rested my forearms on the table as I fiddled with a paper napkin. "He's not an asshole."

Not even close.

"He just . . . doesn't normally let people get to know him."

Nikki's brows rose. "And you know him?"

"We're . . ."

"You're what?" This from Lillith. She shifted forward. "Are you and Rex seeing each other?" Shock lined every syllable of the question.

Uneasily, I glanced down the street, not sure how to describe what Rex and I were. What we had.

Not when it felt like everything but still lacked a name. "We've been spending time together," I settled on.

Nikki smacked the table then pointed at me. "I knew it!"

"You're dating Rex Gunner?" Lillith drew in a sharp breath, totally taken aback.

"Is that such a surprise?" I didn't mean for it to come across as defensive. But it did. I was feeling protective of Rex and the misguided reputation he had. As if he wasn't deserving of love. Or maybe there were those distorted doubts that I wasn't good enough.

Not to mention those specks of insecurity I felt at the mystery that remained hidden in his eyes, this needle of discomfort that poked and prodded and warned there was something he was keeping from me.

I was right there and he was terrified to let me the rest of the way in.

Lillith softened. "I am surprised, but not in a bad way. Rex deserves to find happiness. He's had it rough. I couldn't imagine a better person for him and that little girl than you."

My lips pursed, and I decided to go with blatant honesty. Because Lillith and Nikki made me feel that I could. "I'm sorry. Sometimes . . . there are times when an old defensiveness appears out of nowhere. High school wasn't exactly easy for me, and trust comes hard sometimes."

Lillith glanced at Nikki. "I don't think it was easy for any of us."

"Oh, Lillith and I are no strangers to the high school bitches, are we Lily Pad? Believe me, we get it, and I promise you, our circle is safe. We invited you into it because we *like* you. That's it."

Gratitude throbbed, and a soft smile pulled to my mouth. "That really means a lot to me. I hope you know that."

"Of course we know it. We're awesome." Nikki capped it off with a wink.

I laughed lightly. Truly loving that they had welcomed me into their circle.

My phone buzzed on the table. Excitement pulled across my ribs. I was biting at my bottom lip as I grabbed it from where I'd placed it face down, beating back a smile when I saw the text from Rex on the screen.

Rex: You still hanging out with your girls?

He'd teased me this morning when I'd tried to leave my bed, which he'd been gloriously stretched out in the middle of. The best kind of topping for twisted sheets. Naked and perfect and turning my world upside down. He'd told me he could think of much better ways to keep me entertained. It'd taken about all I had to rip myself away and force myself into the shower.

He'd just followed me in there.

I tapped out a quick reply.

Me: Finishing up soon. Will I see you later?

I set it back down. Obviously, I hadn't done that great of a job containing my grin.

Nikki and Lillith stared back at me. Then Nikki howled. "Oh girl . . . you have it bad," she drew out. "You should see your face right now. You are in so much trouble. Put a fork in that pie because you are done."

"Stop it," I whispered, laughing at her reference to pie and trying to hide the emotion that pressed in. This shimmery pulse that throbbed and vibrated, stretching out spindly fingers to find purchase in those secret places. Those places that were reserved for when it was right.

For when you just knew.

"So are you two like, together, together?" Lillith asked.

"Yeah." As soon as I said it, those questions brimmed. Ones that hovered around the darkness that would dim his eyes.

"What?" she pressed.

Uneasy, I hesitated, hoping I wasn't sharing something with them that would upset Rex. But I didn't know who else to turn to. Because when I truly thought about it, it scared me.

"His ex-wife . . ." I blinked, choked around the words. "I don't know if he's over her."

Just the thought gutted me.

A hollow, vacant space that radiated pain. He said he hated her. But there was so much pain around it, it made me itch.

"That bitch didn't deserve either of them." Nearly every word that came from Nikki's mouth was light, filled with a tease and the easy way she looked at life. Not this. It was hard. A little bit bitter.

I hated the idea of crossing a line. Invading his privacy by asking for details he hadn't offered.

But there was an ugly part of me that was shrouded in doubt. Turned out, old insecurities were hard to ditch. "What was she like?" I'd barely managed the choppy question when my attention caught on a big white truck that passed us, did a U-Turn, and pulled to a rumbling stop at the curb beside us.

"Holy shit," Nikki mouthed, laughing under her breath. "Is that actually Rex Gunner? Looks like you're not the only one who's done for."

My heart surged to my throat when both passenger side windows glided down. Rex slanted me an almost shy smile that was every kind of sexy from the driver's seat, that expression alone seeping into my spirit and finding a home.

From the backseat, Frankie waved frantically. Milo on her lap, yipping as he tried to paw his way out the window to get to me.

"We's goin' on a picnic, Rynna! You wants to come?" Frankie shouted.

Rex had offered to keep an eye on Milo for me when I was getting ready to leave this morning, claiming Frankie would love to see him when he picked her up this morning from her grandma's.

Wasn't that a sign? It had to be. I soared on it.

"It was all Frankie's idea," Rex said, voice gruff. The sound raked my skin and brought up chills. "She wants to spend the day at the lake, and we thought maybe you and Milo might want to join us."

"We gots all the food, Rynna, but we ain't gots no Pepper Pies. Is that okay?"

Oh my heart. That little girl was undoing me. Just as quickly as her dad. Affection thrummed, fluttery and thick and somehow light.

"That's just fine, Sweet Pea," I told her.

"Hey there, Rex," Nikki sang, grinning as she rocked back in her chair. Leave it to Nikki to put him in the hot seat. "Tell Ollie hi for me."

An exasperated, "Nikki," was the only response she got.

His gaze shifted to Lillith for the flash of a second, his chin lifting in a subdued hello, discomfort ridging the lines of his expression.

But still, there was something significant about him sitting there, all rough and burly in his huge truck.

Something sweet in his offer.

Because this?

This was an offering.

"I would love to go." I glanced back at Lillith and Nikki. "You don't mind me cutting this a little short, do you?"

Nikki waved me off. "Get out of here. The lake sounds way more fun. Besides, Lily Pad over there is getting antsy to get back to Brody. It's totally fine. You know, just leave me here all by myself. I don't mind. Not at all."

Lillith laughed. "So dramatic."

Nikki's eyes widened. "And how else would I get any attention around here? Seems everyone has all their attention trained somewhere else." Her widened eyes slid back to me, all a meaningful tease.

I dropped the peck of a kiss to her cheek. "Thank you. Next time we get together, I'll make you dinner. How's that sound? I need all the practice I can get if I'm going to make the restaurant a success."

Her eyes rolled back in her head. "Girl, don't tease me. Tomorrow? I'll be at your house at seven."

I chuckled. "It's a date." I shifted my gaze to Lillith. "Are you in?"

"Wouldn't miss it. Have fun."

I hopped into the front seat of Rex's truck.

He threaded our fingers together, clutched them tight on the seat between us.

It felt like a claim.

A statement.

I peeked back at Frankie and down to our hands, before I looked up at his gorgeous face, mouthing the words, "Is this fine?"

He squeezed my hand tighter. Like I was his and he was mine.

"This is more than fine, Rynna."

Joy.

I'd never known the full truth of it.

Not until then.

We'd swung by my house, and I'd pulled on a swimsuit, sliding on a pair of shorts and a tank over it, and changed into more appropriate shoes.

Twenty-minutes later, Rex's truck jostled on the dirt road that was nothing more than a worn path carved by the vehicles that traveled the winding road. It curved as it climbed deeper into the forest that lined the lake, which was tucked at the base of the mountain on the outskirts of town.

I'd thought I was prepared. That it didn't matter anymore. That I could keep them at bay. But memories kept breaking loose the deeper we trekked into the forest. The closer we got, the harder the betrayal churned my stomach.

The louder the phantom laughter became. Even eleven years later, I could hear Janel's words floating through the forest.

"You're such a fool. Did you really think he wanted you?"

I swallowed back the tingle of tears that burned my throat and threatened my eyes. It was a long time ago, and I wasn't that same girl who'd run barefoot through these trees. Sobbing. Hurting in a way she'd never known existed until she'd been taught the harsh realities of this world in the cruelest of ways.

None of that mattered.

Not now.

Not with Rex running his thumb over the back of my hand, Frankie belting out the silliest song I'd ever heard from the backseat, and my little puppy secure on my lap.

"Sorry this is so far off the beaten path. Frankie and I kind of like the place to ourselves when we come to the lake, don't we, Frankie Leigh?"

"Yup! We gots our own secret spot that no one knows about. Juss for us."

Rex tossed me a small wink.

My heart, already filled too full, gave an extra wayward beat.

God, he was gorgeous with the sun shining through his opened window. Rays of light speared through the leaves of the trees, sending bright flashes of light against his face as we wound through the thicket. The longer pieces of his dark blond hair were lit up like a blaze of white fire, the hard curve of his jaw and scruff defined by the glowing outline, those earthy eyes a perfect match to the trees.

"Here we go," he said. He pulled to a stop where the path came to a dead end. We climbed out, and I helped Frankie down while Rex grabbed the cooler from the bed of the truck. I kept ahold of Milo's leash and Frankie's hand as we followed him down a narrow trail.

Lush bushes and towering trees lined the twisty path. A gentle breeze rustled through, dragging with it a fragrant bough of wildflowers and leaves and earth.

In the distance, a trickle from a stream cascading down from the mountain could be heard, and birds chirped overhead.

Tranquility and peace.

I inhaled, breathing all of it in, struck with the memory of why I'd always loved this place so much.

Two minutes later, the trees opened up in front of us, revealing the lake.

A glassy expanse of blue.

Calm.

Craggy rocks made up the low cliffs the area was well known for, and the trail weaved down around them, guiding us to a secluded cove and beach.

Awe stoked that fire that continued to grow in my spirit.

"This is gorgeous."

I'd almost forgotten the draw of this place. The stark beauty that gave Gingham Lakes its name.

Frankie jumped up and down at my side, yanking at my hand to lead me closer to the water. "It's our super special secret place. And nows you know! You can't tell any ones! Promise?"

Releasing her hand, I ruffled my fingers through the unruly mess of hair on her head. "I wouldn't dream of telling anyone you and your daddy's secret."

She grinned up at me, flashing me a row of tiny teeth and so much belief. "It's your secret now, too, silly. Right, Daddy?"

She looked to Rex for confirmation. He was setting the cooler down beside the small ring of rocks that had been made for a fire.

He looked over at me.

Meaningfully.

Powerfully.

"Yeah, Frankie Leigh. Now it's Rynna's secret, too."

A shiver rocked me. A different kind than the flood of old memories that had threatened to dim this day.

This was a river of hope.

He was letting me in. Letting me be a part of them.

I looked down at Frankie, who was still grinning at me. "This is exactly the kind of secret I like to keep." I said it to her, but I think I was making that promise to Rex. A promise that I wanted more. That like I'd told him outside their house the other night, I wanted this.

Them.

Us.

That I would protect it just as fiercely as he protected Frankie.

Milo barked his tiny bark, jumping all around, chasing after a butterfly that flitted by.

"Can we go swimmin'?" Frankie asked. She pranced over to her dad, wearing that hot pink tutu over a one-piece bathing suit. The little girl so adorable she caused that secret place to ache.

I guessed maybe I held secrets close, too.

"What do you say we eat first, and then we'll go? Rynna might like to take a hike to our super, super special place."

"Our secret, secret place?" she whispered through barely contained excitement.

He nodded.

Her attention whipped over to me, the child dancing back my direction. "You wanna, Rynna? You wanna go to the super, super special place? Daddy said we could!"

His expression was tender when he tore his gaze from me and turned it on his daughter, a smile fluttering around his full, full lips.

I wondered if he had the first clue the kind of father he was. Amazing, wonderful, and kind.

"I'd be honored to go to your super, super special place," I told her, and Frankie did a twirl, spinning me up tighter. My heart winding up in the fibers of this sweet child. Knitting and weaving and uniting.

I could feel it.

The impact of Rex's daughter becoming a permanent part of me. "Let's go!"

"Give me just a second to get things organized, Sweet Pea," Rex said, tossing a few sticks into the ring of rocks.

I walked over and knelt down beside him. "Anything I can do to help?"

A smirk pulled at the corner of his sexy mouth, voice a rough, muted whisper. "Could you do me a favor and lean in closer?"

I was confused before I followed his line of sight to where my shirt was drooped open, cleavage on full display.

I smacked his shoulder. "Rex." I chuckled beneath my breath.

He laughed from his belly and into the air. It bounded against the cliffs. Ricocheting back.

Boom after boom that rocked my heart.

"This way." Frankie raced ahead of me, hauling me along, her excitement infectious. There was no stopping the permanent smile on my face.

We followed an even narrower, isolated trail than the one we'd taken to get to their picnic spot. Sunlight poured in through the super high trees that towered over us, their trunks slender and their bark gray. Dense branches covered us overhead and soft dirt padded our feet.

We hiked higher, my legs burning from the exertion as we climbed. Five minutes later, we shifted course, the trail guiding us back around to where there was a break in the forest.

My breath caught.

A thundering roar filled my ears, and a cooling spray brushed my skin. We stood on an overhang of rocks that jutted over the lake. Just to the right of us was a rushing waterfall fed from a stream running from the mountain.

It poured over the cliffs and pounded into the lake twenty feet below. Farther away, the cliffs rose in height, fifty or sixty feet high, three more rivulets cascading over the side.

"Whats you fink?" Hope framed Frankie's features when she grinned up at me.

"I think this might be the most beautiful spot I've ever seen."

"Me, too! You fink Milo likes it? I fink he does. Look at him sniffin'."

I laughed. "I'm sure Milo loves it. How could he not?"

She tugged at his leash, taking him from my hold. She took off with him down another trail that wound down closer to the lake.

"Be careful, Frankie Leigh," Rex warned, that voice hitting me from behind. "Stay up here away from the water."

"'kay, Daddy. I knows all the rules. You don't have to keep tellin' me. Sheesh."

I laughed again. But the sound was stolen when I shifted to look over my shoulder to where Rex stood.

He was watching me.

That gaze piercing.

Penetrating.

Hungry.

He slowly edged forward, shards of loosened rock crunching beneath his boots. Power radiated from each predatory step.

Chills flashed across my flesh when he edged up behind me, erupting like a storm, a current of electricity. His callused palms just grazed the surface of my arms from the caps of my shoulders gliding all the way down to my hands.

He laced our fingers together, wound his arms around my waist, and pulled my back against his chest. His hold possessive where he had our hands fisted at my shaking belly.

Leaning down, he planted a soft kiss at the side of my jaw, right over my pulse point that thrummed like the wild, before he released a contented breath and hooked his chin over my shoulder.

Bliss.

It was the first time he'd pulled me into a full embrace out in the open.

Where Frankie could see.

Frankie blushed through a giggle. "You two a huggin'? Grammy said Daddy gots it bad. You gots it bad, Daddy?"

He told his mom about me?

"Guess I do, Frankie Leigh." His voice was gruff when he inclined his mouth to my ear. "Daddy gots it so bad."

Shivers rolled.

Wave after wave.

"Come here," he said. He guided me down to sit on the rocks and situated me between his legs so we could still keep an eye on Frankie. Then his arms were back around me, his nose in my hair. Frankie and Milo played, running around, darting from each other, tumbling on the soft earth beneath the trees.

"Thank you for asking me to come with you two. It means a lot to me."

I chanced peeking back at him, my head rocking against the thunder beating from his chest.

"Don't think you have the first idea what it means to me that you're here, Rynna."

He pressed a kiss to my forehead.

Tender.

So tender it sent a tumble of emotion spiraling through my body. They crashed through me like the river that rushed just in the distance.

"I've never done this before," he admitted.

"Bring someone out here with you and Frankie?"

One small nod, but it seemed a lifetime's admission. "Yeah. Not even my mom."

"Because it's your secret." It was almost a tease. All except for the affection packed in it.

Those eyes slid to Frankie, who tossed a stick for Milo, before he returned his attention to me. "Yeah, it's our secret. Something shared just between Frankie and me. Because she's my life." He hesitated. "Want you to be a part of that now, Rynna."

My life.

Everything pressed down. So much joy. "I want that, too," I barely forced out around the emotion that clogged my lungs.

He threaded our fingers together on both hands, hugging me closer, our fists solid where my heart hammered at the confines of my chest. I could feel him gulp for air, the heavy bob of his thick, strong throat. His words were gravel. "Did you ever dream of it? Want it? Being a mother? Because it's a lot, Rynna, what I'm asking of you. I understand that, and I don't want to push you into something you're not ready for."

I slowly shifted, the hard rocks cutting into my knees, his piercing eyes spearing the rest of the way into me.

Hope and fear radiated back.

"Always, Rex. I always wanted to be a mother. To have a family. And it might have looked different in my mind. But this . . ." I glanced back at Frankie. "You and Frankie are the most wonderful things to ever come into my life. No. I didn't expect you. Not at all. But now that I have you? I'm not letting either of you go."

Almost frantic, Rex pulled me into his arms, his face pressed to my neck. "Fuck, Rynna. How's it possible you make me feel this way?"

A scream jolted us out of our bubble. Our heads whipped around to see the last second of Frankie tripping, her toe caught on an exposed root. She flew forward, her little body tumbling down a rocky incline that sloped down on the far side of where she'd been playing.

Dust flew. Before it'd even settled, Rex was on his feet, sprinting that direction, and I was right on his heels.

"Frankie," he shouted, voice panicked.

Anxious energy stirred the air.

He bolted for her, taking the fastest route, straight over a slippery ridge of wet rocks. Water splashed beneath his shoes as he jumped from one large boulder to another then down to the dirt trail, at her side faster than I could process the entire scene.

"Frankie," he shouted.

Two seconds later, I was there. My heart pitched and churned. Terrified, I peered over his shoulder where he dropped to his knees at her side.

Frankie was sprawled face down in the dirt, head just barely missing a sharp rock where she skidded to a stop.

"Oh God," I whimpered.

And Rex.

Rex was shaking everywhere. Shock slammed his body. These visible, palpable ripples of horror that seized his body. He kept screaming, "Frankie!"

Agony.

It blistered from him, impaling me with each harsh breath he heaved from his lungs.

Uncontrollably, he shook, his hands a mess when he cautiously set them on her back. "Frankie Leigh, Oh God. Baby girl, are you okay? Tell me you're okay."

Frankie moaned, and my breath caught when she flopped over to stare up at the sky. My eyes rushed over her, searching for injuries, while Rex sat up on his knees with his hands rushing over her without touching, as if he were searching her for those same wounds but scared he might make it worse.

Frankie blinked toward the heavens, her voice raspy when she spoke. "Whoa. You see that, Daddy? That was the biggest fwip I ever did."

Relief heaved from my lungs in an audible gush, adrenaline draining fast. I dropped to my knees just as Rex was gathering her in his arms.

Where I felt relief, Rex seemed to be in . . . shock.

Frenzied, he pulled her against him, hugging her tight, refusing to let her go.

I inched closer to them. Dread sank into my spirit when I glanced at Rex again. When I glimpsed his eyes.

Turmoil and fear and desperation.

I wanted to reach out and touch him. Tell him it was okay. Promise him that Frankie was fine. Erase whatever had condemned him to this kind of torture. But he was hugging her to his chest, his jaw clenched so tightly I was sure he was fighting tears. Fighting whatever chaos raged inside him.

So instead, I turned my attention on Frankie. Gently, I reached out and brushed back the tangle of hair that had fallen across her eyes. A slick of mud covered her from her chin up the side of her face, but I didn't see any blood.

"Are you hurt anywhere, Frankie?" My words were scratchy.

Frankie crooked her arm, showing off the flaming-red scrape on her elbow. The shallow wound was quickly filling with blood. "I fink a need a Band-Aid."

Rex winced.

I looked back up the trail, realizing she couldn't have rolled more than four feet. That she'd just tripped. Something little kids did all the time.

Taking a chance, I set a hand on Rex's arm, hoping it would break through the terror that tremored through his body. Muscles twitching. Jaw clenching. "Hey . . . she's okay. She's okay. She didn't fall far. It was just an accident. She's okay. It's okay."

He didn't respond. He just shifted and climbed to standing, keeping her cradled in his arms. His cautious movements seemed at complete odds with the intimidating power of his stance, with the almost vicious steps he took when he headed straight for the trail.

Unsure of what to do, I rushed and grabbed Milo's leash where he'd scampered just off the trail. I followed close behind, surprised when Rex headed directly for his truck instead of going back to the picnic spot.

He loaded Frankie in her booster seat, peppering a bunch of kisses on her forehead and murmuring, "We're going to get you checked out, baby girl. You're fine. I promise, you're fine."

He said it as if he were trying to convince himself.

Still, he said absolutely nothing to me when I slid into the cab.

He turned over the engine. It roared to life. We rode in silence back in to town, tension wound tight as the truck jostled back over the crude path. He drove straight to the emergency room where we'd taken Frankie that night weeks ago.

Somehow, it felt as if years had passed since that night.

So much had changed in such a short amount of time.

Rex killed the engine. Silence descended, so thick it stole the air. I could almost feel the magnitude of the breath Rex inhaled as he stared through the windshield at the ER sliding doors. His gaze remained trained on that spot when he finally spoke. "Told you before I don't take chances."

I reached out, hand trembling as I set it on his forearm. Corded, sinewy muscle flexed, bunching and straining beneath the tanned skin and tattoos that wound down his arm.

"It's about taking the right ones, Rex."

He swallowed. My eyes traced the tremor of his throat, my gaze going soft when he looked over at me.

There was something there.

A plea.

The man begging me for understanding.

To *get* it.

I thought maybe he was waiting on me to run. To spook. To leave him like the woman who was supposed to be Frankie's mother.

In that second, I hated her a little more.

I nuzzled the top of Milo's head. "Take her inside. I'm going to call Nikki and see if she can pick up Milo, then I'll be in."

I'm not going anywhere.

A reluctant, disbelieving smile pull to one side of his mouth. The man so brilliant and good it wasn't fair that all that life was hidden behind whatever had beaten him down.

"Okay," he said.

He hopped out and unbuckled Frankie, and when I looked back at them from over my shoulder, Rex was pulling his daughter into his arms, her head on his shoulder.

She stretched her little fingers toward me.

I did the same.

Our fingertips met.

A flash of energy.

That connection profound.

"I'll be right in, Sweet Pea," I promised through a murmur.

"Hurry . . . I needs you."

"I need you, too," I whispered.

I'd never been playing games.

But now I was playing for keeps.

Rynna – Seventeen Years Old

"You bitch," Janel whispered her hatred from behind me, and I jerked to look over my shoulder. Janel stood in the doorway, seething mad with tears in her eyes. Janel's momma had just rushed out, pressing a hand over her mouth, as if she were either trying to accept what I had just told her or was wanting to reject it.

"I'm sorry, Janel. But I . . . I can't continue keeping these secrets for you. Lying for you. You need help."

"I need help? You don't know anything."

"I know you've been stealing from my gramma, I know you stole from the dance fund at the school, and I know I've been covering for you, and I'm not willing to do it anymore. Your momma needed to know."

Janel scoffed out a hard laugh. "You just want to make yourself look good, same way as you always do." Her voice sing-songed with bitterness. "Rynna Dayne, angel of Gingham Lakes. Holier than thou when she's nothing but a self-righteous bitch." She sank back, shaking her head. "You're gonna pay for this, Rynna Dayne."

twenty-eight

Rex

*D*usk hovered in the atmosphere, and the sky had dimmed from pink to gray.

I sat on my front porch on the rocker watching this clusterfuck of a day slip away. Bugs droned from the stilled trees, the air calm while my heart still banged around, lashing with unstable beats.

I looked up when the front door slowly creaked open. Rynna's footsteps were quiet as she stepped outside into the encroaching night. "I just checked in on Frankie. She's asleep."

I nodded at her, and she stepped all the way out, Milo trotting out beside her. She drew the door closed, all but an inch so we could hear if Frankie needed us.

She'd been fine. Of course, she was fine. My freak out uncalled for, which was something Kale had been all too eager to tease me about. I'd demanded he check her for any unseen injuries that we could have missed just by looking at her. He'd shot off some statistic on the average number of falls a kid Frankie's age had a day, pointing out that it wasn't like she'd taken a tumble over the cliff.

I didn't care. When it came to Frankie, I didn't take chances.

Rynna handed me a fresh beer. "Thought you could use this."

My laughter was soft. Incredulous. Disbelief that this girl could come battering into my life and the only thing it took for her to knock down my walls was all that kindness and faith. "Thanks," I muttered.

After twisting off the cap, I took a long pull.

Ice-cold amber glided down my throat.

Rynna eased out onto the porch and sat on the steps. Her back was to me, her arms wrapped around her knees as she stared out at the peace that hummed around us.

Lost in thought.

Contemplation.

The girl was so damned gorgeous I was having a hard time differentiating the emotions that thrummed and danced and glowed. It was a war against the ones that screamed and warned and howled. The chaos in my heart and mind made me want to rip the hair from my head.

Crazy how everything I'd lived my life on suddenly felt like a lie.

With Rynna, I knew it was all or nothing. I couldn't keep shutting her down and shutting her out. Couldn't keep giving her these warnings without giving her a reason.

It was time I gave her all of me.

I needed to fess up the bullshit that haunted my life. Tell her everything. I just didn't fucking know how to drag it all out into the open. If she would run. Hate me like I deserved for her to.

Agony cinched down on my chest, and my mouth flopped open and closed. The words too thick on my tongue. Finally, I forced them out into the stilled, deepening night. "Warned you that you don't want my mess." It came out hoarse. Choked.

Rynna didn't look back at me. She just sent all that belief floating out to the stars that were beginning to blink in the sky. "And I told you I wasn't afraid."

I sat forward on the rocker, elbows on my thighs as I rolled the beer bottle between my palms. "Lost the first girl I loved when I was seventeen."

Fuck.

A lid had been ripped off, and all the torment that'd boiled inside, contained and hidden, escaped.

Bubbling out and spilling over the sides.

Overflowing.

Burning and singeing and scalding.

Pain shocked through me. As shocked as the breath that left Rynna on a gush of air.

Waiting patiently. So goddamned kind and understanding.

A soft puff of laughter rippled out. Dubious and low. "I loved her, Rynna. I fucking did. Can still feel exactly the way my stomach would feel any time I thought of her. The way I felt when I touched her."

She glanced back at me. I worried I was giving her too much. Being too honest. Maybe I couldn't burden her with everything. Not yet. But she needed to know *this*.

Of course, because it was Rynna, sympathy lined her striking features, her mouth and those eyes that always seemed to see so much deeper than I wanted them to.

My chin fucking trembled. "Ollie's younger sister, Sydney." It left me like the whisper of a confession. "She was a year younger than us."

Surprise flashed before she tamped it down. She just sat there. Twisting her fingers. Listening.

"He would have killed me if he knew." My voice drew tight. "That I'd been living in his little sister for the past six months. Sneaking off with her every chance I got. Two of us lying through our teeth about where we'd been when we'd been in each other."

Pain slithered up and down my throat.

Constricting.

Suffocating.

Could almost feel the ghost of her. The faint brush of her hand. Couldn't tell if I welcomed it or hated it.

"We were all out at the lake. We were drinking, sitting in the bed and on the tail of my truck. Kale was off doing God knows what with his girlfriend, and Ollie had invited a few other girls out. One of them was coming onto me. Sydney—"

Her name hitched on my tongue.

My stomach coiled in knots.

White-hot agony.

"Sydney was there. Watching. Hating it. Hating that I couldn't say a damned thing and that girl was straddling my waist. I laughed it off like it wasn't a big deal while Ollie goaded me. Telling me I was nothing but a pussy and it was about time I saw some action. About time that I got my dick wet."

"Rex," Rynna whispered. Pain radiating from her. Or maybe it was just mine echoing back.

I blinked against the memory.

"She jumped out of the bed and stood next to my truck, demanding I take her home. She was so mad, Rynna. So fucking hurt. And I laughed at her and kissed that girl because that was what I thought Ollie expected me to do."

My eyes squeezed closed.

It didn't matter.

That same fucking vision flashed.

The last time I saw her.

The words dripped. Soured. Old decayed wounds. "I won't ever forget her face, Rynna. I'd broken her right there, and I didn't even mean it. Ollie shouted at her to just go home, telling her she didn't belong there, anyway. She looked at me one last time . . . torment in her eyes. Then she turned and started down the dirt road. And I let her go."

I let her go.

Fuck.

I let her go.

"No one ever saw her again." Guilt stampeded through me. Over me. Trampling me into the ground.

Rynna gasped. "Oh God, Rex,"

"I just watched her storm off into the night, Rynna. I fucking watched her go. I didn't chase after her. Had no fucking clue she was even missing until the next day."

She shifted onto her hands and knees and crawled the short distance across the boards of the porch until she was at my feet.

Tears shined in her eyes.

"What happened?"

A tremor rolled my throat. Horror. Hate. Fear. I'd carried it for twelve fucking years. That girl chasing me through the days and haunting me in the night.

"We searched. Searched and searched and searched for what felt like forever. I hunted through that forest every day. Months. A year. Maybe more. Screaming her name. Begging her to come back. She was gone, Rynna. Fucking gone. No trace. No suspects. No clues."

In agony, I looked at her, fighting the moisture that had gathered in my eyes. "Now I do it in my dreams. I hunt for her. Scream her name. Desperate to find her when I know with every part of me she's gone." My teeth ground. "Buried in some shallow grave."

Tears streaked her cheeks. "Oh God, Rex. I'm so sorry. I'm so sorry. I can't . . ."

She gulped around the tragedy. Like maybe the magnitude of it was slowly sinking in. Her arms wound around her stomach like she might be sick. "Oh God. Oh My God . . . Ollie. Oh God," she whimpered. Looking up at me, she set one of those tender hands on my jaw, her face pinched in anguish.

How was it even possible she was looking at me that way? Grief striking her cheeks and sympathy in the warmth of those eyes?

"Did you ever tell Ollie? Does he know you loved her?" she almost begged.

My head shook. "He'd kill me, Rynna. He'd fucking kill me. I just let her walk away. She's gone *because of me*. I was responsible, Rynna."

"No."

"There's no lie you could tell me, no lie I could tell myself, that would convince me otherwise. I know it, Rynna. I know if I hadn't have done what I did, she would still be here."

It sliced through us. A double-edged sword. Piercing through the atmosphere.

My gaze traveled out into the night, to the duskiness that held to the sky, trees gusting in the wind.

Swore I heard Sydney's spirit howling back.

"You'd think what happened would have driven the three of us apart. But it tied us together some way. Ollie's been . . ." I gulped around the barbs spiked in my throat. "He was a goddamned mess, Rynna. Blaming himself for that night when the blame has always been on me, and I'm the bastard who can't bring myself to tell him. He tries to pretend he's okay, but he's not. None of us are."

Tenderly, Rynna touched my chin. Her lips trembled and her tears wouldn't stop falling.

I almost managed a grin. "Kale is like a rock. Think he's the one who held Ollie and me together when we were falling apart."

"Does he know?"

I gave a regretful nod. "Yeah. He called it the second things started up with Sydney and me. Think the asshole manages to see everything before it even goes down."

Rynna gave me the softest smile before she laid her cheek on my knee, watching me, holding on to my leg like she could keep me from splitting apart. The girl my strength when that was all I'd ever wanted to be.

"Tell me how you met Frankie's mom," she whispered, encouraging me to go on.

"Was lost for a lot of years, Rynna. Fucking *lost*. But the wilderness gets lonely, you know? So, I fucked around. And that was messed up, too, because any time I touched another girl, when I closed my eyes, only thing I saw was Sydney's face."

Rynna flinched, but I continued, unable to stop the train wreck from tumbling from my mouth. "Then Frankie's mom . . ."

Rynna's spine went rigid.

"It was just the same as always. Met her at a bar on the other side of town. Went back to her place. Whole time, that same guilt ate me up because the only thing I could think was I wished she was Sydney. Then one day, she showed up at my house, telling me she was pregnant."

My voice dropped low, and my mouth angled at Rynna like I were offering her a dirty secret. "I freaked out. Accused her of lying. Claimed it wasn't mine . . . because fuck, I couldn't have a kid. Not with her."

Rynna tried to subdue a sob. But it tore free. A partner to the ripping wind. "She'd told me fine. She'd get rid of it. No problem. She took off down my driveway. Next thing I know, I was chasing her, pleading with her to come back, promising her we'd figure it out. She told me the only way she was going to keep it was if I married her."

The words deepened like a plea. "My mom always taught me to do the right thing, Rynna. So, I did. I married her. I didn't even know her, didn't even like her, and I fucking married her."

"Rex," she whispered.

My gaze turned to where she was still on her knees, staring up at me. Emotion throbbed all around. Circling us. Drawing us in.

My body shook, every part of me overcome. Overwhelmed. "And then . . . I'm holding this baby girl in my arms . . ." I held out my hands, palms up, like somehow Rynna might get it. Like she could see me holding Frankie Leigh for the very first time. Like she could experience what that felt like. "And suddenly, it's not just the right thing. It's the *very best thing*."

More tears streaked from the warm well of those shimmering eyes.

My voice was gravel. "Never thought I could love like that. Not after Sydney. And I thought I'd gotten lucky. That maybe I'd been given another chance. So, I let myself love them both. Let them become the center of my world, just like they should be. I had my dog, Missy, and my girls, and we got this house and everything was fucking perfect."

I blinked around the confusion. Around my mistakes. "Don't even know where I went wrong. Working too long. Too many hours. Thinking I was doing what was right for them. And Frankie's mom . . . she was suffering, and I didn't even know it. I came home just as the sun was going down one night—"

I was numb as I stood by the side of the road, staring blankly as the taillights disappeared in the distance. I tried to blink through the squiggle of red, neon lines that lit up against my bleary vision. It was like looking at the sun and then closing your eyes. Or maybe I just wished they were closed. But they were open wide, my gaze sucked down.

Down.

Down.

Missy dead at my feet.

The words wouldn't even form on my tongue, wounds ripped open wide. Gaping and bleeding. Garbling the confession because I just didn't know what the fuck I'd done wrong.

Just didn't understand.

Still didn't.

And her hands. Rynna's hands were on my face, and she was leaning on both her knees, wedged between mine, forcing me to meet her eyes. "She abandoned you and Frankie. That's not your fault."

"It doesn't matter, Rynna. I still lost her. Every girl I've ever loved has left me. After Sydney disappearing? Anytime something happens to Frankie . . ." I fisted my hand, pressed it against the raging of my heart. "I'm terrified, Rynna. Terrified of her slipping away, too. Terrified of something horrible happening to her. If I lost her . . . fuck . . . I can't. I won't. I'll die first before I let something happen to her. Do you get it now? Why I'm terrified of you? Why I'm terrified of the way you make me feel? This afternoon, I—"

Her words were muted but desperate. "I need you to listen to me. What happened this afternoon with Frankie wasn't your fault. It wasn't neglect. She was playing, loving the amazing life you've given her. Experiencing it the way she should. Living it to its fullest because that's what she is. She's life. She's joy. She's rambunctious and curious and perfect, and the last thing you want to do is limit that. You can't keep her from falling, Rex, but you can be there to pick her up when she does. That's what matters the most."

My forehead dropped against hers, and I whispered into the darkness. "After Frankie's mom left, I waited for her, Rynna. Waited because I thought that was what I was supposed to do."

Loyalty.

Distorted and confused.

It spun around me like a bad fucking dream.

"Truth is, I didn't want anyone, anyway. Didn't want to repeat it. Refused to ever fall into that trap again."

I gathered that gorgeous face between my hands. "And then there was you. There was beautiful you standing across the street, and every promise I'd made myself suddenly felt like a lie. You make me feel again, Rynna. You make me feel like every chance is one worth taking. Like you're leading me out of the darkness that's ruled my life. When I close my eyes, who I see is *you*. Show me the way, Rynna. Show me the way out of it. Fuck. Please, show me the way."

She pressed her mouth to mine.

Hard.

"Rynna," I moaned.

Fucking Rynna.

Little Thief.

twenty-nine

Rynna

Strong arms wrapped around my waist, and the rocker groaned when Rex pushed to standing, taking me with him. He hiked me up into the strength of his arms, my legs immediately cinching around his narrow waist.

With one arm locked around my waist, he gripped me by the jaw with the other hand, controlling our kiss, ruling my mind where I disappeared into the abyss of this complicated man.

My spirit roared.

A thunder of grief and torrent of love.

I wanted to sing it. Sing it for him. For this man who'd lost so much and deserved every good thing the world had to give. Instead, I poured it into him. Into our kiss and into every desperate touch.

He gripped me tighter, wedging open the door, carrying me inside. With his foot, he held the door open, breaking away for the briefest flash when he called, "Milo, come," his voice gruff.

My tiny puppy scampered past his feet, trotting right over to the bed Rex had set up for him in the corner of the living room, already knowing his place.

Then Rex got right back to kissing me. A hand wound up in my hair and the other locked around my waist.

I ached for him in a way that was only possible when someone's joy mattered more to you than anything else. When you'd give up yours to see them smile. When you'd sacrifice to make them happy.

When you were so far gone the only thing that mattered was them.

My gramma had told me I'd just know.

That it'd be magic.

And that was what this felt like.

Magic. Magic composed of so many threads. Layers of wounds and grief and tragedy. All of it bound by a seed of hope that had been planted somewhere along the way.

It bloomed.

Bloomed so big and bright that this man was the only thing I could see.

It felt too powerful to be one-sided. Too vast to be warped.

Lives pieced together precariously. Fragilely. A tender, loving, imperfect balance.

He carried me down the hall, only pausing for a moment to look in at Frankie, who was fast asleep. The man smiled up at me when he partially drew her door back shut, his expression so profound as he swept his hand back into my hair, his words a grumbled rasp. A root that had blossomed from that hopeful seed. "Want to do this every night, Rynna. Want to tuck my baby girl in bed then take my other girl to mine."

He walked us the rest of the way into his room. He kicked the door shut and tossed me onto his bed. I bounced on the mattress, a wave of need capturing me. Chasing away the fears and the questions that had plagued us since we'd met.

Nothing left to stand in our way.

He reached back and clicked the lock before reaching down and peeling his shirt over his head, revealing the overwhelming strength of his chest and the ripple of his abs glowing in the wispy tendrils of moonlight that flooded his room.

I heaved out a breath.

"Every night, Rynna. I want to take you. Fuck you. Love you. Keep you."

My entire body shook, the impact of his words tearing through me like an earthquake.

I pushed up onto my palms, squirming on his bed. "I'm not going anywhere."

He flicked the button of his jeans and shoved out of them.

Baring all.

Oh God.

He was magnificent, his cock jutting free, pointing to the sky. Needy for me.

Me.

"Gonna make you a moaning, sweaty mess, Rynna Dayne, then I'm going to do it all over again."

"I'm yours."

The air crackled.

Alive.

Fire and heat and flames.

I writhed as I stared up at him.

Muscle and strength and that amazing heart underneath.

He inched forward, making me insane when he reached over from the side of the bed and dragged my shorts and the bathing suit bottom off. He dropped them to the floor, ran his fingers between my thighs. "So fucking sweet."

"Rex, I need you."

"You have me, baby. Anytime. Anywhere. Always."

He climbed onto his knees on the bed, slowly dragging up my tank and setting it free, quick to do the same with my bikini top.

He tossed it over his shoulder, a wicked gleam lighting in his eye. He leaned closer, framing me in with his big body, mouth blowing across my breasts.

Instantly, my nipples budded into tight, pebbled peaks.

My hips jerked. "Rex. Please."

I needed him more than I'd ever needed him before. I felt closer to him than I ever had. All his exteriors ripped away, shields down. It was just him and me.

I set my palms flat against the hard, defined ridges of his abdomen, and he rubbed his cock against my center.

A slow, sensual tease.

A shiver slipped down my spine. It dove straight into the pool of desire that grew to a boil in my belly.

My hands slid up his smooth skin.

Greedy as they explored. Savoring every inch. "You're so beautiful, Rex Gunner. Inside and out. Thank you for letting me see it. For trusting me with it. With who you are."

I let my fingers trace across the tattoo on his arm that so clearly wept.

Finally understanding what it meant. The kind of loss that would go on forever.

He cupped my face in the palm of his hand, something so serious blanketing his expression. "Who I am is yours, Rynna. I'm going to fix the bullshit in my life I should have fixed a long time ago."

My mouth dropped open to ask him what that meant, but he took it as an opportunity to delve his tongue between my lips in a kiss that seared my soul.

All thoughts evaporated.

"Rynna." My name was a plea. A prayer. I don't think either of us could tell the difference anymore.

He wedged deeper between my thighs. His cock so big, trapped between us, begging for release.

Need throbbed, and he suddenly grasped me by the knees, spreading me wide as he edged back onto his. He dove in, licking through my folds.

I moaned, writhed, fisted my hands in his hair. "Rex."

His only answer was to devour me. Fucking me with his tongue. Long laps and sweet, dizzying sucks.

Pleasure wound. So fast that I restrained a scream. That I writhed and moaned and whimpered his name.

It built to a pinpoint. Ready to burst.

The second before I did, he was over me. One hand planted next to my head as he hooked his other arm under my right knee.

He pinned my leg up high on his arm, pressing our chests together.

I could feel the beat of his heart where it raged against mine.

Wild. Wild and free.

He slowly pressed himself into my body. Never looking away.

Taking.

Owning.

Obliterating.

My mouth dropped open while his jaw clenched.

He began to move. His thrusts slow. Each rock of his hips deliberate. A slow, steady conquering. Winding me right back up.

He teased me with the most exquisite kind of torture. Passion stretched taut. Palpable and alive.

It was too much and too little and I begged him for more.

The physical and emotional that had waited anxiously on opposite sides suddenly charged toward the other.

The two crashed in the middle.

Sublime devastation.

Body and soul.

Tears pricked at my eyes and streaked down my face.

Because I was again overcome.

Overwhelmed by this man. I inhaled and filled my lungs with the magnitude of him.

Lake and earth and the clearest sky.

He moved in me in barely contained thrusts, slow and hard in his claiming command while I spun through the brightest kind of bliss.

Blinding.

Where I basked in this unfathomable beauty.

In that place that had become us.

Real and whole.

His mouth brushed against mine. "You changed everything, Rynna. Where I found an end, you saw a beginning. You saved me. Called me from the shadows. You changed everything the day you walked into my life. You are my heart's second chance."

I floated on the ecstasy of that chance.

Elevated.

Tossed into our perfect harmony.

Where I'd fall forever.

Weightless.

Rex clutched me by the shoulders, his rocks turning frenzied as he clutched me against him, as he burrowed his face into my hair, as he whispered my name.

"Rynna."

And Rex.

He fell with me.

Exactly where he'd always belonged.

thirty

Rynna

Peace swam through his room, a dusky quiet broken by the milky moonlight streaming in from the window. I didn't think there could be anything more perfect than being nestled in the crook of his arm with my head resting on his chest.

Tangled together.

Basking in the afterglow.

He gently brushed his fingers through my hair, and I sighed, so content, and I could only pray this incredible man felt the same. I rolled a fraction so I could place a kiss over the thrum of his heart. "You're my heart's second chance, too," I told him through a murmur.

He shifted me to lay on top of him. Nudging me back, he peered up at me. "How's that?"

I played with one of the longer locks of his hair. "The entire time I was in San Francisco, I felt as if I was missing something. When I left . . ." I blinked through the memories, searching for what to say, wondering if I should even bring it up.

The past was the past.

But he'd shared his, and I needed him to know mine.

"I won't pretend what happened to me comes anywhere close to what you went through. To what you and Ollie and Kale lost that day. But I lost a piece of myself when I left. More than one piece," I admitted in a hurried whisper. "I left behind my dreams and my innocence and my hopes. I left behind my grandmother. My only family."

The loss of her drummed through me. A woeful ache.

He threaded his fingers through my hair and cupped the side of my head.

"You don't have to minimize what you went through, Rynna. Yeah, what happened with Sydney was brutal. So goddamned brutal. But I know I'm not the only person in this world who's suffered."

Rex wavered for a moment, before his words dropped low. "What happened, Rynna? What sent you running?"

Blinking into the distance, I let my thoughts slip back to that time. "There was this girl . . . we were friends." I shook my head, my voice going even quieter. "But really, we weren't. I told you before how I never quite fit in. I was always on the outside. Lonely. Looking back now, I see how she took advantage of that. That I was willing to take any abuse if it meant I had friends."

I could feel the flinch of his fingers he held against the side of my head. "It got worse as I got older. Much worse. I found out she'd been stealing, and maybe it was stupid, but I was actually worried about her." Regretfully, I looked at him. "So I told her mom."

My head shook. "She was so angry. So angry. I should have known when she warned me I was going to pay for it that she meant it. But I was naïve that way. I never suspected cruelty because it was so far out of the realm of anything I'd ever wish against someone."

"What happened?" His voice was a low rumble, and I could feel his unease. I could feel anger sifting through him, shaking out and taking hold.

I eased down onto his chest and laid my ear against the soothing thrum of his heart. I wasn't sure I could look him in the eyes when I made this confession. Distractedly, I traced over the tattoo on his arm and shoulder, whispering the words into the dense air.

"I'd had a crush on this boy for as long as I could remember . . . middle school at least." It was almost sorrow that formed on my mouth, though it was brittle with hurt. "I never thought he'd look my way, then one day . . . one day he asked me out."

"You want to grab a bite Friday night?"

I stood behind the long counter at my gramma's diner, looking behind me, around me. Was Aaron really talking to me? Every one of the butterflies in my stomach held their breath. My heart shook so hard I was sure everyone in the diner could hear it.

"Rynna?" he prodded.

Mouth dropping open, I stared blankly at him, my tongue not cooperating. "You . . . you want to go out with . . . me?" I finally managed to stutter around the shock.

"Yeah. Why wouldn't I?" He shrugged a muscular shoulder, and my wide-eyed gaze got transfixed on the motion. This had to be a dream, right?

"So what do you think?" He angled his face down to capture my attention. "Don't break my heart, Rynna."

Don't break his heart? Oh God. Oh God. This was really happening. "Um . . . yeah . . . yes. Definitely. I definitely want to go out with you." I nodded frantically.

He grinned and those butterflies scattered, a frenzy in my belly. He smacked the counter before pointing at me. "Pick you up at seven."

I tried to keep the tears out of my voice while I let the story bleed free. "God, I was so excited, Rex, that this boy actually liked me."

A growl stalked his throat. I could feel it, hear it all the way to my soul. He tightened his hold on me. As if he didn't want to hear it but needed to, the same way I needed to tell him.

"I was on cloud nine. He picked me up and took me out. He kissed me right across the street in front of my gramma's door. It went on like that for three weeks. The two of us together. Kissing and touching and me feeling like I finally was important." A sob threatened at the base of my throat, words hitching as I forced the last out. "That I wasn't invisible."

"Rynna." It was a shaky breath that blew between Rex's lips.

I angled up so I could look down at his face. "I was so tired of being invisible, Rex. Of feeling stupid and unattractive and unlovable. So tired of being alone. But I should have known. God, I should have seen it coming a mile away."

I stood at my full-length mirror, twisting this way and that, looking at myself from every angle, trying to convince myself that the dress I wore looked good. That my rolls didn't show. That Aaron liked what I looked like, and it didn't matter if they showed, anyway.

It was my birthday.

My eighteenth birthday, and I was so finished being scared. Finished with all the doubts and insecurities that threatened to explode and send me cowering under the covers of my bed. I was going to live this life, and live it to its fullest.

That was what Gramma had always taught me to do.

It was time to start embracing it.

Hurrying out of my room and downstairs, I bounced into the kitchen.

Gramma turned away from the new recipe she was testing by the stove. "My, my, look at you, child. All grown up."

In the center of the old kitchen, I spun around in my dress. "Thank you for buying it for me, Gramma."

"Of course. Every girl needs a dress to celebrate their eighteenth birthday. You're a woman now, and as gorgeous as ever, if I say so myself."

I felt the blush climb to my cheeks. Because after tonight, I really would be a woman. In every sense of the word. "Thank you, Gramma, so much."

She looked at me softly, and I gazed back. Love spun through me with the intensity of the sun. "I hope you know everything you mean to me, Gramma. I hope you know I appreciate every single thing you've done for me. Everything you sacrificed. That you raised me. That you've loved me the way you have. I know you always worried it wasn't enough, but I could never ask for anything more than you."

Moisture shined in her grayed eyes, and she smiled. Smiled a smile that encompassed the meaning of both of our worlds. She reached out a weathered hand and twisted one of the curls I'd ironed into my hair. "We've made quite the team, haven't we?"

"The best team," I said, reaching out to wrap my arms around her. "Thank you, Gramma. Thank you so much," I murmured at her ear, inhaling the sweet scent of vanilla and sugar that somewhere along the way had become a permanent part of her.

She hugged me tight, so thin and frail yet so incredibly strong. "I love you more than you'll ever know, Corinne Paisley. You have been the greatest light of my life. It has been the greatest honor raising you into the woman you are."

Tears slipped free, and I sniffled.

She pulled back and wiped them away. "Stop that, now, or you're gonna mess up that makeup you spent the last two hours perfecting." She nudged me toward the door. "Go on, have fun."

I stepped back and squeezed both her hands in mine. "Thank you. I love you so much."

Sight bleary with tears, I swallowed around the knot of hurt wedged at the base of my throat. "I left the house so happy that night."

"Fuck, Rynna. I can't . . ." Rex itched beneath me, muscles straining, as if he had to stop himself from jumping up and going back to that day to stop it from happening. But that was the thing about the past. It was over. All except for the scars it left behind.

"He picked me up at the end of the street. I hopped in his truck. I can still remember how he squeezed my hand, told me that tonight was just him and me." Agony wheezed from my throat. "And for a moment, I felt beautiful."

"Fuck, Rynna." It was grit from Rex's mouth. Hate bound with the protectiveness he so clearly felt for me.

"He took me to the lake. I was nervous and excited. There was this . . ." My brow pinched at the memory of it. "Old shack. Barely standing. So secluded I don't know how he ever found it. There was a fire already burning in a pit near the shore. He said he'd come out and set it up for me. It was the first time I felt uneasy about everything. Something about it felt off. I should have listened to that flicker of intuition."

I turned my stare down to Rex, who was grinding his teeth, hands tightening, holding on to me.

"I should have listened." It left me a on a grated rasp.

Aaron led me into the shack. Immediately, his mouth covered mine. I kissed him back, fighting the quiver of fear that slicked beneath the surface of my skin.

I liked him.

I liked him so much.

I was just nervous. It was my first time. Everyone was nervous when they left themselves vulnerable to someone else. When you gave them this kind of trust.

I'd been enamored with him for all of forever. I finally had this chance, and I'd be an absolute fool if I let anxiety and insecurity get in the way.

Not again.

I'd been doing it for too long.

But when he led me to the small cot backed against the far wall and started to undress me, I couldn't stop shaking. Shaking and shaking and shaking. Nerves skittered free and fast. Naked, my stomach tightened, and I couldn't relax. I pressed my knees together, suddenly wanting to cover myself. It didn't let up when Aaron undressed in the muted darkness.

I should have been watching his muscular body in the shadows. Instead, I squeezed my eyes closed and fought tears.

"Shh," was all he said when he climbed over me and wedged between my thighs. My legs shook. I squeezed them against him, because something about this felt all wrong. My fingers dug into his shoulders and a whimper escaped my lips.

A sharp pain stole my breath when he thrust into me. I tried to hold it back, but a small cry escaped.

And those cries—they wouldn't stop coming, though, I bit them back, keeping them subdued as he kept driving into me, his head shifted to the side, away, never looking at my face

Tears flowed, almost silent as I stared at the ceiling, wondering how his kisses had felt so good when this felt so . . . wrong.

I knew it.

My gut told me.

Wrong. Wrong. Wrong.

Something was so unbearably wrong.

I just didn't know the extent of it until he groaned and pulsed before he quickly pushed off me and climbed to his feet. His naked body was lit up in oranges and reds against the lapping flames reflected in from outside.

Then Aaron, he smirked.

I blinked down at this amazing man who lay completely still, listening, knowing he wouldn't judge me. But that didn't mean my voice didn't quiver with shame and agony. "He gave me this look before he ducked down and grabbed my clothes from the floor. He balled them against his chest and just . . . walked out with them. I couldn't stop crying, Rex. Couldn't stop crying. I kept calling for him. Screaming for him to come back. Not to leave me. Never in my life had I felt more alone than the moment when he walked out on me after he'd taken my innocence. After I thought I meant something to him."

"That piece of shit." His words barely made it between his clenched teeth.

My tongue darted out to wet my lips. "I stayed in there for so long. It was horrible. It was dark, and I was naked and alone. Finally . . . finally, I stumbled out to find him, trying to cover myself when I did."

Grief clamped down on my heart. "I stumbled out and . . . there was . . . there was a bunch of kids from school," I finally managed. Every word was filled with the disgrace I'd felt that day. "They were waiting for me to come out. They all just started laughing, like my standing there naked . . . hurt . . . terrified . . . was the funniest thing they'd ever seen."

The group of about eight laughed. Laughed as I stumbled on my feet. My body sore.

The trickle of something foreign ran down my leg.

My head dropped, not wanting to meet their eyes.

Oh God.

Help.

I twisted awkwardly, bending over and pressing my thighs and knees together, my arms crossed over my chest.

As if it might shield me.

Shield me from the insults.

From the jeers.

From the laughter.

I barely peeked up, gasping when I saw Janel at the center of it. With Aaron. One of his arms was wrapped around her waist, her body plastered to his side, her hands on his chest. He'd pulled on underwear and was casually draining a beer as if he hadn't just degraded me in the worst way.

Oh God. No. My head spun with dizziness. Nausea churned in my stomach. I was going to be sick.

I stumbled a step backward, trying to quiet the cries that were tearing from my aching throat. Raking from me like broken glass. "Aaron," I mumbled the plea.

"Oh, Rynna." Janel took a step toward me, her blonde hair lit up light a ring of flames from the fire behind her. "You poor, pathetic thing. Did you really think he'd actually go out with you? Did you actually think he wanted you?"

"Oh my God . . . look at all that fat. Dude, did you really just put your dick in that? Not sure how you stomached it." I didn't want to acknowledge it, but I couldn't help but look at Remi, Aaron's best friend, who was laughing hysterically where he stood by the bonfire.

Aaron looked at him with a grin before he planted a kiss on Janel's temple. "Like I wouldn't do anything for my girl. And it was dark." He hefted a shoulder. "Didn't make it all that bad."

Janel smirked at me.

Horror.

It spun around me in whipping, rending lights. The world canting.

Oh God.

Oh God.

"Ah, poor, Rynna Dayne, always such a good girl. But look at her now, nothing but a filthy, fat slut."

Another string of lights. Flashes from a camera.

Picture after picture.

"Janel," I begged.

No.

I tried to cover myself, wrenched over as I sobbed.

Janel just sneered. "You should have known better than to fuck with me."

Then it hit me. A pie. Splattering. Blueberries in my hair, streaking down my chest, dripping on my belly.

Howls of laughter.

"Happy birthday, Rynna," Janel mocked. She tossed me my dress.

I gasped out in relief, scrambling to gather the fabric that landed two feet in front of me and hugged it against my body.

Jeers and abuse struck me from all sides, and I clutched the material to my chest, as if it might stand the chance to shield me from the torment.

Take it away.

Hide me.

The confession tumbled from me on a downpour of tears. Rex clung to me, horror in his posture as he held me as close as he possibly could.

"I ran home. Mortified. Knowing those pictures were going to be plastered all over the school the next day. Knowing my gramma would see them and know what I'd done. So I ran. I ran and ran and ran and I never stopped running, Rex. Not until I came back here."

Not until I'd collided with this mesmerizing man.

"Rynna, what's going on?" The sleepy voice filled with concern hit me from behind.

Torment lashed like the crack of a whip. My eyes slammed closed, and the words trembled from my mouth. "I'm so sorry, Gramma, but I've got to go."

The floor creaked with my grandmother's footsteps. She sucked in a breath when she rounded me, shocked by my battered appearance. "Oh my lord, what happened to you?" Her voice quivered. "Who hurt you? Tell me, Rynna. Who hurt you? I won't stand for it."

Vigorously, I shook my head, finding the lie. "No one. I just . . . I can't stay in this stupid town for a second more. I'm going to find Mama."

I hated it. The way the mention of my mother contorted my gramma's face in agony.

"What are you sayin'?"

"I'm saying, I'm leaving."

A weathered hand reached out to grip my forearm. "But graduation is just next month. You've got to do your speech. Walk across the stage in your cap and gown. Never seen anyone so excited about somethin' in all my life. Now you're just gonna up and leave? If you can't trust me, then you can't trust anyone. Tell me what happened tonight. You left here just as happy as a bug in a rug, and now you aren't doing anything but runnin' scared."

Tears streaking down my dirty cheeks, I forced myself to look at the woman who meant everything to me. "You're the only person I can trust, Gramma. That's why I've got to go. Let's leave it at that."

Anguish creased my grandmother's aged face. "Rynna, I won't let you just walk out like this."

She reached out and brushed a tear from under my eye. Softly, she tilted her head to the side, that same tender smile she had watched me with at least a million times hinting at the corner of her mouth. "Don't you ever forget, if you aren't laughing, you're crying. Now, which would you rather be doin'?" She paused, and I couldn't bring myself to answer. "Wipe those tears, and let's figure something out. Just like we always do."

Sadness swelled like its own being in the tiny room. Loss. Regret. Like an echo of every breath of encouragement my grandmother had ever whispered in my ear. "I can't stay here, Gramma. Please don't ask me to."

With the plea, my grandmother winced. Quickly, I dipped down to place a lingering kiss to her cheek, breathing in the ever-present scent of vanilla and sugar, committing it to memory.

Then I tugged my suitcase from the bed and started for the door.

Gramma reached for me, fingertips brushing my arm, begging, "Rynna, don't go. Please, don't leave me like this. There's nothing that's so bad that I won't understand. That we can't fix."

I didn't slow. Didn't answer.

I ran.

And I didn't look back.

"I just . . ." The words whispered from me on a regretful plea. "I just wish I would have come back sooner. I just wish I would have realized it didn't matter what they'd done to me. My gramma would have never looked at me differently. She loved me, no matter what, and I let them steal eleven years of that."

Fingers sank into my flesh, rage barely contained. "I want to hunt that little fucker down and kill him, Rynna. Who the fuck would do that to you? And that bitch? Fuck. I can't even fathom it."

Aaron's name threatened on my tongue, the fact that I'd seen him on the sidewalk in front of the restaurant a couple weeks before. But there was no use in saying names. On laying blame. I just wanted to let Rex in, let him see me, understand me, the same way as he'd allowed me to understand him.

"It was a long time ago, Rex."

"But it doesn't take away what they did."

"No." My head shook, a tweak of hope lifting the corner of my trembling lip. "And you're right. I spent a long time being terrified of them. Just the idea of ever seeing them again had kept me chained to San Francisco. But maybe they regret it now. Maybe the years passed, and they recognized the depravity of what they had done. Maybe they look back, and they're struck with shame and remorse and would take it all back if they could."

Rex touched the side of my face. "You are nothin' but grace and good, Rynna Dayne. Forgiving them that way."

"Holding on to hate would only hurt me more."

It was almost a grin that lit on his face. "Am I allowed to hate them for you?"

I bit my bottom lip, fighting a smile. Again, overcome by him. By that beautiful exterior and the amazing heart beating its own kind of grace underneath. "If it makes you feel better."

He clutched me to him, burrowing his face into my neck, pressing his lips against my skin. "Yeah, it makes me feel so much better."

Then he nipped at me, and a giggle slipped out.

Because Rex Gunner made me feel completely free.

I moved to stare down at him, and I swore his eyes saw all the way to the depths of me.

The air shifted.

Hit with that charge.

A bolt of electricity.

I sucked in a breath, and he placed his palm at the center of my chest, nudging me back until I was sitting up, straddling him.

He gripped his length in his hand.

Already ready. Wanting more.

Which was just fine, because everything I had belonged to this man.

thirty-one

Rynna

Morning light flooded through the window. Bright, white, and glowing.

I thought maybe I was, too.

I watched Rex, the man lost to sleep. Peace floated around him like a full-body halo where he lay face down on his bed. Twisted in his sheets. A hint of his perfect, round ass peeked out from above the satiny material, the ridges of his muscular back on display, his shoulders so deliciously wide.

My gaze traced every inch of exposed skin.

Even though he'd been so lost, he'd opened up, willing to be found.

Redness rushed across my chest and up to my face, this feeling that was so heavy and warm and light fluttering through my senses. Everything so incredibly right.

Not even trying to stop my smile, I quietly dressed and slipped out of his room.

I peeked in at Frankie. I had to stifle a laugh when I found her facing the opposite end of her bed, sprawled out across it. She had one arm thrown over the side and a leg bent at an odd angle so her foot rested against the wall.

Not even sleep could keep that rambunctious child tamed.

My heart thrummed.

Love. Love. Love.

Pulling her door closed a fraction, I continued to edge down the hall, eager to start the day. Milo would need to be taken out.

On top of that? I figured Rex would love to have a fresh pot of coffee waiting for him when he woke.

Or maybe . . .

Maybe I would have one of Pepper's breakfast pies ready. The kind my gramma had been known for most. It was close to a quiche, but the entire thing was topped with a flaky, delicious crust. People had come for miles to have it start their days.

A grin gripped my entire face when I thought of Rex's reaction. The way he'd look at me when he stood all rumpled and sleepy at the end of the hall, finding me in his kitchen.

That man and his pie.

When he heard me approaching, Milo scrambled to his feet. Nails scratching at the wood floor, he scampered over to me. His tail and hind-end wagged all over the place, his whole body shaking.

"Morning, sweet boy," I said. I scooped him into my arms. "I bet you need to go potty, don't you?" I cooed, nuzzling my nose against the top of his head. He licked my chin.

I slipped on the flip-flops I'd left by the couch and grabbed his leash.

Right as I was reaching for the knob, light knocking sounded against the wood. It stopped me short. Ears perking up, Milo twisted in my arms, his attention trained that direction. I fumbled my fingers through his soft fur. "It's okay, sweet boy. Let's see who it is so they don't wake up the whole house."

I glanced at the clock. It wasn't even seven in the morning. Frowning, I quickly and quietly twisted the lock, careful as I eased it open.

Confused, I blinked, trying to see through the bright sunlight that poured in from behind the figure on the porch.

A blazing silhouette just on the other side of Rex's door.

I attempted to shake myself from the hallucination. To focus clearly. Desperate to find who was really there and not what my mind was taunting me into believing.

Bewilderment stirred through my brain, nudging at the recesses of my mind, prodding at every hurt I'd triumphed. Every fear that had attempted to hold me back. I could feel the trigger being squeezed. Shooting me straight into the worst kind of dream.

No.

I blinked at her.

No.

Movement at the end of the hall tore my attention from the figure standing on the porch. My mouth flapped open, questions wanting to pour out when I found Rex standing there, wearing only his jeans.

But I couldn't say anything.

His own shock had frozen him in place, those sage eyes wider than I'd ever seen.

"Janel," he finally rasped. Her name was barely audible, but it struck my world like an atomic bomb.

Detonating.

Exploding.
Destroying.
Slowly, I looked back at her. My knees went weak.
And the entire world dropped out from under me.

Rex

I could barely see through the fog. Through the haze of my mind.

Clouded.

Confused.

Hurt and hate. They spun through my spirit, a goddamned cyclone that blistered my blood.

I stood at the end of my hall staring at the woman who couldn't be anything more than an apparition.

A fucking ghost. A demon cast from hell to torment the living.

Or maybe that was just where I'd been condemned.

Hell.

Punishment for giving up and giving in.

Because Rynna stood there, as shocked as I was, her knees going weak when Janel's name finally tore through my lips like lead.

It might as well have been a bullet.

Rynna fumbled back a step. Her hand shot out to the wall to keep her from falling. Janel stared at her. Shocked. Angry. Jealous. I didn't fucking know. All I knew was she finally said her name.

"Rynna?"

She said it like she knew her.

"What are you doing here?" Janel all of a sudden demanded, words a harsh breath.

Guessed that was what finally knocked me from the trance. The fact she had the audacity to come into my house and make any kind of claim. I angled forward, head cocked to the side as I stalked across the floor of my home.

My home.

Frankie's home.

The home I had every intention of becoming Rynna's, too.

"You really gonna fucking stand there and demand to know who's in my house? Are you fuckin' kiddin' me?"

"Rex." Janel's blue eyes found mine. Wide and innocent. The way she'd always looked at me when she wanted something most. Which was usually about all the time. Maybe I didn't recognize it until then. But there it was, the truth of it glaring back at me.

Three fucking years, and she was going to stand there looking at me like that?

"Get the fuck out." My voice was grit.

Rynna reeled at my side. Gasping over a breath. She barely caught herself before she fell to her knees, clutching Milo to her chest.

"No." It was a whimper from her mouth.

Grief.

"Rynna," I whispered, arm going out to gather her up. To steady her. To let her know it didn't matter this fucking bitch was standing at my door.

Panic surged through me when she dodged my touch and lurched forward, grabbing her purse from where she'd set it on the floor the night before, and then bolted out my door.

Janel stumbled out of her way as Rynna blew by.

No fucking way was I letting this happen.

I darted after her. "Rynna. Stop. Don't leave. Don't . . . fuck, don't leave."

Don't leave.

She didn't seem to be able to focus when she looked back at me. She kept moving, stumbling down the steps of my front porch and clinging to the railing with one hand and Milo with the other, her eyes glazed over with confusion.

With horror.

With disbelief.

Like she was running from her own ghosts.

"Rynna," I begged it again, desperate where I stood at the edge of my porch. Right where I'd confessed to her all my secrets last night.

"Please . . . just . . . don't," she pleaded. Her eyes flashed to Janel for a beat before she had a hand up to stop me. Frantic, she swallowed. "I have to . . . I have to get out of here."

"Rynna."

With a sharp, erratic shake of her head, she turned, fumbling as she shot forward.

Every part of me wanted to chase after her. Last thing I wanted was to be standing there, helpless, watching her flee across the road and disappear inside her house.

But I had an issue I needed to manage.

Hands clenched, I slowly turned to look at where Janel stood at the far end of the porch. She was twisting her fingers, throat wobbling, just as sure as her bottom lip. "I'm so sorry. I didn't mean to just show up—"

My head cocked, words nothing but fiery darts that cut her off. "You're sorry?" I took a menacing step forward. "Three fucking years, and you're sorry?"

"Rex . . . I . . . I can explain."

"I don't want to hear anything you have to say."

My heart dropped to the fucking floor when Frankie was suddenly there in the doorway, tiny fists rubbing at her sleepy eyes. "Daddy? Who's is here?"

"Baby," Janel suddenly said. She lunged forward, going right for her.

Anger.

Disgust.

Disbelief.

They roiled.

I reached out and gripped her by the upper arm, probably harder than I should have. "Don't you dare."

She looked at me as if she couldn't believe I would stop her. As if she had any right. I pushed her behind me and dropped to my knees in front of my daughter. Almost frantic, I brushed back that unruly disaster of hair from her face while I felt everything inside me bust apart. "Need you to do Daddy a big, huge favor."

She grinned, and I fucking cringed when she glanced over my shoulder.

And I fucking saw it.

The recognition. The goddamned pictures I used to show her, thinking her seeing her mother's face might comfort her. Back when I promised my daughter that her mother would be coming back. That everything would be all right. Knowing someday Janel would come to her senses and return.

When I'd remained devoted.

I'd prayed for it.

Begged for it.

Motherfucking loyalty.

"Is that's my mommy?" She seemed confused by it, not exactly excited.

Wary.

That panic lit in an all-out frenzy.

"Yes, baby. Yes. I'm your mommy."

Every muscle in my body seized, and I wanted to lash out. Shout at Janel. Tell her to go right back to hell where she'd come from.

I shifted so Frankie could only look at me, and I begged her with my eyes. "Daddy needs you to do me that favor, Sweet Pea."

She nodded at me. Like she'd just caught on to my turmoil.

I squeezed her by the hips. "Need you to go into your room and shut your door. Don't come out until I come get you, okay? Can you do that for me?"

She nodded with all that trust. "Course, I can."

"Good girl," I told her, hoping my words didn't shake.

I didn't rise until she turned the corner at the end of the hall, only pausing to peer back at us once, curiosity and a shot of fear in the wells of her brown eyes.

Like she could feel mine.

Years of suppressed, barely checked hate.

It was all there in the clench of my fists when I finally pushed to my feet. My teeth ground so hard I was sure they were grating to dust. And Janel? She just stood there with a pleading expression on her face. A face I'd once thought pretty.

Gorgeous even.

This woman, who I'd allowed to twist me up and tie me, left me hanging out to dry.

Tears sprang to her eyes and raced down her face. "She's so big." Her words hitched.

"It's been three years. What did you think?" Mine were nothing but spite.

Her head shook, and she looked away, dropping her gaze. "I don't know. It feels like it's been forever and like it was only yesterday."

A huff scraped my throat. "Yesterday? She was barely walking when you left. She starts school next year. You don't get to come here and pretend like you didn't miss anything when you missed *everything*."

My head shook. Harsh. A jolt to clear the chaos. The disorder that tumbled and shook.

I angled back on her, bitterness bleeding out. "What do you want?" This woman could come in and rip apart our unstable world.

Standing there, wearing all that bullshit innocence written in her features. Holding all the power in the palm of her seedy hand.

"You're my husband."

She might as well have punched me in the face. Kicked me in the gut. Her statement blew through me like a grenade. "Don't fucking call me that." It dropped out in a low, slow threat.

"It's the truth."

Hostility shook my head. "You haven't belonged to me in a long time."

"I never stopped belonging to you. You didn't sign the papers, remember? That was your choice. A choice I let go."

Fuck.

Mother. Fuck.

"Doesn't mean anything," I grated.

She took a pleading step forward. "It means everything. I—"

Hopeless, she looked to the house that was supposed to be our home. The one she'd set afire. Burned it straight into the ground, leaving that bullshit note about how it was all my fault before she just fucking took off and left us behind.

Right then, I might as well have been back there. A prisoner to that day. Missy lying dead at my feet and my wife driving away.

Leaving me.

My attention moved across the street, to the impenetrable silence that hovered like stone around Rynna's house.

Don't leave me.

A sob erupted in the air, stealing my focus, my purpose. I jerked my head back to Janel, who pressed her hands over her heart. Like she was trying to keep it inside. "You're with her? With Rynna?"

"How do you know her?" I demanded.

Apparently, last night I'd ripped off the lid to Pandora's box. Every demon in my past flying out. Guess it only seemed fitting one stood on my front porch. Seeking a way in when I'd been so diligent at keeping everything out.

Rynna.

Fucking Rynna.

Little Thief.

The second she'd stepped into my life, she'd turned everything upside down.

A frown crossed Janel's brow, hesitation thick, before she quietly spoke, "I didn't know her well, but I knew her well enough to know she's Corinne Dayne's granddaughter. We didn't run in the same circle, though. It just . . . caught me off guard that she's here. I'm . . . I know I don't have any right to be jealous, but I can't help it. I thought when I came back we . . ." She trailed off, her intentions hanging in the air like a thick shroud of dread.

"Well, you thought wrong. You left us. You can't come back and expect anything to be waiting for you."

"You know I couldn't stay any longer. I was dying inside. You—"

"Then what are you doing here?" My biting words cut her off.

"I . . . I got help. A counselor who helped me see we just needed to work through our troubles. Courage to fight for it. For my family."

Fight for us?

Mocking laughter rocked from my lungs. "You're here to fight for us? To win me back?"

"Yes." She said it so simply. So easily. Like I should just let go of three years of hurt. Like I should just let go of Rynna.

"It's a little late for that."

"It's never too late." She reached out. Both hands circled around my wrist. "At least I need to see Frankie Leigh. I can't go on without her, Rex. I have never been the same since I walked away from my child. Never have known a torture like the one I've been livin'. Please, I need to try to make it up to her. She needs to know her momma."

Agony crawled over my body.

A devouring beast.

Fangs sinking all the way to bone.

How long did I pray for that? Beg and plead and cry out to the emptiness of the night? Nothing but a beggar on his knees, willing to give up anything for his daughter's life to be whole. Fulfilled. For her to never feel an ounce of the betrayal that I'd worn around like a second skin.

And there was her mom. Without my permission, my gaze moved back to the open door. To my kid. I'd always done what was best for her. Problem was, right then I had no clue what that was. What was right.

"Not sure I can give you that kind of chance, Janel."

"She's my daughter."

"Who you abandoned," I bit out, voice muted so Frankie couldn't hear.

A sob tore from her. A loud, guttural moan. "I'm so sorry," she whimpered. "So sorry. I'll do anything to make it up to her. Anything. Please give me a chance. I just need to see my daughter."

thirty-three

Rynna

I stumbled into my house, drawing in big, sucking breaths. Trying to keep it together when I already knew that was impossible.

Janel.

Janel.

Rex.

Frankie.

Oh God.

Agony sliced through my being, cutting me in two. Clutching Milo to my chest, I tipped my head back toward the ceiling. Tears slicked down my face and dripped into my hair.

Why?

Why did life have to be so cruel? Fate twisted. Warped and perverted.

I set Milo on his feet and frantically dug in my bag to find my phone. Uncontrollably, my hands shook when I tried to find Macy's contact. Finally, I managed to push send. It rang twice before her groggy voice came onto the line. "Hello?"

It was three hours earlier there. No doubt, I'd pulled her from sleep. But I needed her. Had no one else to turn to. Sorrow wrenched from me on panted, shattered cries. No words but the tumble of frenzied, horrified confusion that gripped my mind.

"Ryn . . . is that you?" I could picture her shaking herself out of the haze of sleep. Panic surged into her voice. "Ryn, what's wrong? Tell me what happened."

"She's here." It was a whimper.

"Who?" she demanded before she caught on. Silence eclipsed the flood of worry that had been rolling from her mouth. "Shit," she muttered. "Where'd you run into her?"

"She's . . ." I struggled to find the explanation, choking over the revulsion at even having to say it. "She's Frankie's mom."

A moan slipped from my tongue.

"Oh God, Rynna . . . sweetheart . . . shit. I'm so sorry."

"I can't believe it," I whispered.

Rex. The man I'd lost myself to.

She'd belonged to him. I couldn't stomach it. The picture of her touching him. Of him touching her.

Sickness spun.

Spun and spun and spun.

Riding an agitator that fully wrung me out.

"Does he know?"

Grief constricted my chest. "No." It was a wheeze. "I finally told him last night what'd happened. But he has no idea it was her."

That was when I hadn't thought it would matter. When the name and face meant absolutely nothing because the only thing remaining had been the scars.

Those scars had been ripped wide open.

"What are you going to do?"

"I don't know. She's . . . she's over there now, and I don't have a fucking clue what I'm supposed to do. She's her mother."

It dropped from me like a stone.

Sorrow.

Dejection.

Regret.

Janel was Frankie Leigh's mother. That was a fact I couldn't change. One I couldn't stand in the way of, no matter how much I loved that little girl.

"Ryn, I'm so sorry. Tell me what to do. How can I make this better?"

"I don't think there's anything you can do."

"I can't stand the idea of you clear across the country hurting and no one there to feed you gallons of ice cream."

I choked out a soggy laugh. "I wish you were here, too."

"If you need me, you know I'm on the first plane. You say the word, and I'm there."

"I know, thank you."

"Just . . . hold tight, Ryn. He's probably as shocked as you are. See what comes of it. What he has to say."

I nodded. It was the only rational thing I could do.

Wait.

And I thought the waiting just might kill me.

Three hours later, I was at the diner. It turned out I couldn't wait. Couldn't sit idle while Janel was directly across the street with Rex and Frankie. Not when I couldn't see through the walls or hear what they were saying.

Torture. I couldn't find another word to describe the turmoil that seethed within. Pulling and ripping and grinding. It felt as if I were being torn apart, rended by white-hot agony.

So, I went to the one place I would find solace. I stood holding a sledgehammer in my hands, blinking into the dimness of the old restaurant as if I had any clue what to do with it.

As if I could make a difference.

A thick coat of dust had settled on the floor, and plastic sheets covered the booths that had been moved against one wall, waiting for the contractor who'd been hired to reupholster them. The old tabletops ripped out, the empty spaces waiting for new tables to be delivered.

It was amazing what Rex's men had already accomplished.

It seemed almost a dream now. The excitement and hope I'd felt the last time I'd been in this very spot just a couple of days ago, envisioning its completion. The day I would finally be able to turn on the neon open sign I'd ordered. When customers would begin to pile in, eager for a taste of my grandmother's legacy that would become my own.

It shivered around me, a haunting reminder that these walls still held their secrets. My past an echo that had hit its end and came bounding right back.

I turned toward the old counter, hands fisting around the wooden handle. At least it gave me something to hold on to.

I froze when awareness struck me from behind.

The door slowly creaked open. It was instant, the way the air thickened and the tension pulsed.

It slammed the walls. Amplifying. Lifting. Increasing. Pulling and pulling and pulling.

Gravity.

I swore I could feel his wary footsteps tremor across the floor and climb my legs. That connection streaking free. Though this time in a frenzy.

Slowly, I released the sledgehammer to the ground, turned around. The man had the power to reach right out and pluck the breath from me. My lungs heaved at the sight of him, and I whispered, "Rex."

"Rynna." He shifted on his feet, an agitated hand jerking at the longer pieces of his hair. He looked at the floor as if it might hold an answer, his tone low, laden with guilt. "God, Rynna . . . never in a million years would I have expected what we woke up to this morning. I'm so fucking sorry."

Lightheadedness spun, and I gulped for air, trying to focus. To see straight. To focus on what was most important. "Where's Frankie?"

He swallowed when he met my eye. "Took her to my mom's. Didn't want her in the middle of this. Not when I don't have the first clue what the fuck I'm supposed to do."

"What does she want?" The question broke in desperation.

What do you want?

I wanted to ask it, but I was terrified. Terrified of the answer. Terrified of how this man made me feel. How he'd consumed me entirely. Everything that was mine, his.

My body.

My heart.

My mind.

Mouth trembling, he stared at me, expression distant, the man shaken from his own axis. "Frankie. Me. Fuck, I don't know."

A strangled sob sprang from the depths of me, and I clutched my stomach. "And what do you want?"

In a second flat, Rex rushed me. Those big hands were on my face, forcing me to look at him. "I want you. God, Rynna, I want you."

The relief was almost as fierce as the pain. As fierce as the stark grief that passed through his eyes. Eyes that swam with the deepest guilt. "Need to tell you something, Rynna."

I blinked at him. Strung up. My world hinging on what he might say.

He squeezed his eyes closed, his expression pinching in regret. "I . . ."

"What?" I begged.

Shaking his head, he slightly angled it to the side and pulled me closer, as if he were pleading with me to understand. "She's still my wife, Rynna."

My heart froze.

Froze in horror. In disbelief.

"What?" I begged again, but this time because I didn't want the answer he'd given. I wanted him to tell me I'd misunderstood. That he didn't mean what I'd heard.

I struggled to break out of his hold, and he held me tighter. "I never signed the papers, Rynna. I'm so sorry. I should have told you. God, I should have told you."

Another rush of dizziness swept through me. This time it was so intense, it nearly knocked me from my feet. "You're . . . still . . . married to her?" The last came off as an accusation.

After everything we'd shared? After everything I'd told him and he'd told me? And he'd failed to mention this?

My mind flashed through a barrage of memories. The things Rex had eluded to. The way he'd first reacted when we'd met. The fact he'd never been with another woman after Janel left. Not until me. He'd kept warning me and warning me he didn't have anything to give.

Horror flooded the words. "You were waiting for her. The whole time, you've been *waiting* for her to come back."

Tears streaked free, and I struggled to break out of his hold. "We never even had a chance, did we?" It barely made it out over the sobs that clogged my throat. The grief that clenched my chest, making it hard to breathe. "You were always waiting for her."

Now she was here.

Janel.

Oh God.

I pressed my hand over my mouth, trying to keep it all in. To keep from spewing the hatred that had blazed back to life the moment I'd seen her standing in his door. Tell him who she really was. What she'd done.

But she was Frankie's mother. How could I do that? I couldn't be that person. One who maligned Janel's name because she had what I wanted. Who was I to know if she'd changed? Like I'd told Rex, it'd been more than ten years.

My spirit thrashed, rejecting that notion, convinced I knew exactly who she was. But was that because of my jealousy? Was it because she was Frankie's mother? Because she was Rex's wife?

Wife.

Nausea crawled through my senses, a sickening poison injected straight into my veins.

Rex fumbled to get his hands back on my face, eyes so intense, his presence powering straight through my body. It only ruined me all the more. "No, Rynna. No. Fuck. Of course, we have a chance. You and me? We're supposed to be." His tone was despairing.

I blinked at him, trying to make sense of the situation. To sift through every horrible emotion. My anger. My hurt. The love that shined far too bright. Trying to look inside myself and find what was right.

But the betrayal glared, blinding. Both Janel's and Rex's. How could I make sense of the two? "You lied to me."

"No, Rynna. I was going to tell you. I promise, I was going to tell you."

"You had plenty of time to tell me last night. You're married, Rex. *Married,* because you chose to be. Because you were waiting for her to come back to you. Oh God." A whimper burst from between my lips.

"I swear, Rynna, swear to you."

Frantically, my head shook. "You need to figure out what you want from your life, Rex, because I can't be with you. Not when you're with her."

"No," Rex grated, shaking his head. "There's no chance of me bein' with her, Rynna. Not when it's you I want."

"I can't—" He cut me off with a kiss. A kiss so desperate I nearly got lost in it. I wanted to let go. Let him take me and love me and capture me. Pretend it was real. Pretend this man wasn't married and his wife wasn't waiting for him back at his house.

Hands still on my face, he pulled back. "Please."

I gripped him around both wrists, staring at him through bleary eyes. Hot tears streaked down my face and into the webs of his fingers.

This beautiful, intricate man who wasn't mine.

Misery.

Agony.

So much hurt.

It whirled around us. A tornado that screamed.

"I can't keep you when you never really belonged to me."

A moan pulled from his throat, and he gripped me. His voice was a rasp. "Don't do this, Rynna. You promised me you wouldn't run. That you wouldn't leave. *You promised.*"

Janel's face taunted me. The idea of her touching him. Of him touching her.

"I can't," I whispered my heartbreak against the top of his head.

He made a choking sound, as if I were causing him physical pain, before he turned and walked away. He pulled open the door, paused to look back at me, grief scored across every line in his face. "You promised you'd stay."

My head shook. "And I trusted you not to lie to me."

His throat bobbed as if he were swallowing the reality down.

He was married, and he'd never thought it important enough to tell me.

What did that make us?

Then he turned and was gone.

Rex

I had to pry myself from her, force myself to walk out her diner door when it was the last thing I wanted to do, fucking agony clamoring along behind me the whole way.

She'd promised me.

I stalked out into the blazing day, squeezing my eyes against the harsh reality, wondering if this was what it felt like to be eaten alive. If you could feel every part of yourself being devoured and destroyed, helpless to do anything but accept that you were getting ready to die a slow, painful death.

Bit by bit.

Because I was. I was fucking dying inside, all those pieces I'd offered into Rynna's hands shriveling into nothing.

It just left more room for the bitterness.

More room for the anger and hate and questions to flood and inundate.

In a daze, I climbed into the cab of my truck, slammed the door, and turned over the ignition. The engine roared. I pulled out onto the road.

Torn.

Wanting to turn right back around and beg Rynna, when instead I headed in the direction of my house.

I still couldn't believe my wife had shown up at my door.

Fuck.

My wife.

I scrubbed a hand over my face like it might give me some kind of clarity when nothing had ever looked hazier.

She was back and she wanted Frankie and me and I had no idea what to do with that.

Reject it was what I wanted to do. Send her fucking packing so Rynna and I could get right back to where we'd been last night. Tangled and bound. Perfectly tied.

Memories of the pledge I'd made pressed in, taunting me in the periphery of my mind, that vow I'd stood and taken.

Could I just disregard it? Shun it? The commitment I'd made? And why did I feel even an ounce of it when she'd been the one to up and disappear?

Motherfucking loyalty.

She was the one who'd broken the vows we'd made. Betrayed and abandoned and deceived. I mean, fuck, I had no clue where she'd even been for the last three years. What she'd been doing. Most sickening was realizing I really didn't care.

But it didn't matter anyway, did it? Rynna had made her decision. Pushed me aside just like I deserved for her to.

God. What had I been thinking would happen when I didn't tell her? Those words locked on my tongue like some dirty secret. Rynna had been right. I'd waited. I'd waited for years for Janel to come back. But the part Rynna was missing was she'd changed everything. Once she'd shown up, the hole Janel had left behind was no longer vacant. Not when Rynna had inhabited every inch.

Now that space was a pit again—deeper, darker, suffocating. Nothing but a hollow chasm, sucking me down where I'd be forever falling in an endless black hole.

I made a left onto my street. I drove passed the rows of happy houses shaded by towering trees, the perfect family neighborhood.

Slowing, I eased into my drive, flinching at the sight of the same beat-up car Janel had taken off in three years before still sitting there. Grim and foreboding beneath the cheerful rays of summer light.

Everything that should have been right was nothing but a contradiction.

Because Janel returning was a prayer I wished would have remained unanswered.

Dropping my forehead to the steering wheel, I exhaled a heavy breath before I forced myself to man up and climb out. That didn't mean I didn't hate every step that brought me closer, my footfalls slackened with dread.

I slid the key in the lock and cracked open the door. There wasn't a whole lot left but resignation when I stepped inside.

Janel was in the kitchen, and she whirled around, wringing her hands together and looking at me expectantly.

I tossed my keys to the small table by the door. "You can stay," I told her, voice hard.

She exhaled a relieved breath and started for me. Repulsed, I gave a harsh shake of my head and took a step back. She stumbled to a quick stop. Was she actually so clueless she didn't get why I'd push her away? Did she not grasp what she'd done?

"You can sleep in my room, and I'll sleep on the couch." Might as well have spit the words at her. But I couldn't help it. That anger was slipping and sliding, sinking in deeper, the freedom I'd found in Rynna binding me in chains.

Disappointment flashed across her face, and she went back to twisting her fingers. I kept on, giving her what I could, feeling like I didn't have another choice. "I don't want you alone with Frankie."

"But—"

"You don't get a say in this, Janel. You left, and if you want to see Frankie, then it's gonna be on my terms. Or else you can walk right back out that door." I pointed at it, hoping she'd take it as an invitation.

She gulped, nodding for me to continue. "Okay. I told you I'd do anything."

"She's going to be confused, so you need to be respectful of that. Let her get used to you. And you're going to have to prove to me that you actually want to be here. That you've changed before I can trust you with her."

Her blue eyes widened in sincerity, her blonde ponytail swishing as she took a surging step forward. "I will. I'll do whatever it takes. Maybe . . . maybe I can go to work for you in the office. Do something with my hands. Show you I'm responsible. I've changed, Rex. I've changed."

Mine widened in disbelief. "I think you're getting ahead of yourself, don't you?"

"I just want to make things right. What . . . what about us?"

"There's no us, Janel."

She stumbled over a whimper. "Because of Rynna?"

Pain pierced me, a straight shot right through the center of my heart. I tried to hide it, but I knew Janel saw it. "It's none of your business what I've got going on with Rynna."

"You're my husband, Rex."

I stalked passed her and into the kitchen. I grabbed a beer from the refrigerator, doing everything I could to keep myself in check. "Who you left."

"And now I'm back. I came back to you because I missed you so much. Every single day," she begged.

I cringed. Didn't want to hear it. It didn't matter what she had to say. "It's too late."

Her voice was a plea behind me. "It's never too late."

Rynna

I'd thought I'd timed it right. I'd mastered peeking out the window to make sure the coast was clear before I raced from my door to my car. Making sure our paths didn't cross.

But there they were, Rex stepping outside and turning around to lock his door, Frankie bounding down the steps, calling my name. "Rynna, Rynna! What's you doing? We's goin' to the lake. You wants to come?"

Janel was between them, at the top of the steps. Arms crossed over her chest. A sneer on her face when she met my eyes.

I gulped around the agony. Fumbling, I tried to hurry and unlock my SUV. I had to get away. Escape. Instead, my hands were shaking so badly I dropped my keys. They clattered to the ground. The only thing I managed was to draw more attention to myself.

I snatched the key ring up, trying to steady myself, my heart and my hands and my voice. "I don't think that's a good idea, Frankie."

"Ah, man. But I misses you."

I miss you. I miss you. I miss you.

The world spun around me. A circuit of torment. I inhaled, blinked, my words barely a whisper. "I miss you, too."

So much.

"Does Milo wants to come and play?"

Behind Janel, Rex slowly turned around. His entire being flinched when he saw me, and instantly, he cast his eyes to the floorboards of his porch. As if I'd broken him every bit as much as he'd broken me.

The hate in Janel's expression shifted, and she looked up at him, beaming, before she set her hand on Frankie's shoulder. "Come on, sweetheart. We'd better go before it gets too late."

I floundered to get into the driver's seat before slamming the door shut. I choked back tears as I pulled out of my drive, refusing to let her see me fall apart, my teeth clenched as I took the three quick turns to get out onto the main road.

I lost it just down the street, my eyes blurring over. I pulled into a convenience store parking lot, whipped into a parking spot, gripped the steering wheel in both hands. Head dropped. Gasping.

He lied to me.

Maybe this was the way it was supposed to end, anyway.

Maybe Janel had changed. What if she was exactly what they needed? The one who would make them whole again? Who would chase away the darkness that lingered in the depths of Rex's eyes?

Every part of me rejected it. The fact she was Rex's wife. That he belonged to her. Not when my heart screamed he was mine.

I jerked when the diner door swung open. But I wasn't struck with the presence I'd been aching for over the last five days. Instead, I was slammed with a stark, radiating anger.

I'd been sweeping up some of the mess left behind by the resanding of the long countertop, again looking for something to keep my idle hands busy.

Knowing if I kept still for too long I might go insane.

My mouth dropped open when a woman stormed into my restaurant. All bristling fire and animosity.

She wore jeans, boots, and a flowy, whimsical blouse. Her blonde hair had been darkened underneath and curled into long waves, the woman beautiful in an earthy, natural way, aged by the faint traces of smile wrinkles at the edges of her mouth.

But her eyes.

Her eyes were warm and sincere, even though they were raging mad.

Sage.

My heart clutched.

This was Rex's mother.

She crossed her arms over her chest and looked me up and down. "Well, you must be Rynna Dayne."

I set the broom and pan aside. I tried to straighten myself out, to keep myself from falling apart, my voice shaking when I finally spoke. "I am. You must be Jenny Gunner."

Still, her name tripped on my tongue.

Standing there, she seemed to war with something, and she blew out a strained breath from her nose and lifted her chin when she came to whatever conclusion she'd been looking for. Some of that anger slipped away. "I wish we were meetin' under different circumstances," she said. "Honestly, I came over here thinking I was gonna knock a little sense into you for breaking my boy's heart, but from where I'm standing, looks to me like you're suffering from that breaking, too."

I choked out a laugh. Wow. She was . . . something. Confident and brazen and sweet. Country to the bone. So much like the women I'd been surrounded with all my years growing up.

I forced myself to smile, though it came out weak. "Yeah . . . I think I'm dealing with a bit of a heart breaking."

A bit.

My stomach tumbled with the shards of jagged, broken glass that coated my insides, gouging into my flesh. Deeper and deeper with each breath.

It was a constant, excruciating pain.

She cocked her head. "So, what's the problem then?"

That choked laugh turned into a cry. "What's the problem?" My head shook, and I blinked at her through the motes that floated through the haze of light streaming in through the windows. "Rex is married. His wife is at his house right now. What kind of person would I be if I stood in the way of that?"

I went back to the same justification I'd been trying to feed myself, the rationale that they might be better with Janel. All week, I'd been trying to persuade myself maybe it was meant to be. That it was best if I walked away.

But I was beginning to wonder if I wasn't trying to cover the hurt, the fear of finding her there, and what that would mean for Rex and me. If I could ever rid her face from my mind if I ever allowed him to touch me again. Or maybe I was just afraid of facing that same kind of rejection that had chased me away in the first place.

Jenny Gunner didn't even hesitate. "Just the fact you'd even consider it proves to me that you are the exact kind of person he deserves."

For a beat, I turned away, gathering myself, before I turned back to her. "She's Frankie's mother, Jenny. I—"

"You love them." It wasn't a question. It was a solution.

My hands pressed against my chest. "So much. Which is why I'm willing to let them go."

She turned away from me and began to wander around my restaurant, her fingers tracing across the new tables that had been installed this week. Her voice dropped into a slow musing, "You know, I raised my son to be good. To respect whoever crossed his path. To honor his promises. Maybe it was because his father up and left me the second I told him Rex was on his way, but I drilled that loyalty into him so deep. And I won't ever regret that. The man he became."

She turned to gaze at me from over her shoulder. "He's a good, good man. Honorable and noble. And when he loves, he loves with all he's got. And that love has come back to bite him in the ass time and time again."

She looked toward the ceiling. She inhaled deeply and a tremor slid down her spine. "When Sydney disappeared, I was terrified I wouldn't ever see my son again. Physically, sure, he was there. But the rest of him? His amazing spirit? His smile so wide and his belief so big? It was gone. And then there was Frankie . . . Frankie Leigh. She rekindled a part of him that'd gone dim. Lit him up. He'd sacrifice anything for her."

She glanced back at me. "And Janel? She's always been a sacrifice. He chose to love her because he should. And I won't diminish that. Say it was wrong. Not when my son was tryin' to do what was right. But the bad seed in that equation was Janel. She's always been nothing but a leech." She looked around the restaurant, shaking her head. "Honestly, can't believe your grandma tolerated her so long."

Strangled confusion fell from my tongue. "What did you say?"

She turned back to me. "Your grandmother . . ."

My brow pinched. "I know you said my grandmother . . . but Janel . . . she worked here? When she was with Rex?"

Her eyes narrowed in confusion. "Don't really know a time she lived in this town when she didn't work for your grandma. From what I know, she started out when she was in high school."

Oh God.

My arm went around my belly. I had no idea why I'd assumed Janel no longer worked at Pepper's. That once I left, my grandmother would have let her go.

Regret churned.

Once I'd gotten to California and called Gramma to let her know where I was, I'd told her I didn't want to hear a thing about what was happening in Gingham Lakes or its people. I'd told her the only person I cared about was her.

I'd wanted to shun it and hide it and pretend the rest never existed.

Of course, life here had just gone on.

Gramma had no idea what Janel had done to me. There'd been no reason for her to cut her loose.

"What's wrong?" Jenny asked, taking a cautious step my direction.

"I . . . I didn't know she was still working for my gramma. That she was here. It feels . . . wrong."

So wrong.

So off.

Awareness pressed in. A thread tickling my consciousness, vying to make itself known.

"You knew her?" Jenny asked.

I barely nodded. "I lived with my gramma growing up."

Jenny huffed. "Everything about Janel is wrong, Rynna. Make no mistake about that."

She approached me, touched my cheek. Her expression turned pleading. "My son deserves to be happy. And my grandbaby? She deserves to be safe. Both of them deserve to be loved. The right way. And I know I don't know you all that well, but I've always considered myself a good judge of character, and I'm betting you deserve it, too."

I felt jarred when she suddenly stepped back and began to walk away. Just as she pulled the door open, she looked back at me. "I don't trust her, Rynna. And you and my boy . . . your hearts are in the right places. But any sacrifice you and Rex are trying to make are only opening the door for her to hurt them all over again."

My head was still spinning when I left the diner. Streetlamps shined down, twilight the deepest blue where it took to the sky, the Alabama air cooled by the shallow gusts of wind that blew through the quieted corridor, the shops lining the street shut down for the night.

I'd spent the entire day inside.

Working and cleaning and trying to process what Jenny Gunner had been trying to say. It'd felt like a warning. I'd pondered it until the windows had dimmed and darkness had begun to take hold.

I stumbled toward my Jeep parked at the street, my mind five miles away on that little house across from mine. I jerked back when I saw the man at Pepper's windows, hands cupping around his eyes as if he were trying to get a better view inside through the tinted windows.

Slowly, he peeled himself back, ambled my direction.

Aaron.

Why was he looking in my restaurant?

Terror bottled in my throat, and I took a step back when he took one toward me.

He smirked, every slimy inch of his arrogant face lit in the lamps. This time, the asshole clearly knew who I was. "Well, Rynna Dayne. Thought you looked familiar before. Just couldn't place you. You look good. Real good."

He grabbed me by the wrist.

Something took me over. The fear gone, replaced by something fierce. I wrenched out of his hold. Disgusted. Anger burst free. "You didn't recognize me? Why's that? Because I wasn't naked, letting you take advantage of me? Because I wasn't following you around like a fool? Because I lost a few pounds? Which is it?"

He let loose a low, amused whistle. "Ah, I see the way you look isn't the only thing that's changed. Feisty. I like that."

He went to touch my hand, and I jerked it back. "Don't touch me. Don't look at me. Don't come around me. In fact, stay off this street. Don't want to see you in front of this diner ever again."

I ducked around him, trying to keep it together, pretending as if I weren't shaking all over the place. I was seconds away from coming unglued. Unhinged.

A chuckle rumbled from his mouth, and he looked back at me, shaking his head. "Always in Janel's way, aren't you? Brave girl. Just wonder who she's going to hurt most this time."

I whipped around. "What did you say?"

He just smirked then he turned and sauntered down the street.

By the time I made it home, I was trembling so hard I could barely see. I killed the engine and sat in the darkness of the cab. I clutched the steering wheel, sucking in breaths.

What was I supposed to do?

What did any of this mean?

I forced myself out into the night. Wind gusted and worry climbed through every inch of my body. Despite all my efforts, my attention tuned to his house. It was lit, all the windows shining with a soft yellow glow.

Janel's car was in the driveway, but Rex's truck was gone.

At least there was some comfort in knowing they weren't together. It was Friday night, so Rex would be at the bar and Frankie would be spending the night with her grandma, who so obviously had Frankie's best interest at heart.

I forced myself up the steps, across the porch, and fumbled to get the key into the lock. The door swung open.

Dread echoed back from the silence.

God. I was losing it. I had to be.

But everything felt . . . off.

I swore a disorder tumbled through the air, a disturbance ricocheting from my grandmother's walls that hadn't been there when I'd left this morning.

I flicked on the light. Eyes jumping around. Calculating as I took everything in.

Nothing seemed out of place. But my gut? It warned me someone had been there.

Fear slithered beneath the surface of my skin, and I stepped all the way inside and locked the door. I went into the kitchen and flicked on the light.

Empty.

I was alone. Somehow, that didn't make me feel any better. I warmed up some leftover pot pie in the microwave and sat down at the table by the window. It was like sand in my mouth, but I forced it down since I hadn't eaten in days.

Forty minutes later, a loud engine rumbled down the street. Approaching. Coming closer.

A frenzy climbed to the air.

Awareness.

Confusion.

Dread.

Headlights sliced through the darkness before Rex's big truck turned into his driveway, way earlier than I'd have expected him to.

That frenzy roiled.

The breath got locked in my lungs when he finally stepped out, and I couldn't look away as I watched him, his head drooped between his shoulders as he ascended the porch steps and made his way inside.

My eyes squeezed closed, and I pressed my hand over my heart.

God. What was I supposed to do?

thirty-six

Rex

I sat at the bar, tossing back beer after beer. Olive's was packed, same way as it was every Friday night. Hoards of people were out living it up, having the time of their lives, their laughter and voices and conversations ringing out.

It only amplified the hollowness.

The vacancy that wept.

That turmoil I'd stumbled into the day Rynna had pushed me away had only grown with each moment that passed. Janel's presence had gotten harder and harder to bear. Every single time I opened my goddamned door and she was there, it hit me anew.

It made my stomach clutch and my heart wrench, hating that I wasn't coming home to Rynna. Hating that Frankie still didn't know how to act around her mother, uneasy and unsure and a little bit scared. Hated that it made my skin crawl every goddamned time Janel took my baby girl in her arms.

I just fucking . . . hated.

Ollie appeared in front of me, popping the cap off a fresh beer. He slid it across the shiny bar. "Don't know whether to keep feeding you these or cut you off."

I lifted it to my lips and took a long pull before I tipped the neck his direction. "I'm pretty sure the answer to that is to keep them coming. You know what they say, it's all about who you know."

Chuckling beneath his breath, he planted his hands on the bar and stretched his tattooed arms out between us, dropping his voice when he leaned in close. "Yeah, well that might be the case, but that also means I know you. And I know you're fucking miserable, man. This isn't healthy."

I took another sip. "Not much to be done about that now, is there?"

Ollie's face screwed up in concern. "Not sure wasting away at my bar is the solution."

"Just . . . can't go back there, Ollie."

He sighed and wiped a palm over his mouth before he turned his attention back on me. "So, you let your ex-wife back in your house, and now you can't go back to it? You not seeing an issue with that?"

Oh, I was seeing plenty of issues.

Harsh laughter rolled from my tongue. "That's the problem, Ollie. Janel's not my ex. She's still my fucking wife."

A frown pinched between his brows. "Only thing claiming it is a piece of paper. And you know what that piece of paper says? It says the two of you would cherish each other, love each other, respect each other for all of your lives. It says the two of you would stay true through thick and thin. Through the good and the bad. I was there, remember? You really think Janel has been faithful to you since she left? You think her running off on you was fueled by her respect?" Quiet outrage shook Ollie's head. "Pretty sure any contract you two had is expired."

I jumped when a hand clamped down on my shoulder. My head jerked that way. Kale was there, grinning down, sliding into the stool next to me.

"Oh, do tell me I'm just in time for the conversation about the fucked-up situation our boy here has gotten himself into."

Just fucking great.

All I needed was the two of them razzing me. Teasing and taunting me with what I already knew.

Ollie lifted his chin to Kale. "Yep. Right in time, brother. Pretty sure this asshole thinks he's going to sit here all night and actually manage to drink his cares away." Ollie turned back to me. "But believe me, when you wake up in the morning? They're going to be right there waiting for you."

"Comforting," I grunted, taking a quick swig.

Ollie shrugged. "Just telling you like it is."

"And what the hell do you expect me to do about it? Rynna already made her decision." Didn't mean to come off so pissy and irate, but I couldn't stop it. Because I was.

I was angry.

Hurt.

This raging storm billowing inside of me where I was lost, going down in the middle of the sea, getting swallowed by the waves. No goddamned chance of being saved.

"Yeah?" Kale challenged, angling to the side in his stool so he was fully facing me. "And why's that?"

"Because she knows it's not worth getting involved in my mess."

"Really?"

"Really."

"I call bullshit."

A huff of frustration bled out. "I went to her, Kale, I went to her and I begged her and she sent me away. I betrayed her, man, withholding that truth. She doesn't trust me, which I can't expect her to. I fucked it up, just like I always do."

"Yeah, because she got railroaded by the truth that you're still married. You think that whole thing wouldn't have gone down differently if she would have been prepared? If you would have already been taking the steps to end that bullshit marriage that never should have existed in the first place?"

"Or maybe she should shut me down. I made a vow, and for once in my life, I need to stick to it."

"Once in your life?" he bit out like he couldn't believe his ears.

"Yeah. You think I didn't make the same damned promises to Sydney—"

I slammed my mouth closed, a fence going down in front of the words that wanted to keep rolling out.

Ollie looked like I'd punched him. "What does Sydney have to do with any of this?"

Fuck. Fuck. Fuck.

I'd slipped.

Just like I'd been saying all along, ever since Rynna had come into my life, things had spun out of control. In the best of ways. In the worst of ways. I had just ripped open the locks to a past I didn't want to unleash. A goddamned train wreck, no consideration to who was going to get in the mix of it.

Last thing I wanted was to hurt Ollie more than I already had. He didn't need this. Fuck, he didn't need any of this. Never had deserved it.

"What did you say?" Ollie's voice was muted and strained.

I hopped up, hands gripping my hair, trying to reel it all in. Tossed out a few more lies. Not like they made any difference anyway. "Nothing . . . just should have stopped her that night."

I drained my beer and slammed it down on the bar. "Gonna get out of here."

Throwing a handful of twenties down, I spun on my heels and wound back through the crowds, shouldering through the bodies packed tight, their laughter and joy grating in my ear. A fucking grinding pad against my consciousness.

Swore I was close to a panic attack by the time I stumbled out into the night. I sucked down the cool breeze, lifting my head to the sky, wishing on any goddamned star that might appear.

I cringed when the door swung open behind me.

Didn't need to turn around to know it was Kale.

"Just go back inside," I told him.

"You really think I'm going to turn my back on you? Now? When you need me most? You might have done a bang-up job of convincing yourself all these years that you didn't need anybody, but I think it's plenty clear by now you're wrong."

He took a step toward me. "Tell me what you want, Rex. Tell me. Who?"

Frankie and Rynna. Frankie and Rynna. Their names spun on a circuit. Nonstop.

I shook my head. "This is all so fucked up, Kale."

Slowly, I turned. "So fucked up, and I don't have a fucking clue what to do."

"Yes, you do. You know exactly what to do."

Air puffed through my nose, and I looked away, raking a hand through my hair. "And what's that?"

"You probably should start by forgiving yourself for Sydney. By finally letting go of what you've been carrying. Tell Ollie. He deserves to know."

Fear clamored through my nerves. "Sydney doesn't have anything to do with this." Could barely force out the defense.

Kale took a step forward, angling his head. "Really? You're really going to stand there and act like it doesn't have everything to do with every damned decision you've made since it happened? Are you really going to act like it didn't have everything to do with Janel in the first place?"

I blanched, attention swinging back to him, anger filling the words. "What? I'm not seeing how the two relate."

"You settled, man. You settled because you thought you didn't deserve to be happy. Because you thought you shouldn't ever get to love again. And then Frankie, that sweet baby girl, came into your life, and you didn't know how *not* to love anymore. So you gave in, opened your heart, loved. You loved, man, and then Janel destroyed it all over again. And now she's back and you're settling again."

He edged forward, voice dropping low. "You really think Rynna's not worth the fight?"

Anguish fisted my heart. "Of course, she's worth the fight."

"Then fight for her, Rex. Fight for her and fight for Frankie, and for goddamned once, fight for yourself."

Every muscle in my body recoiled. "What if I don't deserve it, man?" I swam against all the emotions that came rushing in. "I fuck everything up. Every single time. Lose the people I love. I thought this time . . . I thought this time with Rynna I'd finally outrun it. That I'd gotten a second chance. And the next thing I know, she's gone, too. She doesn't want me, man. She doesn't want me, and I don't know how to stop it. I don't know how to stop it."

The last left me on a wheeze, and I pressed the heels of my hands into my eyes.

Fuck.

I didn't know how to stop it.

I drove back home in a blaze of pain. I'd sat in my truck for two fucking hours, letting the booze run their course, before I forced myself to move. I pulled into my drive, trying not to look behind me to Rynna's place. Maybe if I blocked it all, I wouldn't feel it anymore.

Frankie and Rynna.

Maybe if I managed to go numb, it'd erase all the pain. Maybe then I could float right through the days.

I heaved out a couple of breaths before I forced myself from the cab. Footsteps dragging, I made my way up the porch and to the door.

I was in a daze when I walked through it, and I squinted when I stepped inside and let the door fall shut behind me. Like I was watching the scene through a dream. Everything distorted.

Janel was in the kitchen.

Cooking dinner.

Frankie and Rynna.

The smell of pork chops hung heavy in the air. But it felt all off. A knot formed in my throat, and I tried to swallow.

Her blonde hair swished around her shoulders when she turned to look at me, taken by surprise. She quickly tucked her phone in her back pocket, hands shaking. "Oh, you're here early."

She dipped into the fridge and grabbed a beer. "Here. You look like you could use this."

She was all care and concern when she sauntered over to me, twisting the cap from the beer, leading me to the couch.

"Did you have a bad day?" she asked, sinking to her knees on the floor, staring up at me.

I choked out a laugh. A bad day. She had no clue what her returning had done to me. Had done to Rynna. The toll it was taking on Frankie.

And I still had no idea if this was right, letting her into our lives, giving her a chance to be a mother.

She'd gone to dance with Frankie twice, done everything I'd let her, taking her to the park, playing with her every chance she got, even though every time they were in the same room, I wanted to rip my hair out.

But she was trying.

Shouldn't I?

"You might say that," I told her.

She pressed both her hands on my knees and leaned up, her voice going quiet when she reached for the fly of my jeans. "Then let me take the bad away. Let me take care of you. Please, Rex, let me take care of you."

I groaned, head rocking back on the top of the sofa, breath a hiss on my

tongue.
    Frankie and Rynna.

thirty-seven

Rynna

I paced my kitchen.

I felt as if I were stuck in limbo.

A path set out ahead of me that I didn't yet know how to take. Stuck in a purgatory of worry and jealousy and loss. A shimmery anger that lit up at the edges where it kept me enclosed.

Helpless.

And helpless was the last thing I wanted to be.

Milo was asleep on his bed in the corner, and I shuffled around in my kitchen, trying to distract myself from it. Maybe baking would give me a little clarity. Insight to the right decision. A calm in the midst of the worst kind of disturbance that still rattled my walls.

I tried to reject the shiver of unease that slipped down my spine, still unable to shake the idea that someone had been in my house when I was away.

Wondering if it was just me being foolish—jealous and petty and needy— or if the foolish part was me ignoring it.

Gramma had told me to always, always trust my gut.

But my guts were tied in one of those impossible knots. The kind where you couldn't tell what was what, where one loop started and another ended.

"Gramma . . . I wish you were here. You would know what to do," I murmured under my breath, pulling the ingredients for an apple pie from the pantry and refrigerator. Night pressed in at the window, the globe light on the ceiling a hazy hue of yellow that lit the dated kitchen.

I had just set everything on the counter when I stilled.

A prickle of awareness flashed up the nape of my neck. Though this was an entirely different kind of fear.

This was hope and excitement and the worst kind of confusion. Sucking in a breath, I took a step backward and craned my head out the arch and into the living room.

Listening.

Silence echoed back. But that silence was thick. Weighted. Heavy.

Like a tether was tied around my waist and anchored in my belly.

Drawing me closer.

I edged across the room, my footsteps subdued, my breaths shallow when I inched toward the door.

One solid knock rattled against it.

It rang out like a call.

A beckoning.

A plea.

My hand was trembling when I reached for the lock. Maybe it made me a fool, but I twisted it, anyway. The scrape of metal pierced the bottled quiet. For a flash, I squeezed my eyes closed before I turned the knob and pulled open the door.

He was there.

Standing on my deck.

A scatter of stars stretched across the heavens above, and gusts of wind whipped up the long pieces of his hair, his expression pained where his face was cast in a haze of milky moonlight.

A perfect picture of hope and despair.

It was instant, the way tears streaked free from my eyes.

"Rex."

His hands were balled into fists, jaw clenched, eyes hard.

Dominant and dangerous and somehow chained by all his doubt.

Energy lashed. Whipping and inciting.

Compelling.

And God, I wanted to fight. Fight with him for lying to me. Fight for him because I wanted him so badly. Fight for what was right. The problem was, I wasn't certain of exactly what that was.

Rex's nostrils flared, and we stood there staring at each other. Captives to all those questions that bounded between us. Coming faster and faster and faster.

I saw the second he finally snapped. He pushed across the threshold, on me in a flash, the heat of his strong body lighting me up like a furnace.

My heart fluttered and drummed.

He wound a big hand in my hair, tugging, forcing me to look up at him.

"Little Thief."

The accusation was gravel, and I sucked in a staggered breath. It only drew him deeper, his presence sinking in, penetrating every cell. Emotion swelled just as the pain of my past went rushing through my veins. A raging river that threatened to drown.

The fact of who Janel was. What she'd done.

I gasped over a cry. Unable to keep it in any longer.

"I married her, Rynna, I married her, and I knew all along, I shouldn't. Maybe I was ashamed to admit it to you or maybe I was just afraid of your reaction when you found out I hadn't severed it. But I promise, I promise you I was going to. When I told you I needed to get some things in my life in order, that's what I was referring to. Ending that marriage like I should have years before."

Another cry wrenched free.

He took my face in his big hands, fingers in my hair. "Rynna . . . baby . . . Rynna. Don't cry." He was kissing me through a tumble of frantic words he mumbled at my mouth. "I'm right here. I'm right here. I'm not going anywhere. I told her to go. I told her I was leaving and would be back in an hour and she and her things needed to be gone when I got back. I told her, Rynna. I told her my heart belongs to you, even if you won't take it. But I want you to. I'm gonna fight for you, Rynna. I'm not giving us up. Not ever. You and me . . . we're what's right."

I choked over a cry, and he kissed me deeper. The only thing I wanted to do was succumb.

Get lost in this man.

In his presence and his power and his overwhelming heart.

Another ripping sob tore from my throat. Unstoppable. Wounds fresh and raw. Too much. "It hurts so bad, Rex. I didn't mean for it to. I thought I was over it. Bigger than it. And it's right there. I don't know how to handle what happened. It's just . . . I think about it and it hurts all over again."

Framing my face in his hands, he edged back, confusion a flash across those striking features. "What are you talking about, baby?"

A car engine churned to life from across the street. A reminder of who we were and what we were battling.

I could hear the car crunch on gravel as it backed up, accelerate when it took to the street.

Janel. I knew it was her. It only made me cry harder.

"Janel," I hiccupped over her name.

He looked over his shoulder. "I've been outside pacing your lot for the last hour. I came home tonight, thinking that was the only thing I could do. Condemn myself. Walk away from you and pretend like this thing we've got doesn't matter. I almost gave in because I thought it might be the right thing to do. But it's not, Rynna. It's not, because you and me? We're what's right. I'm not willing to settle or turn my back or act like I'm not dying for you. I walked out on her and right to you. And this whole time, I've been trying to get up the courage. Trying to find the words to convince you that *we're* what's right. Please, Rynna. Please put me out of this misery. I can't lose you. I can't lose you, too."

"Janel." Another whimper, and I knew I wasn't making any sense, because none of this situation did.

"She doesn't matter to me, Rynna. I promise you. Yes, I was waiting for her all those years. Stayed loyal because I had some messed-up notion that one day she was going to come back, and it was on me to keep our family intact. And then there you were, Rynna. My second chance. You changed everything. You became my loyalty. My heart. You and my Frankie. That's all I need."

"Janel hated me, Rex. She hated me so much. And what she did . . . I don't know how to get past it. Forgive her and move on, because I know she's going to be a part of Frankie's life."

He jerked back, holding my face tighter. "What?"

A ramble of incoherent words slid free. "Janel . . . she was the one who hated me so much. I think I pushed you away, clung to your omission, because of her. Not sure how I could handle the fact that the two of you had been together. So I tried . . . tried to hope that she'd changed. For your sake. For Frankie's sake. But I don't—"

"What did you just say?" Rex's words were a growl, menacing and fierce. His demeanor shifted in a flash. From pleading to completely on edge.

"Janel. Janel's the one who's responsible for what happened to me. She set the whole thing up. She had Aaron pretend like he wanted to date me. I didn't know she was your wife, Frankie's mom. I didn't know until I opened that door."

Rex blew back like he'd been struck by a bomb. "Aaron? Aaron who?"

I blinked at him. Aaron didn't matter in the end. "Aaron Reed."

Shock blanketed his face before it turned into panic. He began to pace, back and forth, ripping at handfuls of hair. "Fuck. I knew it. I fucking knew it. I knew it."

I reached for him, his frenzy breaking into mine. "Calm down, Rex. What's wrong?"

"Aaron Reed used to be my business partner." His head shook through his stupor. "He and Janel . . . they acted like they didn't know each other. But he was at the bar with me across town the night I met her. He was the one who'd suggested that bar to meet up at after work. He was the one who noticed her . . ." Rex whipped around, grabbing me by the arms. I wasn't sure who he was steadying—me or himself. "He pushed me toward her. Told me to go for it. That she looked exactly like my type. And Janel . . . she was instantly all over me. Like . . . she'd been expecting me."

He pulled away, back to gripping fistfuls of hair. "They were together the whole time, weren't they?"

Rex punched an aimless fist into the air. "Fuck. They were together the whole goddamned time, and I didn't have the first clue. Or maybe I did."

His gaze dropped to the floor, his head shaking as if he were adding it all up. "When Aaron was arrested for embezzling from the company, there was something off. I got this feeling . . . this feeling that there was something more to the whole thing. That he couldn't have been acting alone. All those documents that had been tampered with. The money that had gone missing."

"Oh God." I pressed my hand over my mouth.

Rex looked at me. Panic streaked through his expression. "She left the day before he went to jail, Rynna. He got his sentence, and I thought things were finally going to be okay, and then I got home to find Janel leaving me."

"Oh God," I said again. "Aaron . . . he was outside the diner this evening. About a week ago, too. He said something about me getting in Janel's way."

Rex stared at me for a beat before his eyes went wide. Then he was bolting out the door and flying across the street.

Rex

sprinted across the street, taking the porch steps in two bounding leaps. I barreled through the front door. I had no clue what I was even searching for, but an overwhelming anxiety pushed me forward.

I'd felt nothing but relief when I'd heard her car taking off ten or fifteen minutes ago. But right then? Nothing made sense. Everything I'd thought I'd known as truth had only been some kind of twisted fabrication. All these years, and I'd fucking thought I'd done something wrong. Neglected Janel. Didn't treat her well enough. Didn't give her enough time. Made her feel less than worthy. Because in truth, in my heart, she'd never been.

Had every second of it been a set up?

My eyes darted around the room, hunting for anything that might be amiss. Dishes littered the kitchen from the dinner Janel had been preparing, the trash bin out in the middle of the floor, pork chops dumped inside. Like she was pissed at me for suddenly sending her away.

That, I understood.

The idea that she might have been an accomplice to the bullshit Aaron had pulled all those years ago I did not.

I couldn't grasp it. Accept it. But the truth of it rang out in my consciousness. A promise she was guilty. That she'd been using me all along.

Anger spiraled, and I clenched my teeth, turning to head down the hall, going directly for my room.

It was just like I'd expected. It was torn apart. Ransacked. The contents of all the drawers were dumped out onto the floor in a mad search for anything of value.

Blankets pulled from the bed, mattress shoved to the side, the small safe hidden under the bed gone.

"Bitch," I seethed.

I should have known.

I should have known better than to let her back into my damn house. Into our lives so she could just turn around and make another mess of it. But honestly, the only thing that mattered right then was the fact she was gone. I'd gladly accept the loss of the bit of cash in that safe if it meant Janel was eradicated from our lives.

A plague eliminated.

Extinguished.

"Rex!" Rynna's scream flooded my ears. I pushed back out of my room and into the hall.

She was at Frankie's door, her hand pressed to her mouth, the girl staring inside.

For a beat, I froze in terror.

Frankie.

I sprang into action. Rynna stumbled out of my way when I rounded the doorway. I jerked to a stop in my daughter's room.

In a fleeting glance, you'd think nothing was out of order, her bed made and her stuffed animals still lined against her pillows.

But the closet—clothes were pulled from the hangers and some of her shoes were gone. Frantic, I rushed for Frankie's dresser. The drawers . . . they were empty.

The worst kind of terror took hold of me.

All the fears I'd ever had of losing my child rose to the surface.

Rising above.

Pulling me under.

I couldn't fucking breathe.

My hands were shaking when I dug into my pocket for my phone. It was already ringing before I had the chance to dial, my mom's name lit on the screen.

I answered it, and every part of me twisted in two.

My mother . . . she was screaming. Screaming and screaming and screaming. "She's gone. I don't know where she is, Rex. She's not here. Frankie's gone."

Rynna

Jenny Gunner's cries poured through the phone. Begging and screaming and weeping.

And Rex? Oh God, Rex made an inhuman noise. Wailed this wail that came from his soul.

Agonized.

Devastated.

Crushed.

It reverberated from the walls and pummeled through my senses.

I wound my arm around my stomach as if it might staunch the pain that split me from the inside.

Frankie Leigh.

I could feel my heart shredding at the same second my spirit moaned.

I should have done something, said something earlier.

My fault. All of this was my fault.

Right from the beginning. I should have stayed that first night when Janel had cut me apart. I should have stood my ground and stood up for myself. Exposed Janel for who she really was.

But I'd let her get away with her sins as if they hadn't been committed at all.

Rex spouted a bunch of incoherent words to his mother before he ended that call, quick to dial 9-1-1. I could hear the moment the operator came on.

Rex had made another switch, pulling himself from the spiral of torment. His shoulders rolled back and determination set on his face. Refusing to allow his worst fears to happen. His voice was gritted—direct and hard—as he quickly relayed the information to the operator. Her name. The make and model of her car. Description of both her and Frankie. The last time both of them had been seen.

Then he ended the call and came striding across the room and into the hall, all power and barely contained intensity. He grabbed me by the outside of my shoulders, his voice a plea. "Stay here, Rynna. In case they come back, stay here. Have your phone ready to call 9-1-1." He gave a gentle shake. "Okay?"

"Of course," I told him, but the words were barely a breath. He pressed his lips to my forehead and then he was gone, the only trace of him the sound of him gunning his truck and it roaring down the street.

Silence swooped in like a cold, steely drape. Clamoring against the walls and trembling across the floors.

Ominous and foreboding.

I wrung my fingers, and my feet took the hall. Back and forth. Back and forth. Desperate to do something. Intuition promised there was no chance Janel would come back here.

My mind rolled. I couldn't quiet it, the way images flashed and blipped, the way voices murmured as if someone were right there, whispering them in my ear.

Jenny Gunner's words when she'd come to Pepper's Pies.

"Don't really know a time she lived in this town when she didn't work for your grandma. From what I know, she started out when she was in high school."

My mind flashed to Aaron on the street, the way he'd been peeking in the window.

"Always in Janel's way, aren't you?"

All of it spun and spun. Winding to a sum.

That thread of awareness finally took hold.

It'd hadn't been by chance that Aaron was outside the diner, peering in. It wasn't out of curiosity or the interest of an old restaurant reopening.

He'd been spying. Wondering exactly what was going on inside.

A slow chill trickled down my spine.

Freezing ice.

Cold.

It seeped into every cell. I could barely breathe. Lungs heaving around it, breaking its bindings, I fumbled for my phone. I was already racing out the door and across the street when I put it to my ear.

Rex's phone went straight to voice mail.

"Shit," I mumbled, trying to balance the phone between my ear and shoulder so I could unlock the door. I was jumping into the driver's seat when the message beeped. "Please don't be angry, but I'm going to the diner." The words were a ramble.

I threw my SUV in reverse and backed out, quick to shift into drive. "It's probably just a hunch, and God, the last thing I want to do is distract you, but

I can't ignore this. I need to make sure Janel isn't there. I just . . . have this feeling, and I have to act on it. I'll let you know if anything seems off."

I ended the call, tossed my phone to the passenger seat, and flew. Flew through the neighborhood and onto the main street. Streetlamps blurred past, streaked in my eyes and sent my heart into overdrive. I took the three turns required to get me into the middle of town faster than I should, until I finally made the last left onto Fairview.

The entire street was shut down for the night except for the single bar on the end, and only a few exterior lights shined from the awnings of the rest of the businesses that had been closed for hours.

I slowed when I reached Pepper's and swung into a parking spot. My headlights sprayed across the long pane of darkened windows. Glinting, blinding light reflected back.

I killed the engine, cracked the door, and stepped out. The construction site directly across from the restaurant was dark.

Vacant.

The only movement on the whole street was a foreboding breeze that blew through.

I was scared.

Terrified, really. I'd walked in this diner a million times, and never before had it evoked this type of reaction in me. But I couldn't ignore what was screaming out from inside.

I grabbed my phone, 9-1-1 already programmed to dial, my footsteps slow and cautious as I edged around the front of my SUV and along the sidewalk that ran in front of the restaurant. Holding my breath, I slid the key into the lock and quietly nudged open the door.

Silence rained down.

Ominous and thick.

Too thick.

So thick, dread flashed across my flesh. It sent a tumble of goose bumps across my arms and tingling in my hands, awareness a prickle of needles across my neck.

I inched inside, each footstep measured as I tried to keep completely silent. I eased through the dining room, my breaths shallow and panted as I wound around the long counter and pushed open the shiny metal swinging door.

I inched forward, vigilant as I stepped into the kitchen.

A footstep crunched. A reverberation through the dense, dim air.

A footstep that wasn't mine.

Every cell in my body seized in fear. Slowly, I attempted to slide my finger across my phone.

A swish of blonde hair flashed at the corner of my eye. Fear sped and my finger fumbled. I sucked in a breath when I heard the *whoosh,* felt the shift in the air, before something metal cracked against the back of my head.

Pain. So much pain. I tried to hold on to consciousness. I needed to fight. Fight for Frankie. But I could feel darkness pressing in, taking over, and everything went black.

forty

Corinne Dayne – Three Years Ago

Anger burned through my old, brittle bones. Apprehension sank into the pit of my stomach, my veins drumming with sluggish, burdened blood, a shrinking fear that vibrated out to take hold of my already shaky, weathered hands.

I should have realized it a long time ago. There'd always been something off about that girl. But I'd been the fool that'd ignored it, thinking people were different and I didn't have any right to make judgments about them.

But this?

I did.

When her car pulled in across the street, I moved out the door and onto my porch. For the first time in a long time, I wished I were younger. Stronger. That I didn't do it with a limp and my body didn't protest every step.

She pulled that sweet baby girl from the backseat and kissed the side of her head as if she weren't wretched all the way through.

The sky had darkened to a dusky blue, the horizon holding the last vestiges of oranges and pinks as the day fully melted away. Ambling across the street, I held the evidence tight against my chest, voice shaking, no longer able to hold back the accusation. "What did you do?"

Janel's head whipped my way. She huffed out a breath. "Corinne, I don't have time for your nonsense ramblings today. It's been real rough around here, with all that's been going on at Rex's company. Need to make him supper. He'll be home shortly." She turned her back on me, Frankie Leigh hooked to her hip, and started for their porch steps.

"That's awfully convenient, isn't it, fact that Aaron boy you were always so chummy with growing up is getting sent off to prison for doing your husband wrong? Stealing all that money. What a shame. And here you are, playing the innocent card. Guess that's the way it's always been, hasn't it? Playing us for fools while you ran around manipulating everything to get your way?"

Regret slithered through my spirit. Should have known it back then, in the days when my Rynna had run away. Oh, how my girl had pined after that Aaron boy, eyes always dreamy anytime he wandered in for a piece of pie, her whole world made when she'd finally caught his eye.

Wasn't until I was watching this video that I realized those two were to blame for her running.

Janel and Aaron.

Same as they both were to blame for what was happening to Rex.

This time I wasn't about to turn a blind eye.

Janel froze at the door that she was pulling open. Slowly, she edged around to face me, her voice going dim. "What did you just say? Because it sounded to me like you were accusing me of something you shouldn't be."

The videotape felt heavy in my hands. An overbearing weight. "You know . . . all these years the register has been coming up short. So many times that I thought I was goin' crazy or maybe I just couldn't count. But I figured I needed proof that it was time to shut the place down and retire if I couldn't handle running the day-to-day. Imagine my surprise when I sat watching the video from last night."

Janel blanched. White as a ghost.

She knew as well as I did what was on this video. Had considered telling her about the new cameras going in, but thought better of it, figuring I was either going senile or somebody was stealing right from under my nose.

Just had no idea of the enormity of the stealing that'd been going on.

The blip of video had been caught in the middle of the night in the back office, Janel and Aaron arguing about the fact Aaron was going away for embezzling from RG Construction.

"You're the idiot who went and got yourself caught," Janel seethed.

"And you're the one who put me up to it. You're the one who has the money, and I'm the one who's gonna land in jail? I don't think so, Janel. This was all your idea, and you're gonna tell him. You've been controlling things for years. It's about time it stopped."

"The hell I am. Rex doesn't know shit, and it's going to stay that way. You do what you're supposed to do. Follow through, like a man, because from where I'm standing, you don't look like anything but a pussy."

She edged closer to him, slid a hand up his chest. "Besides, it won't do either of us any good if we're both behind bars. We still have all that money they never accounted for. I'll hide it, and when you're out, we'll pick back up right where we left off. Now that you're out of the office, Rex is gonna need someone to take over. Who better than his loving wife?"

Then they'd been kissing—along with other unsavory things that'd made my skin crawl. I'd been flooded with sympathy for that poor man who'd not done anything but work himself to the bone to take care of his family, Rex having no clue he was being betrayed.

Janel set Frankie on her feet. The cute thing toddled forward, barely keeping balance as she blabbered around the two fingers she had stuffed in her mouth. Janel rolled back her shoulders. "Messing with me would be a mistake, old lady."

Probably so, but I couldn't regret it. Not when that little girl squealed, innocent joy. Not when I knew the woman standing over her was nothing but poison. The only thing Janel was good for was destruction, and I wasn't gonna stand aside and watch her ruin anyone else.

"Seems I'm holding all the cards this time, now, doesn't it?"

In a flash, Janel came blazing down the steps and rushing my direction. I rasped out in surprise when her fingernails dug into the skin of my wrist. "Give it to me."

Even though she was hurting me, mocking laughter rolled from my tongue. Anger for my Rynna. Anger for Rex. Anger for any other person she'd done wrong, because I was betting these two weren't her only victims. "Take it. Plenty more where that came from. All set up and ready to go straight to the police."

She stumbled back a step. "I think you're bluffing, Corinne Dayne, because if you had anything on me, you would have already run and snitched to the cops, just like your prissy granddaughter did when she went tattling to my mom. Two of you are just alike. What is it you think you want from me?"

But that was where she was wrong. I wasn't bluffing. I just wasn't taking the chance that the cops would disregard the video or deem it inconclusive. Wasn't taking the chance this schemer might go and convince that trusting man that I'd construed it all wrong. Take her back or give her another chance.

I just wanted her gone.

"What I want is for you to go. Go pack your things before Rex gets home and get out of town. Don't ever come back."

Her blue eyes flamed with hate. Ice cold. "Are you insane? I'm not doing a thing you say."

"Then I'll gladly forward this along. And if something happens to me, who knows where one of these videos is going to pop up."

Steam might as well have been rolling from her ears, her jaw sharp and clenched, hate pouring out. "You bitch, just like your snot of a granddaughter."

"Maybe, but it sure beats being a thief and liar and a cheat. I'm thinking your husband might agree."

She paled, as if she were only just then realizing I was serious. The words were choppy when she released them from her vile mouth.

"You're asking me to leave?"

"Oh, I'm not askin' anything. I'm tellin' you."

"So what . . . I get out of town, don't come back, and that video isn't ever gonna appear? You're saying those are your terms? You aren't angling for anything more?"

Leave it to the thief to think I was aiming to steal from her.

"That's it. Just go."

She laughed a sour, hostile laugh, before she squared up, lifted her chin as if it didn't hurt her none. "Fine."

She spun around and flew back up the steps, door banging as she rushed inside. Rex's dog, Missy, yelped when she slid out the door, door catching her tail before she went to stand guard at Frankie's side. Frankie giggled and pushed her fingers through the dog's hair. I took a couple steps into the driveway, figuring I best be guarding, too.

Ten minutes later, Janel came barreling back out, wrangling a big suitcase in both hands. She fumbled down the steps and heaved them into her trunk before she went running back up the stairs.

She scooped Frankie Leigh off her feet and raced back with her to the car. Missy scrambled down at their sides, whining, sensing that something was wrong.

Panic just about squeezed my heart into a million pieces, and I rushed that direction just as Janel was shoving Frankie into the backseat. She slammed the door shut and rushed to get into the driver's seat before I could get there. Gunning it in reverse, she started to peel out of the drive.

I barely caught onto the back handle and jerked open the door. Hating the idea of putting Frankie in danger, but I couldn't allow her to drive off with her.

The car screeched to a stop as I was hauling Frankie into my arms. Janel's door flew open, fury on her face when she jumped out. "You might want me gone, but I'm not leaving without my daughter."

She tore at my arms, skin breaking under the claw of her nails. Frankie started crying. Crying and crying. A jumble of confusion and fear. A baby who deserved none of this.

I fought her, backing down the driveway and holding Frankie protectively against my chest. "You're not taking her, Janel. You are the devil and I'm not gonna allow you to taint this child. Leave her or I'll gladly die showing Rex exactly who you are."

Missy jumped around us. Yipping and barking. Not sure who she was supposed to be fighting and who she was supposed to be protecting. Janel continued to try to rip Frankie from my arms, two of us scuffling closer to the road.

And I tried to hold on. Not to let Frankie go. But Janel was stronger than I was. She finally tore her free, a sneer of victory on her face. That was right when we heard the loud rumble of the ever-distinguishable truck, the powerful engine rumbling as it turned onto the far neighborhood street.

For a second, Janel froze. I took the opportunity to lunge for her, grasping for Frankie, arm locking around her waist. I dislodged her from Janel's hold just before Janel shoved me just as hard as she could. Both Frankie and I tumbled to the ground.

A wail of a cry rose from Frankie, and she climbed to her feet, wobbling at the back of the car. I skidded across the gravel, coming to a stop just to the side.

That engine roared in the distance. Coming closer and closer.

Panicked, Janel jumped back into the front seat and threw her car in reverse. Caring about nothing but setting herself free.

I screamed, "No!"

Tires screeched and dust billowed. It was so loud, the engine and my screams and Frankie's cries, and I couldn't make sense of the picture, nothing except her car hitting the street, shifting into drive, and then tearing down the road in the opposite direction of Rex's truck.

No. Frankie Leigh, oh God, no.

It was a prayer from my soul. A cry from my lips.

A strangled sound of relief left my throat when my eyes landed on Frankie. She was crying, sprawled face-down on the dirt where she'd been thrown.

My eyes drifted back, and horror took to my throat.

Missy was dead in her place.

A heap at the side of the road.

Missy had saved her. Pushed her out of the way.

Rex's truck jerked to a stop in the middle of the road, and he stumbled out, the glare of headlights cutting into the descending night. A cry wrenched from his mouth. "Missy. Oh . . . no . . . oh God . . . what . . .Frankie!" Second he saw his daughter, he went rushing her way. Stunned, he looked over his shoulder to the taillights disappearing in the distance, his expression shattered when he turned back to the scene.

But that was the thing. This loyal man had no clue just how much worse it could have been.

Rynna

$\mathcal{P}$ain throbbed at the back of my head. Blinding. Excruciating. I fought it, swallowed the nausea and forced myself to climb to my knees. My hands fumbled around, searching the floor for my phone.

Gone.

It was gone.

Mumbled voices echoed from the depths of the kitchen. They were coming from the old break room and office.

Fighting the terror lining my veins, I pushed myself to standing and squinted through the darkness. I pressed my back against the commercial ovens just inside the kitchen. I fought to stay as small and quiet as possible.

Slowly, I edged toward the voices.

Sinks lined the far back wall. A huge dry storage pantry was to the right of them and the old office was down a short hall to the left.

Keeping myself plastered against the metal, I shifted so I could peek into the murky depths.

A flashlight and the flickering flame of a candle cast the small room in leaping shadows. Two people were inside, their silhouettes striking against the wall as they moved.

Where was Frankie?

A cold sweat broke out across my nape, and I squeezed my eyes again, gathering courage, calculating whether I could make it to the phone that rested on the old desk that sat right inside the office.

I eased down the short hall, those voices coming clearer with each step I took. Panicked whispers, frantic as they searched.

"Where is it?"

"The question is, where the fuck did you hide it?"

"It has to be here . . . I . . . it's been a lot of years. I'm not leaving without that money. That money and my daughter and that goddamned tape."

"You think they aren't already going to be looking for you since you took that kid? That was so stupid, Janel. I warned you that was the dumbest thing you could do. Going back to his house. What were you thinking?"

"I'm not leaving my baby behind. Not again. It wasn't supposed to turn out like this."

"Yeah, and what'd you expect? Me just to sit on the sidelines while you cozied up with that arrogant asshole again? Taking what's mine? You're insane if you thought I was going to let you stay there."

"Just shut up and help me find it. None of that matters anymore."

I kept edging closer, footsteps subdued, my heart threatening to pound right out of my chest.

"Yes! Here it is . . . it's here!" Janel suddenly shrieked, coming into view when she jumped to her feet with a box in her hands. A box she had to have found beneath the floorboards.

I knew I didn't have any more time. I rushed for the phone that was four steps away. I grabbed the receiver, fumbling to hit those three simple numbers.

I made it. I made it. One second before the receiver was yanked out of my hand. I started to spin around, caught off guard when I was shoved in the side.

Hard.

My feet flew out from under me.

I slammed against the wall. But this time, I was ready. Ready for this fight. A fight that'd been coming for years. For what felt like forever. I was fighting for Rex. For Frankie. I was fighting for me. "You coward, taking a little girl."

I charged her. Rammed my shoulder into her chest as hard as I could.

Pain splintered through my head, but it was worth it. It was worth it because Janel stumbled back, arms flailing and hair whipping around her. The box she'd had in her hands went sailing through the air and crashed to the floor.

I dove for it. A hand fisted in my hair, yanking it back. "You stupid bitch, always in my way. Not this time. Not this time."

I threw an elbow back and caught her in the ribs.

She heaved out a cry.

I spun around and rushed her just as she was rushing me.

Our bodies collided.

A clash of souls.

I hooked her around the neck, trying to pin her, hold her.

She jerked free, so frenzied that she reeled, her footing gone. She stumbled back until she hit the desk.

I dove on her, and we slid across the slick wood, knocking everything that had been on the top to the floor.

Papers and the phone and the candle.

And we fought. Arms and fists and ripping hair. Fought until a big body was yanking me off. I screeched and kicked and fought. Fought in fury. In hate. In the desperate need to get to Frankie.

Frankie.

Frankie Leigh.

Aaron's cologne filled my nose, the memory of it making me gag. I struggled to break out of his hold, but he was too strong. He tossed me aside. As if I was nothing.

Trash.

Just the same as he'd treated me before.

Aaron grabbed the box from the floor and then snagged Janel by the wrist. "We have to get out of here. Right now."

My attention caught on the floor across the room. A tiny flame leapt to life. The candle a match to a piece of paper that'd floated to the floor.

Part of me wanted to go for it. Stamp it out. Protect my gramma's legacy. But none of that mattered if they got away with Frankie. I couldn't—wouldn't allow it to happen.

Hand-in-hand, Janel and Aaron ran down the short hall and escaped out the back door. The door they'd most likely broke in through.

Frankie was my only concern. Not a building or its memories or the hopes of what it may be one day.

Only that little girl.

Crying out in pain, I struggled to get to my feet, chasing right after them. By the time I made it out the door, they were sprinting toward a black Durango parked in the back lot. In my periphery, I could see the spark of fire.

And I knew my grandma's restaurant was getting ready to go up in flames.

I didn't slow, only pushed myself harder, desperate to get to Frankie.

Aaron tried to force Janel around to the front passenger seat, but she diverted and wrenched open the back passenger door. "Frankie . . . Frankie?"

Janel started to panic, shouting it again. "Frankie!"

Struggling to jerk out of his hold, she whirled on Aaron. "Where's Frankie?"

I stumbled to a stop halfway across the vacant lot, heart crashing against my ribs.

"Warned you, Janel, but you wouldn't listen. We're not taking that fucking kid. We're getting out of Gingham Lakes and out of this country, and I won't have anything slowing us down. Now, let's go."

"Where is she?" she screamed.

Even though he seemed to avoid it, Aaron's attention darted back to the diner, expression twisting in the briefest flash of guilt.

Guilt aimed at my gramma's diner that was going up in flames.

No.

Oh my God.

Slowly he shook his head. "Didn't expect the fire. That's not on me. Now get in or I'm leaving you behind."

Janel's expression froze in horror. And I thought maybe it was the first time I saw any true humanity in her. Any true care. Just as fast, it was gone, and Janel started around to the front of the SUV.

She was just going to leave her.

I spun around in my own horror. Flames licked out from the back window and glowed through the gaping door.

For a flash, my eyes squeezed closed, my gramma's voice a whisper in my ear. Her presence overwhelming, so much I could feel her belief penetrating to the depths of me.

All moments matter. We just rarely know how important they are until the chance to act on them has already passed.

I'd always known Rex and Frankie were worth the chance. This one might cost me it all. Everything. But they would always, always be worth it.

My feet pounded against the pavement. Adrenaline and fear were a thunder that stampeded through my veins and whooshed in my ears.

I held up my arm as if it might protect me when I barreled through the doorway and into the kitchen.

Smoke swallowed me.

Taking me whole.

Black.

Thick.

Suffocating.

Holding my breath, I tried to get as low as possible as I began to search.

When I couldn't do anything else, I tugged my shirt over my nose and gave in.

Inhaled.

It burned.

Burned so badly that my lungs wept, just the same as my insides.

Heat licked across my skin, so hot I wanted to scream.

Scream for help.

For sanity.

For Frankie.

Most of all, for Frankie.

I groped along the walls. Trying to find my way. To make sense of where I was.

Disoriented, I fumbled, trying to focus.

A wall.

An oven.

The pantry.

Oh God, the pantry.

The door was closed.

When I'd left this evening, it'd been wide open. I was sure of it. I'd been moving things in and out and had propped it open.

I slid my hands over it, feeling, searching. Relief wrenched from me when I found the latch. I managed to drag it open.

Smoke billowed inside. It was at the same second I heard Frankie's cry.

"Frankie!" It was a shout.

Joy.

Solace.

Fear.

Each emotion rushed me. One after another.

Because I couldn't breathe and I couldn't see and everything hurt so bad.

The radiating heat and the asphyxiating smoke.

But there was no chance I was giving up.

Flames bloomed just outside the pantry door, consuming the kitchen, eating away the plaster and wood and memories.

I dropped to my knees and crawled across the floor. My hand came into contact with something that moved. A foot. A leg. A tiny body that I pulled into my arms, holding her against my chest, burying her face in my shirt.

Because I'd do anything to protect her. To save her.

Dizziness swept through my being. Head. Body. Soul. I fought to stay coherent. To stay awake. To fight.

I clutched Frankie to me, rocked back, and screamed.

Rex

I rushed through the doors of the police station. I'd been on the phone with my mom the whole way over, trying to get as much information from her as I could and settle her down at the same time. Which was a ridiculous notion in and of itself, considering how close I was to coming unglued. Torn limb from limb. Janel's fist punched right into the center of my chest, the bitch ripping out my still beating, bleeding heart, holding it hostage in her corrupt, vicious hand.

Never in a million years would I have imagined she'd stoop this low. Of course, I'd had no clue how deep her betrayal went, either.

Treason.

Treachery.

It was nothing less.

Lieutenant Seth Long was already coming out of his office when I skidded to a stop in front of it. We'd gone to school together, had been friends for as long as I could remember, the guy devoting his life to the greater good.

"Rex," he wheezed, amped up, whole station already on red alert. "APB has been issued, and I have every available cruiser already on the streets. We're going to get her back. I promise you, Rex, if it's the last thing I do, I'm going to get your daughter back."

I nodded, though it was choppy, jerky with hatred and fear. The two together were a dangerous combination. They itched my fingers in direction's they shouldn't go. Thoughts of vengeance and retribution skating my skin, a twine that bound my body.

"I just . . . I've got to do something."

He set a hand on my shoulder, head dipping down, eyes meeting mine.

Like he was trying to get through to me. To get me to see reason when all I was seeing was red. "I know you do. But I need you to make an official statement first then you can ride with me, okay? I don't want you running off doing something stupid."

Another spastic nod, filled with reluctance, but what the hell else was I going to do? "Okay," I agreed.

"Come on, let's get this moving so we can get out of here."

I started to follow him into his office, when my phone chirped with a message. I pulled it from my pocket, squinting when I realized it'd come in close to fifteen minutes ago, during the time I'd been talking to my mom.

Rynna.

Apprehension pressed against my ribs, and I quickly thumbed into the message, pushing the phone to my ear. Rynna was on the other end, sounding panicked and worried and a little shamed, telling me she was sorry but she was going to Pepper's.

That was at the same second a radio bleeped in the station, a code issued and an address given, an officer asking for backup.

It was to an address I knew all too well.

My gaze locked with Seth's. Time froze while awareness shot between us. Then I was running. Running back out into the night and into my truck. Seth was right on my heels, sliding into the front seat of his cruiser. I floored it, didn't care that I was breaking about fifteen different laws as I sped toward the diner.

Toward Rynna.

Toward Frankie.

Toward my entire life.

The center of my world.

Felt like it took me forever to get there when not more than five minutes could have passed. I skidded around the last corner, taking a sharp left turn, roaring down the road.

All the breath left me when the building came into view.

Pepper's ravaged by fire and smoke.

No.

No. No. No.

I didn't slow. Instead, I accelerated, truck careening, everything lurching and jostling when the tires hit the curb and jumped the sidewalk. Second before I hit the brick wall, I rammed on the breaks and jumped out without bothering to put it in park.

Anguish pulsed through my veins. Spurring me faster and harder.

I went right for the front door and flung it open.

Desperation makes you do desperate things.

And there was no hesitation. No thought except for getting to them. I knew they were in there. Knew it with *every part of me.*

A thick plume of smoke gushed out when I rushed in.

It felt just like I was stepping into a furnace.

Seth was there, screaming at me to stay. Not to move.

But there was no chance of him stopping me.

Lifting my shirt to cover my mouth and nose, I edged in, following the smoke that was coming from somewhere in the kitchen like a target.

I made it to the swinging door. My eyes burned when I pushed it open, every inch of me swallowed by the heat.

An inferno.

I refused to let it become our hell.

"Rynna!" I shouted. Beside me, an avalanche of metal clattered to the floor, and I jumped back, dodging it two seconds before I became a pile of rubble right along with it.

God. It was so fucking hot. So hot, I swore I could feel my skin melting from my bones. But I pushed forward, adrenalin thrumming through me like a bullet. I screamed again, "Rynna!"

It was faint, barely discernable. But I heard something rise above the thunder. A foreign sound just to my right. Or maybe it was just some kind of sixth sense. An acute kind of awareness. A need inside that became my greatest strength.

Blindly, I fumbled that way, dropping to my knees, teeth gritted against the flames.

My hands, they searched, running over everything like the diner was written in Braille. Each bump and dip telling me to hurry. That every second that passed brought me closer to running out of time.

Then my hand, it ran over something solid but soft. Something sweet.

And I was struck with so much goddamned relief, because it was my girls huddled at the foot of the back door. Rynna was slamming a pot against the floor, guiding me.

I tried to push the heavy metal door open, but it was wedged shut, surely why Rynna hadn't been able to get out.

I felt like my lungs were exploding, but I gathered all of me. All my love. Every devotion. Every hope.

I reared back and kicked it.

When it didn't give, I kicked it again.

It burst open.

I wanted to shout in victory. In hope. I rushed, grasping Rynna from behind, my little girl still in the safety of her arms. I dragged them out onto the pavement of the back lot, as far as I could get them away from the fire, before I collapsed to my knees beside them.

I choked and coughed while around me voices shouted and sirens blared.

Someone was on a radio, calling for help in the back lot, three victims down.

But the only thing I could focus on was their ash-covered faces. Frankie clutched in Rynna's arms. I didn't want to touch them, worried I'd cause more damage, but I was certain my baby girl wasn't breathing.

My already failing heart stalled.

Oh God, please, no.

Rynna dragged in violent, choked breaths, eyes wide, no coherency in their depths.

"Help!" I screamed. "Somebody help."

Footsteps pounded around me, rushing in. Someone pulled me away. I fought to get back to them, but hands were on me, restraining. "Let them take care of them, man. You've got to let them take care of them." Seth's voice was grit in my ear.

I slumped forward, dropping back to my knees.

Fireman and paramedics swarmed. Working. A controlled, frantic storm.

My world spun, and one was in front of me, taking my pulse and asking me questions, if I was in pain or if I was having trouble breathing.

He just had no idea all my breaths were wrapped up in them. That I'd gladly give mine. Every breath. Every heartbeat. Everything. Just as long as they were okay.

I sat hunched over in the hard plastic chair, elbows on my knees, exhaustion in my bones. People hustled on the other side of the door that'd been wedged open a crack. But inside this room? Time had stopped. Nothing less than a mind-altering waiting game.

Dimness floated on the feigned peace, and that steady beeping of the monitor lulled me into a sense of security I was praying wasn't faulty.

"You should go get some rest, man."

I jumped when the muted voice hit me from behind. I scrubbed a hand over my face, trying to clear the daze, and shifted to look over my shoulder.

Kale stood there in his scrubs. Dude looked just about as weary as I felt. Since the second we'd rushed through the emergency room doors, he'd been running nonstop, making sure every test possible had been run on my daughter. Ensuring nothing was missed.

He'd been up all night and all of today.

"Think it's probably you who should be taking a break," I told him.

He let a smirk ridge his mouth. "Nah, I'm basically a super hero. Can't keep me down. "

Cocky asshole.

A light chuckle rumbled from my tongue. "That so?"

"Come on, look at me, you know it is." He was all affable grins.

I turned my attention back to my daughter. Frankie was lost to sleep, tiny body tucked beneath stark white sheets.

Resting.

Whole and right.

According to Kale, things could go south up to two days after prolonged smoke exposure.

Which left me an unwilling player in this waiting game.

But Kale kept insisting I shouldn't worry. That she was going to be fine. That he'd make sure of it.

She'd been dosed with precautionary antibiotics and breathing treatments, and Kale promised not a single base had been missed.

I'd always known it, but it wasn't so clear what a damned good doctor Kale was until then.

"Thank you, man," I muttered quietly. "No way I could ever repay you for what you've done."

He made a sound of rebuttal. "I was just doing my job, Rex. You know she wouldn't be here if it wasn't for you and Rynna."

Rynna.

Beautiful Rynna. This girl who'd become my orbit. My sun. My gravity.

Rynna had saved my daughter's life. She'd put herself on the line. She fought for her. For us. She loved her in a way that was absolute.

"Almost at the cost of her own."

Everything pressed and pulled.

This gratefulness that had taken up residence in every part of me, up against this blistering agony at the thought of almost losing her, too.

"I won't pretend to know Rynna all that well," he said. "But from what I do? I'd bet she doesn't regret rushing into that fire any more than you do. Which is why I'm here. You can see her now."

My body swayed with the harsh heave of my breath. "Can you sit with Frankie for a while?"

"It'd be my honor."

He shuffled in, his own exhaustion making itself known. I stood and then hesitated before I reached for him. I gripped him tight, hugged him hard, hand fisted in the middle of his back. "Couldn't do any of this without you. Thank you, man, thank you so much."

He hugged me back, saying nothing, both of us giving a moment of silence. A moment for grief. For what might have been.

Then he stepped back. "Go. Frankie's in good hands."

I started for the door when Frankie shifted and released a tiny moan. Instantly, I changed directions, going straight for my daughter, who hadn't been awake for more than a total of an hour the entire day. Kale clapped me on the shoulder. "I'll be right outside the door. Let me know when you're ready for me."

"Thanks."

I slowly sank back into the chair, every inch of me glowing when I brushed my fingers through my daughter's hair, staring down at my world.

"Hi, Daddy," she said, so close to managing her precious grin.

I ran my thumb over her squished-up brow, my voice so low. "Hey, Sweet Pea. How are you feeling?"

"My's froat hurts."

Anger pulsed, but I tucked it down.

"I know, baby. Uncle Kale is working on fixing you up so you're good as new. Better than new. You just need to get lots of rest, okay?"

She barely nodded, her brown eyes wide in the muted light. I hated that I saw fear in them. That she'd been subjected to evil and greed. I kept brushing my thumb over her brow, letting her know I was there, that I wasn't going anywhere.

Finally, she broke the silence, her words the barest whisper. "Daddy, I gots a secret."

My heart fisted, threatened to fail, terrified of what she might say. Of what she might have experienced during the short time Janel had her.

Couldn't stomach it, and honestly, I was a little worried about what I might do. What I already wanted to do. But I held all that back, because my daughter was the most important thing, not the rage boiling inside me. "What, baby? You can tell Daddy anything."

She hesitated, like what she was going to say might get her into trouble. "I wants Rynna to be my mommy. Nots Janel."

I choked over a quieted laugh, blinking at my sweet girl and wondering how I'd managed to get so lucky.

Edging forward, I pressed a kiss to her temple before I pulled back to meet those wide, trusting eyes. "How about we don't keep it a secret? I say we tell the whole world."

I'd been terrified of falling in love. Of losing someone else. Knowing there was no place inside me left to lose. Those vacancies went too deep.

But Rynna.

She filled them. Saved my world and gave me back my heart.

Rynna.

Fucking Rynna.

Little Thief.

forty-three

Rynna

The door creaked open. I rolled my head that direction and tried to keep the tears out of my eyes when I found who was standing there. But I couldn't. They escaped, hot rivers streaking down my face.

"Hey . . . you're awake." His voice was a murmur, cautious and low. Still, the magnitude of him hit me like a flashflood. Overpowering. Overwhelming.

"Frankie?" Her name felt like fire where it grated from my raw, blistered throat.

Fear and anxiety and hope.

The second I'd awoken, I'd begged the nurse for an update, for her to tell me that she was okay, for any news.

Because the last thing I remembered was Rex standing over the two of us while I'd held on to Frankie.

Instead of an answer, she'd promised me she would let them know I was awake so someone could come talk to me.

For a beat, he stared at me, his lip trembling while that powerful gaze bore into me. Then he smiled. This slow, amazed, adoring smile. "Because of you, Rynna. Because of you, Frankie's going to be just fine."

More tears fell. But these were pure, unbridled relief. I released them as if I were pouring them into the heavens. Gratitude for the prayers I'd been granted.

Rex angled the rest of the way into the room, footsteps eating up the floor, the bed shifting when he gingerly eased down at my side. He brushed back the matted hair stuck to my forehead, voice cracking when he repeated, "She's okay . . . because of you."

All the turmoil I'd held back suddenly came spilling out.

"I should have told you from the beginning. If I had, this never would have happened. I'm so sorry."

Rex gave a harsh shake of his head, big hand cupping my cheek. "Don't you dare apologize, Rynna. I could accuse myself since I should have known the whole time Janel was no good. That only a fool wouldn't have known she'd been stealing from me from day one. Our relationship, *our daughter*, nothing but a ploy for her to get close to me. To gain access to my accounts so she and Aaron could embed themselves deeper into my life."

His hold tightened on my face. "But all the blame? It's on them. What they did to both of us is on them. They're the ones who are guilty, and they're going to be paying for it for the rest of their lives."

"Did they catch them?" My voice quivered.

He gave a slight nod. "Twenty miles out of town. Cargo area loaded down with cash that most definitely didn't belong to them. Apparently, there was a tape, too, one that implicated Janel in the original embezzlement charges that Aaron went down for."

Tone laced with the significance, Rex continued carefully, "The video was from right before Janel left and was recorded at Pepper's, Rynna . . . in the back office. Both she and Aaron were there."

His statement hovered in the room. Permeating. Seeping into my consciousness.

Realization settled slow. "My gramma knew," I finally said.

He nodded. "Yeah, I think she did. Now that I got a few more details, everything makes sense. The fact your grandma was right there the day Janel was driving away, shaken up, supporting me with the blow of both Janel leaving and finding Missy on the street. I think your grandma might have scared her away, probably why Janel came back after she heard she passed."

Sorrow bloomed, weaving through that hollow space, the loss of my gramma a wound I was sure would never go away. But in it was something sweet and tender and gentle. Knowing. Just like my gramma had always been.

Rex's jaw ticked. "I just . . . I'm not even sure I want to know what happened that day. Leading up to that moment. And even though it destroyed me at the time, the only thing I'm doing right now is thanking your grandma for everything she did. For protecting my daughter. I might not know exactly what happened, but after Janel tried to take Frankie tonight? Pretty sure I would have lost my daughter a long time ago if it wasn't for your grandma."

Adoration pulled at the corner of his mouth. "All the Dayne women, saving my little girl. Both coming into our lives exactly when we needed you."

And that spot inside? It glowed. Warmth and light.

A soft smile fluttered at my mouth, and I shifted, ignoring the pain that burned hot on my left arm. "Maybe my gramma knew it all along, Rex. Maybe she knew it was supposed to be us. Maybe that's why she was so insistent I come back here. She had a way of seeing things long before they happened."

He smoothed his hand over the side of my head. Comforting. Soothing. I wanted to fall into his touch. Forever disappear. "You think she knew you were meant for me?"

My smile was timid, and I gave a slight nod. "Gramma always said we'd just know. That it'd be magic when it happened. Maybe she felt that magic long before either of us could."

"It is magic, Rynna. Frankie's here. You're here. We're together. And that's all that matters."

As soon as he said it, he winced, and a hard gush of air left his lungs. "I'm so sorry, Rynna. About the restaurant. So goddamned sorry."

Reaching up, I wrapped a hand around his wrist, brought his palm to my mouth and kissed him there before I tugged it flat against my beating heart. "I would have given up anything to save her, Rex. Anything. The restaurant. My heart. My life."

I clutched him a little tighter. "And I thought I was going to. I thought both of our lives were slipping away. And then you were there. Saving me. Saving Frankie."

His expression tightened, almost grim in its emphasis. "Maybe that's what being a family is all about. I've always been terrified of losing Frankie. Knowing I would never survive that kind of loss. When it became a possibility—losing either of you—I would have sacrificed everything. Anything. Sold my soul. Lost my life. And you . . . you, Little Thief . . ."

Thumb brushing across my cheek, his head angled to the side. Those sage eyes speared me, finding their way to my soul.

"You saved my daughter, Rynna." He blinked at me, as if he were struggling for the right thing to say. "I knew the moment I met you that you were different. I fought it and fought it while you just continued to fight for me. To fight for us. But every time our paths crossed, I knew my life changed a little more. Truth is, I was terrified to take the chance. But like you said, it's all about taking the *right* ones."

He edged in, so close that our noses brushed and his breaths became mine. "You and Frankie? You were the best chances I ever took. And I was terrified both times. But if something doesn't scare you? Maybe it's not important enough. You are my life. You and Frankie are what it means to be a family. Do you understand what I'm telling you?"

My heart went wild, flailing against its boundaries.

He dipped in and pressed his lips to mine. So sweet. Before he pulled back, pinning me with that mesmerizing stare. "I love you, Rynna Dayne. I love you so much, and I'm not ever going to let you go."

Love. Love. Love.

It surged and spread and flowed. Filling every crevice. Every void. And my heart. I think maybe it did manage to split in two. Held in the hands of two people. Two people who'd become my center. My focus. Etching themselves into my being.

Mounting Rex Gunner's walls had seemed impossible. Those towering obstacles insurmountable.

Impenetrable and impossible.

But my gramma had always told me that life was just one long string of possibilities.

That chances were worth taking.

And this man and his baby girl? They were worth every single one.

the epilogues

Epilogue One – Rex Gunner

"Are your eyes closed?" I asked, unable to keep from peeking over at her. At the incredible woman who rode in the front seat of my truck.

Just looking at her had every inch of me tightening.

In need.

In want.

In this mad kind of love.

She was beautiful.

So damned beautiful she was hard to look at. Rynna was the kind of beauty that shined and blinded and radiated. Inside and out. Flush with goodness and grace. That body still my greatest temptation.

Though, I had zero qualms about giving in.

"Yes. And you put this blindfold on me." Rynna pointed at the strip of purple fabric, like I wasn't already well aware it was there.

I suppressed a chuckle while she continued her little rant.

"Seriously, I'm not sure what you think I'm going to see because it's pitch black in here." Rynna almost whined, all of it done behind the most brilliant smile, the girl biting at her lip, totally failing at trying to keep her excitement contained. "And I'm pretty sure you've been driving in circles, trying to throw me off. Or get me sick. There's that."

But she was grinning so wide that I knew she was loving this every bit as much as me.

"Hold tight, baby. Your surprise is right around the corner."

I eased the truck into a parking spot and killed the engine. I leaned across the cab, enjoying the way she inhaled sharply when I got close to her face, the way a shiver rolled down her spine when I leaned around her and gently untied the purple silk fabric from her eyes.

Slowly, I eased it back. The girl blinked, reoriented herself, needing time to grab on to her senses. Nothing made me happier than the fact when she did, she was looking directly at me.

I'd become her focal point. Just the same as she'd become mine.

"Hey," she murmured, her expression soft.

"Hi, beautiful." For a few seconds, we floated on the moment, just loving being together. Then I grinned and angled my head, urging her attention out the windshield.

She laughed. Laughed loud before she looked back at me like I'd lost my mind.

Truth was, the only thing I'd lost was my heart.

"You brought me to Pepper's? After I was here all day, slaving away? Tell me we aren't here for me to bake you a pie." Every word that fell from her mouth was playful, filled with a tease.

A chuckle rumbled free. "Wouldn't dream of it, baby. Come on." I unlatched the door, hopped out, and jogged around to her side. I was already there, helping her down when she opened her door. I threaded our fingers, brought her hand to my lips, brushed them across her knuckles. "Tonight's all about me taking care of you."

Six months had passed since the fire.

This day could have been somber.

But no.

Rynna and I? We were celebrating.

I led her across the sidewalk to the door, and she giggled, struggling to keep up with my long strides in her heels. I was quick to insert my key, unlock it. I pulled it open a fraction and stood in the middle of it, turning around to face the girl who'd changed everything.

The one who'd knocked free all the bitter, broken pieces of my heart and found what was hiding underneath.

"This building, Rynna . . . this building has come to mean so much. That fire—" My throat grew thick and moisture gathered in Rynna's eyes, her gaze so intent as she stared back at me. "You and I, we almost lost everything in that fire. This building. Your dreams. *Frankie. Each other.*" Each word that fell from my mouth came more intense with each one that passed.

That energy lapped, blazing to life. Inciting that never-ending desire.

"But from those ashes rose the greatest hope. My greatest joy."

I'd never thought I'd truly love a woman again after I'd lost Sydney. But Rynna changed all of that. Rekindled places in me I'd thought had gone forever dormant. Even though I hadn't told Ollie yet, I would. I was no longer afraid of him hating me, I was just worried that I'd bring him more pain.

But Rynna and I had also learned that keeping those kind of secrets only hurt us more in the end.

I gathered both her hands in mine, pulling her inside, quick to lock the door behind us.

It was dark, all except for the hurricane lamp I'd placed on a blanket on the floor in the middle of the room. Beside it was a bucket, chilling our champagne. It was all set up right where all the new booths would be installed next week. This afternoon, me and my crew had raced in after Rynna left and hung pictures on the walls.

They were pictures I'd had enlarged, all in black and white, and set in giant frames.

They were images of Rynna's grandmother in this place, serving her pies, baking in the back, working the register, and making customers smile where they sat at the counter. The old pictures had been in a box in Rynna's bedroom closet, waiting to be reclaimed. To be given a voice.

Overwhelmed, Rynna looked around. Tears glided down her cheeks, glistening in the faint electric light that danced in the lamp.

"Rex," she whispered, biting down on her lip, trying not to cry. "This is amazing."

I pulled her a little farther into the room. "Nothing has made me happier than giving this building back to you, Rynna. There's been no greater honor than resurrecting each brick. And I've never been prouder than being at your side while you've brought this place back to life."

Another two steps, and her chest was heaving while my heart was running wild, blood a thunder in my veins. "Six months ago, we could have lost it all, and instead, we were given everything. We were given another *chance*."

I blinked at her. Overcome by emotion. By feeling. "You came into our lives, Rynna, and you made everything better. I was filled with so much fear and hate, and you taught me how to love again. You showed my daughter what it is really like to be loved by a mother. You gave us a joy unlike anything we've ever known. I see you with her—"

I gulped around immensity of it. Rynna and my little girl. The way it felt when Frankie called her Mommy. The way Rynna adored her with all her soul.

I squeezed Rynna's hands. "I see you with her, and every single thing in my world is right. Because you and Frankie, the two of you are my world. My entire world, and I don't ever want to be without you."

I dropped to a knee and shock jetted from Rynna's mouth.

Tears came in a free fall, the wet streaks doing nothing but illuminating that gorgeous face.

I pulled the ring from my pocket and held it up between us, my hand trembling while I offered this girl all of me. "Marry me, Rynna Dayne. I want to give you all my days. My heart and my life. Tell me, you're always going to be mine."

A tiny cry erupted from her, and she stood there staring down at me for the longest time, the smile lighting her mouth soft and soggy and so goddamned sweet. "And you . . . you gave me everything, Rex Gunner. My dreams. My hopes. A little girl to call my own. You and Frankie, you are the parts of me I hadn't known I was missing. Both of you, you are my heart and my life. And I promise you, I will always be yours."

Overcome by emotion, blinking back my own tears, I slid that ring on her finger, and Rynna dropped to her knees on the blanket in front of me. Those eyes searched me, flitting all over my face. "I knew today was a special day, and I've been saving you a surprise of my own."

I cupped her face, tracing my thumb along the curve of her jaw. Just needing to touch her. "You've got a surprise for me, huh? Not sure I need anything but what you've already given me."

Her eyes fluttered, and her head dropped, and she set both her hands on her belly. Then she peeked up at me with a timid smile, wearing eternity on her face.

My eternity.

My forever.

My second chance.

I pressed my hands over hers, hardly able to speak. "You telling me I'm lucky enough that you're going to make me a daddy again, too?"

Quickly, she nodded. "I know, I know it's soon, but you and I, we haven't exactly been careful all this time . . . and . . . and . . . oh God, Rex, I'm so happy. This baby makes me so happy."

She was rambling. Nervous. Excited.

Wondering how I'd react.

Crazy thing was, we'd never had this conversation, but all along I'd been taking that chance with her.

I dropped my forehead to hers, her hair wound through my fingers, our noses touching as I murmured, "Nothing could make me happier than growing this family with you. I'm so happy, Rynna. So goddamned happy. You're my second chance, Rynna, and I'm not afraid of what this life will bring."

Little Thief.

She'd stolen my heart.

And I was going to give her everything.

Epilogue Two – Rynna

I paused just outside the swinging kitchen door—a fresh cherry pie in my hands—staring out into the dining room.

Every person I loved was there for the grand re-opening of Pepper's Pies.

There for me. Because of this legacy. A private party just for my family and friends.

My husband.

My sweet daughter, Frankie Leigh.

The woman I'd come to adore, to claim as my own, Rex's mother, Jenny. She was such an important fixture in our lives, there to give me advice and an encouraging word when I needed one, or simply being a friend at other times. Fun and caring with that wild streak I was sure she'd never outgrow. Loving us unconditionally, in her own perfect way.

Ollie and Kale, Nikki and Lillith and Brody were all there, laughing where they stood by a few tables we'd pushed together in the middle. Seth Long, the officer who'd worked to put Janel and Aaron away, and a few of the guys from RG Construction I'd gotten to know were there, too.

Macy had flown out just for the celebration, and she mixed in just fine, laughing at something Kale had to say, which was probably something entirely inappropriate.

And I swore, as I looked around, my gramma was there, too. Her spirit always so strong. Her presence so profound.

Forever guiding me with the whisper of her encouraging words. Comfort covered me, a warmth that lit me from head to toe, her voice a murmur in my ear.

"Someday you'll understand what I'm talkin' about. Someday you'll know what it's like to be in love . . . You know you're in love when their happiness counts more than yours. The key is your happiness meaning most to them, too. Put those two together? That's magic, Rynna. That's what real love is. It's two people giving all they have."

Magic.

That's what Rex and I were. Two people giving it all we had.

We both loved the other first, their happiness before our own. Approaching our relationship that way? That happiness could only grow as it was poured out in the day to day, amplified in the little things and strengthened when life threw obstacles in our way.

Frankie suddenly looked my direction, wearing that grin on her face that always managed to touch my soul, the word falling from her mouth making my spirit thrum with joy. "Mommy!"

"Yes, baby?"

"Is that a Pepper's Pie?"

"Of course it's a Pepper's Pie. I made your favorite kind."

"Dids you know my Gramma C'rine used to make me all the Pepper's Pies?" she turned and continued to ramble at Macy, who seemed to be her new best friend. "She used to works here, too, but now my mommy does and she makes me pies and they're soes good, and my daddy eats them all, all, all gone and I have to race him to even get a piece."

"No!" Macy said in mock horror.

Heart so full, I wound around the counter, heading their direction. My man shifted, like he felt me approaching.

Those sage eyes pinning me.

Capturing me.

So beautiful.

That coarse, rough exterior with the most beautiful, giving heart underneath.

He no longer kept it hidden.

He'd welcomed me into it.

Wholly.

No questions blocking our path.

Rex took the pie from my hands and placed it on the table, turning to me wearing that sexy smile riding the edge of his full, full lips. The one that tipped my tummy and sent that attraction rushing free. Then his hands were on my stomach, over our son, his love pouring from him in shattering waves. "I love you, Rynna Gunner," he murmured.

"I love you so much," I told him.

Our gazes tangled for a moment, before he swiveled me, tucked me to his side. He lifted his glass just the same as he lifted his voice over the perfect clatter of voices. "I think a toast is in order."

Everyone turned their attention to us. Their smiles so bright, brimming with the bonds of friendship and family.

Rex glanced at me, then back to them. "To Gramma Dayne. For the woman who loved this restaurant, but loved the people of Gingham Lakes so much more. To her courageous, gracious heart. I'm not sure where I'd be right now if it wasn't for her."

He lifted his glass higher.

Toward the heavens.

"You'll always be a part of Pepper's Pies. More so, you'll always be a part of our lives."

It was a chorus of cheers.

Cheers to Gramma Corinne.

To the woman who'd given us her all.

For her love and her inspiration.

All moments matter. We just rarely know how important they are until the chance to act on them has already passed.

Because of her I'd acted. I'd taken the chance.

The chance on love.

The chance of forever.

And I was never looking back.

Follow Me

Back

Disclaimer

Follow Me Back has the use of American Sign Language within its pages. In order to give better ease of reading, they are not written in true ASL format.

prologue

I stumbled out the sliding door and into the sunlight, which streaked like daggers through edges of the sky. It cast the last, fading moments of the day in a blaze of glittering red and blinding oranges.

Everything felt too bright. Too harsh. Too real.

Shedding the darkest light on what I'd done.

Hair fisted in my hands, I careened across the street. No destination when I no longer recognized where I belonged.

Still, a desperation took me whole, the need to get away when there would never be an escape.

With every faltering step, I felt the bond I'd thought would last forever stretching thin.

Prying and pulling until it snapped.

Until I had nothing left but the failure I held in the palm of my hands.

A mark forever left on my heart.

I'd tried.

I'd tried with every part of me, with everything I had to give.

But it wasn't enough.

The sun shimmered around me. A glowing, dissipating orb.

Dissolving on the horizon until it dwindled to nothing.

That was the moment my world went dim.

one

Kale

"Kale, congratulations! You deserve it, even if you are nothing but a pain in my ass!" Ollie shouted over the din of the busy bar, finishing his toast, which basically was a roast.

Not like it wasn't expected.

I fought an affected grin as I lifted my glass to join the ring of shot glasses that met in the middle of the round table.

I sat surrounded by my friends, who I considered more family than anything else.

Rex and Rynna.

Lillith and Brody.

Nikki.

Ollie.

They all shouted, "To Kale!" before all those little glasses were clinking together and shots were being tossed back.

Expensive tequila burned down my throat and pooled in my stomach. It landed in a splash of flames that licked and jumped, igniting in my veins.

Head to toe, a rush of satisfaction washed through me.

Contentment seeping all the way to my bones.

Smiling wide, I blew out a gratified breath as I slammed the empty down on the table. "I have to give it to you, man. That was a fine example of what your bar has to offer."

Ollie smirked. The guy was nothing but burly muscle and tattoos. A fucking giant made up of solid stone.

"Now you can't say I haven't done anything for you," he tossed out. "That was *the* best bottle of liquor in the house, asshole. Been keeping this baby stashed in the back for a special occasion or a rainy day, whichever came first. Guess the latter won out."

"Well, it's good to know my little accomplishment was deemed worthy of this level of praise."

Ollie held up his thumb and index finger, leaving a centimeter of space between. "Barely."

My body shook with laughter. "Always such an asshole."

His expression lost some of its mischief. "You do deserve it, man. Hope you know that."

Grief flashed.

A streak that blazed through me before it was gone.

Tucked back away where I kept it safe as a reminder of what I was living for.

"Thanks, man."

I let my gaze rove over the faces of my friends, who were chatting, voices elevated so they could hear each other. It was the bar Ollie owned on Macaber Street, super cool and constantly packed. People flocked through the doors to get a taste of the most popular lounge in our small city of Gingham Lakes, Alabama.

It was located about a block down from my loft, and I'd be a liar if I said I didn't frequent the place. If someone was looking for me and I wasn't at work, they wouldn't be too far off base looking for me at this bar, indulging in all the revelry it had to offer.

It was set in one of the old buildings that had been renovated during Gingham Lakes's revival. Rex's company, RG Construction, had been responsible for the restoration. It boasted red brick walls and atmospheric lights, and the never-ending rotation of local bands gave it the aura of somewhere you wanted to be.

But tonight wasn't just any night that I was out looking for a reprieve from the rigorous demands of working in the ER.

Tonight, all my friends were there to celebrate this new stage in my life, which would take me in a direction I'd been feeling the call to all along. Hoping to give back. Help the most helpless and innocent among us.

Rex tilted the neck of his beer bottle my direction as his wife, Rynna, snuggled under the arm he had draped around her shoulders. "Seriously, Kale, I'm fucking proud of you. Always knew you were an amazing doctor . . . now you've got the office to prove it. Don't let it go to your pretty head." The last came out with a quirk of his brow.

"You just wish you looked this good." I shot him my best grin.

"Cocky bastard," he returned, chuckling and dropping a kiss to Rynna's temple.

Gratefulness pulsed through my chest. Rex, Ollie, and I? We'd always had each other's backs. Together through the worst of times and the best of times. And honestly, life had dealt out some damned bitter blows.

From Ollie's sister, Sydney, going missing when she was sixteen, never to be found, to Rex's first wife leaving him to raise his little girl, Frankie Leigh, on his own, to my devastating failure.

But somehow, it'd only made us stronger. We gave each other nonstop shit, but our bond was unshakeable. Did my best to always look to the bright side for them, be the strong one they could count on even though sometimes that felt like deceit.

Truthfully, it wasn't so hard to put a smile on my face.

I enjoyed my life.

I was . . . content.

Really, damned content.

I had everyone who surrounded me tonight.

A career that I gave everything to, where my heart wholly belonged, and I did my best to make that change.

All except for the piece of my heart that belonged to Frankie Leigh and Ryland—Rex and Rynna's kids. My godbabies.

Frankie Leigh had me wrapped around all her wily little fingers, and when Ryland was born just six weeks ago, it was instant. The way I loved that kid.

"Are you about ready to get out of here?" Rex asked Rynna.

Lillith and Nikki both booed. "No, it's early!" Nikki whined.

The guys and I had all gone to school with Lillith and Nikki. We'd known them forever, hung out now and again, but they hadn't been a part of our tight-knit group until they'd become good friends with Rynna, which of course meant Broderick Wolfe was part of the mix as well since he was married to Lillith.

"Says the girl who doesn't have to get up at five in the morning to nurse," Rynna deadpanned.

"If you stay a little longer, I promise I'll be there at five to take on the morning shift so you guys can sleep in and do whatever else it is you want to do." She waggled her brows. Pure suggestion. "And I volunteer Lillith to join."

She nudged Lillith with her elbow. "You'll come, won't you?"

"Um . . . for some Frankie and Ryland time? Absolutely."

Rex glanced at Rynna. "I do believe these two have just been promoted to my new best friends."

"Nice, write me off so easily. And on my big day," I said with a quirk of my brow, lifting my tumbler of whiskey to my mouth.

Rex cracked a smile. "Hey, man, there are few things more important in life than sleep and sex. Nikki here is allowing me both. Boom. Best friends."

An incredulous huff shot from my mouth. "Um, hello. This I know firsthand. I was an emergency room physician for the last three years, remember?"

Sleep had become my unicorn.

And sex had become my prize.

I allowed myself that pleasure. Getting lost in a willing body to forget about all the stress and trauma and horrible shit I saw every fucking day.

For a few hours, I'd let myself get lost.

Unbound and unchained.

No promises or commitments or loyalties that I couldn't make.

Just . . . freedom.

Then I'd pass the hell out for hours.

It was enough to recharge and reboot. The push of knowing I could actually make some kind of difference in the middle of a fucked-up world. A world that continually marched forward in time, meting out tragedy after tragedy.

Truth was, I'd come to realize there were just as many miracles buried beneath the rubble as there were the disasters that had caused them in the first place.

For every heart broken, one was mended.

For every life lost, there was one to be saved.

So, my life was dedicated to *saving*.

Ollie shook his index finger at me, tatted knuckles flashing under the light.

Funny, how we all looked so different sitting around this table. Brody and I in suits. Clean-cut and shaven. Rex and Ollie a little rough. Clearly, not ones to be fucked with.

"Told you, you were gonna be a doctor when I broke my ankle out by the lake when we were twelve and you set it with a damned stick and your shirt. Think you actually owe me all the thanks since I was the one with the foresight to send you that direction."

Amusement rippled across my lips. "Dude, you wish."

"No wishing about it. I expect royalties."

My brow lifted. "What, you think I'm some kind of celebrity?"

Laughter moved across his face. "Nah, man. Not even close. But they sure as hell seem to think so."

My gaze moved over my shoulder in the direction he'd gestured to. A rowdy group of women took up the entire opposite end of the bar. Five or six high-top tables had been pushed together to accommodate them, cheers and toasts going up, their laughter and voices ringing through the atmosphere.

Winding with the band that played behind them.

Celebrating and free.

With a grin, I started to turn back to Ollie, to tell him I was refraining tonight, when my attention snagged, tripping up and tangling on a girl in their party.

Like there was a goddamned chance I could look another direction.

A mass of lush red waves rolled all the way down her back. Not the kind that came from a bottle. But the kind that told me there was a smattering of freckles across her milky skin. Skin I was instantly itching to know whether it felt as soft as it looked.

From my vantage, I could see her from the side. The warm, muted lights that poured over her from above illuminated her profile—button nose and pouty lips and dimpled chin.

A knockout.

Because God knew she'd knocked the breath out of me.

But where the rest of her party was having a blast, she was sitting on a stool like she'd rather be any place than there.

My eyes traced across the cream-colored blouse, the crisscross V-neck lined in a wave of ruffles, and down the black skirt I could only imagine hugged perfect hips. Her ankles were crossed, heels hooked in the rung of the high stool. The girl was sipping a glass of rosé like she was terrified the next sip might be the one that put a hole in her rigid armor.

If anyone needed to be shown a good time, it was her.

Nikki sidled up between Ollie and me. "Looks like we're about to lose tonight's guest of honor. Look at you, drooling all over that poor girl sitting over there minding her own business."

Tsking, she shot me a teasing smile. She was always goading me about the girls I followed home, saying one of these days one of them was going to stick.

She didn't need to know that was never going to happen.

I threw a hand over my heart. "Nikki Walters . . . do you think so little of me? I was doing nothing of the sort."

"Right," she drew out, shaking her head and smiling as she gave a little shove to my back. "Well, go on, what are you waiting for? You never know, that might be the girl of your dreams waiting over there for you."

I cocked a grin. "You know me better than that. This guy is not looking for the girl of his dreams." I slammed the rest of my drink and smacked my lips. "But I am most definitely looking for a good time." One look at the girl sitting across the haze of the dingy bar? *Bam.* The whole idea of refraining for the night had been sacked.

Nikki gave a little mock scoff of disgust. "One of these days, you're going to get tired of the games you play."

She stole a glance at Ollie. Pain pierced her expression before she covered it with a bright smile. Poor girl'd been head over heels for Ollie for all the years I'd known her. Sure, she dated here and there, but it was clear she was waiting around for Ollie to come to his senses.

I knew Ollie well enough that I wanted to tell her to move on. Live her life. Find someone who would appreciate her for who she was—this loving, free spirit who had the world to offer and deserved it in return.

Dropping a big kiss to her temple, I hugged her to my side. "And sometimes the only thing we've got time for are the games."

She shook her head. "Yeah, yeah, yeah. Married to your work. I get it."

Only she didn't. Only Ollie and Rex knew. The two people in this world I trusted with my secrets and my life and my shame.

"Go on, then. We'll just be over here polishing off this awesome bottle of tequila Ollie was so kind to share." She dragged Ollie back by the wrist. "You know where to find us . . ."

"In about an hour, it'll be with your head buried in a toilet."

She pointed at me. "Oh, dude, I'll drink your ass under the table any time. But not tonight. I'm on auntie duty in the morning."

"You're on. A hundred bucks."

"Hell no . . . I win and you go on an actual date."

I gasped. "The cruelty. And here I thought we were celebrating me?"

Her smile turned wry. "Oh, we are."

The two of them turned back to the rest of our friends, who were laughing and chatting around the table, and I strode to the bar, got a refill of my whiskey, and asked for a glass of bubbly pink stuff.

When I turned around, I damned near stumbled again.

It was a flash.

The girl looking at me.

Eyes the greenest green.

A grassy plain.

Mossy, warm earth.

For a second, I lost my footing.

Lost ground.

Lost sanity.

Because just looking at her felt like something profound.

Before I could evaluate the feeling, I shook it off and twisted my mouth into the smile my ma said I'd always wielded like manipulation.

And I strode her way.

two

Hope

He caught me staring.

Crap.

He caught me staring.

I jerked forward, trying to hide myself in the fall of my hair.

It was no use.

I could feel him approaching.

Shivers trailed down my spine. I stiffened it, gnawing at my bottom lip when I felt the presence roll over me from behind.

Potent.

Powerful.

Persuasive.

That was what the man looked like. Persuasion and dominance and sex.

Like one of those models in a suit with a single hand tucked in the front pocket of his pants, an understated watch showing off his masculine wrist, his face hard and chiseled and angled.

If he didn't scream *all man*, he'd almost be pretty.

Turbulence shook my spirit.

I knew his type.

The type that oozed arrogance and pretension and ego. I knew to stay as far away from his breed as possible.

What made it worse were the chills that skated across the surface of my skin when he was suddenly right there, his essence a breath across my shoulder. My senses were slammed with a woodsy, citrusy scent. Like an orange zested on a pile of maple leaves and whipped up in a vat of sugar, the concoction doused with the warmth of a sweet whiskey.

Goodness. The man even smelled smooth.

A new glass of the same wine I'd been sipping slid in front of me while the man slipped into the vacant stool next to mine. "Thought you could use a refill."

I turned to face him, and I had to fight to keep my jaw from dropping right to the floor, because the glimpses I'd been stealing from across the room did absolutely nothing to prepare me for what he actually looked like up close.

So tall. So obscenely tall. Muscle packed on his long, lean frame. Blond hair short, the front a smidge longer, styled in a polished, immaculate way. Lips plush and soft and dangerous.

He looked like discord.

Chaos with an easy, arrogant smile.

A perfect, controlled disorder.

I shook my head to break myself from the stupor.

What he looked like was a damned broken heart. I lifted my chin. "Is that so?"

As if it were evidence of a crime, I glanced at my glass that was still half full.

"Mm-hmm. I'm a guy who's all about being prepared. What kind of man would I be if I ran the risk of you running out?"

"How chivalrous of you." I tried my best to force the words from my tongue like darts of sarcasm. But with the way his lip twitched in amusement, I was sure the man picked up on the way my response shook.

God, I had to be careful, or else I'd be wrapped right around his finger. My gut told me it'd be easy to do.

Round, round, round, and I'd be nothing but putty stomped beneath the sole of his expensive shoe.

I traced my fingertip around the rim of my own glass. "But completely unnecessary. I have a one-drink limit."

His brow lifted, and something playful danced around his flirty, sensuous mouth. "Ah . . . I see . . . you got wrangled into being the designated driver for your friends? Drew the short end of the stick?"

I fought the unease that welled in my chest and turned away as I admitted, "Something like that."

Truthfully, I would never consider my circumstances as a negative. The short end. A chore or a saddle. But that didn't mean I had free space to flit my days away. Especially with a man like him.

Angling his head around, he captured my attention with that potent stare. As if he'd immediately caught on to the current that ran through the center of me. I shook when I got the sense that maybe he was searching for a way to see it, to find what it was made of.

His brow drew together. "Or this just isn't your scene?" The flash of a moment passed before he seemed to settle on a conclusion, his eyes dimming in some kind of softness. "I'd put down bets on the latter."

Something about his response made my tummy twist and dragged my attention to my best friend.

Her laughter floated through the air, her voice buoyant as she talked with a few of our other friends, her smile free.

Everyone there to celebrate her.

There was no question she was having a great time. Kind of the way she'd been hoping I would when she'd convinced me to come. "It's my best friend's birthday. Jenna," I explained. I turned to look at him, unable to keep out the wobble of affection that fell into the words. "It was kind of mandatory that I show."

The flirtation rimming his lips turned to straight seduction, and he edged forward, his words a murmur two beats from the shell of my ear. "And what would she say if I whisked you away from here?"

There was nothing I could do to stop it. The attraction that throbbed in the center of me.

Its own entity.

It lit in the air between us. Heat and a lusty kind of desire.

There was no denying this beautiful stranger affected me.

But even sitting there talking with him was reckless. "*She'd* probably say go for it. *I'd* say you're wasting your time."

Almost chuckling, he rubbed one of those massive hands over his defined jaw, grin growing wide behind it. "I promise you . . . I'd make sure it wouldn't come close to being a waste of your time. I'd make good use of every second."

The other thing I didn't like about his arrogant, pretentious kind? They were also presumptuous. They thought they could reach out and take whatever they wanted without it costing them anything. Without a thought toward what it might cost you.

Ignoring the attraction that blazed at my insides, I rode on the offense and inched in a fraction. My words dropped to the hiss of a breath. "Do I look like the kind of girl who follows a complete stranger out of a bar? You might be on the prowl, but I'm here to celebrate with my friend. Give her *my* time, because she pretty much gives me all of hers. And honestly, I'm kind of tired of the idea that a man can just snap his fingers and a woman will start peeling off her panties."

He jerked back, intense blue eyes going dark. Like the sun setting on Bora Bora, tossing its turquoise waters in a glittering black. As if he were shocked by the rejection and liked it at the same time.

Or maybe he was just envisioning exactly what that might look like, because his gaze was tracing down, over my skirt, and to my ridiculously high heels I'd had to crawl to the back of my closet to find.

Slowly, he dragged those darkened eyes back up to my face. A flush pulled across my chest as he went.

His tongue licked out to run along his bottom lip while I sat there watching the flip.

The way his entire demeanor shifted into something playful and casual.

"Well then, as much as I *love* the idea of you peeling off your panties, you can see I'm not over here snapping my fingers. You just looked like you were having a horrible time, and I thought maybe I could rectify the situation."

"Which I can only imagine included the two of us ditching our clothes." I wanted it to come off as hard. Confident. Instead, it sent a rush to heat my face.

Ducking down, I bit my lip, cursing myself under my breath. I was so absolutely terrible at this. So out of my element. That alone was enough to remind me I didn't belong there.

At a bar where all the rules changed.

Chuckling under his breath, he stood, towering over me. I shivered when he leaned down, his words just a whisper at my temple. "If that was what you wanted? Me to wrap you up and steal you away from here? I'd be a fool to pass up the chance. You're wound up so tight, I'd spend the entire night undoing you. Time and again. But I would never ask you to do something you aren't comfortable with."

His response took me by surprise, and when he straightened, I was a shaky mess. The man cast me a smile and pointed at the full wine glass. "If you get the inclination, drink up. Let go. Just for a little while." He looked around the bar. "I get the feeling you deserve it more than any one of us."

Something gentle swam through the depths of those icy eyes, and my chest tightened in an almost painful way.

Kindness.

I saw it there, hiding underneath something so powerful I didn't have the strength to fathom it.

"Thank you," I said.

He dipped his head and turned away without another word.

I tried not to watch when he strode back across the bar. But I couldn't help the furtive peeks, enthralled by the way the man weaved through the high-top tables.

All causal ease and confidence.

He got right back to living it up with his group of friends, instantly laughing as if he hadn't missed a beat, slinging an arm around a big guy's shoulders as if they'd been friends forever.

At the yank on my arm, I jerked to find Jenna standing there.

Brown eyes wide and intrigued, her voice was laced with the scandal. "Who was that tall drink of deliciousness? Good lord, if I knew what this bar was serving up . . ."

I shook myself out of the daze the man had me in and forced myself back down to reality. "He was nothin' but a train wreck avoided."

"Oh, come on, Hope." She flung my arm all around with the plea. "You promised me you'd have a good time. One night, remember?"

Peering up at her, I worried my lip. "I'm sorry. Last thing I want is to be a downer on your party. But you know I have to be careful."

"You think I don't know that, Harley Hope? But that doesn't mean you have to pretend like you're dead. I mean, look at you! You are the prettiest girl in the whole damned place, and here you are, wastin' it." She hugged my head against her chest, basically burying my face in her boobs as she petted my head as if I were a brand-new puppy.

There was no stopping my grin.

"And for the record, the only way you could possibly be a downer on my party is if you weren't a part of it. Now, get that gorgeous ass up and do a shot with me."

"Are you crazy?"

She hauled me up onto my ridiculous heels, her grin wide and her gaze hazy. "Tonight I am."

I hesitated. Sympathy lined her features.

Because Jenna?

She got it in a way no one else could.

She squeezed my hand. "It's fine, Hope. I promise. You deserve to have a little fun, too."

I shook my head, and I gave, letting myself get lost for a little while. Because I knew that, come morning, reality would be waiting for me. It wasn't going anywhere.

Two hours later, I stumbled out the front door and into the slowed warmth of the Alabama night. Streetlamps poured a dingy glow across the sidewalk, the area still busy with people moving from one place to the next, the bouncer still at the door standing guard.

Jenna had insisted she'd walk me out, but I'd refused. The last thing I wanted was to break into her fun. But it was time for mine to end. I'd already indulged in a way I never allowed myself to do.

Head down, I rushed toward the street where a small line of cabs waited to whisk away the revelers of the night.

My heel caught in a crack in the sidewalk. My senses dulled, too slow to process it. The way it tipped me and sent me fumbling forward.

I gasped, nothing I could do but anticipate the nasty faceplant.

That gasp only grew when a big arm was suddenly around my waist, hauling me back onto my feet, steadying me there.

My chest heaved, and I already knew by the time he turned me around that it was him.

Those eyes searched me, carefully, the man almost out of breath as he demanded, "Are you okay?"

I stepped back, trying to get my bearings.

I blinked so many times the man had to think I was crazy.

But Mr. Panty Dropper was right there.

Hands on the outside of my arms, the contact sending tingles flying across my flesh.

The worry in his expression shifting to a wry grin. Face so beautiful I couldn't help but stare.

Damn that shot.

Because ideas thrummed through my mind. The dangerous, dangerous kind. Ones that made me question and want and wish I could have something more in my life.

But I didn't need *more*. I had *enough*—more than enough—and I knew I had to be content with that.

"You look fine to me," he said, smirk kicking up at the corner of his mouth.

Squeezing my eyes closed, I clamored around for my senses, for something to say, mortified the second it came tumbling out. "Are you stalking me now?"

Amusement played all over that mouth. "Uh . . . you're serious?"

I crossed my arms over my chest, trying to put up a wall, a shield, because I could feel this man everywhere. "Of course, I'm serious?"

Leave it to me that it came out a question.

A disbelieving chuckle rolled from him, and he hooked his thumb toward the door behind him. "I was standing right here when you came out. Just put my friend in the cab to make sure she made it home safe. You're the one that came blundering out, Princess. You're lucky I was out here to save you."

He took a single step forward, filling the space.

Fear tumbled through me.

Not in a way that made me concerned for my physical well-being. But for the fact this man made me feel things I couldn't. Not yet. Someday, maybe. But right then, I didn't have that luxury.

"Someone's feeling a little full of themselves tonight." It was all a rumbly tease.

"Not even close," I managed, gulping around the words.

His expression was back to doing that gentle, knowing thing. His head tipped to the side, and the gorgeous man appeared as if he might actually have the capacity to understand. As if he could see right through me to the heart of the matter.

I didn't know if that comforted or terrified.

"I really need to go," I told him.

He reached out, tender when he barely grazed my chin with his knuckle.

I gasped.

Shocked by the zing that raced through my nerves. Blooming and tugging right through my middle.

Hooked.

A tether drawing me in his direction.

A magnetic force.

Powerful and potent and somehow soft.

Tucking his bottom lip between his teeth, he seemed to contemplate before he nodded and stepped back, tucking his hands into his pockets. "Yeah. I know. Go home, sweet girl. You don't belong here. Just . . ." He wavered and then said, "Can you do me one favor?"

Unnerved, I blinked.

Waiting and unsure, because I was sure this man was so utterly different from my first impression of him. So much more than the assumptions I had made.

"Take care of yourself. Let yourself off the hook once in a while. You deserve to be happy."

I let the emotion wind to my mouth. "I am happy."

"But fear is holding some of that back."

And I knew it then.

He could see straight through me.

"There are some things important enough they are worthy of that fear," I told him, not sure why. Not sure how he made me want to split myself right open and reveal it all to him when I didn't even know his name.

His chin ticked up in a quiet kind of understanding, and I gave him a small nod before I turned and opened the door to the cab waiting at the curb.

I stalled when I heard his voice hit me from behind. "I truly hope whatever is holding it back resolves itself quickly."

From over my shoulder, I cast him a small smile. "Don't worry. My heart is always hung on hope."

Before I allowed myself to say anything else, I hopped into the backseat of the cab, slammed the door, and didn't look back when it drove away.

I gave the driver my address, my thoughts all over the place as we traveled the short distance to my sleeping neighborhood. He pulled up in front of the one-story house on the left, the grassy yard literally hedged in a white-picket fence.

My emotions warred between satisfaction and dread. This little place rang with hope. I just had to make sure it stayed that way.

I tossed a twenty into the front seat, mumbled a, "Thank you," and then stepped out. The click of my heels echoed against the walkway that cut down the center of my yard, the towering trees swaying overhead as I made my way up the two steps to the covered porch.

I already had my key out, ready to slide it into the lock as I approached the door, when I sensed the movement.

The hairs lifted at the back of my neck.

Shivers raced.

A flood of dread. A sea of apprehension.

Slowly, I turned, watching as the shape emerged from the shadows.

Ominous.

Cold.

My heart roared, an erratic crash that thundered through my body, lifting to a deafening pound in my ears.

I took a step back toward the door. "What are you doing here?"

He laughed a malignant sound.

That was what he was.

Malignant.

Set on destroying the best part of me. For years, I had kept faith that one day he would see. That the stones of anger that lined him would finally crack, and his eyes would be opened to what true beauty actually looked like.

That he'd understand the world's definition of perfection was nothing but a falsity.

Now, I knew better.

He approached, his steps slow as he moved. "I think the better question would be, what are you doing just getting home?"

"I don't think that's any of your business."

He laughed again. As if I were ignorant. Small. Foolish. "Anything you do *is* my business, Harley. Do you really think running off is going to change that?"

"Yes." I said it with as much power behind it as I could manage, the sound of the word reverberating through the dense air.

"I won't let you walk away." He edged forward. "Tell me where you were tonight."

I didn't want to give him the honor of an answer. But the last thing I wanted was to give him ammunition to feed his twisted mind. Funny, how he demanded perfection, *respect*, when he'd lost all of mine so many years ago. "You know it's Jenna's birthday. And why do you even care? I'm giving you an out. I'm not asking you for anything other than to leave us alone."

Desperation wove into the last. All I wanted was for him to leave us alone.

His eyes blinked black fury, and he inched closer, his voice dropping to a threat. "You think you can take my say away? Leave me to look like a fool? I won't allow it."

Disbelief pulled from me in a scoff. "That's all you've ever cared about, Dane. Appearances. Control. Inheriting your grandfather's goddamned business as if it were the only important thing in the world. I told you when I left that I was finished, and there's nothing you can do or say to change my mind."

I turned my back to him and pushed my key into the lock, needing to escape. Working it open, I started to push the door open but he clutched me by the wrist. I whirled around to the anger on his arrogant face.

But his arrogance was cruel.

Proud in the most twisted kind of way.

"This ends now, Harley, or you're going to regret it."

I yanked my arm free. "You've already made me regret every single second I willingly stayed in that house. That I willingly stayed with you."

I shoved away from him, quick to slip through the door and slam it shut, fingers frantic as I worked the deadbolt.

Never before had I been physically afraid of Dane. Was I terrified of him? Yes. But I was terrified of the kind of control he'd always wielded. The disgust that had only grown in his eyes with each year that had passed. The hardness that had stamped out his spirit.

I had no idea what lengths he would go to keep that power.

three

Kale

At a red light, I drummed my thumbs on the steering wheel and glanced down at the clock on the dashboard screen.

Six fifteen.

I scrubbed a palm over my face.

Early.

Way early.

But I hadn't been able to sleep. I'd spent the entire night tossing and turning. Nothing but a jumble of nerves.

Anxiety and excitement penetrating all the way to my bones.

Like a kid on his first trip to an amusement park who was terrified to get strapped into the ride.

Well aware the coaster was going to twist and swerve and flip. That it might jerk and jar and hurt.

Still, I knew it was well worth any amount of pain.

Blowing out a breath, I searched along the street that I was traveling.

Fairview—right smack dab in the oldest part of town.

The sidewalks were laid with old, gray bricks, and massive trees grew from planters, their lush branches outstretched and shading the two- and three-story historic buildings that housed businesses and apartments.

Colorful fabric awnings jutted over the doors on the bottom floors, and big windows showcased what was to offer inside.

I was up a couple blocks from Pepper's Pies, the diner Rynna ran and the trendy hotel Broderick Wolfe and his company had brought to Gingham Lakes.

The two of them had been like a straight shot to the economy. Jolting things into action.

New shops, restaurants, and bars had been popping up all over the place, much the same as the revitalization over on Macaber Street where Ollie's bar and my loft building were located.

My new office was just up the road, to the left on McAlister where a bunch of new private-practice medical offices had sprung up in the midst of the city's rejuvenation.

Admittedly, I wasn't all that familiar with everything Fairview had to provide this far down the street.

But there it was, calling out like a beacon sent to save my ass, written on one of those rustic chalkboard signs that had been set up outside a small shop.

Coffee.

Hell yes.

When the light turned green, I accelerated through the intersection, quick to jerk my car into one of the open parallel spots lining the curb right out front.

I hopped out and strode toward the coffee shop, glancing up at the mint-green awning, the name scrawled across the top in a flowy font.

A Drop of Hope.

The logo beside it was a coffee cup tipped to its side, a drop of coffee falling free.

A bell dinged from above when I swung open the door.

It was instant. The strike of my favorite aroma.

That bold scent of a fresh brew.

Damn, if it didn't almost make me lightheaded, my mouth watering with anticipation.

I blamed my addiction on med school.

My stomach was quick to catch up to the reaction, rumbling a greedy sound when I caught onto the subtler aroma—rich cream and decadent sugar—something sweet baking in an oven.

Score.

I stepped farther into the quaint shop. A bunch of round and square tables with mismatched chairs were set up in the open space.

Bookshelves, which were filled with a mess of knickknacks and games and worn hardbound books, lined the back wall.

The place rustic and quaint.

Of course, none of that was what captivated me. My attention homed in on the huge display case attached to the front counter.

Every kind of cupcake and muffin a man could hope to imagine teased from behind the glass.

Behind the counter were about ten different industrial-sized silver coffee urns.

Heaven.

I'd just stumbled upon my new favorite place.

Big chalkboards hung from the ceiling, and I looked up, checking out the specialty coffee drinks and flavors they had to offer.

Movement rustled from the back kitchen before the swinging door flew open.

A tiny gasp echoed through the air.

For a beat, I froze. Somehow knowing it was familiar. That I'd heard it before.

My attention, which had been wrapped up in the menu, was suddenly completely otherwise occupied.

Swore, my eyes had to have doubled in size.

No fucking way.

The same girl I couldn't get off my mind since Friday night, the one I didn't think I'd ever see again, stood in front of me.

All flowing red hair and pouty lips and freckled nose.

Body as mouthwatering as the cupcakes displayed in the case.

Both times I'd walked away from her that night had left me with this odd sense of regret. Something about her had just . . . struck me. Made me want to get inside her pretty little head just about as badly as I wanted to get inside her tight little body.

She stood there staring at me with those green eyes that had to be as wide as mine, shock freezing her mouth into a perfect "O".

Tension bound the air, and that crazy attraction that had haunted my dreams all weekend was right there.

Simmering between us like one of those chaotic summer thunderstorms that gathered over the lake. The kind of storm you knew was going to rock your entire world.

Blinking, she inhaled a big breath and seemed to shake herself out of it. She ran her hands over the tiny black apron tied around her even tinier waist, smoothing herself out. Rolling back her shoulders, she plastered the fakest smile I'd ever seen across her pretty face.

"What can I get for you this morning?" The slightest country drawl tumbled out with her words.

She was fucking adorable.

One side of my mouth lifted in a smirk. "You really know how to hit a man where it hurts, don't you, Princess? Acting like you don't remember me? Come now, don't break my heart. Tell me I'm really not that forgettable."

Her eyes narrowed like she was trying to figure out what to make of me. "Actually, I'm trying to decide if you really *are* stalking me."

A light chuckle rumbled out. "Someone seems to be feeling a little full of themselves again this morning."

There was no way I could stop myself from baiting this girl.

Her eyes roamed over my best suit—the one I'd donned for the day, knowing I would be stepping through the doors of my new office for the first time in partnership with a group of physicians who had years of experience on me.

The day would be nothing but meetings with staff and reviewing cases that I'd be taking on, intermingled with the few patients they'd already scheduled me to see.

Let's just say those nerves I'd been riddled with all last night had me putting my best foot forward, because in my world, there was always, always something to prove.

Still, I felt like a king with the way she gulped as she took me in, the air flaring with the track of her gaze, her hands visibly shaking.

She seemed to swallow it all down and pasted on an expression of decided indifference. "Says the guy with the five-thousand-dollar suit."

I tsked. "Seems someone loves to exaggerate. It was only four."

She pressed her hand to her chest. "Oh my, you must excuse my naivety."

So fucking adorable.

Taking a step forward, I set my palms on the counter in front of the register and leaned in. My voice dropped. "I think there's a chance you can be forgiven. I'm not above a bribe."

So what if I injected about as much suggestion as I could into the simple words.

It worked.

Because this gorgeous girl was fighting a genuine smile as she ducked her head to the side to try to hide the flush splashed across the milky expanse of her chest.

That exquisite color rode up and lit on her cheeks.

Seemed as hard as she tried to front a brash exterior, all I had to do was peel back a single layer to expose the shyness underneath.

She barely peeked at me when she whispered back, "How kind of you."

Clearly, she was still trying to play along, but I got the feeling this girl didn't typically flirt or tease. That she felt completely out of her element.

And damn, if I didn't like that, too.

"Are you?" she suddenly asked, her question an uneasy murmur, not even a hint of playfulness in it.

Confusion drew my brows together. "Am I what?"

Her voice dipped even lower, the girl whispering out of the corner of her mouth. "You know . . . stalking me?"

Soft, amused laughter escaped, and I scratched at my temple, shaking my head.

She was something else, all feisty fire and soft-spoken uncertainty.

"Um . . . I'm pretty sure that's a question anyone would answer as no, truth or not. But for what it's worth, I promise you that I'm not. I'm starting a new position up the street this morning. I was a little early, so figured I'd check out what A Drop of Hope had to offer. Name's Kale. Kale Bryant."

A small gust of relief blew from her lungs, and she fiddled with her fingers. "Hope. Hope Masterson."

Hope.

A Drop of Hope.

That feeling was back again. It was the same one that had forced me to walk away from her Friday night. The sense that this girl was way too good to be chased and hunted and played. The game was totally unfair if she didn't know how to play it back.

She shocked me again when she asked, "So, Mr. Bryant, tell me what kind of bribe you had in mind."

She said it with the hint of a smile dancing around that soft, plush mouth.

Answer to that was easy.

Exactly the kind there was no chance this girl would entertain.

"How about one of those cupcakes?" I suggested instead, angling my head toward the case.

She chewed at her bottom lip, the hard exterior gone. Like it was so heavily fabricated she didn't have the strength to hold it up. "Do you see something you like?"

There was nothing but innocence in her expression. In her voice. She had no idea what those kinds of words would do to me. The way it sounded like she was offering herself up on a platter.

My gaze traced over her plain black V-neck tee, jeans, and flats she wore today. Her height dropped about five inches from Friday night.

Petite and delicate.

Apparently, good things did come in small packages, and I was about two seconds from telling her that she was what I wanted.

But there was just something that stopped me from saying it.

Something inside me that screamed to turn on my heel and get the hell out of there before it was too late. Warning me she was different in a way I liked far too much.

I guessed I shouldn't have been surprised the really reckless side of myself was begging for a couple more seconds.

I forced my attention from her and turned it to the treats in the display, gaze roaming across the selection, basically salivating at the sight. Each cupcake was oversized, topped with swirls of rich, colorful frosting, finished with little pieces of candies and fresh fruits that matched the flavor and names of the cupcakes.

How the hell was I supposed to choose?

A grin twisted across my mouth when I saw it. Because really, there was no other choice.

I eyed her from over the case, the girl so dainty she was barely peeking at me from over the top.

I inclined my head. "I'll take one of those."

Strawberries and cream and everything sweet.

Hope slid the door open, ducking down, hand reaching in. "Which one?"

"Strawberry Shortcake." I said it like it meant something else.

She heard it, too, and her entire being froze for a fraction of a second, and then she drew a sharp breath before she pulled one out. "Good choice," she muttered.

"I've been told I have good taste." My voice dropped low with the allusion.

She straightened, and for a beat, our gazes tangled.

Attraction wound tighter and tighter with each breath that passed.

She cleared her throat and turned to the back counter where she placed the cupcake in a clear plastic container. She spoke without looking my way. "Is there anything else I can get for you?"

Right.

What I'd stopped for in the first place.

Clearly, this girl had the power to make me forget myself.

"Just a large black coffee will do. Medium roast."

She filled a paper cup adorned with the shop's name and logo on the side and placed a lid on it.

It was at the same second a clamor sounded from the back. The swinging door banged open as someone came bustling out.

Jenna.

Instantly, I recognized her from the bar.

The sex kitten from Friday night was gone, replaced with nothing but rumpled clothes and messy bun, potholder gloves on her hands as she carried out a large tray of steaming hot muffins.

When she caught sight of me, she stumbled in her tracks.

She recognized me, too.

I stood there trying not to laugh while a completely silent conversation transpired between the two of them.

Widened eyes. Tilted heads. Purses of lips.

Got the feeling they were arguing about me, though I had no idea which side either of them was bickering for.

Jenna stepped around Hope, and I was pretty sure it was a warning glare she shot me when she ducked down to start filling the bottom shelf in the case with muffins.

There was no missing the protectiveness that blazed in her brown eyes. Though I was pretty sure that was only the half of it, and she was restraining herself from grabbing Hope's wrist, dragging her around the counter, and shoving her in my direction.

Go for it. But if you hurt her? I'll gladly cut off your dick.

I heard it loud and clear.

Apparently, all three of us were proficient in silent communication.

Hope turned back around, slid the cup of coffee my way, and put the container into a brown paper gift bag.

I dug in my pocket for my wallet. "What do I owe you?"

She shook her head. "It's on the house." She offered me the sweetest kind of smile before it turned wry. "It is a bribe, after all."

That grin on my mouth was growing wider with each second that passed. There was just something about this girl that put it there. So damned easily. Flickers of a blaze that'd been dead a really long time.

Before I went and did something stupid, I pulled a twenty from my wallet and stuffed it into the tip jar. "Thank you for the cupcake and coffee, Hope. I think this was exactly what I needed to kick off this new adventure in my life this morning."

"Kale, that's completely unnecessary," she said, eyes dipping to the jar.

Clearly, she wanted to refuse the small offering. Still, there was an undertone of gratefulness that there was no chance of missing.

"Sure it is, Shortcake. You made my day."

She just stood there, staring at me, strawberries and cream and all things sweet.

I sent her one last smile before I spun on my heel and headed for the door. All this shit on the tip of my tongue. I pulled the handle, and the door opened to the sound of the bell jingling overhead.

My guts twisted in the same second I was spinning back around, striding to the counter in a flash. Faster than I could process just what it was I actually thought I was doing.

"Go out with me."

Startled, Hope blinked in surprise, her pretty mouth trembling at the edges. "I . . ."

"Just dinner."

What the fuck?

I hadn't asked anyone to dinner in . . .

I slammed a lid on the thought, hammered it down with a bunch of rusted nails, swallowed hard. "Just dinner."

Head shaking in regret, she took a step back, like she needed to put space between us. "I'm sorry, but I don't think that's a good idea."

She was completely, one hundred percent right. It was a terrible idea. But fuck . . . I wanted it.

I let a grin tweak up one side of my lips. "How could hanging out with me ever be considered a bad idea?"

That stunning face flushed again, an affected smile wobbling around her delicious mouth. That was right before a sorrowful kind of regret took hold of her features. "I have a lot of stuff going on in my life right now. It wouldn't be right."

I nodded around the impact of the rejection, hating the way it bit and stung. At the same time, I did my best to convince myself it was for the best. I'd just dodged my own damned bullet. Because, really, what was I thinking? "All right, then."

Awkwardly, I lifted the bag and the coffee in front of me. "Thank you again for these."

She wrung her fingers. "You're welcome. I hope you have a really great day at the new job."

I didn't respond, just pushed out the door and into the spill of the bright, morning sun, the bell chiming as it swung shut behind me.

I rushed for my car, feeling all kinds of shit I hadn't felt in such a long time.

The whole way, I wished at least one of those feelings were relief.

four

Hope

"Harley Hope Masterson."

I jerked my attention from the big window that overlooked the sidewalk running the front of the shop, ripping it from the vacant spot where the sleek, dark gray car had just pulled from the curb.

The driver was nothing but a shadowy silhouette in the blacked-out tinting.

I blinked to clear the daze.

Jenna stood there with her fists propped on her hips.

Turning away, I started scrubbing down the counter where the coffee had dribbled from my shaky hands. Apparently, Kale had that kind of effect on me.

Which was just dangerous business in and of itself.

"Don't you start on me, Jenna. And you know I hate it when you call me by my full name. You act as if you're my mama or something."

"I might as well be because someone needs to knock some sense into you. Hell, I'm gonna call her down here right now so we can tag team you."

"You wouldn't dare." I shot her a death glare. Because seriously, her and Mama? That was what nightmares were made of. "And were you not the one who just gave me the we-have-a-creeper alert?"

I didn't even need to air quote it. It was an expression Jenna had patented all the way back in high school. The single look told me, "*Let's get the hell out of here,*" because she wanted to ditch some guy who was coming on too strong.

It'd recently been translated to, "*Send this weirdo packing,*" since we opened the shop together two years ago.

"He caught me off guard, that's all. I mean . . . it was kind of weird that he just showed up here after he was so clearly into you Friday night."

I shrugged it off. "He's not into me. I bet he acts like that with every woman he runs across."

"Um . . . I'm pretty sure he was picturing doing you right there on the counter." She pointed to where Kale had just had his big hands pressed beside the register. "Maybe while eating one of your cupcakes off your tits. And believe me, he sure as hell wasn't picturing doing it with me."

For a second, I got dizzy picturing it before I snapped out of it and slapped at my best friend. "What is wrong with you? Why do you have to be so danged crass all the time?"

"Don't tell me you weren't thinking about it. I mean, that man is blistering hot. One touch, and I'd bet you'd go up in flames. That boy would leave a sunburn worse than the summer when we told your mama we had a school camping trip, but we really spent the weekend at Cotton Bayou Beach with our friends."

I rinsed out the rag, wringing it a little more aggressively than necessary. "And you know that burn nearly killed me. No thank you. I've got enough pain in my life. And I'm not exactly free to go chasing after a man who smiles and asks me out."

"Pssh . . . those papers sitting on your desk say otherwise. You shouldn't let Asshat's inability to keep it in his pants keep you from enjoyin' yourself. It's his fault you're here in the first place. It's time you took time for yourself, Hope."

Turmoil fisted my heart. Every selfish betrayal meted at Dane's hand. Thing was, I really didn't care about the cheating.

"You know him stepping out on me was the least of my concerns."

I'd actually been relieved to know he'd been seeing other women except for the fact he'd continued to come to me.

It was everything else that made the coil of hate glow hot where it throbbed deep within me. A feeling that was so foreign and gross and wrong I wanted to purge it from my consciousness.

It was there, this ominous cloud that followed me day to day. Just waiting for the downpour.

I got the unsettled feeling after his unexpected visit this weekend that the storm was about to make landfall.

Helplessly, my head shook. "Besides, you know exactly what Dane would do with that information."

Really, all it would take was one rumor, and Dane's lawyers would have all the ammo they needed to bury me. Even if that weren't the case, I wasn't sure I was ready to make myself vulnerable again, either. If I was ready to open myself up. Once I did, I knew I'd be all in.

She huffed and pointed toward the door. "Tell me you aren't attracted to him."

Images flashed.

The man at the bar.

My breath gone.

My stomach twisted and twined in an overpowering kind of desire.

It was a feeling I hadn't felt in so, so long.

Too long.

I'd loved the way the idea of it had tasted on my tongue.

The way I'd thought about him when I'd crawled into the cold sheets of my bed.

The way I'd touched myself and pretended as if I were finally completely free.

The way butterflies had stormed and scattered and flapped when I'd looked up to find him standing there this morning.

Tall and confident and so damned pretty.

Polished, immaculate chaos.

An epiphany.

"I know you, Hope," Jenna continued with her badgering, all gall and exasperation. "And you haven't had a reaction to a man in years. Not since limp dick came weaseling his way into your life when you were twenty."

I started to refill the sectioned basket next to the register with napkins and coffee stirrers. "It doesn't change anything, Jenna." I lifted a droll brow. "And I'm pretty sure his dick being limp was not his problem."

The problem with Dane was he wasn't just a dick.

He had an ugly soul.

A warped kind of soul he hadn't shown me until it was too late.

"Might as well have been with the size of it. Pathetic." Jenna was fighting a smile. That was just Jenna's way.

She completely caught me off guard when she suddenly reached out and grabbed me by the outside of my arms, forcing me to face her and giving me a little shake.

"Life's dealt you some tough blows. I'm not discounting that. But I'm not about to stand aside and watch you forget how to live. That's what Dane wants. You to be so terrified you don't know how to live anymore. I refuse to let that happen. Not when you finally got up the courage to leave."

Emotion clogged my throat and tears burned my eyes. My brow pinched in a pleading way. "I've got plenty to live for, Jenna. You know that. And right now, I have to protect it. Please don't ask me to compromise that."

Grief struck across her face. "I know that . . . I just . . . the point of you leaving was so he was no longer in control. I don't want to see you give him any more."

"He was waiting for me at my house Friday night after I got home from your party," I admitted way too fast.

Shock slammed into Jenna's expression before twisting into anger. "That bastard. What did he want?"

Bitter laughter tumbled free. "What he always wants. His way. To look like he has a perfect little wife and a perfect family. I told him there was no chance of that ever happening. Now I just have to make sure I'm smart enough to keep that promise a reality."

I was beginning to wonder if it was going to be the greatest fight of my life.

Both of us jumped when the bell above the door jingled with a new customer.

It was just past six thirty, right when it typically got busy with people grabbing coffee and a quick bite to eat on the way to work.

I angled my head and gave her a smile that promised I was okay. "It's about to get busy . . . let's do this."

Kale

After our morning meeting, I reviewed the few patients I would actually be seeing today. The whole time, I'd been trying to shuck the memories of Hope from this morning. Doing my best to rid myself of the impression she'd left on me, this feeling that I'd stumbled upon something significant when I knew better.

I didn't have time to allow myself to get wrapped up in someone, and if I spent any more time with her, I got the feeling that I just might.

I needed to focus on what was important.

Why I was there.

The reason I lived my life.

When I signed on at Gingham Lakes Children's Center, I already understood the load I would be carrying.

The burden I was accepting.

My patients would run the gamut, almost a reverse referral system from specialists who wanted their patients seen in-house for continuity. From easily controlled chronic illnesses that families barely considered once they walked out these doors, to the kids whose entire worlds revolved around their diagnoses.

Some of these kids? They were sick. Really fucking sick.

Looking at the scope of cases I'd be seeing broke pieces inside of me I tried to pretend didn't exist.

Quadriplegia.

Cystic fibrosis.

Cancer.

I knew this was where I'd been being called all along.

But what made me almost stumble in my damn tracks was my first patient.
My first patient.
Of course.
Life was only a test, right?
As hard as I tried to stop the onslaught of memories, it was no use. They were there.
Emergency room lights glared from overhead. Panic. Fear. Compression after compression after compression. That fucking flat line.
I swallowed it all down. Knew this wasn't even close to being the same, but it didn't mean every single goddamned time I was presented with a heart patient of any kind, I didn't crumble a little.
The reminder that I'd failed.
That I'd never be the hero.
God knew that I got up every single day and tried anyway.
I took a second to get myself under control before I gave a couple small taps to the door then pushed it open.
Josiah Washington.
An eight-year-old with a congenital heart defect. The defect had been fairly simple to treat with a balloon stent procedure when he was an infant. The boy was living without symptoms and bi-yearly cardiology visits.
See.
Not even close.
I shut down the shudder that rattled in my ribcage and put on a smile, introduced myself to him and his father, and went through the typical questions of any patient establishing care.
By the time I was in the middle of his exam, I knew without a doubt that this was in fact what I was supposed to do.
The kid so cool. Laughing. Joking. Living the happy kind of life every kid deserved.
"Are you pulling my leg right now? I think you're really just making this up because you were picturing yourself behind one of those wheels. Looks like we have a future race car driver here," I told him as he sat there telling me about what he'd witnessed last week that had definitely made an impression on him.
Josiah howled with laughter, holding his stomach as he sat on the edge of the exam table. I was on a low, wheeled stool, sitting right in front of him, basically distracting him as I did his well-child examination.
Everything seemed normal.
Especially his heart, which I'd spent an inordinate amount of time listening to.
Wasn't about to take any chances.
"Not even. You should have seen it. It was a Ferrari *and* a Maserati. Both of them floored it at the light, right here in Gingham Lakes. Who has cars like

that around here, anyway? Swear, they had to be going at least one fifty. Maybe one sixty. Right, Dad?"

He looked up at his dad for validation. His dad was leaning against the wall with his arms crossed over his chest, watching protectively over his kid. "You got it, son. Right on the other side of the river at the end of town. Would have called the cops myself had they not disappeared five seconds later. Heck, they probably would have already been crossing the Georgia line by the time I made the call."

"Whew, they were faaa-ast," Josiah emphasized with a whistle.

Chuckling, I stood and grabbed the scope so I could peer into his ears. "So what else is it you like to do around here besides for dreaming about racing cars, Mr. Josiah?"

"Me and my best friend, Evan, like to go fishin' at the lake. Dr. Krane introduced us because we both have bad hearts."

Mine twisted again. I shoved it down, refusing to go down that path, and continued smiling as I listened to the cute kid go on about his friend. "He goes to a different school, our moms always take us to each other's houses, so it's no big deal. And my mom and dad *finally* let me get Snap," he said with an annoyed roll of his eyes. "So now we can send messages on our iPads."

"You know not to accept any requests from anyone you don't know, right?"

Yeah, I went there. Too many freaks out there to let that one slip by.

He sighed in exasperation. "Of course, I know. My mom told me like a million times."

"She sounds pretty smart."

"Yup. Best part about me and Evan?"

"What's that?"

Josiah grinned. "I'm taller."

Six

Kale

As soon as I left the office, I headed straight for Rex and Rynna's house. After spending the day meeting some of my new patients, I had this itchy feeling.

Needing to hold my godbabies in my arms. Feel them whole and healthy and strong.

Which was crazy, considering the day had left me feeling more fulfilled than I'd ever imagined and entirely wrecked at the same time.

I pulled into the gravel drive of the family's little house. The larger house across the street that Rynna had inherited from her grandmother was currently undergoing a full renovation. As soon as it was finished, they'd sell this place and move over there since they needed the room.

I bounded up the porch steps, Milo barking like crazy as he hopped up and pawed at the window.

The door flew open before I even made it there, Frankie Leigh barreling out. The kid was wearing the black tutu I'd given her for her birthday over a pair of shorts and a sweater, her brown hair just as wild and free as her spirit. "Uncle Kale, Uncle Kale! Yous came to see me. What you been doing? I've been missing you!"

I scooped her off her feet, tossed her in the air as she squealed with delight. I hugged her close. "I've been missing you, too. How's big girl school?"

"It's so, so fun! I learned all my letters, and I can write my name. You want to see?"

"You know I do."

I set her on her feet, and Frankie was rounding the couch and flying down the hall before I closed the door. Rynna was bouncing Ryland by the dining room table, looking a little frazzled, the tiny baby boy facing out and releasing all these tiny, gurgled cries as he attempted to stuff his whole fist into his mouth.

Rex was in the kitchen making dinner.

I grinned at him. "About time you made yourself useful . . . what are you making me? Just don't burn it because it actually smells delicious. I mean, seriously, what miracle is this? Last time I checked, your specialty was pizza from a box."

He tossed me a middle finger with his hand still wrapped around the paring knife he was dicing potatoes with. "Don't even start, man. My family needs a good dinner, and the last thing my Rynna needs is to go worrying about making dinner after she's been taking care of the kids all day."

With an exaggerated sigh, she kissed the top of Ryland's head. "Who would have thought taking care of an infant would be a hundred times harder than running a diner all day? I'm not complaining, but I think I could sleep for a week straight. Thank God Nikki decided to take the general manager position. I don't even know what I'd do right now if I had to go in and oversee things."

Nikki hadn't been in love with her previous job and had jumped on the opportunity when Rynna had suggested she come work at Pepper's Pies.

Rynna knew she wouldn't be able to devote as much time to the diner once she had Ryland, and she wanted someone she could trust to handle the little diner that had been her dream, her grandmother's legacy.

It had been a good transition for both of them.

I approached her, dropped a kiss to her forehead, and ran a tender hand over Ryland's head. He leaned into it, the kid loving the contact, a sweet coo coming from his mouth. "No one until they're standing right in your shoes, that's who." I lifted my hands for Ryland. "Here, let me take him for a while. Looks like you could use a break."

She beamed at me as she shifted Ryland into my hold. "You're a godsend."

I quirked a brow. "You mean a god?"

"You wish, asshole." Rex was eager to supply. "And it's about time you showed up for Uncle duty."

"Hey, I've been busy, man." I held Ryland's teeny body against my chest, bouncing him lightly.

Affection went sliding through my veins. Was crazy how much I adored these kids.

"Oh, I bet you've been busy. What's her name?"

"Is there ever a name?"

Of course, there was one dancing at the tip of my tongue.

Hope.

What the hell it was about her, I didn't know. But all day, she'd been taking possession of my thoughts without my permission, my mind continually traipsing back to the heat lighting on her cheeks, that sweet shyness I wanted to dip my fingers into, desperate for a taste.

Rynna grinned at me as she headed into the kitchen to help Rex. "Oh, I'm sure there are plenty of names. You just forget them before you're on to the next one." She washed her hands, looking back at me. "And that baby looks good on you, by the way."

"Only because I get to give him back when he starts crying." I shot her a wink. "And, well, I always look good. It's kind of impossible for me not to."

Rex's expression was nothing but adoration when he gazed over at her, amusement playing around his mouth. "Can you believe this guy?"

She giggled with a shake of her head. "He's your friend. You're the one who decided to keep him around all this time."

"Hey," I drew out, fighting the laughter. "Don't be knocking my presence. Doubt very much the two of you would be together if it weren't for me. I was the one who knocked some sense into his stubborn ass."

Rynna pushed up onto her toes and pressed a kiss to Rex's jaw, her voice not meant for me. "I'm pretty sure he would have found me either way. Some people are just meant to be."

She almost did a double take when she looked back and found Ryland was already conked out in my arms.

"Oh, make it look easy, why don't you? He hasn't slept a wink all day."

"Magic touch right here. Kids love me, and you know I love them." My brow lifted. "Just as long as they aren't mine."

Frankie was suddenly right there at my feet, a box of fat markers in one hand and a frilly pink notebook in the other. A pout pursed her lips. "Uncle Kale, you said I was always gonna be your favorite girl. That means I belongs to you. You don't want to keep me anymore?"

I looked down at the adorable thing, who was growing way too fast, her sweet lisp starting to sort itself out but still evident enough to fist me right in the heart with the sweetness of it.

Swore, the kid had me wrapped around her little finger.

Rex was grinning as he was rinsing the potatoes in the sink. "Now tell me how your gonna dig yourself out of that one, my friend. And don't you dare go breaking my Frankie Leigh's heart."

"Never."

I shifted Ryland into the crook of one arm so I could rustle my fingers through Frankie's hair. "What are you talking about, Sweet Pea Frankie Leigh? Do you have beans growing in your ears? Here, quick, let me take you to the office so I can look in there, because you heard me all wrong. I said you're always going to be mine, not *as long as they're not mine.*"

Giggling, she wiggled all over the place. "I don't gots any beans growing in my ears, Uncle. I think you're teasin' me."

"And you know I only tease my favorite, favorite girls, right?"

"Uh-huh," she agreed as she scrambled onto a dining room chair so she could show me how she wrote her name, completely assuaged, not another thought about me leaving her behind.

"Smooth," Rex said with a shake of his head, dumping the diced potatoes into a pot of boiling water.

"Skilled," I tossed back.

"So, tell us about this new position. What did you think?" Rynna's demeanor had shifted, all concern as she looked back at me.

I roughed a hand through my hair.

Didn't want to tell her I had to come straight from the office because I needed reassurance that Ryland and Frankie were just fine. That something horrible hadn't crept up in the time I'd been away.

It was funny because, for years, I'd given Rex crap about being too overprotective of Frankie, always rushing her to the ER whenever the slightest things went wrong. I'd continually made light of it and razzed him that he was ridiculous.

Truth was, I'd been in knots while I'd waited for them to arrive, terrified something was seriously wrong.

I saw so much bad shit come through the ER doors every single day.

Had experienced it firsthand.

Had felt death's claws tear right through my skin to rip my life apart.

Like it was teaching me a lesson.

But the last thing I wanted was to make him worry more than he already had been. He was coming to me for reassurance, not to be launched into some kind of tailspin.

So, I took it upon myself to make sure she was healthy, trying to take some of the burden from his shoulders. I would do the same with Ryland.

I pushed out a sigh, trying to find the right words. "It was amazing. Hard and exhausting and trying, and still the best thing I've ever done."

"It must be incredibly difficult . . . seeing all those sick children. Caring for them. Worrying about them. And still knowing it's worth it, making the difference that you do."

I guessed Rynna got it anyway.

Made me so happy she'd found Rex and he'd found her, two of them needing each other more than anyone I knew. She was right. Some people were just meant to be.

"You're right. It is really difficult. Only thing I can hope for is that I really do make a difference."

Rynna looked at me seriously. "Kale . . . of course, you make a difference. I think probably more than you know." She walked up to me and touched her baby's cheek as her eyes flicked between me and him. "I just want you to promise me one thing . . . no matter what you see or what you deal with . . . don't lose you. Don't let it break you. And don't ever, ever give up on hope. Because it's always there, no matter how dismal things might seem."

Emotion clutched my chest, that terror that I was right there, at the ledge I'd stumble and fall over.

Fail all over again.

I refused to ever repeat it. Because I knew that this time there was no chance I'd be able to get back up.

I forced a smirk. "Come now, Rynna, do I really look like I could be broken?"

Her expression said *yes, you do*. But Frankie Leigh was calling my name, and I was shifting my attention, her little hand scribbling across the page. "That's 'cause you're a superhero, too, rights, Uncle Kale? Wonder Woman and Cap'in 'merica, right? We're the bestest team."

"Heck yes, we're the best team."

And this little team was all I was ever going to need.

Seven

Hope

The door swung open for what had to have been the thousandth time that morning.

But this time . . . this time, my entire being took note.

The breath burst from my lungs in a rattled gasp, and my feet wanted to give out from under me.

It sent my heart taking off at a sprint, banging around in the confines of my chest like a big spoon whipping up something sweet in a metal bowl.

Jarring and vibrating.

Penetrating all the way to the bone.

I tried to swallow around it and focus my attention on where it should be—the customers lined up at the front register during our normal morning rush. Today it seemed as if the traffic had been multiplied.

Jenna, Claire, and I had been hustling nonstop, trying to keep up with the demand.

But as soon as he walked in the door, it seemed impossible. All my eyes wanted to do was get lost in the sight set in front of me.

Kale was back.

All tall, lean body and easy, casual way. His grin was pure confidence as he strode through the door. His crop of blond hair burned like white fire in the rays of bright morning sun that poured in from above him.

Lighting him up. Making him glow.

As if the light couldn't help but be drawn to him, too.

I blinked through the daze, scolding myself under my breath as I finished swirling the whipped cream on the café mocha I'd been making, quick to move on to the plain coffee that went with the order.

I was being ridiculous, wondering if he was back for any other reason than coffee. He'd told me he had started a job just down the street. It wasn't as if him swinging by would be out of his way.

Still, three days had passed.

Three days, and I'd begun to think I would never see him again. Oh, I knew the overwhelming sense of disappointment that thought left me with made me a fool.

Just asking for trouble when every time the bell jingled over the door, I looked that way.

Like a beggar who was looking for anything to hope for.

Even if it was just a spec of his time.

A moment in his day.

Because I'd forgotten what it was like to feel this way.

To have my tummy turn and my pulse race. To have someone make me toss sleeplessly in my bed, imagining what it would be like to be touched by those big hands.

Adored.

And there he was.

His fancy suit from the other morning had been ditched in favor of a crisp, white button-up, dark gray dress pants tailored to fit and accentuate every immaculate inch of his body.

A shiver traveled my spine, spreading out, drenching every cell.

No man should be that gorgeous. Or that sexy.

It was just unfair.

He shot me a knowing smirk.

I jerked, realizing I was just standing there.

Staring.

I hopped back a step to keep from spilling a cup of coffee straight down my blouse when I realized the cup I was holding had tipped to the side. The splash I'd dodged hit the floor.

"Sorry about that," I muttered to the customer, turning to make a new coffee.

From the corner of my eye, I kept watching him, the way he began to meander around my shop rather than get into line.

His fingers drummed over the displays, as if he couldn't fully appreciate something without touching it. The imported boxes of teas and packaged goods in gift baskets wrapped in clear cellophane and big bows.

The large cups with inspiring quotes.

Tumblers with the store's logo.

Not that I was paying attention or anything.

Jenna squeezed by to get to the latte machine. She elbowed me in the ribs when she did, and her voice lowered conspiratorially. "Looks like someone has a visitor. Look at all that deliciousness standing right there. Told you he'd be back."

"I'm sure he's just here for a cup of coffee," I defended under my breath, facing away as I filled a medium cup with hazelnut.

"Well, you just keep on thinking that, Harley Hope, but that man right over there is thinking about you naked."

I swatted her. "Stop it."

Her eyes went wide with innocence as she dipped into the case to get two pumpkin muffins. "What?"

"You know what. I swear that you are nothin' but a pain in my ass."

"What you need is a good kick in the ass."

"I need nothing of the sort," I mumbled, lidding the three cups. I turned and slid them to the customer waiting for her order. "There you are. Have a great day."

She uttered a thank you and moved on her way. I was quick to fill the next customer's order, trying not to pay attention to Kale, who'd taken note of the big lollipops displayed in a pink wooden decorative box. To keep them all standing, the sticks had been stuck in Styrofoam, which had been hidden by the fake moss that covered it.

So what if Pinterest had become my lover, keeping me company in the lonely nights.

From the side, I took in the way his blue, blue eyes narrowed in curiosity, the way he pulled one out.

I bit down on my lip.

Damn it.

Normally, I wanted everyone to buy them up. But there was something about the man holding one that made a rush of unease slip and slide through my body. That achy place throbbing and needy.

As if he was holding a piece of me that was sacred.

All of them were the same. Colorful swirls with a clear wrapper and a white label on the front.

It was just my luck Jenna noticed at the second the last customer I'd been helping walked away with his coffee and half dozen muffins.

"Those are for charity," she called over the counter.

Cocking his head, he studied the label before he looked up at me. "Anything's possible if you have a lick of hope?"

He asked it like a question.

As if he were wondering if I really believed it.

Heat flooded my cheeks. The uneasy kind. The kind that had me shifting on my feet.

"Yep," Jenna said. "Hope here makes those herself. Every last cent goes to charity."

For a moment, he stared at me, something soft fluttering around his lush mouth before he tucked the stick back into the Styrofoam.

I didn't know if I was relieved or disappointed.

That was right before he scooped the entire box up under his arm. "In that case, I'll take them all. I think I have an idea of where I can put them to good use."

"If you're taking them all, you should come back and help Hope here make some more. You know . . . philanthropy . . . not at all because you want to hang out with her or anything."

I sent a glare at Jenna. *What are you thinking?*

What? She mouthed back with an innocent shrug.

If she *what-ed* me one more time when she knew exactly what she was doing, I was going to strangle her.

I would have right then, but I was too busy trying not to shake when Kale approached the counter, filling the air the way he did.

All potent, persuasive power.

The space between us growing so thick it made it difficult to draw a full breath.

"Why do you need all those, anyway?" I all but demanded, feeling out of sorts. Hopeful and eager and awed, and that made me scared.

Because him standing there with those lollipops made me feel as if he were stepping into an area that was off limits.

As if he'd dipped his fingers in the places of my life that I protected most.

Touching on the things that were most important to me when he couldn't come close to understanding.

"Maybe I just have a sweet tooth."

"You don't be careful, and you're going to rot them all out." I tried to form it a tease, but it came out breathy and almost pleading. He had no idea just what that box tucked to his side meant to me.

He smiled a smile that pierced me straight through my center.

An arrow that nearly dropped me to my knees.

Because that knowing kindness was back. The one that made me feel vulnerable and exposed.

"I think I'll take my chances," he said.

I sucked in a breath. Set off kilter. Lightheaded. "All right, then. Is there anything else I can get for you?"

"Large regular coffee."

I swiveled away, going for the coffee urns, thankful for the moment of reprieve. Looking at him was making it impossible to stop the foolish notions from racing through my brain, especially when I couldn't help but wonder if maybe he were different.

If there were something intrinsically good at the heart of him.

Caring and . . . and . . .

Giving.

My hands were shaking as I filled the cup, my smile probably more so when I turned back to him and slid it across the counter. He already had his wallet out, pulling out a stack of crisp one-hundred-dollar bills.

He set them on the counter.

Another tremble.

"What is this?"

"For charity." The depths of those turquoise eyes deepened in a way that promised he saw too much.

Part of me wanted to refuse because something about it made me feel weak.

But the money wasn't for me.

"Thank you," I offered. "That's really generous of you."

He took out a five and placed it on top of the other bills, tapping it as he let that grin ride to his lips, which were getting more and more difficult not to reach out and trace. "And that's for the coffee, which is delicious, by the way. Though, not nearly as delicious as the cupcake."

"I'm glad you enjoyed it," I told him. A rush of that shyness pulled fast, getting all mixed up with the crazy desire that thrummed through my body.

It seemed unfair attraction was always immediate.

Natural.

Easy.

It was what came after that left your world in shambles. Battered walls and broken windows, your house falling down around you. It was taking everything I had to rebuild mine—to reconstruct and restore and revitalize. I had worked tirelessly to fill the spots that had been dredged out by cruelty, and I couldn't falter or misstep.

He hesitated for a second, as if he were struggling to find what he wanted to say, before all that easy confidence came riding back. "Thanks, Shortcake."

A short laugh escaped, and I shook my head, unable to keep up with him. "You're absurd."

"And here I'd thought you'd implied I was cocky?"

"That, too."

He laughed, though, the sound was soft. So different from the guy I'd thought I'd first run into at the bar on Friday night. This man revealing something good every time he invaded my space, making me want to dig deeper, see more.

I was drawn to him in a way I couldn't fathom.

He blinked at me, and I leaned forward, drawn, unable to stop myself from reacting to his presence.

Then he shook his head as if he needed to shake himself out of a dream.

He jarred me out of my own.

A smile was pinned on his lips, and he hiked the box up a little higher on his side, grabbing his cup and lifting it in the air. "I hope you have a great day, Hope."

I sucked in my bottom lip. "You, too."

I watched him stride across the café toward the door, hating the way everything tightened when he did. The way something like regret rippled through the atmosphere when he pulled open the door.

His or mine, I wasn't sure.

But it was there.

Heavy.

Pressing on my heart.

I couldn't stop from watching him through the big windows as he started down the sidewalk, the man a scorching silhouette in the blaze of the day.

But he didn't climb into his car that was parked at the curb.

He began to pace.

A pace that looked like indecision and turmoil.

Back and forth right on the other side of the window.

His head tilted back toward the sky, as if it might hold an answer, before he set his coffee and the lollipops down on one of the open tables, dug in his pocket, and pulled out his phone.

"You're an idiot," Jenna hissed from beside me. "That guy likes you, and he's literally the hottest thing to ever walk through that door. And he bought All. The. Lollipops."

Maybe that was part of the problem.

"I don't get simple," was my response.

"What if he doesn't want simple?"

I would have answered her, told her that in the end, everyone did. They always took the easy way out when the going got tough. Except the café phone rang. I moved for it, thankful for the distraction, something to keep my feet from rounding the counter and running after him.

Because what the hell would that accomplish?

I lifted the receiver from the wall and pressed it to my ear. "A Drop of Hope. How can I help you?"

"Go out with me." His gravelly voice echoed through the line.

A surprised sound whispered from my lips, and Kale was suddenly at the window, his face pressed to the glass, hand shading his eyes so he could see inside. His other hand was holding his cell to his ear. "Go out with me, Hope. Just dinner. Because I can't fucking stop thinking about you. Couldn't after I saw you the first time at Olive's on Friday night. It only got worse after I saw you here Monday morning. I don't know what it is about you . . . but there's something that makes me want to figure it out."

My breaths were hard pants, my heart a jackhammer in my chest. "My life's complicated, Kale."

"And I'm offering you a night away from it. Don't you at least deserve that?"

I wanted to beg him, what then? What happened if I fell for that smirk and that smile and those tender eyes?

Fast and hard?

I could already feel myself slipping. My heart tipping his direction.

What happened if Dane found out?

What then?

But I was so tired of that man controlling every aspect of my life, even after I'd made the decision to cut him from it.

Jenna was suddenly in my face, gripping my wrist, her voice a hard, demanding whisper. "You tell him yes, Harley Hope. Don't you dare hang up that phone without telling him yes. You deserve something just for you. Just for you."

Indecision swarmed, questions and worries and want.

But it was the feeling balled in my stomach that trembled the floor beneath my feet.

The urge to reach out and touch on the beauty and tenderness that swam in his eyes. To discover if it was real.

The throb of desire that begged, a whisper in my ear that goaded—*just one touch.*

The hidden need to feel those hands skating my flesh.

I guessed I'd thought I'd never crave that again, my life fulfilled, my spirit content in knowing I was living for what was right.

Jenna squeezed tighter, my bossy best friend mouthing the word as she angled her head with the demand. "Say yes."

It was at the same second Kale fisted his hand against the window, his forehead rocking against it, his own words a petition. "Come on, Hope. Say yes. I promise you, you won't regret it."

A hint of playfulness came out on the last, but it didn't matter, because I was agreeing.

"Yes," I murmured, wanting to feel something good even though I wasn't so much a fool that I didn't know I was making a mistake. That in the end, it wouldn't hurt.

Because it already felt as if *this* mattered.

As if *he* mattered.

"Okay. One night. Just dinner," I reiterated.

He breathed out in what sounded like relief. "Just dinner."

Kale

I fumbled for my phone when it dinged in my pocket. "Shit," I muttered when the damn thing nearly slipped from my hand.

Didn't help that I was all kinds of overeager and terrified like some kind of pathetic fucker begging for a bone.

That was what I'd become.

Pathetic.

Because my stomach was tied up in knots, anxiety lining my insides, nerves rattling through me like an earthquake that hit from out of nowhere in the middle of the night.

The last two days had been spent wondering what in the hell it was I thought I was doing.

What I thought I expected to pull off here.

I was so far out of bounds that I had not a single clue where I stood.

Standing around, waiting on a girl.

Wanting her.

Both her sweet little body and her sweet little mind, wondering what it was that made her reserved and shut off and shy.

What ignited that fire that so clearly burned underneath.

What brought the flush riding to her cheeks.

Why those places that had gone dormant inside me found it fit to light up when we got in the same room.

It fucking terrified me that they did. That I felt something I was sure had died with *her.* Something that had been obliterated into nonexistence that suddenly had a flicker of a heartbeat again.

Was it worth it?

I sucked in a breath. I didn't fucking know. But there I stood anyway, waiting, praying that she showed.

The guys were going to have a field day if they found out where I was tonight.

On a motherfucking date.

It wasn't even as a consequence of Nikki drinking my ass under the table.

No bets or wagers other than the one I'd lobbied against myself.

I mean, I'd made it all the way out the door of A Drop of Hope without letting the words that had been begging on my tongue free.

All the way out the damned door.

All I'd had to do was get in my car, drive away, and never look back.

Then, like a fool, I'd looked up the café on my phone.

Brilliant, right?

Taking the pussy's way out. The whole time I'd been muttering a million warnings under my breath. None of which had been heeded. I'd just gone right on ahead and pressed send.

Guessed maybe my subconscious had gone for the call since I couldn't take another rejection delivered to my face.

This girl had shot me down at every turn, and each time, I got up for another round. Something feeling like maybe she needed me to fight for her.

Like I said.

Pathetic.

Guts in knots, I read the message.

Hope: Sorry, I got hung up. I'm on my way. Be there in five.

I breathed out in relief.

I'd been doing my best not to lose my cool where I stood outside the chic restaurant on the sidewalk on Macaber. The street was all lit up on a Friday night, people coming and going, their laughter rippling through the warm Alabama air.

Waiting.

She'd insisted on taking an Uber and meeting me here. That this was just dinner. Nothing more.

Ironic.

Considering all I wanted was more.

I tapped out a quick reply.

Me: No worries. I just got here.

What bullshit. I'd been here for fifteen minutes.

This girl had me feeling outside myself.

Interested and intrigued.

Wanting to fist my hands in that lush, red hair, sure it'd be as soft as it looked.

Wondering if she tasted like strawberries and cream and all things sweet, the way I'd put down bets that she did.

Shortcake.

Couldn't help but imagine her in the shadows of my room. Wild. That sexy modesty evaporated as she begged my name.

The craziest part was I thought I might just settle for seeing that shy smile light her face.

I drove all my fingers into my hair.

Fuck.

She really had gotten under my skin.

Five minutes later, a black car pulled to the curb. I didn't know what it was, but the way my heart thundered and boomed, sped with an unsteady beat, told me it was her before the car came to a full stop.

I pasted on a confident smile, strolled that way with a hand in my pocket, and opened the back door to help her out.

I dipped down, and I swore my thundering heart came to a full stop in my chest.

On all things holy.

What the hell did she think she was doing to me?

My head spun with a rush of uncontained lust.

Fast and hot and hard.

Sloshing through my blood like an out-of-control demand.

Those knots in my stomach notched tighter, a constricting band around my chest, the easy air suddenly thick.

Heady.

Rippling with need.

That dress.

She was wearing this black dress that was super short, the backseat full of nothing but silky, toned legs. My throat went dry when I noticed the pair of black heels wrapped around her ankles.

So damned high.

So fucking hot.

Who was this girl? Because she was peeking out at me, biting back a smile that danced between shy and seductive when I reached down and offered her my hand.

A streak of lightning bolted up my arm when she accepted it.

Motherfucker.

What was happening to me?

She shifted to slide out, that fall of red cascading down around one shoulder.

I somehow managed to shoot her a grin as I tugged her toward me.

She stumbled to a stop two inches away. A gush of surprise heaved from her lungs, our bodies close to touching, the space between crackling, no doubt two seconds from catching fire.

Clearly, she wasn't anticipating me being so forward.

But if this was the only night she was giving me, I was going to make it count.

Those green eyes blinked up at me. I swore they were the same color as the moss that lined the bank of the river, deep and brimming with life.

"Hi," I told her, a smirk flitting across my mouth.

"Hi," she whispered back between her plush lips that were coated in only shiny gloss. "I'm so sorry I'm late."

For a beat, she took in our surroundings as if she was looking for someone, but then she finally turned back to face me. Her expression now held something that almost looked like worry or fear that threatened to break loose. She beat it back—buried it—and smiled at me in a way that moved through me like warmth.

"I really am sorry I'm late," she said again.

I kept her fingertips threaded with mine, unwilling to give up the connection, having the urge to tell her to trust me. That whatever the fuck was going on, she could *trust* me.

But I didn't know how to make that promise, so I tucked it all down and focused on the kind of night I had promised her.

One that was only about her. Making her feel good.

"It's fine." I arched a brow, sending her a look that told her how bad I was dying to eat her up. "Though, I thought I was going to have to track you down because you were going to bail on me. I don't think my fragile ego could take it."

A bit of that fire lit on her face.

God.

I liked that, too.

The feisty redhead ready to spar.

"You were going to track me down, huh? Tell me you aren't really stalking me." Her voice had dropped an octave, dripping with excitement and nervousness, the words a low, throaty tease.

"Is it working?"

She chewed at her bottom lip, and it took about all I had not to reach out and brush back the lock of hair that swooped across her forehead, obscuring one of her eyes. "I'm here, aren't I? Against my better judgment."

"Why's that?" I played it off as unimportant. Like I wasn't wanting to dig deeper into her. To discover all those things I couldn't get off my mind.

The low laughter that rolled from her was completely at her expense. "I already told you my life is complicated . . . hence my being late."

"Are you going to tell me about that?"

For a flash, her gaze went to the far side of the street, her profile soft beneath the glow of the strands of lights strung up overhead. Face innocent while her body looked like nothing but sin wrapped in this slinky black dress.

She was a walking contradiction.

The perfect kind of fantasy.

Sexy and soft.

Hot and sweet.

She looked back at me with a silent plea riding her expression. "Do you remember what you asked me? You asked me for one night. And this night is for me."

She swallowed and averted her gaze again, like she was gathering her thoughts, and then she set the power of those green eyes back on me. "So, no, I'm not. I just . . . want to enjoy myself and not think about anything else except for the fact I'm out with a man. A man I can't help but want to spend more time with. That, for one night, I get to experience it. Can we do that?"

Unable to stop myself, I reached out and ran the pad of my thumb across her chin, right over the cute little dimple I kind of wanted to lick.

She shivered at my touch.

"Yeah, Shortcake, we can definitely do that." A smirk kicked up at the corner of my mouth. "You want a good time? Then I promise to show you a good time."

There was almost a warning behind it. The caution that my body was already way ahead of us.

Imagining her against the wall, that short, short skirt hiked around her hips.

Back at my loft, the girl writhing on my bed.

Or maybe it was just a promise.

She must have seen every single salacious thought play out in my eyes. Because she chuckled this sound that shot straight to my dick, a hand flattening on my chest. "Oh, back it up, Cowboy. We aren't gonna be having that *good* of a time."

Grabbing that hand, I kissed across her knuckles. "Are you sure about that? And cowboy?" My brow arched. "Come on now, do I look like a cowboy to you?"

She laughed a little deeper, her expression going light, sparking with the freedom of the moment. "Mm-hmm . . . I am most definitely certain of that."

Her tongue darted out to lick across those glossy lips, the girl cocking her head with a type of mischief I hadn't recognized in her before.

Lust knotted my insides.

"Such a bad boy. I knew it back at the bar, the trouble written all over you. And don't you know all boys from Alabama are cowboys at heart? You can dress yourself up like a city boy, but it doesn't change a thing."

A chuckle rippled free. "Actually, I was thinking more like knight in shining armor . . . you know, since I am rescuing you tonight."

"Thinking awfully highly of yourself, are you?"

I guided her into the restaurant ahead of me, mouth dipping down to brush across the shell of her ear as she walked through the door. "Hell yeah. As long as that means I get to make you my princess."

She glanced at me from over her shoulder as we stepped into the restaurant. "My hero."

She delivered it with a tone of flirtatious sarcasm.

Having no clue that statement sliced through me.

A double-edged sword.

Did my best not to reveal the cringe that jolted through me and told myself I wasn't going there tonight.

Because if this was the only one we had, I was going to make it count.

nine

Hope

Chills skated my spine, and I shivered with the slow release of his breath that washed across my jaw when he leaned in.

The heat of him took me whole.

Overpowering.

Too much and somehow not nearly enough.

"How was your dinner?" he asked.

The man was conflict.

Persuasion and dominance and sex.

Kind and perceptive and intuitive.

I didn't know what side of him was more dangerous. The only thing I knew was I could barely breathe when he set one of those big hands on my knee underneath the table.

All night, he'd been touching me. Just tiny brushes and caresses.

Flutters of fingertips that sped my heart in a needy kind of anticipation.

It was as if he were issuing little promises—assuring me I was interesting and beautiful and he wouldn't want to be anywhere else.

I took a sip of red wine, still unable to fathom I was actually sitting across from this man. "It was wonderful. I think I've had more fun tonight than I have in a long, long time. I wish I could tell you how much that means to me."

His brow quirked. "Says the girl who basically made me beg to get a little bit of time with her."

Thank God it was dim where we were seated at the back of the upscale restaurant. Because I could feel the heat rise to my cheeks. The way he managed to slip right under my skin with that easy smile, the man nothing but seduction where he casually rested in the high-backed upholstered chair.

One big hand was wrapped around the crystal tumbler he'd been sipping from all evening, the other still caressing my knee.

Back and forth.

Back and forth.

Embers flickering to life in the deepest parts of me.

I wondered if he had the first clue each stroke wound me higher. Higher and higher until it felt as if I was floating with the stars. Or maybe he knew exactly what he was doing.

"I guess sometimes we all need a little push," I admitted quietly.

His eyes crinkled at the corners. "Well, I guess it should be me saying thank you for giving you that little push."

I tucked my bottom lip between my teeth, trying to figure out what to do with the magnitude of this man. "I'm just glad you were the one to do it."

He sat back a little, head tilting to the side as he offered a casual expression. "What about last Friday? It seems like your friends don't hesitate to have a little fun."

I laughed lightly. "No, they definitely don't. Jenna is always trying to drag me out."

"Why don't you let her?"

It was the first time Kale had let our conversation traipse in the direction of personal. His eyes narrowed, studying me with a new kind of severity through the flicker of the candles that lapped and licked at the center of the table.

It cast that strong jaw in shadows, that turquoise gaze glinting in the flame.

During dinner, we'd kept to safe subjects. Reminiscing about growing up. My life in Texas. His in Gingham Lakes. I told him how I'd been a total drama geek in high school, living my life for the next play, while he'd laughed the sweetest kind of laugh and told me nerds were always the best before he'd gone on to tell me he'd won first place in the Alabama State Science Fair all four years of high school.

I guessed nerds really were the best.

Now, beneath his scrutiny, I felt compelled.

I felt looser and freer than I had felt in so long. Before I could stop it, I was pushing right past the promise I'd made to myself that tonight was just for me and I was leaving everything else behind.

The words dropped like a bomb from my mouth, my frustration and bitterness bleeding free.

"I doubt very much my husband would approve of that."

I watched as the admission penetrated Kale.

As he jerked back as if he'd been kicked in the gut.

The breath knocked out of him as he resituated everything he'd thought about me in his head. Eyes going wide before his jaw clenched tight. Slowly coming to the realization that when I told him my life was complicated, I meant it.

My life was in transition, a hard, painful transition. In the end, it would be the best decision I'd ever made. I just had to make it through to the other side.

Where I was didn't change the reality of what was happening right then, though. It didn't change the fight I had ahead of me.

I cleared my throat, knowing I'd made a mistake by telling him that way.

That was the problem when you started to feel comfortable with someone. When you started *liking* them in a way you couldn't allow. You started telling them things you shouldn't trust them with. Letting them go deeper than you should.

I tossed my fabric napkin on the table. "We should probably get going. It's getting late. The day starts really early for me."

It was stupid of me to even think this was okay when I had no idea the lengths Dane might go to. I searched for a breath, feeling like a complete fool. All I'd wanted was one night. I should have known not even that was possible.

I pushed from the small, round table, giving him my back, unable to face him.

Not after I'd sent our night spiraling.

Ruining it with just a dash of the truth.

Warily, Kale stood, and I could sense him slowly signing the credit card receipt and then tucking the card back in his wallet.

He was probably realizing that I was no princess just as I was realizing I was an idiot to hope for a knight.

Then his hand was back on the small of my back, stealing my breath, and a tiny whimper was breaking free from my lips. His words were uttered so close to my ear that I couldn't help but cling to the security of his hold.

"Let's get you out of here," he said.

He wound us back through the lavish restaurant and out onto the sidewalk. Crowds moved around us, people darting here and there to enjoy their Friday nights, laughter ringing on the Alabama night.

I inhaled, filling myself with the calming, familiar scents of this city, the river and the trees and the thick, intoxicating scent of honeysuckle that rode the air on provocative waves.

But I guessed it was the sheer potency of him that made me feel lightheaded—drunk—when he shocked me by wrapping an arm around my waist and tugging me close.

Citrus and spice and the lingering scent of whiskey.

His lips were a murmur against my temple. "I know you're getting ready to run from me, Hope. Don't. Stay with me . . . just a little while more."

I could feel the confusion pressed into the lines of my forehead when I pulled back to look at his face. And the man . . . the man had let that knowing smirk climb to his pretty, pretty face.

My knees nearly gave when he threaded his fingers back through mine.

Tenderly.

Possessively.

"Come," he said, a glint in his eyes before he darted us across the busy street. A surprised gasp ripped from my lungs, and I struggled to keep up on my too-high heels as he hauled me in the direction of the bar on the opposite corner.

The same bar our paths had first crossed just last week that now felt as if they were being impossibly tangled together.

"What are you doing?" I demanded, the words a breathy plea.

Hope and reservation.

A giddy giggle rolled out right behind it.

Because this man made me feel so free. Unshackled after years of being chained. Years of trying to change our situation and not knowing the right answer to finding that solution. Of course, my conclusion had been swift and without question that day one year ago when I'd packed our things and left.

There are just times in your life when things become crystal clear and you know the path you need to run down, the situation you need to run away from.

Jerking open the door, Kale sent me one of those smiles that blasted through me with the power of a hurricane.

Annihilating.

Exhilarating.

Because when Kale Bryant looked at me that way?

I felt as if I were the only person in the world.

"I promised you a good time, and you're gonna get a good time."

He pulled me into the intensity of the bar. People were packed wall to wall, voices lifted above the mayhem, the vibe so much rowdier than it'd been last Friday.

Tonight, the band was the focus, commanding the attention with their distinct country flare. Tables were pushed back out of the way to create a makeshift dance floor beneath the risers that had been brought in to create an elevated stage.

My heart rate latched on to the intensity. An erratic thrum, thrum, thrum that hammered and beat.

Kale ran his hand down the center of my back.

Chills.

Fire.

Heat.

His palm hit home right above my bottom, his pinky finger just skating into the vicinity.

Oh God.

Maybe it had been too long.

Because that simple touch had me flying.

Wanting things I knew full well I shouldn't. Not when so many things were still left unresolved.

His mouth landed at the edge of my ear, voice lifted to be heard above the chaos. "Carolina George is playing tonight . . . they travel around the South, hitting cool venues and dives alike. Ollie, the owner here? He and the guitarist go way back, so once a month, they come to play here. People flock through that door in droves whenever they do."

"I take it you're a fan?"

He glanced around with a grin. "Think it's safe to say just about everyone around here is. Not a whole lot not to like."

I patted his chest, feeling bolder in his presence. "Told you all Alabama boys are cowboys at heart."

He pulled me closer. "Knight. Don't forget it."

"Whatever you say, Cowboy."

Carolina George's singer was this stunning, dainty creature, who belted out her song at the microphone. Her face was the perfect match to her gorgeous, mesmerizing voice.

It vibrated through the speakers, somehow both sultry and upbeat as it kept time with the quick rhythm that pounded from the drums.

In perfect harmony with the guitar that strummed at her side.

Clearly, it was the jaw-dropping man playing that guitar that had brought a herd of women squealing to the foot of the elevated stage.

I could feel Kale's playful smile when he saw me gawking. "Now, don't go getting any ideas. Rick seems to be a little popular with the ladies. Don't understand what they see in him, actually, when they could be looking at me."

There it was. That cocky arrogance the man wore so well, the words nothing but a tease that oozed from his mouth, which was still close to my ear.

Inching back a fraction, I stared up at his face. Because while I understood Rick's appeal, Kale was the only one I wanted to be looking at. "You don't have a thing to worry about. I'm a one-man kind of girl."

I tried to make it come out light.

Playful.

But those blue eyes saw straight through me, glinting and sparking in the hazy glow of the bulbs that hung from the rafters. Searching me for the answer he so clearly wanted to reach in and pluck out of me.

He set one of those big hands on the side of my face, cupping my jaw, making me shake. "You think I don't know that? That I can't see it shining out of you? What do you say we grab a drink, and you tell me a little about that?"

He said it as if he'd gone right ahead and sifted around inside me and found his answer anyway.

I gave him the smallest nod. "Okay."

He ran his thumb across my lips, and my tongue darted out without my permission, grabbing the tiniest taste of his flesh.

Oh God. How easily could I get wrapped up in this man?

I swore I could hear Kale's body hum with a tremor of desire. Swore I could feel every inch of him grow hard.

Ripples of lust vibrated.

They struck in the space between us, shockwaves of heat that blasted across my skin.

I jerked when a man was suddenly there, clapping him on the back.

A man who was shockingly good-looking in an intimidating, almost frightening way.

Where Kale was tall with lean, packed muscle, this guy was a monster. Nothing but hulking muscle covered in tattoos, a mess of designs running down across his arms and hands and fingers.

But his eyes. They were soft with some kind of unknown affection when they landed on Kale.

"Well, well, well, look who's here. Texted your ass fifteen times to try to convince you to show tonight, and each time you hit me back with some kind of lame excuse about being busy. And here you are. Not busy."

Kale cocked his head, halfway toward me, his voice a little hard. "Do I look *not* busy to you?"

Burly guy laughed, drummed his fingers across his lips. "Honestly not sure what you look like tonight."

There was some kind of conversation that transpired between the two of them, the giant of a man giving Kale a look as if he'd caught him stealing from the till and was going to offer him a prize for doing it.

Gaze traveling to me, the man's eyes lit in recognition. A victorious grin pulled to his bearded mouth.

He'd seen me before.

That night.

That was right.

I'd seen him, too.

Maybe I'd been too busy stealing peeks at the splendor of the man who right then was slipping his arm around my waist and tugging me tight against his body. But it dawned on me that this guy had been there, in Kale's group that had been huddled around a back table.

Kale roughed his free hand through his hair. "Hey, just be thankful I'm gracing you with my presence tonight. I did have better things to do than seeing your ugly face, but then I thought I'd introduce Hope here to one of the best bands in the South.”

"Pssh. Ugly? You only wish you could look as good as me.”

"Keep dreaming, man.”

The guy stretched out his tattooed arms. “I *am* a dream.”

I bit back a laugh, and Kale glanced down at me with a wide smile, gesturing to his friend.

"Hope, this is one of my best friends, Oliver, but everyone calls him Ollie. Ollie here is the owner of this fine establishment. Also, as you can see, a royal pain in my ass.”

Ollie’s brow lifted. “Pain in your ass? Says the guy who thinks he holds the answer to every last one of the world’s problems in the palm of his hands.”

Amusement danced across Ollie’s face when he turned his attention my way and hooked a thumb in Kale’s direction. “This asshole thinks he knows what’s best for everyone. Always tossing out advice like we actually wanna hear it. Singlehandedly going to save the world.”

Kale chuckled under his breath at the razzing and scratched nervously behind his ear.

Part of me wanted to ask more about the whole saving the world thing, considering tonight he’d set out to rescue me, but Kale was already tossing out a hand of entreaty between them.

Or so I’d thought.

"All right, all right, man. We get it. You think I’m the smartest guy around. No need to run it into the ground. It is kind of common knowledge.”

A scoff from Ollie. “Such a cocky bastard.”

"Says the guy who thinks he’s a dream.”

"Just keeping it real.”

"Right,” Kale drew out.

There was no holding the laughter back any longer, amusement rolling from my mouth when I finally pushed my hand toward Ollie, feeling more comfortable than I ever could have imagined. “It’s really nice to meet you, Ollie. My best friend tells me this is the place to be.”

He shook my hand, gentler than I would have imagined he could manage. “Ahh, she sounds like my kind of girl. And you have no idea just how great it is to meet you.”

Without releasing me, his eyes darted between the two of us. “So, tell me what you two were up to before you stepped into my house.”

"Dinner,” I immediately answered.

I had to wonder if it was the wrong one when Kale flinched.

Ollie’s eyebrows shot to the sky. “Is that so?” This was all directed at Kale.

Kale hesitated for a second before he met his friend’s demanding eye. “What, I can’t have dinner with the most gorgeous girl in Gingham Lakes?”

Puddles.

God, he left me a mess of gooey puddles right at his feet.

How did he manage that?

In disbelief, Ollie shook his head. "Nah, man, it's no problem. No problem at all. Just comes as a surprise someone as pretty as her would want to hang out with the likes of you."

"Jealousy." Kale muttered it under his breath before he looked at me, mischief playing all over his striking face. "Pure jealousy. Do you see the nonsense I have to deal with?"

But there was no tension between either of them, and Ollie was all smiles when he stepped back, placating hands set out in front of him. "Sorry to cut this short, but duty calls. Need to go check on the band and see if they need anything. Cece's manning the bar. She'll take good care of you."

"Shit," Kale mumbled, rubbing a hand over his face.

Kale started to lead me toward the bar.

"What was that all about?" I asked.

"Seems you and I are both stepping out of our comfort zones tonight. When's the last time you were on a date?" he basically shouted as he wove us through the horde of people jammed shoulder to shoulder.

"Um . . . I'm not sure you want the answer to the question."

"What if I wanted you to tell me anyway?"

"Then I'd tell you I was twenty-one and naïve."

The look he gave me from over his shoulder was one filled with guilt. Maybe regret. I didn't know. All I knew was it twisted around my chest like a band.

Constricting.

Cinching tight.

"What about you?" I hurried to say, still keeping up with him as we jostled through the crowd.

"Twenty-two." Somehow it sounded like a warning.

As if he were telling me something intrinsic about himself when I'd already made my own conclusions. That I saw this devastating kindness radiating from him, and it didn't have a thing to do with my naivety.

Without giving more, he angled his way right up to the front of the bar, and the woman behind the bar sauntered right up. She was tall and curvy and wearing a leather corset, tattoos covering the flesh exposed on her chest and shoulders and arms.

Oozing sex, she flashed him a red-lipped smile. "Kale Bryant. I've missed you. You haven't been around to visit me lately."

Her eyes dropped to me when she said it. Sizing me up.

Unease spun through my senses, and Kale squeezed my hand in reassurance. "Ah, Cece, I'm sure you've been keeping yourself plenty busy since the last time we ran into each other."

She threw her head back and laughed, smile widening with a wicked sort of glee. "Oh, you know I have, but none of these other boys are nearly as fun as you. But, clearly, you aren't here for me tonight. Tell me, what can I get you."

"I'll take my regular."

No. It shouldn't have. But that stung, too. And I knew I was getting myself in far too deep, getting attached the way I would. Wanting something that just wasn't there, wondering how it was possible I wanted to claim him when I'd been the one to tell him I could give him absolutely nothing more than just one night.

And a short one, at that.

Not the kind I was sure this beautiful man was accustomed to.

But then Kale was looking at me that way again. With that tender knowledge.

The man my conflict.

"What would you like, baby?"

Baby.

Damn him. Because I was nobody's *baby*. I had to be strong.

Fierce to face each day.

But the only thing I felt then was fiercely vulnerable against the word, the part of me that wanted to be taken care of for once, adored, begging for it to mean something.

"A red would be nice."

He looked back at her. "Get my girl some red."

Cece smirked, and I knew Kale was making a statement in front of her, and she seemed to mind less than I did when she poured his whiskey into an ice-filled tumbler and pushed it his way, when she jerked off the cork of the half-empty bottle of Freak Show and filled me a glass to the brim.

"Enjoy," she told me because, clearly, she already had.

"Thank you," I barely managed, taking a long sip while Kale tossed two twenties to the bar.

It was in that moment that I realized there was so little I knew about him.

Nothing, really.

As little as he knew about me.

And part of me wanted to push him away and keep him there while the other side was begging for him to turn around, face me, and let me see inside.

Because I kept getting this feeling that he might need me the way I was beginning to feel as if I needed him.

That maybe it was okay to lean on someone once in a while.

He grabbed my hand again, not saying a word as he led me back through the crowd. I expected him to find a table around the dance floor, but he bypassed it, heading toward the stairs that led to the second floor.

The voices filtering from above were raucous, even wilder than downstairs.

The reason for it quickly became evident as we mounted the last step and found the rows of pool tables lining the back wall, country boys and city boys alike out shooting a few rounds, beers flowing as freely as the laughter.

My mama had always told me boys would be boys. Didn't matter what fabric they were cut from.

She'd meant it as comfort.

After Dane, I'd taken it as a warning.

But I knew in my heart of hearts that no two were created alike. That no one person was a blanket statement. And someday . . . someday, I'd find the one who was created for me.

Kale didn't pause. He just led me to the far left where a wall of windows blocked off a balcony.

A sign was set on an easel in front of it declaring that the balcony was closed, but Kale wasn't deterred. He headed to the far end where the wall could be fully opened like an accordion, opened it just enough so we could slip through, and tugged me forward.

"Kale," I whispered almost desperately, feeling as if we were committing some terrible crime.

A deep, dark chuckle rolled from him, the man dripping sex when he turned to tug me through the crack he'd made. "Call it the perks of putting up with Ollie."

"You seem to have a lot of perks to offer."

The chuckle that rumbled from his chest should have been illegal. "You have no idea."

Those shivers were back, racing my flesh. There was no mistaking what was in his words.

The desire that soaked them. Drenched in gasoline. The mere brush of his hand a match.

That need was only stoked with each second that passed.

He shut and latched the partition, shutting us away from the rest of the world. Elevated above it.

The loud, boisterous voices had become a dull hum, just an echo of revelry that filtered through the glass panes. From below, I could feel the rumbling beat of the band, a vibration that traveled my legs and settled into my bones.

Only a trickle of the singer's mesmerizing voice made it through, carried on the breeze that blew through the quieted, secluded space.

I released an awed breath.

I felt as if I'd been removed. Lifted from the realities of the world and was watching it in slow motion.

The city set out below us, the river a black, twisty, shimmery rope where it snaked behind the buildings on the opposite side of the street.

I edged up to the railing, leaning against it as I took in the view. "It's gorgeous up here," I murmured, never more unsure of what I was doing than right then.

Because I could feel that power blister over me from behind.

Hot, heated energy.

Billowing in waves and wrapping me whole. His voice enveloped me from behind. "I'm sorry about what happened down there."

I almost laughed, and I bit my lip, gazing down at the couples that strolled along the sidewalk. "It's none of my business who you sleep with, Kale. We just had a dinner date. That was it. Remember?"

It felt like a lie forced through my teeth.

"Was it?" he asked, inching closer, making me shake. He ran a hand from my shoulder down my arm.

I blew out a quivering breath.

Complicated. I could feel it compounding, amplifying in the dark.

"Because every time I get around you, it feels like something else."

I gazed over at him for a long beat before I turned back to look over the twinkling lights. "My life is a mess right now, Kale."

"Are you going to tell me about him?" There was no missing the hardness that lined his words.

He eased around the side of me and leaned against the ornate metal railing. He lifted the crystal to his mouth, the amber liquid glinting in strands of lights that crisscrossed like a starry ceiling above.

But his face.

His face was cast in shadows, eyes dimmed but no less intense.

So magnetically beautiful.

I took a steeling sip of my wine and fought to keep the tremor from my voice "What do you want to know?"

"You said husband. Not ex-husband."

"I'm working on that." I shifted my gaze to study him, searching for an answer. "You knew I was married and you still brought me up here."

His head shook. "You're no cheater, Hope. I may not know you, but I do know that."

"No. I'm not," I admitted, not sure how much to give him. Because some things were sacred and should only be trusted in the hands of those who'd earned it.

"So . . . you're separated?" he hedged.

"Yes. For the last year."

I might as well have been seeking refuge in the middle of a battlefield. Because I could feel myself rushing out onto uneven, treacherous ground. Where each step was perilous. Landmines underfoot.

His comfort unsustainable. Fleeting. If I weren't careful, I'd be carving out a place for him, giving him those pieces that were sacred, the most important parts of me.

But giving him this little bit felt right.

I looked down at the red fluid dancing in my glass and wet my lips. "We're in the middle of a divorce. You could call it nasty. He . . ."

He's cruel and wicked. Appearances are the most important thing to him, but he's the one who's truly blind. The one who can't see the beauty right in front of him. The one who'd rejected the miraculous gift he'd been given.

A strained breath seeped free, and my voice lowered with the admission. "If he found out I was here with you . . ."

Anger bristled through the air. It strangled the words in my throat. I could feel it radiating from Kale. A severe kind of protectiveness I was unaccustomed to.

"Do you miss him?" he asked, something fierce barely checked when he issued the question.

Casting my attention to the street, I pushed out a weighted sigh and whispered, "No."

I lifted my gaze to the potency of his. "Is it wrong that I lost faith in him a long time ago?"

I'd wanted to believe. Believe he would come to his senses. That he was just in shock and dealing with the blow life had issued. That he would see perfection came in all forms.

But there were some lines that couldn't be uncrossed.

The smile that turned up the corner of Kale's mouth was soft. So soft, and I was trembling when he reached out and brushed his fingertips across my cheek. "No, Hope. It isn't wrong. Not if he can't see you for who you are."

I searched him in the flickers of light that danced against the darkness, illuminating the stunning lines of his face. "You don't even know me."

"Some things are just written on a person. You can't hide who you are, just the same as I can't hide who I am."

"And who is it you think you are?"

He sighed with my question, as if this time it was me who was getting too close. Digging in too deep.

Straight on, he met my gaze. "A guy who probably shouldn't be standing here doing this."

Grief.

I saw the stark flash of it take him whole, the impact of it so severe it jarred me back a step.

I blinked at him, trying to make sense of this complicated man and piece together his complex layers. "What does that mean?"

"It means I don't get close to women, Hope, and the only thing I fucking want right now is to get closer to you."

Everything inside me took flight.

Kale set his tumbler aside before taking my glass and placing it next to his. Then he pushed to his full height, towering over me, pinning me with the power of his presence.

He framed my face in both of his hands.

Gently.

Tenderly.

That conflict raged inside me.

The push and the pull.

Gravity.

"Is there any chance you'll take him back?"

"No." It flew from my mouth like a curse. "Never."

He stood there, staring down at me, rocking on his heels. "Good. Don't settle, Hope. Don't fucking ever settle."

"I won't," I promised, swallowing over the lump that had grown thick at the base of my throat.

His forehead dropped to mine, and I reached up, wrapping my hands around his wrists, the man still holding me while I clung to him.

His breaths mine. My heart reaching for his.

He groaned a needy sound before he tilted up my chin, searching as he stared down at me.

Slow . . . so slow . . . he leaned down and brushed his lips across mine.

Fire.

Everywhere.

Racing my flesh. Hijacking my veins.

His tongue tangled with mine. Stroking, dizzying as he edged me back, deeper into the darkness that lined the far recesses of the balcony.

His kiss no longer gentle.

An all-consuming demand.

My heart rate kicked, drumming wildly.

I swore his caught, too.

Because the very air around us started to thrum.

Heads spinning and spirits soaring.

I gasped when I was suddenly propped on the very edge of a small bistro table that was tucked against the far wall, Kale's fingers sinking into the outside of my thighs as he broke the kiss and dropped into a chair in front of me.

"Kale . . . what are you . . ."

I couldn't think, couldn't speak, not when he ran his thumbs over the flesh. "You said we had one night. I want to give you this. I want to make you feel good." His voice deepened, so low it sounded like a threat. "Is that what you want? For me to make you feel good? Tell me, Hope. Tell me you want this. Let me make you feel good."

My breaths came short, needy pants rising into the dense air, my heart manic where it pounded in my chest.

"I—"

He yanked me closer, my ass barely clinging to the edge. "Do you want me to touch you?" It was a demand.

Oh God.

There he was.

The confident, arrogant man.

Dangerous and perfect.

"Yes," I whimpered.

He caressed his hands over the tops of my thighs and down to my knees. He started gliding his palms back down the inside of my legs.

Spreading me wide.

My pulse thundered.

I wasn't sure I'd ever felt so exposed.

His thumbs traced along the inside edges of my underwear. Curling my fingers around the edge of the table, my head dropped back on a breathy moan.

I swore, I felt the ground quake.

"You are so sexy. So beautiful. Do you know, Hope? Do you have any idea the way you affect me?" he murmured, just a finger teasing over the lace that covered me. "Did you know the first time I saw you, you knocked the air right out of my lungs? For a fleeting second, I literally couldn't breathe. How's it possible you do that to me?"

I throbbed, overcome with the ache that pulsed at the juncture of my thighs.

The ache to be touched. To be adored. Just for a little while.

"I couldn't stop looking at you." My wispy admission carried on the breeze. "Wondering what it might be like to be wanted by a man like you. Wondering what it would be like to go home with you. Wishing for a little while, that girl could be me."

"She is you, Hope. I want to get inside you so badly, it's painful. But the last thing I want to do is complicate things more than they are. I get it. So, let me give you this."

Did he get it?

Because the man was so absolutely complicating things when he nudged the fabric aside, his fingers slicking through my folds.

"Oh God." Jerking forward, my fingers burrowed into his shoulders, my forehead dropping to his.

His mouth pressed up under my jaw. "Is this what you need?"

His free hand wound in my hair as he kissed down the column of my neck. He tugged my head back, demanding more.

"Yes."

His breaths came harsh when he pushed two fingers into me.

"Kale." I shook around the intrusion, fingers fumbling to hold on tighter, my belly in knots, white-hot coils that glowed bright and blinding.

Jerking back, that dominating gaze raked over my body. Purposed when it dropped to watch where he touched me. "You are perfect. Look at you, always so shy, all spread out for me."

He drove his fingers in slow, deep, maddening thrusts, and his thumb . . . I gasped and writhed as he began to rub it back and forth across my clit.

"Please . . . don't stop."

"That's what I thought. Knew you'd like it hard and slow and a little rough. You deserve a man who'll take the time to do it right. Give me that time, baby, and I promise you, the only thing you'll regret is the fact you didn't let me take you sooner."

And God, I should be mortified, the way he was talking to me, that same arrogant, overconfident man who'd approached me last week making a reappearance.

But instead, I stared at him through the dimness. Through the shadows and questions and madness that swirled around us. As he stroked me and touched me so intimately. In a way that was one-hundred percent unlike me.

But with him . . . I felt different.

I felt confident.

Beautiful.

Brave.

Reaching out, I trembled my fingers across his lush, sexy mouth, felt the needy breath he released against my palm.

He wrapped his free arm around my waist, nearly pulling me from the table, his stare severe. "Kiss me," he demanded, and I did, nearly desperate as I wrapped my arms around his neck, our tongues coiled, winding and teasing and tasting.

While this man drove me straight toward ecstasy.

Pleasure. It gathered from the ends of the earth.

Speeding as it converged.

Tightening to a pinpoint.

Kale curled his fingers.

My frozen world ignited in a burst of flames.

The most intense orgasm ripped through my body. Unlike anything I'd ever experienced.

Wave after wave. Crash after crash.

Staggering.

Kale continued driving his fingers as I rode them. As I let myself completely go for the first time in more years than I could remember. Flying.

I begged for him to never stop. To never let go.

But that was the thing about trusting someone. Wanting them in a way you shouldn't. You started searching for ways to make them fit into the mix of all your complicated things. Wishing there was a way to carve space for them without sending that precarious balance toppling over.

My chest heaved, and Kale held me steady, edging back to eye me with satisfaction.

While I clung to his shoulders, a gasping, heaving mess.

And just for a little while, I allowed him to hold me up before the weight of my world could come crashing back down.

He straightened my underwear and my skirt while I bit my lip and fought the creeping awkwardness that began to seep into my veins, climbing my chest and heating my cheeks.

Laughing a rugged sound, he gripped me by the chin and forced me to look at him. "You aren't going to get shy on me now, are you?"

"I don't know . . . it seems you have me at a disadvantage."

He laughed lower, pushed back his chair, his grin easy when he gestured to the huge bulge straining at his pants. "You're the one with the disadvantage? I wouldn't be so sure about that. Look what you've done to me."

His words were playful.

No expectation behind them.

My hands flew up to my face, and I frantically shook my head, the mortification finally taking hold. "I'm so sorry."

Kale pried my hands away. "I'm not."

A line pinched my brow. "You aren't?"

"No, Hope. The only thing I asked of you was to let me make you feel good."

A smile pulled at the corner of my mouth. "I think it's safe to say you accomplished that."

"Yeah?" he asked, voice winding into a tease.

I couldn't help but utter my own. "Gold medal. Perfect ten."

He pulled me onto his lap so I was straddling him. "What, you think this is the Olympics? I know you didn't get to experience my stamina firsthand, but I was thinking more like this knight deserves a promotion from his princess. Maybe then he'll get to make her his queen."

I ran my fingers through his hair and played along, though I couldn't keep the tenderness out of my voice. "I think you may already be royalty, Kale Bryant."

Because that was the way he made me feel. Special. Wanted. The girl who got her fairy tale.

But the clock was getting ready to strike midnight. "I'm sorry, but I really should get home. I wasn't planning on staying out this late."

His lips flattened, though he nodded in understanding. "Okay then, let's get you home."

He stood and gathered my hand, leading me back the way we'd come. Out through the riot of voices that shouted where they played and drank, down the stairs, and through the murky haze.

Confidently, he guided me through the crowds, which again broke for him, by the band that continued to play, the singer's sultry voice a soft encouragement against my ear.

Someday.

Someday I'll find what was meant for me.

That day you'll find me, too.

Just don't let it be too far away.

"Someday." I let the silent promise move across my lips as I snuggled into Kale's side.

He led me out onto the same sidewalk where I'd parted from him a week before. When I'd thought I'd never see him again.

My chest wanted to cave with that idea now.

With the cruelty of that distinct possibility.

But I had to protect what was important, and standing out there with him was a recklessness in itself.

He lifted his hand in the air, hailing a cab approaching from down the street.

It pulled to the curb. Kale opened the door for me.

Cavalier in his perfect, arrogant way.

"Thank you," I told him, my heart in my throat and tears suddenly burning behind my eyes.

Damn it.

This was the kind of complication I didn't need. The new kind of trouble this boy had ignited in me.

I climbed in.

Grinning, he slid in beside me.

"What are you doing?" The words were panicked.

"Getting you home. You really think I'm going to send you off by yourself in the middle of the night?" Mischief danced across his face, his brow arching high. "What kind of knight would I be then?"

I fiddled with the hem of my dress. "That isn't necessary."

"It is," he said. This time his tone left no room for argument.

Resigned, I gave the driver my address, and Kale held my hand while the car drove through the city. Night pressed down through the bottled silence, broken by the streetlamps that flashed through the windows and the loud thrum of my heart.

This was so stupid.

Giving in this way.

Because my gut had warned me that one night would never be enough.

And if Dane was waiting for me again?

Anger and a shot of fear churned in my gut because I was so tired of playing by his rules.

It wasn't fair.

Not at all.

The cab made the last left into the quiet, sleeping neighborhood. Big, dense trees stood guard over the small homes, their windows cast in darkness and wrapped in the comfort of the night.

The driver cut across the road, pulling up alongside the curb in front of my house.

I looked over at Kale, and I knew I shouldn't, that I was only prolonging the inevitable. Making it hurt a little worse.

It didn't matter.

I leaned in and pressed a soft kiss to his full lips.

So gentle beneath mine. As if they might be able to promise all the things I wanted most.

A second later, I pulled back. "Thank you," I murmured, my fingers regretfully fiddling with the top button of his shirt.

When I started to slide toward the door, he snatched me by the wrist. "Let me come in."

I sent him a small, sad smile, ran my thumb along the defined curve of his cheek. "I had an amazing time tonight. The best time. Thank you for rescuing me for a little while. I won't ever forget it."

For a moment, he stared across at me before he gave a tight nod of reluctant acceptance, his smile slight, his voice wistful regret. "Good night, Shortcake."

I would have giggled if everything didn't suddenly hurt so much.

Clicking the door open, I let myself into the vacant loneliness of the waiting night.

ten

Kale

"Fess up, asshole." Ollie flicked the bottle cap he twisted from a beer at me where I was sitting out on the balcony of my loft.

I dodged it, not surprised to see him waltzing into my place like he owned it after I'd ignored the two calls he'd made this afternoon and the ten texts that'd come in after.

Dude was worse than a stage-five clinger.

"Fuck off, man."

His eyes widened in mock horror. "Such a foul mouth for a kiddie doctor. Shame. And here I thought you'd be classier than that. You sound like some kind of lowlife loser."

I rolled my eyes and took a sip of the beer I'd been nursing for the last two hours. "Gonna blame that one on the fact I hang out with you. They say you are the company you keep."

He dropped down into the lounger beside me, kicking out his legs, crossing them at the ankles. He let out a satisfied sigh.

My brow lifted. "Make yourself at home, why don't you?"

He smirked. "What do you think I'm doing?"

"Ruining my life?"

"Oh, come on, dude. You know you were just begging me to make a surprise visit when you ignored my calls, especially considering you showed up at my bar last night *after* you'd had dinner with the same chick who'd shot you down the week before. Far as I'm concerned, you were shooting SOS flares in the air. Man down. I came running."

He sat up on the side of the lounger, elbows resting on his knees with his beer dangling between them. "So let's hear it, because I'm pretty sure either my best friend has caught some kind of horrible disease or that heart of his is finally thawing out. Which is it?"

I exhaled heavily, eyes trained on the view that was basically exactly the same as the one from Olive's balcony. Lights stretched out across the city, the river winding behind the buildings just on the other side of the street, carefree voices lifting from the sidewalk below.

My place was just a half block down from Ollie's bar. It was located in another reclaimed warehouse that Rex's company, RG Construction, had been hired to bring back to life. I'd been looking for a permanent place to call home at the time, and he'd told me he was working on a project that might interest me.

Even though it'd been nothing but bare bones and rotted wood when I'd viewed it, I'd bought it on the spot.

Pretty much for the view alone since the unit was located on the fifth floor.

Though, I had to admit that my pad turned out to be better than I could have imagined. A cohesive flow of rustic and modern, antique and industrial.

Rex and his crew were skilled, that was for sure.

Too bad the only thing missing from the view tonight was a redhead propped on a table. Like one of those hypnotizing sirens playing you for help when you were the one who was gonna end up dead.

I roughed a hand over my face, trying to clear the vision, to purge her from my mind.

"So," he prodded.

"So, what?"

"So, why are you moping around like some kind of pathetic pussy when you had that gorgeous girl hanging on your arm last night? Even you have to admit, she's way out of your league."

I drove my fingers through my hair. "Guess maybe she is."

"She send you packing?"

"Something like that."

I knew I'd pushed her too far and too fast last night. Touching her, thinking it was the only chance I was going to get. But it'd felt impossible not to after what she'd confessed. It hadn't even been all that much, but I could see the betrayal and hurt written all over her.

The fear.

Without a doubt, the piece of shit was the reason she didn't think she had anything to offer.

All I'd wanted was to make her feel *more.*

Treat her like the queen she deserved to be.

Ollie sobered, rocking back when he finally caught the magnitude of my mood. "Whoa . . . you actually really like this girl."

I sighed out some of the frustration that'd been nagging me all day. "I don't fucking know. There's just . . . something about her I can't shake. She owns this little coffee shop and bakery right down the street from the new office. Stumbled in there last Monday morning, and I couldn't stay away. And you know I sure as hell don't have the time or space for a girl, but I was asking her out before I could stop myself."

"So, last night was, like, a for real date?" He said it like the idea was a mystery dangling somewhere in the universe.

I rubbed my forehead before raking my hand to the back of my head. "Yeah."

"Are you going to see her again?"

"Nah, man."

One night.

It was the only thing either of us could afford.

"And why not? Because your mopey ass does not seem to be happy about it. Which doesn't fit you, by the way."

"You know why." I angled my face away from him a fraction when I said it.

Normally, I was the guy who looked to the bright side. The one who found the good buried in the rubble. But there would always be this one part of me where the sun had gone missing.

That place that had gone dark and dim.

That place I didn't have the capacity to revisit.

I could feel the weight of his frown. "That was ten years ago, Kale, and you know it doesn't have a thing to do with that girl. You've got to quit blaming yourself for something that wasn't your fault. Quit thinking you can't move on."

My laughter was hard. "Not my fault?"

It didn't matter that everyone around me had told me it wasn't my fault. That I'd done everything I could. My heart had convicted me on the spot that I was the only one who should shoulder the blame.

"You made a mistake, man."

A mistake?

"And someone died," I spat.

The girl I loved fucking died because of that mistake.

Because I'd missed it.

Because I'd been too wrapped up.

Busy.

My guts clenched in pain. In the kind of regret that would never fade.

It was right at the second Ollie flinched with my statement. A lightning bolt that ravaged his body.

"Shit," I muttered in apology, knowing where his mind had gone with the callus way I'd thrown it out there. Our situations were different, but in the end, we both were culpable for the same damned thing.

He'd sent his sixteen-year-old sister home from the lake in the middle of the night. Telling her she didn't belong.

She hadn't made it home that night.

That was the kind of guilt that could eat a man alive. Make him hard and callus and coarse.

Ollie lifted his head to the night sky. "We are a fucking pair, aren't we?"

A low chuckle filtered free. "Yeah. Guess we are."

He dropped his head back down to look at me, eyeing me seriously. "Don't let the past keep you from today, man. I know you loved her, and I know a piece of you died with her. But what about the rest of you that's still living? You're the coolest fucking guy I know. You love with all you have. You give every part of yourself to your career and still manage to give more to the rest of us after there shouldn't be anything left. You deserve to live, Kale. Really live."

That was the problem. It was those dead, dark places that didn't know how to move on. If I even wanted to.

Hope's face flashed behind my eyes, and I wasn't quite sure where the fresh bolt of regret was coming from.

The lump that rose in my throat was nothing but cragged, pitted rocks. "Doesn't matter, anyway. Hope's got her own shit."

Standing, he drained his beer and then pointed at me with the same hand wrapped around the empty bottle. "Then pull her out of it." He smirked. "And why don't you pull yourself out of yours while you're at it."

It was Monday morning, and I sat at the red light, drumming my thumbs on my steering wheel as if it might keep me busy enough not to notice where I was.

Like I could drive right by and pretend the little coffee shop wasn't tucked under the quaint, three-story building or keep the colorful umbrellas that were shading the small tables out front from singing out in welcome, begging me to stop in.

Hell, the little A-frame chalkboard sign literally read: It's a beautiful day. We're about to make it better. Come on in.

Motherfucking sunshine.

I accelerated through the intersection, a war going on inside me, knowing she was fighting one of her own. I tried to convince myself to let it go. To just man the fuck up and get to the office because God knew I had plenty to do.

Leave all this nonsense behind.

Because all Hope had given me was one night.

I kept my attention facing forward as I passed, the logo calling out to me where it was printed on the large plate glass window.

A Drop of Hope.

"Fuck it." I whipped my car into an available spot and jumped out into the warm Alabama morning, probably a little quicker than necessary.

Like I said, pathetic.

My insides were nothing but a jumble of nerves, but I pasted on a smile and roughed an easy hand through my hair as I jerked open the door, figuring what the hell.

Some things were just worth a second try.

The bell jingled overhead, and movement rustled in the back. The door swung open, and Jenna rushed out while drying her hands on a dishtowel.

A little too eagerly, my gaze jumped around the small space, across the tables littered with people enjoying their morning coffee and a muffin rather than taking it on the go.

"You lookin' for someone?" The question was delivered with an undercurrent of laughter.

I jerked my attention back to Jenna, who stood there grinning.

Like she didn't know exactly why I was there. It was written all over me. "Just wanted to grab a cup of coffee before work."

It wasn't like I was going to admit it, either.

"Is that so?"

"It is the best coffee in town. It says so right there." I pointed at the little plaque proudly affixed to the wall.

She grinned. "I guess it does, doesn't it?" She turned away and grabbed a large paper cup, talking as she did. "If I remember right, since you seem to just keep stumbling in for our award-winning brew, you prefer a regular ol' cup of Joe. Nothing fancy." She shot me a look from over her shoulder. "I mean, unlike your clothes and your car and that face."

My chuckle was two-parts unease and one-part amusement. "Hey, I was born with this face."

She turned back around, head angled in scrutiny as she slid the coffee across the counter in my direction. "Really. Here I was thinking it might have been cosmetically enhanced."

"I don't know whether to take that as a compliment or not."

Her eyes went wide. "Well, probably depends on who you're talking to."

I laughed again, this time lighter. "Which would you be?"

She leaned against the counter. "Depends."

I pulled a ten from my wallet and passed it to her. "On what?"

"On what you're really doing here."

I pushed out a breath, eyes darting around, searching for that fall of red. "Is she around?" I asked. Clearly, Jenna already had my intentions pegged.

"No, she has an appointment this morning."

Disappointment.

It was there in the way the anxious tension in my shoulders slumped in some kind of defeat.

That should have been warning enough.

"I love her like a sister, you know? So you probably should be aware I'll happily cut your dick off if you hurt her."

Apparently, I really was fluent in silent conversations. I'd gotten that one spot on.

"She's the one who said she could only give me one night."

"Did she?" Jenna handed me the change, looking at me like I was dense. "Or was that her asking you to be careful with her because she's terrified of getting herself mixed up in another situation that isn't healthy? But you need to know that when she tells you her life is complicated, she isn't exaggerating or feeling sorry for herself. It's because her life is really that damned complicated."

I pushed out a sigh. "Last thing I want to do is hurt her."

A puff of air shot from her nose. "That's what they all say in the beginning, isn't it? It'd be nice for a guy to actually prove it for once." She headed for the back, sending a flippant wave over her shoulder. "See ya around, Sir Bryant."

Laughter burst from my chest, and I pressed my fist over my mouth, shaking my head as I tried to keep it contained.

But with the thought of Hope talking about me to her friend?

It made hope come bubbling up inside.

Because maybe Ollie was right.

Maybe it was time for me to move on. And maybe Hope needed help moving on, too.

White lights glared from above. Blinding. The emergency room stark and barren and cold.

Arms aching.

Compression after compression after compression.

Desperation bursting in my blood.

Sweat ran down my brow and soaked the back of my shirt.

And I tried and I tried and I tried.

A flat line . . .

I sucked in a breath against the phantom hum of the machine.

That fucking flat line.

I gave a harsh shake of my head to clear the pictures from my mind and forced myself to focus on the chart I was studying on my laptop.

Telling myself not to freak the fuck out. This wasn't the past trying to test me.

Taunt me and tease me.

This was shit that just happened.

Uncontrolled.

While doctors did their best to control it.

I'd come to accept it was cases like this that got me most, but that didn't mean it didn't shake me to my bones.

My eyes moved over the screen.

An eight-year-old boy who'd been born with a genetic defect that had required a heart transplant when he was an infant. That genetic defect had also affected other organs and caused complete deafness.

It wasn't like I hadn't constantly dealt with life-threatening issues in the ER.

But when kids had come through those doors, I either patched them up and sent them on their way or referred them to someone who specialized in what they were going through.

Or in the worst cases, which thank God were rare in this town, a child was rushed in, already so far gone there'd been nothing anyone could do.

Twice, I'd lost a kid on my table in the ER.

Both times, I'd thought I might lose myself.

That was somehow different. Part of this boy's permanent care was being placed in my hands when I'd signed up to become a part of this team.

Evan.

Josiah's best friend with the "bad" heart.

But I didn't think Josiah understood the full extent of what that meant for Evan.

Another swell of dread tumbled through me, and I knocked it down, refusing it. Seemed the more time I'd spent with Hope, the more unearthed that feeling was becoming. That girl making me face the reasons why I couldn't give myself wholly. The reasons I couldn't risk it.

Why I had to keep my focus on what I'd devoted my life to.

But knowing it didn't seem to make a difference. Not with the way I'd gone running into her shop earlier today. Not the way I just kept wanting more.

Because fuck.

Ollie was right. Maybe it was fucking time, and that scared the shit out of me.

Pushing to my feet, I forced myself to leave my office and get this over with. I knew that no matter how much this was going to affect me—make me remember—I was still going to pour myself into this kid and his case.

When I stepped out into the hall, my nurse was calling over her shoulder as she flew by. "Vitals are all logged. He's ready for you."

"Thank you," I mumbled before I lightly knocked at the door with my knuckle, mentally preparing myself. I pushed open the door, ready to meet him and his family for the first time.

And my own heart . . .

It stalled in my chest.

Before it bottomed out and spilled onto the floor.

Breath gone.

Shock racing my veins.

Eyes wide as I tried to process the scene in front of me.

Because there was this adorable kid, sitting on the exam table, legs swinging over the side, kicking the heels of his shoes against the metal drawers.

Massive grin on his face like he didn't have a care in the world. Or like maybe he had every care, and he embraced what life had given him, anyway.

He wore these thick glasses that made him look like a cute little bug because his sight had also been affected by the congenital malformations.

But his eye involvement hadn't been nearly as severe as the defect of his ears.

His hearing loss complete and profound.

As profound as the deformity of his heart.

His chart had told me he'd had his heart transplant when he was six months old. The last-ditch effort that had saved his life.

When he sensed my presence in the room, his attention snapped my direction, his messy red, wavy hair flopping over with the action.

Attention landing on me, he grinned even wider.

The sight of it clutched me everywhere.

I had this instant, overwhelming sense of affection.

And fear.

So much damned fear I didn't know how to process the two.

To make sense of the two of them together.

Because there was also his mother.

She was standing in the middle of the room. Like she'd barely just made it to her feet a second before I'd opened the door.

Gasping for air and backing away.

Clutching the business card with my contact information my nurse had undoubtedly just passed to her, the same way she did with every new patient I'd taken over for Dr. Browning.

Her horrified gaze bounced between me and the card and the fucking lollipops that were still in the basket, left like a tease or a prize or maybe an outright bribe, on the counter at the back of the exam room.

"Hope," I breathed, my hand still clutching the knob, frozen in the middle of the doorway.

God. In all my hunting for crucial information in Evan's chart, I hadn't even taken note of his last name.

Everything came crashing down.

The things she'd said, and everything she'd implied. The fact she had nothing left to give and no time for herself because she was giving all her time to this little man who needed her most.

She swallowed hard and blinked at me as if she were begging me for something.

Problem was, I didn't exactly know what that was, and I thought maybe she didn't, either.

We stood there staring.

Held.

Bound.

The air between us alive. Thick and tense and aching.

Fuck. What was I supposed to do?

Finally, she broke the connection. She dropped her gaze and sank back into the chair.

Every single thing about her movements were riddled with anxiety. It was as if she was teetering between reaching out and stopping me and heaving all her hope and trust into my taking care of her son.

Because all those amazing things I'd been thinking about her?

They were suddenly right there.

Brought into the light.

Whole.

Flickering with the goodness I saw surrounding her every time I got in her space.

Her *reason*.

And that reason was right there, grinning this bright smile that lit the whole room.

Clearing my throat, I moved the rest of the way through the door and snapped it shut behind me. "I'm Dr. Bryant," I said, feeling totally off-kilter.

Hope made a little choking sound, and my attention darted that way. Trying to tell her I was sorry for putting her in this uncomfortable position. That I had been caught just as much off-guard as she was.

Fuck, I had this intense urge to tell her that her son was everything that terrified me the most. What made me question and made me fight to be the best damned doctor I could possibly be.

"Dr. Bryant," she whispered, as if she were processing that fact.

Cautiously, I went to the little wheeled stool and dropped down onto it, sucking in a breath as I used my feet to wheel closer to Evan.

I felt the frantic movement off to the side and behind me. For a flash, I cut my eyes that way.

Hope.

Hope was signing, her hands and fingers moving in this choreographed dance. The sight of it pierced me somewhere deep.

God. It was beautiful.

She was beautiful.

And I had no fucking clue how to process the turmoil raging inside me.

Evan smiled a wide smile at her, nothing but adoration and belief, before he was looking at me, freckles speckled across the bridge of his nose and his cheeks. He lifted his hand, fingertips to his temple, drawing it out to the side in a wave.

"He said hello." A hoarse explanation from Hope.

Which I got because my own throat had grown thick. I offered an awkward wave to this adorable kid.

And Evan.

He laughed.

It was a quiet sound that scuffed from the depths of him, a laugh from his belly that shook his entire body.

He reached out, all excited like, and grabbed my wrist, pulled my hand up, and showed me how to do it right.

I repeated it.

He smiled again, touched his chin, fingertips coming out toward me like he was blowing a kiss.

"Good." I saw the word form on his lips when he did.

GOOD.

He was telling me I did a good job.

But I knew that was the furthest from the truth.

Because everything inside me was screaming that I'd already fucked this up beyond repair. Of all the people I couldn't get involved with, Hope owned the number one spot.

Goddamned forbidden.

Because my insides were clenching and all those fears and inadequacies were rushing back.

A smile tweaked at the edge of my mouth, and I eyed him carefully as I spoke. "I bet you are way better at it than I am, though, yeah?"

He nodded enthusiastically, green eyes glinting beneath the lights.

A mossy, earthy green.

Just like his mom's.

His hands suddenly went wild, speaking a language I was ignorant to. Somehow, it made me feel like some kind of illiterate asshole.

Tinkling laughter filtered from Hope, the woman so in tune with her kid that it sent a tumble of affection through the center of me. She shifted forward so she could look at me, her expression so damned soft as she said, "He said there's no way you can keep up, but he might be nice enough to let you try."

I turned back to him, cocked my head, mouth moving with the tease. "Is that a challenge?"

Another emphatic nod, the kid's grin so wide I could have counted his teeth.

"Oh really . . . I'm the doctor here. You don't think I can beat you at your little game?"

He made a gesture across his body, a swipe of his hand as he pinched his fingers together, his mouth moving in time.

NO WAY.

I hefted out a breath. That was what I thought.

Evan could read lips.

Of course, he could. This sweet kid who oozed love and faith and intelligence.

A kid whose chart promised he was fragile and breakable and weak, when really his spirit was big enough to fill the entire room as he prepared to outwit me.

"Well, then, I'll do my best to keep up. How's that sound?"

GOOD, he signed again.

And my insides were twisting again because I had no idea how the fuck I was going to get through this. But I had to suck it up, act like the man I'd been trained to be. How I was going to pretend I hadn't had his mother propped on a table a mere three days before, touching her and wishing things could be different, was beyond me. One thing at a time, though.

Because this was the reality.

I was Evan's doctor.

His doctor.

The one responsible for his care.

And I wasn't about to fuck that up.

Stark lights. Cold. Barren. Flat line.

I jarred against the sudden vision, blinking the cruelty away, voice rough when I said, "All right, then, Evan. Let's check you out."

If I wasn't paying such close attention, I probably wouldn't have noticed the way he flinched.

Wouldn't have noticed the fear that went racing beneath the surface of his skin.

Or the way his mother cringed in sympathy of it. Swore, I could feel her having to physically restrain herself from reaching out and gathering him into the safety of her arms.

This amazing woman so clearly desperate to shield him from the things she didn't have the power to protect him from.

No doubt, he was no stranger to needles and pain or being poked and prodded.

Even though I knew he couldn't hear me, I kept my voice soft, filled with assurance. "I already checked out your records, Evan. You don't need any shots, and you did all your heart tests for Dr. Krane last month. That means,

I'm going to give you a really fast checkup. Make sure everything's going just right. No needles. How's that sound?"

His trusting face flushed with relief, tension draining from his body.

While mine curled with the yearning to be able to take everything from him.

Make it better.

Promise him he would never hurt again.

Wishing I could be the hero I could never be.

Another part of me wanted to tease him about monsters growing in his belly. Make him laugh the way I did Frankie Leigh and my younger patients, but the boy was eight years old. If I did that, he would probably demand a new doctor because the one he'd been assigned had lost his mind.

Sounded about right.

"I'm going to take your shirt off, okay?" I made sure to keep my mouth in view of his eyes when I asked it.

Without any reluctance, his arms flew over his head.

I chuckled, reached down, and worked it over his head. Had to beat down the urge to ruffle my fingers through his hair when I did. "There we go," I said, setting it beside him.

From behind and to the side, I could feel the weight of his mother's stare against the side of my face.

Could feel the weight of her burden and her fear that I was sure never went away.

The anticipated prominent scar ran from the top of his sternum to about two inches above his belly button. I ran my fingers across his breastbone, palpating the area and familiarizing myself with his scars and the way his surgical wound had healed.

I moved back to make sure he could see my mouth. "Do you ever have any pain in this area? Anytime you're playing or trying to sleep? Anything that makes you feel funny?"

He'd had a cardiology checkup with Dr. Krane recently. His chart affirmed his transplanted heart was functioning well. But as his primary care, I would cover all the bases.

That was what the clinic was all about.

Ensuring nothing was overlooked. If one doctor missed a sign, chances were, the next would pick up on it. And I sure as fuck wasn't going to miss it.

Evan gave an assertive shake of his head.

Clearly, he knew the importance of that answer.

"That's good. Why don't you lie back so I can check your belly?"

He didn't hesitate. He shifted and laid on his back, and I stood over him, my fingertips checking his abdomen for any lumps or bumps, examining all the quadrants, watching his face for any kind of reaction. "Anything feel funny when I do that?"

He smiled when he gave another shake of his head.

And the examination continued that way. Like he was any kid who walked through my door. Which of course, I cared about every single patient I saw.

They were the reason I lived.

Why I devoted my life.

But this one . . . this one left me with a lump the size of a grapefruit in my throat and my heart battering my ribcage.

I stood over him, pretending like I didn't want to drop to my knees and tell him I'd make it better if I could.

Pretending I didn't want to say a million things to his mom and demand a million things of her in return.

Instead, I carried on like this was perfectly normal while tension I hoped Evan didn't notice bounded through the tight space, ricocheting from the walls and echoing in the air.

Swore, I could taste the woman on my breath and hear her moan in my ear.

God. This was brutal.

I patted his knee when I finished. "All done."

Rolling the stool to the counter, I set my laptop on it, cleared my throat, and tried not to really look at her when I started going over all the shit I normally did first with the parents but had been too shocked to focus on when I'd found her there.

I asked Hope about his diet and exercise and if she had any concerns while thousands of unsaid questions roiled between us.

I told her he was at the fifth percentile in height and weight, to be expected for his condition, that as long as he was eating well, it was nothing to worry about.

Right.

Nothing to worry about.

Because worry surrounded her like a dark, ominous cloud. But with a simple glance at her kid, that storm was obliterated with the force of a thousand suns.

"Thank you, Dr. Bryant," she said, eyes downcast as if she couldn't physically bring herself to look at me.

She stood, took Evan's hand, and helped him down. She ran a tender hand through his hair and then signed something I didn't understand.

He beamed up at her.

Clearly, she hung the little boy's moon.

Watching it felt like I was being shredded in two.

I looked at him, trying to loosen my jaw. No doubt, he'd recognize if I was grinding my teeth.

"It was great to meet you, Evan. I . . ." I hesitated, suddenly feeling like a fool. Like maybe I was the brunt of a cruel, sick joke. So out of sorts, I had no clue how to decipher up from down.

Still, I didn't want to treat him any different from anyone else, so I plucked one of the lollipops from the box and bent at the knees to offer it to him. "Here. This is for you . . . if your mom says it's okay."

His face lit up, and Hope choked over a tiny sob that I knew she was doing her best to hide. I paused, reluctant to turn and look her way. I'd told Hope that night that I didn't know her all that well, but some things a person couldn't miss. And I knew without a doubt that Hope was at her breaking point.

She'd warned me her life was complicated. I guessed I couldn't really grasp what that really meant until right then when all those threads I could sense her hanging by started to weave together. Taking shape in my mind. The fact she was in the middle of a nasty divorce.

Dread settled over me like a sheet of ice, awareness taking hold. Suddenly, I was sure all that *nasty* had to do with the well-being of this kid.

Evan yanked at her arm, signed something quickly. Casting him a soft smile, she nodded, and he took the candy, grinning at it like he was in awe before he pushed past me toward the counter.

Hiking up onto his toes, he grabbed the pen and the pad with the clinic info at the top, tongue sticking out at the side in concentration as he scribbled something across the paper.

When he was finished, the beaming was directed at me, the kid getting under my skin as quickly as his mom had as he stood there with the pad of paper lifted up to me like an offering.

Unsure what to do, I glanced at Hope.

Her voice scratched. "He wants to be able to talk to you himself. Not through me. He said it's a secret."

My throat was nothing but sheers of broken glass when I accepted the pad. My eyes moved across the messy marks scored deep on the page.

> *I helped my mom make those. She said a nice man came in and bought them all so we need to make more. We gave all the money to the babies with bad hearts like mine. Was it you who bought them all?*

My nod felt like a confession of a crime.
He grabbed it back and scribbled some more.

> *You are nice. I'm glad you're my new doctor. If you think I'm going to die, don't tell my mom. I don't want her to be sad.*

Emotion screamed through my throat. Racing the length. Winding down to fist my heart and crush my ribs. With a shaky hand, I took the pen from him and wrote my own message below his.

I'm glad I am, too. Really glad. And you aren't dying, Evan. Not even close. I promise I won't let that happen.

I thought he might be more alive than anyone I'd ever met.

His grin lit up the room when he read my answer. He gave me a thumbs-up. Apparently, he thought that was simple enough for me.

When I'd never felt so *complicated* in all my life.

Hope gathered him by the hand. She cast me a remorseful glance, those green eyes telling a million secrets that I knew she wouldn't allow her tongue to speak. The two of them started out the door. Evan dashed out ahead of her.

Before she could make it all the way out, I snatched her by the wrist, unable to keep it back.

"Why didn't you tell me?" It came out harder than I intended.

An accusation. A demand.

I didn't know.

She spun around, all that red hair swishing around her like a red, violent wave. It was almost terror that rippled across her gorgeous face.

It wrenched through me.

Tripping me up.

Bringing me to my knees.

"What was I supposed to tell you? I told you what you needed to know. I told you my life was complicated, and I didn't have room for anything else."

"You could have at least told me you had a kid."

Disbelief pinched her eyes together. "And what then? What difference would it have made? He's my priority. My only priority."

Her tone swung into desperation. "And right now, I'm fighting for him. I've *been* fighting for him since the second he was born, Kale. But this fight I'm in the middle of right now? It's one I didn't see coming. One that's going to take all of me to win. *Sacrifice.*"

Instead of releasing her, anger tightened my hold, none of it directed at her.

"What does that mean?" The question hissed between my teeth as all those threads had suddenly laced together became clear.

Venom seeped into my veins.

The implications of her confessions.

"He wants to take everything from me."

I suddenly understood what kind of fight she was talking about.

Motherfucker.

I could feel the emphasis of it twist across my brow. "He's trying to get custody?"

Fuck. I didn't even know who *he* was. But I hated him. Hated him more than I thought I'd ever hated anyone in my life.

And that shouldn't be possible.

Her entire being winced, her chin trembling before she gave me a small nod. "The suit is asking for joint."

She pressed her hands to her chest. "Which I know sounds fair to most people, but if you knew . . ." She inhaled a sharp breath. "If you knew how unfair that is to my son . . ."

I gritted my teeth, fighting the rage that bloomed in my blood.

She swallowed hard. "Do you get it now? Why I can't do this? Why I can't risk it?" Those green eyes moved across my face, searching for understanding.

And I got it.

I got it on every level.

That didn't mean I wasn't seething inside. Wanting to hunt the piece of shit down.

She blinked, like she was trying to break the connection, the band of understanding that stretched and pulled between us.

"We never should have done what we did, Kale. I shouldn't have. That's on me. It was selfish, but I wanted to experience it for a little while. Being with a man like you. But it was a mistake."

It was.

I knew it was.

But I wanted to counter her claim.

Refute it.

Tell her I'd just been getting started.

But Evan was my patient.

My fucking heart-transplant patient.

"Shit." Dropping my hold and the power of her gaze, I ran a frustrated hand through my hair.

"Shit," I mumbled again.

What had I done? How could I have let myself get into this position again? But that was the way it happened. Without your knowledge. Without your permission. You got caught up, and before you even knew it, you were in deep.

Swept away.

Hope reached out to caress my jaw with her fingertips.

Sweet.

Soft.

Heat.

Her lip trembled as she traced across my chin before she tilted her head and looked up at me with the warmth of those green, earthy eyes.

Need and something else I didn't want to recognize tumbled through my body, a flare in my spirit that lit.

"I told you I'd never forget that night. I meant it. But now . . . now I'm going to walk away and pretend it didn't happen, and I'm going to trust you to take care of my son."

eleven

Hope

"You've got to be shittin' me."

I glanced over the back of the couch and toward the hallway to make sure the coast was clear before I turned back to Jenna, who waited impatiently, legs crisscrossed under her and hugging a frilly throw pillow to her chest. She looked seconds away from pressing her face to it and releasing a frustrated scream.

Or maybe that was what I was imagining.

Because it was the truth. I wanted to scream.

Or maybe cry.

I wasn't sure.

So, I opted to clutch my wine glass in my hands.

Maybe it wasn't healthy, but tonight, it was my lifeline.

"Do you really think I'd joke around about something like that?"

"You'd better not. Good God almighty, Harley Hope. He's a doctor. I should've seen it all along." She fanned herself.

My eyes narrowed, my voice dropping to an incredulous whisper. "Why are you acting like this is a good thing?"

Hers widened, her brows disappearing behind her bangs. "Um . . . have we not established that man is nothin' but straight deliciousness? He's sex on a stick and should be licked up and down. I'd eat that boy with a spoon. Hell, you could name a cupcake after him and put one of those little stakes in it with a picture of his face. *Bam*. Bestseller. *And* he's a doctor. Honestly, the only thing I'm seein' here are the positives."

"He's *Evan's* doctor."

She shrugged. "So."

"So I'm going to have to see him for basically all of forever."

It was hard enough to resist him when he kept coming into my store.

Seeing him care for my son?

Those puddles he'd left me in during our date had up and boiled at the sight, leaving me a shaking, quivering mess of awe and desire. I'd sat there watching him from behind, my stomach clenching in need and my heart doing wild, wild things.

My subconscious had been quick to offer up all kinds of excuses to convince my mind why seeing him again would be just fine. A whisper that urged me to reach out, caress his striking face, to run my fingertips across that magnificent jaw.

And maybe, just maybe, it would be okay to reach out to touch on the beauty of his kind, genuine heart.

Shivers raced my spine.

That was definitely going to cause all kinds of problems I wasn't sure I knew how to deal with.

"You don't see the complication?" I asked.

She huffed. "You and your *complications*. What it seems to me is *convenient*. One-stop shopping. You *are* the one who's always sayin' she doesn't have time."

"This isn't about having time, Jenna. You know that. This is about Dane."

"Who you need to stop letting control you."

"I'm not letting Dane control me. I'm trying to protect my son."

"That's it? You're not going to see Kale anymore?"

I gave her a resolute nod that made a rush of sadness billow through my spirit.

Someday.

But as of right then, I had to make the sacrifice. This wasn't about me, and I had to put my son first.

"That means you wouldn't mind if I went for him then?" Jenna tossed out, sipping her wine as if I shouldn't reach out and smack her just for suggesting it. "You know, I wouldn't mind a little of that *royal treatment*."

She waggled her brows. Goading me.

God, I never should have told her that. I was never gonna hear the end of it.

"You're disgusting and crass and no longer my best friend," I told her as petulantly as I could.

She laughed, set her glass down, and then scrambled across the couch, hugging me to her side. "You know you love me. Just like you know I love you. Which is why I want you to take care of you, too. You give and you give and you give, and you never know when that giving is finally going to bleed you dry."

Tears pricked at my eyes, and I rested my head on her shoulder. "Evan is enough for me, Jenna."

The only thing I needed, at least for a little while. Until life sorted itself out. Until we were free, and we could move on and leave the ugliness behind.

All I wanted was a safe, secure home for my son. That was what I'd strived for all along. I was determined to give it to him. The rest would fill itself in. I had faith that it would.

Jenna ran her fingers through my hair. "I know. I just want you to promise me you will remember that it's okay to love, too, especially if you're doing it because you want to instead of because you have to. You deserve it."

"I know that. But right now, with Dane showing up here, I need to be careful."

Honestly, I shouldn't have been shocked when I'd received the papers that he was going after joint custody.

It was nothing but a show, I knew that. The vile man wasn't doing anything but keeping up appearances and then turning right around and hating me for having the *audacity* to actually leave him.

I should have left him as soon as he'd reacted to the news of Evan's heart the way he had, our son only a couple days old.

But I'd believed in him, in the man I'd thought I'd married, and had been certain it was only shock and grief and fear making him behave the way he had.

Rejecting our precious child as if he were a stain.

The years had whittled away that faith until there'd been nothing left before the proverbial final nail was driven into the coffin, the one that still made me sick to my stomach.

"Not all men are pricks, Hope. You just happened to marry one."

"He definitely set the bar, didn't he?"

"Yeah, so low the snake couldn't even slither under it."

Light laughter escaped me, and I let her hold me up for a little bit. When I heard the clatter of footsteps smacking the floor behind me, I shifted, turning to look back over the couch.

Evan stood there, dripping wet and making puddles on my wood floor, clutching the ends of the towel, which he hadn't taken the time to actually dry with, to his chest.

He was grinning that smile that decimated me. My heart so full I was sure any second it would burst.

He hooked his towel under his chin and chest.

FINISHED, he signed.

GOOD BOY, I signed back.

Jenna shifted all the way around. "Come give Auntie a hug good night."

Evan scrambled around the couch, throwing himself at her. My best friend squeezed him and wiggled him around. She roughed a hand through his wet hair. "Who's my favorite little man?"

EVAN THE GREAT! he signed.

"That's right," she said. "Because You. Are. Great."

Grinning from ear to ear, he nodded emphatically.

My miracle boy.

They say there is no love like a mother's, and I'd never claim to love my child more than any other mother loved theirs. But what I did know with everything inside me was I couldn't love mine more. That I'd never know a love greater.

He'd been written on me.

In me.

For me.

I knew I'd been the one created specifically for his care because I loved him in a way that no one else could.

In a way that was ours.

Whole and complete.

I pushed from the couch and set my wine on the coffee table.

TIME FOR BED.

He made an *oh-man* face, before he was trotting off toward his room, and by the time I made it there, he had already pulled on his underwear and tee. He jumped into bed, and I dimmed the light, crossed the room, and lowered to my knees beside him.

He pulled the covers up to his chest and wiggled beneath them.

COZY?

A nod, Evan still oozing love and smiles.

GOOD.

I hesitated, considering what to say. If I even should. I bit my lip as I stared down at my incredible son.

WHAT DID YOU THINK ABOUT TODAY? I finally asked.

In the dim light, his green eyes danced, his lips and hands quick with their reply.

ABOUT MY NEW DOCTOR?

We always mouthed the words to each other when we signed since Dane had refused to learn. He'd claimed we were only giving Evan a crutch. If he worked *hard* enough, *listened* better, if we didn't coddle him, he might be *normal.*

What an asshole.

YES, I gestured.

I THINK YOU WERE RIGHT.

I frowned. ABOUT WHAT?

THAT HE'S NICE.

BECAUSE OF THE LOLLIPOPS?

He didn't hesitate with his response. *YES. THAT, AND HE'S GENTLE, AND HE DOESN'T WANT TO HURT ME.*

My guts clenched. *I DON'T THINK ANY OF YOUR DOCTORS WANT TO HURT YOU. SOMETIMES THEY HAVE TO. TO KEEP YOU HEALTHY.*

With honesty, he blinked up at me. *BUT SOMETIMES THEY GET USED TO IT, AND THEY FORGET TO BE CAREFUL.*

My son saw things in a different way.

As if he were years older.

Insightful.

Quick and keen.

Kind and knowing.

Maybe it was because the constant noises most of us were inundated with were silenced for him. Because he could observe people without having to listen to the things they said. Actions always spoke so much louder than words.

I WISH YOU NEVER HAD TO HURT, I told him. *IF I COULD, I WOULD TAKE IT ALL AWAY.*

I KNOW, M-A-M-A. He signed *Mama* instead of *Mom*, which he only did when he wanted to make me feel special. I could feel the affection in it, his love as he spelled out the letters.

I smoothed my hand out over his chest, felt the steady thrum beneath my palm. *My heart,* I mouthed.

Evan reached out and set his on mine. *My heart,* he mouthed the same.

Smiling down at him, I brushed my fingers through his hair, leaned up, and pressed a lingering kiss to his forehead.

I leaned back so he could see my mouth. "I love you."

I LOVE YOU THE MOST, he signed.

ARE YOU SURE ABOUT THAT? I teased.

Because it wasn't possible.

Not when he was my center. My earth, moon, and sky.

Night seeped in through the window and branches scraped at the eaves in the slight breeze. The tiny lamp on my nightstand cast my bedroom in a golden glow.

Basking it in warmth.

I lay propped against the white fabric headboard, surrounded by pillows and huddled under my comforter, reading some smutty novel Jenna had shoved at me and insisted I read.

It wasn't helping things. Not with the riot that had been ignited in my body. Not after Kale had taken me to a place where I'd touched on the most intense kind of beauty.

My phone lit up on the nightstand, vibrating on the wood.

Unease slammed me when I glanced at the clock.

Twelve thirty-three.

It wasn't all that late, but . . . still. I hated that I was instantly on guard. Continually on watch. God, how I was counting the days to that court date circled on the calendar. Two months and all of this would be over, and then Evan and I could finally fully move on.

But Jenna was right.

It was time I stopped tiptoeing and allowing Dane to control me in the way only he could—through fear and apprehension. The asshole knew my weakness.

And my weakness was my son.

Taking in a steeling breath, I prepared myself to fight another battle in this war and swiped my thumb across the screen.

The air left me on a shaky exhale.

Not Dane. Emotion pulled tight across my ribs when my eyes moved over the text.

Kale: Your son is amazing.

That emotion climbed my throat and trembled across my lips. My tongue swept out to wet them, unsure of how to respond, wondering what good any of this would do.

Still, I found myself tapping out a reply.

Me: He's the best thing that's ever happened to me.

I almost jumped when my phone buzzed in my hand.

Kale: He looks like you. He has your eyes. Your hair. Your smile.
Kale: Your heart.

That one came in a few seconds behind. As if he'd hesitated to say it.

Hands shaking, I replied.

Me: If I could, I would give him mine.

Time spun on, me staring at my phone, wondering why the man made me feel as if I could tell him anything.

It was probably stupid that I'd even returned his text. Because we'd already established that we couldn't do this. That the timing was all wrong. And even if the timing were right, I really had no idea what Kale's intentions would be. If he even wanted to date a woman with a child. Because Evan and

I? We were a package deal.

But that didn't mean my heart wasn't fluttering in its confines, legs trembling with the rush of excitement that stampeded through my body, warming my flesh.

I sucked in a breath when he responded.

Kale: I think you already have.

A wistful smile lifted my mouth. Gratefulness a shaky heave from my lungs.

It was as if he got it.

Understood the sacrifice.

I should have shut the conversation down, but instead, I was typing out another reply.

Me: He likes you.

His response was instant.

Kale: I like him, too. A lot.

A second passed and then another text came in.

Kale: Problem is, I like his mom as well. Not sure what to do about that.

Butterflies scattered.

God, what was I doing? But I couldn't stop the way my bottom lip quivered, the way my belly flipped, or the way my fingers were all too eager as they tapped across the screen.

Me: Then I guess it's an even bigger problem that his mom likes his doctor, too.

I bit my lip, knowing I needed to rein this in, so I sent a second behind it.

Me: But we can't do this, can we?

I didn't know if it was a question or a plea. Because my mind was back there, on that balcony where he'd made me feel like a woman for the first time in years. As if I'd been exactly where I was supposed to be.

As if maybe I'd belonged there all along.

His breath on my neck and his hands on my body.

My name on his tongue.

A shiver rolled down my spine and need became an achy appeal in my core.

Kale: What? Text?

I could almost see him lifting that strong brow, biting his lip as he fought a mischievous smile. It took everything I had not to imagine him doing it on his bed with his shirt off.

Me: This isn't a joking matter.

Kale: No?

Me: No.

Kale: You're right. It's not. But tell me one thing. What's the second-best thing that's happened to you? I'd bet my bank account it went down on that balcony.

Redness flushed my cheeks, and I typed out my response and hit send before I could think better of it.

Me: No man has ever made me feel the way you did.

Kale: That's because you deserve a man who will treat you right. Guessing that fucker didn't come close.

Wow.

I shouldn't have been surprised.

I'd seen it in Kale's eyes when I'd watched him come to the realization in the office earlier today. When it dawned on him exactly what was at stake.

Rage had burned across his face and tightened his hold, as if he didn't want to let me go.

Then he'd realized he had to. That we might be drawn to each other, but our paths couldn't connect.

Me: I can't do this with you. There's too much on the line.

Someday.

Someday, I could let myself get lost in the sea of a brilliant, beautiful man. Swept away. No need for solid ground because he would be my footing.

It took the longest time before a response came through.

Kale: I know. I know better. I'm sorry. I keep crossing that line when it's clear neither of us are allowed to have what's waiting on the other side. But you make it really damned hard not to try to jump over it.

Neither of us.

I frowned at that, wondering what he meant. What would hold him back—his own circumstances or my baggage? Maybe he didn't have the capacity to be with someone like me.

Even if I weren't in the middle of a divorce, my life would always be hinged on the most perfect complication.

The center of my world a red-headed, freckle-faced boy.

A bunch of texts blipped through in quick succession behind it.

Kale: Shit.
Kale: I'm sorry.
Kale: I'm fucking this up.
Kale: I just wanted to check on you both. Tell you, you have an amazing kid.
Kale: See what you do to me? You make me lose control.

An affected smile lit on my face. I had the unsettled feeling this man could be the completion of my joy.

I let the feeling take me over, gaze moving back over his words, wishing for a way.

Then I did what I knew I needed to do.

Me: Good night, Kale.

Kale: Good night, Hope.

I started to set it aside, but it blipped again.

Kale: Good night kiss?

Oh, this man. I was right all along. He really was trouble.

Me: I don't think that's a good idea.

I hoped it came across as stern and he couldn't tell there was a giddy grin threatening to light on my mouth.

Kale: Boob shot? I'll reciprocate.

It was no longer a threat, affection racing out, twisting my lips in a ridiculous smile, my heart beating overtime.

Me: You're out of your mind.

Kale: I was thinking more along the lines of blowing yours.

Sitting in my bed, I laughed, out loud. It was as if I could actually feel his playfulness behind it. That easy confidence that had slipped into his tone.

Me: Go to sleep.

I was still wearing that silly grin when I hit send.
If only Jenna could see me right then.

Kale: If you won't blow me a kiss, tell me you'll at least dream of me?

I would not be admitting to that, though, the chances were good.

Me: Stop it.

When the next one came through, my heart grew heavy.

Kale: You're beautiful, Hope. Seriously. That's the last thing I'm going to say. Now I'm gonna back away.

I held his message to my chest and looked toward the ceiling, cherishing the words, fighting the urge to beg him not to.
Finally, I forced myself to set my phone aside.
I flipped off the lamp and curled on my side, hugging the comforter to my chest.
And it shouldn't have been possible.
Not with everything that was going on.
But that night, as I drifted to sleep, I did so with a smile on my lips.

twelve

Hope

I tucked a receipt into the register and glanced up to the next customer in line. "Can I help you?"

The man stepped forward. "Harley Hope Gentry?"

It was instant.

The apprehension that bolted through me, forcing me back a step. The fact that he used *that* last name, the one I was trying to purge from my conscious and my life and my reality, set off a deafening scream of warning sirens in my ears.

Still, I was nodding, a painful lump growing up in my throat, obstructing any words that might have passed. He shoved a large envelope my direction. "You've been served."

Tears burned, and the room spun. Violent trembles rolled through my body because this was so much like that day six months ago when Dane had rocked my world, contesting my divorce claim that would grant me full custody without support.

All I wanted was to cut ties.

Be done with it.

Give Evan the life he deserved.

I could barely clutch the envelope, my hands were shaking so bad.

"Jenna," I tried to call but my voice cracked, coming out as little more than a whisper.

She was in the seating area wiping down tables, and she jerked her attention to me. As soon as she caught sight of my expression, she started moving toward me.

What had to be fear and dread and hate contorting my face in pain.

"Can you take over for me?" I all but begged, angling my head toward the long line of customers waiting at the counter.

"What's going on?" she demanded instead.

"I don't know . . . I just . . . I need a minute so I can find out."

Her attention dropped to the envelope. Her brown eyes turned sharp as daggers, as if her glare might set it on fire.

I could only wish.

"Excuse me," the lady called at the counter, patience clearly not her strong suit.

Jenna gave me a regretful look. "Go on. I'll be right here."

With a jerky nod, I fumbled through the swinging door and staggered toward the small office area set up at the very back of the kitchen.

Barely able to stand.

I set my hand on the desk to steady myself, drawing in a few deep breaths before I forced myself to rip open the letter. My eyes raced over the words drawn up by Dane's attorneys.

Terror ridged my spine, that dread igniting in the worst kind of horror.

"Asshole," I gasped, choking, my vision turning black.

Scrambling for my purse I'd left on the desk, I dug for my phone. I could barely get my hands to cooperate enough to pull up the number I needed.

I squeezed my eyes closed as I pushed send.

I didn't have to wait long.

Dane answered on the first ring. "Ah, I see you got my present."

Present.

What did he think? That this was a joke?

Fun?

A competition?

I swallowed around the razors that lined my throat, forced out the words that scraped and ground. "Why are you doing this?"

"I told you I was finished playing your games, Harley. I warned you that if you didn't come home and stop this foolishness, you were going to regret it."

"This *isn't* a game, Dane. The furthest from it. I'm giving you an out. You and I both know you don't want Evan."

I flinched just saying it.

The years of silent abuse.

The rejection.

The disgust.

Everything was hoarse and choppy as it flooded from my mouth. "And now you're asking for full custody and a review of his medical records? Stating I'm an ill-fit mother? You don't have the first clue what his care requires."

"Hiring help has never been an issue, Harley. I think you know better than that."

Sickness roiled. "Help."

He wanted strangers to raise my son.

God. Knowing Dane, he would probably lock him away. Hide Evan and pretend he didn't exist. Put him in some institution as if he were shame.

Humiliation.

When my son was beauty and life and joy.

"When you married me, you promised you would be mine for all your days, and be clear, all your days belong to me. You think I'm actually going to let you walk away from me? You knew you had a role as my wife . . . now stop being foolish and fill it."

"I didn't marry you for that role. I married you because I *loved* you. And you promised to cherish and love me in return. In sickness and in health."

The words crawled from my throat, venom and a plea. Not for him to have a change of heart. But for him to let us go.

Dane laughed a morbid sound. One that echoed with his own grief. "I never stopped loving you."

"And you never started loving him."

Silence moved through the line, and the tears I'd been holding broke free. Hot veins streaked down my cheeks. Years of holding out for this man and the hatred that loss had left in that void.

I could feel the shift, the detached control that filled his voice. "You know how to resolve this, Harley."

Bitter laughter rumbled somewhere inside me. The disbelief. "Do you not know me at all? Do you think I will ever give in? Allow your disgusting, vile demand?"

The final stake had been driven into my faith in him that day a year ago when I'd opened our front door to find a mailman, holding out a certified letter. One that had to be signed for.

A DNR that had been drawn up for Evan. Without my knowledge or consent.

"It's time to stop propagating his suffering."

That was what Dane had said when he'd tried to force me into signing it.

Evan and I were gone the next morning.

"Why fight the inevitable?" he said indifferently, as if it didn't matter at all.

Pain leeched into my pores. Because I knew he wasn't talking about my losing Evan to him. He was talking about me losing him forever.

"I will never, ever give up hope on my son. Never. I'll die first."

I rushed to end the call, unable to listen to him for a second longer. Slipping from my shaking hands, the phone clattered to the desk, my weak knees finally giving. Back pressed against the wall, I slid to the ground. My face in my hands.

It didn't matter how hard I tried to contain them.

Sobs broke free, ripping from my throat, fed from my soul. And I swore, I was right back in the hospital on the day my entire world was ripped apart.

I shivered when the door to the private room we'd been whisked to on the maternity floor edged open.

I had no idea what was happening, though every cell in my body warned it was bad.

I'd been waiting for hours. Days, I thought. I wasn't sure. The only thing I knew was my world had stopped the second they'd taken away my infant son.

The doctor who came through the door was older, hair gray and thin, his expression stoic. Yet, I could read people well enough that I could see beneath it.

To the grim lines that had been checked. Held. As if it might make the delivery of horrible news more bearable.

Slowly, he sat next to me.

My husband was on the other side of me, the heel of one of his expensive dress shoes bobbing incessantly.

Waiting silently. Swimming in his own turmoil.

"Mr. and Mrs. Gentry . . ." the doctor broached.

I clutched my trembling hands on my lap.

"I'm sorry I don't have better news. We've discovered a severe abnormality of your son's heart."

Dizziness whipped through my head, whooshing through my body. A vortex of dread and fear and grief. The man continued to speak, attempting to explain the deformity.

But the only thing I could hear was my soul screaming, "No, no, no!"

"What does that mean?" I finally whispered through the anguish.

"We are going to have him transported to Camden Children's Hospital in Tennessee. One of the best in the nation. He'll need to undergo surgery as soon as possible. We hope to repair the abnormality, which may make it so a heart transplant isn't required."

I blinked as the term penetrated.

Heart transplant.

I jarred forward.

Unprepared.

How could this be happening? It couldn't. It couldn't.

The doctor continued speaking, "Not all of the tests are back, but we believe this is due to a genetic defect. If he survives, this will most likely present itself in other ways in the future."

If he survives.

Horror burst in my blood, and I curled in on myself, no longer able to remain upright, the overwhelming joy and love inside me shattering.

Splintering out.

I squeezed my eyes closed as the tears fell. And I issued up a million prayers. Begging for this not to be real. To go back to hours ago when I held my tiny, healthy baby boy in my arms.

"Evan," I rasped, clutching at my chest as I whimpered his name.

"I'm sorry," the doctor offered, pulling himself back to standing. "A case manager will

be in to talk with you about making arrangements to get him transported by air to expedite his care."

The door swung shut behind him.

Dane jumped to his feet, the first reaction out of him since the doctor had begun speaking. But I was unprepared again, jerking in fear and surprise when I heard the crash.

The punch of his fist against the wall and the sound of his guttural shout. Then his dark head of hair dropped between his shoulders as he gasped for the air that had been sucked from the room.

I forced myself to stand. To go to him. I set my hand on his back, needing to comfort him, desperate for it in return. Needing him to hold me, support me, whisper that it would be okay.

We had to have faith. We had to. Otherwise, we'd have nothing left.

But he shocked me again when he twisted away from my touch, spinning into the middle of the room and facing me. Hatred glinted in his eyes. "Don't fucking touch me."

"Dane," I gasped, eyes pinching, a terrified kind of confusion sinking like lead to land with the fear and grief.

He hesitated for a moment before he pointed at me. "Don't fucking touch me."

He whipped away, anger and fury in his stride. He flung open the door and didn't look back before he disappeared down the hallway, leaving me standing there by myself. Knees week. Foundation gone.

I slid down the wall and onto the ground, my hands clutching my chest that ached and moaned.

And I was sure, never in my life, had I ever felt so alone.

"Finally got the last of the customers out of here," Jenna said as she blew through the swinging door.

Shaken from the horrible memory, I jerked my head from my hands. Through bleary eyes, I stared at her. The second she saw my state, she rushed for where I was crumpled on the floor.

"That asshole. What is he spoutin' this time?" she demanded, sinking onto her knees beside me.

Unable to answer, I gasped over another sob.

"Fuck," she muttered, shifting to sit on her butt. She pulled me to her chest, wrapping me in her arms. "What did he do now?"

"He's trying to take him from me." It left me on a coarse, whimpered cry.

Anger ripped through her body, and she hugged me tighter, her mouth at the top of my head. "What's he sayin'?"

"That I'm not a fit mother. That he wants full custody." The last broke. "Oh, God—" I choked, burying my face in her neck.

"That's not gonna happen, Harley Hope. I promise you, there is no way any court is going to give that man custody."

"Why is he doing this?" I whimpered.

She squeezed me. "Because *he's* scared. Because he knows you have the upper hand. He's a pathetic rat bastard who's scared he's gonna look bad. That you're gonna expose him for the kind of man he really is. That, for once in his life, he's not gonna win. You know he can't stand the thought of that."

Unease spun through my spirit. I couldn't escape the feeling that it was more than that. That his intentions were different from what I could see.

Crueler.

Uglier.

He wanted me back in that house, and I didn't know why. Not when I knew he wanted us gone.

Swallowing hard, Jenna drew me closer. "I promise you that those courts are going to see him for what he is. You have given up your entire life for that little boy, and that piece of crap hasn't given up a damned thing. And every single person who knows is gonna sit up on that stand and testify to it, including your son. And where do you think he's gonna want to be?"

I knew it. I knew all of it.

"What if he finds out what we did?" The words were nothing more than the gasp of a breath.

Wisps of terror that spun through the atmosphere and clawed at my spirit. My spirit that burned to be set free. Gone to a place where I might land in the arms of a man who would hold me up rather than beat me down.

God.

It was stupid for me to even be thinking about another man when I was in the midst of mayhem. But every day that'd passed since Kale had last texted me made me wish for him a little more.

Someday.

Someday.

"He won't," she said vehemently, though there was no missing the spark of fear in her eyes. "He won't. Okay?"

"I've always had to be the strong one, Jenna. The one who had faith." I fisted both my hands over my heart. "I never stopped believing my son would live when everyone else had. And somehow . . . somehow this time, I'm petrified I'm going to lose him in a way I never imagined."

"That's because you're being attacked. Your heart and your faith and your family, all your beliefs, everything you've worked for . . . it's being attacked. But this is a battle you and Evan are going to win. And we're gonna fight it however we have to."

I pressed my fingertips into my eyes and gave a sharp shake of my head. "I can't even stand the thought of Evan having to spend one night in that house."

"He won't have to. And seriously, this is Dane we're talking about. He'd probably have Evan for one hour, and the pussy would send him home to you. Evan always did put a cramp in his style. Honestly, I don't think he ever thought you'd let it get this far, and he's just trying to put the pressure on you.

I'd bet my life he's too much of a coward to see this through."

Anger blew out of me on a rigid huff. "Or *Mommy Dearest* will pay to have someone come in and care for him full-time." Locked away like some modern-day flower in the attic. "Or send him away like she suggested we do when he was born, you know, because Evan is a 'bad representation of the Gentry name.'"

I could feel the consequences of what we'd done barreling forward, the memory of the moment I'd felt so helpless I'd been left without a choice.

"That's crazy," I had said.

But it didn't matter how crazy Jenna's suggestion had seemed, my heart had screamed it was the only way. That I had to take action and do it then. I could no longer sit around and wait.

"How?" I'd begged through my tears while I'd peeked over at my precious son who'd been fast asleep on Jenna's couch since we'd gone to her house to find escape.

She'd grimaced. "I might know a guy who can help."

I'd started down a path I thought I'd had to take. My actions illicit as I tried to hide Evan away from the clutches of Dane.

Illegal things I never could have imagined myself doing a few years ago.

Getting myself in deeper and deeper each day that passed.

But protecting my son was worth any crime or sin on my part. But Dane was asking for the records.

Dread coiled and twined. A downward spiral.

God.

What was I going to do?

"Hey. This doesn't change anything. You don't let him beat you down or scare you, because that's what he wants. You and Evan are gonna keep moving forward. Do you understand what I'm saying?"

I nodded minutely, the tweak of my lips thankful. So grateful for my friend who'd stepped up, my rock when I'd needed to be Evan's.

She brushed back the hair matted to my face. "Okay, then. It's settled. No more tears. What do you say we go pick up Evan the Great? I'm taking you both to dinner. My treat."

Sniffling, I nodded again. "Okay."

thirteen

Kale

Willpower was a tricky bitch.

Out of the gate, you felt strong in your resolution. Confident. Insolent, even.

You could so absolutely do this.

No question.

It was in the bag.

Easy-peasy.

Whether you had committed to quitting smoking or cutting your calories in half or giving up the bottle, that first moment you made that promise to yourself?

You were almost on a high. On top of the world. A champion.

Your only focus was why you should do it and why it would benefit you and the people around you.

No thought given to how hard it was actually going to be.

You hadn't considered that when you woke up in the morning, it'd be the first thing on your mind or that it'd track you through the day. No deliberation of the niggling sensation at the back of your brain, constantly whispering that you were missing something.

And you definitely hadn't given thought to the reality that when you tried to go to sleep at night, it'd be the only thing you could see when you closed your eyes.

But I did it.

I drove past that little shop every damned day for nearly two weeks and barely gave it a glance. And by the time I passed by it in the evening, I'd gun the accelerator, flying right on by, jaw rigid and teeth clenched, refusing to look that way.

Not allowing myself to wonder if she was still behind the doors. If she was smiling. If Evan was with her.

When I crawled in bed at night, I pretended she wasn't the only thing I could see. Pretended I didn't wonder if she was wet and thinking of me.

It was for the best.

It was stupid to even want her, anyway. It wasn't like I was going to make something with her and that kid. A life like they deserved.

If I could even if I wanted to.

Just being around them had dredged up too many memories. Made me *remember,* and remembering fucking hurt. Gut told me if I got any deeper into Hope, any deeper into Evan, it just might ruin me.

So, I shoved that little obsession aside, buried it with the flickers of worry that kept flaring up when I thought of her shit-pile of a soon-to-be ex-husband, who was probably still giving her a hard time.

Restrained myself from looking him up so I could pay him a little visit.

None of my concern.

Right?

Right.

And then . . .

Then there was this little girl.

Five years old.

Tiffany.

Fucking adorable, black curly hair that was all kinds of wild around her chubby face.

She'd returned for her second visit with me, being worked up for intermittent high fevers that we couldn't pin down the cause of.

The whole time, she'd been completely cooperative, smiling, following my requests.

In hindsight, maybe she'd been a little too cooperative.

Because the second we'd finished, she'd looked up at me with wide, hopeful eyes and told me she'd been a good girl during her examination and she wanted to know where her lollipop was.

Of course, she did.

With my mouth flopping all over the place, I'd finally managed to tell her I'd run out.

You'd think I had single-handedly taken down the entire Disney franchise.

That'd been my breaking point.

At least I was blaming it on that.

I scrubbed a hand over my face and looked to the Alabama sky, so blue with the day. "You're an idiot," I mumbled beneath my breath before I spun on my heel and moved the rest of the way down the sidewalk.

I didn't hesitate at the door. I pulled it open and stepped inside.

Hoping I was making the right choice.

But I had no idea what else to do.

The bell chimed above when I stepped into the small shop. The second she saw me, Jenna grinned like she'd won the lottery.

But she wasn't who held my attention.

It was Hope whose mossy gaze snapped up to meet mine when she felt my presence, those full lips parting in surprise.

Hope.

Fucking Hope.

The air got thick, and I felt a little dizzy while I was standing there just inside the doorway, looking at this girl who had to be the best thing I'd ever seen.

Red hair twisted into a loose braid and pulled over one shoulder, pieces falling out everywhere, those eyes so damned green. And she was wearing this floral dress that did funny things to me, twisting me up in knots of need.

Fuck.

I wanted her.

I wanted her so damned bad I could taste it.

"Kale."

"Hey," I said, taking one step in from the door, feeling flustered and hot. So unlike me, but this girl had me outside of myself. My attention darted to the spot where the lollipops had been, a bunch of coffee mugs filling the space. "I'm out."

Hope frowned in confusion. "What?"

"I need more," I stammered.

Her frown deepened.

Brilliant.

If only Ollie could see me, he'd be giving me shit for the rest of my life.

I drew a circle in the air with my index fingers, starting at the top and meeting at the bottom.

She looked at me like she was concerned for my sanity.

Yeah.

Me, too.

"The lollipops. I'm out of the lollipops," I finally managed.

"Oh." Disappointment or surprise, I wasn't sure, but she blinked like she was rearranging the idea of why I was there around in her brain.

I guessed maybe I should have been doing that, too. Too bad all I could think about right then was stalking around the counter and propping her on it.

Kissing her and touching her and sinking inside.

All the reasons why I couldn't slammed against the visions.

Cold, stark lights. That fucking flat line.

My heart shivered in my chest, and then I was thinking about why this was bad for her, too. The fact she was fucking terrified of whatever that dickhead was demanding of her.

I'd seen it. Written all over her when she'd made that admission in the examination room. When she'd told me what she had to lose, which was so much more than I could even comprehend or imagine. Knew I wasn't even close to understanding what she was going through.

The thought of that sent a fresh round of rage rushing through me.

I had this intrinsic need to know what that asshole was demanding of her, of Evan, all the while I was contending with all these images of what their lives might have been like when he was in them. If it was good or bad. If she missed him or was glad he was gone.

If he'd *hurt* them.

My nerves zapped with the threat of rage.

Fuck. I couldn't even tolerate the thought.

She smoothed her hands over her apron nervously. "I'm still out. I was planning to make some over the weekend at the house. If you want to come back on Monday, I'll have them ready for you to pick up."

Right then, the swinging door to the kitchen swung open and Evan came bounding out.

Joy.

Life.

Hope.

It swirled through the air. Filling the space.

Radiating and vibrating and confusing.

It made it difficult for me to stand, the solid ground suddenly unsteady, those memories trying to press themselves into the forefront.

His entire face lit up when he saw me, and he pushed his glasses farther up his nose with both his hands like he was making sure it was really me he was seeing.

God, the kid looked like the cutest little bug when he blinked at me from behind the thick lenses.

Heart squeezing in a fist, I lifted a hand to wave at him.

HI, he gestured. Now that I could read.

He gestured a bunch more while he mouthed, *Dr. Bryant.*

All of a sudden, he darted back into the kitchen, the door swinging behind him. In a flash, he was bursting back through, holding a big spiral-bound notebook and a marker. He went straight to the counter and started writing on the notebook.

He held it up.

What are you doing here?

Hope fidgeted beside him, her expression nearly unreadable because it said too much.

Why are you really here?

You're only making this harder.

I wish things were different.

Stay.

Carefully, I edged across the space, eyeing Hope as that energy lit between us. That insane attraction I felt when we neared.

Flares.

Fire.

Flames.

I wanted to lick her up and down. Touch her and fuck her and maybe hold her afterward.

That right there was the reason I should hightail it out the door.

Among a million others.

Instead, I accepted the marker Evan offered.

I'm out of lollipops. All the kids love them. I need more.

His attention dropped to read it and then he looked back up at me.

I swore the magnitude of his smile knocked me back a step.

REALLY? he gestured. I got that, too.

"Really," I said.

He went back to writing.

That's good because me and mom and Aunt Jenna are going to make a lot. How many do you want? Maybe we'll sell enough that there will be no more bad hearts.

I rubbed at my chest, having to wonder exactly what it was this kid was doing to mine.

That depends on how many you can make.

Lots. Do you want to help? I bet we can make a million.

Hope cleared her throat and touched his shoulder to get his attention. Apparently, she'd been watching the interaction over his shoulder. "I don't think that's a good idea. The kitchen is already going to be pretty crowded with the three of us."

She didn't even sign. She was talking to me. Expecting her son to pick up on what she was saying.

"That's okay. I get it."

Jenna made a dramatic gasping sound. Her phone was held out in front of her, her eyes wide in an exaggerated way. "Oh goodness, Harley Hope, I am *so* sorry . . ."

Harley Hope.

A smile edged my mouth at her full name, and I tucked away that information for another day.

Jenna continued without pausing, "But I just got word Maw-Maw needs her hair done up real nice for bingo tonight, and I'm not going to be able to help like I promised. Apparently, there's a man she has her sights set on. I'm afraid I'm going to have to bail. I feel so bad."

Hope shot her a look that promised she *was* going to be sorry before saying, "Evan and I can handle it. No worries."

Jenna's brow twisted in horror. "Are you sure? That is a lot of work."

"Completely sure. We have all weekend."

"Oh, I have a good idea!" Jenna turned her gaze on me, forged innocence written all over her face. "Why don't you help? You're the one who needs them, after all. Plus, Hope here is gonna have all these supplies she needs to carry in, and they're super heavy, and she's had a really long day here at the shop. It might be nice for her to have a big, strapping man help her out."

Could the girl be more obvious?

She shot me an exaggerated wink.

Apparently, she could.

Hope hissed something under her breath and smacked Jenna's hip. Clearly, she thought I couldn't see it, so I stood there trying not to laugh.

But it was Evan who was suddenly jumping up and down and waving his arms, the nod of his head about as overdramatic as the ridiculous story Jenna had just told.

That was what nailed me to the spot.

The little lip-reader.

Had the feeling he always knew more than people gave him credit for.

I rubbed a hand over my mouth.

Not knowing what to say.

Because there was Evan basically begging me to, and Hope begging me with her eyes to stay away.

I glanced around at all three faces that were waiting for me to respond.

It didn't seem all that hard to figure out.

How could devoting a Friday night to helping out a single mom ever be considered bad?

I had been the one who walked through the door, asking for the favor. The one who'd come here after I'd committed to stay away and put Hope on the spot, telling her the kids needed more candy.

I'd lend a hand. Help out. Put a smile on the kid's face and make a fat contribution to their charity when we finished.

That was it.

Nothing more.

Easy-peasy.
Because just like that willpower?
Right then, I was riding a high.
Resolved.
Confident.
I could do this . . . said every addict trying to give up a vice.

fourteen

Kale

It was five after six when I pulled up in front of Hope and Evan's house.

The sun was a blazing halo that hung low on the Alabama horizon. Hazy rays glinted through the leafy trees and cast the air in shimmers and shadows.

The second I stepped from my car, the overpowering scent of honeysuckle hit my senses, the muggy summer in full bloom.

My heart rate kicked. A jumble of nerves and uncertainty.

That didn't stop me from heading for the white-picket fence that enclosed the perfectly hedged lawn.

Still, each step wound me tighter, ribbons of anticipation and greed.

I opened the short gate and strode up the walkway that cut through the center of the front yard, passing by the two massive trees on either side of the sidewalk that stood like proud soldiers guarding the quaint house.

Never slowing, I bounded up the two steps and onto the white porch. Potted plants were set up all over the place, vines growing over the railings, the door painted a bright red to give it a splash of color.

The little house screamed charm and comfort. It was the kind of place where you liked to imagine a happy family rested behind its doors, all of them curled up on the couch where they watched a show together.

My chest tightened, my mind wandering with questions, knowing I didn't really have the first clue about their lives. Wondering if it was good. If they were really happy.

This antsy need lit up my veins with the drive to offer them some of it.

Fuck. I really was losing my mind.

I rapped at the door.

A riot of footsteps thudded on the other side, frantic fingers flying through the locks. I thought maybe I had some of my answer to that when what had to be the happiest kid in the world grinned from the other side when the door swung open.

Wavy red hair and freckled nose and hopeful green eyes.

HI, he signed, bouncing on his toes, putting all kinds of emotion into that simple gesture.

My heart did that wobbly thing in my chest. Like it no longer fit. I gave an awkward wave. "Hey, Evan, how are you?"

He gave me a thumbs-up, and I had no idea why I found that so cute.

Felt like he was trying to make things as simple for me as he could— because God knew I was the one who had no clue what the fuck he was doing—the same as when he waved his hand in the air, indicating for me to follow.

I glanced around, quick to take in their home.

The front door opened to a small foyer that faced an arch that led to the living space, which was lined by crown molding.

An overstuffed couch covered in pillows and throws took up most of the room, two armchairs situated on either side, and a plush area rug covering the dark hardwood floors. All three pieces of furniture were angled so each seat had a good view of the television.

But none of that was the focus. No, because it was abundantly clear where all Hope's attention was aimed.

Pictures of Evan as far as the eye could see. Every surface and wall. A mismatch of frames and sizes.

Organized like art.

Like praise.

Evan darted down a short hall to the right, and I tore myself away from the scene in front of me and followed.

My stride easy until I damned near tripped over my feet when he led me through a smaller arch and into the kitchen.

Because Hope was bent over, wearing that same lust-inducing dress she'd had on earlier at the shop. She was digging into a bottom cupboard, her perfect, round ass swaying from side to side.

That ass I wanted to sink my teeth into.

Mouthwatering.

Every bit as much as whatever that insanely delicious smell was that filled the air.

Hearty and thick and warm.

She jerked around when she heard us walk in behind her. Green eyes went wide in her own kind of shock, like even though she expected me, she was still unprepared.

And that unbridled connection I felt to her every time I was in her space . . .

It surged.

Free and fast.

Rushing across the floor before either of us had the chance to find our footing.

Invading and penetrating and capturing.

Attraction and need.

This insane desire that threatened to get the best of me.

But that wasn't why I was here, so I tamped it down.

Clearing my throat, I pinned on an easy expression. That was the only way I was going to make it through this without having her on that counter, her legs around my waist, mouth devouring every inch of her.

"Hey, Shortcake." I stretched out my arms, the sleeves of my button-up rolled up my forearms. "I'm here and at your disposal. Whatever fits your fancy. Don't be shy. Use me up."

For a few beats, she breathed deeply. Like she needed to find her axis the same way I just had to do.

Beating the attraction down.

Both of us coming to the same place. The reason I was there.

To give something back when these two so clearly gave and gave.

I watched as her shoulders relaxed and amusement fluttered across those plush, pink lips. "Watch yourself, Dr. Bryant. You call me Shortcake one more time, and I'll have you out back mowing my lawn."

"Is that a threat? Come on, tell me you can do better than that."

She grabbed mitts and opened the top oven, because even though the girl's house was modest, the kitchen was not.

Gourmet might have been an understatement.

She had one of those huge industrial refrigerators and a double oven to match. Everything white and country and oozing the same kind of charm that seeped from her pores.

She leaned over and pulled out a casserole dish.

Good God. I almost blacked out.

Lush red hair falling around one shoulder as she leaned down, back arching just a fraction, the profile of her face revealing that button nose and pouty lips and dimpled chin.

She glanced at me from over her shoulder. "Oh, Dr. Bryant, you are heading into dangerous territory . . ."

My eyes raked over her body. Didn't I know it.

"I just might have a to-do list that is begging for attention. Considering I have no 'Honey,' it's grown about fifteen miles long," she teased, and I realized how much I liked it when she did.

When she felt comfortable enough to let go of a little of her worry when she was in my presence.

I flexed my arms. Satisfaction lined my insides when her attention went there, her breaths coming shorter and shorter. "Are you asking me to rescue you again, Shortcake? Bring it on, baby. Sir Bryant, remember? I'm obligated to do anything for my princess. And believe me, I won't consider it a burden."

Evan was suddenly right in my face, holding his pad up for me to see it, jarring me back into the reason I was there.

Which was absolutely not to flirt with his mom.

With all his stealth lip-reading, I could only pray the kid couldn't pick up on innuendo, too.

He jabbed at the page with his forefinger, brows rising high.

Hey, I thought we were making lollipops?

Forcing myself to stop looking at his mother, I chuckled at the way Evan was staring up at me like he'd be all too happy to put me in my place.

This time, I didn't even try to stop myself from ruffling my fingers through his hair.

Grabbing his notebook, I headed over to the island. He scrambled onto a stool right beside where I stood so he could read as I wrote.

Don't worry, buddy. I am here to make lollipops.

Knew he could read my lips, but something about communicating with him this way made me feel like I was talking directly to him.

I looked up, made sure Evan wasn't paying attention, and said, "But if your mom wants to put me to work after we're finished, she totally can. I'm all hers."

Fighting laughter, she narrowed her eyes at me. "I'm pretty sure these lollipops are going to keep you plenty busy. They are a lot more time-consuming than you can imagine. By the end of the night, you'll be regretting agreeing to come help. Begging for someone to put you out of your misery."

"That's where you're wrong. I can go all night."

Damn it all, I just couldn't help myself. Not when it came to her. Not when I knew that redness would go flushing up her neck and splashing on her cheeks.

Sweet.

Heat.

"Awful sure of yourself, aren't you, Dr. Bryant?" The words fell from her lips, throaty and low.

As she rounded the island, my attention swept from her legs, to the swish of her hips, and to the sway of her ass. She hiked up on her toes and grabbed three plates from a high cupboard.

"I'm one-hundred percent confident in myself, Ms. Masterson. I wasn't granted *knighthood* without reason. And I believe we've already talked about my stamina."

This time, she did laugh, shaking her head. "You are the cockiest man I've ever met."

She glanced back at me. Playful and sexy and the best thing I'd ever seen.

This woman was a vision. The kind of face that hit me right in the gut. Because there was no question she was stunning.

But it was the sheer goodness radiating from underneath that absolutely made her glow.

"Don't ever mistake confidence with arrogance. They are two very different things," I told her. Tension throbbed, clinging to the air and rippling with unspoken things.

Like she was issuing a secret, saying she'd really like to experience what that might be like.

"Shall we get to work so I can prove it?" I asked, not even sure what I was asking anymore. Knowing I just kept getting myself deeper and deeper. But I didn't know how to stop myself when I was around her.

She walked back to the island. Evan had his head down, scribbling something across the page. She set the plates on the counter and pressed her hands to either side of them, the swell of her tits just peaking over the neckline of her dress.

"Dinner first. You're going to need your energy."

Favorite food?

Reading his question, I pursed my lips in playful contemplation before I said, "Pizza."

I made sure Evan, who was sitting next to me at the table, could see my lips clearly.

Favorite car?

"Uh . . . foreign or American?"

He studied me through his thick glasses, so damned cute I was having a hard time focusing on making the candy. Having a tougher and tougher time keeping it at bay, the affection for this kid that just kept growing and growing.

American.

"Well, that's easy then. A 1968 Shelby Mustang."

Whoa, he mouthed, nodding his agreement. *Mine, too.*

"Really . . . are you sure you're not just trying to copy me?" I would have written it down, but I was wearing plastic gloves that were covered with melted sugar.

Across the table from us, Hope was over there, grinning this affected, sweet grin as she worked.

Her expression beneath the light pouring in from above shot straight through the center of me. The girl looked so damned happy while she listened to the interrogation Evan had been giving me for the last twenty minutes.

I'm not a copier!

He angled the pad of paper in my direction before widening his eyes and giving me a little shake of his head.

Like I already should have known.

I grinned at him. Of course, I did.

My expression must have assuaged him, because he was tapping the end of the marker on the pad, considering his next question.

Favorite ice cream?

"Strawberry."

It was out without a thought, and my gaze immediately darted to Hope across the table.

Maybe just so I could catch the blush heating up on her cheeks.

Obviously, she knew exactly the direction my thoughts had gone spiraling.

To strawberries and cream and all things sweet.

The way I wanted to lick her up and down. Go back to that night when she'd been in the palm of my hands and my name had been a whimper on her tongue.

A curl of lust threatened, and I tamped it down, refusing to go down that path, yet somehow, feeling like *going there* was inevitable at the same time.

Evan's hand flew across the page.

Are you my mom's boyfriend?

Okay, then. Apparently, I wasn't doing that bang-up of a job keeping my thoughts to myself.

I stopped what I was doing and shucked off the gloves, eyeing him as I grabbed the pad.

Why would you say that?

His answer was swift and honest.

Because when you look at her, you smile like you think she's pretty.

Damn, this kid saw things in a way unlike no other kid I'd ever met.
Keen and smart and discerning.
I hesitated for only a second before I wrote out my response.

That's because she is pretty.

Evan was grinning when he looked over at her before scratching something on the pad.

My mom is the prettiest mom in the whole world.

"What are you two over there gossiping about?" Hope asked, leaning farther over the table so she could sneak a peek at our private conversation.

That subtle blush blossomed when she saw the truth of what her son and I had been discussing.

"Oh, you two stop it. Every eight-year-old boy thinks his mama is the prettiest in the world until he gets to be a teenager, and then he decides to pretend like she doesn't even exist." It was all a gentle chiding.

NO WAY, he signed. *MY FAVORITE* was as close as I could get to figuring what he'd said.

Which made perfect sense, considering her smile turned so damned soft I felt something inside me melt just looking at the two of them.

MY HEART. That I got, without question, Evan's little lips moving as he looked at his mother, his little hand fisted over his chest.

Hope gestured the same, touching her chest, her gaze adoring.

My insides clenched almost painfully. Something that beautiful was hard to take in. The bond they shared. How was it possible I was goddamned terrified of it and drawn to it at the same time?

Evan looked back at me before he scribbled quickly.

Is she?

Was it regret I felt when I took back the marker and started to write?

No, Evan. We're just friends.

Another pass of the marker.

Are you my friend?

This kid.

Yeah, Buddy. We are definitely friends.

Sitting there, I didn't know why that didn't seem like enough.

I shoved the feeling off and poked him gently in the side. "Now get to work, little slacker."

He laughed, that rasping sound coming from his mouth, his smile so bright, his lips moving between the juts of laughter as he wrote.

I'm not a slacker.

No.

Not even.

But if I spent more time in their space, I was going to be a goner.

And I wasn't sure *my heart* could take that.

"You were not joking." I glanced over at Hope, who was standing hunched over the table and carefully winding the long ropes of colored candy into circles before she pressed sticks into their bases.

Why I was whispering, I didn't know.

But somehow it fit the mood the long night had slipped into.

The quiet vibe that had taken over the space.

"Where's that stamina you were bragging about a few hours ago?" It might have been a tease if the words hadn't have been so strained, so weighted in her own exhaustion.

A light chuckle rumbled out. "Guess I shouldn't be so sure of myself, after all. Some things are harder than they look."

She flinched with the double-meaning of it.

Both of us painfully aware of the other.

Like each of our movements barreled across the table.

Ricocheting and compounding.

We'd been at it for hours.

My fingers were sore, and my back hurt from leaning over for so long.

Heating the sugar and corn syrup on the stove.

Adding the flavor and the colors.

Rolling it into ropes.

Twisting them into circles.

Pressing the sticks into the bases.

It was tedious and time-consuming, and we most definitely hadn't come close to making the *million* Evan thought we would.

Still, we'd made a ton. Trays of them sat on every surface in varying degrees of readiness. Cooling before they could be wrapped in clear wrappers so the ribbon and stickers could be affixed, which was actually Evan's job on this makeshift assembly line.

Evan, who was fast asleep on the couch. Three hours before, he'd claimed he needed a break. Thirty minutes later, I'd tiptoed to the living room to check on him, only to find him curled under one of the throw blankets on the couch, his glasses askew, mouth open as his small breaths filled the air.

I'd taken his glasses and set them on the coffee table, somehow knowing I was crossing far too many lines when I pulled the blanket over his shoulders, affection so thick in my chest I could almost taste it.

I couldn't stop it.

Not after having what had to be the most amazing night of my life.

Hours spent with him and his mom. With his trusting smile and open, incredible mind. With their amazing connection. Their love so free. Unconditional.

With Hope's heart shining so bright, her body a stunning distraction.

Light and life and belief.

Yeah. I loved seeing it with Rex and Rynna. Their happy family. Didn't know of many people who deserved it the way they did.

But that experience was always me on the outside looking in. Doing my best to be there for them when they needed me.

Tonight, I'd felt right in the middle of it.

A partner to it.

A part of it.

It was stupid.

I hardly even knew them.

But standing there looking down at him, I'd been wishing things could maybe be different. I'd been wishing that fate wasn't such a cruel bitch to send me these two when I couldn't keep them. Shouldn't keep them.

Because everything felt too close and too raw and too real.

Besides, I knew Hope was struggling to deal with something bigger than I fully understood.

My bones howled with the warning that I shouldn't even be there. But my spirit was demanding I stay. That I explore whatever was happening between us. It felt too important to ignore.

The awareness of it had seeped into the atmosphere when I'd come back into the kitchen and told Hope he was asleep.

All the playful easiness from earlier had been erased.

In its place was an intensity that slowed the atmosphere. The room echoing with what-ifs and questions and hunger. This blinding need that tugged and pushed and bound.

"It's really late, Kale. You should go home. I never expected you'd stay this long."

I glanced at the clock. "It's barely one a.m. on a Friday night. That's still early."

I attempted a smirk that fell flat.

She gave a little huff. "I bet. Though, I'm sure you are much more accustomed to putting that stamina to better use on Fridays in the middle of the night. You regretting it yet, Cowboy?"

My mind blazed right back to that Friday two weeks ago.

I could hear her.

Taste her.

I angled my gaze her direction, pinning her with my stare, voice going deep. "My only regret is you not having the chance to experience it yet."

"Kale," she whispered, her fingers fumbling as she wound the candy. "Don't do this."

"I'm not the one who's doing it, Hope. Seems to me it's already there, whether we give it permission to be or not."

She blinked, trying to concentrate on finishing one of the last lollipops. I still could see the small tremble on the corner of her delicious mouth. "You're right. It's there. I just wish it would have come at a better time." I could see it, the fear that suddenly blistered across her flesh, the way those eyes glinted beneath the light with the moisture that had instantly gathered.

Rage.

It burned.

Immediate.

Hardening every place inside me. The sudden, consuming need to wrap both of them up and protect them.

"What is he asking?" I pushed out through gritted teeth, trying to keep myself cool and composed.

Impossible.

She exhaled a harsh breath, eyes moving to the archway to ensure Evan was still asleep before she looked back at me. "I'm not sure I should be telling you any of this."

I blinked, swallowing back the fury, something that was typically so foreign for me. I was the laid back one. The one who found the good in all situations.

But whoever that piece of shit was had the power to obliterate that.

My teeth gritted. "Why not?"

A small gesture of her chin as she said, "For starters, you basically look like you want to up and murder someone at the mention of my ex."

"That only seems natural."

"What's that?"

"Wanting to protect you."

She dropped her gaze back to her work, and I reached out, touched her hand from across the table. "I want to know, Hope. You can trust me."

Her eyes squeezed closed, like she wanted to disagree, or maybe like she wanted to run and hide, obviously struggling around the fear that had taken her whole.

"He wasn't a good dad?" Obvious, I knew, but I needed the verification. Her proof. Because I was feeling things I hadn't ever felt before.

A wild kind of protectiveness.

A savage kind of possessiveness.

She rasped a hoarse, unamused laugh, as she peered over at me.

"No, Kale, he wasn't a good dad."

Violence curled my fists. The itch to get up. Hunt him down.

"And I know what you're thinking . . ." she rushed. "It wasn't physical. It was . . ."

I attempted to keep my voice steady, but it tremored with barely contained fury. "What? You can tell me anything."

Fuck.

Deeper and deeper.

I couldn't stop.

She looked over at me.

Hopelessly.

Which just about fucking killed me.

"He rejected him as his child the second we found out about his heart condition."

My curled fists tightened. The tight rein I had on my anger slipped, just a fraction. "How could he do that?"

It wasn't even a question. I just couldn't fathom a father rejecting that kid.

That amazing kid.

An old kind of sorrow shook her head. "At first, I thought he was in shock. Processing it in his own way. But time wore on, and it only got worse and worse. The only thing he cared about was inheriting his grandfather's company, working day and night, his life consumed with earning that spot. Wanting the *money*. That became the only thing his life was about. I tried to hold out faith until there wasn't any faith left to hold on to."

Her tongue darted out to wet her lips, and she pressed the stick into the last lollipop, sinking into a chair from where she was standing.

Like she couldn't remain on her feet anymore.

"He—" She slammed her lips together and harshly shook her head, like she was about to admit something and then stopped herself. She hesitated for a couple seconds before she tentatively cut her gaze my direction, admitting what she thought she could, "It all finally came to a head a year ago, and I knew I couldn't keep my son in that house for a second longer."

Without a doubt, she was keeping the details veiled. Hidden. But I wanted to know it all. Every element. Fuel for the hatred that coursed and raced.

She cleared the thickness from her throat. "I packed our things and left. We were hiding out at Jenna's house, and of course, he showed up there demanding for us to come home. She threatened to call the police if he tried to get through her door. I petitioned for divorce. I asked for full custody and nothing more. I'd saved enough that I could put a down payment on this little house. I didn't want his support or his time or anything because he has never wanted anything from Evan. All I wanted was a quiet separation and our freedom."

Lines of pain tweaked all over her face, her voice rough. "I did what I thought I had to do, Kale."

There was so much in that statement. Something she wanted me to know and couldn't bring herself to say.

Anger swelled in the room. A swilling wave threatening to take me under.

Because this? I didn't know if I could handle it. Hearing about someone doing either her or Evan wrong.

Her inhale was sharp. Cutting. "He fought me from the beginning . . . saying I would regret it if I left him. I told him the only thing I wanted was my son free of his influence, so he did the one thing he knew would hurt me most . . ."

Head dropping, she choked as tears streaked down her face. When she finally looked up at me, her eyes were nothing but devastation. "This last week, I received a counter to my divorce claim. He's asking for full custody. The whole point of my leaving was to remove Evan completely from his life, protect him, and now he's trying to take him away from me."

My teeth ground as that rage clattered around my ribcage, and I couldn't remain sitting any longer. I was moving around the table. My discarded gloves hit the floor a split second before my knees did, and then I was cupping her face, urging her to look at me. "There is no chance on this earth that any court would declare you an unfit mother, Hope. None. I don't want you to worry about that."

Sniffling, she gave me one of those believing smiles, the kind that made her glow.

Sunshine.

Could feel it heating those vacant, dead places inside me. That place riddled with fear when all I'd ever wanted to be was the one who was brave.

The goddamned hero.

Or maybe it was the hatred that flamed. Hate for a man I hadn't even met. A man who was the one who was going to be feeling all the *regret* if we ever crossed paths.

"That's what Jenna keeps saying, and I'm trying to cling to that belief."

I ran my thumb under the hollow of her eye and then dropped my hands. "Good. Believe it. Hold on to it. Don't ever, *ever* give up on hope."

She smiled this wistful smile. "My heart has always been hung on hope."

My chest squeezed. Because I got it. She was an incredible woman who carried her entire world on her shoulders. And, fuck, I wanted to bear some of that weight.

I knew I didn't deserve the jealousy that raved through my insides. But it was there. Alive and thriving. "So, if he rejected Evan, why the hell would he want custody?"

A shrug of her dainty shoulders and a tug of her bottom lip between her teeth. "Part of it is because I left him. Because of his pride. But I can't help but feel it's more than that. He says he still loves me, but then he always blamed me."

"That Evan was sick?"

Her nod was shaky. "We didn't know anything was wrong until Evan was two days old. He was this perfect, tiny thing. Small. So small. But the doctors didn't seem to be all that concerned. Until the nurse listened to his heart on his final check when we were being discharged from the hospital."

Her voice trembled, taken back to that day. "They flew him to Memphis to the big children's hospital there. He had his first heart surgery when he was five days old. *Five days old.*"

Hope clutched her chest. "I've never been so scared in all my life. They tried to repair his abnormality, hoping it would be enough for him not to need a transplant, but they didn't give us a lot of reassurance that it would. They told us to prepare for the worst. They told us his condition was typically caused by a genetic defect, and that if he did live, then we should expect it to also present in other ways."

Images flashed. My greatest loss. My biggest regret.

I sucked in air against the memories, trying not to compare the two. But it was so fucking hard. So close. Too similar. Still, it didn't seem to fucking matter because all I wanted was to move closer, hold her, take the turmoil away.

"Hope," I murmured, shifting farther around so I could see her better, see the brilliant love that shined on her face.

Really, I didn't even have to look.

Because I could feel it.

Bounding from the walls. She gave a soggy smile. "I didn't accept what they said, Kale. I knew my baby would be just fine. That he would grow and love and live. And that the world might see him differently, but he was exactly how *he* was supposed to be. I won't lie and say it was easy, because those were the most difficult, terrifying months and years of my life. But never—not once—did I give up hope."

"And that hope shines right out of him," I said.

Her face pinched. "But his father . . . his father didn't get the perfect son he demanded. He refused to be tested to see if he carried the gene. Telling me it was bullshit. That we should *let him go* and try again."

The last tore from her throat on a cry. On the hurt and wounds the bastard had inflicted.

That rage.

It blistered.

Blinking through her tears, she dropped her gaze, her chest heaving, before looking back at me.

Destroyed.

Her expression was nothing but desolation.

"I took Evan away because he wanted me to sign a DNR. If Evan falls ill again, he doesn't want us to fight to save him. I can't let that happen. I did what I *had* to do." She begged the last. Like she was pleading for me to understand.

I choked out this sound that verged somewhere between horror and the threat of revenge.

"Fuck," I muttered, trying to process. To make sense of what all of this really meant.

Monster.

That vile bastard was nothing but a monster. I hated him.

But I didn't know how to say it. How I would get out of it if I stepped in the middle of it. But that was what I wanted to do. I wanted to get in the ring and beat the piece of shit bloody.

Her expression shifted into one of stark vulnerability. "But you've probably already read all of this in his records, haven't you, Dr. Bryant?" She said it like she wanted to attempt a tease, before she fell back into somberness. "You probably understand it better than I do."

I let a small smile tweak the corner of my mouth. "Well, I knew some of it. But his records never said anything about his father being a douchebag who needs to be taught a few lessons about being a man."

She stumbled over a small laugh. "Well, I wish they did. I could use it in court."

"Done," I said, forcing a grin before I sobered again, studying her expression.

"So, really, he's just doing all of this to threaten you? To force you into doing what he wants?"

He wanted her.

But not Evan.

What a sick fucker.

A tremor raced her throat when she swallowed. "I have no idea what he really wants, Kale. I don't even think he knows. And the only thing I want is him to leave us alone. Let us live."

I took her face between my palms again, making sure she was looking directly into my eyes before I said, "You are, Hope. You are living and giving your son the best kind of life. He's the happiest kid I've ever seen."

"He's the best thing that ever happened to me," she whispered. I did my best to tame the overwhelming feeling that raced my veins.

Possession

Greed.

Not because I wanted to control her the way that prick tried to keep her under his thumb but because the need to protect her was almost a riot where it clamored to take hold inside me.

Raging and growing and stirring.

"Don't let him scare you. I know that's simple for me to say, but I promise you . . . you don't have anything to worry about. No judge would ever find in that bastard's favor. And if you need me to sit up on that stand and claim it, as Evan's doctor, I will."

Fuck.

This was getting messy.

So damned messy.

Because all those lines were blurring and crossing and tangling.

A fresh round of tears streaked down her face. "Thank you, Kale, but I don't know if I can ask you to get in the middle of this mess. It goes deeper than you know." Grief and fear struck on her face. "When I told you my life was complicated, I meant it, but I refuse to regret a single choice I've made in my life that I've made to protect my son. No matter what it costs me"

"Maybe you should stop questioning the lengths I'd go to in order to protect the both of you."

"You don't know what you're getting yourself into," she whispered softly.

It was like a zap to the air.

Energy.

Need.

That tether of awareness cinching and cinching, pulling us closer until it felt like there was no space between us at all.

My fingers slipped into the silky strands of her hair.

I wanted to kiss her.

God, I wanted to kiss her so damned bad, and I knew if I did, there would be no going back.

I thought maybe she saw the hesitation in my eyes, because she cleared her throat and inched back to put some space between us.

"Let's call it a night. The rest of these need to cool before they can be wrapped, and I need to get Evan into bed. He and I can finish them in the morning. I'll drop them off to you so you don't have to bother on Monday morning."

I quirked a grin. "What, you don't want to see me walking through your shop's door on Monday morning. What if I'm having a terrible craving for A Drop of Hope?"

I let my voice twist with the tease, a distraction from the chaos staging a war in my spirit. The selfless war raging in her.

Heat rushed across her cheeks, and she peered at me, that vulnerable expression laying siege to her face.

Faith and belief.

The girl was so gorgeous that it was hard to look at her.

She let her fingertips roam the collar of my shirt, staring at the action before she met my gaze again.

Words a breathy confession. "Am I a fool to admit that the favorite part of my day is watching you walk through that door?"

"Think maybe both of us are guilty of that . . . being fools," I told her, gentling my fingers through a long strand of her strawberry hair. Through the silky softness.

Relishing.

Wanting more.

Something darkened in her gaze, and I knew she was about to dive deeper than I was ready for her to go. That she was getting ready to ask me things I wasn't ready to answer.

Because the girl could read me, too.

I edged back, hating being the asshole who shut her down after she'd just completely opened up to me. Trusted me.

But I wasn't ready to bring the darkness that lived deep inside me out into her light.

"I should go," I told her.

She nodded. "Okay. But please . . . let me bring the lollipops to you. It would make me feel better after everything you've done."

For a moment, I just stared, blinking, assaulted by the urge to ask her to let me stay.

But I had to go. I knew it. I needed to get the hell out of there before I did something I couldn't undo.

"All right then," I told her, smiling slowly as I pushed to my feet.

I stretched my hand out for her, and she accepted it.

Need.

Just that small touch had need racing through my veins, careening and curving and compelling.

My jaw clenched, and I forced myself to let her hand go once she was standing.

Hope followed me down the hall. Her presence covering me all over. Skating my skin and spinning my head.

Intoxicating.

I tried to hold my breath because I swore this girl floated on the air.

So damned sweet.

I paused in the doorway to the living room, hesitated for a beat before I went for the couch.

Before she could stop me, before I could stop myself, I scooped the kid into my arms. He made a grumpy, grumbling sound as he looped his arms around my neck and snuggled closer.

Shit. Shit. Shit.

"Kale." More fidgeting from beside me, Hope anxious and restless.

"Let me help you get him to bed," I managed, no longer able to see how the lines holding me back made any sense.

Resigned, she nodded, and I followed her when she headed through another arch and down a separate hall that led to the back of the house. We passed by one small room that was set up as an office, and she turned into the last door at the end of the hall.

I followed close behind, unable to stop myself from grinning when I saw his room.

Decorated in everything comics. From Marvel to Conan to the completely obscure.

It so utterly, completely fit this adorable kid that my heart was thumping again.

Mind spinning with impossibilities.

I laid him on his bed and stepped back so Hope could pull his covers over him. She pressed a kiss to his temple and then ran her fingers through his hair. Neither of us said anything as we tiptoed out of his room, back down the hall, and through the living room.

For a flash, my gaze darted to the far back of the living space. To the double doors I knew had to lead to Hope's bedroom.

I wanted to take her there. Lay her out. Treat her right.

Lust curled my guts. Almost painfully. No question, Hope knew exactly where my thoughts had gone. Hers right there with mine.

Desire a flood in the room. Rising so high that there was no doubt we were getting ready to drown.

Both of us going deeper and deeper into that territory where it was so abundantly clear we couldn't go.

Fisting my hands in restraint, I forced my feet to move the rest of the way across the room, back through the foyer, and out the front door.

When I stepped out onto the porch, I inhaled the cool air that brushed my heated skin and prayed it might stand a chance of dousing the fire.

I pulled in a couple deep breaths, letting the sounds of the night calm my racing heart, the bugs trilling in the trees and the leaves that rustled in the light breeze.

I turned around when Hope came out behind me and quietly snapped the door shut behind her.

Moonlight poured down on her face. Milky skin a translucent glow.

"Thank you so much for helping out tonight," she whispered, her arms crossed over her chest like she didn't know how else to protect herself.

"No, Hope, thank you. For dinner. For taking the time to make all those lollipops. For letting me experience the best night I've had in a long time."

For being you.

Her head shook, and her brow pinched. "I don't know what to make of you, Kale Bryant."

I let out the tiny huff of a laugh. "When I'm around you, I don't know what to make of myself, either." I smiled at her. "Good night, Harley Hope. Tell your little man I had the best time tonight. And you tell his mom that he's lucky he has her, just as lucky as she is to have him."

Her expression turned almost pleading.

Want and desire and that unbridled hope that radiated from her like it was a second skin.

It took everything I had to force myself to turn away and start across her porch. My footsteps echoing on the dense night.

She retreated, standing in the doorway. I could feel her staring back at me.

"Kale." I heard it at the same time that intensity swept through the air.

A bolt of lightning.

Combustion.

I turned around just as the girl spun in the doorway, coming for me.

I was already moving back that direction.

We collided.

Fire.

I hoisted her up, and her legs wrapped around my waist as our mouths crashed together.

Her tongue swept against mine.

That sweet, sweet tongue.

Frantic.

Needy.

Desperate.

Laps and licks and frenzied strokes.

Winding a hand in her hair, I kissed her just as wildly as she was kissing me. Without breaking it, I carried her back across the porch and into the foyer. Held in the protective shadows of the short hall, I pressed her against the wall.

Ground my hard-on against her center, her skirt riding up, just her underwear and my jeans separating us.

Her pussy as hot as her fingers that sank into my shoulders.

As hot as her tongue that tangled with mine.

I had no idea how I was going to make it back from this. How I was ever going to stop craving it.

"Fuck, Hope. One touch, and you are already killing me. I want to disappear in you. Sink deep inside. Get lost in your body. Tell me you want that."

God. What the fuck was I saying?

I rocked again.

Hope moaned. "Kale. Yes. Please."

"What do you need?" I mumbled against her mouth, and she was mumbling back, "Make me feel good. You make me feel good. How is it possible you make me feel so good?"

"Because I know how to take care of you. You deserve a man who will treat you right."

And I pressed myself harder against her, rubbing and rocking and driving her mad.

Which was the best kind of torture.

Complete, utter torture as she writhed and pitched and begged, the urgent thrust of her hips against my jeans and the delicious sounds from her mouth as she kissed and begged, bringing me to the edge.

That greedy, selfish place inside me roared, telling me it would be fine if I ripped open my fly and sank right in.

That she was right there.

I shoved the urge down and gave her what I knew she needed.

My hands moved to her hips, and I rode my palms up, cupping her ass so I could angle her just right.

Hitting her clit with each roll of my hips.

I was so hard I swore I was going to lose it right there.

Her nails cut into my shoulders and scratched at the back of my neck, and she whimpered, her back arching off the wall. "Kale, oh God . . . again."

I dipped down and bit her tit through her dress.

Harley Hope caught fire.

Trembles rocked through her body, vibrating through me.

Her pleasure.

The sweet, sweet heat.

I could feel it radiating from her body and into mine. And I didn't even care that I was in physical pain or that I was going to go home with the worst case of blue balls I'd ever endured.

Because watching her glow?

For a moment, the girl free and riding on ecstasy?

That was all that I needed.

She whimpered and moaned these tiny, perfect sounds, trying to keep quiet as she flew.

A stark reminder that we needed to hide.

That there was some pussy bitch out there who wanted to hurt them. Maybe not physically. But the kind of wounds he wanted to inflict cut just as deep.

I was right there to catch her when she came back down.

She was gasping tiny, uncontained breaths, her chest heaving from the wall as she struggled to find her control.

Swallowing hard, she stared at me through the shadows with a mix of awe and regret. "I lose myself when I'm with you. I am so sorry."

I think I'm already lost.

I didn't say it. I just peeled myself from her body and carefully set her on her feet. I touched her face. Softly. Hoping she got it. "For once in your life, Hope, I think it's time someone took care of you."

She set her hand over mine, pressing it tighter into her face. A blaze of affection smoldered in her eyes as she looked at me. "It feels good, Kale. You feel so good. You make me want things I know I shouldn't ask you for."

A smirk ticked up at the corner of my mouth. "I certainly hope it feels good. Wouldn't want my knightly duties to be lacking, would we?"

The redness bloomed, the freckles across her cheeks sparking against her soft, soft skin.

I ran my thumb over her swollen lips. "And believe me, Hope. You have me wanting things I know I shouldn't ask you for, either."

I looked around the enclosed space, the house blanketed by the deep, deep night. "I don't want to do anything that hurts you."

And I didn't even know what I was referring to. Putting her in a situation that might cause trouble with her ex or putting her in a situation where I bailed.

Because there I stood, tempted to tell her that her son terrified me but that I wanted to wrap him up and protect him anyway. Wanted to tell her I was terrified of failing again. That I might not be enough when I'd been struggling to be that man for all my life.

Instead, I backed away, still looking at her, my smile gentle. "Now go . . . sleep. Rest. You deserve it."

She gulped around the emotion that rippled between us.

I shoved my hands in my pockets so I wouldn't reach out and take more and headed back out the door.

"Thank you, Kale," she whispered, her soft voice riding on the night, hitting me from behind where she'd followed me out.

From the gate, I glanced back at her, at her silhouette on her porch.

The girl the best thing I'd ever seen.

"Good night, Princess," I called quietly into the night.

Then I turned and forced myself to get in my car, start it up, and drive away.

Hope

I didn't even have to look to know who it was when I heard the rustling in the foyer.

"Oh, now you decide to show up," I called, glancing at her when I felt the force of energy burst in the room.

Jenna stood in the archway to the kitchen, arms stretched out and braced on the jambs, grinning from ear to ear. She glanced around at the disaster that had become my kitchen. "Looks to me like you had it all under control."

Under control.

Right.

I didn't think I'd ever felt so out of control in all my life.

Without an invitation, she waltzed in and went straight for the coffee maker. "Besides, some people need a little nudge in the right direction."

I eyed her as I slid the wrappers over the lollipops. "And just what direction do you think you're sending me?"

She poured coffee into a big mug and then grinned at me from over her shoulder. "With the way that man looks, I'm hoping to the moon. Or maybe the stars. He does have big hands, after all . . . you know what that means."

She wiggled her fingers out in front of her.

"Jenna," I hissed. My eyes darted to Evan, praying he hadn't been paying attention. I'd already been feeling itchy this morning, unable to believe I'd let that man bring me to orgasm right out in the open.

Twice.

This time in my foyer.

A shiver blazed a path down my spine, landing in that well of desire in my belly that was getting fuller and fuller. I had no idea how much more I could take before it overflowed.

Thank God, Evan was completely occupied where he sat in the built-in booth at the breakfast nook that curved under the big window.

His focus was trained on his iPad and whatever goofy pictures he and his friend Josiah were sending back and forth over Snapchat.

Their favorite way to communicate.

"What?" Jenna defended, giving me that look. "I already checked to make sure he wasn't paying any attention."

"But still."

Her brows lifted as she dug into my fridge and pulled out the creamer. "But still, you need to lighten up. You're strung up so tight that I bet one touch really would send you rocketing for the moon."

A rush of heat flushed my skin. My thoughts were back there. To last night. God, I didn't recognize myself around that man.

Jenna cocked her head, eyes going wide before she squealed in vicarious delight. "Oh my God. Did you two do the deed? Give me the details. I want them all. Don't leave anything out. Please tell me it was right here on this counter." She smacked it with the palm of her hand. "So hot."

I shushed her, waving my hand in her face, my voice dropped to a manic whisper. "We did not do the *deed*."

It wasn't as if Evan could actually hear, but that didn't mean he wouldn't *hear*. My son was about as clever as they came and could read body language almost as well as he could read lips.

"But you did do *something*. You would not be lookin' like that otherwise, so don't try to lie." She circled her finger around me, her expression pure glee.

For a second, I hesitated before the muted words tumbled from my mouth. "He kissed me."

Okay, so he'd kissed me before. But this kiss . . .

This kiss.

There was something between us last night that hadn't been there before. Something beyond the attraction. Strong and fierce and overpowering.

My insides shook and, suddenly, I couldn't breathe. I reached a shaky hand out to steady myself on the table.

Jenna loosed a knowing smile before taking a sip of coffee. "Whoa. That must have been some kiss."

I nodded. "It was some kiss."

Kale had kissed me in a way I hadn't ever been kissed before. As if I was beautiful and right and he wanted me more than anything else.

With respect.

With adoration and desperation.

As if maybe I could be everything.

Was it foolish to want him to be that for me in return?

I sank into a chair. "I've never felt anything like it."

Jenna washed her hands and plopped down beside me, sliding on a pair of gloves so she could help me put the wrappers on the lollipops.

Her voice was quiet. "You like, *like* him?"

I nodded slowly.

I liked him.

"So much." I gave a harsh shake of my head before I peeked over at her. "Why do the best things have to come into our lives at the worst times?"

"I know sometimes it feels that way. But in the end, it turns out things happen exactly when they're supposed to."

In contemplation, I bit down on my bottom lip, wishing it were true. "Maybe. But I . . ." I glanced over at my son, my reason for living. "I just can't do anything that would put Evan at risk."

Jenna rolled her eyes at me affectionately. "Newsflash, Harley Hope, I don't think you could do anything that would put Evan at risk. Your make up just wouldn't allow it. He's always come first, and he always will. And the fact that you are even considering something with that man should tell you something."

"My instincts weren't exactly spot on with Dane."

"Dane lost his ever-loving mind, Hope. Seriously, that man was himself one day, and the next? *Poof*, he was unrecognizable. I don't think your instincts could have warned you about him."

I blinked, knowing what she said was the truth. Not that it was even close to an excuse, but I'd always known Evan's diagnosis had somehow sent my husband over the edge. Sparked a cold, cowardly wickedness in him that had been nonexistent before.

Jenna eyed me. "What about him bein' Evan's doctor."

A sigh pushed free. "I don't know. I would think . . . I'd think he'd have to stop seeing him as a patient if he were to get involved with us in any way. And the records . . ."

I gulped, fighting the sick, clawing feeling that took to my blood when I thought of the consequences of anyone finding out.

"No one's gonna find out. We're gonna make sure that divorce is final and then it won't matter, anymore. It was just temporary, Hope. You know that."

I did.

But I realized the closer Kale got, the more he knew, there was a chance I might be putting his career on the line, too.

Besides that, I hated the idea of Kale no longer caring for my son.

He was a *good* doctor.

I'd seen it the second he sat on that stool in front of Evan in the exam room.

We'd been through enough physicians that I instinctively knew when they actually cared. When they felt for their patients and would do everything possible to keep them healthy rather than treating them as another number or dollar sign.

"But honestly? My biggest concern about all of this is what Dane would do with the information if I started seeing someone. He wouldn't hesitate to use it against me. Call me a cheater."

Not to mention, the unease and obscured fear I couldn't help but notice flicker in Kale's eyes. A part of him I couldn't really see. A demon of his own. Gone before I could establish exactly what it was. As if that sea of blue suddenly went murky, muddled with questions and reservations and panic before he forced it down into a secret place.

Maybe we both were complicated.

"Pssh . . . that asshole has been cheatin' for years, Harley Hope. If he tries to use it against you, it won't take much to dig up evidence to throw down your own accusation. Maybe you returning the favor and calling him out on in it court is exactly what Mr. Limp Dick needs."

A wry grin took to Jenna's face. "Hopefully his *mama* will be there for support so she can have a front-row seat. Dane Gentry III. Heir to the Gentry fortune and lousy cheater shoots himself in five seconds. Every. Single. Time. Poor boy wouldn't know a clitoris if it smacked him in the face. Think we can bribe anyone to add in those few minor details? They may not be admissible in court, but I think it's about time someone brought that horrible *obstruction of justice* to light."

A giggle slipped free. "Could you picture his mama's face?"

Jenna made a face like she was sucking on a lemon. "Well, I never," she feigned the rich Southern accent, her hand pressed to her throat.

"I bet she never." It slipped out before I could stop it, and my eyes bugged as my hand slapped over my mouth.

Jenna busted up laughing. "Oh my God, what has gotten into you, Harley Hope?" She leaned in closer. "Tell me it's a big, huge, yummy dick."

This time I did smack her, unable to keep myself from laughing. "Jenna. What is wrong with you?"

"The question is, what is wrong with you? A man like that wants you, and you're sitting over here wrapping lollipops on a Saturday morning? Here we went through all that trouble to hire a manager to run the cafe on the weekends so we could have them off, and we are both still working. You should be spending this time *wrapping* something else."

"Oh, I think I have plenty of *wrapping* to do. We need to get all of these packaged by noon so Evan and I can drop them off at Kale's place."

She jostled her shoulder into mine. "Swapping addresses now, huh?"

I sent her a playful scowl. "Yeah, because of your meddling."

And because of the meddling, the few evenings I'd spent with Kale Bryant had come to feel more profound, more *important*, than all I'd spent with Dane combined.

"Give that man a chance. You really need to move on and find what's right for you and Evan."

The concept of that flared in my chest, pressing out, wrapping me in warm, perfect ribbons. But I had no idea what Kale really wanted. Why he kept coming through my door, shaking up my world, tempting me with the kind of pleasure I'd never known before.

And if he did want it? Us? Would it be me who hurt him in the end?

"I'm not even sure he wants a chance. He said it himself when he asked me out. He wanted one night."

"Yet, where was he last night? Here, with you, working on lollipops for your son's charity, on a Friday night nonetheless. Doesn't sound like a one-night thing to me."

Warmth fluttered in my belly.

Wings of hope.

Still, my reservations were like an updraft. "And you know me dating isn't only about me. Especially when Evan gets involved, which he already is. That man is his doctor. And Evan and I are a package deal."

"Maybe he likes the look of your *package*."

"Jenna." It was pure exasperation.

"Just sayin'."

I looked up when I felt the movement from the side. Evan was scrambling out of the nook, eyes wide with excitement as he bounced over to me, already signing frantically.

CAN I GO TO THE PARK WITH JOSIAH? PLEASE. PLEASE. PLEASE.

My phone started ringing before I had the chance to answer him. I held up a finger for him to give me a second, picked up my phone, and smiled when I saw the name on the screen.

"Chanda, hi, it seems our boys have been scheming again," I said warmly.

Chanda laughed on the other end of the line. "Well, Josiah has been begging me to get together with Evan for the last week. Richard and I thought we'd take them to the park and then have a sleepover, if that's all right with you?"

Evan was jumping around, flapping his arms, begging me. I smiled at him. "I'm thinking Evan is excited by this prospect."

I could hear Josiah shouting in the background, "Can he, Mom, can he?"

"Put me out of my misery, Hope. Tell me Evan is free today," Chanda said, nothing but affection in her voice for her son, who had to be just as eager as mine.

Light laughter tumbled out, and I ran a loving hand through my son's hair. "Of course, that would be great. I have a project I need to finish up really quick, but I can drop him off at your house in an hour."

"Sounds good. See you soon."

I ended the call, my hands quick as I spoke with my son.

PACK YOUR THINGS. YOU'RE SLEEPING OVER, TOO.
YES!

He gave a victorious pump of his fist before he was flying out the kitchen, the entire house shaking as he banged down the hall and into his room.

"Someone must be excited," Jenna said, taking a sip of her coffee.

I angled my head when another clatter echoed through the walls. "Apparently."

Jenna grinned. "I wasn't talking about him."

sixteen

Hope

I pulled into the parking lot tucked behind the rows of old buildings that ran the length of Macaber Street.

An anxious shiver ran my spine.

Nervously, I glanced between the address Kale had texted and the copper-hewn letters affixed to the back entrance of the building.

This was it.

Opening the door to my Suburban, I hopped out, doing my best not to shake like some kind of giddy fool as I rounded to the back and opened the hatch.

But that was what I felt.

Giddy.

Jenna was right.

Someone was excited.

And it was me.

He lived in a building that had to be more than a hundred years old.

Gorgeous.

Stoic.

Proud.

It was five stories high, the red bricks aged to a roughened, blackened patina. It was obviously one of the old, historic buildings that lined this street that had been reclaimed and repurposed into trendy, downtown living spaces.

Trees grew up all around its perimeter, thick trunks and spindly branches stretched wide as they lifted toward that blue Alabama sky, the everlasting scent of wild honeysuckle wafting through the warm, heated air.

I felt flushed beneath it, but I was sure it didn't have a thing to do with the sun.

I grabbed the big box, which held five hundred lollipops, balanced it against my stomach, and pressed the fob to lower the hatch.

My heels clicked against the pavement as I walked toward the building.

Yep.

I was wearing heels.

After I'd dropped Evan at Josiah's, I told myself I was just hopping into the shower to freshen up since I'd gotten a little hot and sweaty. Of course, since I was in there anyway, I shaved just about every inch of my body. Then I spent way too much time on my hair and another hour standing in front of the mirror deciding what to wear.

God, I really was in deep. Getting reckless and eager and hopeful in a way I wasn't sure I should be.

But it was there. Spinning around me. The need compelling me to step forward and take a chance. Urging me in a direction that might be foolish.

I knew I had to be careful.

But I refused to live my life walking on eggshells. A prisoner to Dane's will. I was living for Evan. I was living for myself. I was living for *us*.

At the security door, I situated the box onto my left hip and punched in the code he'd given me. There was a buzz and the metal lock gave. The door popped open an inch. I pulled it the rest of the way open with the toe of my shoe and angled through.

Inside, the bricks remained exposed, and a bunch of leather couches were set up in a common area that took up a good amount of the bottom floor.

An old-style elevator with a half-moon dial waited behind the sitting area in the middle and an open-well staircase zigzagged back and forth against the right wall.

Elevator.

Definitely the elevator.

When the door slid open, I stepped in and hit the button for the fifth floor with my elbow. The elevator lifted, bouncing and jerking as it climbed, grinding on its cogs, winding me tighter and tighter the higher it went.

By the time the opposite side of it opened at the top floor, I was a shaking mess.

I didn't know why.

But coming there felt like taking a leap.

Stepping out on a limb.

On faith.

Landing on this shimmery, fluttery feeling that promised Kale was intended to be something special to me.

Even if it might be dangerous.

I advanced into the quiet, dimly lit hall. Choking on my nerves, I turned right, passing the first apartment and heading to the second and only other one on the floor.

I paused, gathered my wits, and shifted the box to my hip before gently rapping on his door.

Two seconds later, it flew open. The sight of Kale standing there made me take a stumbling step back.

The man so beautiful.

So tall and commanding.

Jeans snug and his T-shirt tight.

Arrogant.

And somehow so fundamentally sweet.

It was written all over him when his confused gaze bounced around me, searching the hall for my son. "Where's Evan?" he asked when his attention landed back on me.

"He's spending the night at a friend's," I answered, the words rough as they pulled from my throbbing throat.

Kale's expression transformed, disappointment melting to something severe when he realized I was alone.

Seductive.

"Ah, my princess has made it to the tower. All by herself. Awfully brave."

A shy, affected smile tweaked the edge of my lips, and I peeked up at him. This man.

He made me feel . . . different.

More beautiful than I had in a long, long time.

Wanted in a way that was right and not filled with cruel intentions.

I did my best to play along with his ribbing, widened my eyes. "Um . . . I think you might have this backward. Isn't it the knight who's supposed to save the princess who's locked in the tower?"

He grinned that grin that made me weak in the knees. "Who said I'm not about to lock her up and keep her here forever?"

My tummy tightened, affection pulsing from within while I tried to maintain the playfulness this boy exuded. "Should I be scared? Here you promised you weren't stalking me. *And* I thought you claimed to be the one who wanted to save me? I'm confused."

"Yet, here you are, standing at my door, searching for a way to break into my castle and looking like that while you do it."

His gaze swept me from head to toe.

It elicited a rush of heat that climbed into the thrumming air. Awareness spun like an exotic dance, twisting through the motes that floated in the rays of sunlight that speared through his door and lit him up from behind.

A spotlight.

Undoubtedly, that was where he belonged.

Everything about him was distracting. That body and those eyes and his giving, beautiful heart.

That was the part that had me snared. Happy to get caught up in his trap.

"Touché." It played from my mouth on a flimsy, shuddered breath.

He edged forward, voice growing darker. "And don't you worry yourself, Princess, I'm all about the saving. Why don't you come inside, and I'll show you exactly what that's like? I think you might have been misinformed."

That well of desire in my belly sloshed, threatening to overflow. A few fat droplets splashed out like a drenching tease, fuel for the ache that begged for more at the juncture between my thighs.

Because he was right. All these years, I had been brutally misinformed. He'd showed me just how much so that first night out on the balcony. Again, last night. And I had no idea how much more of that education I could take before I completely belonged to him.

Before he owned me in every way.

He felt so much bigger than my tiny world. As if he were expanding it. Filling it with possibility.

So obscenely tall. Overpowering in his casual, confident way. Lean muscle that bristled when he worked with those big, big hands.

Lips full and soft and lush.

So lush my mouth watered standing there looking up at his provocative face.

I'd been right at the beginning.

The man was discord.

Chaos with an easy, arrogant smile.

A perfect, controlled disorder.

I could almost feel that broken heart already making its first, tiny crack.

A splinter that creaked through me like a warning.

Because I could resist a pretty face.

But it was the tenderness and care lined beneath his gorgeous exterior that made him truly dangerous. What had drawn me to him all along.

"I don't think that's a good idea. I think you already showed me plenty last night."

Kale pressed his hands to either side of the doorjamb, leaned in close, and whispered, "Oh, Shortcake, that was me barely getting started."

Tingles spread. A flash fire of need that raced through my veins.

That was the thing about Kale Bryant. He knew exactly how to get to me.

I pushed the box his direction. "Here are the lollipops. Thank you so much for helping with them. I wish I could express just how much that means to me."

I wished, too, that I could express to him how I was feeling more. How I felt desperate to explore and test and tease him the way he'd been teasing me.

He took the box and set it on the floor just inside his door, one of those smoldering smirks lighting at the edge of his alluring mouth when he straightened to his full, towering height.

Oh, he was dangerous to me when he got that way. Steadily winning me over. Second by second. Grin by grin. The heart beneath that chipped all the brash away.

"I can't believe I left you standing there holding that. I'm really slacking on my knightly duties, aren't I? Letting you stand there with that heavy box. The atrocity. Have to admit, I was a little distracted by the very stimulating conversation I was having. Let me make it up to you."

It was all mischief and mayhem from between those flirty lips, because he knew as well as I did that box didn't weigh all that much.

His eyes glinted in playfulness while his pupils dilated in a distinct kind of wickedness.

His expression alone invited me to partake in a thousand scandalous acts.

I wavered, rocking back on my heels. "I think I should go."

Before I fell.

It was instant, the way his hand darted out to cup my face, his voice gruff. "I think you should stay."

I watched the plea play out in his eyes.

Let me touch you.

Let me take care of you.

Let me be your hero.

Just for a little while.

A tremble ripped through my body. His touch gasoline.

Instant.

The inferno raging inside me.

My tongue darted out to wet my suddenly dry lips. "If I sleep with you, there won't be any going back for me, Kale Bryant. Don't make me fall in love with you. I don't think either of us are ready for that."

There was zero provocation in the words, no hint of a tease, just my stark vulnerability. I wrung my fingers in front of me, waiting for his reaction. The air thick. So thick I couldn't breathe while Kale stood there staring at me as something flashed across his gorgeous face.

Both vivid and obscure.

And I couldn't stop myself from letting the words tumble free. "I know what I deserve, Kale. I know who I am, even though it's only been the last couple years that I've finally stood up and demanded it."

I inhaled a harsh breath, my eyes darting across his face to make sure he understood. "What I'm afraid of is you leading me down a path I'm not sure I can travel. Because maybe I *am* the fool who loves too easily. The one who sees the best in people. The one who sees what *they* deserve. Evan's dad didn't leave me jaded. He left me knowing exactly what it is I want. And what scares me most is I see so much of what I want in you, and I'm not sure you see the same in me."

My heart clenched, and I felt another piece of my world shatter when he stepped forward and pushed his fingers into my hair. His hand weaved all the way around to hold me by the back of the head, angling me back as he pulled me closer.

Holding me up. As if he'd never let me fall.

"God damn it, Hope. You really think I don't see that in you? I have no idea how to make sense of this. How to understand what it is you make me feel. What you make me want. But it's there. Haunting me. Chasing me. Demanding more."

He gathered me closer, his nose brushing mine, his words quiet and rough. "I don't know how to stop thinking about you. About Evan."

A tremor rolled through him, and his hold tightened. "I want you in a way I've never wanted anyone. Not ever. But I'm afraid I'm not capable of being the man you see because there isn't a whole lot of that guy left. I lost him a long time ago. I live for the people around me. For my job. My friends. Their families. *My patients.* I've walked that line for a long, long time. The straight. The narrow. Never veering from my path. But as hard as I try to stop it, colliding with you feels unavoidable."

God. This incredible man.

So beautiful and giving, radiating a selfless kind of devotion behind that stunning, devastating exterior. Haunted by something he wouldn't allow me to see.

Staring up at him, I let my fingertips trail across the sharp curve of his jaw. "What about living for you?"

The chuckle that rumbled in his chest was almost dark, words back to flirting with a tease, skirting that subject that hovered around him like a dark, condemning halo. "How about I just keep showing you what you've been missing out on?"

"That hardly seems fair," I whispered, the words wisps and tendrils that got hung up on his seduction that spun around us.

He gently plucked the pad of his thumb across my bottom lip. "Just getting to touch you feels like the best thing in the world."

My heart shivered.

In affection.

In want.

In something that almost felt like despair.

"Kale." It was a murmur.

Praise.

A spark.

Because his mouth crashed against mine.

His arms wound around my waist, and he pulled me into his apartment.

He kicked the door shut behind us without breaking the kiss.

Hot hands explored. Gliding down my back. Palming my bottom.

Roaming up my sides.

A moan rippled up my throat, and his tongue swept into my mouth, tangling with mine.

Needy and desperate.

Overpowering.

Overwhelming.

My head spun, and I was suddenly in his arms.

My legs wrapped around his narrow waist.

Second nature.

Exactly where I belonged.

"Hope," he mumbled at my mouth as he carried me through his massive, open loft.

The floors echoed with his heavy footsteps as they thudded across the worn, dark planks and toward the massive leather couch set up in the middle of the living space.

Pure masculine style and impeccable taste with the need for comfort at the root of it all.

Just like the man.

Setting me down on the dark cushions, he dropped to his knees on the plush white rug.

Expression predatory.

No doubt, he was preparing to devour and destroy.

He palmed my knees. The simple contact made me arch and gasp.

"It's getting harder and harder to resist you," he murmured, voice scraping and raw.

"Then why are you trying?"

Because I was already so far beyond that point. The second I stepped through his door, I knew it was over. That there was no longer any resisting.

I was tumbling.

Plunging.

Falling.

He groaned, as if my statement caused him physical pain, his blond hair striking in the late afternoon light, the curves and lines and definition of his striking face bold.

His expression enough to tear through me.

Flames licked across my skin, and just the sight of him had need coiling inside me so tightly I could barely see.

"Fuck, Hope. I want to give. You make me want to fucking give." He blinked, sucking in a breath. "Let me make you feel good. Please. I want to make you feel good."

I arched. "Nothing feels better than you."

That smirk resurfaced, whatever reservations that had lingered in his eyes eradicated, that brazen confidence riding back.

Taking hold.

"This dress. What are you wearing, baby?" He ran his hands up the outside of my thighs, under my flimsy, beige dress, the material loose but the skirt short. "God, you are the sexiest thing I've ever seen. What do you think you're trying to do to me?"

He dipped down and ran his lips along the inside of my thigh as he whispered the words. "Showing up at my house looking like this?"

I whimpered, threaded my fingers through his hair while I sank back into his couch, head rocking on the cushions as he made a delirium-inducing path upward.

Kissing up my bare thigh.

Shivers.

His mouth continued its assault, traipsing over the top of the material while his hands moved under it. He grabbed me by the outside of the thighs and dragged my bottom to the edge of the couch as he edged up, kissing higher and higher.

Over my belly that shuddered and shook.

Nose running across the top of one of my breasts.

Dipping between.

He kissed a path over my heart, which thundered and roared, until he buried his face in my neck and carved out a spot for himself between my knees at the same time.

I could feel his heat where he pressed eagerly at me.

The outline of his cock where he nestled between my legs.

Desire tumbled.

A violent twist.

Because I had never wanted a man the way I wanted him. I wanted to beg him to put me out of my misery. To release the ache. Wholly trusting in him that he would.

He leaned back down on his knees, taking me by surprise when he kissed across my belly.

Something about it so erotic that desire flooded, the feel of his mouth moving over the material driving me wild.

Both of my hands were in his hair, tugging lightly and caressing gently.

A whimper tumbled from my mouth.

"I don't know what this is, Hope." His mouth kept moving higher, whispering into the thin fabric.

My heart kicked. Bucked against its confines.

"What's happening between us. All I know is that you're making me feel things I haven't felt in a long, long time, and it terrifies me."

He pulled back and looked at me. His expression grim.

As if saying it brought him some kind of physical torment.

I wanted to ask him to show me what was hidden in his eyes. Trust me with it. Why this flirty, easygoing guy would suddenly lose himself to a place where it was dark and dismal.

I traced my fingers along the prominent curve of his powerful jaw. "Take me, Kale. Show me."

A tremor rolled in his throat, and he shook his head, dipped his face away so I couldn't see his expression.

As if he were pulling himself together. Getting himself back on that line he walked. When he looked back at me, his eyes glimmered.

Lust and need.

"You know that isn't what you really want, Harley Hope. I refuse to become your regret. But I am going to set you free. Make you scream."

He burrowed his face up under my jaw. He nipped and kissed at my pulse point, his body pressing deeper between my legs as he edged up higher.

My head rocked back, and my fingers sank into his shoulders.

A dark chuckle rumbled from his throat. "Look at you. Barely takes a brush of my body and you're already about to go off."

My arm curled around the top of his head. "That's because you make me feel something, too."

He inched back and set his hand over the thunder that beat at my chest, the intensity of his gaze meeting with mine. "Hope."

I gulped around the emotion that suddenly felt prominent at the base of my throat. "When did you lose yours?"

Because that was what came in flashes.

From the depths of this man.

Grief.

I wanted to hold it, the way he was holding me.

He groaned almost painfully before he was back to kissing between my breasts, giving me no answer, hands riding back up the outside of my thighs.

He tucked me close. Rocked against me.

Sparks and shimmers lit up behind my eyes.

He kissed across the V neckline of my dress, inching it lower with each pass. Licking across the top swell of my breast. His fingers adept as he undid the three little buttons. He showed no hesitation when he pulled the fabric down, exposing me.

Cool air hit my sensitive flesh.

I gasped.

Kale glanced up at me with a smirk, running his thumb around a nipple that pebbled with his touch. "Perfect, Hope. Fucking perfect."

"Kale."

He was going to ruin me. Save me. I didn't know. The only thing I knew was he held me in the palm of his hands.

To crush or protect.

"Hmm?" he hummed as he bent down and blew across the delicate flesh before he bit down lightly, tugging it between his teeth.

"Oh," I whimpered, arching toward him. He must have taken that as an invitation because the next second had him sucking and lapping, and both my arms were curled around his head, hugging him to me, begging him for more.

For the kind of *more* I'd had no idea I needed until Kale swaggered into my life.

He was right.

That was exactly what this felt like.

Like I was colliding with what had been missing all along.

He released my nipple with a *pop*, his thumb back to circling the tight bud before he eased back and set both hands on my knees.

I sat there panting toward the ceiling, eyes cut down so I could take him in.

Blue eyes gleamed as he slowly ran his hands up the tops of my thighs. This time, they disappeared beneath the fabric.

Like a warning.

A promise.

Because the dress gathered on his forearms the higher he went before he hooked his fingers at the sides of my underwear.

Deliberately slow, he dragged them down.

"Shit," he hissed.

His thick throat bobbed, lust radiating from him as he watched himself peel them off.

Lace grazed my legs, tingles sprinting across my flesh as he pulled them down.

Shivers skated my skin, and my breaths turned ragged as he unwound the fabric from my ankles and heels.

He peered up at my face when he did. "You are perfect, Hope. Sweet, sublime perfection. The first time I saw you, I knew it. Had this feeling like I'd been struck. Like maybe I wouldn't ever be the same. Know now that I never will."

Then there was that grin. That wicked grin as his tongue swept across his bottom lip. "Not sure I really want to be."

Then he spread me. Pressing my knees apart the way he'd done that night at the bar. But this time, there was no barrier.

My body completely exposed.

And he was diving in without further warning, his hot, hot tongue sweeping into my folds.

I yelped and desire tumbled.

Pleasure spiked on all sides.

Magnified.

Compounded as he licked through my sensitive, engorged lips, dragging up and circling around that achy spot that throbbed and glowed.

"Kale." A whimper.

"I know, Hope," he rumbled. "I told you I know what you need."

But that was where he was wrong. Because I needed all of him. Every inch and every word and every smile.

A flicker of a warning rose up in my consciousness, telling me I was spiraling too fast, tripping into a free fall while Kale continued to drive me higher.

Higher and higher and higher.

His kiss so intimate I would have blushed if my skin weren't already covered in a flush of heat.

Red from the flames that licked up inside me. Flames that spiked and flared and grew hotter with each decadent stroke of his mouth.

Igniting into a full-body blaze.

Blistering.

He tucked me closer, his hands on my bottom as he lifted me from the couch, his thumb doing magical things to the most private part of me.

Circling.

Teasing.

Easing into my ass.

"Oh, God. Kale . . . what—" The words were thready. Thin with the rasp. My fingers slipped frantically across the leather of the couch, searching for something to hang on to.

"Relax, I've got you," he murmured. His low command reverberated through me. "I've got you. Trust me. I've got you. Want to make you feel good. Let me give you this."

"I trust you."

I did.

I trusted him with every part of me.

With the recognition, the *acceptance*, my heart clattered in my chest, and I whispered, "Please."

Though I knew he didn't know I was begging for so many things.

I gulped for the nonexistent air when he dipped his head back down and burrowed back between my thighs. With his other hand, he pressed two fingers into the well of my body. He moved in perfect sync with his thumb.

My walls clenched around him.

With his tongue, he laved at my clit, suckled and licked and tempted me into a boiling frenzy that gathered to a pinpoint.

It was unlike anything I'd ever felt.

An avalanche of sensation riding on every nerve.

Filling every crevice.

My head swished back and forth on the back of the couch, pleasure gathering fast.

Flashing of bliss. Flickers of ecstasy.

Then everything split.

Breaking wide open.

Streaking and spinning and spiraling.

Euphoria.

I wanted to stay there for all of forever, and I couldn't help but whimper as I tumbled back down.

A weightless dive through limbless bliss.

When I landed, Kale was right there, placing gentle kisses along the inside of my thigh, holding me steady as my body twitched and jerked with the most powerful kind of aftershocks.

There was nothing I could do, my hands were on his face, pulling him up to me.

His jeans ground against my bare center, and I almost went off again.

I kissed him. Kissed him frantically. Maniacally. A frenzy that had taken hold. "Kale. Take me. I'm yours. I want to feel you. I need to feel you. Please."

He groaned a sound of pain as he kissed me deeper, and his eyes squeezed shut before he palmed the side of my face and pried himself back. "You know you don't want that."

"I do."

"No, Hope, you don't. You told me you couldn't afford another complication. And you know that's exactly what I'd be."

But he already was the most intricately exquisite complication.

I kissed across his jaw and up to his ear. "What if I want to take care of you, too? Make you feel good?"

Another groan, but it was one of those belly-flipping smirks that hitched up at the corner of his sexy mouth when he pulled back. "What exactly did you have in mind, Shortcake?"

This time, I did blush. Heat rushed to my cheeks. But I tried to remain bold, confident as I nudged him back. He eased onto his knees.

Fumbling beneath the hem of his shirt, I pressed my hands up under the soft material, inching it up.

My palms gliding over carved, defined muscle as I went. "I want to see you," I confessed.

He shuddered and shook, but he was grinning when he lifted his arms over his head and let me draw his shirt from his body.

I blinked when I dragged it free.

Stunned.

Struck dumb.

Left in staggered awe.

Holy crap.

Jenna may let a ton of nonsense roll out of her mouth, but she'd had one thing right.

This man was delicious.

I let my fingertips run up his chiseled abdomen, fluttering across his huge, bulging pecs, running over both of his shoulders and down his arms, watching the path I made the whole time.

Sucking on my bottom lip, I peeked up at him. "And you said I was perfect."

"You are, baby. So goddamned perfect. Just looking at you makes my guts hurt. Nothing should be that beautiful. But you are."

My blush deepened, my hands shaking, unsure of where to go from there.

But Kale, he knew when he needed to take control.

When I wanted him to.

He slowly pushed to his feet, straightening to that towering height of security where he stood right in front of me.

Potent.

Powerful.

Persuasive.

While I still sat on his couch, nothing but a fumbling mess of need.

"You want to touch me?" he grated.

I could barely get out a spastic nod.

Staring down at me, he started flicking through the buttons of his jeans. "You sure?"

He almost grinned, but it was weighted with his own desire, held back by the tight clench of his jaw as he freed the last button.

Oh goodness.

My insides trembled.

A tiny earthquake.

"Yes," I whispered.

He pushed his jeans and underwear down over his hips, and the little air I had left in my lungs jetted out on a panted heave when his cock sprang free.

Massive, thickened, and throbbing with his need.

Pointing toward the sky, it bobbed in front of my face, swaying just to the right, just as arrogantly confident as the rest of this mesmerizing man.

"This is what you do to me, Hope. This. Every time I see you. Every time I think of you. *This.*"

A shiver rocked me to the core.

My core, which had been sated to a simmer, was stoked into an all-out blaze again.

My tongue darted out to wet my dried lips, my fingers shaking and shaking when I reached out and tentatively traced them down the velvet skin.

His hips bucked, and his stomach clenched.

"Hope, baby, are you trying to embarrass me?"

I peeked up to find him gazing down at me, as if he were riveted by the feel of my hands on him. Touching him.

"I don't think that's possible, Kale Bryant. I don't even know what to do with you." It came on the huff of a breathy laugh, a tease and the utmost truth.

The truth was, my stomach was twisted in a million intricate knots when I took him in my trembling hands, circling him at the base. The crash in my heart an uncontrolled bang, bang, bang.

A groan jutted from his mouth. "I think you're doing just fine starting right there."

"This is okay?"

"Yes." It was a long moan when I ran my hands up and back down before I picked up a slow pace, letting one hand glide over his dripping head each time.

"Just like that," he said.

Leaning forward, my tongue darted out, flattening across the tip.

Tasting him.

"Or that. Yes, that. Fuck, Princess. I think it's me who doesn't know what to do with you."

But he did.

Because his hands landed on either side of my face, and I held him while I looked up at him.

The man lit up in the blaze of the sun.

A conqueror.

A champion.

"Suck me, baby." It was a grunt, his tip nudging at my lips. "Let me have that sweet mouth."

I wanted to tell him I would give him anything, but he was already tugging me forward, begging his own plea.

My lips parted, and I drew him into my mouth.

My insides clenched.

Why did I love the feel of his flesh on my tongue? Why did I ache with the impact of his soft grunt?

He drove his fingers into my hair. They dug in deep, spreading out, all the way over the back of my head until his fingertips were brushing the back of my neck.

"I'm going to fuck your mouth, Hope. Hold on, baby." His hips surged forward, my hands and mouth and heart full of him.

Overflowing and somehow wanting more.

More.

I whined around him, trying not to gag as my trembling hands spread out to clutch his hips.

He drove deeper and deeper with each of his slow thrusts. As if he were carefully claiming me while I felt frantic to demand all of him.

"Fuck . . . so good, baby. Just like that. Your mouth is perfect. So perfect.

Just like the rest of you." It was a muddled jumble of pleasure that tripped from his tongue.

His wicked, delicious tongue.

More.

My spirit sang, and those hidden places that Dane had beaten down danced.

Freed.

There was some kind of magic in touching Kale this way. Power in making him moan. Power in hearing his pleas rumble from somewhere in the depths of him.

Both of us unchained and unbound.

His stomach tightened just the same as his fingers tightened in my hair. He gave a little yank, and I tipped my gaze toward his magnificent face.

I was literally brought to my knees by the magnitude of what I saw there, my body slipping from the edge of the couch to kneel on the floor.

Held by the raw, unbridled possession.

The passion and the need.

Hunger.

Never before had it been so fiercely directed at me.

"I'm getting close. Can you take it?" It was a warning that pressed between his lips, grit and lust and desire. Every inch of him trembled in restraint, muscle rippling and twitching as his own pleasure gathered.

My hands moved to his chiseled ass, gripping him, my eyes wide, begging him to let me be the one to give him what he needed.

To be the one who believed in him. To hold all his secrets and hidden desires. To be the one to cherish him in the highs. To stand beside him on the lows.

Because I wanted him to be a part of all of mine.

"Sweet girl," he murmured. So softly. As soft as his gaze that traced over my face.

Riddled with affection.

Lined with fear.

One second later, Kale let go.

I let him possess me as his hips began to snap, desperate in their play.

His thrusts wild.

Unhinged and uncontrolled.

And maybe I was a fool, thinking I could have stopped it. Kept it away. The chaos that rose and lifted and shivered in the bright, blinding light that poured in behind him.

But I should have known better.

Because I was already lost.

The room spun and the ground shook and lights flashed where I knelt before him on my knees.

An offering.

His.

Kale gripped me as if he were determined to never let me go. His beautiful, glorious body stretched taut. Muscle keening, twisting, covered in a light sheen of sweat.

"Hope, baby, oh . . . fuck . . . yes."

His hips surged forward, and I took him as deeply as I could. Tears pricked my eyes as he pressed all the way into my throat.

He throbbed and jerked and poured in my mouth.

And that spinning room canted, my axis knocked.

I felt almost frantic as I swallowed around him.

Because all I could see was hope spread out in front of me.

seventeen

Kale

Struggling for a breath, I stared down at her staring up at me, my hands still twisted in that perfect mass of red, lush hair.

Affection.

It pulled and taunted and teased. Stretched tight across my chest. The squeeze in my lungs was almost painful, already lacking breath and looking at her stealing more.

I had no fucking clue how to make sense of what I was feeling. How to understand how this woman had singlehandedly made me question everything.

What I wanted and where I was going and what I stood for.

I wasn't supposed to need anyone, my devotion all locked up on the fact my patients needed me. My fate sealed the day I'd failed.

Yet, there she was, looking at me like I might be something better. Something more than just the *Dr.* tacked to the front of my name.

Fear tumbled through my spirit.

Because I couldn't—wouldn't—allow myself to fail.

Not ever again.

And I'd molded myself into accepting being a doctor was my only identity, but this girl was making me wonder if I might have a chance to find something more in the middle of it. Something good and right that might be meant for me.

Or maybe fate really was a cruel bitch. Teasing me in the worst of ways. Putting this woman and her kid in front of me. Knowing I'd never make it through a repeat.

Hope's chest heaved as her tumultuous green eyes watched me like she wanted to crawl around inside me to discover all that I was. Though, hidden deep, flickering right on the recesses, was a spec of that shyness, that uncertainty of where to go from there.

She dropped her gaze and gathered the top of her dress, covering herself and fumbling with the buttons because those exquisite tits were still exposed.

All it took was a glance of her, and I was kicked in the gut with a fresh bolt of lust. Didn't help that her panties were crumpled on my floor, the memory of getting my first real taste of Harley Hope Masterson forever ingrained on my mind.

Strawberries and cream.

Sweet, sweet heat.

The girl was calm and a raging fire.

Peace and a hurricane.

Modest and demure with straight shot of vixen.

Quickly, I pulled up my jeans and readjusted myself, figuring the last thing I needed was to be standing there looking like some kind of pathetic fucker caught with his pants around his ankles.

Not when she kept stealing peeks at me. Wondering where we stood when every time we crossed paths, we just got deeper and deeper. Running faster and faster down that path she wasn't sure she should follow me down.

I had no answer, but I no longer knew how to stay away. Wasn't sure if I wanted to.

I stretched my hand out to her. "Come here."

With an affected smile, she accepted it, and I helped pull her to her feet. She wobbled on her heels and shaky knees.

I tucked her against my chest, wrapped my arms around her, and pressed a kiss to the top of her head. "You just blew my mind, Harley Hope. Where exactly did you come from? Because if you disappear, I'm pretty sure I'm gonna have to hunt you down."

"Stalker," she mumbled on a breathy laugh.

My own laugh was full. Hearty. Happy.

Because right then? That was exactly what I was.

I wrapped her even closer, swaying her slowly in the pour of light that tumbled in through the windows behind us.

Those dark places inside me light.

She released a contented sigh, her breath lifting chills that sped across my chest.

"I liked doing it," she finally whispered like a confession right over the thunder that was my heart.

Another chuckle rippled free, my lips murmuring against the crown of her head. "Have to admit, I liked you doing it, too."

She glanced up to meet my eyes. The warmth held in that mossy green swept through me like a caress. "Are you sure you aren't just telling me that because you don't want to make me feel bad?"

"Uh . . . considering I'm probably going to be begging you to do it again in about ten minutes, think you can safely assume that was no platitude." Then I glanced around my loft, eyes going wide with the tease. "See . . . no blowing of smoke anywhere." I hugged her back to me. "You're the only fire around here, Shortcake."

I could feel the force of her smile, and she gave a fake cough. "Oh, I smell smoke all right. Seems as if someone is trying to butter me up."

Fantasies flashed, and I grabbed her round ass in both of my hands, giving her a good squeeze. "Don't tempt me, Hope. You have no idea just what I could do with that."

She choked over a surprised laugh. "I swear, you are worse than Jenna. I think maybe you should be hanging out with her, instead. She'd probably handle you a whole lot better."

I gathered her close, her heart beating against mine.

Wild in its content.

Filling me with more of that joy that spun through the center of me. Winding up and taking hold.

"Sorry, Shortcake. That isn't gonna work for me. Seems I've acquired a taste for you. Don't want anyone else."

I meant for it to be playful, but it hit the air like a sonic boom. It thundered and roared through the sudden silence. Dense and deep and heavy with questions.

Her blunted fingernails scratched across my chest, inciting a new kind of storm that was building inside me. "I don't want anyone else, either."

For a few minutes, we just stayed there, lost in the other.

Swam in the possibilities.

Finally, I cleared my throat, stepped back.

"I'm starving."

Really. We needed a distraction. Because I had none of those answers.

But what I did know? I wanted her like I wanted the sun to keep rising in the morning. And if I didn't put some distance between us in the next five seconds, I would have her tossed over my shoulder and laid out on my bed.

And going there would change everything.

For her.

For me.

Since I'd lost Melody, I'd spent my life living casually. Easily. But there was nothing casual about this girl, and if it went there, it was going to mean something.

And I didn't want to be that asshole.

The one who took and took and took when I wasn't sure what I could give in return.

What I could offer.

I mean, fuck, if I kept seeing her? I was going to have to write a report. Have Evan's care transferred.

But if I was being honest, that was the easy part. Not a big deal except for the fact I hated the idea of not being able to treat him. Relinquishing the kid's care to someone else.

Trusting his health to them.

Unease slithered through my senses. Hooks and lines, drawing me closer to the realization of how much I fucking cared.

Problem was, I didn't know if I wanted to protect him because I couldn't stand the thought of missing something again or if it was simply because it was this kid.

I was getting attached to him just as swiftly as I was getting attached to his mom.

Fuck.

I was.

I was falling.

Ripping myself from her, I locked down that train of thought because none of that needed to be entertained right then. I cleared my throat and started for the kitchen. "Are you hungry? Let me feed you."

A moment's hesitation brimmed around her, her gaze jumping around my loft before she gave a quick nod. "Sure. Something to eat would be nice. I'm never quite sure what to do with myself when Evan isn't around."

I glanced at the spot where we'd just been tangled, letting a smirk climb to my mouth. "I'd say I approve of your most recent choice of activities. Great use of your time, Shortcake."

She tucked her bottom lip between her teeth, like she didn't know whether to be embarrassed or laugh. "I bet. It seems you really do have me at a disadvantage, Dr. Bryant. And here I thought I'd finally graduated to princess and ditched the whole Shortcake thing."

"Ah, there's no ditching the whole Shortcake thing . . . not when you're so damned sweet."

She stood there with that blush riding to her cheeks while I stepped up to the sink to wash my hands.

She angled her head toward the hall. "Do you mind if I freshen up a little bit?"

"First door on the right. Make yourself at home."

She gave a slight nod before she reached down and covertly snatched her underwear from the floor. She tucked them in a ball to conceal them in her hand, like I hadn't been the one just peeling them from her body.

I chuckled, shooting her a grin. "Feel free to leave those here if you want."

"Kale," she admonished, flustered, as she shook her head and fought a smile before she bolted down the hall. The door slammed behind her, shaking the panes of the windows.

And my smile?

My smile was wider than I thought it'd ever been.

Giggles floated through my kitchen. Wrapping around me like soft, lulling waves.

I smiled back at her from over my shoulder where I was digging something out to make for an early dinner.

Hope was propped up on my island, that dress bunched up around her thighs, her lush legs swinging over the edge.

Feet bare.

Sun shining all around her from behind. Lighting up that red hair. Setting it aflame.

Swore, the girl was like curling up in front of a fireplace on a cold winter's day.

I pulled an onion, fresh garlic, and tomatoes from the crisper. Spaghetti was the one meal I cooked well, which wasn't surprising since that shit was what I'd lived on in medical school.

I rinsed everything, set a cutting board beside her, and started dicing so I could start the sauce.

I glanced over at her. "If I make you dinner, that means you're making me dessert, right?"

"Oh, I see how this works. A favor for a favor, huh? And here I thought you were making me dinner out of the goodness of your heart."

She sat up there like her weight had been lifted. The girl was lost in the mood, relaxed, catching on to the vibe of the sun slowly sinking in the sky.

My phone was synced with Spotify and set to one of my favorite playlists. Mellow and gritty, the guitar-driven beats pumped quietly from the speakers set up all through my loft, the hypnotizing lyrics setting the mood.

I feigned an offended gasp. "This is out of the goodness of my heart, Shortcake. But, seriously, have you tasted your cupcakes? You can't blame a man for trying. Call it self-preservation. The instinct to survive kicking in. Because I might die if I don't get another taste."

"The dramatics," she teased.

"The truth," I shot back.

Amusement flitted across her features, and she placed her palms on the stone counter behind her, leaning back, hair swept over one shoulder. She stared at the ceiling like she was really contemplating what she was going to say. "And what flavor would you pick if I was kind enough to make you something? On my day off, mind you."

She dropped her gaze back to me, that mesmerizing green swallowing me whole.

My brow lifted. "Do you really need to ask?"

My eyes raked her. Head to toe. Not even attempting to hide the fact I was already ready to devour her again.

Strawberries and cream and all things sweet.

A soft giggle floated from her delicious mouth. "You haven't even tried anything else. Strawberry shortcake might be your least favorite and you don't even know it."

"Oh, there are some things a man just knows." I leaned in closer to her, letting my nose graze her jaw, my voice rough. "And this I know. Don't need to taste anything else when I already know I've got the fucking best thing sitting right in front of me."

Truth was, I'd *tasted* enough in my lifetime to know when I'd never stumble on anything better.

Goose bumps spread across her flesh, and a shiver rolled down her spine as I pressed a gentle kiss behind her ear. "Got it?" I murmured.

"Well then, I guess I'd better stock up on strawberries." A tremor rolled out with her wispy response.

I chuckled, swiveling around and digging out a large saucepan from the bottom cupboard and placing it on the stove. "I like the way you think. But I have to wonder if you're thinking big enough. Not sure simply stocking up will suffice. I'm thinking maybe we need to invest in some stock in one of those fields up north. Maybe buy it outright."

While I spoke, I flicked on the burner, a ring of blue flames jumping to life, and tossed some olive oil in the pan. I let that heat before adding the onions and garlic.

"You think so? Sounds to me like someone is getting a little greedy."

Filling a pot with hot water, I smirked over at her. "Hard not to be when I want it all."

There I went, running down that path, not sure how to stop myself.

Knowing if I reached out my hand, she'd be right there running along beside me. Or maybe it was the girl who was out front, hair flying all around her as she looked back at me from over her shoulder, smile so wide and welcoming.

Tempting me into chasing after that blinding, blistering hope. Wanting the striking, stark beauty of it. Hungry for something I've always wanted for the people around me, but never thinking I could keep any of it for myself.

I focused on getting the pot on the stove instead of all the thousand thoughts and temptations dangling right there.

Within reach.

The whole time, knowing if I were to grab on, every single one of them might be covered in spikes and spurs and barbs.

The onions and garlic began to sizzle. The thick aroma rose in the air.

"God, I love that smell," Hope murmured, her head dropped back and her eyes closed.

Savoring.

Lust twisted my guts.

So tightly, I could feel it climb all the way to my chest and squeeze my heart.

"Yeah?" I asked as I dumped a can of premade sauce into the pan, tossed in the diced tomatoes to add a little extra texture and flavor.

"It's my favorite."

"Onion and garlic?"

She laughed that mesmerizing sound.

Sex and innocence.

The score of this girl hypnotic.

"No, spaghetti. It's my favorite."

A short chuckle rumbled deep in my throat. "Good. Because that's about the only thing I know how to make."

She hummed softly, lost to some kind of memory. "When I was a sophomore, my grandparents took me to New York City to see one of the Broadway shows. They said they were feeding my love of the theater. I think what they really were doing was feeding my love for Italian food."

A gentle smile pulled at one side of my mouth as I poured the noodles in. "And how is it my little actress turned into a baker?"

A giggle slipped free, hair swishing around her as she shifted. "Sometimes dreams are only meant for a moment. They mean the world to us, and then sometimes something takes their place, and they're not quite as important to us anymore."

Slowly, I turned and rested my back against the counter facing her. "What happened to that dream?"

She shook her head, her shoulders lifting in the smallest shrug. "I can't really pinpoint exactly when it happened, but somewhere along the way, it stopped being a burning need inside me. I loved theater in high school. I think it was an outlet. A way to express myself. And I guess I got to a point where I no longer needed to express myself that way."

"So . . . how did you end up here?"

Lines crossed. I wasn't even jumping over the hurdles set between us. I was barreling right through them.

The hint of a smile edged her mouth, made up of regret and honesty. "In college, I fell in love, and I followed him here."

I flinched.

A stake driven through the center of me.

God, that was stupid, but just her even mentioning the idea of that dirtbag, the thought of another man touching her, made my skin crawl.

Unable to tolerate the distance, I slowly crossed the space, awareness thrumming between us. I took in a shuddered breath when I planted myself between her knees, staring at her through the glittering rays of lights that glowed against her gorgeous face. "Do you ever regret it? Not going to New York? Not following that dream? Chasing it even after it was gone?"

Her head shook. Zero reluctance behind it. "No. I don't. Because Evan *is* the reason I dream."

I set my hand against her cheek. "Hope." It was praise from my mouth. Sure a girl as selfless and giving as this one didn't exist. "You are amazing. The most incredible woman I've ever had the honor to meet."

Redness flushed up her delicate neck, splashing on her cheeks, and she pressed deeper into the well of my hand. Hungry for the touch. Relishing in me. "I think I could say the same thing about you."

My brow pinched a little, not sure how to handle a girl like this saying something like that.

Catching it, her eyes narrowed, and she was reaching up and softly trailing her fingertips down the side of my face. "Who are you, Kale Bryant? Because you *are* the most incredible man I've ever met, but there's something inside you that you try to keep hidden. And I wonder if that's the part of you that I'm drawn to the most."

Eyes falling closed, I swallowed around the painful lump that was suddenly prominent at the base of my throat. Throbbing and tormenting.

And I wanted to lay it all out.

Tell her everything.

"You can trust me, Kale," she whispered.

I blinked at her. "But I'm not sure if I can trust myself."

She searched me. Gently. In all that belief. "How is that?"

I gathered both of her hands between mine, forcing the tweak of a smile. "I always wanted to be a doctor. My dad was a general practitioner. I basically idolized him my whole life. Couldn't wait to walk in his shoes."

A wistful smile pulled at her mouth, her eyes tracing over me like she was trying to imagine what I was like when I was little.

Drawing an image in her mind of a blond-haired boy who wanted to be just like his father.

"He must be so proud of you. You are the best doctor I know. And I'm not just saying that. The second you sat in front of my son, I knew what kind of doctor you were."

I winced, the words flooding out before I could stop them. "I try to be, Hope. I try to be the best damned doctor I can be. Making sure I never get so wrapped up inside myself, distracted, or focused on things I shouldn't be that I start missing or neglecting the things that are most important. And what's most important are my patients."

Something flickered through her features.

A kind of understanding I wasn't sure she could possess. A tiny sound fell from her tongue, and she was back to caressing across my lips.

Sadness and grace rippled through her.

"You're scared of getting involved with someone." She didn't even ask it as a question. It was just a statement. An awareness. No judgment. Just her quiet compassion.

That didn't mean I didn't see the tiny flame of hurt in her eyes. Her want for something more for me, *from* me, was clear. Only, I didn't have a fucking clue if I could be man enough to offer it in return.

Thing was, I was wanting to. Fuck. I wanted it more than I'd wanted anything in a long, long time.

"I . . ." For a moment I wavered before I surrendered, giving her a little of what I could. "When I was in med school, I fell in love for the first and only time in my life."

My mouth tweaked up with the old memories. Before they were horror and regret and shame.

Hope's almost matched. That green glinting.

This girl.

I could feel her cracking me wide open.

A small puff of air jolted from her lungs, but she looked at me, filling me with silent encouragement.

"I met her at a fundraiser on campus. It was before I even started my clinicals . . . basically spending my time in books and labs."

My head slowly shook as I was assailed with the memories, my lips pulling with the old affection. "She had the biggest spirit. She lit up any room she stepped into. She kept . . . complaining that she didn't feel well. That she was tired. I should have known. I'd learned enough by that time that I should have known." The words scraped from my throat.

Emergency room lights glared from overhead. Panic. Fear. Compression after compression after compression. That fucking flat line.

"She was sick, Hope. She was fucking sick, and I didn't even see it. I thought she was just tired. Exhausted from classes and studying and always wanting to be a part of everything. I missed it."

I was unable to admit to her why Evan petrified me. Why the situation was so fucked up. Why it was different and still felt so goddamned much the same. That I was there. That I tried to save her.

I tried.

I tried.

"You lost her." Grief rang from Hope's tongue. Spinning through the room. Wrapping me in her warmth.

Those dead places flickered, and I dropped my head to her chest, nodding against the steady thrum of her heart as I struggled with the crushing wave that slammed into me.

The regret and remorse and the old feelings I'd done fine at keeping locked down, all being unleashed at once.

"Oh, Kale, I'm so sorry," she whispered, fingers gentling through my hair.

I buried my face in her neck.

Ashamed.

Stricken.

She hugged me to her for the longest time, her scent all around me, strawberries and cream and calm.

It felt like an eternity before she edged back. She framed my face in her delicate hands. Sympathy and that stunning understanding ridged every line of her expression. "You still love her?"

Oh fuck. This girl was going to destroy me.

Hope

My hands trembled where they rested on his striking face.

But it had shaken me.

Being able to finally see all the way past the gorgeous exterior. Down, deep inside this miraculous man with his huge, beautiful, bleeding heart.

To the man who had lost, who remained terrified and hurt. The one who had somehow taken on some of that responsibility when it clearly didn't belong to him.

The one who was so clearly scared of repeating it again.

And my son.

He was sick.

I understood it in a way I wasn't sure I wanted to.

I wanted to ask him so many things.

How?

What happened?

I wanted to tell him it would be okay.

That it was all right to hurt.

That I understood.

Instead, I just sat there, waiting for him, needing this answer, knowing if I had it, I might be able to understand him on a level I hadn't before. That maybe we could make sense of what was going on between us.

He peeled himself away and looked at me. Grief swam in that turbulent sea of blue. "Part of me will always love her, Hope. But what torments me is she didn't get the chance to experience life. That I missed her symptoms and took that chance away."

Sorrow clenched down on my chest, sorrow that he could possibly think he was responsible for his first love's death.

His Adam's apple bobbed heavily as he swallowed. "Then the other part of me wonders . . . wonders what my life would have looked like had I been able to save her. Would we be married? Would we have kids? Would she be an anesthesiologist like she'd wanted to be? Or would her dreams have changed, too?"

His voice cracked as he continued, "She deserved to experience everything life had in store for her, and I stole that from her. Failed her when she needed me most."

I could feel my heart splintering under the devastation in his expression.

"I've been told that sometimes it's the what-ifs that hurt the most. What haunt us the longest. But there is absolutely no chance you were responsible for her death, Kale. You have to let that go. Live and find joy. Because I promise you, you deserve it, everything life has in store for you."

He flinched as if he wanted to refute my claim, so I was quick to add, "Believe it. I do."

He took my hand and pressed his face in to my palm, kissing the flesh before he moved to kiss the inside of my wrist. "Incredible. Told you, Hope. You are incredible. And I don't know how to make sense of it."

"Do you want to try?" I asked him. Stepping out, that limb teetering beneath me, threatening to splinter.

And God . . .

The smile he sent me?

It rocked me to the core.

Confidence and naked vulnerability, the contours of his face lit up in the glow of the fading sun.

"I do . . . but the last thing I want to do is fail you. Fail Evan."

I blinked at him, my chest tightening, and I started to tell him I didn't think it was possible for him to do that.

Fail us. But then the sizzle and hiss of water boiling over onto the stove hit our ears.

"Shit." He spun away and rushed that direction. He drove a pasta spoon into the pot, stirring quickly to settle the roil down.

I almost giggled when the sauce started to bubble and spit all over the place.

"Shit," he said again, this time with an amused huff that came at his expense, his strong back bare as he worked to salvage our dinner.

Cute.

Confident.

Chaos.

He glanced back at me, the heaviness from moments ago gone. "Can't even get spaghetti right."

I ignored the questions still looming around us and slid off the counter. I slinked up behind him and pressed a gentle kiss to the warm, bare flesh at the center of his back.

He shuddered, the quiver of an arrow straight through the center of me.

"You are the most incredible man I have ever met, Kale Bryant. I am so sorry you had to go through that. I hate it for you. If I could take it away, I would," I whispered against his spine, which stiffened the barest fraction.

I knew I needed to give him space, let him process. He had probably shared more with me than he had with anyone in a long, long time. I moved to stand beside him, nudged him with my hip, and sent him a smile. "Here, let me help with that."

Kale laughed. "What? You don't trust me in my own kitchen?"

I widened my eyes up at him. "Should I?"

He hesitated for a second before he busted up laughing. "No . . . no, you definitely should not."

I shot him a grin. "That's what I thought." I snagged the spoon from his grip. "Give me that before someone gets hurt."

He took his turn knocking me with his hip. "Fine. I relinquish these duties. Thinking they're not so knightly, anyway."

I gasped a horrified sound that was completely feigned. "And just what is it you're implying?"

He laughed again. A bellowing sound that came from his belly, making his abdomen ripple and flex. "Absolutely nothing, Princess. Nothing at all."

I poked him in the side. "I'll let you off the hook this time. Just because I like you."

His eyes smoldered when he looked down at me, the edges brimming with something brilliant.

Something beautiful and whole. "You like me, huh, Shortcake?"

I didn't know why I adored it when he called me that. That coaxing tease that clearly meant so much more.

I kept my focus trained ahead, stirring the noodles, the confession a breath on my tongue. "Yeah, Kale, I like you."

I think I'm in love with you.

Sitting out on his gorgeous balcony, we shared our meal beneath the blaze of the setting sun. Engines hummed from below and voices carried on the breeze. The Alabama air thick and warm, comforting in a way I didn't know it could be.

Or maybe it was just Kale.

The man who steadily stole more and more, each laugh and tease and smirk shackling another piece of me.

"That was delicious," I told him, sitting back in the chair, my stomach so full it was close to painful.

He arched an eyebrow. "And just who are you complimenting?"

A giggle floated out on the air, every shield and guard ripped away, my ribbing so easy. "I was complimenting you, but I guess I really should give the credit where it belongs."

"Is that so?"

"Mm-hmm," I drew out.

Flying from his chair, he lunged for me, and I squealed, jumping to my feet and racing through the open doors.

He chased me. And God, I loved it.

Loved it when he caught me from behind. When he lifted me from my feet. When he hugged me against his bare chest.

Loved it when he kissed the back of my head. Loved it more when he started leaving dizzying trails of kisses down the side of my neck, nipping at the corner of my jaw, his cock growing thick against my bottom.

Oh.

He was undoing me.

My phone rang from within my purse, and I held back the groan at the interruption.

He set me back on my feet.

"Don't think just because you have a phone call that you get a free pass. I'll be waiting for you."

I glanced at him from over my shoulder, putting an extra sway into my steps when I moved toward my purse, grinning wide. "Is that a promise?"

"Oh, Harley Hope, you are in so, so much trouble."

I was.

I already knew it.

And I loved that, too.

I was grinning when I dug into the side pocket and found my phone. I glanced at the screen. A frown pulled across my brow when I saw Chanda's name.

Quickly, I answered it, sure it was nothing.

But it took only the flash of a second before I knew it was something.

Dread curled through my insides when I heard her voice coming through the line. Frantic. Words so rushed, I couldn't make out what she was saying.

"Evan . . . breath . . . hurry."

My insides trembled. Panic blew through me. Pummeling and beating.

A gale force.

"What?" I asked, eyes pinching shut as my fingers drove into my hair, yanking, struggling to process what she'd said. "What are you saying? Where are you? What happened? Slow down and tell me what's happening."

Chanda sucked in a breath. Trying to calm herself. "We're just pulling up at the ER. The boys were tossing the football with Richard. The same as they always do. He was fine, Hope, he was fine, and then all of a sudden, Evan said he couldn't breathe."

A hand landed on my shoulder, grabbing hold, maybe holding me up.

Tension wound tight. Round and round and round.

"Is he okay?" I didn't know if she could hear me, the words choked where they locked in my throat, not prepared for what she might say.

"I think so. I think so," she rambled. Frazzled. Frenzied.

Or maybe all that frenzy belonged to me. Because I could feel it shaking through my system.

Speeding through my veins.

Seeping into my spirit.

Penetrating to my bones.

"Okay, we're here. We're here. I'll call you back," she said.

The line went dead and dread pressed down on my chest.

Too heavy.

Too much.

I couldn't move.

Frozen.

Kale spun me around and pried the phone from my hand, setting both of his on my shoulders. He gave me a tiny shake, trying to snap me out of the daze. "Hope, what is going on? Who was that? Tell me what's happening."

"Evan."

His name.

It was a plea.

A prayer.

Kale's face blanched.

White as a ghost.

Or maybe I could only see what was reflected in me.

Tremors rolled beneath my skin, my muscles trembling as the freeze finally thawed.

It gave way to a raging river. Sweeping me away. Taking me with it and shooting me into action.

I fumbled into my shoes, grabbed my purse, and jerked open the door.

I could sense the torment of the presence behind me. The anguish in his silence. And maybe I did understand him better. His walls higher than mine. Why he couldn't do this with me.

I didn't pause to look back when I floundered with the latch and flew out the door.

The only thing I knew was I needed to get to my son.

nineteen

Kale

The door slammed closed behind her.

I gripped fistfuls of my hair, staring at the spot where she'd just been.

Air gone, my lungs squeezed tight.

What the fuck was I supposed to do?

Fear spiraled. Slammed and howled. It beat against this overwhelming sensation that welled.

Growing bigger—more powerful—than anything else. Constricting my chest and shattering every reserve.

I was moving before I let myself think through the consequences. Because the consequence of standing there like a worthless piece of shit were so much greater than going after what had just fled out my door.

Bolting into the living room, I nabbed my shirt from the rug. I was pulling it over my head at the same time as I was grabbing my keys and wallet from the entry table. Not wanting to take the time to go to my room, I shoved my feet into some ripped-up Vans and then went racing out.

I didn't bother with the elevator.

I pounded down the stairs, taking them three at a time. I blew through the big metal back door and flew out into the lot.

Twilight had taken hostage of the sky, the heavens streaked with darkened clouds, a single star blinking on the horizon above the copse of trees.

My eyes hunted.

Immediately, they landed on Hope. She was across the lot, stumbling through her panic as she tried to run in her heels.

She jerked at the door handle of her big SUV, fumbling and shaking as she struggled to get inside.

Sprinting her direction, I caught her just before she was all the way in. "Hope."

She gasped a pained sound. "I've got to get to him."

My voice was grit at her ear as I hauled her back from around the waist. "I know. I know. But I can't let you drive like this. Come on, baby, let me help you. It's going to be okay."

She gasped another sound. This one a guttural cry, her terror that had been bottled spilling out.

"I've got you. It's going to be okay," I told her, anxiety gripping me like a vise.

It is going to be okay.

He'll be okay.

I promise I won't let anything happen to him.

I shifted her around, slamming her door shut as I did. Quickly, I guided her to my car parked two spaces over. Opening the passenger door, I helped her in, darted around the front, and hopped inside.

The second the engine turned over, I threw it in reverse and whipped out of the spot. Half a second later, I had it in gear and was gunning the engine, tires squealing when I skidded out onto the street.

Teeth gritted, I weaved in and out of traffic, trying to remain calm.

Cool.

Which was impossible since my heart was a fucking throbbing mess where it was lodged in my throat.

When all I could think about was that kid.

That kid.

I struggled to focus, to breathe in the dense, dark air that had taken hold.

Hope fisted her hands on her lap, choppy pants heaving from her shuddering chest.

Terrified.

Doing my best to keep it together, to be there for her, I reached out and set my hand on her leg. I gave her a soft squeeze. "He's going to be okay, Hope. I promise you, he's going to be okay."

The oaths I'd kept silenced before came tumbling out.

Her nod was jerky. She set her hand on top of mine, squeezing so hard I was sure she was drawing blood.

Leaning on me.

Relying on me.

Silently begging me to keep that promise.

Five minutes later, I skidded into the parking lot at the ER.

The same ER where I'd been a resident for the previous three years.

I jerked into a vacant spot, killed the engine, and was already out and at Hope's door by the time she had it open and was climbing out.

"Thank you," she rasped, clutching my shirt. She was shaking all over, so I wrapped my arm around her waist to support her.

Together, we rushed for the entryway doors.

They swished apart as we approached.

Once we got inside, I let Hope run ahead of me, feeling like a complete asshole for dropping my arm.

But I felt so tied.

Those memories too close. Too real. Too much.

I rubbed an anxious hand over my jaw, watching Hope as she went for the triage station, her son's name a plea from her tongue.

The door leading into the back buzzed and swung open. Hope went right for it.

And I stood there like a chump.

Fuck it.

I hurtled after her, barely grabbing the door before it closed. I hurried to catch up to her where she raced down the hall that was lined with curtained exam spaces, a big nursing station in the middle.

She headed straight down the hallway and toward the room number she'd been given.

This place was so familiar. So much of my time had been devoted to this emergency room. But it was always me caring for the patients that came through the doors.

My complete dedication given to them.

But this time . . . this time it was different. The tables turned.

I passed familiar faces, and a couple of nurses offered confused hellos as I passed.

Frantically, Hope jerked open the door of one of the enclosed exam rooms reserved for higher-risk patients. Equipment at the ready for testing and treatment that might need to be rendered urgently.

And that chaotic world spinning around us?

For a moment, it completely froze.

It gave Hope a second to catch up.

A chance to take in her son, who was in the middle of the room, partially propped up on an elevated hospital bed with an oxygen mask covering his nose and mouth.

He was alert, those green eyes scared, but they shimmered with relief when he caught sight of his mom.

For a beat, Hope was locked in that suspended moment where only her son existed.

Then she jolted forward. "Oh . . . God . . . Evan."

Her hand was on the side of his face, the other going straight for his heart. *My heart. My heart.*

From behind, I could see her shoulders sag in relief when she felt it beating.

When she felt the life that pounded through his veins.

And there was nothing I could do but step up behind her, touch Evan's cheek, his forehead, fingers trembling as I felt along the steady pulse in his neck.

It was the furthest from an exam. It was simply a man needing to be reassured that someone he cared about was okay.

From under the mask, Evan smiled his wide smile, and I ruffled my fingers through his hair, barely able to mouth the words, "Hey, buddy."

He was okay.

He signed *HI.*

A breath pressed from my lips, a million pounds of worry let loose in the sound. I glanced at Hope, touched her cheek, praying she could see it in my eyes.

He's fine. I promise. He's fine.

A throat cleared, and my attention jumped up to meet the confused gaze of a woman I'd never met, but knew had to be Josiah's mother. She stood on the opposite side of the bed, watching over him, dried tears still staining her cheeks.

She tore her eyes away from me and turned them on Hope. "Hope . . . I'm so sorry to scare you this way. I think . . . I think he just got out of breath, and I panicked—" She fumbled, hesitated, her worried gaze turning to Josiah, who was huddled in the corner, sitting on his father's knee.

Josiah's eyes were wide and terrified and confused. Worried about his friend.

"You know . . ." She said it like an apology riddled with empathy.

Because Josiah's mom understood all the things Hope was feeling perfectly.

"It's okay," Hope managed, stare still locked on her son. "It's okay. I'm just . . ." She forced herself to look at Josiah's mom, offering a soggy smile. "I'm so grateful you brought him here, Chanda. It isn't worth the risk. I would have done the same thing."

Chanda gave a reassuring tip of her chin, her eyes flitting to me before they jerked away. As if she thought she was invading on something private.

At the exact same time, her husband's brow was pinching together in his own confusion, clearly working to figure out where he'd seen me before.

I roughed a hand over my head, blinking, calculating, trying to figure out what the fuck to do. I had no idea how Hope would want me to handle this.

How I wanted to.

That was right when I noticed Dr. Laurent Kristoff standing just off to the side, studying the readout on the portable ECG machine, checking the rhythm of Evan's heart.

In all the upheaval, I hadn't realized the emergency room doctor I'd worked next to for years was right there. Seems Hope wasn't the only one with tunnel vision.

Laurent did a double take when he noticed me. "Dr. Bryant?"

Nodding, I forced myself to give him a cordial smile, but I didn't get anything out before the door opened behind me.

Dr. Krane, the cardiac specialist at GL Children's Center, stepped inside.

Obviously, he was the pediatric cardiologist on call this weekend.

Shit.

He grinned when he saw me. "Dr. Bryant, I didn't realize you were on call."

That's because I wasn't.

I grimaced. "Not on call," I admitted.

His expression shifted for a flash, morphing into confusion or concern, I wasn't sure, before he shrugged it off, moved across the floor, and turned his attention on Evan.

The reason we were all there.

That didn't mean I couldn't feel the weight of Josiah's dad's stare. The questions that were coming from everyone.

Because I was responsible for the care of both of these boys.

They were supposed to be my single focus.

No distractions.

I'd lived my life on that rule.

And here I was, so goddamned distracted my insides were in knots and my spirit was roaring, wrapped up in a way I'd never let it before.

Sure. I'd examined Frankie Leigh. But always on the side. As a bolster for Rex. A second opinion. Reassurance. Her pediatrician was the one who was truly in charge of her care.

Hope sent me an apologetic glance.

I shook my head.

Don't be sorry.

Because the truth of it all?

I wanted to be there.

I wanted to be there for her.

And goddamn it, I needed to be there for him.

twenty

Hope

"Ms. Masterson, I would think it would greatly benefit you to apply for our state health care program."

I blinked at the woman behind the desk, who was speaking to me about the fact my son had been rushed into the ER. Uninsured.

What she didn't understand was that he had to be, for just a little while longer.

My head shook, and I fought the new kind of panic that clawed through my spirit. "No, I'll be paying out of pocket."

She looked at me as if I were crazy, which admittedly, was exactly how I felt, never having imagined I would ever go down a path such as this. But my son was worth it.

He was worth any debt. Any sacrifice. Any lie.

It was only for a year. Until the day I could ensure Dane would never be a threat to Evan again.

"You're looking at, at least five thousand for this visit alone, Ms. Masterson."

My throat constricted at that number, but I managed to force a bright, fake smile. "It's fine, I have the funds."

Or really, I would find a way to get them.

Another loan taken out against the coffee shop.

A rush of guilt made me cringe. I hated that I was putting Jenna in this position. A Drop of Hope was every bit as much her dream as it was mine. But she'd promised me she was willing to make any sacrifice she had to. Promised she was in this with me. Whatever it took or cost.

The woman pushed out a confused sigh. "Okay, then, but I'm including these pamphlets for you to look over. I'm sure there's a plan that's a good fit for your son."

I reached over the desk and took them from her. "Thank you, I'll look through them," I promised, telling another lie, tossing it right on the mounting pile. The shorter the paper trail, the better.

Pushing to my feet, I left her office, feeling shaky all over as I went. Adrenaline dumping from my veins, leaving me drained, the remnants the fear of this day had evoked almost too much to bear.

My emotions precarious. So close to breaking me.

Desperate.

That was what I was.

Desperate for my son to be okay. Desperate for this charade to go away and Dane to leave us be so we could live our lives.

Rounding the corner, I peered into the examination room through the small window in the door, just needing to get a peek at my son.

A buoy to give me the strength to keep fighting. To gain the confidence that he was really okay. The doctor had spent a half hour trying to reassure me that he'd just overexerted himself. That it was typical. That there wasn't anything to worry about.

Still, Dr. Krane had made an appointment for him to follow up in two weeks to do a thorough workup of his heart to make sure it was functioning fine. Covering all the bases.

My frantic spirit eased when I gazed in, taking in the sight in front of me.

Evan was fully propped up in the hospital bed, his mop of messy red hair flying all around as he laughed.

Laughed because Kale was sitting at the end of his bed, angled with his knee under himself so he could face Evan, scribbling something on the pad one of the nurses had brought in for ease of communication.

My heart clenched.

Painfully.

Beautifully.

Because my son looked so free and content and comfortable with Kale at his side. And Kale was looking at my son the way a child deserved to be looked at.

Protectively.

Adoringly.

And now I knew the source of Kale's unease. His fear of loving someone and taking the chance that they might be violently, savagely ripped away. The barriers and shields he struggled to maintain to protect himself from that chance.

And he had stayed.

That meant more to me than he could ever know.

Kale met my eye through the small window.

That protective possessiveness extended out to me, searching through its own confusion and uncertainty. The man holding me up with a simple glance.

I'm here.

I blinked, swallowed, no steel left around my heart. Because in that blink. I was right back in that day. The day I'd been left alone . . .

"Mrs. Gentry, has your husband returned?" He looked around the room where I sat alone. Clutching my arms over my chest.

Rocking.

Trying to be strong.

Jenna had just left to get coffee, and my mama was on her way from Texas. Promising she would get there as quickly as she could.

"No." I swallowed around the ball of agony cinched tight in my throat. Cutting off circulation. Shutting down belief. I didn't know how much more I could take.

The doctor who'd first given us the news tried to hide his surprise when I told him I was still alone, but it was there. He shook his head in what I knew was supposed to be sympathy. "All right, then."

He sank to the chair beside me. "We would like to have your blood drawn so we can try to determine the exact genetic defect your son suffers from."

Jerkily, I nodded, rushing my hands over the chills that lifted on my arms. I was cold. So cold.

"Of course."

I would do anything.

Give anything.

The doctor paused, as if he were waiting for me to snap. Break. Then he issued almost carefully, "It is important we get your husband's as well."

I blinked, trying to stay upright against the force of the walls that spun and spun. "He's not here," I said, somehow feeling as if that statement was on repeat.

The words leaving me through the stark numbness that echoed from that hollow place inside.

He hadn't been there since he'd stormed out the day before when I'd refused to leave.

Refusing food.

Refusing sleep.

"Just as soon as it's possible is all we ask."

I nodded again. "I'll do what I can."

I couldn't understand it. How he could leave us there. He'd doted on me through my entire pregnancy. I could never forget the amount of pride on his face and love in his eyes when we'd found out we were having a boy.

Then he had just . . . disappeared.

Abandoned us.

But Dane was the least of my worries right then.

"The arrangements have been finalized for his transfer, and the heart team will be ready to perform his surgery as soon as he arrives. Transport is scheduled for three this afternoon."

I nodded again, clutching myself tighter.

"You can go in and see him now, and I will send someone to come to draw your blood while they prep him for transfer."

The only thing I could process was that I could see him. I could finally see him.

"Thank you." The words left me on a gush of air.

Kindly, he patted my knee. "I know things look bleak right now, and I know you're scared, but don't stop praying. I've seen a lot of miracles in my lifetime."

Gratefulness pulsed through my being, thankful this doctor had taken the time to step outside of his duty and offer me kind words when it felt as if the world only had cruelty to offer.

"I won't," I promised, though I was terrified it might be a lie.

When he stood, I followed, my knees weak and my body swaying.

I followed him out and down a long hall and then another before I was cleared through a set of imposing double doors.

I was taken to a preparation area and instructed on how to wash, before I was led into a darkened room. The large area was only illuminated by dim, unobtrusive lights, sections curtained off, concealing the isolettes behind each.

Some of the curtains were opened where I could see mothers nursing and fathers cradling their babies in the rocking chairs.

I gulped again when the nurse led me toward another sectioned off area. My heart raced in its confines.

Fear and grief and hope.

They constricted and squeezed, my chest so tight I thought my heart might be physically crushed.

The nurse drew the curtain back slightly so I could slip through.

At the sight in front of me, a tiny sound climbed from my throat.

Love.

The impact of it was staggering.

My infant son lay riddled with tubes and lines, attached to monitors, tape concealing the lower half of his face to keep the oxygen in place.

But I saw none of those things.

I saw the child that'd been given into my care.

I saw a little boy running on a playground.

I saw a future.

Slowly, I edged forward. Tears blurred my eyes as I looked down on my son. Hand shaking, I reached out and caressed my thumb across the back of his tiny hand.

Those tiny fingers searched, tightly wrapping around my finger.

He stared up at me.

I was certain that connection was greater than anything I'd ever felt.

My mouth trembled, overwhelmed with affection. With my free hand, I reached up and softly ran my knuckle down his plump cheek.

"My heart," I whispered, and the little boy stared up at me as if he'd known me for a million years.

The little boy who would forever hold my heart.
And I murmured a million of those prayers into the air.
Believed.
And knew, right that second, with every part of me, I would never, ever give up on hope.

Blinking out of the reverie, I ran my fingertips over my eyelids, clearing the tears. Refusing to allow myself to spiral into hopelessness.

I just needed to focus on the fact Evan was okay. Spend this time in gratefulness.

Knees shaky, I opened the door.

Instantly, Evan was frantically signing my way, his eyes still dancing with his laughter. *DR. BRYANT SAID HE WAS A NERD IN SCHOOL. DID YOU KNOW THAT? HE SAID NERDS ARE THE BEST. THEY GROW UP TO BE DOCTORS.*

Nerds are the best.

The memory of him teasing me about being a nerd that first night hit me.

This man. He had completely demolished me in the best of ways.

A sound that was half a sob and half laughter tripped from my mouth. It originated somewhere in my spirit.

The sound made up of the remnants of terror I'd felt this afternoon.

The astounding relief when I'd found Evan was really okay.

The million emotions Kale had taken me through earlier at his loft. The need and the desire and the beauty.

The pure adoration I felt then.

It was all there.

Compounding.

Kale stood from the bed, and I sucked in a shattered breath.

"Come on, let's get your little man home."

I felt him in the doorway behind me.

His presence thick and potent and powerful. It surged into the room, a crashing wave, taking me whole.

It was late, close to one in the morning.

I'd been kneeling in the same spot on the floor beside Evan's bed for the last three hours. Watching him sleep. Just . . . feeling the beat of his heart.

My amazing son, who'd fallen asleep on the way home from the hospital.

Kale had carried him in from the car and laid him in his bed. The way he'd done the night before.

Only this time, he'd stayed while I'd changed Evan into his pajamas, brought me hot tea when I'd refused to leave Evan's side, and then paced my house for hours as if he were searching for a purpose when I knew he could already feel his purpose echoing from the floors.

Footsteps shuffled behind me, quiet and subdued, before the man knelt next to me. Fingers ran the length of my hair, massaging into my neck, as his nose pressed into the locks as he inhaled.

I shivered with the whisper at my ear, "You need to get some rest. You're exhausted."

I glanced back at him, gazing into the depths of those caring, kind eyes that glinted and shone in the muted light that glowed from the lamp on Evan's nightstand. My mouth trembled, my lips soaked with the silent tears I could no longer hold back.

As if I was purging every negative thing from the day and casting up a million prayers of gratefulness at the same time. "I don't know how to leave him after a day like today."

We'd been assured he was fine.

Still, I felt chained to my son's side. Unable to move.

Kale wrapped his strong arms around me, pulling my back to his chest. I could feel the thrum, thrum, thrum of his magnificent heart. The sound reverberating and seeping into me.

"Let me take care of you. Let me take care of him," he murmured.

Shifting, he pushed to his feet, bringing me with him, sweeping me from the floor and cradling me in his arms.

I held on, sinking into the staunchest kind of security, and pressed my face up under his chin, feeling the warmth and the life. Inhaling the woodsy, masculine scent.

"I've got you," he said for what had to be the hundredth time that day.

And I trusted that he did.

He carried me out of Evan's room, through the house, and into my bedroom.

A room he'd never seen.

I could feel it when his sight landed on my massive bed, the heft of the breath that pressed from his lungs.

He moved through my room and set me down on one side. He didn't say anything, just quietly worked through the buttons of my dress. Though this time it was different. This time, it was with care and deference.

He slowly lifted it over my head. Cool air skated my skin. His gaze swept over me, but there was no smirk. No tease.

He moved to my dresser and pulled open the top right door, as if he already knew what he was looking for. Silently, he moved back through the space, his hands winding the silky soft pink nightgown over my head, gliding it over my body where it barely landed at the top of my thighs.

Everything felt so intimate.

Our breaths and his touch and his care.

"Kale."

I didn't know what I was asking for.

He cupped the side of my face and ran his thumb along the hollow beneath my eye. "I know."

He kissed my forehead once, twice, and then lifted my covers. "Get in, sweet girl."

I sank back into the comfort.

Not just of my bed.

But the feeling that swam through my spirit. The promise that everything was going to be all right. He pulled the covers over me, and his fingertips danced across my cheek. "Sleep well, Hope."

Exhausted, I slumped into the welcome of my pillow, my body relaxing beneath the blankets, only a fluttered breath before I was asleep.

I jolted awake to the silence. To the thick darkness of my room.

I reached over, switching on the lamp on my nightstand. I blinked, adjusting to the shadows before I pushed off the covers and slid from my bed.

Barefoot, I padded across the wooden floors. Drawn. Silently moving through the living room and back down the hall.

At Evan's door, I paused.

Kale lay on the hard floor next to the bed, a pillow from the couch under his head and a tiny throw barely covering his torso, still in his shirt and jeans.

His arm was slung up onto Evan's bed, his palm resting across my son's heart.

And that feeling—that affection that compounded and churned and swelled—it burst.

I'd known this man was *more*.

Now I knew he was everything.

I tiptoed over to the side of Evan's bed and gently ran my hand over my son's forehead.

He sighed from the depths of his sleep.

Content and safe and perfect.

And Kale's hand that was on Evan's heart? I gathered it in mine and threaded my fingers through his. Those eyes popped open, twilight on the sea.

He looked up at me before he climbed to his towering height.

He followed me without a word.

Without a sound.

The only voice the energy that rumbled beneath our feet.

twenty-one

Kale

Silently, I followed behind her. Our footsteps subdued as we waded through the tension that climbed into the atmosphere, amplifying the closer we got to her room.

Energy lapped, mounting and building in the dense, dense air.

Severe.

Intense.

That storm I'd felt coming for weeks was suddenly overhead. Battering at the walls and howling at the windows.

Hope didn't look back at me as she led me through the living room, her head bowed, her motions somehow deliberate. Like she was moving through honey.

The minutes set to slow. Like we didn't have to rush.

But there was no doubt, no hesitation in her decision.

I could feel it galloping ahead of us. This girl already riding toward a divine destination.

Inviting me to join her.

Part of me screamed and raged, tearing at my insides, shouting at me to go. To tell her this was a horrible idea. It was four in the morning and our walls were down.

I needed to leave because I had no idea where this path was going to lead us, and if I hurt her, I wasn't sure I'd make it through this time.

Because she brought every old feeling back. Ones I'd never thought I'd feel again. Then she multiplied it by something that was brand new. Bigger than anything I'd felt. Not once. Not ever.

Only her.

Blips of the day flashed through my mind. The girl blowing my mind. Confessing to her that I'd lost the first and only girl I'd ever loved. The sheer terror I'd felt over Evan. The fact I hadn't been able to walk away when I'd brought them back here.

And I knew.

I knew.

I wanted to try.

God. I wanted to try. Hope's breaths turned shallow when she guided me through the threshold of her doorway and into the dimmed, shadowy glow that clung to her bedroom.

Golden shadows and a lusty haze.

Just inside, she dropped my hand. Slowly, she swiveled around to face me, her chin lifting on a lurching breath. I saw the offering just as clearly as I heard the plea.

Her legs were bare beneath that tiny slip of a gown.

Every damned inch of me grew hard at the sight, my chest tightening and my dick thickening, begging at my jeans.

I shifted to quietly latch the door shut and flicked the lock.

The promise of it hit the room like a sonic boom.

I stepped forward, erasing the distance between us, my fingertips reaching out to flutter along the delicate column of her neck.

Her pulse thrummed an erratic, reckless beat. I trailed them back up, over the divot in her chin, and ran them across the pout of those lush, full lips. "You are so beautiful, Hope. So beautiful that I think I have to be dreaming right now."

"I need you, Kale," she whispered across my fingertips.

It sent a spiral of need curling through me.

Lust.

Greed.

Possession.

"I need you," she whispered again.

Every muscle in my stomach clenched when she stepped back and gathered the hem of her nightgown in her hands. Slowly, she peeled it over her body.

Exposing herself. Inch by delicious inch.

After tugging it over her head, she dropped it to the floor.

That mass of hair fell around her bare shoulders, caressing over her collarbones. Kissing her tits.

Pink, pert, pebbled nipples peeked through the long strands like the most brutal kind of tease.

Her belly flat and her waist narrow, hips flared and wide, thighs full.

Pussy covered by the same scrap of underwear that had earlier been on my floor.

That felt like a lifetime ago.

Like everything had changed. Like time had shifted and I no longer knew where I was.

A shudder took to my spine, lighting up my insides.

I ran the back of my knuckles across one peaked nipple.

She emitted a tiny moan.

"Is this what you need? You need me to touch you?"

She looked up at me. Baring herself. "I just need you. The only thing I need is you."

"Hope," I murmured, knowing exactly what this girl was saying.

Her heart and spirit soaring through the room.

Spinning around me.

Sucking me in.

I gripped her by the back of the head, my fingers splaying wide, drawing her to me.

I kissed her slowly. Deeply. Because right then, I got that this girl needed to be treated delicately.

Carefully.

That in her amazing strength, she was fragile and vulnerable, and she needed someone to hold her up. Treat her like a queen.

And I wanted to be him. That guy she said she saw when she looked at me. The guy who might make her better rather than destroy her a little more in the end.

"I need you," she muttered again, a sigh against my lips.

"I need you, too, Hope. Fuck. I need you, too."

There was so much in that statement. Things that burned in that cold, dark place. Impaling the numbness I'd surrendered it to.

Her light threatening to bring that dead place back to life.

My kiss was a slow claiming, as I backed her across her room until she butted against the bed. She didn't hesitate to crawl on top.

Our breaths heaving into the dense air when we broke apart.

The girl watched me through the shadows that jumped and danced against her bedroom walls while I stood there, taking her in, all lush milky skin and fiery red hair and hopeful, trusting eyes.

So damned gorgeous where she rested on her elbows with her knees bent and feet planted on the bed.

Rocking softly.

Touch me.

Love me.

Protect me.

Body singing with the appeal.

"If I sleep with you, there won't be any going back for me, Kale Bryant. Don't make me fall in love with you."

Another shudder ripped through me at the thought because the way she was looking at me promised it was already too late.

"Are you sure this is what you want?" I asked her, gritting my teeth, hands fisting in restraint.

"You already know my life is in turmoil." Her words were wispy tendrils that left her sensuous mouth. "I hate that I'm dragging you into the middle of it, not knowing what's going to happen. But if I'm sure of one thing? I'm sure of you."

Heart clattering with her words, I tugged my shirt over my head and ticked through my fly, shoved down my jeans and underwear, shrugged them free of my feet.

Lust knotting my insides.

A needy sigh puffed from her lungs when she looked at me, those eyes wandering with a greedy awe as they roved over me. The girl doing her own claiming. Raking my chest. Moving down my abdomen, muscles flexing and bowing, taut with need.

Her attention dipped lower, those pink lips parting when she let her heated gaze trace over my cock.

I was hard.

So damned hard.

Harder than I'd ever been.

Because this felt different from anything I'd ever felt.

Her eyes flicked back up to mine, her words soft adoration. "How is it possible you're standing there? You are magnificent, Kale Bryant. Better than any dream. Better than any fantasy. Inside and out."

I didn't know what it was about those words. But they crushed my reservations and made me forget any old devotion and any lingering fear.

Without thought, I was reaching down, fisting her underwear in my hands, dragging them down her gorgeous legs as I dipped over her to kiss at her belly.

She squirmed and sighed.

Body reaching for mine.

And I was wondering what it really meant to dream. To hold them and possess them and never give them up.

If she and Evan could possibly become the reason for mine.

Because my heart was careening in my chest, knocking at my ribs like some kind of beast when I climbed over her, when I made a spot for myself between her thighs.

Her pussy bare. Fire against my cock that barely kissed through the slick warmth of her lips. I hesitated for a second before she whispered, "I'm on the pill."

I brushed my fingers through her hair, staring down at her. "Princess," I murmured.

Her expression shifted, so soft and tender, voice sweet affection. "Hey, Cowboy."

And fuck. I wanted to tell her I'd be her anything. Her cowboy or her knight when the only fucking thing I wanted was to be her hero.

She looped an arm around my neck, our chests pressed together, hearts beating wild against the other.

Little pants of anticipation escaped from her mouth.

"Are you ready for me?" I asked.

She blinked at me through the shadows, the fingertips of her free hand running the line of my jaw. "I think I've been ready for you my whole life."

I grabbed the hand tracing my face, kissing her fingertips, her wrist, the inside of her forearm, hoping she knew that this meant something to me. That it was *more*. Then I hooked that arm around my neck, too. "Hold on to me, sweet girl."

I edged back a fraction. Just enough that I could watch her while I began to tuck myself deep in the tight, clutching grasp of her body.

Her walls hugging my dick perfectly as I spread her.

Sweet, sweet heat.

"Fuck . . . Hope . . . baby." It was all a guttural rasp from my mouth.

Heaven.

Didn't think I'd ever touched on it until right then. Because she was warm and snug and felt a little too close to home. Like maybe this girl had been meant for me. Like right here . . . with her was exactly where I was supposed to be.

She sucked in a sharp gasp, and her chest arched into mine.

"Kale." It was a shaky, unstable prayer.

Slipping my arms under her back, I gathered her tighter, wrapping her whole. Holding her as close as I could get her.

Our hearts battered against each other's, almost frantically, and I swore, I could feel the beats catching time. "I know. I've got you. I've got you," I told her.

And that energy—that feeling that had made me stumble the first time I'd caught the full impact of her face back at the bar—it combusted.

I should have known it that night that she had the power to change everything.

Because it spun the room and my head, licked through my veins, and knocked something loose inside me.

My spirit thrashed when it touched those dark places. Kindling and sparks.

Pushing up onto my hands, I pulled almost all the way out, until the tip of my dick was just hanging on.

My eyes swept over her sweet, sweet body where she was laid out beneath me, and her knees hugged my hips eagerly. Her nails sinking into my back. "Kale."

I pressed back into her heat.

Slow and sure.

Deep and promising.

Until I was filling her, the girl taking all of me the same way I was taking her.

Wholly.

"You are perfection. So goddamned perfect."

She whimpered, her perfect tits jutting toward me as she arched.

Demanding more. Emotion thick as it washed across her gorgeous face.

My hips dragged out then surged forward.

Possessing.

I quickened with each thrust, and Hope met every one with the needy roll of her body. Her hips lifted from the bed to meet mine, my name a constant prayer from her lips.

I dropped back to my elbows, every inch of us pressed together because we no longer knew how to be apart.

I fucked her and consumed her and murmured her name. Kissed her mouth. Her neck, her jaw, her tits. My lips everywhere I could reach.

She whimpered and begged and moaned, nails scratching deep into my skin. Sinking in until we were a blur of rocks and moans and twined bodies.

And I wanted to make a million promises.

Promise it all.

Pleasure threatened at the base of my spine, my balls tightening as I drove deeper and madder and faster.

Hope grasped at my shoulders as her moans and pleas increased.

Until she was begging, "Please. Kale. Oh, God, I'm close . . . please."

I edged back, pushing up onto a hand, giving myself a second to let the other smooth over her unforgettable face.

Then I dipped my thumb into the well of her mouth. She sucked it, tongue grazing the flesh, nearly sending me flying right then.

Tugging it free, I cupped her round, full breast and ran my thumb across her nipple.

She mewled a tiny plea.

Slowly, I dragged it down the valley of her stomach, winding her up, before I slipped it lower and against her clit.

I circled and flicked and teased as I climbed to my knees. The new position let me take her deeper.

And this time . . . I took her hard.

Her head rocked back on the mattress, and her hips lifted from the bed.

Every fuck of my hips drove her higher.

Higher and higher and higher until I could see it.

The second it split.

The orgasm ripping through her being.

Hope tried to mute her scream. To control the way the quivers of bliss ravaged her body.

It was the exact same second that ecstasy went streaking through mine.

The most intense kind of pleasure rocked through my body. I held back a roar when I came, pouring inside her, not giving a single thought to consequence except for the one where I might get to keep her.

I panted over her before I slumped down, resting most of my weight on top of her. Hope wrapped her slender arms back around me and held on as I rolled us to our sides.

She smiled at me.

Smiled this smile that demolished me.

"Are you okay?" I asked her.

Her fingertips danced across my brow, my jaw, my lips. It wasn't shyness that blossomed on her cheeks, just soft, sweet affection. "I think you ruined me."

There was a tease in it, mixed with a heavy dose of awe.

I let the smirk ride to my mouth and pulled her naked body flush with mine. "You think *you're* ruined?"

A giggle slipped between her swollen lips. "Really?"

I ran the palm of my hand over the top of her head, cupping it from behind. "Yeah, really, Hope. That was . . . I don't know how to properly describe what I feel when I'm with you. And getting to be with you like that? Inside you? You own me, Princess."

Redness flushed her cheeks, and she drummed her fingers over my bare shoulder. "I'm pretty sure it's the other way around, Kale. I've never experienced anything like that."

I ran my nose down her face, nuzzling up under her chin. "So, you're telling me you like my stamina after all?"

Another giggle. "If I tell you I do, will it go to your head?"

I laughed, pressing my hips to hers in a playful way, my dick already perking up with the contact. "Uh, I'm thinking that's a possibility."

Smacking at my arm, she laughed, keeping it quiet, so much easiness floating through the air. I gathered her closer and locked my arms fully around her, loving the way she felt against me.

All warm, silky flesh and lush curves and tender spirit.

Light.

Rolling again, I pulled her on top of me, and more of those giggles slipped free. And fuck. I loved being her haven. Giving her some reprieve.

She pressed her palms to my chest and pushed up, red hair falling all around her, lighting up in the dawn of the day that was barely breaking at the window.

She stared down at me, all that belief shining around her like a halo.

And this gorgeous girl?

Looking up at her?

I was gone.

Incinerated.

"What you did today, Kale . . ." Sincerity took hold of her expression, and she chewed at her bottom lip, like she was searching for what to say. "I want you to know how much that meant to me. You staying with us."

"I wanted to be there," I told her, threading my fingers through the fall of her hair.

Her eyes searched mine. Honestly. "I wanted you to be there, too."

A heavy sigh pressed between my lips. "I hate that I have to, but I'm going to need to put in a transfer of care for Evan. It isn't a good idea for me to see him as my patient if you and I are together."

It was a tweak of joy that pulled at the corner of her lush mouth, though concern swam in her eyes. "Is that what we are . . . together?"

I bucked up a little. "Sure feels like it to me."

Heat bloomed on those sweet cheeks, her freckles prominent in the wash of the sunrise that glowed against her face. Hesitation rimmed her words when she said, "But you do this all the time."

I shot up to sitting, framing both sides of her face in my hands. "No, Hope. I don't do this all the time. Not like this."

"It feels different, doesn't it?" she asked, voice almost whimsical as she chanced meeting my eyes.

I cupped the side of her neck. "Yeah . . . it feels different. It feels better."

It feels right.

A sad smile tweaked her mouth. "I hate the idea of you not seeing him. You're a good doctor, Kale."

"I want to be."

"Does this scare you?" There she was, once again, so goddamned open. Vulnerable and honest and real. No games.

I refused to play them, either. "Yeah. It fucking terrifies me."

"I don't ever want to put you in a position you don't want to be in, Kale. I'd never back you into a corner. But you need to know, Evan is my life, and every choice I make affects him. I have to be careful, especially with what's going on with his father right now. Most of all, I need you to know I will do whatever it takes to protect him."

There was almost a warning in her words.

Anger flamed, and I pushed it down, refusing to let that bastard come into our sacred space.

Instead, I wrapped my arms around her slender waist and tipped my head back so I could read her expression better. "I'm not here to yank you around, Hope. You already made yourself perfectly clear, and I knew what I was doing when I followed you into this room. I get it. I know what's on the line."

With her, I wanted to walk it.

She wrapped her arms tighter around me, pressed her mouth to my neck. "I didn't expect you, Kale Bryant."

I hugged her body against mine, our hearts synced, beating in time. "I definitely didn't expect you, Hope."

I glanced at the clock on her nightstand. "I should go before Evan wakes up."

"Yeah," she agreed, albeit reluctantly.

I shifted so I could toss her onto her back on her bed. Giggling, she bounced, red, red hair splayed all around her, her smile brighter than the sun that rose through her window.

My chest clenched. Never thought I could feel this way.

I climbed off her bed, feeling the heat of her gaze as she watched me dress from behind. When I turned back to her, she had her sheets pressed to her mouth, blushing all over the place.

God. This girl.

I leaned over and planted my hands on her bed, kissed her mouth. "You can ogle me any time you want, Princess. You don't have to be shy about it. I've been ogling you since the second I met you."

"It's just . . . you're gorgeous, Kale. Such a beautiful man. Inside and out. I don't think I ever want to stop looking at you."

I dipped down closer. "And you're the best damned thing I've ever seen."

I let my gaze rake her body. "Fair warning . . . next time I get you in bed, I'm not gonna be so easy on you."

Because there I was, wanting to climb right back onto her bed and take her again. My mind running wild with fantasies. The ways I wanted to have her. Wanting to incite that sweet little vixen.

Redness splashed those cheeks when she grinned. "Is that a promise?"

I growled, buried my face in her neck before I pushed back, smirking down at her. "You are in so much trouble, Harley Hope."

She ran her fingers through my hair. "Figured as much. I knew you were trouble the first time I saw you."

I pecked her mouth again. "I'll swing by later, if that's okay? Check up on Evan?"

Her expression grew soft. "Yeah, that would be nice."

"Why don't you try to get some more rest? Yesterday was a long day."

She tucked her bottom lip between her teeth, gave a nod. "Okay."

"Okay," I told her in encouragement before I straightened. Wavered.

Looked around her room, not really wanting to leave but knowing I needed to.

She was right.

We had to be careful with Evan. Their lives were riddled with complications, and I definitely didn't want to make a single one of them worse.

I headed for her door where I slowly and quietly released the lock. The door barely creaked when I opened it. I tiptoed out, leaving it open a crack behind me, heading for the door.

I froze when I saw the mess of red hair sticking up all over the place from over the top of the couch.

I wondered if it'd make me a horrible person if I tried to sneak out, taking advantage of his disability that way.

But he'd already noticed the movement, anyway. His eyes keen and knowing, the kid always picking up on more than I thought he would.

He scrambled from the couch, going for the pad that was on the coffee table like he'd been waiting for me.

Furiously, he scratched something on the top sheet, and I slowly eased around to the front of the couch. I sank down onto the edge of it, the coward's side of me wanting to bolt.

Somehow sitting there made me feel like I was fifteen and had been caught sneaking out the window of my girlfriend's bedroom in the middle of the night, her dad standing with a shotgun on the lawn, waiting for me.

Which was ridiculous.

Or not.

Because my eyes bugged out of my damned head when I saw what he'd written.

Did you and my mom do it?

Evan's green eyes were hard and demanding behind his thick-rimmed glasses, his demeanor a little mad when he shoved it at me.

I roughed my palm over my face. Apparently, that feeling hadn't been so off base.

Warily, I eyed him, watching him carefully when I took the pen and wrote out a response.

How do you know what that is?

He seemed annoyed when he snatched it back.

I'm 8. Almost 9.

"Exactly," I said, knowing he was reading my lips.
He scribbled more.

Do you even watch TV?

A disbelieving laugh jolted free, nerves and caution and unease.
He scribbled again.

Did you sleep in her bed?

How the hell was I supposed to answer that? I didn't want to lie. Fuck, I didn't want to lie to this kid.
Because I saw it all over him.
He thought he was the one who was supposed to be protecting his mom.
Looking out for her.
The man of the house.
And I didn't think he really knew exactly what he was asking me, but I knew it was wholly important to him.
My chest tightened, and I swallowed around the lump in my throat, leaned over, watching him as I wrote.

That's private between your mom and me.

I knew in his expression that answer brought him to his conclusion.
In a flash, he was on his feet in front of me.
Tears of anger and frustration glistened in his eyes when his hands frantically signed.
No. I couldn't read it.
But I knew exactly what he said.
BUT DO YOU LOVE HER?
Everything clenched and crushed, and I was rubbing my mouth again, dropping my hand to make sure he could see.
"It's complicated, Evan," I said.
He was back to the pad, the pen cutting deep into the paper.

You have to love her if you live here. That's the rule.

And God, he was so innocent and wise. Smarter than I was. Seeing the world so simply.
I reached out and grabbed him by the outside of the shoulders, dragging him a step toward me, wishing with all of me he could *hear* me. That I could communicate with him better. That I could make him understand something that I didn't fully understand, either.
"I care about your mom, Evan. I care about her so much. And I care about you. Okay?"
Without warning, his tears were running free, and I had him in my arms, hugging him against me.
I suddenly realized so many things about those complications that Hope

had warned me about.

This kid and his mom had been through hell, and he was terrified of a man taking them there again. I pulled back, dried his eyes. "I won't hurt her."

He swiped his forearm under his nose. "Promise," he said. His lips formed the word, but the sound he forced from his throat was unintelligible.

But I heard.

I heard.

"I promise."

He stared at me for a beat before he nodded. *OK.*

Okay.

I huffed out a breath, hit with a distinct rush of relief.

I grabbed the pad and wrote out the question.

How are you feeling?

Hungry.

I chuckled.

All right then.

Breakfast.

I stood and offered him my hand. And there weren't a whole lot of things in the world that felt better than when he took it.

twenty-two

Hope

It was early afternoon when I heard a clatter in the foyer. The front door banged open then slammed shut. Two seconds later, Jenna stumbled through the kitchen archway.

Hair a mess. Clothes splattered with dough and streaked in frosting.

Frazzled and unnerved.

Her gaze darted to Evan, who was sitting on his knees on the stool next to me with his elbows propped on the counter as he Snapped with Josiah.

As if he hadn't been through the trauma of yesterday.

Jenna had been at the coffee shop this morning when I'd called to let her know what had happened. The weekend manager had been short-staffed, so she'd gone in to pick up the slack.

She went right for him, hauling him into her arms, hugging him tight and peppering a bunch of sloppy kisses all over his head and face.

"Is he okay?" she asked, her eyes cutting up to me from over his head.

I nodded, fighting that rush of terror I was struck with when I thought of what might have been. Instead, I forced myself into focusing on the fact he was here.

Whole.

Healthy.

"He got a little out of breath. Chanda and Richard were concerned, so they rushed him in. He was fine by the time I got there."

No. It hadn't been our first urgent trip to the ER, and I hated to accept that it certainly wouldn't be our last. But it was the life we lived. But it sure didn't ever get any easier. Terrified that one day the diagnosis wouldn't be so simple. That our worlds might be rocked once again.

"Thank God," she said, squeezing him tighter. He pulled back, sending her a huge grin, shaking his head as if he thought she was being ridiculous.

She set him back on the stool and ruffled his hair before dropping down low to be sure he was watching her face. "You have to stop scaring me like that."

He gave her an indulgent nod, signing, *I DON'T MEAN TO SCARE YOU, AUNTIE.*

Jenna only signed well enough to pick up on whatever my son was trying to say.

She ran a tender hand down the side of his face. "I know, sweetheart. I know."

Evan immediately went back to his iPad.

Straightening, she ran both her palms over her face and blew a big puff of air between her lips.

She gave me that look, the one asking if I was okay.

I grimaced, not sure how to answer that question. Yesterday had been horrible, bad enough to drop me to my knees, and still one of the best days of my life.

I was struggling to process all the emotions roiling inside me.

I could still taste Kale on my breath and feel him on my skin.

"Yesterday was rough," I told her, "but I promise I'm okay. I'm just thankful it turned out the way it did."

I turned to make sure Evan couldn't see me speaking before I set my attention back on Jenna. "You know I'm going to have to borrow more money to pay for that visit."

We'd figured paying out of pocket for Evan's medical care for a year was going to be steep. But we hadn't prepared for any emergencies, praying we could eke by on the bare minimum, going with it, riding on the hope that it would all work out in the end.

"Don't you dare mention money, Hope. I told you from the start, I'm in this with you."

I blinked, pushing out the words around the heavy emotion in my throat. "I just hate that I'm putting your livelihood on the line, right along with mine. It isn't fair to you, Jenna."

"Pssh." She waved me off with a wry grin. "Don't give yourself so much credit. Who do you think the criminal mastermind is around here? If I hadn't have come up with the idea, you never would have been in the middle of this. Just be thankful I'm your BFF—best friend felon."

My brows lifted. "Best friend felon?"

"Um, I did go into a dark alley to make that happen. Doesn't get more gangster than that."

"So hardcore," I teased her, letting myself latch on to her mood. Because she was right. It was all gonna work out. I just had to hold out a little longer.

"Hey, that dude was scaaaary," she drew out, before she fanned herself. "And hot. On all things holy, that man was hotter than Hades. Hell, he might have been Lucifer himself."

Only Jenna.

She dropped her smile. "But seriously, the last thing I want you worrying about is money. We'll figure it out, no matter what. We're almost to the end. We've got this, okay?"

"Okay."

"Good."

Shucking off the heaviness, I grabbed a coffee mug from the cupboard and waved it toward her. "You want?"

Her eyebrows disappeared behind her messy bangs. "After a day like today? That cup had better have wine in it."

I laughed, shaking my head. "Wine it is."

Ducking into the fridge, I pulled out a chilled bottle of rosé. I hunted in the drawer for the opener, focused on tearing off the foil and popping the cork.

"So, why didn't you call me yesterday?" she asked. "You know I hate the idea of you having to go through something like that on your own. One call, and you know either me or your mama would be there in a flash."

There was a hint of hurt in her tone. A little bit of conniving, too.

Because Jenna knew me so well that I was pretty sure she'd waltzed through that door and saw everything about me was different.

That my insides had been rearranged to make room for something new.

Something beautiful and wonderful.

Magical.

I could feel the flush race up my neck, and I dropped my face toward the floor, trying to conceal what was probably written all over me, anyway.

"Harley Hope Masterson, you better fess up right now . . . because I see that pink hitting your cheeks, and you haven't even had a sip of your wine."

I peeked up at her. "I didn't have to go through it alone."

"And who might it have been at the hospital with you?"

Evan caught my attention in my periphery when he sat upright, nonchalantly signing, *K-A-L-E*.

Little stinker. He had a knack of knowing exactly when to start paying attention, picking up on the little bits I might want to keep hidden.

But there had been no hiding what I felt this morning when I'd gotten up and could hear the deep tenor of Kale's voice echoing through my walls.

After I'd thought he was sneaking out when I'd wanted to beg him to stay.

I'd tiptoed out to find the staggering sight of the man in there with my son. Cooking for him. Laughing with him. Caring for him.

After the night we'd shared together, seeing him there like that had almost been too much.

Triumph glinted in Jenna's eyes as they slanted from Evan toward me. "Oh, really."

Evan was back to divulging all my secrets. *YUP. AND HE SPENT THE NIGHT AND MADE ME BREAKFAST. HE'S HER BOYFRIEND.*

The last he said with a little shrug.

No big deal.

Jenna choked, sputtered over her laugh, that original triumph shifting to an all-out celebration of victory. "You little slut."

"Jenna," I hissed, glancing at Evan, who'd decided we were boring after all, his attention wrapped up in watching Josiah dancing around the screen with his face the center of a flower.

She stalked toward me, a gleam in her eyes, and then turned so her back was toward Evan. "Was he good? Oh, God, I bet that doctor is amazing with those big hands. I told you all you needed was a big, yummy dick and all would be right with the world."

Her words deviated from a salacious secret to a breathy wisp to the worst kind of tease.

"A lady never tells," I tried to defend.

Though I might as well have been shouting it from the rooftops with the way heat went flushing over every inch of me, the memory of the way he'd touched me. Bringing me to ecstasy as if he were the one who'd always possessed my pleasure, the one sent to deliver it.

"Oh, come on, Hope. That's a total crock, and you know it. You've at least got to tell me if the man knows where the clicker is."

How she and I were friends, I didn't know. When I didn't answer, her grin just grew, yet, her voice turned soft. "At least tell me he knows how to treat you right. That's the only thing I want for you. Don't ever settle. Not again."

I cracked, whispering, "He definitely knows how to treat me right."

In every way.

We were all hushed secrets behind the corner Jenna had backed me into. "How right?"

"So right." My tummy flipped at the thought.

"Like . . . how . . . how right?" She angled her head, prying the truth out of me.

"Like, so very right. Like I've never felt anything close to the way I do when I'm with him. Not in all my life."

She squeezed me in her arms like a miracle just had happened. "Praise Mary."

Then she pulled me back, staring at me as all the prying tease left her voice. "Are you okay?" she asked me again. Though this time, the question was entirely different.

Because when I said she knew me, she knew me. She knew I'd never have slept with him if it didn't mean something to me.

I searched around inside myself for what to say. How to express what it was I really felt. "My life is crazy with Dane right now . . . I feel like I'm running faster and faster, trying to outrun him, praying he doesn't catch us."

All the while not fully understanding why he was chasing us in the first place.

My words started to become breathy, the horror of what Dane might actually do, what he might actually want.

"I'm terrified of what's coming. But somehow . . . that world? Right now, it feels like it's stronger than it has ever been. Like maybe Kale is holding some pieces together I might have lost if I had to do this alone."

"He's good with Evan?"

"He's amazing with him."

She rubbed her thumbs where she was still holding me by the arms. "But you know it's got to be more than that, Hope. This can't just be about Evan. And I know you live for that boy, as you should, but you deserve to find happiness in the middle of that, too. Real happiness."

I knew she was prodding. Digging deeper. Forcing me to evaluate everything. That was Jenna's way. Goading and coaxing and shoving me toward something she might think I needed and then urging me to look at it for what it was.

Playing devil's advocate. "It's so much more than just that."

I glanced at Evan before turning back to her. "Evan will always be my first priority, and I'll never allow a man into our lives who doesn't care about him. But this . . . what I feel?" I splayed my hands flat across my chest. "It's overwhelming and wonderful and terrifying, and what happened between us last night? It was bigger—more powerful—than anything I could have imagined."

Magical. A fantasy that shouldn't have been real.

"I want to feel like this, every day, for the rest of my life. And I want to get to do it with him."

She huffed an affectionate breath and edged back. "Oh, Harley Hope. You're already in love with him."

Maybe it made me a fool.

Naïve and unsuspecting.

"I don't think I could have stopped myself from falling for that man if I'd tried."

She quirked a playful brow. "He is delicious. Sex on a stick. Tell me we are naming a cupcake after him."

"Watch yourself," I tossed at her with a small laugh.

My phone chirped on the island. I went for it, unable to stop the force of my smile when I read the text.

"Look at you over there, grinning like you just swallowed a big ol' canary,"

Jenna teased. "Don't think I need to ask you who it is. What's he sayin'?"

"He wants Evan and I to go over to his place for pizza and a movie this evening. He said he'd pick us up since my car is still over there."

"Oh, Harley Hope. I think that man just might be a keeper."

"I know."

He was so, absolutely a keeper. I could only pray he was really ready for it. For us. That he understood what being with us would be like.

Because Evan and I? I knew we were a big decision. What I knew would be a huge change to his life . . . his previous lifestyle so different than the kind of life we had to offer.

But I knew, with all of me, that Evan and I could fill his life with so much joy. The kind of joy he had evoked in me.

And my heart?

It was always hung on hope.

And all I was hoping was Kale could see it, too. That he really wanted it.

That he would take a chance on us.

twenty-three

Hope

A rim of light blazed at the edge of the horizon as the day sank away. The twinkling lights that were strung between the buildings sparked to life and spilled in through the bank of windows that overlooked Kale's balcony and the bustling city below, casting his loft in a warm glow.

Or maybe the warm glow was actually radiating from Evan and Kale where they sat facing each other on the expansive plush rug on the floor.

We'd just finished eating pizza, our bellies satisfied and full.

I watched them from where I was curled up on the same couch, in the very spot Kale had undone me yesterday afternoon.

God, that seemed like a lifetime ago. Another world. As if a stake had been driven into time, segmenting and dividing it, giving us a new direction and a new day.

A new chance.

A chance that maybe the three of us could become one.

A rush of nerves streaked my spine. Hope and a niggle of fear. Because Kale and I were moving fast. So fast that I was still struggling to wrap my mind around the fact I'd given myself to him last night.

Fully.

Wholly.

But somehow, despite everything that was going against us, every worry and every complication, I knew this beautiful man with that huge, magnificent heart was meant for me.

Because there he sat, grinning at my son, his right hand lifted as he attempted to copy the sign language letters Evan was trying to teach him.

"Like this?" he asked aloud, concentrating and still getting it horribly wrong.

Emotion pulsed in my chest, lost to the adorableness of it all. The man, who was larger than life and seemed as if he could accomplish anything, couldn't seem to manage to get his fingers to cooperate.

Evan rapidly shook his head and reached out and tried to move Kale's hand into the correct position.

Like that, Evan mouthed.

Kale's hand curled into some kind of deformed ball as he struggled to keep the position. "Got it!"

I bit back my amusement at his fumbling because he *so* didn't have it. Honestly, it seemed downright absurd, considering I knew firsthand the type of *magic* those fingers could evoke.

Evan laughed that scraping sound. I could feel the echo of it ripple across the wooden floor. Joy and life. Vigorously, Evan shook his head while he leaned over to write on his notepad, all too eager to hold it up for Kale to see.

Dr. Bryant, you're not even close.

"What?" Kale defended playfully. He sent me a roguish wink that made my tummy tumble before he let his expression wind into a goofy face that he directed at my son. "What are you talking about? That was perfect. I mean, how hard can making an 'A' be?"

Evan wrote some more.

Too hard for you!

In mock horror, Kale's mouth dropped open. "Hey, I thought you told me the first time I met you that you were going to let me try to keep up with you?"

Evan's little hand flew across the page.

I said you could TRY to keep up with me.

"And you think you're too fast for me?"

A downpour of love flooded me as I watched Kale interact with my child. These overpowering, stunning emotions hitting me from every side.

They were feelings that were foreign, though, I intrinsically knew I'd been missing them all along.

Emphatically, Evan nodded, grinning big enough to fill the room.

"Oh, little man, you better run, because I'm about to show you just how fast I am," Kale warned.

Evan's eyes widened in both surprise and delight, and he scrambled to his feet at the same second Kale leapt to his. Evan darted across the living room and Kale was hot on his heels.

Always *just* missing him as they zigzagged and weaved.

Evan's sock covered feet slid on the slick floor as he rounded the island in the kitchen and came running back for me, arms thrown above his head and face tipped toward the ceiling, silent laughter pouring free.

I stretched my arms out for Evan. "Hurry, Evan. Mom's home base!" I called.

Right before Evan made it to me, Kale scooped him up from behind and tossed Evan onto his back, galloping around the room with him, Kale's deep laughter ricocheting against the walls.

Both of them were smiling these smiles that blasted through me.

So wide.

So happy.

So right.

I pressed my palm over my mouth. Overcome. Because I'd had no idea I'd wanted this so much.

No true idea how much I'd been lacking until Kale had filled that vacant place. I had to wonder how much my son had been lacking, too. I'd spent years trying to compensate. To fill all the holes Dane's rejection had to have carved into his innocent spirit.

Suddenly, I hungered for it, this feeling of completeness that took me over and set me free when Kale looked at me that certain way.

As if I were his everything and he would always crave more.

Added and multiplied to that was the way he treated my son.

Accepting his disability and still acting as if it weren't there to begin with.

Adoring him in spite of it.

Loving him because of it.

Love.

Is that what shone when Kale grinned up at my son, holding him in the security of his arms and still allowing him to fly?

"Got you," Kale sang.

Evan kicked and flailed and laughed before Kale settled him on his feet and ruffled his fingers through my son's mess of red, red hair.

Somehow, I understood exactly the way Kale felt in that moment. Evan was eight, yet still so vulnerable. I always had this incredible urge to pick him up and hold him. Protect him forever and never allow anything to happen to him.

I could see the exact same feeling written all over Kale's face.

Evan began to frantically sign, hands flying in front of him.

Kale looked over at me for help, and a shiver raked across my flesh when the power of his gaze landed on me.

"He said you're stronger than Superman," I told him, trying to keep the needy tremor from my voice.

Kale chuckled and looked back at Evan. "Superman, huh? My goddaughter, Frankie Leigh, would argue with you. She insists I'm Captain America."

Evan signed again.

"He wants to know who she is," I said, emotion tightening my throat.

Kale widened his eyes in emphasis. "Wonder Woman, of course."

Evan grinned, his own eyes going wide with excitement. This conversation had definitely taken a turn down Evan alley.

WHO AM I? he signed and mouthed at the same time.

"That's a no brainer. You've got to be The Hulk. Smart as a whip and look at these muscles."

Kale squeezed Evan's tiny bicep.

Evan's whole body rocked with his glee, and he forced out the rasping words, as if he couldn't hold back his praise. "Dr. Bryant."

Slowing, Kale's gaze turned tender. "What do you say you start calling me Kale instead of Dr. Bryant?"

Affection burst in my chest.

Evan signed quickly, his head cocked to the side with the question.

"He asked if that's because you're his friend now." My words were choppy.

A warm smiled pulled to Kale's lips, something so genuine and sincere. "Yeah, buddy, because you're my friend. Because I care about you."

Evan signed, *OKAY*, beaming at the man who continued to weave himself deeper and deeper into my skin.

Into my heart.

"Good," Kale said as if what he'd just done didn't matter all that much. "I think it's movie time. What do you say we put us on some superheroes, and we can decide exactly which we are? I have just about every Marvel movie ever made."

YES! Evan signed, giving a little fist pump in the air.

A small giggle fluttered from my lips, but my tone was coated with the emotion that gathered thick. "Careful, Evan won't ever want to leave."

My insides fluttered when he began to stalk toward me.

Potent.

Powerful.

Persuasive.

That was what the man looked like. Persuasion and dominance and sex.

Most of all, right then, he looked like he was mine.

I sucked in a breath when he leaned over me, his mouth coming to my ear. "Maybe that's my intention."

"Don't say things you don't mean," I whispered.

He pulled back and stared down at me, those blue eyes intense. "What if I do?"

That crazy attraction I felt around him climbed to the air. This time fuller. Denser. Brimming with *more*.

So badly that I wanted to lean forward so I could press my mouth to his.

Touch him and claim him as mine.

But we'd decided to take it slow in front of Evan. Working him into the idea of us, especially since Kale and I hadn't quite established what that meant.

But it was Kale who pushed it further, inching closer, the words a breathy murmur that sent a shiver down my spine. "I can't wait to be inside you again. I've been dying to touch you since the second you walked through my door. Second I get the chance? You're mine."

Oh.

Butterflies scattered in my belly and desire pooled. There was nothing I could do but press my thighs together.

Kale edged back with a smirk. "That's what I thought, Princess."

As if he hadn't just made my knees knock, he stood straight and shifted his attention back to Evan.

"So, what movie do you want to watch?" Kale asked. He grabbed the remote, flicked on his big television, and switched it to the long list of his downloaded movies.

He hadn't been joking when he said he had about every Marvel movie ever made.

Boys.

Evan grabbed his pad.

We have to take a vote. That's the rule.

An affectionate chuckle rumbled from Kale. "You are just full of all kinds of rules, aren't you, little man?"

Only good rules.

Contentment seeped into my pores.

More so than I'd ever been.

Darkness swam through Kale's loft, broken by the flickers and flashes from the television as the movie played on.

We were on the second Avengers movie, and my son lay across Kale's couch, still facing the screen, his breaths soft snores as he slept the movie away.

His head was on Kale's lap and Kale was running his fingers through his hair.

I was on the other side of Kale, curled up so I could rest on his shoulder.

He pressed his lips to my temple, his voice a rough murmur. "I'm so glad you're here."

Shifting to face him more, I peered at him through the shifting light. "I'm so glad I'm here."

He traced his nose down the curve of my jaw. "You'd better be."

A tiny moan left me when he kissed down the slope of my neck. "Is that so?"

I could feel his grin against my skin. "You know it's so."

"Stalker," I whispered with a smile fluttering at my lips, the word nothing but affection.

"Knight, Princess. Knight. After last night, tell me I get to be your king."

My head tilted back, and the smile that had been threatening lit in a full bloom. "Hmm . . . I don't know," I teased, my fingers twining in his soft hair.

"Ouch, Princess. You know exactly where to hit a man where it hurts, don't you?" It was all mischief on his tongue as he kissed and nipped. "I guess you don't need me after all."

A giggle slipped free before I pulled back and cupped his face, sincerity weaving into my tone. "Yesterday was terrifying, Kale, and somehow . . . somehow you turned it into the best night of my life."

Those soulful eyes glinted in the light, his throat bobbing as he swallowed. "I don't think I've ever felt the way I felt last night," he admitted his voice gruff.

I tucked my bottom lip between my teeth before I asked, "What are we doing, Kale?"

His fingertips fluttered across my cheek. "I think we're needing each other." He blinked. "I had no idea I needed anyone or anything until I met you."

And that need . . .

I could feel it compounding and expanding and shifting.

Restoring.

"Stay with me tonight," he said.

My gaze moved to my sleeping son. "I don't think he's ready for that yet. Plus, I need to be up early to get to the shop in the morning, and Evan has his summer program."

The words flooded out like excuses I didn't want to have. But they were there, and they were real.

"I have a guest room. You both can sleep in there. I just want you near me. I need to know you're safe. I have to be at work early, too. I'll wake you first thing."

"This is getting so very complicated."

A grin tweaked his striking face. Goodness, no man should be that pretty.

It just wasn't fair.

"I promise that if you stay, I'm going to take you in my room and really complicate you."

Oh, and neither was that. Not at all.

Desire exploded in the air.

Hot, heated energy.

But it was bigger than ever before.

Because I could feel it.

The love that shined all around me.

Powerfully. Brilliantly.

But looking at Kale? I was too scared to let it escape from my tongue. Afraid to put it out in the world. I knew once I said it, it was going to ring so true that I'd never be able to hear anything else.

"Stay with me," he coaxed in that magnetic way.

There was nothing I could do but relent. I guessed I'd been relenting all along. Giving and giving because I couldn't stay away. Last night, I'd fully succumbed. I should know any reservations would be futile.

"Okay," I whispered.

"Need me after all, huh, Princess?" That tease was back.

"I think I'll always need you," I murmured.

A soft smile fluttered across his sexy mouth, before he shifted around so he didn't disturb Evan. He climbed to his feet and carefully pulled my little boy into the well of his arms.

Kale hugged him to his chest.

And it spun and spun.

The love that whipped through the room like a hurricane.

The strength of it was so massive that a slice of terror cut through my center.

Awed by its beauty and intimidated by its force.

Kale started for the hall, and I climbed to my feet and followed him through the darkness.

Angling Evan a bit, he dipped down so he could turn the knob.

The room was obviously reserved for guests. The ceiling high, coffered and finished with crown molding and massive windows that overlooked the city beyond.

A rustic, four-poster bed, covered in plush, luxurious bedding, sat against the right wall.

Kale went right for it, dragging down the covers and nestling my son in its safety. He ran his fingers through Evan's hair and pressed a tender kiss to the top of his head.

Evan sighed and sank into the comfort.

I swore that I felt the ground shake beneath my feet, felt the tangle of emotion lodge in my throat.

Tears threatened to strangle me.

Overwhelming. The way Kale's aura was suddenly everything. Wisps that wound.

Vapor.

Kale headed back my way, the softest kiss pressed to my cheek. "Hold on one second, I'll be right back."

He slipped by me, disappearing for a few moments into his bedroom before he returned with a baby monitor. "I have this for Rex's kids. I know Evan's not a baby, but it will make me feel better that we can hear him if he wakes up and needs us. I set up the speaker in my room."

And that love?

That was the moment it shattered me.

He plugged in the monitor and then slowly moved back toward me. He threaded his fingers through mine and led me back into the hall, leaving the door open a crack.

A breath jutted free when he shifted and moved toward me. My back hit the opposite wall of the hall.

He pushed his fingers into my hair, his nose back to running along my jaw. "I haven't even gotten to kiss you yet. I've been going out of my mind thinking about last night. About you spread out under me. Your sweet body. Want to get lost in it, Hope. Get lost in you."

A whimper left me, and I fisted my hands into his T-shirt. "I will never forget feeling you for the first time . . . the way it felt the moment you took me."

That piece that would always belong to him.

He lightly swept his lips across mine.

Fire.

I swore that one brush was all it took for this man to set me on fire.

My phone blipped from my back pocket.

Kale dropped his forehead to mine. "Someone has awful timing."

"Whoever it is can wait because I'm not sure I can."

A sexy chuckle rumbled from his chest. "Ah . . . there she is . . . my little vixen hiding under all that sweet. I love it when she comes out to play."

My phone blipped again.

"Shit." He pulled back, those blue eyes glimmering, hovering somewhere between playfulness and lust. "If that's Jenna, you'd better get it."

The smallest laugh jolted free. "Don't tell me you're afraid of my best friend."

A smirk ticked up at one side of that delicious mouth. "Not scared. Terrified. You know she threatened to cut off my dick."

"No," I wheezed, embarrassment riding to my face.

She had no shame.

Kale ran a thick lock of my hair between his thumb and forefinger, flirty play moving across his features. "It is my best asset. I don't think I can risk it . . . for your sake."

He grinned one of those earth-shattering grins. The kind that was cocky and arrogant and did funny things to my insides.

Heat flashed to my face, flutters lighting in my belly and making my hands tremble. I fumbled to reach for my phone, the words a wisp. "You're ruinin' me, Kale Bryant."

He nuzzled under my chin, leaving a trail of kisses across the sensitive skin. "Oh, baby, trust me, I plan on it."

Oh God.

This man.

I quickly slipped my thumb across my screen, sure Kale was right and it was Jenna checking on us. Hell, knowing her, she was probably wanting a play by play.

When I saw what was on the screen, it was instant. The way fear cinched down on my chest like the tightest band and sickness clawed at my spirit.

Nausea churned in my gut.

Unknown: Last chance, Harley, before I see to it that you never see your son again.

Kale edged back, eyes slanted down so he could read me in the darkness. "What's wrong?"

Anxiety climbed my throat, clotting and suffocating. I tried to force it down. Play it off. "It's just my ex."

Anger.

In a flash, it had taken Kale hostage. His entire being vibrated with rage.

Fierce and brutal and savage.

His voice was grit. "What does he want?"

I had a feeling if I told him the whole truth, he would go flying out the door. Set on destruction. Intent on crushing anything that might stand as a threat to Evan or me.

But I couldn't hide this from him. Not when I'd already dragged him into the middle of it. I turned my phone toward him so he could see what it said.

Fury.

It ignited on Kale's face.

Kerosene.

This was not a knight dressed in shining, unblemished armor. Not the kind fairy tales were made of.

This was the kind that filled history books.

The kind that fought to the death for what they believed was right.

Kale pressed a fist to the wall at the side of my head as if he was barely holding on, coming unhinged, words gravel as they scraped from his throat.

"I want to erase him, Hope. I want to hunt him down and destroy him. Make sure he can never hurt you or Evan. Not ever again."

"I hate him," I admitted over the clot of horror and fear bottled like acid in my chest.

Kale dropped his forehead to mine, this time in a tortured, rattled rage. "Who is he?"

I blinked, pressed my mouth to the roar of his heart that pounded through his shirt. "You can't do something crazy, Kale. You can't. You have to trust me that I'm doing everything to end this and end it for good."

I'd already gotten myself in deep enough without drawing more attention.

I needed to do this quietly and swiftly.

And God, I wanted to tell Kale, admit it all. But he was still Evan's doctor, and I wasn't sure I could risk putting him in that position.

Endanger him that way.

It wasn't fair.

It wasn't right.

So instead, I pushed my phone into my back pocket and wound my hands back into the fabric of Kale's shirt. Clinging to him. Hoping he could hear the beat of truth in my words.

"I'll do whatever it takes to keep him away from my son. But the next months are going to be difficult. I'm up for the greatest fight of my life. I need you to know, I will do anything, sacrifice anything, to make sure I win that fight."

I was gathering evidence.

Each text.

Each message.

Each threat.

My attorney was sure that would be all the proof of abuse we needed. The callousness and carelessness.

Kale groaned, as if it caused him pain. "And what if I want to be the one to do it? Protect him. Save him." His big hand slid to my face. "*Save you.*"

My words were a breath. "You're already savin' me. In so many ways."

Kale groaned again. But this time, it was in need. "God damn it, Hope. God damn it, what have you done to me?"

His mouth slanted over mine.

Commanding.

Demanding all of me.

Tangles of tongue and nips of teeth.

He didn't break the kiss when he hoisted me from my feet and pressed me deeper against the wall, his hands on the outsides of my thighs as he made a place for himself between my legs.

He rubbed himself at my center, his cock hard, as desperate as his touch.

I ached and whimpered, my fingers sinking into his shoulders. As if I might be able to hold on to him forever. "Kale."

"I won't let him hurt you. I won't. Not you or Evan. You're mine."

Need tumbled through me. A raging storm.

This man too much.

Too perfect.

He pulled me from the wall and carried me the rest of the way down the hall and through the double doors at the end of it. He stepped inside, nudged the door shut with his foot, and fumbled to click the lock behind him.

He pulled back, staring up at me as he carried me into the center of the enormous, darkened room, the only light filtering in through the wall of sliding doors that overlooked the city below.

His room luxury and peace and comfort.

Masculine.

Sexy.

That was what I felt when he kneaded his big hands into my bottom, kissing me again and murmuring, "I'm losing myself."

I framed his face in my hands. "And I'm finding myself." He carried me toward his bed, which was massive and imposing, just like the man. Slowly, he slid me down his body, my feet unsteady when he set me on the floor.

He pressed a hand on either side of my neck, and I was sure he could feel the raging thunder of my pulse beating through me.

The way my heart went pound, pound, pound. "I want you, Hope. Want you in a way that scares me."

I searched his face. "Fear never negates hope. It just means we want something badly enough that we're terrified we might not get to keep it."

A groan rumbled in his chest, and he was pulling me flush against all his hard and heat. "Sweet girl."

"I need you," I returned.

The air stretched taut around us. Pushing and pulling and demanding.

That attraction alive.

A thriving, breathing entity.

We panted through it. Sucking it into our lungs, inhaling each other as all our pieces fell together.

Forming something complete and whole.

Kale stared down at me. Eyes that intense, fathomless blue.

It felt as if I were jumping into the coolest waters, floating in the deepest sea, soaring through the warmest sky.

He gripped me tight. "Told you next time I had you, I wasn't going to go easy on you."

His voice grated with the warning.

Desire boiled my blood. "Don't you know what they say . . . nothing good in life is easy."

There was no longer any question about what had gotten into me. It was this magnetic man. Seeping into my skin. Dripping into my veins.

That was the only invitation he needed. Kale was on me in a flash. His mouth swooping in to capture mine the same way he'd captured my heart.

Swiftly.

Madly.

Wholly.

Plundering—body, mind, and soul.

I felt beautiful in his arms.

Bold and sexy.

My mama would call it risqué.

She'd be right because, with Kale, I was ready to take every risk.

He flattened his hands under my shirt, running them up my back and lifting it higher and higher.

"Strawberries and cream. So fucking sweet," he murmured.

Those words sent a rush of chills skating down my neck and scattering across my flesh.

He tore my shirt over my head and dropped it to the floor before he flicked the hook of my bra and dragged it free of my arms. His eyes swept over me. Head to toe. "Look at you, Hope. You are a vision, baby. I think every fantasy I've ever had was of you, and I didn't even know it."

My spirit danced, and I was pressing my hands under his shirt, running them over the hard, defined planes of his abdomen, needing to discover him, expose every inch of smooth, tanned skin.

He stepped back and yanked it the rest of the way over his head.

A sharp breath left me at the sight. "I close my eyes, and this is what I see. You, Kale. Beautiful you. I never thought it would be possible to want a man the way I want you."

I leaned forward and pressed my lips to his chest right over his beautiful heart that thundered and sped.

Every part of this man was stunning.

Captivating.

Kale suddenly dropped to his knees in front of me. Adept fingers were quick to work free the button and zipper of my jeans. He pulled them down a fraction and dragged me forward to kiss me on the lace fabric that covered my center.

He inhaled. "So, so sweet."

My fingers twisted in his hair, and I swore I couldn't breathe. "You undo me."

The air grew thicker when he peeled both my underwear and jeans down my legs. My legs that shook as he stripped me, leaving my clothing a discarded pile on his floor.

The way he looked up at me was staggering.

He nudged my legs apart and dragged his fingers through my lips, spreading me.

I gasped.

"So sweet and wet and hot. Your pussy is perfection. Want to live in it. Fuck you day and night."

A blink of that shyness gathered on my chest and climbed to my cheeks. A part of me was shocked that I was turned on that he was talking to me this way. Shocked that I was standing there letting him touch me this way.

My world flipped so quickly.

No longer recognizable.

But those thoughts were chased away when he slowly drove two fingers into my body.

So deep that I shuddered, my knees giving, close to buckling.

The man knocked me from my feet.

Kale pushed to his and set me on the edge of his bed. Free hand smoothing up the inside of my thigh, he spread me wide for him while he continued to pump me with the other.

"Kale," I whispered like a plea.

He dipped down and licked against that spot where I needed him most. Where I felt needy and achy and desperate. My fingers dug into his covers. "Kale . . . that feels so good. How do you make everything feel so good?"

I whimpered when he pulled his fingers free, and he edged back, leaving me a wet, quivering mess where he had me lain out on his bed.

He sent me one of those smirks as he began to shrug out of his jeans and underwear. "I'm just getting started, Princess."

He kicked free of his clothing.

An earthquake rocked me to the core, looking at him standing there that way.

Arrogant and bare and bold.

His cock jutting for the sky.

He stroked himself once.

I swore, I nearly lost it right there.

"On your hands and knees, baby."

Oh.

Oh God.

My insides trembled and shook.

Watching him, I slowly rolled over and climbed to my hands and knees. I started to crawl toward the middle of the bed.

Hot hands landed on either side of my waist, and Kale hauled me back to the edge. "Not so fast, Shortcake."

Standing behind me, he smoothed his palms over my bottom.

He groaned. "Perfect."

And I knew I'd been right all along.

I was in trouble.

So, so much trouble.

Because from behind, the man licked through my crease.

I jumped then moaned, pushing back, my body begging for more.

I had the errant thought that I'd never been so exposed.

Had never given myself so freely.

Had never been so vulnerable.

But then that thought was gone, overpowered by the sensation of his tongue.

His tongue that was working the most mind-blowing bliss as he suckled and lapped, his thumbs running up and down my slit before he was easing his big fingers back inside me.

I shook, his name a whimper as he worked my body into a frenzy.

I wanted to cry when he pulled away, unable to make sense of the way this man made me feel. What he made me need. "Kale, please."

I couldn't seem to keep up, never knowing if he was coming or going, my head spinning.

Desperate for him.

His chest was suddenly plastered to my back, his penis nestled against my bottom.

This time it was two of his fingers that were pressing deep into my mouth, his mouth at my ear. "Suck, sweet girl. Taste how delicious you are . . . everything about you."

I did. I sucked them into the well of my mouth.

Unsure why it sent a rush of euphoria ripping through my body when my taste hit my tongue.

Why I felt so powerful when I was pinned.

Why I felt so confident in his hands.

Cool air hit my back when he again jerked away.

I wiggled and squirmed, my hands fisting in his bedding, not even ashamed when I panted a frenzied, "Please."

His hands were back on my bottom. Caressing and kneading. Winding me higher. "I love this sweet ass, Hope." He gripped two fistfuls in his hands.

He started running his thumb around that sensitive spot.

"Kale," I whimpered.

"Need you to know, I'm an ass man, sweet girl." His thumb pressed into that tight hole, and I clenched around him. "Not tonight, but I'm going to want to fuck it and lick it and bite it."

He shocked me again when he leaned down and sank his teeth into the flesh of one cheek. Not enough to hurt. Enough to send my stomach tumbling with the decadent, dark threat.

From over my shoulder, I looked back at him, floored by the sight of him. My spirit reeled with the impact.

Winding us. Wrapping us. Bonding us.

I gave him my truth. "I'm yours."

He groaned, and I could feel the fat head of him broaching my lips, nudging in, spreading me. "So sweet. So fucking sweet."

Then Kale slammed into me.

Filling me full.

So full.

All other sensation lost. Nothing but him.

Taking me. Owning me the way only he could.

He clutched me by the hips when he pulled out and then took me again.

I jolted forward, my heart frantic, my need escalating as I gripped at his comforter to keep myself grounded.

Fearing I just might float away.

He began to pound into me, his cock so massive he stole my breath with each powerful thrust.

He fucked me exactly like I knew he would when I'd seen him that first time in the bar.

Arrogantly.

Confidently.

Relentlessly.

And he still felt like a broken heart. Because I had no idea what I would do if I lost him.

It was true.

I needed him.

Needed him not because I would fail without him but because he perfectly fit that hollow spot that had been carved out inside me. Filled it till it was close to overflowing, the way he was filling me right then.

Stroke after stroke.

Too much, and somehow, I wanted more.

Pleasure glowed all around me, this needy feeling that was desperate and shaky.

Sweat slicked my skin and light flickered behind my eyes.

"Is this what you wanted, Hope? Is this what you wanted? Tell me."

"Yes," I rasped, rocking back to meet every dominating thrust. "Yes. I want this. I want you."

Everything sizzled and sparked.

Kale's palm slid around to my chest, and he pulled me up, my back against his chest. I reached up and hooked my arm around the back of his neck.

Our bodies pressed together.

Sweat slicking our heated skin.

Through the reflection in the plate glass window, I met his eye. "Look at you, Hope. Look at you . . . what I see every time I look at you."

I gasped a tiny sound when I did, my body all stretched out, my breasts heavy and peaked. Flesh flushed and hair a mussed-up mess.

Kale's stunning, chiseled face gazed at me from over my shoulder. The man so gorgeous I felt the earth shake.

And I was sure I'd never felt so wanted in all my life.

So sexy.

So adored.

Kale fluttered his fingertips down over my trembling belly, before he strummed them where I throbbed, rolled those magic fingers around my clit.

He continued to drive into me from behind.

The angle almost more than I could take.

Thrust after obliterating thrust.

He spun me into the tightest knot.

And the light.

It was brilliant when it shattered.

Crashing, crushing waves.

Radiating through me. Taking me under.

I writhed and pitched and begged as the most tortuous kind of bliss flooded my body.

Kale grasped my breasts in both hands as he bucked into me.

Hard.

Desperate. He buried his face in the fall of my hair to cover the roar of my name when he came.

He pulsed and I soared.

We rode through ecstasy. The two of us lost to each other.

He held me against his shuddering body until I slumped facedown onto his bed.

"Stay," he told me. Naked, the man walked into the en suite bathroom and flicked on the light.

His gorgeous body was set on display, the sight of him sending a fresh round of shudders through me. He grabbed a washcloth, wet it under the sink, and sauntered back out.

Leaning over my back, he kissed my temple, brushed back the damp hair from my face, and pressed the warm cloth between my legs.

"Are you okay?" he asked, crawling up and lying on his side facing me. Those blue eyes swam, all his goodness pouring out, darkened pools of adoration.

This man.

This man.

I let my fingertips trail down the side of his face. "I don't think I've ever felt better than I do right now. Right this minute. With you."

He grabbed my hand and kissed across my fingertips. "Good. Because I don't think I can let you go. Not ever."

His tone was playful, but his expression flickered with something serious and sincere.

"Stalker," I let myself rib, though I knew there was no way he missed the soft affection that tripped from my tongue, knowing I was exposing everything I was feeling right then.

Love.

It sang all around us.

Whispering and thrumming and spilling into the sanctity of his room.

He wrapped an arm around my waist and pulled me flush against him, fingers brushing through my hair, the peace that echoed through my body swift and whole. "If that's what it takes for me to get to keep you. Keep Evan."

A knot grew heavy at the base of my throat, and I searched him in the shadows. "You can't keep saying things like that if you don't mean them."

His voice was rough. "What if I mean them, Hope?"

Hesitation billowed in my spirit. All the things we didn't know about each other suddenly felt like a chasm between us.

Bottomless.

Fingers fluttering across his full lips, I let my whispered question hit the air. "What do you want from your life, Kale? Before you met me . . . where did you see yourself tomorrow? In five years? Where do you picture yourself when you're growing old?"

Awareness filled his expression. Clearly, the man knew exactly what I was asking. Words faltered on his lips before he got a distant look on his face.

When he finally spoke, his confession was hoarse and choppy. "I think we need to go back to what I used to want, Hope. Not yesterday and not a year ago."

He grimaced in pain. "But ten years ago? I'd pictured that by now, I'd be married. Have a horde of kids who'd come running out of the house to meet me at the end of the day."

A sad smile kicked at the corner of his mouth, and his voice turned wistful, as if he were lost to the image in his mind. "They'd be shouting 'Daddy' and tugging at my pant legs and driving me crazy in the best of ways."

He swallowed hard, his gaze filled with longing when he set the sincerity of those eyes back on me. "I thought I'd have a wife, who'd be waiting on the porch after her own long day, and we'd meet in the middle. Our lives would be chaotic and busy, but they'd be perfect because we were living for the right things."

A tremor ran his thick throat. "Then that picture was shattered. And it destroyed something in me. From the day I lost her, I thought I'd be going my life alone. And I was okay with that."

No longer was his gaze distant, but he was right there, with me. "That lonely picture remained the same until the day I met you."

My heart pressed and thrummed and battered at my chest.

Agony.

The words caught, and I had to force them from my lips. "You know I can't give you that . . . a horde of kids."

He blinked in confusion. It only took a second for the man to come to understanding, and I thought maybe it was anger that flashed through his features. "I know what his records say, Hope. They don't know where his disorder stems from."

I blinked my own tears. "And you know I can't take that risk."

He rolled me to my back and propped himself on an elbow, staring down at me as he wound a lock of my hair around his forefinger. "And if you knew . . . what would you want?"

Wetness seeped from the corners of my eyes. "I'd always dreamed of a big family . . . but Evan will always, always be enough for me."

His smile turned tender. "You think the two of you aren't enough? You two are more than enough. So much more. Which means I can't help but want to give you everything."

Dreams and faith. They spun around me, wrapping me whole.

Because to Dane, Evan and I had never been enough.

And I swore, right then, Kale Bryant had become everything I needed.

twenty-four

Kale

I glanced at her from the corner of my eye.

Sitting in the front seat of my car like she'd been meant for that spot.

My chest clenched in an almost painful way. Reverberating with a deep-rooted sort of pleasure. The kind that promised it might last forever and, still, you were terrified of letting it slip through your fingers.

That didn't mean my muscles weren't knotted in anticipation.

I was heading in a direction I'd never gone. Taking a girl to hang out with my friends, who I considered family.

I'd asked Hope and Evan to go to Rex's with me for a barbeque.

Not since Melody had I invited someone into our intimate circle, and even then, she'd only hung out with them once or twice because I was attending medical school in Birmingham.

That was where I'd met her.

Where I'd lost her.

I clamped down on the morbid thoughts that threatened to rise from that dark place inside me and, instead, focused on Evan, who was bouncing with excitement in the backseat, his smile bright as he strained to see out the windows.

Funny how all those questions and what-ifs were rambling around me, and I still felt completely at peace.

It was like that frantic lust and greed and want that had flamed inside me since I'd met Hope had become aware that feeling was actually an everlasting need.

An undying devotion.

And it wasn't ever going to go away.

I felt the weight of her questioning stare burning into the side of my face. I took a right-hand turn, and I let myself peek over at her for a second as I accelerated down the road.

Fuck.

She was gorgeous.

So goddamned gorgeous.

All that red hair aflame, a halo of fire where it was lit up in the streaks of light that blazed through the passenger window.

Body tight and skin soft. Pale with that smattering of freckles.

Like she was sprinkled in some kind of fairy dust and she held her own special brand of magic.

Enchanting.

Entrancing.

That was what she was.

"What?" I asked, word scraping from my throat.

She bit down on that plump bottom lip and fiddled with the skirt of another one of those sundresses I was pretty sure she'd figured out were the ruin of me.

"I'm nervous," she admitted in that sweet, shy way.

"Why are you nervous?"

She laughed a disbelieving yet hopeful sound. "You're taking me and my son to meet your friends . . . the people who mean the most to you. You've got to know that's kind of intimidating."

I arched a brow. "As intimidating as your best friend?"

Her laughter rippled through the cabin of my car.

Swore the sound made me glow.

She tried to hold back a grin. "She's not that bad."

"Oh, believe me, Shortcake. A girl starts threatening the most important parts? That ranks her up there with arsonists and serial killers."

She laughed outright, her gaze so soft. "So dramatic."

I sent her a reassuring smile. "Seriously, though. They're amazing. You're going to love them just as much as they're going to love you and Evan."

Tenderness moved through her expression, that feeling rising high between us.

Alive.

I think both of us knew we were embarking on something new. It was no secret I wouldn't be inviting anyone to meet my family unless I intended for them to become a part of it, and it was palpable in the air, the fact that everything was getting ready to change.

Truth was, my world had changed that night at the bar. I'd thought it was simply because I was changing careers. Taking the partnership at the children's clinic. Maybe all along, that coming change had been Hope.

I made a left into Rex's gravel drive, my tires crunching on the rocks as we came to a stop.

The houses in his neighborhood were spread out and elevated from the ground by several steps that led up to the porches of the modest homes.

Yards hedged in towering trees, which gave them a private feel.

Secluded and quiet.

Like they were in the middle of the woods and might not have a neighbor for miles, when in reality, they were in the middle of the town.

I killed the engine. "This is it."

Hope sucked in a breath, and Evan freed himself from his seatbelt. Grinning, he scrambled to poke his head between the two front seats. That innocent gaze darted between us, excitement rolling from him in waves.

My chest tightened. Affection and that fluttering feeling. The one I was terrified to give a name.

I turned so I could face him. "You ready, little man?"

An energetic nod, and then he was yanking open the back door and flying out. Chuckling, I was quick to follow, wrapping his hand up in mine, running my thumb over the back of it.

Giving him the encouragement he didn't seem to need but I wanted to offer anyway.

He and I wound around the front of the car just as Hope was ducking into the backseat to grab the container of cupcakes she'd insisted on bringing, her sweet ass swaying in the air, sending all kinds of thoughts and ideas skating through my head and licking across my skin.

She whipped around. A blush rushed to her cheeks when she caught what had to be the salacious expression on my face.

Busted.

"You are nothin' but trouble, Cowboy," she said with a jittery giggle, smoothing her rumpled self out.

Affected.

I let a smirk climb to the edge of my mouth. "Don't act like you aren't begging for it. Wearing those dresses that you know are gonna drive me straight out of my mind."

Hope was shaking her head with sweet disbelief while Evan's attention jumped between us, confused.

Chuckling, figured I'd better stop that train that was quickly speeding out of control and do it fast.

"Come on, let's go meet everyone."

Keeping Evan's hand in mine, I tucked my other arm around Hope's waist and pulled her to my side. I pressed my lips to her temple and murmured, "Thank you so much for coming with me. It means more to me than you could know."

Those green eyes found mine. Tender and real. "Just you bringing us here says so many things," she whispered. "I'm honored to be a part of your world. To get to know the people you love most."

Fuck.

This woman had undone me. Unchinked all the armor I hadn't even realized had been there until it toppled to the ground.

An offering at her feet.

Instead of going up the porch steps to the front door, we headed around the side of the house where carefree voices echoed from the backyard, riding on the humidity that was hot and thick and sticky this time of year.

Evan trotted along at my side, continually looking up at me, almost like he was asking for approval, those adorable bug eyes huge behind his thick glasses, wearing that blameless smile that completely destroyed my heart.

Putty in his trusting hands.

We rounded the corner, listening to the easy laughter of my friends, and strode into the grassy, sprawling yard at the back of Rex and Rynna's house that was fenced in by soaring trees.

A big wooden porch ran the back of the house, and a few round tables and chairs sat in the middle of it, covered by colorful umbrellas that stretched out to protect from the searing heat of the Alabama sun.

A built-in grill and outdoor kitchen had been built at the opposite end of it. Smoke already puffed from the closed lid, twisty plumes of white rising into the air, carrying with it the divine scent of grilling steaks.

Hope leaned a little closer to me.

"You're with me, baby. You don't have a thing to worry about."

She peered up at me. "I know. It's ridiculous, but I just always worry when I get Evan in new situations. How he's gonna react and how people are gonna react to him."

I slowed to a stop, tucking Evan to my side before I dropped his hand and turned to take his mother by the face. My hold emphatic. "I would never bring him somewhere he wouldn't be welcome. Would never put him in danger. Not ever."

She blinked up at me, her hands winding around my wrists. "And that's why we're right here, with you."

I wanted nothing more than to drop everything right there and kiss her wild, this woman who'd do anything to stand up for her son.

Protect him.

All I wanted was to hold her and keep her and tell her that bastard was never going to hurt either of them.

That I'd make sure of it.

That I'd never let her down.

It was getting harder and harder to ignore what was going on in her life. Something I hadn't seen firsthand but saw the same as if I was standing in the middle of it.

Her ex a lowlife fucker I wanted to beat down with my bare fists. Destroy and ruin the way he intended to ruin them.

I shoved the urge back, my voice gruff when I murmured, "I can't wait for them to meet you."

A tender smile fluttered across those full lips, and I hugged her closer before I gathered Evan's little hand back in mine.

Fighting the shudder that ripped through me because I loved the way it felt against mine so damned much.

I led them up the side steps to the porch. Everyone was already lounging beneath the umbrellas, enjoying the Sunday afternoon.

Rynna noticed us first. The second she did, she pushed from her chair and hopped to her feet, all welcoming the way she always was. "I'm so happy you're here."

That chatter quieted to nothing, and about five different pairs of eyes snapped our direction.

Sure, it was unnerving, but it was totally expected.

I knew showing up this way was going to shock the hell out of them. Each of them was doing their best to play it cool when really it was clear their minds were working at a hundred miles an hour.

Because I'd been completely straight up with Hope.

This was a first for me.

Rynna crossed to the edge of the porch where we'd stopped at the top of the stairs. Her sincere gaze moved over us before landing on Evan. When they locked eyes, Evan's hand moved in an exuberant wave.

Her expression grew tender, and she knelt down and signed *HI.*

"Oh," Hope breathed at my side, awe oozing out at Rynna's display of welcome.

It was at the same second that one simple gesture made joy light on Evan's face.

A goddamned sunburst.

Because the kid was so damned sweet.

"I'm Rynna. You must be Evan," she said, her lips moving a little slower than usual.

When I'd called to tell her I was bringing guests, she'd launched into a thrilled-sort of third-degree, badgering me for as much information as she could possibly dig out.

I'd told her about Evan's disability, giving her what I could without revealing too much, telling her he could read lips and not to treat him any different from Frankie Leigh.

Which was ridiculous I'd even felt the need to say it.

Evan gave her one of those enthusiastic nods, his little hand still wound up in mine, swaying at my side.

"Well, it is so great to meet you, Evan. I hope you have a blast at my house today."

With an affectionate touch of his chin, Rynna pushed to her feet and extended both her hands toward Hope. "I'm Rynna Gunner. Welcome to our home. Thank you so much for coming."

Hope pushed the plastic container out in front of her like a peace offering. "Thank you for having us. I brought cupcakes."

Rynna accepted them with a generous smile. "Oh, my goodness, this is exactly what we needed. The only treats my family gets around here are my pies, and I'm pretty sure they have to be getting sick of them by now."

"That's impossible," Hope said.

The girl was so genuine there was no question of her sincerity.

She tucked a strand of that red, red hair behind her ear almost nervously and offered a smile. "I've eaten at Pepper's Pies plenty of times to know it never gets old."

Rynna grinned from ear to ear. "You've been?"

"Of course. Those pies are legendary."

"Well, I can't exactly take credit. They are my grandmother's recipes."

Frankie Leigh suddenly came barreling out the back door with her dog Milo hot on her heels, the screen door smacking shut behind them. "Uncle Kale! Uncle Kale! You came to see me!"

She threw her arms in the air, feet clattering on the planks as she scrambled around the tables, flying for me. She came to a grinding stop when she saw the little boy's hand wrapped in mine.

Her eyes went wide in excited interest.

"Is this mys new friend Evan?" she asked me, looking up at me hopefully.

I knelt beside them. "Sure is, Sweet Pea. This is Evan, and he's really special to me, so I hope you spend the whole day playing with him because he doesn't know anyone else here."

Of course, she would. The kid was a force field of joy.

But I never expected that my Frankie Leigh, my goddaughter and the girl who had always held every inch of my heart, would sign *HI* just like her mom had done, probably more awkwardly than I'd done when Evan had been trying to teach me the alphabet.

But that didn't matter.

Nothing did except that my family had made sure to make this little boy feel welcomed.

Emotion fisted my heart, not expecting to feel this way when I saw the two of them together.

Overcome and a little overwhelmed.

Evan signed with a huge grin, and I looked over my shoulder to Hope. She chewed at her lip, the woman so fucking stunning standing there with the sun shining all around her that I was having a hard time seeing straight. "Wonder Woman," she said, her voice a wisp.

A smile flew to my face, and I looked back at Evan. "Yeah, buddy. This is

Wonder Woman."

I turned to Frankie. "And this is my little Hulk."

Mine.

My chest tightened.

All of this was so goddamned new but so goddamned right.

Frankie Leigh giggled like crazy. "I likes the Hulk . . . but he's not as strong as my daddy and my uncles! Thor and Cap'in 'merica."

I felt Rynna staring at me, and I glanced up to meet her eyes.

I'm happy for you.

He's wonderful.

I'm so glad you brought them.

"Wanna play? I gots my puppy and he's so fast and he likes to jump and lick and he's so funny," Frankie Leigh rambled out, pushing the wild, wild locks of her hair from her face with both hands.

Evan didn't even hesitate. He dropped my hand and was rushing down the stairs, clambering behind Frankie and Milo out onto the lawn.

Frankie squealed, dancing all around like the carefree thing she was, and Evan's smile was as big as I'd ever seen it as he tried to follow her lead.

I took Hope's hand.

She squeezed mine back.

Her emotions leaching into my veins.

Gratefulness and joy and that feeling that terrified me kept nudging me more and more.

"Guys, I want you all to meet someone."

All those pairs of eyes that'd been watching us scrambled to their feet.

I introduced Hope to everyone, pointing to them as I said their names.

"Lillith. Brody. That's Nikki, and that little thing sleeping on her chest is my godbaby, Ryland."

Hope gave a tiny wave, still clinging to me with the other hand. "It's nice to meet you all."

Rex, who was grinning as he manned the grill, welcoming her to his home, sending me a bunch of looks on the sly that told me we would definitely be talking about this later.

No shit.

I knew showing up like this was signing myself up to stand in front of the firing squad.

Especially considering the last time I'd been here I'd been claiming my old ways. Certain I didn't need anything more when, really, I'd been lacking everything.

I was ready to face it.

Of course, Hope had already met Ollie. He sauntered up and pulled her into a big, burly, overbearing hug.

Like they were the oldest of friends.

My girl looked like some kind of rag doll when he flung her around, brows climbing to the sky when he peered at me from over her shoulder, silently telling me I had some explaining to do.

So maybe I'd been dodging all his texts and calls for the last two weeks. Didn't show at the bar on either Friday night the way I always did, deciding to trade in a night of carousing and revelry for hanging out with Hope and Evan.

Crazy how quickly things could change.

Finally, he set her on her feet. "So, I see you decided to put up with this asshole, after all."

Hope glanced at me. "Yeah, I guess I did."

Two hours later, we'd eaten, our stomachs were full, and everyone was sitting around talking and relaxing the lazy day away.

Easy.

I had to admit, my gaze was probably a little too eager where I sat on the porch nursing a beer, watching Hope where she was hanging out with the girls over at the far end of the lawn in the shade of a lush, sprawling tree.

Laughing.

Chatting like she'd known them for years.

Ryland was on a blanket, kicking his little arms and legs, and Rynna was propped up on an arm, sitting protectively at his side.

Nikki, Lillith, and Hope had gathered around the little makeshift play area, lounging on chairs and sharing a bottle of wine.

Frankie Leigh and Evan were still racing around the yard, playing hide and seek, Milo basically giving them away each time, all too quick to sniff them out.

Broderick had to bail to take a conference call with his office in New York.

Rex tipped the neck of his beer bottle out toward the yard. "This is all so very domestic of you," he said, broaching the subject I'd felt coming all afternoon.

He cut me a glance from the side, taking a long pull of his beer as he studied me.

"You about ready to talk about what's going on? Because this is so far out of left field, I'm wondering who you are and what you've done with my friend."

His brow lifted. "You know, the one who's insisted since he finished medical school that he didn't need anyone in his life other than his patients and us. A warm body without a face to keep him company on the nights he wants to get his dick wet right before he goes on his merry way."

He gave a sharp shake of his head. "Then my wife shocks the shit out of me last night by telling me you're coming over with some chick and her kid. That's enough of a one-eighty to make any man's head spin."

Wasn't that the truth.

I drummed my fingertips on my knee. "It's complicated."

Apparently, I had been hanging out with Hope too much.

Rex's expression turned incredulous. "Think you'd better figure out exactly what that means, because there isn't room for fucking around when there's a kid involved."

His words were hard, and there was no mistaking it was fueled by a threat.

He got it on a level many couldn't.

"You really think I'd fuck around with her if I didn't get that?" My tone was a little harsher than I'd intended.

But fuck.

His warning hit me in all the wrong places. In those places where my own terror was held. The worry that I might fail this kid.

"No. I didn't think you would," Rex said with a shake of his head. "Which is why I'm wondering what the hell is going on in that head of yours."

Ollie rocked forward in his chair, leaned his elbows on his knees as he looked over me. "Last time I talked to you, you were still hung up on the past. Thinking you didn't deserve the chance. That you couldn't take it."

His brows drew together. "That neither could she."

My attention landed on Evan, who was in the middle of the yard. His arms were thrown up over his head and he was spinning in a circle as he let the sun rain down on his precious face.

My heart throbbed. Pulsing and pressing and pushing.

"They happened."

A snort puffed from Rex's nose. "Women. When we meet the one, they make us forget ourselves, don't they?" he mused as he sipped his beer.

Ollie scoffed. "Uh . . . no. I can assuredly say I don't know what that's like, man. But this fucker sure seems to have caught the same plague that your sorry ass did." He hooked his thumb my direction.

I smirked at him. "Hey, man, go ahead. Rub it in. Know you're just jealous."

"Fuck no," he said with a laugh, not even realizing his attention immediately drifted to Nikki, who was cracking up in her chair, rocking forward as she clutched her stomach.

Her eyes flashed up to meet his like she felt the weight of his stare.

Just as fast, he jerked his attention back, the way he'd done for too many goddamned years.

Asshole didn't know what was right under his nose.

Or more likely, he just did a damned good job of ignoring it.

Ollie scrubbed a tattooed hand over his face like he was breaking himself from the trance.

I didn't think he knew how he'd gotten there in the first place.

"But seriously . . . are you ready to let it go? Give *her* up? Because you've been clinging to her memory for years. And that girl . . ."

He pointed at Hope, who'd taken Ryland in her arms.

She stared down at the tiny thing as if she were looking on beauty while at the same second it broke her heart.

Ollie's features shifted, not even a remnant of a tease. "She doesn't deserve to live in the shadow of Melody's ghost, man. She doesn't. And neither do you."

Unease slithered beneath my skin. Melody's face a sequence of flashes in my mind.

Stark, blinding lights. Compression after compression. That fucking flat line.

Smiles and laughter and grief.

Never thought I could love anyone again.

Had never entertained it.

"I'm terrified of it," I admitted. "That I'm always going to be haunted by her ghost. That I might fail again. But I don't think I can stop this, either."

Silence fell over us for a beat, my eyes watching Evan as he played. He caught me staring, waved over his head.

This kid.

This kid.

I gulped around the thick emotion that swelled in my throat. "He has a bad heart."

Rex's attention whipped my direction. "Fuck, man."

Yeah.

Fuck me.

twenty-five

Hope

held the tiny baby in my arms.

It spun my heart into intricate knots.

Because I could almost remember Evan this way.

The way he'd felt when I'd held him.

Tiny and soft.

But he had been so fragile.

Broken.

While I did my best to breathe belief.

To fill his little soul with it so he'd know he was loved. Cherished and adored. Even though he spent months in and out of the hospital attached to wires and monitors. Even though he'd endured so much pain.

He was loved.

In my periphery, I could see Rynna's smile. "You should see your face right now."

Confused, I looked up at her, blinking.

"With that baby," she sang as if I was ridiculous. It was a soft tease. A gentle coaxing. "Seems you need another one of your own in your arms."

The reality of life squeezed down on that faith. On that hope. I forced a smile that I knew wobbled, my voice more hoarse than I meant for it to be. "No. No more babies for me."

The deepest frown pulled across Rynna's brow, and I could sense Lillith and Nikki shifting forward, as if that minor movement was them standing and taking guard. There for me when they'd barely just met me.

These women were all so different from each other, but each so incredibly kind.

Welcoming Evan and I into their mix as if we'd always belonged.

No wonder Kale talked about them the way he did. The camaraderie and intimacy and devotion they shared.

Ryland cooed and pursed his little lips. He twisted his tiny fingers in front of his face, eyes bulging at the magic of his trick.

I attempted to clear the heaviness from my heart, to shuck the weight from my chest. "Evan's hearing and heart defects were genetic. I can't risk passing that on to another child."

I felt like a hypocrite saying it. Because my son was perfect in my eyes. Yet, I couldn't fathom being so selfish to curse another child to this life.

A muted, whimpered sound wheezed from Lillith.

As if she'd tried to hold it back and it'd bled free anyway.

She inched closer to me. "Oh God, Hope." She splayed her hands out over her heart as if my confession caused her a sharp, sudden pain. She looked over to where Evan played on the lawn. "I can't imagine. He's such an incredible little boy. One smile, and I was in love."

Tenderness had me chewing at the inside of my cheek, fighting the emotion that threatened to moisten my eyes. "He's the greatest gift I've ever been given," I murmured softly.

"But you hate what he's been through," she continued in complete understanding.

No judgment.

Kale was right.

These were amazing, incredible people.

"I completely understand that." She hesitated for a moment before she asked, "You're the carrier?"

Rynna shifted forward, winding her arms around her knees, listening intently.

I hefted a resigned shoulder. "They deemed my testing inconclusive."

Nikki jolted forward. "Wait . . . you don't know for sure?"

I shook my head. "No."

Her blue eyes widened, and I could tell she was holding it back, fighting a question she figured was out of line. But it didn't matter. I could already see it all over her face, written in big, red, blinking letters.

I went ahead and answered, more comfortable with the three of them than I could have imagined. "His biological father couldn't *possibly* be a carrier, now could he? Not with his dignified Southern bloodline. Testing would be nothing less than an insult to his masculinity and his heritage."

It rolled out in a tirade of sarcastic bitterness and disdain.

So unlike me.

But it'd finally all caught up to me.

The festering mess of anger and disappointment and grief.

It was all doused with the hatred that burned for the fact he could possibly think Evan wasn't worth the fight.

Gasoline to my battling soul.

Finally, I felt ready to face it. Head on.

I didn't know if it was Kale who'd given me the last measure of courage.

Either way, I was so thankful for his promise. That he would be there at my side. That I didn't have to go this alone.

Nikki bit down on her lip, butt shimmying in her seat, before she burst out with, "Oh my God, I can't stand it. Someone please tell me this is where we get to call the wanker names and talk about how horrible he is in bed and how his breath always stinks. Oh, oh, oh, and how he got piss-ass drunk and stepped out in front of a speeding car and now *poof.* Gone. Problem solved."

Her hands made an exploding motion out in front of her.

Lillith smacked at her. "Nikki! I swear. You are always trying to scare the good ones away with that mouth of yours."

She turned an apologetic smile on me. "You'll have to excuse her. This one was never taught that sometimes it's better to hold your tongue. You have to get used to her. She's kind of an acquired taste," she needled a little more, playful admonishment in her words.

Laughter rumbled, and I let my eyes widen conspiratorially when I looked at Nikki. "Oh, there's nothin' wrong with speaking truth where it's due. Unfortunately, all except for that whole speeding car thing was on point."

Nikki squealed in glee. "Oh . . . I like her. I think I just found my new best friend since Lily Pad over here thinks I'm too much to handle." The last came with a feigned pout.

Lillith rolled her eyes. "I can handle you just fine. It's the people around us who I'm worried about. You remember I'm an attorney. I deal with crazies all the time."

"Pssh. Crazy? Who me?" Nikki waved her off, leaning my direction, clear scheming in her tease. "This one just can't stand it that I'm the ultimate matchmaker—that I'm responsible for all the orgasms Brody gives her and she doesn't want to give me any of the credit. They'd still be each other's worst enemies and sending hate emails if it wasn't for me."

A light giggle floated from Rynna. "Watch out, Hope. If you aren't careful, Nikki here will be taking credit for getting you and Kale together. She definitely thinks she set things in motion for Rex and me."

Nikki waved her hands at herself. "Um . . . hello . . . I did set you up with Rex. If I hadn't invited you to Ollie's bar, you never would have hooked up. *And* I was there that night when Kale first saw Hope at Olive's, remember? Of course, I'm responsible. I'm head matchmaker. I just walk through a crowd and all those love-connecting darts start flying out of me, striking whoever I walk by."

"You do remember I first met Brody at Olive's?" Lillith pointed out, trying not to laugh. "It has nothing to do with you. The bar is definitely the tie."

Nikki gasped. "Shut your face, Lily Pad. Stop looking for solutions when the answer is right in front of you. Head matchmaker." She circled a halo around her head. "Orgasm fairy."

She slanted a knowing grin my direction. "Tell me the last rings true."

Oh.

Redness bloomed on my cheeks.

I was pretty sure I needed to introduce Nikki and Jenna. They had to have been separated at birth.

Lillith smacked her again. "I swear, Nikki."

"What?" she defended, totally innocently before she turned back to me.

Laughing under my breath, I ducked down when I admitted, "It definitely rings true."

Her mouth popped open, and she leaned in closer to me, eyes wide with excitement. "Lovestruck?"

I let my attention slide to where Kale sat on the deck. Evan had scrambled behind Frankie Leigh up to the porch, and my son was now in front of Kale, communicating something to him that I couldn't make out, but he was red and flushed and happy.

So content and free.

My spirit thrashed.

That feeling settled over me.

Because it was true.

I was totally and completely . . . lovestruck.

The day played on in a blur of laughter and joy and easiness. Kale and I sat on the grass with his friends as the sun began to sink in the sky, his arm slung around my shoulders while we watched Evan run through the grass, my son's head tipped back in his silent laughter that I swore I could hear ring through the air.

It was late evening when we said our goodbyes. I accepted all the hugs that were offered and agreed with the girls that we all would hang out together soon.

Joy pressed at my ribs. It was a kind of wholeness that seemed almost foreign where it throbbed within the depths of me.

Kale helped Evan into the backseat of the car and ensured he was buckled before he slid into the driver's seat.

Immediately, he leaned in and kissed me over the console.

In front of Evan.

It felt like a gentle claiming.

A statement.

A promise.

From the backseat, Evan made that scraping, laughing sound, and Kale and I both peered back at him. He was grinning that earth-shattering smile, his cheeks red with a certain kind of embarrassment that manifested the greatest joy.

"Is it okay if I kiss your mom, little man?"

Evan was quick to write on his pad he had on his lap.

You're supposed to kiss her if you're her boyfriend. That's the rule.

I flushed, and Kale leaned his forehead against mine, his voice a murmur. "Then I guess I'm your boyfriend. The kid says it's the rule."

He looked back at Evan. "I'm her boyfriend, and she's my girlfriend. Right?"

Evan nodded vigorously, then his little hand went flying across the paper.

Yep. So, what am I?

Kale stilled, contemplating, before he said, "You're my favorite."

Evan beamed. His entire being lit with a profound joy.

You're my favorite, too.

Every inch of me warmed.

Kale glanced at me as he turned back, a small, adoring smile gracing his striking face. "All right, then. I think that's settled."

He started his car, backed out, and hit the road.

He held my hand as he drove back through our small, quaint city.

A quiet peace filtered through like a murky haze as twilight gathered fast, the moon climbing to the sky from behind the mountain in the distance.

Kale made the last turn onto our street.

We parked at the curb and everyone climbed out.

Rounding the front of his car, Kale swept my son from his feet. "Come here, little man, you look tired."

Evan nodded.

Lines of worry pulled across Kale's brow, and he ran a hand over Evan's forehead. "Are you feeling okay, buddy?"

I watched the two of them, my chest so full as Evan signed.

"He says he's just tired because he had so much fun today."

"Oh, yeah? What did you think about Frankie Leigh?"

A giggle slipped from between my lips when I saw my son's response, my expression so soft when I turned my attention on the man who'd changed everything.

"He said he's gonna marry her."

A grin split Kale's face. "Is that so? You like her that much, huh?"

Evan gave a flourishing nod.

"She's awfully pretty. Seems it's always the ones who are a handful that snag our hearts, isn't it?"

Somehow, I knew he was no longer talking to my son, that smirk washing me over like a slow promise, raking my flesh, making me blush.

Complicated.

Never would I regret letting this man complicate me even more.

I headed up the walk, carrying the empty plastic cupcake container, continually peeking over my shoulder at Kale who trailed close behind, holding my son in the security of his arms.

I balanced the container on my hip, worked the key into the lock, and pushed open the door. I looked back at my son when I did. "We'd better get you a bath and into bed."

Evan pursed his little lips in a pout, and Kale chuckled, ruffled his hair. "Get your bath, little man, and then we can read that Spiderman story you've been telling me about."

Promise? Evan mouthed.

"Promise," Kale returned, setting him on his feet. Evan took off for the bathroom.

Kale took the container from my hands. "Let me take care of that while you give him his bath."

"You better be careful, Cowboy, or I could get used to this," I teased, though the words were fluttery, my heart and my spirit tied to his.

No longer afraid to hope.

Wanting him a permanent part of our world.

I started to follow Evan when Kale snatched me by the wrist.

Heat sped up my arm, and shock rasped from my lungs when he pressed me against the wall. And the man kissed me.

Softly.

Tenderly.

Stealing my breath.

That energy rose up at our feet, climbing higher.

On a rumbly groan, he dropped his forehead to mine. "I'm such a goner, Shortcake. Don't think you understand the way you've gotten to me."

My eyes dropped closed, the words screaming from the depths of me.

Love. Love. Love.

I didn't say it. I just relished it. Let it surge and dance and swell.

Penetrate those places where it'd last forever.

I heard the faucet turning on in the bathroom. "I better go check on him."

Kale nodded and pressed a tender kiss to my forehead. "I'll be right here."

Kale

From where I stood at the sink washing the container, I could hear Hope through the walls. Her words indistinguishable and ambiguous.

But that didn't matter. I could hear what was important, anyway.

Joy.

There was so much of it. Because that was what these two were.

Joy.

My chest tightened when I realized the magnitude of what that actually meant.

That somehow they had become *my joy.*

My home when I hadn't realized I'd been looking for one.

It should scare me. Terrify me that I had gone into territory I'd sworn I'd never go.

But standing there in the comfort of Hope's kitchen, being all sorts of domestic like Rex had pointed out?

Nothing had ever felt so right.

I'd denied myself even the idea of this.

Family.

Thinking I couldn't have it.

Didn't deserve it.

Old fear trembled in my bones.

I went rigid against it.

Rejecting it.

Because I refused to fail these two. The past was the past and I was leaving it there. Hope and Evan were my here and now.

My future.

After finishing washing the container, I rinsed it and placed it on a dishtowel, drying my hands at the same time.

In my periphery, my sight caught on the stack of mail that rested at the far end of the counter. My head jerked violently in a double take.

I wasn't trying to be nosy. I wasn't. Overstepping my bounds.

But the name . . . the name on the top envelope was all wrong.

Dread sank like a stone to the pit of my stomach, and a freezing cold chill slicked like ice down my spine.

My vision turned hazy, and my eyes narrowed. I swore, my damned heart was beating so hard I could hear the roar of it thundering through my veins.

I inched that direction, my subconscious flailing and thrashing in a disturbed awareness.

The closer I got, the more that distress grew, scraping across my skin like a razor-sharp knife.

At the edge of the counter, I froze, gulping around the knot in my throat that cut off air.

Staring down at the envelope on top of the stack.

I gave an aggressive shake of my head. Like it would clear up the picture.

Because fuck.

I had to be seeing things. Making shit up.

It was all those old memories and regrets and sorrow rising and playing cruel, sick tricks.

Tormenting me with a stark, glaring reminder of my greatest loss. It all pressed down, the soul-crushing fear of losing him the same obscene way.

But it didn't matter how long I stared at it.

All the letters remained the same.

Harley Gentry. Harley Gentry. Harley Gentry.

The room spun. Faster and faster.

My new world crumbling out from under my feet.

Hands ripping at fistfuls of my hair, I stumbled back.

No.

Fuck.

No.

Panic surged. Bouncing from the walls.

Ricocheting.

Gaining speed.

I couldn't breathe.

"What's wrong?" That understanding, tender voice hit me from behind, filled with soft concern.

Slowly, I turned to look at her.

Those green eyes went wide with surprise when she got a look at me, my spine rigid and my face pale.

She took a surging step forward. "Kale? Are you okay? Are you sick?"

Care. It radiated from her like the goddamned sun.

My eyes squeezed closed because looking at all the light hurt. It hurt so goddamned much I felt my stomach clench in a roil of nausea that lifted to my throat.

"Who is he?" I demanded, eyes still pinched closed, not wanting to see her expression when she said it.

Not sure I could handle it.

This couldn't be real. It couldn't be real.

"What are you askin'?" she wheezed, a slip of that country drawl seeping into her worry. "We already talked about this."

I shot across the floor and grabbed her by the outside of her arms.

Her eyes widened. A bolt of fear. A vat of confusion.

"Tell me who he is. Your ex. What is his name?"

"Kale," she pleaded, her eyes searching mine.

"Tell me," I grated, losing my goddamned head.

"Dane. His name is Dane Gentry." It was almost a whimper.

A blow.

A gunshot that rang through the air.

Deafening.

I choked over the confirmation. My hands releasing her like I'd been holding fire.

I had. I had. I had.

I'd been holding fire in the palm of my hands.

My head shook. "No . . . no. Your name is Harley Hope Masterson. Masterson," I almost begged.

She winced. "Masterson is my maiden name."

Sucking for nonexistent air, I fumbled away from her. Panic burning me up from the inside.

No.

Oh, God, no.

Hope reached for me, brow pinched tight. "Kale . . . please don't look at me like you don't know me. I don't understand why you're so upset."

Fumbling away, my back knocked into the kitchen wall next to the arch.

"I . . ." Glass abraded my throat, the raw cuts refusing words.

This couldn't be real.

A plea took to Hope's unforgettable face. "I've been trying to erase him from our lives. You've got to understand that. I told you I would do anything to protect my son."

Hope's explanation became frantic, desperate, the woman edging closer, too close.

So close I could taste her on my tongue and feel her on my skin.

Her rushed words fell on my ears. "I didn't tell you his name because I was afraid you'd do something you'd regret later on. Standing up for Evan and me. Because you're a good man, Kale. Such a good man, and I knew you'd do whatever you thought you could do to protect us. I was protecting you, too. It's just a name, Kale. It's just a name. It doesn't change anything."

But that's where she was wrong.

It changed everything.

"I have to go." It raked from my raw throat.

I had to get out of there.

Run.

Melody.

I squeezed my eyes when I was suddenly assaulted with memories.

Her smile. Her laugh. Her pleas. Gone. Horror. Grief.

I choked.

Hope's face pinched in a brutal kind of pain. "What?"

"I can't do this," I told her, nothing but a coward when I tried to get by her without looking at her face.

Without looking in those earthy eyes to see the beauty that waited there.

The hope and the joy and the belief.

She grabbed me by the wrist.

That roar in my veins cracked.

A thunderclap.

"Tell me what's happening," she begged. "What is really going on?"

I blinked at her, but all I could see was *her* face.

Melody.

Compression after compression. That fucking flat line. "You did this. You did this. She's dead because of you."

Evan's sweet face flashed.

Lifeless.

"I can't do this."

Not again.

Hope tightened her hold, refusing to let me go. "You don't get to do this, Kale Bryant. You don't get to just walk out. You promised."

My eyes squeezed closed again.

Looking at this girl and knowing I couldn't keep her was the most brutal tease I'd ever endured.

Just another fucking failure.

Her words dropped to a wispy plea. "Where did you go, Kale? Where did the man go who is wonderful and generous and kind? The man who ten minutes ago told me he'd be right here, waiting for me? Where is he? Follow me back . . . come back to me . . . because I'm right here. I'm *right* here."

Grief crushed me on all sides.

Pressing down.

Destroying.

Because if I could, I would follow her anywhere.

"I'm sorry," I forced out, because I was. So fucking sorry.

I twisted my arm free from her hold and stepped back.

Her expression twisted.

Horror and grief.

The hurt so blatant.

"You promised," she begged on a breath.

My head shook, and I slowly backed away, looking at her standing heartbroken in her kitchen.

A cascade of red hair, tearstained cheeks, bloodshot eyes.

The girl the best thing I'd ever seen.

I committed it to memory.

What I did. The ruin I inflicted.

Hope had spent years fighting the stigma that her son wasn't enough.

But that stigma was meant for me.

Because I would never, ever be enough.

I spun on my heel and bolted.

Out her door and into the fading light.

I stumbled across the porch. Gasping for a breath, the entire world spinning and the ground canting to the side, crumbling out from under me.

I wheezed, desperate for relief. But all the air had been sucked from the sky.

A hollow, vacant vortex that consumed everything in its path.

twenty-seven

Hope

The walls of the entire house shook when the door slammed closed.

A violent blow.

Or maybe it was just my insides ripping apart.

Collapsing and imploding.

A raking sob tore up my throat, and I bent in two. I wrapped my arms around my waist as if it might be enough to keep me standing.

But it wasn't.

A rush of dizziness swept through me like a landslide, and I lurched forward. My hands barely caught on the counter before I fell to my knees.

A loss so intense pounded through me, and my head dropped between my shoulders, mouth parting in a guttural cry there was no possible way to contain.

"Kale," I whimpered.

Thoughts swirled in my mind. Confusion thick. My emotions had been yanked from the highest high to the lowest low.

What just happened?

I couldn't make sense of the sudden shift.

I didn't know how he could do this to me.

Could do this to *us*.

He'd promised he wouldn't leave.

That he'd be there.

That he'd stay.

After he'd sworn he knew what was on the line.

And he'd left me.

Over a name.

Over that vile, cruel name.

My insides twisted again, my stomach revolting, just the same as my spirit. Because this was wrong.

All of it was so very wrong.

The numbers weren't even close to adding up to the correct sum.

A switch had been flipped, and I had no idea what had been the trigger.

Because I'd grown to know this man in the most intimate of ways. I knew I wasn't just being blind or naïve for the sake of falling for a gorgeous man.

I'd seen him for who he truly was—kind, generous, and devoted.

And that man I'd grown to know was not the one who'd just gone running out my door.

He'd been terrified.

White as a ghost.

A slow dread sank over me like bitter cold.

The horror that had been scored on his face flashed behind my eyes. As if he'd stood right there in the middle of my kitchen and come face-to-face with an apparition.

A demon.

Or maybe the devil himself.

That fear I'd so often seen rise up in him, shuttering that beautiful, unselfish heart, had never been so clear than right then.

He'd demanded Dane's name as if my soon-to-be ex-husband was a disloyalty to him.

As if a name alone held the power to confuse and contort and destroy.

If a name alone were enough to send him running, what would he do when he found out the whole truth?

A thunder pounded on the front door.

Shocked, a breath heaved from my lungs, the sound made up of relief and confusion and deliverance.

Because there was the man, who I trusted implicitly, yanking and pushing. Dragging my fragile heart through the mud.

But I had to realize this was all new to him. I'd asked so much of him in such a short period of time. I hadn't been exaggerating when I'd warned him my life was so very complicated.

As much as I wanted it—craved it—deep down, I knew the man had stepped into a position he might not have been fully prepared to take on.

Maybe he needed some time to catch up. But as much as I knew he deserved that time, I couldn't allow him to go running in and out of our home without thought or consideration of what it might do to Evan.

Of what it would do to me.

When another round of pounding hammered from the door, I straightened and sucked in a steeling breath, preparing myself because Kale and I were going to have to talk.

Really talk.

Lay it out.

It was time the two of us shared our true hopes, fears, and reservations.

I wanted him.

God, I wanted him.

But I could admit we'd been moving fast, and I needed him to be ready before he took that final leap. Deal with the fear that would dim his eyes.

Hurt and a quiver of jealousy staked through my heart.

Maybe . . . maybe he wasn't ready to let her go.

His first love.

Maybe he'd realized he didn't have space for me, after all. The idea of letting him go broke me in two, but I was willing to face that reality if I had to.

Raking my forearm across my bleary eyes, I cleared the moisture, headed down the hallway, and took another deep breath before I turned the knob and carefully cracked open the door.

"Dane." A slick of fear lifted my skin in a clammy sweat when I saw him on my porch.

It mixed with an overwhelming disappointment that it wasn't Kale.

"What are you doing here?"

"I want to talk to you."

There was something new in his eyes that prickled the hairs at the back of my neck and sent a rocket of chills shooting up my spine.

"I don't have anything to say to you."

I went to close the door. I didn't have the capacity to deal with him right then. Not after Kale had left me feeling brittle and broken. His arm shot out to stop it from latching, his voice hard as he pushed open the door. "I said I wanted to talk to you."

I stumbled back, and the door swung open wide. I edged away as Dane stepped into my little home for the first time ever.

It was so wrong with him standing there. Black hair and black eyes and black heart.

"And I said, I didn't have anything to say to you."

"Is that so?"

"Yes." It trembled from my mouth.

He took another step forward. "How about you start by telling me who just drove away from here."

I didn't answer, just took another step back as he took one forward, backing me into the opposite wall. Right in the same place where Kale had had me not thirty minutes before.

Again, my breath was stolen.

But this time it was stolen by the clot of alarm that constricted my throat, my heart beating faster and faster with a warning.

He'd seen Kale. Oh God, he'd seen Kale.

His hot words were venom across my face. "Who the fuck was here, Harley?"

"No one." The lie cracked on the toxic air. Splinters and shards.

"Bullshit. I saw someone driving away."

Anger fisted my chest. "What does it even matter, Dane. Are you really gonna stand there and pretend like you weren't stepping out on me all along? You think I don't know about all those women?"

I was long over Dane. But there was no stopping the bitterness that came out with accusation.

His jaw clenched, but he angled his head and his voice turned soft. "You know why, Harley. You know why. You didn't have anything left for me since you gave every second of every day to that kid."

Was he serious? He was jealous of our child?

Pathetic.

God, this man was pathetic.

Flinching, I jerked my chin to the side when he reached out and brushed his fingers down my jaw.

Revulsion pulsed through my being.

"None of that matters now. Come home where you belong, and we'll try again."

"Try again?" My eyes snapped back to him, my tone incredulous.

He ran the pad of this thumb over my cheek. "Another baby. We'll start over. Forget everything that's happened."

"You're insane."

Dane suddenly pressed himself against me, planting both hands on the wall on either side of my head.

Gasping, I tried to block out the feel of him. The smell of him. But I was assaulted by a million memories. His cloying cologne. His vicious words. His hatred of our son.

"Don't touch me," I rasped, struggling to push away from him.

He just leaned in closer, his voice turning hard. Malicious. "Did you let another man fuck you, Harley? Touch what's mine?"

"You're disgusting," I spat.

A horrified yelp escaped when he suddenly fisted his hands in the fabric of my shirt and pulled me against his chest. "You think I'm a fool? Is that what you think? You think you can play me? You think I didn't just see that car pull away from here?"

"It doesn't matter, Dane. It's over. You already know this. We're over."

I don't love you.

Thoughts of Kale flooded my mind. His kiss. His touch. His kindness. And I had to wonder if I ever had loved Dane.

"You're my wife."

My eyes squeezed shut. "No."

He crushed his mouth against mine, his hands on my face as he tried to force me to comply. I flailed and struggled against the unwelcome intrusion, trying to fight him off while an avalanche of fear and hate crashed into me.

I drew back my arm, my hand flying out and connecting with his cheek.

The smack echoed through the foyer.

He snapped back, his black eyes glowering before he released a menacing growl. His hands moved from my face and wrapped around my throat. Not tight enough to constrict airflow. But tight enough to exert just how easily he could.

Any coaxing softness he'd worn before had been stripped away, replaced by his true character.

The man I'd fallen in love with completely gone.

As if he'd never existed.

A vile wickedness bleeding free.

His words dropped to a low, vicious threat in my ear. "You really think I'm a fool, don't you, Harley? Why don't you tell me why my attorney can't find a single medical record on Evan for the last year? You think I don't know you're up to something?"

And I'd thought I'd felt fear before.

But maybe I had never really experienced it until right then.

"He's been healthy . . . he . . . he hasn't needed to go in." The lie fumbled from my mouth. Lurching and pleading.

I was prepared to tell a million more when I was struck with a dread unlike anything I'd ever known.

Fear and horror and the undying need to protect my son at any cost compounded and sharpened.

Because all I could hear was the clatter of unaware feet excitedly banging down the hall and through the living room. My little boy thinking he was running out to find Kale and his promise of a story.

Oh, God.

No.

I couldn't let this happen.

It was at the same second Dane bared back down on me, roaring with my answer.

He fisted my dress in his hands and slammed my back against the wall.

Pain radiated through my body, and I cried out, completely caught off guard. Never before had the danger Dane imposed been physical.

He lifted me by my clothing, spewing the words an inch from my face.

"Bullshit, Harley. You think you're going to get away with whatever you're trying to pull? Do you know who my family is? What I stand to lose?"

His statement sent a jolt of confusion tumbling through my mind. I had no idea what he had to lose other than his overinflated pride, but I was too terrified to process it. Too terrified to ask. The only thing I cared about were the feet that rushed across the hardwood floors.

I could feel Evan's presence break the morbid air as he rounded the corner into the foyer.

I felt the second he slammed into shock.

His iPad slipped from his hands and crashed against the floor, and those innocent eyes grew round with stark, cutting fear.

"Run, Evan! Go to your room. Lock the door," I screamed.

But he wasn't looking at me.

Redness blistered across his face, a sort of anger I'd never seen my son wear before. In horror, I watched as he rushed forward. His gangly arms began to fly. He pounded and pounded and pounded against Dane's leg with his little fists.

Scraping, rasping cries jutted from Evan's mouth, and tears streaked from his eyes.

I knew it was surprise that twisted through Dane's furious expression, and the man staggered back a single step, his head jerking down to Evan who continued to wail on his leg.

"No, Evan, no!" I screamed, my spirit begging with him to look at me. To *understand.*

Dane's surprise turned to rage, and he reached out to grab my son.

Blinding fury surged inside me so intense I was sure my blood physically boiled.

I'd never allow this man to hurt my child.

Not ever.

From behind, I shoved Dane with everything I had.

"Don't touch him!" It was a scream that came from the very depths of my soul.

Don't touch him. Leave us alone. We just want to live.

My effort barely moved Dane an inch. But it was *enough.* It was enough to distract him from Evan and set that spiteful, depraved cruelty on me. Terror rippled through the confined space, crawling across my skin like a shivering omen.

Because I could see it slosh and churn from the depths of Dane's eyes.

A wickedness unlike anything I'd witnessed before.

Menace bounced from the walls.

Trembling, I backed away as Dane stalked forward.

Frantic, I found Evan's frightened eyes where he remained across the foyer because I knew, right then, I was in the kind of danger I'd never fathomed.

The movement of my mouth was exaggerated when I shouted for Evan to call 9-1-1.

Evan met my eyes, his fear almost enough to bring me to my knees. But I stood strong, willing to fight for him, the one I'd always been fighting for.

It took only a flash for it to penetrate Evan's mind, and he darted for my purse where I'd left it on the coffee table in the living room.

Dane shoved me so hard it sent me reeling, my feet unable to find solid ground. I flew backward, my head snapping back and smashing against the wall.

A sharp strike of pain blazed across my skull, blurring my vision for a second.

Dane's vindictive voice filled the chaotic air. "He can't hear you, Harley. That little freak *can't hear you.*"

And I knew I would never get through to this man.

But in that moment, while I stood there helpless, sure he was going to end me, I let the years of pent-up hurt and rage pour from my mouth. "He can *hear* me. He's always heard me, just like I hear him. You just refused to listen. To understand him. To *see* him. You're the one who missed out. And now you don't get us, not ever again."

Dane growled an inch from my face, "He was a mistake."

Defiance pulsed through my veins. "He's the best thing that has ever happened to me."

A clatter sounded from the other room.

Dane's attention jerked that way, and his gaze narrowed in shock when he found Evan with the phone, the screen lit and connected, an operator on the line.

Blanching, Dane reared back.

Shock on his face before it was gone and the monster returned. Revulsion curled his fists. "You think this is over? I warned you, Harley. I will find out what you're up to. And you will come home . . . one way or another."

He blew out the door.

A loud sob wrenched from my body, and I slid down the wall to the floor.

It was too much.

The shock and the grief. The hurt and the fear.

Cracks fissuring through my spirit.

Two seconds after Dane disappeared, Evan ran back through the archway with my phone in his hand.

And I swore, I was crushed by his expression when he found me balled up on the floor, sobbing.

No longer able to stand.

His little face was ridden with horror, confusion, and fear. Maybe the worst was that he was looking at me as if he would give anything to have stopped what had just happened.

"Evan," I whispered, and he rushed to me, his precious face a mess of sticky tears.

Arms stretched out for him, I pulled him onto my lap and against my chest. My mouth went to his temple, my lips moving with the promise as I rocked us. "It's okay, it's okay."

He made a scraping sound, and his tears soaked the front of my dress as he clung to me.

"I'm so sorry, Evan," I whimpered, clutching him tighter. "I'm so sorry."

Sorry he had to see that. Go through it. Feel it.

My little man.

My savior.

My protector.

Sirens echoed in the distance, growing louder and louder as they approached. A gasping, relieved breath tore from my lungs when two police officers finally appeared at my gaping door, their guns drawn as they stepped inside to assess the situation.

I pressed Evan's face to my chest to at least protect him from that, hating to put him through any more shock and turmoil.

"We're okay. We're okay. We're okay," I told them through my cries, which only increased as the adrenaline bled away.

As I realized the magnitude of what had just happened.

As I wondered if my telling them we were *okay* was just another lie because I wasn't sure that we truly were.

Dane had just given me ammunition to fight him. An attack that I'd been unprepared for.

But did that even matter when he suspected, knew something was wrong with the records? I held Evan tighter against me as if that one touch might protect him from every danger.

Still, I could feel it slipping away.

Hope.

An officer helped me to my feet, and I carried Evan to the couch, and I continued to hold him as tightly as I could while I answered the officers' questions.

What happened?

Did anything occur to incite the attack?

Were we injured?

I saw it in their expressions when I told him it was my estranged husband.

This was just another common domestic disturbance to them. The same kind of call they'd probably responded to a million times.

Despair settled into the pit of my stomach when they said they would *attempt* to get in touch with Dane Gentry to get his side of the story.

As if the fact he'd forced his way into my home weren't enough.

After an hour of answering their questions, I followed them to the door to let them out, every muscle in my body feeling as if it weighed a million pounds.

The younger officer, the one who'd helped me stand from the floor, paused on the porch and turned back to look at me from over his shoulder, sympathy in the tight twist of his brow. "Make sure you have that door locked up, ma'am."

I gave him a slow nod and followed his instructions.

Though, I wasn't sure it would make a difference, anyway.

Dane had become unstable. Volatile.

And I still couldn't understand why he would continue to press this.

He'd gotten a free card.

A pass.

He could go on and live his life the easy way. Without being tied to Evan. Without being tied to me. He seemed almost desperate for me to return, and that same flare of warning that something was off lapped at my spirit.

I edged back into the living room where my son sat on the couch with his arms wrapped around his knees.

Rocking.

My heart tremored in its confines, the loss and grief threatening to take me over. Drown me in despair.

But I had to be strong.

For my son.

He'd always been my reason.

What I'd been fighting for.

"Come here, my sweet boy."

Gently, I scooped him into my arms, his weight reminding me he wasn't so little anymore . . . that these were the things he would remember. Horrible things that would be etched and scraped into his consciousness.

I wanted so desperately to protect him from that.

Carrying him to his room, I pulled back his covers and nestled him in his bed.

Getting to my knees, I leaned over him and brushed back his red, red hair.

In silence, he stared up at me.

Turmoil in his eyes. So much fear and so many questions I didn't know how to answer brimming in their depths.

I could feel pieces inside me dangling free. Coming apart.

I signed.

ARE YOU OKAY?

His face pinched as if he was upset at me for asking it.

ARE YOU OKAY? His movements were a frantic demand. Angry. As if he wanted to get up and defend me all over again.

Pain clutched my heart, my soul. I swallowed hard, my own movements emphatic as I signed, praying their importance would get through.

*I **AM** OKAY. BUT IT MAKES ME SO SAD YOU SAW THAT. THAT YOU EXPERIENCED THAT. IT'S NOT RIGHT FOR THAT TO HAPPEN. NOT EVER.*

Tears streaked from the corners of his eyes, and Evan sat up in his bed, facing me.

I HATE HIM, M-A-M-A. HE'S NOT ALLOWED HERE BECAUSE HE DOESN'T UNDERSTAND LOVE. YOU CAN ONLY BE HERE IF YOU LOVE. THAT'S THE RULE. REMEMBER WHEN WE CAME HERE? THIS HOUSE IS L-O-V-E.

So upset, his hands flew through the air, his little breaths pants of exertion.

My son.

My beautiful, wonderful, insightful son.

YOU'RE RIGHT. THIS HOUSE IS L-O-V-E. AND I'M DOING MY BEST TO PROTECT THAT. BUT YOU HAVE TO PROMISE ME YOU WON'T EVER STEP IN LIKE THAT AGAIN, EVAN. I KNOW YOU WANT TO HELP, BUT IT'S TOO DANGEROUS. IF SOMETHING IS SCARY OR BAD, I NEED YOU TO GO TO YOUR ROOM. LOCK THE DOOR. CALL THE POLICE.

His head shook frantically. *I HAVE TO TAKE CARE OF YOU.*

NO. NO, EVAN. THAT'S MY JOB. TO TAKE CARE OF YOU.

A fresh round of tears blanketed his face, so much grief in his green, innocent eyes.

BUT IF I DIE, WHO IS GOING TO TAKE CARE OF YOU? KALE WAS SUPPOSED TO BE HERE. WHERE WAS HE?

Oh God.

Crack.

Crack.

Crack.

I could feel everything splintering. Breaking apart. I did everything to hold it together.

YOU'RE NOT GOING TO DIE, EVAN. DON'T SAY THAT.

Frustration and regret sped his signs.

WHERE DID KALE GO?

HE HAD TO GO HOME.

The lies just kept coming and coming. But my lies had always been forged to protect my son. It didn't matter how hard it was, how much *I* hurt, that wouldn't change.

Evan would always be my first priority.

If it landed me behind bars or put me in the ground, he would *always, always* hold that spot.

Evan's face twisted, and a frown pulled at one side of his mouth. As if he were fighting more tears but was trying to remain strong.

HE WAS SUPPOSED TO BE HERE. HE PROMISED WE WERE GOING TO READ SPIDERMAN. HE SHOULD HAVE BEEN HERE. I WANT HIM TO COME BACK.

He hit his balled fists into his mattress at his sides, so much confusion and sadness in the action tears pricked at my eyes again.

I wondered right then if I'd ever stop crying.

Sorrow shivered through his room.

A new kind of vacancy that had never been there before.

Because Evan could see through it all. My boy always so insightful, clearly knowing Kale hadn't just left, but had run.

Reaching out, I held him by both sides of his face and met his eye. "I want him, too, Evan, but sometimes people are afraid of what they don't understand."

BUT I'M HIS FAVORITE.

His little hands moved like a plea. As if Kale's rejection of him had been his biggest blow.

And I ached. I ached so badly, and I knew my son did, too.

That was the risk of bringing someone into our lives.

Allowing them to complicate us more. We never knew what kind of mess they'd leave behind. But somewhere, somewhere I knew this was bigger than I understood.

"You need to get some rest," I mouthed, and Evan's mouth pursed in reluctance before he relented and settled back against his pillows.

I stayed with him the longest while, running my fingers through his hair as he just lay there, staring at me.

Giving me his own kind of encouragement.

This time, it was my son breathing belief into me.

Time passed before I finally splayed my hand across the steady thrum in his chest.

"My heart," I whispered.

He reached out and splayed his little hand over mine.

My heart, he mouthed.

And mine, it moaned, missing the piece that had blossomed and bloomed. The piece I'd freely given.

Finally, when Evan had been asleep for a long while, I moved back out into the living room and sank to the edge of the couch, my phone in my hands.

Zero pretension.

Zero pride.

I typed out a message and pressed send.

Me: I need you.

But when I crawled into bed to find a restless, tossing sleep, I'd gotten no response. And when the sun finally struck through the window, sending stakes of glittering light into my room, it still remained unanswered.

And I feared that piece I'd freely given was gone.
Hope shattered.
Maybe it was true what they said. Only fools held out faith.
For the first time in my life, I wondered if that fool was me.

twenty-eight

Kale

Tender hands ran down my bare chest, and giggling lips pressed to my jaw. "Kale," she whispered.

"Melody," I murmured back, rolling on top of her, pressing her to my bed. "Melody."

I stared down at her. Smiling at her trusting face, wondering how it was possible to feel this way.

Her sweet, sweet face.

It pinched in horror.

In pain.

Everything shifted, my room gone, cement under my feet.

"Kale," she begged from where she stood at her car across the lot, the sun blazing down on her from above. She dropped to her knees on the cold, pitted pavement and clutched her chest. "I need you."

Fear took me whole. Frantically, I ran across the lot and dropped to my knees at her side.

Her eyes rolled back. "Melody!" I shouted.

I searched for her pulse. For her breath.

Screams echoed through the air.

My shouts for help.

"I won't let this happen. I promise, I won't let this happen."

I pressed my hands to her chest and began to pump.

Compression after compression.

Teeth grinding together, I worked over her, begging, "Don't leave me. I won't let you leave me."

I fought and the sun spun out of the sky.

Darkness.

The world canted and tipped from its axis.
Everything shook.
Evan's face.
His little, broken body beneath my hands.
That fucking flat line.
A scream. A plea. Hope on her knees. "I need you. I need you . . ."

A roar ripping from my lungs jolted me upright in bed.

Searching for nonexistent air, I gasped and panted, pretty sure the life was being squeezed out of me.

My eyes darted around the shadowy darkness of my bedroom as the images faded.

My skin drenched in sweat, and my heart beating like a motherfucking drum.

My shoulders dropped when I realized I was alone. That it was just another dream.

Which should have been a comfort, but the awareness of it just sent grief swooping down, shackling me in its chains.

"Fuck," I gritted.

Hand fumbling through the dark, I reached over to flick on the lamp on my nightstand. The muted light broke through the night, and I pushed to sit up at the edge of my bed. The movement sent a wave of nausea crashing over me, sucking me down, taking me under.

Lost in the deepest, darkest sea where voices pleaded and moaned and begged.

I need you.

I need you.

I need you.

I knew I was losing it. Coming unglued. Standing at the edge of a cliff and getting ready to fall over the side into that abyss of nothingness.

Where I'd drown in dreams and torment and screams.

I'd never known a loss like the one I was prisoner to right then.

Losing them.

Hope and Evan.

But at least I'd gotten out before I could cause them more damage or pain. Because God knew, that was all I knew how to inflict. That didn't mean I didn't fight myself every second of every day not to go back to them. To ask for a fucked-up sort of forgiveness that I would never deserve.

If Hope knew what I'd done, the way I'd failed, she'd never look at me the same.

Hell, I knew it'd haunt her the same way that fucking text that had come in just after midnight nine days ago haunted me.

I need you.

I'd nearly succumbed. Broken down and crawling back on my hands and knees like a beggar, groveling, trying to find any excuse in my mind that would make it okay to be with them.

But I sucked it up. Refused the urges and the need and the sorrow.

Because I was staying away for them.

I need you.

Drawn, my eyes peeled open, and my already choppy breaths turned ragged.

By instinct, I reached for the sheet of folded paper sitting on my nightstand, my hand shaking like a bitch and my stomach threatening to spill onto the floor.

I'd found it sitting on the backseat of my car. I'd wanted to think it discarded. Nothing of importance, but I knew the kid had left it there for me.

A message.

Tonight, I unfolded it for what had to be the millionth time because I couldn't help but torture myself a little more.

My chest tightened when I stared down at the drawing.

A fucking fantastic rendition because the kid was amazing. Clever and talented and smart.

Captain America and a tiny Hulk were holding hands.

My eyes traced what was written at the bottom in the same handwriting I'd come to know so well. Words I heard like a voice.

My favorite.

Regret drove into me like a blunt, rusted knife.

Gutting.

A remnant of Melody's voice clashed with the power of Hope's.

I need you.

I was a goner.

So fucking gone.

And there was no finding my way back.

Every time I'd driven passed A Drop of Hope over the last nine days, I'd gunned my engine and sped by. Refusing to look that way because it brought on more memories and regrets than I knew how to deal with.

But this morning . . .

This morning there was nothing I could do but slow and look that way. Because everything felt different.

An awareness that thundered my heart and twisted my guts in a million knots of need.

My spirit thrashed and screamed.

Because I caught sight of the girl for the first time since I'd left her broken in her kitchen.

Body lush, Hope wearing one of those dresses that drove me out of my mind, the best goddamned thing I'd ever seen.

Considering the fact I was sure my sanity was slipping, I thought for a second I had to be hallucinating.

But there she was. Leaning over and reaching into the back of her SUV to pull out a supply box. That red, red hair whipped around her delicate shoulders when she quickly spun around.

Like she felt me the same way I felt her.

Our eyes locked through the windshield.

The world freezing.

Time suspended.

The two of us lost to a place that belonged only to us.

Grief lined every inch of her unforgettable face, and there was a weight in her eyes that I hadn't ever seen there before.

I could almost hear the plea in the soft part of her full, full lips.

I need you.

Every cell in my body reacted.

Want.

Need.

Regret.

Shame.

The last snapped me back into reality, and I ripped my eyes away from her and floored the accelerator. The coward who had to get away.

It was time.

The way I'd reacted when I'd seen Hope that morning was clear proof of that.

I'd gone astray.

Gotten distracted.

I was pretty sure the second I'd realized Evan was Hope's child, I'd known.

Fate warning me to watch my step. Telling me it'd do me well to take one back.

And I'd just run forward. Careless.

Reckless.

Selfish.

Pushing and pushing for something I wanted, but knew, in the end, I couldn't keep.

The workday had passed in a daze. Every second had been a struggle to focus. A fucking herculean feat to pass out those damned lollipops like every single one of them didn't nearly drop me to my knees.

I finished with my last patient and stumbled into my office.

I sank down at my desk in front of my laptop.

I had to take care of this.

It'd been a constant nag at the back of my brain. Problem was, it'd been met with so much resistance from my heart and spirit that I'd been avoiding it like the goddamned plague.

Maybe I'd been holding out, thinking I might discover the cure before this feeling became a sickness.

Because that was what I felt.

Sick.

Taking this final step.

Snipping the last thread that tied us together.

I'd already spoken with Dr. Acosta about taking over Evan's care. I'd told her there was a conflict of interest, and I'd be more comfortable with her seeing him for his general visits.

The whole time I'd felt like I'd been committing a betrayal. Not because I couldn't be there for him as his physician. But because I couldn't be there for him at all.

I need you.

My chest squeezed when that voice hit me.

I tamped it down and clicked into his chart so I could write up my final notes on his care and transfer them over. That and send Hope the anonymous note that would let her know her son had the same heart defect that his aunt did, even though I couldn't dig deep enough to find the exact records that would confirm it.

Records that should have been there lost.

Purged or hidden.

I didn't know.

Either way, Hope would finally know.

At least I could give her this.

His chart popped up.

Evan Quinn Masterson.

A shudder rolled through me.

Unease.

A shrinking awareness.

Something was just intrinsically . . . off.

I'd been feeling it for days, a disturbance that flamed and lapped on the fringes of my consciousness. No doubt, part of it was the guilt over just walking out of their lives without giving a reason or explanation.

The guilt that I'd left them thinking it might somehow be their fault when

I knew I had to protect them from this. But there was something else. Something just out of my reach.

A light knocking tapped at my door, and my nurse popped her head inside. "I have those reports you were asking for. There is a reprint from two weeks ago that showed it'd been sent from the lab, but I didn't see it come across my desk."

"Who is it from?" I asked, looking at her from over my computer.

"The nuclear radiologist."

"Okay, thank you," I said, reaching out and accepting the small stack of faxes that had been forwarded from the lab and would need to be added to Evan's EHR.

"Anything else you need tonight before I head out for the evening?" she asked.

"No, I'm good. I'm just going to stick around and catch up on some charts."

She paused for a moment like she wanted to say something else. Clearly, she was worried about my state.

But there was absolutely nothing she could do for me to make this better.

I'd brought it all on myself.

She gave a slight nod. "Okay, then. I'll see you in the morning."

She clicked the door shut, and I turned my attention to the printouts, scanning the numbers and tests, trying not to break down in tears like a goddamned pussy.

But fuck.

I missed him.

I missed them both so goddamned much I felt like I was being torn limb from limb. Stretched so thin there was no chance there would be anything left.

I forced myself to move forward. I scanned one page and then another, moving onto the third.

My heart tripped the second my eyes started to move over the numbers.

It was the report from the nuclear medicine radiologist. The results of Evan's cardiac stress test. The numbers that we should have received two weeks ago.

The walls of my small office started to close in.

While I stared at the numbers on the paper.

They were the only thing I could see.

Only interrupted by flashes of Evan's trusting, sweet face.

The episode of severe shortness of breath at the park. The redness on his neck and cheeks that day at Rex and Rynna's. The way I'd asked him if he felt okay, and he'd said he was just tired.

Tired.

Tired because his transplanted heart was not pumping properly.

His records from earlier in the year had shown the very early signs of coronary artery disease, which was to be expected.

But this?

This was accelerated. Progressing at an alarming, dangerous rate.

Panic shot me to my feet, my chair tipping over and crashing to the floor as I clamored to grab my cell.

Frantically, I dialed the number I'd promised myself I'd never dial again.

In the same second, I flew out the door.

You're my favorite.

That promise roared in my ears.

Deafening.

My favorite. My favorite. My favorite.

Fuck.

This couldn't happen.

I wouldn't let it.

Not to him.

"Answer the phone, Hope," I begged under my breath, agitation lighting a path through me as I listened to Hope's phone ring and ring. On the fourth, it clicked over to voice mail.

That sweet voice hit my ear like a song. Mine was grating and hard when it finally beeped.

"Hope, I need you to call me the second you get this. I know you have to be pissed and confused, but this isn't about us. It's about Evan."

Ending the call, I raced down the hall and out the side door toward my car, feet pounding on the pavement.

Adrenaline surged.

A thunder through my veins.

My car blipped and unlocked as I approached, and I already had the engine turned over by the time I had the door closed. I threw the gear in reverse and whipped out of the parking spot.

The second my wheels hit the road, I floored the accelerator.

I weaved in and out of cars, trying to keep it together.

I told myself we'd caught it.

He'd be okay.

But it was that sense I'd been feeling all week—the one that warned something was terribly wrong—that reared its ugly head.

This dark foreboding that crawled beneath the surface of my skin.

Ominous and grim.

Shouting at me to hurry. That this was bigger than I could see.

I flew by the coffee shop. All the lights were off. It was late enough she'd already be gone for the night, so I took a sharp left turn, tires squealing as I skidded around the corner and headed in the direction of her house.

I floored the gas when I approached a yellow light, barreling through, unwilling to stop or slow, zigzagging between cars, pushing it harder and harder.

I careened around a corner and allowed myself a breath of relief when I made the last right onto their street.

I just needed to get there. Needed to know they were okay.

I slowed when I neared their house.

A disorder rumbled in my chest the closer I got.

An awareness.

An unease.

A sixth-fucking-sense.

I didn't know.

All I knew was the hairs prickled at the back of my neck, standing on end and sending a slow ripple of disquiet skating across my flesh.

It was different from when I'd seen the results of Evan's tests.

This was cold.

Protective and harsh.

A midnight blue car sat in front of Hope's house.

It almost blended in with the deepening twilight sky.

Almost.

All except for the fact it was one of those flashy bits. Not just nice. But the kind that screamed pretension.

The kind of car someone bought because they wanted you to know they were better than you in their own fucked-up, inflated heads.

I couldn't see anyone standing around it.

But I knew. I fucking knew.

My chest spasmed. Heart threatening to beat right through my ribs.

I didn't know how I'd look at him without pounding the bastard into the ground for what he'd done to Hope and Evan.

How I'd remain standing when I'd look at him and see *her* eyes.

This had to be the most savage, ruthless reminder of my failure.

But there was no consideration when Hope's porch finally came into view. No hesitation.

Because the fucker had ahold of Evan and was dragging him out the front door.

Hope screaming and trying to free her child.

Panic and terror rippled through the dense air.

And there was nothing but the base, fundamental need to protect these two.

twenty-nine

Hope

I sometimes wondered if people were born evil. If they were bred that way. If they had no chance of compassion. No chance of giving love or providing protection.

Or did life's tragedies and disasters seed it, allowing it to grow and grow until it was twisted and vile?

I wondered it as I came to an abrupt stop at the opening of the hall that led to Evan's room and found Dane Gentry standing in the middle of my living room.

Wearing one of his impeccable suits and hate in his eyes.

My heart climbed to my throat and my stomach sank to the floor.

Nothing but fear freezing my veins in shards of ice.

The instinct to protect Evan swelled inside me, and I pushed him farther behind me, my hand on his arm, trying to give him reassurance.

It did nothing to stop the quiver I felt shake through him, head to toe.

I couldn't let this happen. Not again. I had to find a way to put this madness to an end.

"Get out of my house," I warned.

Dane laughed a morbid sound and took a step forward. "Did you really think you could erase me so easily?"

My eyes went wide at the way he phrased it, my already pounding heart taking off at a sprint.

"I don't know what you're talking about." The defense trembled from my mouth. It might as well have been a confession of guilt.

A smirk ticked up at the corner of his mouth. Cruel and biting. "Always so innocent and pristine. Yet, she doesn't hesitate to tell lies or commit felonies."

An alarm sounded inside my head, so loudly I could hear it blaring in my ears.

There was no questioning it then. He definitely knew.

A shudder rocked my spine, and I gulped, lifting my chin and trying to pretend as if he didn't intimidate me when I was shaking so bad I didn't know how I managed to remain on my feet.

"This ends now, Harley. Get your things and get in my car."

My head shook. "You're insane," I told him again. He had to be. Crazy. Crazy for coming here. Crazy to think I'd just jump and do his bidding.

"Come with me now or rot in prison, Harley. Your choice. It seems like a simple one to me."

Or maybe I was the insane one. The one who had thought going down this road was smart. But at the time, it'd felt like the only way.

"I have no idea what you're saying," I maintained, but I knew it was a losing battle.

I knew there was no way to talk my way out of this with the way his eyes gleamed in victory.

Because he knew. Oh God, he really knew, and the true consequences of that were just sinking in when he took another oppressive step forward, coming closer and closer to my son.

My son who he wanted to reject. Do away with. Toss him aside like garbage.

Try again.

"I warned you that you'd regret it if you took this any further, Harley. And you've gone too far. Now get in my fucking car before I drag you there."

Sickness roiled. I was overtaken by desperation. Every nerve and cell in my body flooded with the wild, violent need to protect my son.

I could feel Evan peeking out from behind me. His small frame shook with fear and confusion, his silent questions ricocheting from the floors as if he were shouting them into the air.

He doesn't belong here, Mama.

This house is love.

My little man who thought it was his job to defend me when I would give my life defending him.

I took a step back, herding Evan with me. "Stay away from us or you'll regret it."

Incredulous, his eyes narrowed as he shook his head. "You think I'm going to regret it, Harley? You have it all wrong. You should have known better than to think you could play me. Now tell that kid to get in my car before I make him regret it, too."

"I'll die before I let you get anywhere near him."

I meant it.

But that didn't mean it wasn't the wrong thing to say.

Because rage lit on Dane's face. A match to gasoline. Two quick steps forward, and he had me by the upper arms. As if I weighed absolutely nothing, he tossed me out of his way and went straight for my son.

Panic seized every inch of my body as I flew across the living room.

It was an awareness taking hold. A deep-seated knowledge that I'd pushed Dane over a line. The same way as he'd done to me a year before. When he'd left me without a choice. When there'd been nothing else I could do.

All I'd wanted was to stop the torment.

To give my son the chance to live the life he deserved to live.

And this man was again exerting his horrible, brutal control. This time . . . this time, he was doing it with the force of his hands.

I screamed out as an excruciating pain splintered through my left side when I crashed into the sofa table set up behind the couch.

Frames that showed off Evan's innocent face fell to the floor. Glass shattering as it struck the wood.

Our best memories scattered across the floor.

I tumbled down on top of them. A wave of helplessness took me over. It was never supposed to be like this. I didn't know how to stand up against it. Fight it.

But that helplessness was eradicated the second I saw the horror blanket my son's face when Dane yanked him by the shirt. He started to drag him through the living room and toward the front door.

Evan's eyes went wide. So wide with an overwhelming terror that I scrambled to find my footing, my words screeching from my raw throat. "Let him go! He's just a little boy. Let him go!"

Dane didn't slow, he just issued his command into the air. "You're coming home with me now. Both of you. You no longer make the decisions. Do you understand me?"

Running after them, I grabbed at Dane's arm and tried to break his hold. "Let him go. He's just a little boy. I won't let you hurt him. Not anymore. Not anymore."

Dane spun around. With a single arm, he locked Evan's back to his chest. He stood there as if my son was a pawn. A twisted ransom held between us.

Contempt dripped from his tongue. "What does it fucking matter, Harley? Why are you clinging to nothing? *Nothing.*"

How could he say that? This was a little boy who was made up of flesh and bones and the brightest spirit. Made up of the biggest heart that beat life through his veins. A boy who was everything.

Hopeless tears streaked down my face, my soul fragmenting as I watched Evan kick and flail, frantic as he clawed at Dane's arm.

"Evan," I whimpered.

His feet kept giving out from under him as he struggled to break free.

His weight held in the palm of Dane's malicious hands.

Dane started backing through my house, his eye on me the entire time as he dragged Evan away. Expecting me to follow. This vile, horrible man using my child as bait.

"Dane . . . don't do this."

"You're out of chances, Harley."

"Why are you doing this?"

My steps were lurching as I moved toward them, and the words flooded from my mouth in a pour of desperation, "Dane . . . please . . . I'm begging you. Let him go. He doesn't deserve your anger. Your hatred. He never has. You are free. We are no longer a burden to you. A worry for you. I don't want anything from you except for you to let us go free. Just let him go and let us live our lives and you can live yours."

At my words, Dane's jaw clenched so hard I could hear his teeth cracking. "I will never be *free*. I will never be free of this."

"What does that mean?" I begged.

For the beat of a second, I wished I could go back to a time when I'd thought I understood this man. When I'd thought our hopes and dreams had been one. Before he'd become *this*.

A monster.

"Please." It ripped through the foyer. Breaking on my pain.

It didn't even touch Dane's rage. He jerked Evan through the door and out onto the porch.

Daylight was giving up its hold. It cast the world in shadows and mist and somehow set everything to slow motion.

A part of me felt detached. As if I were watching it happen from a distance. Removed from the reality that this man was really trying to take my son from me.

It had always been my greatest terror.

But I'd never known how great that terror could truly be until Evan started making these rasping, raking sounds.

Sounds I'd never heard him make.

His lungs brittle. As if my little boy was getting ready to crack.

Still kicking his feet, he stopped clawing at Dane's arm and instead reached for me as if he were begging for a lifeline.

For me to save him.

To keep him safe the way I'd always promised him I would.

"Evan, it's okay. Baby, it's okay. I won't let anything happen to you," I rushed, meeting his eyes, promising him through that connection that I wouldn't allow this to happen. That somehow, some way, I would stop this.

No matter what it cost me.

But Evan's face . . .

It was turning a purpled, beet red. Unnatural. Wrong.

A different kind of panic set in. Stretching out my insides.

Dane spun away and started for the steps. I launched myself onto his back, clawing at his face, screaming in his ear. "You're hurting him, Dane. Oh my God, you're hurting him. Let him go."

I was barely able to see through the haze that clouded my eyes.

This was where we'd come to a head.

Where we imploded.

Where this monster who held a thousand pounds of vile, ugly hate around his heart spiraled into a beast.

"You're hurting him."

I clawed and bit and kicked, but I knew I was no rival for Dane's physical strength.

But that didn't mean I wouldn't fight with everything I had.

I yelped when I was suddenly jarred back, my arms I'd locked around Dane's neck unloosed.

No.

But I was falling. Failing. I crashed onto the wooden planks of the porch.

"No!" The scream tore from my throat as I struggled to get back to my feet.

But it was relief that slammed me when I realized Evan had also been knocked free of Dane's malicious grasp.

It was blinding, cutting relief when I realized it was Dane who was colliding with the ground one second after a fist collided with his face.

A stunned gasp ripped from my lungs.

Kale.

He was there.

Oh, God, he was really there.

Kale dove for him, pinning him down at the waist as he began to pound his fists into his face.

Over and over again.

Shouts and grunts and punches.

Knuckles against buckling flesh.

Dane kicked and grappled. But he was no match for Kale's assault, and his wicked face quickly morphed into a river of blood.

Shocked, I watched wide-eyed and frozen as Kale beat Dane into an unconscious oblivion, my heart thundering so hard and my lungs rasping as I tried to process the scene.

It felt as if it took an age for my mind to catch up.

Kale had come back to me.

He was there.

Saving us.

I finally found a breath for my screaming lungs and managed to tear my attention away from Kale and Dane to look toward Evan. To give him a promise through my eyes.

That even though I'd never wanted him to witness anything like this—violence and bitterness and this savage, brutal war—I wanted him to know he would always be worth it.

My eyes found him where he'd been knocked to the lawn.

The second they did, my heart cracked in the center of me.

Evan was on his hands and knees. His expression was twisted in sheer, confused panic that had him seized.

Locked in pain.

It was one beat before his arms and legs gave.

My little boy fell to the ground.

Face down.

I screamed.

I screamed and screamed. But my screams were silent to my own ears. As if no matter how loud they were, no one would hear. No help to be found.

I crawled for him, half-rolling down the steps as I fought to get there. Everything was weighted, spindly tendrils reaching out from the depths of a nightmare to hold me back.

Because it felt as if I were slithering through quicksand.

Sinking.

Farther and farther away from him with each savage moment that passed.

It was a slowed motion I couldn't breach.

My entire body shivered when I reached for him and flipped him over.

He rolled, completely limp.

I couldn't stop shaking . . . shaking and shaking and shaking . . . when my hand fumbled out to press over his chest.

My heart. My heart.

This time, I heard it.

My scream.

The agony that tore out of me when I could no longer feel the beat of his little life.

My sun and my moon.

I couldn't see.

Couldn't hear.

And I swore, right then, all the stars fell from the sky.

"No," I raked over a sob, my hand pressing harder. Frantically searching. "No. No, no, no. Evan, no. You aren't going to leave me. I won't let you. No. Please."

A cry scraped from my throat when I was suddenly being torn away from where I clung to Evan, hands I'd missed so desperately squeezing me hard for the flash of a second.

Before he'd taken my place.

Kale.

Quickly, the man moved to kneel over my son. He tilted his ear to Evan's mouth then pressed his fingers to his neck.

For the beat of a second, horror struck on his face.

It was the exact same horror I'd seen him wear in my kitchen.

It was the kind of horror that destroyed worlds.

Despairing and desolate.

He started pumping Evan's chest.

My mouth dropped open in another scream.

A plea.

A prayer.

I didn't know.

No. No. No.

Kale's face broke into my vision.

His lips were moving, shouting, but I couldn't hear.

My son, my son, my son.

"Hope. Hope! Call 9-1-1."

Finally, the sound cracked against my ears, penetrating the horrifying daze, snapping me out of my stupor and into action.

I scrambled onto my hands and knees, slipping on the grass before I managed to get to my feet. Clinging to the railing, I fumbled up the steps and raced inside. It felt as if it took a lifetime to get to my room where my phone was charging on the nightstand.

A lifetime flashing.

A tiny infant in my arms.

"I'm sorry, but your son will require a heart transplant. It's the only chance he has."

M-A-M-A, he signed for the first time.

His grin. His smile. His belief.

Love. Love. Love.

Grief fisted me by the throat, and I ripped the phone from the cord and rushed back out, trying to see through the torment as I forced myself to remain steady enough to dial the three numbers.

I was already back outside and dropping to my knees beside where Kale was hunched over Evan when the operator answered.

"9-1-1, what's your emergency?"

"Help, my son. He's collapsed. He's a heart transplant recipient. Please . . . hurry."

I rattled off my address, begging the whole time.

"Ma'am . . . try to stay calm. Can you tell me if he's breathing? Does he have any other visible injuries?"

"No. Just . . . please . . . hurry."

"We have an ambulance in route. Please stay on the line with me."

Kale worked over Evan in a controlled desperation.

Hopefully.

Fiercely.

Grimly.

As if he could pump his own life into my son's body.

While I sat there, helplessly clutching my chest, trying to keep everything from spilling out.

Chills raked down my spine when I felt the shadow looming over us.

It was the evilest kind of darkness.

The man who stared down with animosity and a twisted sort of disbelief where Evan lay on the ground. To where Kale tried to save my son's life.

Then the monster bolted down the walkway and to his car.

His engine roared, and he sped away.

Gone.

The way I wanted him to be.

The sound of sirens whirred in the distance, growing louder and louder as they approached. Red and white lights flickered and flashed through the growing darkness in front of my house as a firetruck and ambulance arrived.

Paramedics swarmed around us, but Kale refused to budge from Evan. He shouted that he was a doctor, making orders, never pausing chest compressions.

Evan's shirt was cut up the middle and a mask was placed over his mouth and nose.

I cringed when an IV was placed in his veins. I hated it for him, how terrified my son was of that specific thing. His fear of needles. The way I'd always wanted to take away all of his pain.

But I'd never, ever been prepared for this.

In a scramble of activity, a defibrillator was set on the ground.

My entire body froze in grief when they set the paddles on his chest and a huge shock jolted his tiny body.

I was certain the entire earth held its breath as we waited for the line on the monitor to blip to life.

But there was nothing.

They administered another.

I could feel all the pieces I'd been trying to hold together fall away when Evan was shocked again and there was still no response. In horror, I watched as Kale went back to compressions as Evan was strapped to a backboard and placed on a gurney.

Kale never stopped his efforts when they moved Evan.

He climbed onto the gurney and straddled my son.

Pumping.

Refusing to give up.

And I prayed. I prayed, and I prayed, and I prayed.

Promising I would never give up hope.

thirty

Kale

Fear took me whole. Frantically, I ran across the lot and dropped to my knees at her side.

Her eyes rolled back. "Melody!" I shouted.
I searched for her pulse. For her breath.
Screams echoed through the air.
My shouts for help.
"I won't let this happen. I promise, I won't let this happen."
I pressed my hands to her chest and began to pump.
Compression after compression.
Teeth grinding together, I worked over her, begging, "Don't leave me. I won't let you leave me."
I fought and the sun spun out of the sky.
Darkness.
The world canted and tipped from its axis.
Everything shook.
Evan's face.
His little, broken body beneath my hands.
That fucking flat line.
A scream. A plea. Hope on her knees. "I need you. I need you . . ."

I bit back the roar that threatened in my throat, a clod of fear and desperation that took up the entire cavity of my chest.

I pumped and pumped and pumped as people moved around the trauma room in a controlled chaos.

I tried to shrug off the hand that landed on my shoulder. "Dr. Bryant . . . you need to step down. We have him. We have him."

"No!" I shouted, continuing to pump through the tears and the cries that raked from my soul.

No.

Evan.

Oh, God, no.

I wouldn't let this happen again.

I couldn't.

Another hand landed on my shoulder, and this time it was Dr. Krane's face that cut into my vision. "Dr. Bryant, we need to move him, and we need to do it now. I will do everything in my power to save him. I promise."

Grief tore through me as I looked down at Evan, to where I was still straddling him on the gurney, the precious little boy's face covered by the mask where one of the nurses pumped the bag.

"We have to move him," Dr. Krane said again in attempt to break through the   mayhem that scattered my brain and scrambled my spirit.

No. Evan.

My favorite. My favorite.

Feeling a piece of me rip away, I let two male nurses haul me off the gurney. Knees weak and my arms screaming from the exertion, I slumped forward, sucking for the nonexistent air.

I tried. I tried. I tried.

I would have given anything.

I'd never be enough.

Grief ricocheted from the walls as the trauma room door slid open, and they quickly wheeled out his tiny, broken body and moved him toward the elevators that would lift him to the surgical floor.

Open-heart surgery.

His only chance.

His last chance.

They'd already gotten Hope's consent. I couldn't imagine what she was feeling right then. The devastation she had to be dealing with.

Fuck. I wanted to take it from her. Shoulder it all.

I staggered out five feet behind them. Hopelessness swooped down, winding around me.

Destroying.

Dizzying.

Overpowering.

I tried.

I tried.

They stopped to wait for the elevator, and my attention was captured by the two big wooden doors that led out to the front entrance as it buzzed and swung open.

That awareness was back. Coasting across my skin like an omen.

A chill.

That sixth fucking sense that knotted my stomach and curled my fists.

Dane Gentry strode through, still wearing the suit he'd been wearing back at Hope's place an hour before, though, his crisp white shirt was smattered with blood and his fucking pretentious face, which he'd tried to wipe clean, was mottled with rising bruises and gaping cuts.

And I wished . . . I wished with all of me I hadn't stopped when I did.

That I'd ended the piece of shit the way he'd deserved to be.

Because there was no missing what was written all over Hope who was right behind him. She was screeching and clawing and trying to jump on his back to keep him away from her son.

The one she'd been living for because she'd always been living for the right things.

The best things.

Dane's voice boomed, a vile echo across the linoleum floors. "Stop what you're doing. That child has a DNR."

Hope screamed. A scream made up of fury and protection. A mother's fight. "He's lying. I would never sign that. Never. Don't listen to him."

Caught off guard, Dr. Krane paused to twist at the waist to check out the commotion behind him. He frowned, confusion and disgust lining his brow. "Excuse me, but I'm afraid I don't know who you are."

When the elevator dinged and the doors slid open, he turned back around and started to move forward, but Dane's voice was bellowing again. "I'm Dane Gentry, Evan's father."

Dr. Krane shook his head. "I'm sorry, but I have no idea who Evan Gentry is. If you'll excuse me, I have a patient to treat."

A blast of hot fury blew through me. I was already moving toward Evan as Dane approached. I'd fight to the end for that little boy.

With everything.

It was all I had left.

What I had to give.

The dickbag had no clue I was there, his attention all wrapped up on one goal. His disgusting ambition that was slowly beginning to make sense.

Those disordered pieces and threads that'd been dangling around me for close to the last two weeks finally coming together.

Seeping into my consciousness.

Dane's words hit Dr. Krane and his team from behind, "If you proceed, I will have your medical license. Your home. Your life. My attorney is on his way, so I suggest you stop whatever she has consented to. This woman's name is Harley Gentry, and that boy's name is Evan Gentry. She perjured his records."

Hope's sweet, sweet voice ripped through the air. Pain. Grief. She tried to scramble around him as she screamed, "No. Don't listen to him. Please, save my son. Save him!"

Her torment pummeled me. Wave after wave, and I didn't know whether to stand guard in front of Evan or rush the motherfucker and make it so he couldn't utter another word.

In the middle of everything, wondering if I would finally truly have something to give.

Because another of those pieces finally took hold. I'd looked through Evan's records what had to be a hundred times. Dane had never been mentioned once.

Not once.

The memory hit me, the plea that had been woven into her tone when she'd told me she'd do absolutely anything to protect her son.

Anything.

This amazing, giving, selfless girl.

Rage churned, and I stepped in front of Dane who was still making his approach.

I didn't give a flying fuck if I lost my medical license. My freedom. Whatever it took.

He tried to keep his arrogant chin lifted, but I saw the way the pussy's knees wobbled, the tremor in his misstep.

I shifted to look over my shoulder at Dr. Krane. "I assure you, Dr. Krane, there is no evidence of a DNR in that boy's file. This man is lying."

It didn't matter if he was or not. I'd gladly go down for this. For Evan. For Hope.

Dr. Krane hesitated, looking between Dane and Evan and me.

"Please . . . save him." I couldn't even manage to get sound into the words. It was just a silent plea.

Issued with every part of me.

Because if I could offer Hope one thing? It would be a chance for her son.

For her amazing, incredible son.

For a moment, Dr. Krane wavered before he cleared his throat and yelled, "Go, get his boy upstairs."

Standing there with my heart battering at my ribs, I watched as they rushed Evan into the elevator. It wasn't until the door closed shut behind them that I sensed the flurry of movement, the whoosh of air before I felt the connection of the fist against my jaw.

Pain splintered across my face and my head rocked back.

But I didn't care.

As long as Evan got his chance.

Hope screamed. Screamed my name so loudly it penetrated my soul, which I swore trembled and shook, stretching out for her.

Wishing it could reach her.

Impossible.

I knew.

But that didn't mean that connection between us wasn't real.

Feet knocked out from under me, I tripped and thudded to the ground. Instantly, Dane was on top of me, going for another blow. Roaring, I caught his wrist just before it connected against my eye.

I tossed him off.

It sent him reeling across the floor. He slammed into a metal file cabinet, head striking against the corner, body slumping to the ground.

I went for him, sitting up high on my knees when I cocked my arm back and let my fist fly. It cracked against his cheekbone. The already fragile skin split and blood poured out.

"Why would you do this?" I demanded, gripping him by the shirt in both of my hands. A new kind of frenzy rose inside me.

Hysteria and turmoil.

A need for Hope. Maybe a need for *me*.

Melody.

I blinked against the images of her face that flashed behind my eyes. That fucking flat line.

"Why? Did you know Melody was sick? Did you know *your sister* was sick?" My own sickness roiled when I thought of the possibility.

Melody falling to the ground, shocked by a pain she never could have anticipated.

I need you.

Hope yelped when I said it. "Your sister? Oh God. Kale. Oh God, the girl . . . your first love who you lost."

No doubt, the girl was catching on to my truth.

The second I'd realized the connection, I'd known the reality would break her in two.

God knew that it'd broken me.

But in the end, she needed to know this more than I did. For Evan. We needed the whole, complete truth for Evan.

I wouldn't stop until we had it.

I could feel her . . . her presence behind me, her cries biting into my skin. Fuck, I just wanted to take it all away. Make it better. Give her back her life.

"Fuck you," Dane spat.

I tightened my hold on his collar, making sure I was cutting off some of the airflow, my teeth gritting as I forced out the low, biting words, "Tell me .. . did you know that your sister was sick? That her heart was bad?"

Guilt streaked across his face before it was replaced with indignation.

He knew. Anger stretched hot across my chest.

"You bastard, you fucking knew." My hands constricted tighter, and his legs flailed, his pathetic hands coming to mine, nails scratching as he tried to break my hold.

"No. You're the one who was supposed to be the doctor. You should have seen it. You should have saved her."

Knives.

They cut and flayed. Slashes across my flesh. Cutting me to pieces.

Because I knew I should have. I should have seen. I should have stopped it.

But I'd ignored all the warning signs. Too busy and too wrapped up in my life to realize their importance until there'd been nothing I could do.

Melody.

My Melody.

"Tell me why, you piece of shit. Tell me."

I cocked my fist back, and he flinched, confession grit from his mouth. "My mother."

Just Dane mentioning Melody's mother threatened to knock me back on my ass, but I kept hold. "Why?"

He roared and struggled to break free.

I curled both my hands around his neck. "Don't assume I wouldn't think twice about ending you. Right now. I've already lost everything. I'd take pleasure in taking you down while I go."

He thrashed, and I tightened my hold, teeth grinding. "Tell me."

His eyes bulged with air loss, his own teeth clenched as he forced out the words. "My grandfather . . . he couldn't know it ran in my mother's family. She had a sister . . . a sister who died from the same thing."

Hope howled.

Dropped to her knees.

The space echoed with her anguished, jutting cries. Horror after horror. "The money. Oh God, the money."

Hope clutched her chest. "It was all about the money, wasn't it? You bastard . . . you bastard, you were gonna let your own son—your own flesh and blood—die over money? That goddamned inheritance? All that talk about your father's prestigious bloodline? It had to remain that way, didn't it? Prestigious and perfect. Without blemish? That's what your grandfather meant? You need a healthy son so you could get your fucking inheritance."

Dane's voice turned almost pleading, the bastard a believer in his own fucked-up, twisted way. "I told you, we could try again."

Hate blistered through my senses.

"You changed his name on his records. You tried to hide his medical records from me." Disgust lined Dane's voice.

Her head shook, lips trembling with the words. "You think I regret that? I'd do it again . . . over and over again . . . no matter what it cost me, so long as it protected him from you."

A sound left Hope.

One of sickened realization.

"Oh, God, you wanted me back because you needed me to have another child. So you could pin the genetic defect on me if you had another child with it?"

Dane's lips pursed.

So goddamned guilty.

But the bastard wouldn't admit it, he only grated, "You'll regret this, Harley," when I jerked him up by the shirt and slammed him down again.

Footsteps pounded around us. It wasn't until then that I realized we were ringed by nurses and bystanders.

Gaping, horrified eyes watched us from the perimeter.

Three security guards and a police officer had busted through the circle and were descending on us.

"Release him," the officer shouted at me, his gun drawn.

I was ripped up from behind.

Arms locked behind my back.

"Let me go," I raged, fighting as the cuffs were locked in place. I needed to get to him. To make sure he could never keep that promise.

End the threat for Hope and Evan once and for all.

Give them something when I could never be enough.

Dane was being hauled up, his knees buckling beneath him when his arms were twisted behind his back. "Twenty-million dollars, Hope. You're willing to let twenty-million dollars go?"

A roar blew from my lungs at his statement.

He said it as if she were the deranged one.

Because the piece of shit couldn't see through his black soul.

Melody.

I gasped over a breath when I realized what it all meant. What they'd been trying to hide.

Hope's face was twisted in the most shocking kind of grief as she climbed to her feet. Her milky flesh illuminated in the lights, glistening with tears.

She took a step toward him.

Red hair flying all around her.

So goddamned strong in her vulnerability.

Her chin trembled, and the words flooded from her mouth. "There was a day I believed in you, Dane. A day when I loved you. A day when I looked at you and I saw the future I wanted."

Her face pinched. "And all you saw was money?"

She blinked, trying to process the blow, before she swallowed hard, gathering herself. "I swear to you, if you so much as think about my son, I will make sure every last person in this world knows who you are and what you did. I will expose you and your disgusting family. I will ruin you, the way you have tried to ruin us."

She took another step toward him.

The girl always standing for what she believed in.

Faith radiating from her.

So damned bright.

"But we *are* not ruined. Not even close. When my son comes out of surgery, because he will—I *know* he will—I will have documents from your attorney relinquishing your parental rights. You will never have a say in his life, or in my life, ever again. Do you understand me?"

His voice was a growl. "You're a fool, Harley."

Mouth trembling, she shook her head. "No, Dane. You are the fool. You were so blinded by greed that you never saw the treasure you already held. The abundant life you could have been given. You are destitute, and I am the one who is rich."

The officer and guards began to haul us toward the entrance doors.

Anger ripped from Dane's chest, and his head jerked back as they dragged him away. "You will pay for this, Harley. You fucked over the wrong person. You won't forget who *I am*."

Just before they pulled me through the double doors, I twisted to look at Hope.

Those eyes met mine.

A mossy, earthy plane. Real and good and genuine.

The best thing I'd ever seen.

In that second, I wanted to promise her a million things.

That Evan would be fine.

That I would protect her.

That she would never hurt again.

Tell her I was so goddamned sorry. That I didn't know. That I would have stopped it if I could have.

That I'd be her hero.

But that just wasn't possible.

Not when I'd already destroyed everything.

Kale

I found her in the deserted chapel. Cast in shadows, the quiet space was illuminated only by the candles that had been lit and remained flickering through the deepest hours of the darkest night.

She was in the very front. On her knees. Red hair all around her where she had her head bowed forward.

That sweet body was shuddering and heaving with silent, wracking sobs.

I wondered if any distance could come between us when I might not be able to hear it.

Because I'd *heard* her through those six excruciating hours it'd taken to be released from the small city jail. My charges dropped, my assault labeled defense of a patient.

The whole time I'd felt like I was losing my mind because I'd heard it in my ear. Heard it in my heart.

I'd heard it through time and space and miles.

Her grief thick and profound.

Ingrained in me.

Marked in me.

I took another step forward.

Energy raced across the floor.

Saw it the second it slammed into her from behind. The way her spine jerked in awareness and that feeling rushed out in front of me.

Thick and heavy.

I took another tentative step forward. I might as well have been wading through quicksand, my steps laboring and heavy and slowed.

Going nowhere.

Or maybe I was just wading through honey.

Sweet, sweet heat.

I took another step down the middle aisle, and she jarred forward, bracing her hand on the floor in front of her as she gasped for a breath.

Swore, the flames on the candles shivered where they licked.

Two feet behind her, I came to a stop.

"Hope." Her name was a tortured murmur.

She choked, and all I wanted was to wrap her up. Hold her and make her all the promises I'd wanted to make all along. Knowing if it did, they would only be lies.

She rose on her knees, her hands flattened to her chest like that action was the only thing keeping her from completely falling apart. "It hurts so bad, Kale. So bad."

My throat was clogged, so goddamned tight and thick I could barely speak. "I should have recognized it. Seen it all along. It's my fault."

"No." It left her on a harrowed breath.

"Yes. I should have seen it. Just like I should have seen it in Melody. But I was too caught up, Hope, too caught up in what I felt for you."

Because of it, I'd done exactly what I'd promised myself I'd never do again.

I'd failed.

Old grief slammed me so hard that I rocked forward. Unable to stand beneath it, I sank down onto the front pew off to the side of her, elbows on my knees as I leaned forward, my face in my hands.

I could feel her peering over at me. Could feel the weight of her unwavering gaze. "You were there when we needed you most. You *came back*. Right when we needed you."

Bile swam. "It never should have come to that. I should have caught it the first time he came into my office. Instead, I spent the whole time thinking of touching you."

Wanting her.

Wishing for things I couldn't have.

I could sense her shifting on her knees, turning to face my direction. Disbelief oozed out on her words. "You're really gonna sit there and make that claim? After everything we shared? After the way you treated him? Like he was somethin' rather than nothin'? Like he might be your world the way you became ours?"

Grief stalked my throat, burning and choking. "I wanted to save him, Hope. I would have given anything. And now he's—"

Barely clinging to life.

I bit down on the words. Unable to even say them even though we both knew exactly what I'd meant.

He was barely clinging to life.

I'd gone straight to the ICU when I'd been released. Dr. Krane had just been leaving when I'd walked in. His expression had been . . . grim.

Worse than grim.

He'd touched my arm and promised me he'd done everything he possibly could. He hadn't filled me in like Evan was just another of my patients. His tone had been cautious, filled with sympathy I actually knew the guy truly felt, the jargon slim.

But I knew well enough what lay in his words and Evan's chart.

Evan had little chance of making it through the night.

A panicked regret swelled, constricting and suffocating. I couldn't breathe. "I tried."

I'd tried to save him.

Had tried to save Melody.

And it wasn't enough.

It wasn't enough.

I would never, ever be enough.

Her soggy plea filled the air. "Don't you dare give up on hope, Kale Bryant. Don't you dare. Not when we're finally free."

I forced myself to look up at her.

At this girl who had changed everything.

Green eyes and red hair and dimpled chin striking in the glow of the candles that sent shadows flickering across her gorgeous, unforgettable face.

The best thing I'd ever seen.

And that spark in the deepest part of me, the one she'd ignited, lapped and danced and begged.

I forced myself to stand, my smile weak. "I think you have enough faith for the both of us, sweet girl."

I'd no longer be the one who threatened it.

I swallowed around the misery. "No matter what happens . . . don't ever lose that. Don't ever give up on hope. It's the brightest thing I've ever seen."

I turned on my heel and started up the aisle.

I could feel her pushing to standing, her presence powerful as it slammed into me from behind, her words choked and rasping, "Don't you dare, Kale Bryant. You promised me."

I kept walking.

"I need you."

I need you. I need you. I need you.

Melody's voice twined with Hopes.

Torment.

Torture.

Agony.

I came to a standstill, breaths panting from my lungs.

"Who is it you're running from Kale? What are you afraid of? That the girl you loved was Evan's aunt? Their hearts? Or are you just afraid of lovin' me?"

I tried to stand upright under the crushing weight of the grief that surged and raged and slammed.

I forced myself to look at her from over my shoulder. "I'm afraid of what I've been afraid of all along. That I would never be enough. That I was chasing after something I couldn't have."

Seeing the heartbreak wash over her face, I turned back around and rushed for the door.

Needing to get out of there before I fell at her feet.

Before I begged her to let me try to be that guy I'd been pretending to be all along.

But that guy had only hurt her. Fucked up time and again.

I squeezed my eyes closed when her voice pierced me from behind. "The only way you can fail me is by walking away."

Grief clutched me in its fiery hold. Incinerating. Blistering.

Ash.

When I tore the door open to escape, I knew that was all that was left of me.

Hope

I'd always wondered how many broken hearts one person could endure.

Broken hearts meted out by unexpected tragedy.

Broken hearts delivered by the ones who were supposed to love them most.

True, physical broken hearts that struggled to continue to beat, marred by fate and health and genetic abnormalities.

Sometimes, I felt as if I could endure no more.

Kale had . . . crushed me.

I'd allowed myself to love him so freely. Love him so easily. Because I saw so much greatness in him. So much kindness in his giving, bleeding heart.

Maybe his heart had been broken one too many times, and he knew he could take no more.

I guessed I'd been right all along.

Had seen it coming the night he'd strode across the bar and slid into the stool next to me.

He'd looked like discord.

Chaos with an easy, arrogant smile.

A perfect, controlled disorder.

Just as I thought, the man had looked like a broken heart.

I sat next to my son—my life—in the darkened room where he lay in the middle of the elevated bed. Lights dimmed in the space. He was connected to a million tubes and wires, face covered in tape the same way he'd been as a tiny infant, the machine he was connected to inflating his chest as it pumped life into him.

Where his tiny body fought and fought and fought to conquer another broken heart.

And I knew sitting there, I would endure a million more broken hearts for him.

With him.

I jerked when I felt the presence behind me. I swiveled to look over my shoulder.

Dr. Krane stood there with a cautious smile on his face. "You're still here."

I almost laughed. "I'm not sure you could drag me out if you tried."

Four days.

That was how many days I'd been sitting in this spot, my mama and Jenna bringing me my meals. Keeping me company while I fought the gnawing that ate me from the inside out. Renewing my energy so I could in turn give it to Evan.

They hadn't expected him to make it through that first night.

I'd seen what was written in Dr. Krane's eyes when he'd come to me after the surgery to give me an update, and then I'd gone straight to the chapel.

I'd dropped to my knees and issued up unending prayers.

I'd given all my belief.

Had fallen on my faith.

My heart had always been hung on hope, and I sure wasn't about to give up then. Not ever.

"How is our little fighter today?" Dr. Krane asked.

Tears blurred my eyes. "Maybe I'm just being hopeful . . . but there's something different today. Like I can feel that he's closer. Like his little spirit is right here with me."

Dr. Krane took another step forward. "Don't sell yourself short. I think you know this little guy better than anyone, Ms. Masterson."

He hesitated for only a moment before he angled his attention my way. "I'd like to recommend that we start testing weaning him off the ventilator tomorrow morning. He seems to be gaining strength, and the last blood tests were stabilizing."

I couldn't tell if it was fear or relief that slammed me at his words.

My hope had never been cautious.

But today it was overwhelming.

A landslide of sensation. Because I'd been whittled raw.

Hurt in so many ways I had no idea if I'd ever heal.

My worry for this little boy, who radiated the biggest, brightest life, even from the depths of the coma he remained in, held there by medicines to give his broken body a better chance to rest and recover.

Not to mention, I was still reeling from what I'd learned, that Dane's sister had had the very heart defect Evan had.

I'd never met her. Dane and I had just married when she died, our courtship quick, a whirlwind I'd believed an intense kind of love. He'd said she was killed in an accident in another state and insisted I not attend the funeral. He'd claimed he'd needed his space to grieve, which I'd been confused by, but I'd respected it.

I'd just had no idea he had been pulling a veil over my eyes. Lying and lying and lying from the start.

Yesterday, I'd received the documents I'd demanded. Dane relinquishing his parental rights. Of course, it'd come with the stipulation that if I ever disclosed any information I had on his family, Dane would pursue charges of my falsification of Evan's medical records, the man vile enough to hold the threat of jail time over my head in order to protect himself.

But the truth of the matter was that I was willing to submit to that provision. Let it go, even though it felt as if I were doing Melody a disservice.

Melody.

My heart broke for her. For the greed that had kept her in the dark. Stolen her life. It broke for the man who had loved her and tried to save her and somehow had taken the burden that belonged to the *Gentry name* and placed it on his own shoulders where it never had belonged.

Then those pieces of my broken heart had been crushed when he'd left me. Because he couldn't stay through the grief. Because he couldn't bear any more. Because I'd fallen so hard and I no longer could picture my life without him in it.

But I'd bleed forever if it meant my son would be okay.

"We'll be monitoring him closely," Dr. Krane assured me. "At the first sign of distress, we'll increase him back until we know his heart is ready to beat on its own."

I twisted my fingers on my lap. Almost painfully as I looked at my son.

My heart.

I peeked up at Dr. Krane, the words laden with a plea. "And what do we do if that time never comes? What if he's never ready?"

Sympathy edged across his stoic features. "Then he'll have to go back on the transplant list. But we can cross that bridge when we get to it. Right now, let's cling to the fact he's doing so much better than we ever could have imagined. Could have hoped for. He is a true miracle, Ms. Masterson. I'm hopeful for a full recovery."

My miracle boy.

A single tear fell, and my chest clenched. So tightly. Gratitude and faith and remnants of fear. I reached out and gathered Dr. Krane's hand in mine. Squeezed it. "Thank you . . . for everything you and your team have done for him."

A soft smile edged his mouth. "Cases like this?" He gestured to Evan with his chin. "They're the reason people like us get up every morning to do what we do."

More tears slipped free, and I swiped at them, overcome. "He's going to be okay, isn't he?"

Dr. Krane gave me a slight nod. "He gets stronger every day. That's the only thing we can ask for." Something passed through his eyes. "And you need to make sure you take care of yourself. Get some rest. You'll need your strength for when he returns home."

Home.

THIS HOUSE IS L-O-V-E.

Everything clutched and clenched.

"I'll try."

"Okay, then. I'll see you in the morning." He gave me a soft smile before he moved for the door. He'd barely cracked it open an inch when he paused to look back at me. "You know he saved his life, don't you? We wouldn't be having this conversation if he hadn't made it to him when he did. If he had given up. He fought for him, and he saved him."

My lungs inflated, so light that I felt as if I might blow away. Or maybe I was the most solid I'd ever felt.

"I know."

His lips gave a slight twist at the corner. "All right then . . . I'll see you in the morning. Hopefully come then, we'll get to see this kid's smile."

When the door closed behind him, I turned back to Evan and gathered his little hand in mine.

Love came in so many forms.

For moments and for lifetimes.

Kale Bryant might have broken my heart.

But he'd left me with the piece he knew I needed most.

And that love?

It'd come to us at the exact, perfect time.

"My heart," I whispered.

Evan's eyes twitched behind his lids.

My heart.

This little boy who would forever hold it.

Kale

Blinding light glinted off my windshield. The Alabama summer was in full swing, the sun spraying darts of warmth across the green, abounding earth.

My driver's side window was cracked so I could take in every sense and sound.

Sweet, sweet heat.

Joy.

The brightest light.

Every cell in my body clenched.

Painfully.

Still, it was possibly the best feeling I'd ever experienced.

From a distance where they wouldn't notice me, I watched them.

My heart threatened to jump right out of my chest when Hope slid out of the driver's side and rounded the front of her SUV.

She helped Evan out from the back passenger side.

His homecoming was met with shouts and cheers from the porch where a ton of balloons swayed in the gentle breeze.

Jenna, Josiah's entire family—and a woman who had to be Hope's mother—were waiting.

Their excitement was palpable. Bubbling and binding to the atmosphere.

Hand-in-hand, Hope and Evan walked through the gate of the white-picket fence and up the pathway.

Their red, red hair glittered in the rays of sunlight that poured over them. It appeared like they were being drenched from above.

Saturated with blessings.

I could see Evan grin from across the space.

I'd been wrong that day in my office when I thought his spirit was bright enough to fill the entire room. Truth was, it was bright enough to fill the entire sky.

To light worlds and spark a million dreams.

They headed up the walk.

Maybe I tried to stop it, pretend it didn't exist, that it wasn't real. But that energy flashed, the attraction that had always been alive between Hope and me since the second I'd first caught sight of her.

It sizzled through the air like a crack of lightning.

I saw her spine stiffen in awareness. I thought maybe she tried to fight its existence before she gave and slowly turned to peer over her shoulder.

Like the girl could feel me the same way I swore I could feel her.

I swallowed around the emotion that knotted in my throat.

Intense.

Overwhelming.

Brutal and beautiful.

She stared back at me. The complexity of her expression was almost more than I could handle.

Sadness and overwhelming, stunning joy.

I met those mossy eyes, everything held in them so genuine and real.

I had to curl my hands around the steering wheel to keep myself from flying out the door and running that way.

Because fuck.

I wanted to go to them.

Wrap them up.

Hold them and keep them.

Instead, I sent her all my thoughts, hoping she could hear them. That she would tuck them away, hold them close to her sweet, sweet spirit.

I'm so fucking happy for you and for Evan. For your amazing, incredible kid. For amazing, incredible you. I'm sorry I couldn't have been better. That I wasn't enough.

My guts twisted as she stared back at me.

Brutally.

Because I wanted her. Wished for all the shit I'd been a fool to wish for in the first place.

But seeing them this way?

It was enough.

It was two when I pulled into the gravel driveway of the little house. I killed the engine and then just . . . sat there. Trying to get myself together. To put a goddamned smile on my face.

Tried to remember that this was what I lived for. My career and my friends that were really my family. They were supposed to be all I needed.

Problem was, the only thing I felt was empty.

Dropping my head, I squeezed the steering wheel and drew in a deep breath before I forced myself to open the door and get out. Milo was pawing and yapping at the window, almost as excited as the little whirlwind who came barreling out the door.

Hair flying.

Hugest smile on her face.

She threw her arms in the air.

"Uncle! You came, you came. I 'fought you forgot all abouts me."

Hit with a rush of that love I had for this kid, I swooped her up and hugged her close to my chest. "Forgot about you? What in the world would make you think that? You know I couldn't forget about my favorite girl."

She giggled like she thought it was the best thing she'd ever heard. "I knows that."

Her eyes went wide, and her voice dropped conspiratorially. Like she was getting ready to let me in on a deep, dark secret. "But Daddy told Uncle Ollie they were gonna have to drag your mopey ass over here 'cause yous were gonna ditch us 'cause you been way, way downs in the dumps."

My brow rose. "They said that, huh?"

"Uh-huh."

"Seems to me those two need to stop gossiping like a bunch of girls," I muttered under my breath.

Frankie Leigh made a horrified sound. "Gossip girls? Auntie Nikki loves *Gossip Girl.*"

Could this conversation spiral any faster?

"You don't love girls, Uncle? I'm a girl. I 'fought you love me?"

Yes. Yes it could.

A sigh pilfered free. How was I supposed to dig my way out of that one? "Of course, I love girls, Sweet Pea. Girls are the best. I just don't love my best friends who act like the gossiping kind."

"Likes my daddy and Uncle Ollie?"

"Exactly." I ruffled her hair. "And you know you shouldn't say that word."

Her eyes doubled in size. "What? Mopey?"

Rynna suddenly appeared in the doorway, holding Ryland to her chest. "You made it."

"Of course, I made it. Where else would I be?"

Rynna gave me a look that said I was full of shit, all mixed with a load of sympathy. "We haven't seen you in weeks. We weren't sure you were going to be able to make it."

Her tone held a distinct undertone of concern.

I settled Frankie Leigh on her feet and shoved a nervous hand through my hair. "Been busy."

That sympathy twisted on Rynna's mouth. She knew full well what my definition of busy meant.

I'd thrown myself into work in an attempt to forget.

It was exactly like I'd done all those years ago. But this time, shoving it all down, hiding it in that secret, dead place, didn't seem to work.

It only seemed to emphasize the hollowed-out vacancy that throbbed inside me.

A festering wound that didn't get any smaller the more time that passed.

It just gaped and yawned and expanded.

Growing bigger each day.

Six weeks had passed since I'd sat down the street from Hope's house and watched Evan's homecoming. Thing was, I couldn't help but seem to torture myself. Thinking about them constantly. My car automatically slowing every time I drove by A Drop of Hope because I was desperate for just a glimpse.

To see Evan whole and healthy.

To see the joy etched on Hope's face.

Every patient I saw only reminded me of the brightest smile, those adorable bug eyes blinking at me from behind those thick glasses, fingers flying with silent words that hit me like the sweetest sound.

Didn't know what was worse—that or the nights I spent tossing and turning through the loneliness. Waking up aching, body straining and hard, wanting Hope in a way that was almost depraved.

Desperate and hopeless.

Seconds from sending me over the edge.

"Come on. Everyone's already out back. Oh, and you're officially on uncle duty," Rynna said. Without a whole lot of warning, she was passing Ryland off to me.

I took him in my arms.

My chest grew tight at the feel of him.

Squeezing and pressing and prodding.

Instantly, he calmed, brown eyes staring up at me like he was trying to figure me out.

Mesmerized.

Or maybe that was just me.

It was amazing the way this tiny thing immediately trusted me to protect him. To take care of him. Always do right by him.

I gulped around the shards of glass that raked my throat.

I wasn't sure I knew what that meant anymore.

"You do have the magic touch, don't you?" Rynna asked over her shoulder as she turned and headed around the patio that wrapped around to the back of the house.

Lillith, Brody, Nikki, and Ollie were already hanging out around the patio tables.

Rex at the grill.

I was struck with how similar it felt to that day all those weeks ago. Yet, every-fucking-thing was wrong.

All wrong.

Ollie grinned at me from where he sat at the table, sipping a beer. "Well, well, well, look who's here. Here I thought you'd forgotten all about us."

I sent him a death glare. "So I heard."

Asshole was worse than a nagging mother, getting all up in my business like he belonged there.

But I guessed the dude had earned a free pass since he'd been the one who'd shown up at the police station in the middle of the night to pick up my pathetic ass. He had driven me straight back to the hospital so I could get to Hope and Evan.

The whole way, he hadn't said a word. He'd just allowed me to be silent in my grief, his voice grating with sincerity just as I'd been jumping out the door. *"So fuckin' sorry, man. Know what they mean to you. What Melody meant to you. Know what you're going through right now. If you need me, I'm just a call away. Don't hesitate, brother."*

I'd given him a tight nod before I'd bolted out.

Because Ollie got it in a way I didn't think anyone else could.

I took a seat under one of the umbrellas and snuggled Ryland against my chest, lightly rocking him. The kid was out cold in about three seconds flat.

Rynna passed by behind my chair, reaching out to touch my shoulder as she went. "I'm really starting to get a complex over that, you know?"

I forced myself to smile. "Apparently the kid knows when he's in the presence of greatness."

"I think he just knows when he's safe."

A rush of grief threatened to strangle me. Suck me in and pull me under where I'd drown forever.

Lost in just . . . nothingness.

I swallowed around it, telling myself that this was the only thing I needed. My career and the people I cared about most.

I settled into it.

The warmth.

The care.

The love.

I enjoyed the afternoon the best way I could.

Rynna had taken Ryland to his crib so he could sleep, and I tried to sit back and relax. Listen to the conversations going on around me.

Join in.

Clearly, everyone was walking on eggshells. Watching me carefully.

Waiting for me to break.

No doubt, it was time I got over this shit. Put it behind me. Because I couldn't go on like this forever.

Rupturing.

Hemorrhaging.

Splintering, day by day.

I ate my meal as if I didn't have to force it down and then sat back to watch as Frankie Leigh twirled across the lawn, doing all these awkward jumps and leaps, which were so adorable it had my chest clenching again.

I loved that little girl so much.

Found it impossible not to think about her out there with Evan.

He said he's gonna marry her.

Hope's expression flashed through my mind.

Adoration.

Evan's emphatic nod when I'd asked him what he'd thought about Frankie Leigh.

A wistful smile pulled across my mouth.

Unstoppable.

That feeling I'd been fighting rose so quickly I was sure it was going to demolish me.

Lay me to waste.

That feeling I couldn't afford to name. The one that kept pressing and prodding and picking me apart.

Limb from goddamned limb.

I sucked in a shuddered breath and tried to rein it in.

Rex plopped down across from me. "You ready to talk about that?"

He pointed at my face like my expression was evidence of some kind of crime.

The conversation happening around me immediately fell into silence. Like every single one of them had been waiting for this moment.

All eyes on me.

I shifted uncomfortably in my seat.

Had to wonder if I'd actually been invited over for a barbecue or if this was some kind of intervention.

God knew, Rex had just put me on the spot.

My head barely shook. "Don't see that there's much to talk about."

"Is that so?" His voice was incredulous.

"Yup." It was sharper than I intended.

"Huh, seems awful backward to me, considering you're the punk who never hesitates to set me straight."

I sipped my beer and turned my attention out across the lawn, to the wall of towering trees that blew in the wind. "And what exactly are you setting me straight about?"

From my side, Ollie scoffed. "How about the fact you're fucking miserable, man. Let's start there."

"I'm fine."

"Really?"

"Really."

Nikki's face pinched, her lips pursing together like she was stopping herself from unleashing on me.

But it was Lillith who spoke from where she was snuggled up to Brody at the next table. "You don't seem fine to me, Kale. Not at all."

Ollie pointed at her. "What she said."

I roughed a hand over the top of my head. "Just . . . don't."

It came out a warning. I was about five seconds from jumping to my feet and bolting.

"Don't what?" Rex demanded, leaning in closer. "Make you open your eyes the way you've always done me? Last time I checked, you were zero bullshit, and now you've got bullshit written all over you."

"Told you a long time ago, all I need is you guys and my job. I was stupid to think that'd changed."

"What's stupid is you thinking you don't deserve to love."

That feeling was back. Pushing and pushing into my consciousness.

Too fucking close.

My heart stumbled in its tracks before it took off sprinting.

Regret cinched down on every cell in my body, and my words dropped to next to nothing. "I failed them, man."

"Did you?" he challenged. "Because from what I know, it sounds a whole lot like you saved him."

"I missed it. I was his doctor, and I missed it."

Nikki exhaled, the sound almost pained as she scrambled around so she could meet my eye. "You think you missed it, Kale, but what if you hadn't been his doctor? What if someone else had missed it, too, and they didn't know him the way you did? What if you hadn't gone to them the day you did? What then?"

Sorrow clutched and gripped and bit. My soul feeling like it was being shredded.

What if I hadn't shown up when I had?

I couldn't process it. Couldn't begin to fathom a fate that cruel.

"It never should have happened in the first place."

Ollie's brow pinched, and he tugged at his beard in frustration. "But it did, man. It did, and you were there, and you saved him. So maybe that's what you need to be focusing on instead of this bullshit excuse that you let them down."

His blue eyes beat against mine. "Unless you were just another asshole with a cold heart who was looking for an excuse to drop some chick and not look like a bastard doing it."

Spears.

Straight through the goddamned heart.

"You know that isn't it."

"You sure about that?" he provoked. "Because I bet that's exactly what that girl is thinking. Hell, she's probably over there thinking you used her up and then tossed her aside. On to the next."

A growl rumbled in my chest.

Rejection.

Anger.

"Fuck you, man, I love her."

I love her.

The heated words were out before I could think through the impact.

A motherfucking bomb that exploded in the air. Decimating me.

Ollie rocked back in his chair. Satisfaction on his face. "That's what I thought."

Unable to breathe, I dropped my face into my hands. Crushed anew. Or maybe I'd been right there all along. Like they thought.

They'd been waiting for me to break.

I guessed they'd gotten their fucking show.

Because I was.

I was fucking broken.

I could feel Ollie leaning in closer, his voice dropping. "You can be pissed at us, man. I get it. Kick my ass if you need to. But I'm willing to take on your wrath if it'll get you to admit the truth."

Bitterness soured on my tongue. "Yeah, and what's that?"

"That you're fucking scared, man. Scared to love again. To fail someone when you're the first asshole to run in and save them."

I opened my eyes to find Frankie Leigh had appeared at my side. She cocked her head in question. "Yous scared, Uncle Kale? 'Cause Cap'in 'merica is never scared."

She tapped her little finger to her chin like she'd just been struck with an epiphany. "Wait a minute . . . maybe he is scared, and he saves all the people anyway."

She looked to Rynna who was standing just off to the side. "Right, Mommy? That's what brave is, being scared and doing what's right anyway because you love someone so, so much?"

Rynna ran her fingers through Frankie's wild, wild hair. "That's right, Sweet Pea. Being brave is being afraid and doing what is right anyway. Just like when your daddy ran into the fire to save us . . . he was scared, but he knew he would do whatever it took to save us. He came right when we needed him most."

Rynna looked over at me. "Just like your uncle Kale rushed in to save Evan right when he needed him most. I just don't think your uncle knows how very brave he really is."

Frankie started hopping across the wooden planks, singing, "Daddys and doctors are so, so brave! They come to save the day! Superhero, superhero, superhero. And I'm Wonder Woman and I'm brave, too!"

She threw her arms in the air with her silly song that to most would mean nothing, when it felt like it just might mean everything. She turned back to me with the biggest grin stretched across her face. "See, Uncle, you don't needs to be sad any more. You are so brave and you did all the right things. Even if you're scared, you are still Evan's bestest team."

My heart thrashed and my spirit soared.

Because, no, I hadn't done all the right things.

But I knew exactly what I needed to do.

thirty-four

Hope

I rushed out from A Drop of Hope's kitchen, my heels clicking on the floors, my knees feeling a little shaky.

I wasn't sure I'd ever been so nervous in all my life.

Sensing the movement, Evan spun around where he was standing by the inside of the cupcake display case. When he saw me, he smiled a smile so powerful it penetrated right through the center of me.

Moving forward, I grabbed him by either side of his precious face, my thumb swiping across his cheek to clean off the smudge of frosting. "Someone's been sneaking into the display case again."

He nodded in my hold, that smile somehow growing stronger, my little man all dressed up in a suit, and his normally messy hair tamed with product.

Just looking at him sent my bottom lip trembling. "You look so handsome."

His little hands flew between us.

YOU ARE THE PRETTIEST MOM IN THE WHOLE WORLD.

"You think so, huh?" I asked, trying to settle the jittery nerves that scattered through my insides, twisting up my tummy in pride and apprehension.

Jenna popped her head in through the front swinging door. "Are you two ready yet? We're gonna be late if we don't get out of here."

ARE YOU READY? I signed.

YUP!

LET'S DO THIS.

I took his hand and wound us around the front counter and toward the entrance. I clicked off the last light in the shop before we stepped out into the evening, the air still full of humidity and warmth.

Still, a chill skated my skin.

Sucking in a deep breath, I moved for Jenna's car, which was idling at the curb, and helped Evan into the back before I climbed into the front passenger seat.

The second I clicked my buckle, Jenna pulled out onto the street.

"This is so gonna wrinkle up my dress," I said, another dose of that worry injecting itself in my veins.

"Don't even start, Harley Hope. You look gorgeous. You're gonna be the prettiest girl in the whole place."

Funny how I'd never had stage fright for a second of my life. But this felt different. As if I was getting ready to let a room full of strangers view the most sacred part of me. But that didn't mean I wasn't incredibly honored to be invited.

To be a part of it.

I fidgeted with the skirt of my designer black dress, the one Jenna had dragged me out to some upscale boutique downtown to purchase for the event.

An event that was being held at Gingham Lakes Children's Center.

The second I even let the thought enter my mind, moisture was threatening at my eyes. I fought off the tingly sensation that raced my throat.

This was definitely not the time nor place to get lost in that vacancy that echoed inside of me.

I only allowed myself it in the darkest hours of the night. When I was alone, and I was free to let the loss I was dealing with consume me. When I allowed myself to miss him. To ache for him. My body pleading and my heart begging for him through the silence.

I gave myself the time to feel it.

The pain.

The loneliness.

Let the *what-should-have-beens* cry out from my spirit.

Just for a little while.

Then I got up the next morning with a staggering amount of thankfulness.

Told myself, *someday*. Someday I'd find the man who was meant for me. The one who completed me.

The hardest part was Kale had fit every single one of those spaces.

Filled them perfectly.

I gave a little yelp when I was poked in the side.

"There you are, Harley Hope Masterson. Here I was, thinking I was gonna have to crawl around in that head of yours and rescue you from wherever you went. Because you sure seem to be going there a whole lot the last few days."

I choked back the thick clot of emotion. "Just thinkin'."

Clinging to the steering wheel, Jenna glanced over at me and then turned back to the road. "And just what are you thinkin' about? Or more specifically, who?"

I gave her a shrug. "No one."

It might as well have been a shout of his name from the rooftops.

Kale. Kale. Kale.

Because it was always right there.

An echo in my consciousness.

The man carved into me.

"Will he be there?" she asked.

Flinching, I shook my head. "No. I saw the guest list. He isn't on there. I'm sure he knew it'd be too hard on us to see him."

Her jaw clenched. "He owes me his dick, you know? Told him I was gonna cut it off if he hurt you. And that man *hurt* you."

A crashing wave of it hit me from out of nowhere.

Covering me whole.

Hurt.

She was right.

Kale had *hurt* me.

A tear streaked free, and my voice cracked when I whispered, "How's it possible to be so thankful for someone and devastated by them at the same time? It feels like I'm torn right in two, Jenna."

"It would be wrong if you felt any other way, Harley Hope. He saved your son's life, but that doesn't give him a pass for walking out on you."

I wiped the back of my hand across my dampened cheek, trying not to smudge my mascara as a shot of frustration took hold. "That's the problem . . . I want to give him that pass, because he gave me back my world. I just didn't know that, in the end, he'd leave such a huge piece of it missing."

A heavy breath pulled from my lungs.

Weighted.

A thousand pounds of sorrow.

I looked at her. "Does that make me crazy?"

Her head shook. "Of course not. It makes you Hope. Who you are. I just wish he would have seen you for what you are."

My attention shifted away, and I blinked out the windshield at the buildings whizzing by. "I'm not sure him walking out had anything to do with me. I just don't think he could handle it. Seeing Evan that way . . . after going through it with Melody."

A quiver rocked through me when the memories flashed.

Evan collapsing.

Kale right there. Fighting for him. Refusing to give up.

Saving him.

My son.

Emotion bottled high in my throat, and I choked around it. "I forgive him, Jenna. I forgive him, and I refuse to regret loving him. No matter what kind of pain he left behind."

She reached over and squeezed my hand. "Then don't. You don't need to feel guilty for loving him. He's the one who's missin' out."

I glanced back at my son, who was drawing another picture of Captain America on his sketchpad.

He'd been doing it nonstop since he'd come home from the hospital eight weeks ago.

Dealing with his own kind of grief.

The man who'd come to mean so much to him had become his own loss.

Evan's heart on the line, the same as mine.

I couldn't count the number of times I'd found him silently crying. Angry and confused by the fact Kale had saved him and then turned around and left us.

HE PROMISED HE WOULDN'T HURT YOU. THAT HE CARED ABOUT US. HE'S NOT SUPPOSED TO HURT YOU. THAT'S THE RULE, he'd signed, driving another stake right into my demolished heart.

Our kinship so profound because he was a prisoner to the same confusion as I was.

This intense, overpowering gratefulness for a man who'd walked away in the end.

But somehow, I understood he couldn't stay and have to face the same ghosts every day. That it wasn't anything Evan or I had or hadn't done. It just hurt him too much to stay.

And I could only be thankful for what he'd given while he was there.

His time purposed.

Purposed for us.

"Someday," I whispered beneath my breath. "Someday."

Two hours later, I was sitting at one of the round banquet tables up close to the stage.

Balloon bouquets were set up all over the enormous space, twinkle lights were strung up across the ceilings, and extravagant floral arrangements were set in the middle of the linen-covered tables.

Our plates had just been removed after we'd finished the gourmet dinner.

Evan was to my right and Jenna was to my left. Dr. Krane and his wife sat to the other side of Evan, and a few people I'd never met before took up the rest of the round table.

The gala had been setup in a conference room, the collapsible walls opened to accommodate the three hundred guests who'd been invited.

The fundraiser was for Gingham Lakes Children's Center, and while some of the guests were staff and families who'd been helped by some of the center's programs, the lions share were Gingham Lakes's affluent, there to open their pocketbooks to support GLCC Charities.

Minus the Gentry's, of course.

"Thank you for all your support," the chairman of the board for NICU Services said as he completed his speech. Those nerves surged and spun, my stomach growing tight.

I was up next.

I'd memorized the program.

William Wright would speak, then Martha Jiminez, one of the event organizers would introduce me. I clapped for William Wright while anxious wings fluttered and scattered through my entire body. My eyes dropped closed for a moment so I could mentally prepare myself for Martha to step out to take his place.

The clapping died off and a ripple of confusion rolled across the room, a quiet anticipation taking hold to each person in attendance.

Though for me, that anticipation thundered and boomed.

A spark to the air.

I pried my eyes open and gasped when I saw who stood at the podium.

That crazy attraction that climbed to the air. It came alive between us where he stood up there dressed in a fitted black tux.

Potent.

Powerful.

Persuasive.

Kale.

The man was a perfect chaos.

My mouth went dry.

His hair was styled in that immaculate way, every part of him put together.

Commanding and bold.

But I saw beneath that gorgeous exterior. Everything about him tonight was abraded and raw.

So intense I could feel the emotion coming off him like a shockwave.

Under the table, Jenna pinched my leg, her eyes wide when I looked at her. "What is he doing here?" she whispered under her breath.

I gave her a short shake of my head.

I had no idea.

Hadn't expected this.

God, I didn't even know if I could handle it.

He cleared his throat. "I know your programs say Martha Jiminez should be standing up here right now to make this next introduction . . ."

He let a small smirk climb to his full lips. "There's a chance I might have bribed her to let me stand up here tonight, but don't blame her, I've been known to be a little convincing when I need to be."

A small wave of laughter rolled through the room.

Because there stood that cocky, arrogant boy.

A second later, a quiet somberness filled his expression. "But the truth is, I would have paid anything to get to stand up here and make this introduction, because this charity is so incredibly important to me. As a pediatric physician here at Gingham Lakes Children's Center, I have the honor of treating patients with many different illnesses and chronic diseases. There is no better feeling than getting to take part in their care. To maybe have the chance to make their lives a little better."

Those blue eyes locked on me.

Penetrating.

Infiltrating and invading.

A shiver rocked through me, and Evan stirred in his seat, his own surprise coming off him in waves.

"And sometimes, it's the patient who makes *our* lives better. The patient who touches us in ways we never could have expected. The patient who teaches us what true hope looks like."

His voice grew thick, and moisture grew heavy in my eyes.

What was he doing?

Ruining me. That's what. I had no idea how I was going to make it through this. And still, nothing felt more right than him standing up there.

He let his gaze bounce around the room. "I'm standing up here tonight with the great honor of introducing our next charity represented here this evening, A Lick of Hope. A Lick of Hope is a foundation created to support children born with heart defects and their families."

He looked down at the folded sheet of paper he'd brought up with him and cleared his throat before he started to read it.

"A Lick of Hope has raised over two hundred fifty thousand dollars this year alone," he said. "Their mantra reads, 'Anything is possible if you have A Lick of Hope.' After having the honor of getting to know this charity's head and its inspiration, an amazing little boy who taught me exactly what that hope looks like, I am now a true believer of this statement."

My ribs squeezed my heart. Or maybe it was just my heart that was struggling to break out. Desperate for its match.

His head dropped for a moment, as if he were gathering himself, before he looked up and met the crowd. "As physicians, we wake up each day with a huge burden on our shoulders. The health and wellbeing of the little people we get to see and treat. Sometimes that burden can be overwhelming. Wearing. Scary."

Overcome, he sucked in a breath. Finally, he pressed on, "A Lick of Hope was created and is headed by an incredible woman and her son who reminded me what being a doctor is truly about. It's about faith and belief and never, ever giving up, no matter how hard it might be. That even through our losses, our failures, we get up and fight all over again."

My blood thundered through my veins, a torrent of emotion when he turned that magnetic, knowing gaze on me.

That connection pulsed.

Alive.

Begging and prodding.

"I am so incredibly proud to introduce the heart of A Lick of Hope, Harley Hope Masterson."

A thunder of applause echoed through the room, and tears broke free of my eyes. Overwhelmed, I pushed to standing on my high heels, still caught in the stare of this beautiful man.

Evan was beaming up at me, getting onto his knees on his chair as he frantically waved his hands in the air.

My child unable to hear the sound but no doubt swept up in the vibration.

I touched his sweet chin before I turned and headed for the steps that led to the stage.

Wobbly.

Lightheaded.

Because this man made me that way.

Vulnerable and shaky as he stared down at me as if I were his world.

Hope.

It threatened to bloom in my spirit.

I beat it back and focused on what tonight was all about.

I moved through the intensity that bellowed from the walls.

At the bottom step, I just . . . stopped. Turned around and stretched my hand out for my son.

He was just as big a part of this endeavor as I was.

Truthfully, more.

The inspiration of it.

The lifeblood of it.

And he'd worked his little fingers to the bone helping me make those lollipops.

His grin was magnetic when he saw my invitation. So huge when he scrambled down from his chair and raced for my side.

The room lit up in *awws* and whistles and sweet sounds for my son.

My miracle boy.

I gathered his hand in mine and we moved up the steps toward Kale.

Kale who stepped back and stuffed his big hands in his pockets and stared at us with this adoring, proud, sorrowful expression on his face.

So sincere.

For a moment, we were stuck there, lost to the other, before he leaned in and brushed his lips against my cheek. "I am so proud of you."

Energy flashed.

Ignited.

Chills racing across my flesh.

He ran his knuckle across Evan's cheek before he turned and headed down the side steps and down the aisle.

Barely able to stand, I moved to the microphone with Evan's hand still wrapped in mine.

I swatted at the tears clouding my vision, clearing my throat as I released a nervous laugh and looked out at the still-cheering crowd.

"Thank you all so much for being here. I know A Lick of Hope is a small charity compared to others here, but it means the entire world to me, and I'm incredibly honored to be invited to speak tonight."

I lifted Evan's hand in the air. "And this little boy . . . Evan . . . he's the reason I'm here tonight."

My tongue darted out to wet my dried lips, still feeling the weight of Kale's stare from where he'd moved to the very back of the room at the entrance doors.

"When my son was born, the first thing I wanted to know was if he had ten fingers and ten toes, and when I held him for the first time, whole and perfect in my arms, I'd never been so happy in all my life. I had no idea that we soon would be in for the fight of our lives."

Emotion swam and churned, and I glanced down at my boy, who was still swaying at my side.

It was easy to find my strength in his bravery.

"I'm not sure there could have been anything to prepare me for learning that he had a severe heart defect. Nothing that could have been said to prepare me for the moment I was told my tiny newborn would need to be flown to another state to undergo emergency surgery to save his life. And there was absolutely nothing that could have equipped me for the devastating news just months later that if he were to live, he would need a heart transplant."

Evan shifted at my side, and I glanced down at him to find him smiling this smile that was so full of love that it nearly bowled me over.

He's the reason I dream.

I looked back to the crowd. "My son might have been born with a heart defect, but it most definitely didn't change the size of it. He's the most genuine, caring little boy I have ever known, and for all the years I can remember since he learned to sign, he's said prayers at night, hoping that no more babies would be born with bad hearts."

I cleared the lump from my throat, so in awe of my child.

For what he'd gone through.

For what he'd accomplished.

For the incredible person he'd become.

"From those prayers, A Lick of Hope was created. And we share that hope with every lollipop we make."

A wobbly, grateful smile pulled to my mouth. "That hope is spread with every lollipop that is purchased and every donation that comes in. Because we will never give up hope that one day, no child will have to go through the pain and struggles my son has gone through. That no parent will ever have to hear the words that their child may not make it through the night. That, through research, congenital defects will be easily repaired, and maybe someday . . . someday . . ."

Someday.

The words stumbled on my tongue and my gaze fumbled to Kale at the very back.

The man just a silhouette.

The most profound thing I'd ever seen.

I finally managed to find my words again. "That maybe someday they won't exist at all. We couldn't do it without every five-dollar lollipop we sell or the amazing donations and contributions that come in every day. So, thank you . . . thank you for your support. And if you're so inclined, we have some of those handmade lollipops available in the auction tonight. Each one is made with love and our gratitude to you."

I stepped back, and applause broke through the room. But my sight was sealed on the man. On his slow, sad smile. The pride behind it.

Then he turned and disappeared out the door.

And I wanted to hate him and hold him. Scream and drop to my knees.

Instead, I fumbled back to my table.

Evan climbed onto his seat and turned to me, confusion and anger and hope billowing across his precious face. *HE CAME BACK.*

My mouth trembled because I had no idea what that meant. Why he'd done what he did.

But hope, it blistered and radiated and beat.

So intense, I kept shifting on my seat, struggling not to come out of my skin as I listened as the next charity head was introduced then the next and the next until finally the auction was opened. The guests filtered out into the next room to bid on vacations and diamonds and a donated car.

And our small offering.

A thousand lollipops.

As everyone filtered out, I looked to my son, who was clearly growing sleepy. I ran my fingers through his hair before I signed, *ARE YOU READY TO GO HOME, SWEET BOY?*

Yes, he mouthed before giving me a tired grin, and the smile I returned was adoring. Because I was so proud and happy, even though there was a huge part of me that was feeling brittle.

Those broken pieces moaning at the sight of Kale.

The man who'd changed everything.

Who gave me the greatest gift and then stole what could have been.

"Let's go," I said, offering my hand, Jenna at my side. We said our goodbyes to Dr. Krane and his wife before we headed up the aisle.

Jenna sidled up to me. "Oh, Harley Hope, you are in so much trouble, my friend."

Trouble.

I'd always known he'd be.

"That man does know how to make an entrance, doesn't he, standing up there looking that way. Mmm . . . all that deliciousness. Think that man sent every woman here into a swoon."

She fanned herself. "He does not fight fair. One look, and he knew you'd be nothin' but putty in those big ol' hands."

"Stop it," I scolded her under my breath, stepping out into the courtyard that fronted the conference building. "He just wanted to be here to support A Lick of Hope. That's all. He left me, Jenna. He left us. Let's just leave it at that, okay?"

"How about we don't?"

That deep, powerful voice hit me from the side.

My fragile heart pulsed.

Kale stepped out from the shadows, his hands still stuffed in his pockets.

Moonlight poured in from above, striking against all the curved, defined angles of his beautiful face.

Evan squeezed my hand almost frantically when he realized Kale was standing right there, two feet away from us.

"What are you doing here?" The words were a frenzied whisper.

"Stalking you, clearly." He fought for the joke, but that mouth only managed to minimally tweak up at the side. Too heavy with the sadness that rimmed his lips.

I could feel my son's own turmoil. The questions coming off him as the man who'd rescued us then abandoned us took another step in our direction.

The air grew thick.

Dense and full.

My pulse thrummed.

Erratic.

My breaths turning choppy.

"I'm just gonna . . . go check out the auction items." Jenna's tone was cautious, her eyes searching when she looked at me to find out if that was what I wanted.

If I wanted to be alone with him or if I wanted for her to step in and intervene.

Problem was that I wasn't so sure I knew the answer to that myself.

Finally, I gave her a tight nod while still staring at Kale because I couldn't seem to tear my attention from his face.

When she disappeared back inside, I finally spoke. "What are you really doing here? Why would you stand up there and say all those things?"

It was a plea. A warning. I didn't know.

I didn't know if I should tell him to stop, not to come a step closer, or throw my arms around his neck and beg him to never leave me the way I was aching to do.

He blanched, and all those defined, distinct curves of his face went rigid in stark vulnerability. "I don't have anywhere else to go . . . not when wherever you are is the only place I want to be. Because I meant every single thing I said when I stood up there. You two taught me what it really means to hope."

"You don't get to do this, Kale Bryant. I told you that day in my kitchen, you don't get to come in and make promises and then just walk away. And you sure as hell don't get to walk right back in whenever you feel like it."

And I knew he had his demons. I respected that. But if he wanted a place in our lives, he had to be certain he was all in. That he could handle my son's disability. His old fear.

He roughed one of those big hands through his hair and looked off into the distance as if he were trying to gather himself.

Evan climbed down onto his hands and knees beside me, his notepad on the ground as he began to furiously write across a clean page.

My son nearly broke me when he turned it toward Kale.

> *You promised you cared about us. That you wouldn't hurt my mom. That she was the prettiest mom in the world. You said you were her boyfriend and I was your favorite. Remember?*

And I knew that it broke Kale in some way, too. Because the towering man dropped to his knees in front of my child.

His hands were shaking when he took the pad and wrote out his response.

> *I did. I was a coward, and I left you. And I know I don't deserve the chance, yours or your mom's forgiveness. But if you can both forgive me, I promise that I will never leave you again. Not as long as I'm living.*

Oh God.

My spirit licked and danced and my body swayed.

Lightheaded.

Evan sat back on his heels, his hands flying in front of him.

YOU PROMISED I WAS YOUR FAVORITE. I THOUGHT I WAS YOUR FAVORITE.

Desperation wove into Evan's movements, and his entire face pinched in grief, the remnants of the rejection Kale had inflicted. He lifted his thick glasses, swiping the tears that streaked down his face with the sleeve of his jacket.

Kale gasped over a sob.

Physical, wrenching pain.

He grabbed the notepad, his back heaving as he leaned over to write.

> *You are my **favorite**. You are my everything. I'm so sorry I hurt you. I never wanted to hurt you.*

Evan's face was completely blanketed by the heartbreak written all over him, soaking wet with the tears that wouldn't stop falling when he read what Kale had written.

I'd warned Kale what was on the line. Did he see it now? The kind of pure love my son had trusted him with?

Evan sat up on his knees and signed more, anger seeded in the emphatic movements.

OUR HOUSE IS L-O-V-E. YOU HAVE TO LOVE IF YOU LIVE THERE. THAT'S THE RULE.

Hardly able to see through the bleariness, I attempted to start to translate, but Kale lifted his own hands.

His motions were awkward and prolonged, off half the time, but there was no mistaking what he was trying to say.

*THAT'S GOOD THEN. BECAUSE I LOVE YOU, EVAN. I LOVE YOU SO MUCH, AND I LOVE YOUR MOM. I WANT TO STAY WITH YOU. WITH HER. BE YOUR FAMILY. BECAUSE YOU ARE MY **HEART**.*

He punctuated the last with a fist against the middle of his chest.

I nearly buckled, watching him sign to my son. That he'd taken the time to learn. That he'd listened. That he could *hear.*

Kale looked up at me from where he was still on his knees. "I love you, Hope. I love you so goddamned much, I can't see. I can't eat. I can't sleep."

Slowly, he pushed to standing, his hand still fisted over his heart. "You warned me your life was complicated, that you didn't have any room for anything else, and I pushed my way into it anyway. I wanted to save you. Save him. Be your knight or your hero or whatever you wanted me to be. But it turned out that you were the one who was complicating me. In the best of ways. Waking me up and making me feel, when I'd never thought I could possibly *feel* that way again. All along, you were the one who was *saving* me."

I tucked my trembling bottom lip between my teeth, and Kale came closer. So close I could feel him everywhere. Racing across my flesh, sinking deeper into my heart.

"It kills me, Hope, kills me that I walked away from you that night when you needed me most. I was scared. Terrified. Filled with grief and guilt. But you awakened that dead place in me. That's a gift . . . you and your son are a gift . . . and I don't want to live my life without it."

He took my face in both of his big hands. "I love you, with all of me, and

I promise, if you can find a way to forgive me, I will live my life for you. For Evan. For *us*. There might be times when I'm afraid, when I fail, but I will never stop fighting for you. You set me on a path that I don't want to stop walking. I will follow you anywhere."

A soggy laugh jolted free, and I sniffled and reached up to scratch my nails across his jaw. "Cowboy."

He gathered that hand in his, brushed his lips across my knuckles. "Princess."

He stared at me for the longest time before he looked back at Evan who was staring up at us, sniffling and wiping the tears from his face. Kale knelt back down and did it for him. "Do you want me to stay?" he asked, his voice ripping from his throat. "With you? With your mom?"

Evan made that scraping, raw sound as he said, "Stay."

I pressed my hands to my chest. Overcome. Overwhelmed.

Kale smiled at him. Tenderly. With so much love it nearly blew me over.

"Is it okay if I kiss your mom, little man?"

Evan turned back to his pad.

You're supposed to kiss her if you're her boyfriend. Lots of kisses. That's the rule.

"Yeah? And what if I'm her husband?"

Evan was quick to write on his pad.

Then you have to give her a billion.

Kale shifted on his knee and turned his gaze on me, the blue brimming with a sea of promises.

Lust and love and devotion.

He dug in his pocket, and my hands flew to my mouth, a gasp flying free when he held out the little black box.

"What do you say, Hope? Can I give you a billion kisses and all my love, every single day, for the rest of our lives?"

I was frozen, shocked.

Wondering if it was all too much, too fast.

"He bought All. The. Lollipops." I jerked to look to the side where Jenna was hanging halfway out the door and shouting at us. "Say yes, Harley Hope. Don't you dare walk away and not say yes. You deserve this. More than anyone I know."

There was my best friend. Grinning from ear to ear in all her brash, pushy encouragement.

"Yes," I whispered, the word soggy, love sliding free.

Because it didn't matter the circumstances. The path we'd taken to get here. This man had led me exactly where I was supposed to be.

"Yes," I said again, this time laughing with the wave of joy that crashed over me.

He slid the ring on my finger. Diamond glimmering in the moonlight, the man stared down at it.

Awed.

Floored.

Finally, he pushed to standing.

The second he did, I threw myself in his arms.

Kale lifted me from the ground and spun me around.

Round and round.

His face buried in my neck while he clung to me.

He set me on my feet and took my face in his hands. He leaned down and captured my mouth in a dizzying kiss.

Soft and tender and slow.

A promise.

A passionate claiming.

And my unstable world . . . it no longer spun.

It danced.

Clapping went wild around us, and Kale dropped his forehead to mine, grinning against my lips. Redness flushing to my cheeks, I peeked out to the side to see Jenna jumping up and down and clapping her hands.

Dr. Krane and his wife were beside her.

His smile was slow.

Knowing.

Kale looked at Jenna. "You wouldn't mind if I gave these two a ride home, would you?"

Jenna smirked. "Like I'd expect anything less from you, Sir Bryant."

She turned her attention to me. "I just expect all the details tomorrow."

Giggling, I rested the side of my head against Kale's beautiful, bleeding heart. "Of course, she does."

"She's going to cause me all sorts of trouble, isn't she?" he murmured down at me.

"Oh, I think you can count on that."

I stretched my hand out, looking at the diamond glinting on my finger. Giddiness swept through me, head to toe. I peeked up at him, a playful smile taking to my mouth. "A ring, huh, Cowboy? Awful presumptuous of you."

He let that cockiness ride to his lips. "Hey, can't blame a man who knows what he wants."

"Is that so?"

"Mmhmm . . ."

He kissed across my jaw and up to my ear. "Besides, I know my girl. If she knows something is right? Then she's going to jump and trust she lands right where she's supposed to."

"With you."

Kale gathered up Evan's hand. "With us."

He wrapped his arm around my waist and leaned in to kiss me on the temple. "Let's go home, Shortcake."

Home.

I couldn't wait to make one with him.

epilogue

Hope

Laughter roared through the dim-lit space. Downstairs, a band played, the music vibrating through the floors adding to the carefree vibe of the private party happening upstairs.

"Are your eyes closed?" Jenna demanded from behind me. "No peeking, you greedy girl, or I'm not gonna let you have any."

I pressed my hands tighter against my eyes and shook my head. A rush of heat lit me up everywhere. "Are you sure I even want to know what this surprise is?"

She'd basically had my skin the color of a tomato since the second I'd mounted the top step to the second floor, with the games we'd been playing and the drinks she'd been plying me with.

She'd said this celebration was for me, and I was damn well going to enjoy myself.

Funny how she didn't have to coerce me into that anymore.

"Oh, I promise you, you're gonna want this surprise," she sing-songed as she leaned around my side and placed something on the table in front of me.

Whatever Jenna was up to was met with a bunch of giggles and laughed whispers rippling all around me.

Nikki nudged me in the side. "Oh yeah, you are definitely going to want this surprise. All of them. But I'm def taking one for myself. I am the orgasm fairy, after all. I totally earned one of those babies."

"Oh God, now I really don't know if I want to see."

From across the table, I heard my mama's distinct laughter.

Mortified.

Yeah. I was so going to be mortified. Still, I didn't think I'd ever been happier about it in all my life.

"Open up!" Jenna shouted, and I was groaning and bracing myself and simultaneously grinning like a fool when I peeled my hands from my eyes.

Then I busted up laughing.

I was right.

Mortified.

Because there in front of me were at least forty cupcakes.

All of them speared with little stakes that boasted pictures of Kale's face, the writing beneath claiming, "Sex on a stick."

"You didn't," I scolded.

"Um . . . you know I did. With a little help from my new friends, of course," she said, glancing at Nikki, Lillith, and Rynna, who kept busting up in fits of laughter.

"Pass one of those down here," Mindy, one of my old friends, shouted from the other end of the long table. "I want a taste of that."

It was a little surreal that I was surrounded by so many of the faces of the women who'd been out to celebrate Jenna's birthday that fateful night nine months ago.

And now, here we were.

My life now looked so incredibly different.

I'd known I was blessed at that time. No question about it. But it'd also come with a weight so heavy there were some days I didn't know if I'd manage to bear it. Stand up under it.

And now . . .

Joy trembled all the way to my bones as I looked around at the faces smiling back at me.

With a grin, I pointed at Jenna's accomplices. "All of you are in so much trouble. Hand in those bridesmaid's dresses."

Nikki gasped and pressed her hand over her chest. "Never. You know you love those cupcakes. I mean, look at all that delicious, creamy frosting. Don't you just want to take a big ol' bite?"

Conspiratorially, she swatted at Lillith. "Tell her, Lillith. She loves them so much she's over there squeezing her thighs together and shifting on her seat just looking at them. Mouth watering. Am I right?"

Lillith sent her a teasing scowl. "Always trying to chase away the good ones, aren't you?" She turned her attention to me. "Although, I guess we officially get to keep you."

I widened my eyes. "You couldn't get rid of me if you tried."

"Says the girl who just told us to pass in the bridesmaids' dresses," Nikki said.

A giggle escaped. "Fine. You're right." I reached out and pulled the tray closer to me. "And I want them all. They're mine. I need all the cupcakes."

"Oh no, greedy girl, those are for everyone. You don't want to go and break Maw-Maw's heart, now do you? After I went over there and got her hair done up real nice just for the occasion." Jenna swung her attention to her grandmother who sat right next to my mama. "Right, Maw-Maw?"

Her grayed eyes glinted. "Only reason I came was to get me one of those cupcakes."

My mouth dropped open in mock offense. "Watch yourself, Maw-Maw. I don't share my man."

"That's good, because I don't share, either." The deep voice hit me from behind.

A shiver raced my spine, and this time, I really was pressing my thighs together. Trying to quell the instant ache.

That's the way I felt. Every moment of every day.

This constant desire for a man who stole my breath and filled up all the missing pieces in my life.

The one who stood by me. My support. My foundation.

Because times weren't always easy, and the fear in our lives could never be fully erased.

But he was there to hold me up through it.

"No, you don't, Sir Bryant. Stop right there." Jenna pointed at him. "No boys allowed. Get that perfect ass back downstairs where it belongs."

He shot her one of those heart-stopping grins. "Don't get your panties all up in a twist. Just need to talk to Shortcake for a quick minute."

Jenna's eyebrows rose so high they disappeared behind her bangs. "A quick minute, huh? That all it takes these days?"

"Ouch . . . you really know how to hit a man where it hurts, don't you?"

Crossing her arms over her chest, she quirked a brow. "Oh, you can count on that."

Kale laughed. "I knew you were going to be all sorts of trouble."

His expression shifted into feigned seriousness. "It's incredibly important I speak with Hope immediately. We have some important business to attend to, and it just can't wait."

"Really?" she challenged.

"Really," he said, dropping those blue eyes to me, mirth swimming in their depths.

Love.

It burst from every cell.

I glanced around at the faces grinning back at me. "Well, if you all will excuse me for a second, my fiancé has something important he has to say to me."

Kale wound my hand in his and helped me to stand.

He started us for the glass partition accordion wall.

From behind, we were hit with a barrage of *Ooo's* and teases and taunts, a *brown chicken brown cow* shouted from Nikki, the little punk.

She and Jenna definitely had to have been separated at birth.

I dropped my head in an attempt to fight the rush of heat that flushed and burned and ignited.

He sent me a smirk over his shoulder as he pulled me through the same gap he'd led me through that night when the only thing I'd planned on giving him was a single *dinner.*

That dinner that had turned into my giving him my body. My heart. My life.

The same way as he'd given me his.

"Oh, Cowboy, I don't know what you have up your sleeve, but I have a party I'm supposed to be attending. Same as you," I whispered through the swell of euphoria that swept through me.

Joy.

I'd never known it could be quite so bold.

Palpable as it surrounded us. Fortified by devotion and loyalty.

He gripped my hand, walking backward as he faced me, watching me with one of those smiles that sent a scatter of butterflies flapping through my belly.

Dominant and persuasive and sexy.

There was my cocky boy.

"Last time I checked, those parties were all about the two of us. Besides, I've got something important to tell you."

He spun me around then pulled me close in an exaggerated, impromptu dance, his arm wrapping around my waist as he tucked me against his body.

His beautiful heart thundered, in sync with mine.

A giggle slipped free, and I stared up at him as he swayed me in the moonlight that poured down from above. "Oh, yeah, and what is that?"

He grinned, but his gaze was soft. "In two days, you're going to be my wife."

I tucked my bottom lip between my teeth, struggled to play along. Because it still blew my mind.

In two days, I would be Kale Bryant's wife.

"Hmm . . . I didn't realize that."

He twirled me again. "No?"

I shook my head. "Must have slipped my mind."

"Slipped your mind, huh?"

Vigorously, I nodded before I was yelping as he dragged me back into the far recesses of the balcony. Right back to that spot that had changed everything between us all those months ago. He hoisted me up and placed my bottom on the table before he plopped down in a chair in front of me.

He gripped me by the outside of the thighs. "Do I need to remind you?"

A tiny moan slipped free from between my grin. "Mmm . . . I think you might."

He shot forward and captured my mouth in a consuming, maddening kiss.

Soft, plush lips and demanding, delicious tongue.

Orange and whiskey.

Smooth.

All man.

My head spun, and my body sang.

Throbbing and needing this man in a way I'd never thought I'd need anyone.

He pushed to standing, and I wrapped my legs around his waist then groaned into his mouth when he pressed his hard cock against my center. "Kale."

"Are you remembering yet, Princess?"

"Almost," I teased, the word both a giggle and plea.

He kissed me deeper.

Passion spiraling around us.

A bind. A bond. Our commitment.

"How about now?" I could feel his smile as he murmured against my lips.

I pulled back so I could look at the defined curves of his face, a perfect silhouette in the shadows. Sobering, I brushed my fingertips across his lips. "I could never, ever forget."

A needy rumble echoed from his chest, all the playfulness gone when he kissed across my jaw and down my throat, words woven in the middle. "Couldn't even stay downstairs for a few hours, knowing you were up here. Only thing I wanted was to get to you. Touch you. I can't believe I've been given this. That in two days, I get to call you my wife. That I get to call Evan my son. Tell me this isn't a dream."

I clung to his shoulders.

Lost to this beautiful, beautiful man.

His devastating body and his extraordinary heart.

"I'm yours," I told him.

Wholly.

Completely.

"I still can't believe it," he murmured, edging back to look at my face as his words rode on the night.

I took him by the face, my gaze locked on his kind, knowing eyes. "Believe it. I believe in us. I believe in you."

Kale had rescued me in so many ways. Filled up all the vacancies. Filled our home with laughter and love.

With security.

He'd worked with his attorneys to ensure Dane could never be a threat to Evan ever again.

And somehow, miraculously, I had received a check for five hundred thousand dollars from the Gentry Trust at the finalization of my divorce.

Almost the exact amount required to cover Evan's emergency heart surgery and ICU stay, plus the debt I'd incurred when I'd made the choice to fight for my son. No matter the cost.

I'd never asked for it, demanded it, my aim only to sever ties with Dane forever. But the truth was, it'd been a lifesaver. Another burden lifted. He'd never admitted it, but I somehow knew Kale had been the one who'd made that happen. How, I wasn't sure. Honestly, I didn't want to know. But I would be grateful for all my days.

He set his big hand on the side of my face. "I love you, Hope. You are my everything. I can't wait to share my life with you. With Evan. Grow our family. I never thought I would get this chance."

I drew in a staggered breath at the thought. I never thought I'd get this chance, either.

Evan would always be enough.

Kale would always be enough.

It almost felt greedy to hope for another child.

Still, that sacred place in my spirit bloomed with the possibility.

But no matter how our family was shaped, I would cherish it.

A tender smile fluttered across Kale's lips and adoration moved across his expression. "I'll never stop fighting for you. Working to protect you and Evan."

"I know that. I love you more than you know," I whispered to him, searching him in the shadows that played and danced across his gorgeous face.

"Princess," he murmured, kissing across my jaw.

"That's queen to you." I let the ribbing weave into my tone before the words softened as I ran my fingers through his hair. "You did say you wanted to be my king."

He released the puff of a chuckle at my neck, chills racing my flesh as he gathered me up.

Held me tight.

"You are my treasure," he whispered.

"And you are my forever," I told him.

My everything.

And I would be the one to treasure every part of him.

Kale had never come to the place where he'd accepted he'd saved my son.

He would tell me it was my faith.

My belief.

My hope that had filled Evan with the strength to fight.

And maybe that was okay.

Because sometimes . . .

Sometimes even hope needed a hero.

And Kale Bryant?

He was mine.

Lead Me Home

prologue

I'd always wondered why people set themselves up for disaster. Why they put their heart on the line when they knew it would only be crushed. Why they led themselves toward the slaughter like blind, ignorant lambs.

Willingly.

I hurried down the short hall of my apartment toward the pounding at my front door. Somehow, I knew that was exactly what I was doing. Yet, there was absolutely nothing I could do to stop myself.

A storm battered the walls, and the windows rattled with a low rumble of thunder.

The door clattered with a fresh round of banging.

The knocking felt a partner to the storm—violent and unyielding yet so utterly distinct.

My heart rose higher in my throat with every pound on the wood. It was as if an accelerant had been poured directly into my blood.

It was close to two in the morning.

Someone showing up at this time of night—in the middle of a downpour, no less—should make me cautious.

If I searched myself, I guessed a little part of me was afraid, but only because I was sure of who was on the other side of the door.

He'd always been dangerous.

Dangerous to my sanity.

Dangerous to my heart.

Obviously, none of that mattered. I was drawn to him anyway.

Tied.

Nothing more than an offering.

I hoisted up on my tiptoes to peer through the peephole, and I sucked in a breath when I saw the tortured face pleading back.

So gorgeous in its hardened, chiseled way. Wind gusted through the longer pieces of his dark-blond hair, his shirt soaked and clinging to his massive body from having to make his way through the deluge that pummeled at the roof.

Quickly, I worked through the lock and yanked open the door.

Chills flashed.

A shockwave.

All brought on by the sight of him.

"Ollie," I whispered, my spirit in an uproar.

Neither of us would ever forget this date.

It was the anniversary of the day his sister Sydney had gone missing.

That was thirteen years ago, and in all that time, he had never come to me. As desperately as I'd needed him . . . as desperately as I'd known he needed me . . . he never came.

He staggered in with a half-drained bottle of scotch clutched in his hand and kicked the door shut behind him.

He dropped the bottle to the carpeted floor, and there was no time to contemplate the *thud* before he was stalking my way.

Body massive.

A burly, beautiful, beast of a man.

I took a startled step back, sucking for the air his presence had stolen. Energy streaked through the room. Those big hands darted out and captured my face in the same second his mouth captured mine.

Lips and tongue and searing heat.

Liquor kisses.

My head spun and need blistered across my skin.

He groaned in misery and released the words between the manic scourge of his mouth. "I need you, Nikki. Need you in a way I haven't needed anything in all my life. Take it away. Fuck . . . please take it away."

If I could, I would.

It was all I'd ever wanted to do.

"Ollie." His name was grief.

Love.

Regret.

"I need you, too. I've always needed you," I told him, the confession striking the air between us with the force of a bomb. Blowing through my tiny apartment. "Why did you wait so long?"

It was a question that had him swooping me into the overwhelming strength of his arms.

He kissed me as he carried me the few steps down the hall. He kissed me when he laid me down on my bed. And he kissed me when he murmured, "You are everything I ever wished I could have."

Desire blossomed in my body.

Full bloom.

So compelling it became its own beat, a thunder in my veins that rumbled as loudly as the storm that raged overhead.

The scariest part was the way my heart sang with the hope of it.

Because I had always belonged to Oliver Preston.

The problem was, he'd never fully belonged to me.

I owned his gazes. His protection. His regret.

But he'd never allow me to possess his broken spirit.

I knew it when he tore the clothes from my body and fumbled with his belt.

I knew it when his pants and underwear hit the floor.

I knew it most when he wedged himself between my thighs and his body met with mine.

I gasped, and he cursed, and for a moment, it was only the two of us. For a moment, we weren't just another casualty of that horrible, horrible day.

Holding me, he moved in me. With me. He panted and touched and whispered, "You take it away. You take it away. You feel so good. So good."

His fucks were deep.

Possessive.

And somehow, painfully tender.

Tears filled my eyes when he pressed his forehead to mine, and a confession fell from his mouth on a low moan, "I miss her. I miss her so much. When will it stop? When will this feeling ever go away?"

I clung to him.

Gave him my body.

If I could, I would have given him everything.

But I guessed maybe I knew better when his body went rigid and he grunted when he came, one moment behind me as he drew out my pleasure perfectly.

Knew better when he slumped to the bed and wrapped me in his muscled arms that were covered in weeping ink.

Knew it when I fell into a dreamless sleep.

When I woke in the morning and he was gone, I realized I'd known it all along.

one

Nikki
One Year Later

"Miss Nikki?" The timid voice hit me from behind.

I stilled where I was refilling my disposable coffee cup at the table. It was set up at the back of the large meeting room in the basement of an office building we rented out every Tuesday night.

I gave myself a moment to gather my composure after the intense session before I turned around with a soft smile on my face.

Brenna.

She stood there, nervously twisting her fingers together, the bruise around her eye finally beginning to fade. She hadn't said a thing the entire session, but the fact that she had even shown up at all had felt like a victory.

"Hey," I told her gently. My heart suddenly felt as if it were too big to fit in my chest. "What did you think of the meeting tonight?"

She chewed at the inside of her lip. "It was good. Everyone is really nice."

"That's good to hear. We want you to be comfortable. It's a safe place."

"I feel safe here." She almost blanched when she said it. As if she never truly felt it or maybe she was scared to. She hesitated and then said, "I wanted to tell you something."

I set my coffee cup aside and fully turned to her. "Of course. You can tell me anything."

There was something about this young girl that got to me. Something that made me want to wrap her up and protect her. Hold her and keep her safe forever.

At barely eighteen with a two-year-old little boy, she'd already been through enough to last her a lifetime. Most of her turmoil was thanks to the piece of garbage who was supposed to be her boyfriend.

"I left him."

Relief.

Sometimes I wondered how it could be so intense.

"I'm so proud of you," I told her, not even trying to keep the emotion out of my voice. "Where are you staying?"

"My momma's. She said Kyle and I could stay with her a bit until I get on my feet."

"That's good. So good. Do you need any money? Anything from me?"

I knew I was making myself too available. Offering too much. But with her, I couldn't help it. All I wanted was to make a difference; although, I was pretty sure Kathy, the doctored psychologist who oversaw the group and mentored me, would tell me I was being a little too overeager.

Or maybe tell me I was straight up breaking the rules.

Call it a pitfall of my personality, I didn't care. I just wanted to do . . . something.

More than something.

Truth was, I'd give absolutely everything I could.

Brenna pursed her lips. "Just you bein' there for me that night meant everything. I don't think I would have had the courage to call anyone else. I've never been so scared—for myself or for my son. You were there when we needed you most. I don't know how to repay you for that."

I gave a tight shake of my head, unable to hold back the moisture that rushed to my eyes. "You don't need to repay me. The only thing I need is to know the two of you are safe. You keep my number close, okay? If you need anything, anything at all, I want you to call me."

"I will," she promised. Her gaze turned to the ground before she looked back up at me. Expression loaded with trust. "I just wanted to let you know."

"I'm glad you did."

Her nod was slight, and I gave her a small smile before she turned and climbed the steps leading from the basement floor meeting room.

Joy filled me full, and I turned back to the table and pressed my palms to it, head dropping as I pulled in a deep breath.

Two years ago, I'd taken the plunge and started accelerated online courses to get my psychology degree. Quietly at first, because I hadn't quite put my finger on why I felt compelled to start down this path. Unsure of where I was going or if I'd stay the course.

Mostly I'd been uncertain of *why* I was doing it.

My purpose.

I'd finally realized I'd just wanted to make a difference.

If I could make one person's life better, help them see the beauty of the world in the midst of so much cruelty and sorrow, it would be worth it.

Maybe I was doing it because of Sydney.

That was okay.

The only thing I knew was I wanted to pour something positive and good into the world after experiencing such a great loss.

That didn't mean the last two years hadn't been rough. It'd been difficult balancing all the online classes and now interning here with Dr. Kathy's women's program while I was still working at Pepper's Pies, the diner my friend Rynna owned.

But after tonight?

I knew it was all going to be worth it.

With a smile on my face, I finished cleaning up the refreshment area while Kathy stacked the folding chairs.

"Are you ready?" she asked.

I grabbed my bag and slung it over my shoulder. "I am."

We flipped off the lights and headed up the stairs. The darkness was thick as we made our way to the ground floor and let ourselves out the front door and down the steps that led to the sidewalk.

The Alabama air was muggy and thick, the summer night sagging with humidity.

The area was pretty much deserted this time of night, the street flanked by two and three-story office buildings that had been around since the beginning of Gingham Lakes.

The drone of cars echoed in the distance, and Kathy's heels clicked on the sidewalk as she headed for her car, which was parked at the curb in front of mine. "Good night," she called.

"Good night. I'll see you next week," I hollered over my shoulder as I rounded the front of my old car to the driver's side.

She paused at hers. "You did well tonight, Nikki. Really well. The women feel comfortable with you."

I looked back at her.

It was funny how I was always the first to laugh. My first instinct to tease and play. But when it came to this, there was nothing but somberness on my face. "I hope so."

A soft smile graced her face. "They are. It's clear you're doing this for all the right reasons. Because you want to be here."

As soon as she said it, she slipped into the front seat of her car and started it. Her headlights cut through the darkness.

I was grinning as I opened my car door and started to slip behind the wheel, only to pause when my attention caught on a small, folded piece of paper tucked under the windshield wiper.

I snagged it, jumped inside, and started my car, only then unfolding what I expected to be a coupon or announcement or sale.

My heart stuttered in my chest.

Deep dents were made in the paper in scratchy letters.

Don't forget about me. I'm coming for you.

Dropping the note, I grabbed on to the steering wheel. My attention darted all around, eyes squinting as I searched the shadows.

There was nothing.

No sign of life other than the brake lights illuminated at the back of Kathy's car as she waited for me to follow.

Dread settled in my gut, and the tiny sheet felt as if it weighed a million pounds as Brenna and Kyle's faces filled my mind.

That little punk.

He thought he could scare me.

He thought wrong.

two

Ollie

What the fuck was I doing? I knew better than this. So much better than this. But I couldn't help it. Couldn't stop myself.

Not when it came to her.

Call it a sickness.

I didn't care.

It was after ten at night when I inched my car up behind her, and that pissed me off, too.

The girl traipsed across the deserted parking lot.

Alone.

Wading through this shithole like a sitting duck.

A tremor of anger ridged down my spine when my gaze moved over the area.

The lot was hidden at the back of the run-down apartment building, like it'd been designed that way specifically for some lowlife to take advantage of the defenseless and vulnerable.

Space nothing but a blanket of darkness except for a couple of dingy, dull streetlamps that barely leaked light in small pools onto the pitted pavement.

Two dumpsters lined the far end, motherfucking shadows dancing out from behind them and across the asphalt like they were restless, eager to become a player in a horror story.

With her head down, she walked toward the exterior stairs of her apartment. She didn't even notice me since she had her attention all wrapped up in her phone that she was staring at in her hand.

Didn't know which was worse.

That, or her other hand being clutched around the handles of this huge-ass bag, just swinging it along at her side like she was begging for it to be stolen.

My chest clenched.

Reckless girl.

Reckless girl who was wearing these tight red pants and some flowery, flowy blouse that I'd expect to see some grandma wear.

How the hell it still managed to get me hard, I didn't know, but there I was, shifting in my damned seat.

Light brown, honeyed locks tumbled a few inches below her shoulders, her hair messy and wild and untamed.

Just like her personality.

As eager as her heart and as bright as her spirit.

Motherfucking sunshine.

The girl was tall and so goddammed skinny. All sharp edges and waif-thin lines. I had to remind myself I liked curves and big tits and handfuls of ass.

Nikki. Fucking. Walters.

The bane of my existence.

Hands gripping the steering wheel, I angled my car right behind her. The spray of my headlights struck her like a spotlight, making her jump about two feet off the ground. She spun around, hand with her phone going up to cover her heart.

Her mouth gaped open in shock.

Well, at least she noticed me.

I rammed the gear of my old Mustang into park and threw open the door, feeling all kinds of pissed off that this girl didn't seem to have a defensive bone in her body.

Self-preservation nonexistent.

She just stood there like a deer caught in the headlights, two seconds from being run down and unable to move to do anything about it.

Hankering for a confrontation, I jumped out.

The fear in her expression transformed the second she realized it was me.

Her eyes were an indigo-blue, like a cracked-open amethyst crystal.

Her own brand of indignant anger burned through the center of them.

Hurt and a fucked-up sense of loyalty.

God damn it . . . I knew better than this.

But with her, I didn't know how to stop myself.

three

Nikki

"Ollie." I rasped his name, trying to steady my wobbling knees. To steady my feet. "You scared the crap out of me."

He'd almost gotten himself a face-full of mace, which would not have been pretty.

And man, oh man, was the boy pretty.

It really would have sucked to muck up that view, even if he would have deserved it. Especially after the note I'd found tonight.

"You should be scared," he gritted.

Beneath the hazy glow of the streetlamps, my heart drummed an erratic beat, and I struggled to slow my ragged breaths that jetted from my lungs. Panic and angered surprise was a blaze that beat through my veins.

My nerves were already set to high-alert, every faint sound enough to have me looking over my shoulder, worried that little asshole would follow me. Threaten me as if I'd just give up and send Brenna back to him. Or maybe he'd go as far to hurt me the way he'd hurt her. Or worse.

"And what exactly am I supposed to be scared of, Oliver?"

He scoffed. "I could have been any asshole out hunting for prey. Some disgusting prick looking for an easy target."

The thing with Ollie? He *did* make me afraid. But not for my physical wellbeing. When it came to him, the only thing in danger was my heart.

He was always sneaking into my life when I didn't have the mental fortitude to resist him. Tonight, I was feeling fragile, and the sight of him just about dropped me to my knees.

I thought I'd made it plenty clear he wasn't welcome. Not anymore. Not after that night a year ago.

Giving comfort did not mean making myself a doormat.

And that was what he'd made me.

Nothing but a place to stomp the dirt off his big shoe.

My head shook. "Yet, you're the only asshole standing there."

A harsh breath of air left his gorgeous mouth. I tried to pretend I didn't notice. "Call me an asshole. Fine. I deserve it. But that doesn't change the fact that you were out here alone. Vulnerable. Someone could hurt you."

With the last, I saw the worry flash across his magnificent features. Maybe the hardest part was how genuine it was.

Which was precisely the reason I couldn't tell him what had happened tonight.

He'd demand I quit. He'd insist I was putting myself in danger and what I was doing was stupid.

Careless.

When I'd never been so full of *care* in all my life.

He stared me down.

Attraction trembled around us like a magnified force. As if the world still spun while we stood still.

The two of us no longer in orbit, and instead, we were strung up in an endless oblivion.

Shivers rolled, and it didn't have a thing to do with the tremble of fear I'd felt a few moments ago.

It was the potent energy that was this man blasting across my flesh like the warmth from a furnace on a cold winter's day.

My attraction to him was so intense I wondered how he didn't taste it in the air.

Bristling and brimming and begging.

Chemistry.

As much as I didn't want it to, it banged between us.

Painfully.

I didn't mean for my smile to come across as sad. There were just some things a person couldn't help. Not when we'd planned for things to turn out so differently between us.

"I don't exactly have someone I'm coming home to who can watch out for me, now, do I?"

He lifted his chin in some sort of defense, and a flash of severity and regret and things I didn't want to read struck through his eyes. "Why do you think I'm here, Nikki. To look after you."

My eyes squeezed shut, and I tried to pretend I didn't want to welcome it. His safety and his protection and his care. But it was right there, surging and spinning like a tease.

It was all compounded by the tight ball of hatred I held for him. He'd used me, and I'd let him.

"You're here to look out for me?" My words were incredulous.

"Yup."

Ollie, who was all rigid anger and glowering scowl where he clung to the top of the doorframe of the black muscle car that was almost as pretty as he was.

He looked like a savage beast with the long pieces of his dark, sandy hair pushed back on his head, the sides cropped short, beard on his face trimmed but full.

The man was this hulking tower of muscle and brawn and intricately drawn ink.

A haunting rendition of the lake had been imprinted on the entirety of his left arm, and a field of the same purple blazing star flowers we'd run through as children swayed from his wrist and up his forearm on the right, those massive, bulging muscles flexed in restraint as he gripped the door.

The position harshly exposed the words etched on his knuckles.

Lost on the left and *Soul* on the right.

It was as if they'd been purposefully tattooed there to punch me in the gut every time I saw them, the permanent reminder of what he'd lost.

Of what *we'd* lost.

My lips pursed. "Maybe I don't want you here."

"Too bad."

Cocky bastard.

I pointed at my apartment behind me. "I don't need this right now, Ollie. It's been a long night, and I just want to go upstairs, pour myself a glass of wine, and crawl into bed."

He stepped away from his car and slammed the door shut.

"Where were you tonight?" he demanded. As if I'd done something wrong.

Every inch of him was rugged and rough and commanding, his body dripping sex from behind a closed-off exterior.

It was all mixed up with this troubled kindness that weighed heavily in the depths of his sapphire eyes, his soft lips always quick to tip into a gentle smile.

He was an enigma.

A veiled mystery.

A cliffhanger waiting to be written.

Who was I kidding?

He was a goddamned mindfuck, that was what he was.

And he'd broken my heart one too many times for me to fall into that trap again.

A resigned sigh pilfered free. "I was at the women's support group. Remember? The internship I have. You know . . . to finish my courses to graduate?"

I didn't mean for the sarcasm to drip out with it, but it did. Ollie had this way of getting under my skin.

"Of course, I remember. I just didn't think that'd mean you'd be running around at all hours of the night." His return came out just as harsh.

"People have lives, Ollie. Jobs and families. It only makes sense for these types of meetings to happen after normal work hours, don't you think?"

"Suppose so. Guess that just means I'll have to drive you." He said it as if it made perfect sense.

Why did he have to constantly do this to me? Pulling and pulling and pulling me closer.

And every time we collided, I only crashed into a brick wall.

"No, thank you."

"I wasn't asking." His voice was gruff.

Hard and demanding.

An extension of the man.

I exhaled heavily. "You have a bar to run. And I'm not a little girl, in case you hadn't noticed. You don't need to worry about me."

"You know that's impossible."

The jab of a knife.

That was what it felt like when he said things like that. A million little cuts over the years that left me continuously bleeding out.

"You haven't shown up here for a year. Why now?"

He flinched, a streak of vulnerability flashing through his face. "Lillith came into Olive's earlier. She said you bailed on her for drinks the other night, and you haven't been to the bar for, like, a week. Texted you to check up, and you didn't text back. Like I said, I got worried."

Shit.

The last thing I needed was this man melting me.

"I rescheduled on Lily because I had a test I needed to study for. She knew that. I turn my phone off during the meetings so it doesn't cause a distraction, and I barely just turned it back on in the car. And it's been three days since I've been in the bar. *Three days.*"

Exasperation filled the last.

And there he was showing up as if he missed me.

But the way that he was looking at me had me wondering if he might. And those were dangerous thoughts I had no business entertaining.

"I'm a big girl, Ollie. I'm home. Safe. You can go on your way."

That intense gaze flashed, and his mouth pinched into some kind of unfound resentment.

"Yeah. You're safe. This time. Thank God, considering you were walking around at this time of night with your face buried in your phone, paying zero attention to your surroundings. You should know better than that. Which is why I will drive you next week."

Annoyance blew out on my breath. He was impossible. "I was paying attention. I already had my phone programmed to 9-1-1 and mace in my hand. You think I didn't notice someone driving like a creeper into the lot?"

"Paying attention? Hardly. You could have been gagged and shoved in my trunk before you even realized what was happening."

I cocked my head. "The gagging I might be up for . . . not so sure about the trunk."

Sometimes I couldn't help but toss his nonsense right back.

Ollie growled. Actually freaking growled, and chills were flashing across my flesh, a whirlwind of energy that skated my skin like a rough, demanding caress.

"Not a joking matter, Nikki," he grated, taking a jolting step forward and getting right in my face.

No.

He was right.

It wasn't. Not after Sydney had gone missing fourteen years ago.

She'd left a chasm right in the center of us.

A black hole in our bright, shining sky.

Gaping and bleeding and pleading.

She'd wandered out into the night and disappeared without a trace.

That night, I'd lost both of them. Sydney was gone and Ollie had all but turned to stone.

Yeah. We still ran in the same circle. A circle that was tight. As close as family, the bonds forged between us just as important. Maybe more so.

The thing was, Ollie and I were on the opposite sides of that circle, keeping each other at arm's length and a world away.

Yet, somehow, after all this time, he continued to remain possessive of me. Keeping me under his guarded watch. As if I were a child he needed to protect. As if he'd forgotten everything we'd been through together.

What we'd almost been to each other.

I'd made the mistake of falling for him a long, long time ago.

When I was little more than a kid.

The problem was, he would never allow himself to fall for me.

Oliver Preston was armor and stone.

Bitterness and venom.

Broken fragments.

Shrapnel waiting to burst.

What made it harder was that there was no missing that huge, giving heart that he kept stunted. Hidden in the darkest kind of shadows.

That made him dangerous to my sanity. Poison to my heart. Yet, I always found myself back in his bar with my friends as if it didn't mean a thing, pasting on a smile and a tease while the man was slowly killing me.

But tonight? It all felt like too much.

"Seriously, Ollie. Don't burden yourself by worrying about me."

He hesitated, throat bobbing. "But I do. Can't change that. No matter how hard I try."

Emotion rushed. So tight. I felt the prickle of the tear blurring my eye before I even realized it was streaking down my cheek.

"Shit," he whispered. One of those big hands darted for my cheek.

I jerked back. "Don't touch me."

His hand dropped like a rock.

"Shit," he whispered again, this time a hiss of frustration. "I'm sorry."

My head shook. I searched his expression, my own frustration bleeding out. "You tell me it's impossible for you not to worry about me, but as far as I'm concerned, I shouldn't even cross your mind."

He flinched, and beneath his beard, his thick throat rolled with his swallow. I got the feeling the man was swallowing a torrent of things he couldn't allow himself to say.

Guard up.

Shields on.

"You're always on my mind," he admitted, voice low, scraping with the admission.

It was so unexpected it knocked the breath from me.

"You don't get to show up here, sayin' things like that to me. You don't get to yank me around, Ollie. I won't let you do that to me. Not anymore."

He swore quietly under his breath before he slowly brought that penetrating gaze up to meet with mine again.

Eyes tangled.

Spirits tied.

Hostages to the intensity that tightened my chest and filled my lungs.

How the hell was I ever supposed to get over him?

"I won't apologize for caring about you. For worrying about you. But the last thing I intended was to show up here acting like an overbearing asshole. I just wanted to check on you."

Tingles raced my throat. Damn him.

I gathered myself and pasted on one of those smiles.

Fake and brittle.

"Don't worry about me. I'm just fine. See." I lifted my hands out to my sides. "All in one piece. So you can leave, go on back to whatever or whoever it is you usually do on a Tuesday night."

Bitterness oozed out with the words.

I didn't mean for it to. Human emotions were such tricky little things. They could be fleeting and fast.

Forgotten before we gave ourselves time to ponder them.

Or they wiggled their way in, so deep that it was impossible to imagine they hadn't been part of us all along.

They came and they went.

They skipped out before they took hold or they lasted a lifetime.

Anger. Joy. Hate. Hope. Fear.

Attractions and crushes and obsessions.

The people who knew me best could say I suffered from any one of those emotions when it came to Oliver Preston. Lillith teased me relentlessly, and I let her, played it off as if it really didn't mean all that much.

He was the one thing I didn't fully let her in on. She believed my feelings for him amounted to nothing more than a mad crush.

The problem was?

I just . . . loved him.

I did, and I had for too many years, and it hurt too much that he didn't love me back.

I took a step back. "I need to go."

I turned on my heel and headed for the exterior steps of my run-down apartment. Even though Gingham Lakes had seen a major rejuvenation over the last decade, this area had not.

I couldn't afford anything else. I wasn't exactly raking in the dough managing Pepper's Pies.

But it was enough.

Enough to get by on until I finished school.

As I mounted the second-floor landing, I peeked over my shoulder.

I shouldn't have.

My heart stuttered at the sight of him. At the fact he kept looking at me in that way I wished he wouldn't. In a way that made hope and need glow hot.

His presence solid as he stared up at me from where he stood beside his car.

So thick I couldn't do anything but breathe him in.

Intoxicating.

The man was a drug.

I jerked my attention away and rushed for my apartment door, only to stumble in my tracks.

A harsh gasp sucked into my lungs.

Shocked.

Stunned.

Then my heart took off racing in a panic of fear.

Horror beating a path through my veins.

Dread took me whole.

My hand went over my mouth, and I choked out, "Oh my God."

I could feel Ollie pounding up the steps. Two seconds later, he was in front of me and pushing me back.

His stance protective when he ordered, "Don't move."

four

Ollie

*B*itch.

It was spray painted in red across her door, and pieces of wood were splintered where a sharp object had been rammed against the door.

Probably an axe.

My heart raced like a motherfucker, anger and protectiveness and fear this blistering heat that churned a thousand tons of adrenaline through my veins.

My chest cinched tighter with every step as I inched forward.

It made it harder and harder to breathe.

Hit with the overpowering urge to make sure she was close, I reached back for Nikki.

Not sure whether to wrap her up and run with her or rush the fuck inside and take out any asshole stupid enough to still be in there.

Take out any piece of shit who might threaten her.

A fucking landslide of jagged rocks scraped at my throat, and I looked back at Nikki who was watching the whole scene through wide, horrified eyes.

Totally shocked.

My insides curled. Every worry I'd ever had surfaced. A surprise attack.

"You still got 9-1-1 up on your dial?" I gritted through clenched teeth, inclining my ear toward the door, trying to listen for any movement inside.

The frame was splintered. Lock knocked loose. Door hanging open an inch.

"Yes," she whispered, voice choked.

"Call it. Tell them to hurry," I urged, nudging the door open with the toe of my boot and taking a quick peek in to look around her tiny apartment.

Stillness echoed back.

But the place . . . it was trashed.

Pictures had been torn from the walls. Lamp knocked to the floor. Couch flipped, ripped apart. In the kitchen, which ran along the far back wall, boxes and cans of food were strewn across the floor.

Ransacked and ravaged.

I roughed a shaking hand over my face, trying to see through the red blaze of hate that clouded my vision.

I could feel my control slipping.

My sanity shifting.

Fuck. It'd been *shifting* all along—since the night my sister had gone missing and I'd become an entirely different man.

My cool had been nothing but a front as I waited.

As I watched.

As I forced myself to hang back, feign patience, until a debt came due.

It was what kept me moving every day. Hunting for my sister.

It was the singular focus of my life. What I'd devoted myself to.

Could feel a splinter of that focus breaking off as my hands curled with the crushing need to chase down any fucker who would even think about hurting Nikki.

Nikki.

Nikki. Fucking. Walters.

This girl threatened to be my undoing.

From behind, I listened to one side of Nikki's conversation with the 9-1-1 operator. "Yes, that's the correct address. The door is busted in, and it has been spray painted."

"It looks like it was splintered with a sharp object."

"Second floor apartment."

I cringed with every detail she reiterated.

Like I was having to see it for the first time.

"No, I don't think anyone is inside."

"No one is hurt. There's no need for an ambulance."

At least not until I found them.

"I'm not sure," she said.

Nikki nodded and whispered at me, "She said to wait outside and not touch anything."

I gave a restrained nod.

It was painful.

I wanted to charge inside. Do a little of that hunting I was made to do.

Protect her.

Just like I'd had the overwhelming need to do earlier, running over here to check on her since she hadn't returned my text.

I was the dumbass who'd showed up here unannounced.

But what if I hadn't?

Dread spiraled through me. A slow stir of something that had simmered forever.

Heat igniting beneath it.

All of two minutes passed before we could hear sirens approaching.

My eyes remained on that indigo gaze, refusing to lose sight, wanting to sink deeper.

Search for the secrets I could so clearly see hiding there.

I forced myself to stand still.

Her lips moved slowly as she spoke into her cell. "Yes, thank you, they're here."

She ended the call and pulled the phone from her ear.

"Who did this?" The question was nothing but shards of hatred from my tongue.

Slowly, she shook her head, blinked in a confused, agitated fear.

Didn't matter. I was certain I saw a moment of clarity doused with worry flit through her expression.

Her own intuition meeting with mine.

"I don't know," she whispered.

I wanted to grab her by the shoulders, shake her, demand more, but two officers were climbing from the cruiser that had just pulled into the parking lot below, their lights spinning through the desolate night.

Couldn't help but feel grateful when I saw the face of the man who started climbing the steps.

Seth Long.

He was an old friend from high school who'd gone into the academy right after graduation. A good guy. A good cop.

Surprise had him faltering a step when he realized who was standing in front of him. "Nikki . . . Ollie . . . God. The last thing I expected was to roll up here and find you two. Are you okay?"

The obvious answer was no.

But true to form, Nikki turned and plastered on one of her smiles. "Yeah. Thank God. We're fine."

Bright, blinding light.

Motherfucking sunshine.

A taste of sweet, sweet lemonade.

That was what Nikki was. Felt myself itching to lean forward and glean some of it. To swim in her calm and her belief.

They said sunshine chases away the dark. I swore, all it did was deepen mine. Amplify why I couldn't take her. Have her.

I was a bastard.

A sinner.

God knew what I was responsible for.

He also knew what I'd be willing to do—vengeance a greed I carried in the palm of my hands.

But that girl? She was a sin I'd never again commit.

Seth and his partner stepped around us, their guns drawn as Seth nudged the broken door open with the toe of his boot.

They edged in, quick to scour before Seth was back in the doorway. "Whoever was here is gone."

"Thank God," Nikki whispered, releasing a huge breath.

Relief.

Wasn't even sure that I felt it.

The only thing it meant was the person who'd done this was still running the streets.

"I need you two to hang out for a bit while we take some pictures and dust for prints."

He swung his gaze to Nikki. "If you're up for it, afterward I'd like you to come inside to see if you see anything missing. I have to warn you, the place is torn up. It's not pretty."

Nikki crossed her arms over her chest. Hugging herself.

My sight snagged on the dragonfly tattoo on the inside of her right wrist. Every time I saw it, it felt like my guts were being shredded.

The way she wore her ghosts the same way I wore mine.

"It never was," she attempted like it was going to lighten the mood.

I wasn't fucking laughing.

The second Seth disappeared, I spun back around.

This girl was so fucking pretty it hurt to look at her. I bit back all those old feelings I couldn't feel. "I need you to go through every single person who might have done this to you."

She sucked her lip into her mouth. "I can't think of anyone."

I wondered if she knew I could see straight through her.

"Don't do this, Nikki. Don't protect someone who doesn't deserve protecting. What is it you're trying to hide?"

Seth popped his head back through the door, interrupting all the demands I wanted to make. "We're ready for you."

"Thank you," she said, sidestepping me and entering her apartment.

I followed right behind.

Nikki started moving through the place, cringing, clearly worrying as she took in the tornado that had ripped through her home.

A storm.

That was exactly what it felt like had hit.

It was the same feeling that had been gathering strength for a while.

Rising and lifting.

The nightmares I couldn't escape coming more often and more intense than ever.

That gut-deep intuition that something was coming.

Something wicked.

I paced her crummy little apartment, yanking at my hair, feeling like I might go out of my damned mind.

Seth was finishing getting her statement where they'd ended up in her bedroom while I stewed and raged in the living room.

I could hear her voice floating from her room. "There was this box my grandma just left me. She said there were some mementoes and keepsakes in there that she wanted me to go through and share with my sister. I only picked it up a couple of days ago. I hadn't had the chance to go through it yet. It was right up there . . . at the top of my closet."

"You're sure?"

"Yeah. It was definitely there."

"You don't know what was inside it?" Seth asked.

I peeked down the short hall, watching him scribble something in his notebook.

"No. But it had a little lock. It probably looked like the only thing in the whole place that was of any value. Whoever it was is going to be sorely disappointed when they crack it open and find it's probably nothing but a bunch of pictures I painted my grandma when I was a little girl. The only other thing I can see is missing is a silver ring I'd left next to my bathroom sink."

Yeah, someone was going to be sorely, sorely disappointed.

Surely, they didn't have the first clue that coming in here and messing with Nikki meant they were fucking with me.

Sometimes lessons had to be learned the hard way. I was going to be all-too happy to teach it.

The three of them moved back out into the living room, Seth talking while they did. "My guess is this is another case of punk kids running the streets and causing trouble."

Seth said it almost casually.

"They probably took off running when your neighbor came out to see what the commotion was. It happens more than I would like to admit. They're looking for anything easy to unload for a little cash, and if they don't find anything, they don't think twice about ruining people's belongings, out of spite or fun, I'm not sure. Either way, it sucks that you have to deal with the aftermath."

She nodded but looked unconvinced.

"Are you sure you can't think of anyone who would have done this?" he asked for the third time.

Nikki's gaze dropped to the floor, off to the side as she ran her hands over her arms and gnawed at that plump bottom lip.

She wasn't saying something. I knew it. *Knew* it.

She accused me of not knowing her.

What bullshit.

I knew her better than anyone.

She went back to hugging herself. "I can't think of anyone. I mean . . . I'm Nikki. Who could hate me?"

She gave a wide grin.

Honestly, it looked a whole lot more like a grimace than anything. Kind of pathetic and awkward and desperate.

She wasn't fooling anyone.

"What about at school or the diner?"

Her head shook. "My classes are all online, and everyone's wonderful at the diner. Who wouldn't be after Rynna feeds them those breakfast pastry pies. Happiest people in the world. I'm sure you're right, and it was just kids," she continued with a resolute nod. "There are packs of them roaming the area all the time. It was bound to happen."

Bound to happen.

I was *bound* to kick someone's ass.

"Luckily, if that's the case, they usually move on once they figure out there isn't anything of value for them to take."

Although Seth's words were obviously delivered to offer her some comfort, he kept shooting me glances on the sly.

Nikki laughed a self-deprecating sound. "Well, then, I'm sure that ring was worth a mint, and unless they were after the VHS player my grandma gave me for my tenth birthday, then they are straight out of luck."

Seth chuckled while he scribbled something onto a fresh sheet in his notepad. "You probably made yourself a prime target with that one."

"I knew I should have gotten a security system with all my valuables. Oh God, what if they'd found my Discman?" Her eyes went wide with feigned horror. "Living the high life is dangerous."

I would have laughed if I wasn't so pissed. Only this girl would make light of the situation.

She'd also be the one to hang on to all those pieces of her childhood.

My insides clutched as I thought about her hopping into her grandmother's car every Saturday morning.

Tagging along to yard sales and thrift stores like it was some sort of epic trip to Chanel.

Couldn't count the number of times the girl had busted into our house with pride in her eyes to show off the latest gadget she'd picked up with her grandma. Half the time, it'd already be obsolete or missing pieces or just plain ugly, but she never cared.

She'd go on about why it'd called out to her. Why it was supposed to have belonged to her all along.

Sentimental to the skinny bone.

Hell, I wouldn't have put it past her to be carrying a beeper in that huge-ass purse of hers, too.

"You should have been born in the seventies," Seth teased.

"I know, I was robbed. Think of all the awesome music I missed out on in the eighties."

He laughed. "Robbed. Vandalized. You really are a target."

Anger soured on my tongue. Knew he was being cool. Setting her at ease. But her safety wasn't a damned joke.

"All right, I think that's all I need for now," Seth said, ripping out the sheet and flipping the notepad closed. "You know where to get in touch with me if you think of anything else. Sometimes things become clearer after the shock wears off. We lifted a couple of prints, so I'll let you know what we find, and I'll send someone over first thing in the morning to get your door fixed."

Nikki sent him a wobbly smile. "Thank you, Seth. I really do appreciate it."

"Just doing my job, though, I have to admit, wasn't a fan of doing it here. You need to be careful, Nikki."

"I know."

He hesitated. "Are you sure you're fine?"

She nodded and pasted on one of those smiles. One of the ones that promised Nikki Walters was just fine.

Having a blast.

Even when the world tossed her shit and problems and trials, she chose to live life large and to its fullest.

"Yeah, I'm totally fine. No need to worry. I knew what I was signing up for when I moved in here."

Seth shook his head. "All right then, I'm going to get out of your hair. Take care of yourself," he told her.

He walked toward me and reached out to shake my hand. With the other, he slipped me the sheet he'd ripped out of the notebook.

Unease rumbled in my gut.

I gave him a tight jut of my chin. "See ya, man."

"Yup," he said before he and his partner slipped out.

Nikki followed them and did her best to wedge the door shut.

While her back was to me, I peeked at the note.

None of this sits right. Call me.

Nikki grunted, trying to get it shut but the wood was too mangled and disfigured.

What if she'd been there? Alone?

What would have happened then?

What had the intruder's intention been in the first place?

Fear tumbled through me like a slow, excruciating burn.

Lava that sprouted from my soul.

Singeing my insides.

It was doubled by a bolt of that rage. A stake through my spirit.

It landed right in the midst of the rest of that bubbling fury, leaving me to barely hang on.

Sometimes I looked in the mirror and was terrified of myself, having no clue who I was gonna be when it happened.

When it all came to a head.

Where she stood facing away from me, I watched a tremble roll through her body. The girl refused to let on that she was shaken up by the incident.

She thought I didn't see her.

Problem was, I could see her too well.

"You knew what you were signing up for when you moved in here." There was no question behind it. Just an accusation.

A frustrated laugh jolted from her mouth, and from behind, she shook her head. "Sometimes there aren't any other options, Ollie."

She slowly turned to face me, and she lifted her chin a fraction.

Defiantly.

Proudly.

That was my girl.

Proud and way too brave and far too sweet.

A dangerously reckless combination.

"We work hard. We make do. We accept that sometimes our lives aren't as pretty as we might like them to be. We accept that our lives don't look the same as we once imagined they would."

Regret tumbled through me at that.

I was the holder of so many of the dreams she'd whispered about.

Dreams she'd trusted me with.

I was the image that no longer looked the same.

"It wasn't like I was going to continue to live with my sister once she got married and became a mom. So here I am."

She lifted her arms out to the sides like her reasoning was going to deter me. "Home sweet home."

She started for the kitchen that was only separated from the living room by a change from old, worn carpet to dinged-to-shit linoleum.

I surveyed the disaster again. Unease knocked at my ribs. My voice was low when I spoke. "Looks personal to me. You sure there isn't anything you want to tell me?"

She kept walking, dipping to grab three boxes of cereal that had been pulled from the pantry and dumped onto the floor.

But I saw it.

The misstep.

The way her spine went rigid in fear.

Hiding.

She was all too quick to cover the ripple of disquiet.

Her words shifted into an overcompensating rant that rode on her breath. "Little punks need someone to teach them a lesson. I mean, seriously, how uncool. Breaking shit for the fun of it. I just never have gotten that mentality. Making life harder for someone . . . because what? They're bored?"

She sucked in a saddened breath. "And my grandma's stuff . . . she's gonna be so heartbroken that I don't have it. It's hard enough that she's fallen sick. People don't even realize the things they do really hurt. Or maybe that's exactly what they want."

There was an undertone to all of it as she tossed the boxes back onto the shelf. Like she was processing.

Like she knew exactly who'd done this.

"Do you have a bat?" she asked, whirling around to face me.

Her expression had turned eager.

Actually fuckin' serious as she looked back at me like she just stumbled on the solution to all the world's problems.

Or at least hers.

Unreal.

She had to be insane.

Or driving me there.

"You're coming home with me." The words were out before I could stop them.

Yeah, it was a bad idea.

But there was no chance in hell I was gonna leave her by herself. Not with the lock on the door broken.

Like a lock made a difference anyway.

"What?" Her brows lifted so high they disappeared beneath the long, wispy bangs that framed her face.

Her goddamned striking face.

Eyes wide and sincere and true. Color that shouldn't be possible.

High, carved cheeks. Smooth, olive skin. Plump, pink-tinted lips.

That smattering of brown freckles that crested the bridge of her nose and dusted beneath her eyes made her appear so damned young and innocent.

But it was that body that bristled with an undercurrent of energy and fire that sent streaks of light radiating from her like the breaking day.

Couldn't stand the thought of her energy fading away. This crazy energy that emanated from her skin like the glow of neon colors.

Couldn't stand the thought of someone touching it.

Snuffing it out.

Dimming that light until it was cast into darkness.

"I said you're coming home with me. You can't stay here by yourself."

Her mouth dropped open in offense, and she propped her hands on her narrow waist, trying to come off as valiant and strong when I saw the panic quiver through her veins.

Yeah.

I was fucking panicked, too.

"Excuse me, but I'm not sure when you decided you got to make decisions for me."

"When some asshole busted in your door, that's when."

She shook her head. "I'm not going to your place."

"No?"

"Nope."

I dug out my cell phone. "Fine, I'll call Lillith, and I'll drop you off there."

Horror crested those pink lips. "Don't you dare, Oliver Preston. It's almost midnight. You're going to freak her out. This is Lily we're talking about, and you know the last thing I need is for her to get all worried over me. She'll have Brody trying to build me my own sky-rise apartment or something."

Sounded like a good plan. I knew there was a reason I liked the guy.

"Rex and Rynna, then. Or maybe your sister Sammie. I'm sure she has a cozy couch."

So what if I was goading her.

"Are you crazy? And wake up their kids?" she screeched as she pointed at me. "And don't you dare say Hope and Kale. Chances are, we'd catch those two right in the middle of something they don't want us to interrupt. They can't keep their hands off each other. I think that was one of my best matches to date."

Her voice got all dreamy on the last. The girl thought she was some kind of arrow-shooting cupid, responsible for every relationship each of our friends had fallen into.

It was cute and eccentric and ridiculous.

Crazy talk.

That's exactly what this was.

What *I* was.

Crazy.

Crazy for even considering this. Crazier for insisting on it. Because I knew she was gonna refuse every single one of my suggestions and the only thing she'd be left with was me.

"Looks to me like your *options* are running out."

She stamped her little foot in defiance. "I'll go to a motel."

I spun on my heel and headed into her bedroom, dragging the duffle bag from the top shelf of her closet. I tossed it onto her bed, doing my best to suppress the images of the last time I had been there.

But they came fast.

An assault of greed and lust.

The girl under me. Skin so soft. Body so warm. Wrapping me in all that comfort.

Sunshine.

Had to grit my teeth to force out the words. "You're coming with me, Nikki. Don't fight me on this because you aren't gonna win."

"Why do you even care?" She was in the doorway, her pretty face pinching. I saw it, her eyes on the bed, picturing the same damned thing as I was.

Hurt hit her, wave after wave.

My stomach knotted.

Regret and need.

I turned away.

Ignoring it, that feeling that struck in the space between us. Something that'd always been there.

Always.

As we'd grown, it'd just transformed and gotten bigger and become something we shouldn't have let it be.

None of it mattered—not the mistakes I'd made, not the way I felt, not what I wanted.

I'd rather die than let something bad happen to her.

"Pack your shit, Nikki, or I'll do it for you."

And the last thing I needed was to be rummaging around through her underwear.

Ollie
Six Years Old

His mom knelt in front of him and squeezed him by the upper arms. "You're such a big boy. I'm so proud of you."

He looked up at the big yellow bus that rumbled at the curb, his belly full of something that felt like wings, and his chest bigger than it'd ever been.

"Now, do you remember what I told you?" his mom asked as she adjusted the straps of his backpack on his shoulders.

He tightened his hold on his little sister's hand. "I've got to take care of my little sister. Always and always."

His mom smiled and it made his chest tighten more. "That's right. You're the biggest and the bravest, so you always watch out for your little sister. She's going to be scared going to school all by herself, but she doesn't have to be because she has you right there to protect her."

Pride swelled inside him. "I'll watch her the best, Momma. Just like Daddy said."

She leaned in and pressed a kiss to his forehead. "I know you will, brave boy."

"Beast Man," he corrected.

His momma laughed a soft sound and brushed her fingers through his hair. "That's right, you're The Beast now."

He proudly held up his *The Beast* lunchbox that his dad had given him yesterday when he'd gotten home from work. His dad told him he was a beast, destined to be a linebacker, bigger than any of the other boys.

Last night, his daddy had come into his room to tuck him in and told him he needed to watch out for his little sister.

Just like his momma was doing right then.

Their momma looked at his little sister, who was swaying in her pretty dress that she had picked out especially for this day. Ollie was worried it was gonna get messy if she played in the dirt, but their momma said that was okay. "You stay close to your brother, okay? He'll help you get to your classroom until you know your way around."

Sydney looked up at Ollie and beamed. "Okay, Momma."

"All right, you two, you'd better get on that bus."

She pressed a long kiss to Sydney's cheek, like the way she did when she was sad.

"It's okay, Momma," he said, "I've got her. I won't let nothin' bad ever happen to her."

She nodded at him and wiped a tear from under her eye. "I'm just sad my babies are getting so big. I know you've got her. Now go on and have a great day. I'll be right here waiting when you get finished."

"We will!" Sydney said, grinning wide and then even wider when she saw another little girl walking up to the bus with her hand in her mother's.

The girl's eyes were so wide and so blue they were almost purple. Like one of those purple flowers that grew thick in the fields and filled their momma's garden.

Though, somehow, they were shiny and iridescent.

Like a big bubble floatin' in the sky and getting caught up in the rays of sunlight.

The girl's mom hugged her before she nudged her toward the bus. "Go on."

The girl's feet dragged on the dirt as she looked behind her.

"You wanna sit with us?" Sydney called out, not the least bit shy.

The girl's mouth tipped in a small smile. "Okay."

Sydney struggled to look around Ollie as they climbed up the bus steps and moved down the narrow aisle between the rows of seats, his little sister trying to get a good peek at the girl. "What's your name?"

"Nikki."

"Hi, Nikki! My name's Sydney. This is my Ollie. You wanna be our best friend?"

"I don't have a best friend," Nikki said.

Nikki looked a little bit scared. Like the way Ollie's dad said Sydney might be because she didn't know her way around.

Ollie puffed out his chest. "Well, you got two now."

Six

Nikki

The powerful engine of Ollie's car roared as we sped down the road. Night passed us by in a blur of city lights that poured in from above, and the silence had its own distinct vibe as it filled the cab of his car.

Hot and heavy and confused with a dash of anger thrown in for good measure.

Seemed fitting considering that was the way this boy always made me feel.

Angry and hot and on edge.

What the hell had I agreed to? I knew so much better than to bend to his will. So much better than giving in.

But how could I not? The truth was, I was scared.

Terrified, really.

I could feel the note I'd stuffed into my bag burning a hole in the bottom of it, flames of fear and worry and dread. They'd ignited the second we'd mounted the steps at my apartment, sure it had to be Brenna's boyfriend Caleb who was responsible for it all.

Should I just say it? Put my theory out there without an ounce of proof?

The hardest part was I didn't know if that would be betraying Brenna's trust. Disrespecting everything she'd offered me in her fragile state.

God . . . I just, couldn't do it. Not with the way Ollie was vibrating beside me like a lunatic.

I'd seen it in his eyes. Felt it radiating from his body.

He wanted to hunt and destroy.

I blew out a relieved breath when my phone finally buzzed with a return text.

Brenna: I'm fine. Is something wrong?

Me: No. I just wanted to check on you to make sure he was leaving you alone. Please text me if you need anything. I'll be there.

I wondered if my demeanor came across as some kind of dirty confession as I tapped out the reply.

Or maybe it was just the way Ollie was looking at me as if he wanted all my secrets. Because the daggers he was shooting were so intense, I could feel them penetrating the side of my face.

Fiery darts.

I thought he might have the power to flay me wide open with the pass of one. See everything hidden inside.

Brenna: Thank you so much for being here for me.

I hugged my phone to my chest as if it might send her a hedge of protection. Send her my hope and belief in her. For her.

Maybe I really had gotten in too deep.

"Who is that?" Ollie finally demanded, shaking me from my thoughts.

I turned to him, taking him in. He barely fit in the space of the seat, his long legs bent and tucked up under the wheel, seat pushed so far back he might as well have been sitting in the back seat.

Bigger than life.

Always, always filling my sight, eyes unable to look anywhere but at him.

He was squeezing the wheel with those massive hands, the muscles in his arms bulging and flexing with uncontainable strength.

I squirmed, and my tongue suddenly felt thick where it stuck to the roof of my mouth.

I didn't know if it was from looking at him or from the fact my gut told me not to let him in on the note. Not to tell him about the day Brenna had called me right after she'd called the police, and I'd run there to support her.

Caleb had called me the very thing that was painted on my door as he was being hauled away.

Bitch.

"No one," I told him.

His eyes darted to my phone. "No one? It's after midnight, Nikki. Don't tell me that's no one. And you refused to call any of our friends. That a guy?"

I almost laughed.

Was he serious? He was jealous I might be texting a man?

That was exactly what I should have been doing.

Texting a guy.

Someone who was totally Ollie's opposite.

Sweet and stable and harmless.

Not a man who could rip me to shreds with nothing but a glance. Not a man who would use me up and toss me aside then turn around and act as if I owed him something.

"What if it is?" I defended, not even trying to keep the outrage out of my words. He deserved it. "Why do you think it's any concern of yours?"

"Everything you do is my concern. I thought we already established that earlier."

"Right." It dripped with sarcasm, and I jerked my attention forward, my jaw working hard, propelled by a surge of fury.

I stared out the windshield. "You've sidelined every single one of my relationships. Convinced me they weren't good *enough,* or you decided it for me and took it upon yourself to scare them away. I told you, you don't get to do that anymore."

Not after last year.

Over the years, I'd dated.

Never seriously. I'd never fully allowed myself to fall because I'd been waiting on him to come to his senses. To see me. To *feel* me the way I felt him.

Or maybe it'd just been *impossible* to fall because I already belonged to him.

My heart too tangled and wrapped up in him to recognize anyone or anything else.

"If that's a guy, then I need a name." His voice came hard, as sharp as a wielded knife. No question, a threat to cut without hesitation.

My laugh was one of disbelief. I gave a short shake of my head. "No, Ollie, you don't."

For the last fourteen years, I'd had to watch him with an endless string of girls.

Painfully pretending as if it didn't matter. I'd done it after he'd broken me when I was sixteen because I'd wanted to give him the space and the time to heal. But when he'd done it again, as if he didn't think it wouldn't destroy me? I was done.

I would no longer allow Oliver Preston to trample all over me. I was moving on, the best I could, the only way I knew how.

"Told you earlier you need someone looking after you. Should be clear enough after that shit went down at your apartment." His voice was gruff like he was scolding a child.

"Um, no, I don't. I'm a grown woman. And yeah, I appreciate you being there for me tonight. That's what *friends* do, but I don't need someone else to approve who I see or who I am with. I've never tried to do it with you, and it's high time I stopped allowing you to do it to me."

Veins bulged in his arms from the pressure he was exerting on the steering wheel, and that energy flared.

Friction and gravity.

Barbed spikes penetrated my skin.

I shuddered around it.

"Just didn't think you were the boyfriend type." It was basically a grunt from his sexy mouth.

Was he for real?

"Since when?" I challenged.

Ollie's jaw clenched in discomfort. Good. Maybe for once he would understand what it felt like.

He doesn't care.

He doesn't care.

I had to keep telling myself that.

What made it worse was the thought of inflicting even an ounce of pain on him made me sick.

He'd always thought he was the one who needed to stand up and protect me, but it was me who ached to protect him. Shield him and hold him, wishing he'd find that solace in me.

"Just tell me who you're texting," he demanded instead of answering my question.

For a flash, he turned that potent gaze on me.

Black sapphire.

Angry and hard.

"There are parts of my life you don't get, Ollie. Some things are private, like the relationships I have with the women who come to sessions. They're trusting in me, and there is no way I can allow you to get in the middle of that. And you know what? If I am dating someone . . . you don't get that, either. It's none of your business. You gave up that right a long time ago. You either need to respect that or accept that I can no longer be in your life."

A breath left him on a hard exhale, and his entire being flinched.

He looked as if he'd taken a swift kick to the gut.

Shocked.

Maybe I should have laid it out between us long ago.

Boundaries and rules.

God knew, I'd been following his for too long.

"Is that what you want . . . me out of your life?" He kneaded the wheel as he said it, agitation coming off him in powerful waves.

I stared across at him.

At his face.

His cheeks and his lips and the profile of his beard.

My beast.

"No," I said quietly. It was the honesty that came out behind it that made it ring in the air.

Slowly, he nodded. "Don't mean to be an asshole every day of my life."

"Are you sure about that?" I said, my voice cracking with the strain as I let myself tease.

A gruff laugh left his sexy mouth. I tried to still the tremor the sound evoked in the depths of me.

There was nothing I loved more than the sound of Ollie happy.

Pathetic, wasn't it? He'd hurt me over and over again, and the only thing in the world I wanted was for him to be happy.

The thing was that I knew the real man. The man hidden by layers of hatred and anger and sorrow. I knew the real heart. The heart concealed by the most devastating kind of grief.

He eased his fingers through his hair and blew out a sigh. "Yeah, I'm pretty sure about that."

"So, you just can't help it?" I ribbed. It was so much easier than being mad at him.

He cracked a wry grin and peeked over at me. "Just comes naturally, I guess."

"Bear," I taunted.

"Brat," he returned.

"Beast."

My heart fisted as we sparred, affection pulling free and spilling into the air.

"Sunshine."

The second he called me that, tears pricked in my eyes.

I beat them back, swallowed the lump that bobbed in my throat, and smiled over at him as if he were my oldest friend.

Because he was.

"Thank you for rescuing me tonight," I told him honestly. "I would have been terrified if I had walked up on that by myself."

"No worries . . . rescuing damsels is kind of my thing." The smirk he gave me was only half forced.

"Well, aren't you just the savage savior?"

He smiled over at me, and I smiled back.

"Saving you was always my job."

My insides shook.

It was so easy to fall back into rhythm with him.

He looked over at me, his expression softening. "Guess I should have known that wasn't a guy."

"Why's that?"

I shouldn't have let him bait me. Not when the subject was such a thin, shaky line.

He tacked on a dangerous smile. "Because if you were my girl, I'd be right there, protecting you. Not texting you like some pussy who doesn't want to get his hands messy."

There was some kind of censure in there.

Possession and a warning.

Yet, here you are, protecting me.

So badly, I wanted to say it, but I bit it back and let a smirk ride to my own mouth. "Um . . . this might be news to you, but being a bossy, overbearing asshole does not make you a man."

The brute grinned wide, his big body overflowing in the seat, hands squeezing down on that wheel as if he knew exactly what it was doing to me. "You sure about that?"

"Positive."

Ollie looked over at me.

The easiness was gone.

Obliterated.

In its place was a desperate man. The one who'd shown up at my doorstep for seemingly no purpose at all but to check on me but had been there the exact moment I needed him.

"Who did you piss off, Nikki? Need to know . . . don't care what it is you've gotten yourself into . . . won't be a dick about it. I just . . . need to know."

My chest squeezed, and I had to force out the response. "You heard Seth. It was probably just some kids."

He turned back to the road.

His big body was slung back deliciously in the seat. Everything about him was wholly overwhelming.

Utterly overpowering.

"Is that what you want me to believe?" He slid the question from between his lips like a low accusation.

That was the thing. Oliver Preston did know me. In all the ways that mattered most.

But even if I wanted to tell him, it wasn't my right. I couldn't break Brenna's confidence.

God knew what Ollie would do if he even *thought* someone was trying to hurt me.

I couldn't risk that.

Contemplating, I stared out the windshield before I murmured, "I haven't done anything wrong, Ollie."

I didn't know if it was an admission or a defense.

"Never said you did, but sometimes doing the right thing puts us in a bad place."

A huff of air blew through my nose.

Wasn't that the truth.

"If I'm in trouble, I'll let you know. I promise, okay?"

His eyes darted across at me, his lips thinning as he pressed them together. "Thing I'm worried about is you're already there."

Two minutes later, Ollie made a quick left turn onto Macaber Street.

Strands of lights twinkled where they crisscrossed over the street, strung between the old renovated buildings to create a cozy vibe.

The area was a destination in and of itself.

The renovated buildings boasted restaurants and bars and cafés on the bottom floors, and trendy loft apartments with views of the city and the river took up the upper floors.

Even though it was after midnight on a weeknight, the sidewalks were dotted with couples that strolled along the storefront windows, wrapped up in each other as if they had nowhere to go, and groups of friends hopped from hot spot to hot spot to drink the night away.

I wasn't surprised to see Olive's, Ollie's bar, was still packed. Curtis, the head bouncer, guarded the door, and a row of taxis waited to carry the revelers home after a night of indulging.

Ollie made the next left turn and whipped around to the back of the building.

He pressed a button, and a large garage door rolled up at one end of the building. He eased his car inside where his collection of restored cars sat in the private garage that took up a small section at the back of the first floor. He pulled the car into one of the open spots, killed the engine, and hopped out without a word.

Almost warily, I unbuckled and climbed out of the car as he grabbed my duffle from the back seat.

Raucous voices carried through the walls from the bar.

Sydney's soft voice floated to me as if she were standing right at my side, whispering it in my ear.

Insightful and real.

My best friend who'd understood the world before any of us could.

I could almost see her with her face tilted toward the summer sky, her legs dangling over the side of the dock, her toes in the cool water.

"I think it's the things that hurt the worst that mean the most, don't you?" she mused, her hair flying around her face as if she'd stirred a new concept that'd been waiting to be revealed. "Good or bad. That's what's gonna shape us. Make us into who we are. Guide us on the path to what we want the most."

She glanced over at me. "I think we'll know it when there's no other direction we can go. And I'm not going to be afraid of walking it anymore."

She wasn't wrong.

I gravitated toward this man.

But what she was wrong about was not being afraid of walking that path.

I knew firsthand it was wrought with peril.

Just spending the night here, being in his space, felt as if he was going to break my heart all over again.

I also somehow understood there was no other place I could go tonight.

He'd found me exactly when I needed him before I'd even realized that need myself.

Maybe Ollie had been following his own path.

All I knew was he'd been there.

For me.

I had to be grateful for that.

He tossed me a look over his shoulder as he strode toward the building.

The man so gorgeous. Big boots eating up the ground with every mind-altering step.

So confident and brash and commanding.

"Comin', Sunshine?"

That was Ollie's way.

Reeling me closer, filling me up, and then cutting me free. Leaving me floating with no safe place to land.

I just prayed this time I landed on my own two feet.

seven

Ollie

Footsteps pounded on the damp earth.

Desperate.

Frantic.

Trees rose on all sides, sentries and witnesses, and branches tore into my skin as I ran through the oppressive night.

Searching.

My eyes blurred in the darkness. Muddied by despair. I stumbled through the forest. Gnarled roots twisted, like spindly fingers that had clawed out of hell to hold me back.

Tears burned my cheeks as the wind blasted my face.

Cruel like the laughter I swore I heard before it was swallowed by a gust of air.

I screamed in the middle of it. "Sydney!"

Voice hoarse, throat bleeding with the pain. "Sydney!"

Sydney. Sydney. Sydney.

I dropped to my knees.

Sydney.

My eyes flew open, and my breaths jutted from my lungs in a panicked rhythm.

Pain lanced through my body.

Physical.

Rending.

Pain.

I deserved it, but sometimes I wished for one goddamned night of peace. I sat up on the side of my bed. With trembling hands, I raked back my hair that clung to my face, matted and sticky with sweat.

Blowing out a breath, I pushed to standing.

Through the faint light that bled into my darkened room, my gaze moved to the corkboard against the far wall. Like all of a sudden it might be pointing to the answer of a twisted, intricate mystery.

Revealing a secret.

Directing me to the missing piece.

All these years, that was what I'd done.

Dug.

Watched.

Waited.

Searching for . . . something.

Someday . . . someday I would find it.

Pushing out a strained breath, I shook off the memories.

Nothing but decay, eating away at my insides. Wondered when there would be nothing left.

I trudged for the door, needing to get out of this room where the nightmares always reigned.

Throat dry and desperate for something to cool the hell living in my belly, I stepped out of my room and headed down the hall.

At the end of it, I stopped dead in my tracks.

Motherfucker.

Motherfucker.

I scrubbed both hands over my face, wondering if I was hallucinating. If I'd thought my throat was dry before, I'd just landed myself in Death Valley.

All the lights in my place were off except for the one inside the refrigerator. The door was wide open, the stark, white light illuminating the tight, round ass that peeked out.

White underwear covered only half of her cheeks, and those long, long legs were bare.

Greed tumbled through me like a landslide.

I fisted my hands. "What in God's name are you doing up?" I grated. My voice was so hoarse from sleep, making the words little more than a grunt. It wasn't like I'd forgotten Nikki had slept in the guest room at the very end of the hall.

Just hadn't anticipated finding her like this.

Gasping, she whirled around. Big, shocked eyes met mine like she hadn't expected me any more than I'd expected her.

"Ollie, you scared the crap out of me," she rasped.

That seemed to be the theme.

Her trembling hand flew to her throat like she was trying to ward off the shock. To reassure herself she wasn't in any danger.

Standing there, I wondered if that was actually true. Because right then, I was feeling dangerous.

Volatile.

Liable to make all kinds of stupid decisions. Like that night close to a year ago, a night I could barely even remember. All I remembered was pulling that bottle from the shelf and trying to drown the grief.

Then I'd woken in her bed.

Her naked body against mine, the smell of her on my skin.

So fucking perfect in my arms.

It was etched and seared and woven with the faint flashes and taunts of memories.

Her sweet, sweet touch, and my desperate greed.

A permanent scar to remind me I couldn't be trusted.

Especially with her.

The only thing she'd paired with those underwear was a thin, white tank top, her tiny tits exposed by the skin-tight fabric, nipples just barely peeking through.

My damned mouth watered.

Those stunning eyes sparked. Purple flames in my kitchen, burning me through as they went skating down my chest and abdomen.

The girl was drinking me in like she was just as thirsty as I was.

Not helping things, Sunshine. Not fucking helping things.

Clenching my fists, I did my best to convince my dick this girl was nothing but a skinny, bony stick and so not my type. Hardest part was convincing my traitor heart I hadn't wanted her for my whole life.

No matter how much shit was piled on top of why I couldn't have her, there was no way I could ever forget her touch. Her smile and her laugh and the way she made me feel like I was a damn king.

Her guardian and shield.

I doubted there'd ever be a time when I looked at her and didn't think she was the best damned thing I'd ever seen.

"Not sure what you expect when you're sneaking around my place in the middle of the night," I finally managed to say, breaking from the spell the girl had me under.

Magic in her fingertips.

And there I was, imagining sucking every single one of them into my mouth.

One by one.

Wondering if she'd groan and go wild or if she'd melt. Didn't know which way I wanted her most.

Sucking in a deep breath, she seemed to gather herself. Her brow lifted in speculation as she set the carton of milk on the island like she'd rummaged through my kitchen a million times before.

Guess there was no need to invite her to make herself at home.

"Middle of night?"

She spun away and hiked up onto her toes to grab a bowl from the cabinet, giving me another flash of that sweet ass.

Little tease.

She spun back around, and there were those tits.

Didn't know which view I liked better.

She really was trying to kill me.

"I have to be to work in thirty minutes."

My attention immediately shot to the huge, curved bay of windows that overlooked the city. Darkness still hugged the buildings, but the promise of something to come was baited in the sky.

"Just because you sleep half the day away, it doesn't mean I get to," she started to ramble, moving to dig through my pantry and my selection of cereals. "Early bird gets the worm—or rather, the breakfast pastry pie. Whatever you want to call it. And I have to be the one to make sure those pies are ready."

Right.

Work.

At an ungodly hour.

"And do you have to do it half naked?"

Couldn't help but bring attention to her state.

It was like only then the girl noticed what she was wearing.

Or lack thereof.

Her full, pink lips stretched into a lust-inducing O, and the shock was punctuated by a tiny sound.

A rash of fantasies rapid-fired through my brain.

Closing the distance.

Taking that mouth.

Devouring that body.

Olive skin and slender curves and cupid mouth.

Fuck.

I wanted her.

Wanted her propped on my counter and spread out on my bed.

She made an offended sound and angled to the side like that might cover her up. She pointed my direction with one hand while she wrapped her other arm over her tits. "Oh, you think this is funny, do you? Sneaking up on me this way?"

I was about to respond, but she didn't let me. That gaze narrowed. "Maybe you really were trying to take advantage of me while I'm here. How the hell a mountain of a man like you sneaks up like some kind of ninja is beyond me."

A chuckle rumbled free, half-pained, half-amused. "This from the girl who decided to parade around my kitchen half naked. Just who is the one who isn't playing fair?"

"You were just asleep. I heard you."

Affection and regret pulsed through her expression the second she realized what she said. With what she'd let on.

She'd heard me.

Fuck. She'd heard me calling out for Sydney.

Shame rumbled through my spirit. It was a feeling she only managed to intensify.

The girl's magic at work again.

Thought she might be the only one who could really understand. Brutal, considering she was the one I couldn't let see.

My life was devoted to finding my sister. Whatever it took. Whatever the cost.

What made it worse was I couldn't look at Nikki without seeing Sydney at her side. Without my mind going to what Nikki and I had done.

I couldn't let her light be dimmed—tainted by that vacant, ugly space that roiled inside of me.

In a moment of weakness, she'd gotten in there once, and look how that'd turned out.

I roughed a palm over my face and down my beard. "You didn't hear anything," I told her. Any amusement in my voice had been extinguished.

That face transformed, and the easy playfulness she normally exuded shifted into some sort of a plea. Because when it was just the two of us together?

The space between us rippled and danced.

Begged to be erased.

That awareness between us became its own, thriving entity.

Rising from the depths.

The girl a crashing wave that was going to take me under.

"Ollie." Her voice was a petition.

Pure understanding.

Come to me.

Too soft and too kind and too full of all the things she couldn't make me feel.

Dropping my head, I lifted a hand. "Don't. Just . . . get dressed. I'll drop you at work. We'll pick up your car after you get off so you have it over here. God knows, I don't need to be getting up before the ass crack of dawn to drive you every day."

She blinked back at me. "You're crazy if you think I'm coming back over here."

"I think we already established that."

Crazy was my goddamned middle name.

Those lips pursed in that wild, impassioned way.

The girl who saw too much.

Too clearly. "I'm not coming back here after work. I only agreed to one night. You know I can't stay here, Ollie."

I didn't ask why. Both of us knew the answer to that. It still didn't mean I was relenting.

Hot air puffed from my nostrils, the same anger from last night slithering beneath the surface of my skin. "It's not safe out there, Nikki."

Didn't matter that she was all the way across the room. I could still feel the weight of her eyes searching me.

I itched beneath it. Tried to shield myself from that feeling that slammed and pulsed and moved.

"What are you going to do, Ollie? Keep me here so you can keep me safe from all the horrible things that happen in this world? Why now? What changed?"

"Are you joking? Some asshole broke into your house. That changed."

"It wasn't a big deal."

"Wasn't it?"

That storm rumbled in the depth of me. A warning. The quake of an omen that ran the length of my spine.

Maybe it was because of the anniversary of Sydney disappearing was inching closer.

But the dreams had become almost unbearable.

Intense.

Vivid.

Every morning, it left me with this gut-deep intuition that something was coming.

Something wicked.

"Just . . . have this bad feeling, okay?" I admitted, nothing but a fool.

I needed to keep my mouth shut.

Put a padlock on what I was feeling.

She took a step forward like she could reach me from across the space. "It's been fourteen years, Ollie."

I stepped back.

Away.

Headed for my room because I couldn't look at her for a second longer without completely losing it. I shouted over my shoulder as I banged into my room, "Be ready in fifteen. This isn't up for discussion."

eight

Ollie
Ten Years Old

"This is a bad idea," Ollie whispered.

If their daddy found out about this, he'd have Ollie's hide.

Sydney grinned. "Are you scared, Ollie Jollie?"

"Course, I'm not scared. This is just stupid."

A frown pinched his sister's brow. "What do you mean, stupid? This is a pact. And a pact means forever. There isn't anything stupid about that."

Nikki shifted beside him where the three of them sat at the back of their yard, their knees touching where they sat in the moonlight beneath the pour of the moon.

He looked that way.

She smiled. Softly. With a tip of her head.

Something tightened in is chest. Tightened in his stomach. She looked like a fairy with those big purple eyes.

Unreal.

So perfect she had to be fake.

"It's a pact, Ollie. Forever," Nikki said, like she was trying to get him to understand.

Forever.

He swallowed hard and picked up the knife Sydney had sneaked out of the kitchen. He turned his hand over to reveal his palm, pushing the tip into his skin.

He sliced a shallow cut into his flesh.

He bit his tongue, trying to pretend it didn't sting.

"Does it hurt?" Sydney asked, scrambling to get closer to watch the droplets of red bead in his palm, interest and awe in her expression.

"Not much." He glanced between the two of them. "You sure you want to do this?"

"Yes!" Sydney giggled, biting her bottom lip, always too excited for her own good. She was always racing off, getting them in trouble because she refused to listen.

Never being bad but never following the rules, either.

And Ollie had promised his mom and dad that he would make sure she did.

He was pretty sure this was breaking that promise in a bad way.

Sydney took the knife and held out her hand, counting under her breath, "One, two, three." She squeezed her eyes shut when she made the slice. Then she giggled wildly. "I did it!"

She held up her hand as proof.

"Your turn," she said, handing the knife off to Nikki.

Nikki's teeth grabbed on her bottom lip. Ollie could feel her getting nervous next to him.

He always could.

Knew she was gonna be scared before she even knew it herself.

"You don't have to do this," he encouraged her, barely tapping her knobby knee with the pads of his fingers.

"I want to," she whispered back, but her words shook. She looked at him, a plea on her face. "Do it for me?"

"I won't know if it hurts."

"Yes, you will. You'd never hurt me."

He hesitated before he took the knife. She was right. He'd never hurt her.

Sydney took Nikki's opposite hand while Ollie took the other, holding the tip of the knife to her palm.

Nikki sucked in a shaky breath, and Sydney squeezed her hand. "Fly, fly dragonfly."

Nikki's lips moved silently when she repeated Sydney's words. "Fly, fly dragonfly."

Ollie slipped the knife across her palm.

Nikki flinched then smiled, holding up her hand in her own kind of awe as she watched the tiny line of red bubble up.

Sydney pushed her hand out to Nikki. "We are three. Forever and ever, you and me."

Nikki smashed her palm to Sydney's. "We are three. Forever and ever, you and me."

Ollie did the same with Sydney, and his sister beamed at him when they chanted the oath Sydney had made them swear back when he was in second grade.

He didn't know why his stomach felt different when he turned to Nikki, but something shivered through him when he pressed his palm against hers.

Their eyes met, and they whispered at the same time, "We are three. Forever and ever. You and me."

Forever.

nine

Nikki

He didn't say a single word to me on the ride to Pepper's Pies.

The infuriating, brooding, fuming asshole who I wanted to wrap up and hold and keep was completely closed off.

As if I was putting him out.

As if he couldn't be bothered.

After he'd been the one making all those overbearing demands.

His dumb, gorgeous face was held rigid, and those sexy, muscled arms rippled with tension, making the field of purple blazing stars shiver across his skin.

I thought maybe if I reached out and traced them, they'd be real. That the small touch would take me back to the days when we'd run through their fields.

Free.

Fly, fly, dragonfly.

Old grief tremored deep in my chest. Thrumming and pulsing out. I swore that I could see it clash with that furious, provocative sort of energy held in every inch of Ollie's delicious body.

As if he rode a fine line between past and present.

Never fully surviving on one side or the other.

I wanted to reach out.

Be his lifeline. His savior when he'd forever been the one saving me.

Ruining me.

Keeping me.

Alienating me.

Push, pull, taunt, tease, take, leave.

My head spun.

Wanting him so desperately and still praying for a way to finally break free of his chains.

I was beginning to think that was impossible.

Not with the way I'd felt looking at him this morning.

The man standing at the end of his hall.

Wearing nothing but his boxer briefs.

Body big and thick.

Burly and intimidating.

His need evident where his cock had pressed so massively against the fabric.

Almost as evident as the power that had blazed between us.

Electricity that spun in sharp, spindly barbs. Stakes to my skin. A hook in my soul.

My wicked savior.

My beast.

Too bad he had to be such a jerk.

He whipped into an angled parking spot in front of the diner.

I yanked at the handle and pushed open the heavy door, fumbling out from the low car and onto the pavement.

Day was just beginning to dawn on the horizon, a gray glow breaking above the mountains in the distance.

I slammed the door shut, freezing when he finally spoke to me through the open window. "Pick you up at three."

"That won't be necessary."

He whipped his face toward me as fast as he'd whipped his car into the parking spot. "Yeah, it is."

"You can't tell me what to do."

So maybe he had me feeling petulant.

Off-kilter.

Could anyone blame me?

"Ah . . . ten-year-old Nikki. My favorite." Mischief moved through those glittering eyes. "Feisty and stubborn. Don't make me throw you over my shoulder the way I used to do."

I shot him a glare while my tummy did a backflip. "You wouldn't dare."

"Wouldn't I? Think you've forgotten who you're talking to."

"You're impossible."

"If you want to call being right impossible, go right ahead."

Ugh. Of all the overconfident, presumptuous, cocky—

"That's what I thought," he said with a smirk, cutting off my internal tirade.

My mouth dropped open, tongue at the ready to protest, but he tossed me a grin, threw the gear into reverse, and revved the engine.

The sound had me stumbling back, and he jerked out of the spot.

Without a glance, he shifted into drive and gunned it.

The man just left me there, staring behind him, wanting to stomp my feet and throw a fit or maybe just scream.

Arrogant asshole.

"What on earth?"

I whirled around when I heard the voice coming from down the sidewalk.

What had I done to anger the gods?

Only a curse could explain this string of bad luck.

When it rains it pours and all of that.

Because there was Lillith with her hands on her hips, wearing one of her fitted pant-suits and heels that made her look like some kind of vixen who'd rolled around in a billion bucks.

Rynna, the owner of Pepper's Pies, was at her side.

"Tell me you didn't have a one-nighter with Oliver Preston." Lillith went all power-attorney lecturer on me.

That's what I got for picking a BFF who was gonna turn out to be a lawyer.

"I mean, I know you're infatuated with him, but seriously, Nikki? That isn't healthy. That man is liable to break your heart."

I had to hold back the dubious laugh.

Too late.

He'd done that a long, long time ago. Had been doing it all along.

Guilt swept through me. I hated that I kept it from her.

She was my closest friend.

Still, the sad thing was, she'd taken Sydney's place. And Sydney hadn't known the full truth either, so how could I tell Lillith? Maybe it was stupid, but that felt like another betrayal.

I forced a playful scowl on to my face. "Oh, stop it. You know full well I didn't have a one-nighter with Ollie. He may star in a fantasy or two, but that's where it ends. I think I'm a little too hot for him to handle."

More like he'd burn me to ashes.

Lillith narrowed her eyes in suspicion. Forever searching for the truth. But I'd played this one off for so long, she wouldn't recognize the lie. "Then why is he driving you to work?"

Rynna gave me an I-second-that look as we turned and headed up the sidewalk toward Pepper's.

I crossed my arms over my chest. "I think the real question is, what are you doing here before five in the morning, Lily? Shouldn't you be back home snuggled up in bed with that hot husband of yours, getting yourself more of those orgasms I was so kind to set up for you? Rynna and I have work to do."

Loosely translated? I knew Rynna wouldn't give me such a hard time.

At Pepper's front door, Rynna turned the key in the lock and widened the door for us to enter.

Pepper's fronted Fairview Street. It was another area that had undergone a massive rejuvenation over the last handful of years, including the luxury hotel Lillith's husband, Broderick, and his company had developed directly across the street.

The entire area buzzed with possibility.

Pepper's served sweet pies and pot pies and breakfast pies.

You know, basically heaven.

Rynna had inherited the little diner from her grandmother and brought it back to life. Her grandmother's unique recipes were the staple that brought patrons in droves every single morning.

Lillith gave a casual shrug. "I thought I'd help set up this morning."

I shot her a dry look. "Dressed like that?"

Another shrug. "So maybe I woke up starving and wanted the first slice of pie this morning."

"Are you pregnant?"

Nothing like a little deflection.

She gasped a horrified sound. "Shut your mouth. You know Brody and I aren't ready for that."

"Yeah, yeah, you have empires to build." I waved my hand dramatically.

Lily's husband, Broderick Wolfe, was the CEO of Wolfe Industries. His company had been responsible for a bunch of the revitalization projects that had been taking place in Gingham Lakes over the last several years.

She scoffed. "Hardly. We're just . . . focusing on us for a while."

"And all those orgasms I earned you. I have to say, my matchmaking skills are on point."

She playfully rolled her eyes Rynna's direction. "She really thinks she set us up with Brody and Rex, doesn't she?"

Rynna smiled. The woman was one of the kindest people I'd ever met. "You know there's no rationalizing with her madness. Let the poor girl have her delusions," she teased.

"Delusions?" I gestured to myself with both hands. "This is the stark, glorious reality. I'm responsible for all your happiness. I think you should give me all the presents as a thank you."

Rynna's light laughter tinkled through the air, and my chest tightened in affection.

I was so happy for her.

For Rex.

That he'd found the love of his life after everything he'd been through.

Rex was one of Ollie's best friends, and I'd known him my whole life. Rex and Kale had become members of our pack somewhere in our childhood, with us nearly as much as Ollie, Sydney, and me had been together.

Rynna had adopted Rex's little girl, Frankie Leigh. Rex and Rynna had a little boy named Ryland who was a year and a half old.

I'd stepped into the role of honorary auntie faster than the doctor could say "one more push."

I adored those babies, my heart overflowing every time I got to be in their space.

Of course, that rule applied to the newest member of our extended family—Evan.

Sweetness didn't come close to describing that little thing. He'd been born completely deaf and had required a heart transplant as an infant.

The thing about him? The child was pure joy, just like his mom, Hope. Honestly, sometimes when I saw Hope and Kale together, I was the deepest shade of jealous a person could be.

I didn't mean to be.

Didn't want to be.

But sometimes it was hard to watch all the things you wanted most, feel them burn inside of you, and have the deep-lying fear that they would never become a reality.

Rynna flicked on the switches right inside the door. Bright lights burst to life in the darkened space.

We all blinked, adjusting to it.

The echo of pots and pans clanged from the very back of the kitchen where Kevin, the head cook, would have already been working for the last two hours preparing for the morning rush.

"Morning, Kevin," Rynna hollered, moving around the counter to start the coffee.

Priorities and all.

His voice was barely heard when he shouted back, "Mornin'."

Lillith slid onto one of the swiveling stools.

"So, what were you doing with Ollie this morning?" Lillith asked, point blank.

Did I really think she'd let it go?

I sucked in a breath, already knowing the riot my response was going to cause.

But there was no hiding this.

"Someone broke into my apartment last night."

Rynna's hand flew to her mouth. "Oh my God."

Lillith flew to her feet. "What?" she demanded while Rynna moved toward me, her hand reaching to grip my forearm, her eyes searching as she whispered, "Are you okay?"

I knew that wasn't going to go over well. But I did my best to downplay it, to shake off just how truly shaken up I was.

Shrugging a shoulder, I leaned against the counter and did my best to sound convincing.

"Seth was the one who responded to the call. He thinks it was just kids running around being punks the way they love to be. They're lucky I didn't catch them. A little ass kickin' would have ensued. Or maybe I would have grabbed them by the ear and dragged them back to their mamas the way my grandma used to do when I was getting unruly. Death by humiliation. I'm pretty sure that's all they need to teach them a lesson. I mean, seriously? Doesn't the world have enough douchebags? Here I'd been crossing my fingers it might skip this new generation."

"This isn't funny, Nikki." A shiver rocked Lillith's entire body as if she'd just been slammed with visions of every single horrible thing that could have happened. "Kids aren't the same as they used to be."

As if I hadn't noticed the downward spiral of decency.

Distress rolled the length of her throat. "They can be dangerous and mean, and they don't think twice about taking someone out if they think it will get them something they want or cover something up to keep them out of trouble."

I deflated.

Because it wasn't a joke.

Not at all.

Deep down in my gut, I knew I'd been targeted. That it was personal, the way Ollie had said.

Brenna and Kyle's faces flashed through my mind.

They were worth it, and I'd learned a long time ago that fighting for what was right wasn't always easy.

I rubbed my palms over my arms. "I know. And I promise I'm not being careless. Which is why I went to Ollie's place."

I could fight with the man about going back to his loft until I was blue in the face. But the truth of the matter was, I was thankful. Thankful that he'd somehow known I needed him.

Rynna moved back to the counter. She pressed brew on the coffee machine before she turned around and propped her hip on the counter. "So, you called Ollie, and he came running?"

"Something like that."

Lily's brow arched. "What do you mean, something like that?"

I sighed.

It wasn't like I was surprised that she'd insist on pushing the issue.

I searched for an explanation that wouldn't cause an uproar. "He . . . he'd stopped by just as I was getting home after the meeting, so he was there when I discovered it."

Surprise and speculation slashed a bunch of lines across her forehead. I could almost see the cogs turning in that analytical brain of hers. "He just happened to stop by?"

An uncomfortable chuckle rumbled in my chest. "He said he was worried

. . . you know . . . since you went and told him I'd bailed on you for drinks when you knew I just needed to study," I tossed out.

The traitor.

She probably thought she was doing me a favor.

The problem was, she didn't have the first clue she was throwing me to the wolves.

Her brows lifted. "Um . . . maybe I was worried, too. Since when do you pass up an awesome bottle of wine on my balcony with your best friend?"

"Since I decided to do something with my life."

"Hey, managing Pepper's is doing something with your life," Rynna pouted through a tease.

A light chuckle rumbled out. "Of course, it is." Turning back to Lily, I cleared my throat. "Correction. Since I decided to do something *different* with my life."

Lily pursed her lips "Uh-huh. Okay. So, you're busy. I get it. That still doesn't explain Ollie showing up at your place. Are you sure there isn't anything you want to tell us?" she pushed.

I shook my head. "There's nothing to tell."

"You have to admit, things have been super weird between the two of you for the last year."

She pointed at me to stop me from speaking when my mouth started to flap with another flimsy excuse.

Because things had been incredibly weird between Ollie and I over the last year.

Worse than ever.

I just hadn't thought she'd noticed.

"Yeah. He showed up, stayed while I dealt with the cops, and then kind of demanded I go home with him since my door was busted in. He said it wasn't safe for me to stay alone."

"Since when do you do anything someone tells you to do?"

Since an overbearing, brute of a man decided he wanted to be my defender.

"Have you met Ollie?" I figured that answer would suffice.

"A sleepover at Ollie's. Sounds to me like you're begging for trouble." Rynna's observation blazed into the air. "There isn't a whole lot that is simple when it comes to that man."

My attention darted to her. A sea of unease lapped and churned in my belly. "Ollie and I are old friends."

Why'd it have to come out sounding like a confession of guilt?

Rynna blushed with whatever thought went racing through her mind, and Lily was looking at me as if she were chipping pieces of me away and labeling each one as evidence.

"That's all you have to say about it? After you've been gushing about that man for all of forever? Dish the goods, lady. God knows you always demand them of me."

I had gushed.

Telling Lillith I thought Ollie was hot and, if I got the chance, I would chew him up and spit him out. At the time, it had seemed like the best way to explain away the longing looks that lasted just a little too long.

Play it off.

Pretend.

It was what I'd done to make it through.

"Believe me, if I had goods to dish, I'd be spilling because that would indeed be a fun story to tell." I lumbered through the lie.

At least I got it out.

"The one where he picked me up and dumped me in his guest room, where I slept alone, and then brought me here this morning? Not so much."

I left out all the million other things that made the situation complicated and so very messy. How I'd woken to hearing him having a nightmare and begging Sydney's name. How I'd wanted to go to him.

Comfort him.

He'd only made it worse when he'd stumbled out of his room, rumpled from sleep, looking so sexy, I'd wanted to toss every single promise I'd made about him right out the window.

Lillith pointed at me. "Um . . . I call bullshit. I know that salacious mind of yours just went to dirty, dirty places. I demand a confession."

I shrugged. "The man's hot, and he was sleeping in the room next to me. Don't blame me for a fantasy or two."

Worry pursed Rynna's mouth. "What do you do now? I'm not sure I like the idea of you going back to your apartment by yourself."

Lily nodded. "Me, neither. The second you told me what side of town you were moving to, I knew it had trouble written all over it."

"Okay, Miss Money Bags," I shot at her.

Her mouth dropped open in offense. "Um, hello. You do remember I had to have Addelaine take me in when I had no place to live. It's not like I haven't been penniless before."

"I'm going to have Rex start looking around for a house that his crew can fix up. It isn't right that you're living in that dump by yourself," Rynna piped in.

And here I thought Lillith was going to be the problem.

Adamantly, my head shook. "There is no way I'm letting you two buy a house for me."

Rynna carried on as if I hadn't said a thing. "We've been talking about getting some investment properties. Really, it would be a favor to us."

"Not a chance, Rynna. I'm no charity case. You know me better than that."

She shook her head as she flipped on the heat lamps in the window. "I do . . . and I know you slave away here at my little restaurant for meager pay. If anyone's getting charity, it's me."

"I think it's a great idea," Lillith agreed a little too eagerly. "Maybe Brody can fund it, and together we can get another rejuvenation project going in Gingham Lakes. There are quite a few old neighborhoods that would benefit from one. It's good for everyone—the community, the economy, the investors. It's a win-win, really."

Excitement bounced between the two of them.

"That would be amazing, Rex and Broderick back on a project together."

"Y'all are out of your minds," I said with a flippant wave of my hand, turning to start filling the little creamer pitchers. "When I said gimme all the presents, I was thinking along the lines of a gift certificate to A Drop of Hope, or maybe a nice Vicky's Secret bra, you know, the push-up kind since my boobs are basically non-existent? I didn't mean a house."

Lily pursed her lips. "Well, you can't go back to that hole, and it isn't like you can stay with Ollie forever. God knows I love him, but that man is a moody bear. He'll eat you alive."

That was exactly what I was worried about. I didn't respond.

"Or has that been your plan all along? Tell me you didn't go into some dark alley and pay some sketchy-looking guy to bust in your door just so you could sleep in the same house as Ollie."

"You got me," I told her, the words scratchy with dry sarcasm.

"Hey, when a woman gets desperate . . ."

She had no idea.

I spun back around and leaned on the far counter, arms across my chest. "I'm not desperate. He's the one insisting I go back over there tonight. That he doesn't want me stayin' alone."

Lillith widened her eyes. "Are you surprised?"

"I guess I am."

Shocked.

Floored.

Stupefied.

I figured the last thing Ollie wanted was to be in close quarters with me.

"He cares about you," Rynna said as if it were as plain as the coming day lighting up on the bank of windows that faced the street.

I shook my head. "No. The only thing Ollie cares about is being a savior."

"Isn't that the same thing?"

No. Not when it was going to destroy me in the end.

ten

Ollie

"Seth, it's Ollie."

He blew out a breath on the other end of the line. "Hey, man. Was wondering if you were going to call."

"You think I wouldn't?"

I paced the concrete floors of my loft in front of the big bay of windows that overlooked my balcony and the city beyond. I had a view of the river twisting through the buildings as it cut through Gingham Lakes.

My loft took up the entire third floor of the building, Olive's existing in the bottom two floors besides for the small bit at the back that was my garage.

The main room was open, decorated in dark woods and even darker leathers.

The entire vibe echoed peace.

Too bad I felt none of it.

Seth chuckled a bit, but there wasn't a whole lot of amusement to it. "Nah. I knew you would. Especially with the way you looked like you were going to lose your mind last night."

That was the problem.

That was exactly what was happening.

I was losing my mind.

"You want to tell me about this line of bullshit you were feeding Nikki about it being a bunch of kids breaking into her place? Because it sure didn't look that way to me."

He sighed, and I could almost see him rocking forward in his office chair at the station to lean his elbows on his desk. "That's exactly what it could be,

Ollie. We see cases like this all the time. But there was something about it that felt purposed. Like someone was trying to send a message."

My hand curled tighter around my phone. "And what kind of message would that be?"

The sound he made was strained. Like he didn't know what to offer me. "A warning."

Anger tightened around me. Chains. Constricting tighter.

"That doesn't mean that's what it was. It's only a hunch." Silence spun for a second before he continued, "Has she made any enemies lately? Maybe broken up with somebody?"

My teeth gritted.

Because I should know. Should know everything about her. Hold her secrets. Her dreams. Her joy.

I was the one who'd crushed every single one of them.

And I sure as shit shouldn't be pissed by the idea of there even *being* someone for her to break up with.

"Not sure. But she's been interning with a psychologist, helping her run some meetings. She was texting someone last night from there on the ride back to my place. Gut tells me it has something to do with that."

He exhaled heavily. "Anything happening there is going to be confidential. You can't get in the middle of that."

"If it means Nikki's safety, I can."

"Ollie," he warned. "I had you call me because I want you to know what's going on. To watch for anything out of the ordinary. Not for you to take off hunting like . . ."

He trailed off.

Leaving the rest suspended in the distance between us.

My mind filled in the blank.

Like Sydney.

I'd hounded that station for fourteen years.

They'd labeled it a cold case.

And I'd labeled that bullshit.

If they wouldn't hunt? I sure as hell would.

"I won't let anything happen to her, Seth."

It was my own warning.

A promise.

Because whoever this fucker was?

He was gonna learn I had a message to send, too.

I heard the bedroom door snap open. Hell, I probably didn't even hear it. More likely, I felt it, the presence stepping out from the far end of the apartment.

That aura she wore was like an additional layer of her skin.

Glittering diamonds and glimmering golds reflecting off the sun.

Swore, I could feel that girl from a mile away.

Bare feet padded on the concrete floor.

That feeling grew stronger and stronger with each step. It'd covered me whole by the time she made her way out into the main living area.

"What are you doing?" she asked.

That sweet voice hit me from ten feet behind. With the way chills went skating across my skin, she might as well have been whispering it in my ear.

I stirred the ground beef I was browning in the skillet, giving her a quick glance over my shoulder, trying not to get wrapped up in her.

Fresh out of the shower after I'd picked her up from work an hour ago and took her back to her apartment to pick up her car.

Now the girl stood there.

Hair wet.

Skin damp.

Expression confused.

Spirit fierce.

That was what always got me more than anything. The way she glowed this unassuming, timid belief, all wrapped up in a wide, bright smile.

"What's it look like I'm doing?"

"Cooking." It was pure, horrified concern.

I chuckled a little. "Seems like we're on the same page then."

Curiosity drawing her forward, she rounded the tall table surrounded by stools that acted as a partition of the kitchen and living area.

Or maybe it was just me.

Because I could feel the tether.

Pulling, pulling, pulling.

"The question is, why are you cooking? Aren't you supposed to be downstairs working?"

"Probably."

She popped her hip on the counter and crossed her arms over her chest.

The stance pushed up her tiny tits, soft mounds of flesh swelling over the neckline of her tight tank. Her olive skin warm, and her innocent face soft, those freckles running across her nose.

No chance could I keep my gaze from dipping from her mouth to that cleft.

My cock stirred and my chest squeezed painfully.

What the hell had I gotten myself into?

Felt like I'd parachuted right behind enemy lines.

Problem was, I had no idea if it was Nikki I was stealing in to rescue or if it was this girl who was going to kill me in the end.

"So why are you up here then?"

"Thought you might be hungry after a long day's work."

Or maybe I felt like shit after being such an asshole this morning.

It was a toss up.

Her brow rose, and she tightened her hold across her chest. "I'm a big girl. I think I can feed myself. If I'm staying here, I can't be interfering with your job. That bar means the world to you."

So do you.

The thought pierced me like an arrow, sheering straight through me.

I hiked what I hoped looked like an indifferent shoulder, trying to fight off this bullshit feeling I couldn't shake.

Couldn't stop the inundation in my mind, though. The idea of what might have happened had she gone back to her place earlier and gotten in the mix of whoever had been there.

My insides clutched.

In pain.

In dread.

Couldn't stop the assault of images. The horror of someone hurting her.

Stealing her away, too.

I wouldn't let it happen.

Not again.

Not to her.

And my call with Seth was not sitting well.

"Was hungry and didn't feel like eating bar food tonight. Thought you might be, too. That's all. Don't always get down there first thing. Perks of being the boss." I shot her a wink with the last, and she was fighting the smile that was twitching across her lips.

"Must be nice," she said, shifting away and opening the fridge.

She dipped down to peer inside.

My eyes landed on her ass, the girl wearing these tiny black shorts that barely covered her cheeks.

Yeah, so, so nice.

Unbearably nice.

Sweat beaded on my brow, and I beat the attraction back, remembered my mission. Why she was here.

"Want a beer?" she asked, digging through my stash.

"Sure."

She straightened, two beers in hand. She twisted the cap off the first one, handed it to me, and then opened her own before tilting it toward me.

"Truce?"

Unease wound through me as I stared at her standing in my kitchen.

"Never knew we were at war."

She laughed a low sound, shaking her head as she glanced at her feet before she peeked up at me. "Don't pretend we haven't been fighting something for a long, long time, Ollie."

I scrubbed a palm over my face and down my beard, searching for an explanation.

Searching for a valid reason for shutting her out.

The truth of why I broke her heart.

Without revealing the part of myself I couldn't let her have. Not when it belonged to Sydney. Not when I couldn't be trusted.

"Think we both know you are better off without me."

A little scoff bled from her mouth. "I couldn't decide that for myself?"

"You really think so?" It was hard to meet her eyes, but I forced myself to, bringing attention to what I'd done for the first time.

Like a dirty secret kept between us.

"Look what happened the last time I came to you."

Pain lanced across her face.

I felt it right at the center of me.

Lash. Lash. Lash.

Ones my selfishness had inflicted.

But that was what it always was, wasn't it?

Selfishness.

Refused to be that way anymore.

For a beat, she looked away, chewing on her bottom lip before she let out a small breath and asked, "Did you need me or were you just using me?"

Hurt leeched out in every word.

Unable to stop myself, I closed the distance between us and took her face between my palms, my voice grit. "I've always fucking needed you."

She jarred, shocked by my sudden movement, and blinked up at me with those eyes that twisted me in two.

I loosened my hold, and my words quieted. "But just because I need you doesn't mean I get to keep you."

For a minute, I just got lost there. Looking at her.

Before I ripped myself away from her and turned all of my attention back to fixing dinner.

Guessed I might as well add foolish to that list of fucked-up qualities.

Because that was maybe the dumbest thing I could have given her. But for once, she deserved it.

A little bit of the truth.

She wasn't looking at me as she fidgeted, those fingers moving out to fiddle with a dishtowel sitting on the counter. "I'm not sure how to move on from that night," she admitted.

Sorrow had taken me whole when I looked over at her. "Which one?"

That was the crux of things. We had no way to move on. Both of us stuck, and I'd only made it worse.

Leaving her when she was sixteen and running back to her a year ago.

"Truce?" I mumbled, reiterating what she'd said.

Light laughter fell from under her breath. "Feels like a shaky one."

I gave a tight nod. No question it was.

Shaky.

But she'd been my friend long before she'd been anything else.

So, I searched for some kind of lightness, the easy yet profound way we'd once been. "Probably. Just hold on to something when you move. One look at me, and you won't be able to remain standing."

It was all a tease with a tip of my lips.

She choked out a laugh. "Wow . . . someone really is full of himself."

"Just keeping things real."

Amusement danced across her pretty face.

So damned pretty.

Painfully pretty.

She was all smiles when she tipped the neck of her beer my direction. "To poor girls who can't keep their heads on straight when they're in your presence. May they forever see through the BS."

I clinked my beer against hers and then lifted it in the air. "Believe me, baby, the outside looks way better than the inside."

I let a little of the cold, hard truth sneak into my ribbing.

She took a sip of her beer before she tucked it up close to her chest as she stared at me, her voice close to a whisper. "I think you sell yourself short, Ollie. I've always been pretty fond of what's on the inside."

I tossed a tortilla onto the griddle I'd had heating with oil. It sizzled and hissed, and I focused on evening it out with the spatula.

"That's an ugly place, Nikki. Believe me, you don't want to get anywhere close to that. Not anymore."

"What if I've just always wanted you for your body?"

Could feel her words take to the air, light and playful, the way we'd spent thirteen years. Acting like we didn't really know each other.

Our interactions nothing more than a breezy tease when the wind that gusted beneath them threatened to be a dust storm.

She was all taunting smirks when I looked over at her.

Little Tease.

Probably the last thing I should do, but I went with it.

"Think I'm more than you can handle."

A sexy twist of her lips had me stumbling. "Well, if that's how you feel."

She nodded, and a flash of sadness twined through her demeanor before she tipped her beer my direction. "Friends."

I picked mine back up and clinked it to hers. "Friends."

Problem was, having to remain friends with Nikki Walters was the hardest thing I'd ever had to do.

A half hour later, the girl's contagious laughter was bouncing against the walls.

She popped the last bit of her taco into her mouth, wiped her hands with her napkin, and rocked back on the high-backed stool. "You're such a liar. That was totally your fault."

My laughter was low, way too amused, barriers down that'd been there for so many years. I shook my head as I sopped up a few pieces of meat that'd fallen from my taco, glancing up at her with a grin when I did.

"My fault? Are you kiddin' me? Every bad idea I ever had was because of you. Tying that rope to that tree included. I said it wasn't gonna hold me . . . and what did you say?"

Guilt twitched all over her flirty mouth. "I don't remember."

A rumble of amusement rolled around in my chest. "Think it went something like, 'Ollie thinks he's the shit, but he's really nothin' but a chicken shit.' On repeat, of course."

"No." Her head shook in vigorous denial, but she was doing her best not to bust up in outright confession. Indigo eyes full of old affection.

The same kind gripped at my chest. Claws wanting to take hold.

I shook it off and focused on being *friends*.

"Yes. You were always the instigator, whispering in my ear, making me think I wasn't a man if I didn't go through with whatever you'd concocted."

I wiped my hands and tossed my napkin onto the table, slinging my arm over the stool back, grinning at her. "Took it on myself to prove to you just what kind of man I was."

Mischief moved across her face, honeyed locks of hair swishing across her cheeks, those freckles so fuckin' sweet.

Had the intense urge to lean out and lick them.

Taste her.

That mouth and those lips and every inch of smooth, soft skin.

"Hey, it isn't my fault you thought you had to be such a badass. Sounds like a personal problem to me."

"More like I had my own, personal troublemaker."

"And look who I was trying to keep up with. If anyone was the troublemaker, it was you."

"And look who I was trying to impress."

A blush kissed across her chest, rising with the energy that danced. Slowly. Quietly. Though just as intense.

Her tone turned wistful. "At least Kale discovered his true calling that day. He got really serious about setting your ankle."

"That shit hurt like hell, too," I told her through a chuckle.

Memories hit me hard.

One after one.

Like they were so close, I could take a step and tumble into them.

They called them the good old days.

For us?

They really were.

She bit her lip. Nikki wasn't shy. She was just real. "I really am sorry you broke your ankle."

I didn't know what I was thinking, but I reached out and let my fingertips trail the defined curve of her cheek.

She trembled, and for a moment, she leaned into my touch before she pulled away.

Like she was just then realizing she needed to stay away from me.

That I was dangerous.

I shook the heaviness off and climbed back into the tease, pretending I wasn't treading choppy waters.

"Oh, sure you are. Who was it standing over me, laughing her ass off, holding her stomach, saying she wished she had a video camera so she could send it in to *America's Funniest Home Videos* . . . thought you were gonna get rich off me."

She tried to hold back a giggle. "Hey, I would have shared."

Couldn't keep my eyes from tracing her face.

Every inch.

I'd *managed* for so long.

Keeping her at a distance while still keeping her close.

It's your fault.

I trusted you.

You were supposed to take care of her.

You promised, you'd take care of her.

Voices resonated from the cold valley planed out inside me.

I swallowed around the grief that thickened my throat, welcoming the reminder.

I couldn't be trusted.

God, I knew I needed to get the fuck out of there, but there was something about being with her this way that made me want to stay.

Just for a little bit.

A few moments of the relief she brought all heaped with a load of torment.

I angled my head toward the television. "You want to catch a show before I head downstairs?"

"Are you sure you have time?"

"Why not? Cece doesn't mind running things."

"You know she's just waiting to oust you from your position, right?" she said as she slipped off the stool, her suggestion a bit of a tease, though I thought maybe there was a true question behind it.

"Nah, Cece might look like a viper, but she's harmless."

"Harmless?" She let out a little laugh. "She doesn't look harmless to me. She basically looks like she could annihilate the bar in one fell swoop."

I plopped onto the couch. "You jealous?"

Nikki dropped down on the opposite end with an incredulous shake of her head. "Of the fact she's stunning and scary and basically can command the bar with a single look? Hell, yes."

Cece oozed sex and radiated intimidation. Men flocked to the bar, salivating and begging for a bone. Her attention the prize, the woman had the power to drop the poor suckers right to their knees.

So maybe she wasn't entirely harmless. She just didn't pose any threat to me.

"I'll be sure to tell her that," I told her with a lift of my brow.

"Don't you dare. Women like that eat girls like me for dinner."

"I think you're safe. As far as I know, she likes men."

Disgust made her scowl. "Tell me you don't know that because you've slept with her. She's your employee. That's just all kinds of wrong, Oliver Preston."

She tried to make it come out as nonchalant, like she was giving a friend advice. But I heard the way the idea of it scraped from her throat. Hurting her.

Always, always hurting her.

I looked at her, hooking up a small smile. "Don't worry your pretty little head, Nikki Walters. I don't sleep with my employees. But you know Kale got a taste of that before he met Hope."

Her eyes went wide with the scandal.

"No," she wheezed.

Had no idea if I was breaking bro code by letting her in on that little bit, but somehow, I couldn't make myself shut the hell up, needing this connection with her, hungry for it. Or maybe I was just trying to shift the attention from myself.

"Yup."

"Freaking Kale . . . he's lucky I love him so much."

"Nah . . . he was just doing his thing . . . biding his time until the right girl came into his life."

She blinked these wide blinks at that, that feeling pulsing at my chest, thrumming in the space between us. "So you really never slept with her?"

"No. Not even close."

Her eyes narrowed for a beat, like she was searching me for the truth, before she relaxed against the arm of the couch and pulled her legs up so she could hug her knees. "Good. You're forgiven. For now."

This time, it was my brows riding high. "And just what are you forgiving me for?"

"Being a gorgeous, brainless, womanizing man." She said it with a jut of her chin. Playful even though I could feel the undertone of severity. The two of us broaching a subject we'd never trusted ourselves to touch before.

An incredulous chuckle rolled out. "Womanizing, huh? Now who's making assumptions about the other?"

Her amusement shifted and fell into something somber. "Oh, come on, Ollie. You don't need to pretend for me. You think I don't see those girls?"

Regret clamped down on my chest. I grabbed the remote and aimed it at the television that sat on the console, voice a little lower than it needed to be. "Those girls don't mean anything."

Her voice was softer. "Everyone means something, Ollie. Feels something. Whether you want to take it into account or not."

This girl.

I turned up the volume. Like it might have the power to mute every mistake I'd ever made.

She was right.

Everyone mattered.

Her the most.

And I'd gone and treated her the same goddamned way I treated everyone else.

Needing a diversion, I flipped through some channels.

A grin took over when I found what I was looking for.

Could feel her amusement ripple from her spirit, the way her mouth twisted up as she attempted to keep herself from laughing. She stretched out her leg and gave me a little kick to the thigh.

"AFV? Are you kidding me?"

My eyes glided up her bare leg.

For a beat, my attention locked on the frayed, braided bracelet made of red thread she still wore around her ankle, the worn metal charm in the middle stamped with the words, "Fly."

I had one to match hidden in my room, unable to bear wearing it.

Seeing it.

The third piece was missing forever.

My guts ached.

I shoved off the thoughts and let feigned innocence lift both my shoulders to my ears. "What? I thought it was your favorite show?"

"Stupid boys," she muttered for what had to have been for the millionth time since I'd known her.

The thing about it?

It was the first time she'd said it in fourteen years.

I pretended I didn't feel contentment go sinking all the way to my bones.

She shifted and groaned a little as she tried to get comfortable on my couch.

Totally should have ignored that sound, considering it spoke directly to my dick, but the question was sliding free before I could stop it. "What's wrong?"

"Legs just get tired from running around the diner for nine hours a day. Feels good to lie down. This couch is Heaven. Seriously, Ollie, when I leave, I'm taking it with me. No need to report a robbery. You know where it'll be."

I let loose a fake gasp. "After all my kindness, you'd go and steal from me?"

She peeked over at me with a sweet grin that slid right through me. "For this couch? Absolutely."

"Here." Reaching out, I dragged both her feet onto my lap and angled to the side a bit so I was facing her better.

Such a bad, bad idea.

She was right.

Stupid boys.

So damned stupid when I took one of her feet into my hands and kneaded my fingers into her heel.

Nikki's gasp was real.

Hitting the air like a motherfucking drug.

Just a moan from her tongue a spell.

For a moment, she hesitated. Clearly, the girl knew this was a bad idea, too. Because she stilled before she relented.

The anxiety firing through her body went lax, and she rolled onto her back to grant me better access.

She emitted another one of those groans.

Throatier this time.

"Don't make me steal this couch and you, too. A girl could get used to this," she murmured.

I had to suck for air because my lungs squeezed.

Constricted with a rush of lust.

Like a dumbass, I continued to massage her foot, my thumbs pressing deeper into her heel before I moved to the arch.

Wishing I was closer.

Needing more.

A sigh pulled from between those pink lips, and the air shifted.

Sizzled and lit.

That'd always been the problem with Nikki.

She was heat and light. A spark and a flame.

Sunshine.

I thought I just might lose my mind because I swore I could see that aura she wore gather between us.

Colors.

Reds and purples and blues.

They thrummed and lapped. It made it impossible to breathe.

I moved to the ball of her foot and then to her toes, which were tiny and somehow delicate, the nails short and painted the same shimmery pink color of her lips.

Did it make me a sick fucker that I wanted to suck one into my mouth? That I wanted to lick up her bare leg? Nibble at the inside of her thigh?

She squirmed, and my breaths came harder.

Harsher.

While hers turned shallow.

She arched from the couch.

Need and pleasure.

I wondered if a girl could go off from a foot massage alone.

Because I thought maybe I could from giving one.

My cock strained painfully as I moved to her other foot.

"Ollie," she whimpered. "That feels so good."

Visions slammed me.

Clearly.

The girl bare.

Laid out under me.

An offering.

Nikki. Nikki. Nikki.

I dropped her foot like a rock and launched to my feet.

Erratically, my chest heaved as lust careened through my body. I roughed both my hands through my hair, trying to calm the fuck down.

Get myself together.

You can't be trusted. You can't be trusted.

Shocked out of the trace, Nikki shot up to sitting. Her eyes blazed as she stared across at me.

With desire and regret.

With the realization she should be protecting herself from me.

She clutched the couch like it was a life raft she was getting ready to get tossed from.

This was stupid.

So stupid.

"Need to get downstairs," I told her, voice rough.

She nodded.

For the first time since I'd known this girl, no smart reply came from her mouth. I didn't wait for her to form one.

I flew for the door.

My own life raft.

Because I was right.

This girl was a wave getting ready to take me under.

And I didn't think she'd ever let me up for air.

eleven

Nikki

It was close to five p.m. when I bounded down the three flights of stairs and out the big metal door into the back-parking lot.

Humidity smacked me in the face, and I was hit with the overpowering scent of honeysuckle that wafted through the dense air.

I jogged across the lot to where I'd parked my car after Ollie had taken me back to my apartment to pick it up yesterday afternoon.

I knew I shouldn't find comfort in staying with him. But I wouldn't lie to myself.

I did.

I wouldn't have been able to sleep last night had I been staying at my apartment, fearful Caleb might return.

All I wanted was to lay low.

Hide out.

Just for a little while.

Until things between him and Brenna cooled down.

Of course, I had to admit I hadn't slept all that well knowing Ollie was once again just a room away.

A wall and a million miles separating us.

But after the evening we'd spent together, it'd felt as if part of that chasm was being erased.

Drawn.

That magnet that would live forever pulling us together.

It was a bad idea to get close to him. I knew it. Of course, I knew it. But sometimes life made it hard to pretend he hadn't once been the most important person in my life.

Anxious to head to my sister's house, I clicked the fob and started to pull open the driver's side door.

Then I froze.

My stomach plummeted to the ground.

The hairs at the nape of my neck lifted on end, and the sweat that was already threatening to gather beaded across my forehead and neck, trickling down my back in a slow slide of dread.

Another note.

It was folded neatly and tucked beneath the wiper.

He'd found me.

Oh God, he'd found me.

I gulped around the rush of terror that glided through my body.

Followed me more likely.

From Brenna's description, he was manipulative in the worst of ways. Yanking her one direction then the other until she thought she was going insane.

Warily, my attention darted around the area, searching beneath the towering trees that lifted to the blue, blue sky, across the line of cars that were parked next to mine since this area was reserved parking for Olive's employees.

Nothing.

Just the whisper of the leaves and the sound of the busy street echoing from the other side of the building.

"Shit," I mumbled. All I wanted was to run right back upstairs. Maybe curl up in the bed Ollie had told me to consider mine.

Maybe curl up in his.

Damn it.

I could not let my brain go down that train of thought.

But it seemed almost impossible.

Not with the way he'd always made me feel safe.

Not with the way he'd touched me last night.

I wanted to fall into Ollie's strong arms and beg him to take it away.

But I wasn't that girl.

One to be frightened away.

Threatened until I backed down so some jerk could have his way.

Brenna deserved so much better than that.

Taking one last glance around the lot, I snagged the note and hopped into my car, quick to slam the door and press the lock.

Heart a riot in my chest, I carefully unfolded it.

Fear slicked across the surface of my flesh.

A cold, cold dread.

You think you can get away so easily? He can't keep you from

what's coming.

Thunder.

It rumbled through my being. A warning. A siren that screamed. Pulse a deafening pound, pound, pound as it echoed in my ears.

I squeezed my eyes closed against the shackle of terror that gripped me.

I'd always known working for the program would require sacrifice.

That it might not always be easy.

Maybe I'd known I was getting in too deep.

I'd just never expected it might make me feel like I was going to drown.

I hoisted myself onto my little sister's kitchen counter.

Sammie gave me a scowl. "Were you born in a barn?"

Playfully, I rolled my eyes at her and tossed another grape into my mouth. "Um, if I was born in a barn, then I'm pretty sure you were, too. Next thing you know, you'll be makin' yo mama jokes. Tryin' to cut me down to size when you're really just cutting yourself off at the knees."

She swatted at me. "Pssh . . . if I wanted to cut you down to size, I wouldn't need to look to our mother. Think I've got plenty to work with just with you sittin' there. We could start with that face."

"Ouch," I said, grinning wide. Funny how neither of us were feeling the love unless we were razzing the other.

Old habits die hard and all that.

"Before you start going down that road, you should probably take a gander in the mirror," I told her.

She laughed. "Oh, God . . . now don't you go talking about how much we look alike. A couple of days ago, I was at that little market over by Grandma's. Remember her neighbor, Margo? I was loading my groceries onto the conveyor belt when I heard someone shoutin', 'Nikki, Nikki, is that you?' I don't know why she even bothered asking the question when she refused to believe I was your sister and not actually you."

"You say this as if looking like me is a bad thing."

She laughed as she flitted around her cozy country kitchen, preparing dinner, the smell of a roast simmering on the stove making my stomach growl.

Her face really was so much like mine that it felt as if I was looking in a mirror.

A few years younger and a tiny bit rounder from the few pounds she was still clinging to after giving birth to my sweet niece two months ago.

"Did you show up at my door diggin' for compliments?"

"Um, no, I didn't show up at your door diggin' for compliments. I showed up at your door diggin' for dinner."

That, and I needed a distraction.

I had to tell Seth about the notes I'd found on my car. I knew I did. But I needed to work myself up to it. Figure out exactly what information I could give without betraying confidence, knowing I didn't have proof.

But my gut?

It was sure.

On top of that? I'd needed to get out of Ollie's loft. Clear my head. Decide exactly what I was going to say to him.

I couldn't just stay there and keep him in the dark about what was happening.

But God knew, I was terrified of letting him in on this.

He wasn't exactly rational when it came to a threat.

Plus, I had to be careful before I lost my heart all over again.

No doubt, that was the most dangerous position I could get myself into.

Sammie pulled out a cutting board and set a head of broccoli on it. "Well, I guess you came to the right place, then, didn't you? Just expecting your married sister was gonna be slaving away in the kitchen for her husband."

"Isn't that what you're doing?" I teased, eyeing the spread she was preparing.

Chuckling, she shook her head. "I do it because I want to do it, not because I'm obligated."

I nudged her with my shoe. "You think I don't know that? And there is not a thing wrong with you wanting to take care of your family."

She glanced over at me. Something about her expression was wistful and sad. "I never really thought it was what I'd want to do. I always envisioned myself in a big skyscraper in an even bigger city, working my way up the corporate ladder, and now all I want to do is spend the day rockin' that baby."

"You always dreamed of getting away from Gingham Lakes, didn't you?"

Her head shook a bit. "Sometimes you think it's the place you need to escape when really it's just your situation."

I stilled at that, something unsettling about her statement. I searched her face. "What does that mean?"

Her posture stiffened, and she pinned on a smile. "Nothing. Just means I thought there might be better things out there waiting for me in the world."

"Why's that?"

She inhaled deeply, biting her bottom lip as she continued chopping. "It's nothing. Just never quite felt comfortable in my own skin."

I shifted to the side so I could see her better. "I don't get that, Sammie. You were always the happiest of us all."

She puffed a little sound. "Not even. You and Sydney and those boys. You were always running free, leaving your poor baby sister behind."

A chuckle rippled out, and I reached over and grabbed another handful of grapes from the bowl. "Ha. Every time I tried to take you anywhere, you didn't want to walk. How many times did Ollie have to carry you home on his back?"

She laughed low and tossed the florets of broccoli she'd just cut into the pot of water boiling on the stove. "Good thing that boy was always the size of a bear, always having to carry all the poor, pathetic girls around."

She grinned. "Of course, you were probably just faking being tired so you could get yourself one of those rides. Anything to get your arms around that man."

Nostalgia moved through me. Joy chased by sorrow. I couldn't stop the sad smile.

She sobered a bit. "You know, I always thought the two of you would end up together."

My head shook. "No. We have too much in common. Too much history to ever make that work."

"Isn't that what makes a good relationship?"

"Not when all that history is filled with pain."

She nodded slowly, quick to change the subject. "So, how are your classes?"

"Good. I'm so close to being finished. I can't believe it."

"I'm really proud of you, you know?"

Light laughter escaped. "It's about time, isn't it? Here I am thirty and barely figuring out what I want to do with my life."

Funny how things were supposed to be coming together and every piece of me felt as if it were descending into disorder.

The apartment.

Brenna.

The internship.

And somehow staying with Ollie felt just as big as all of that.

Maybe bigger.

This was Ollie, we were talking about.

My great big world.

He had taken that world from me for so long, and now I felt as if I was stumbling through it in the darkness.

I chose not to tell my sister any of those things. She didn't need to be fretting over me when she had her family to care for. To worry for.

The important things in life.

She glanced over at me as she started to make gravy in a skillet. I wasn't joking when I said I'd come around here diggin' up dinner. My baby sister knew how to cook. "Mama is so happy you're getting ready to graduate."

My chest tightened with a smidge of pride. "She's always worrying about me. I think she keeps forgetting I'm thirty."

Sammie laughed under her breath. "That's because Mama thinks *she's* still thirty."

Standing at the stove, she looked back at me, concern in her eyes. "I'm worried about how she's handling Gramma falling ill, moving in with her to be her full-time caretaker. That's gotta be hard, seeing her own mama like that."

So many emotions raced through me at the thought, I didn't know how to make sense of them.

My grandma who'd always been so alive and strong.

The summers we'd spent running in and out of her house, the screen door slamming shut as we came and went.

"It has to be the hardest thing any of us ever go through, watching our mother's fall ill. God, I can't stand seeing it with Gramma. Every time I go over there, it breaks my heart a little more."

She nodded through the somberness of it. That cycle of life we'd give anything to stop but never could. It didn't matter how old my gramma was, my mama, my sister. There'd never be a time when I didn't want to cling to them forever.

"At least Uncle Todd is back in town to help around the house. That will hopefully take away some of the stress," I said.

From behind, Sammie's spine stiffened, and I could have sworn I saw her knees sway, losing balance.

"Sammie . . . you okay?"

She nodded. "Of course. Just . . . hate the thought of Gramma being sick."

Just then, the speaker on the baby monitor crackled. A tiny, rattling cry came through, and I slid off the counter. "Let me get her."

"That'd be nice," Sammie said with a gracious smile, though I couldn't shake the feeling something was suddenly off.

I headed down the hall and eased open the door to Penelope's room, which was adorable with its hearts and elephants everywhere.

My chest filled.

So full.

Almost too full.

The feeling only came stronger as I looked down at my niece, who was flailing one fist while trying to shove the other into her tiny mouth. Somehow, she had kicked free of the blanket and was wiggling around, making the sweetest sounds.

I couldn't help but echo them back. "Hey, Angel," I whispered, scooping her into my arms. "How's my sweet, sweet girl? Auntie Nik has been missing you."

I hugged her to my chest and kissed the top of her head, whispering against her crown. "So much."

She cooed, scratched her sharp little nails in my chin as she fisted at my skin.

Was it wrong the little thing made me ache?

It wasn't like I was *old*. But I still felt that time slipping away. A piece of me missing that I'd always assumed would just be there one day.

I could swill wine with my friends and laugh all my nights away. Give back the best I could, live and embrace who I was.

I'd be happy.

That didn't mean something wouldn't be missing.

Maybe it only seemed fitting it was tucked right down in that place with all those pieces that'd gone missing long ago.

"Nik?"

I startled with my sister's voice coming from behind me.

I spun around to find her standing in the doorway. There was something mournful in her expression. As if she'd just heard every single one of my thoughts as if I'd said them aloud.

Or maybe I just saw it projected back, her face like a picture of mine.

I pasted on a thin smile. "She's so beautiful, Sammie. If I were you, I'd want to sit and rock her all day, too."

Sammie gazed at her daughter. "It's funny, just looking at her makes me believe the world could be a better place."

Hugging the tiny thing to me, I kissed her temple.

And I believed it, too.

Outside of my sister's house, I sat in the driver's side seat of my car in the darkness, holding the card Seth had given me between my fingers. With a shaky hand, I dialed the number.

Two rings later, a scratchy voice came on the line. "Hello?"

"Seth . . . it's Nikki."

"Are you okay?" he rushed.

I sucked in a breath, eyes darting through the windows, searching the shadows.

The feeling of being watched sent chills crawling across my skin.

No question, I was being paranoid, but I couldn't seem to stop the dread clinging to me.

I just couldn't take the risk.

"Yeah. I'm fine. I just . . . I have something I need to tell you, but I need you to promise you won't tell Ollie."

twelve

Ollie

I snapped open the door to my nineteen fifties turquoise-blue Chevy truck to the sticky summer air.

Birds flitted across the sky that was painted a bright, brilliant blue, and the lush, towering trees rustled in the gentle breeze blowing through.

I stepped out onto the sidewalk and shut the door to the old truck, which was basically my prized possession.

When I found it, it'd been rotting at the back of this old guy's land, swallowed by weeds and pretty much rusted down to the metal bones.

It was kind of my thing. Taking the dilapidated—the neglected and the failing—and doing my own sort of restoration.

It was where I found my joy.

Taking something that had been left for ruin and giving it a new life. A second chance when I wasn't ever going to get one for myself.

A certain sort of retribution. Like I was desperate to find something good buried in the rubble.

My first love was my bar. Taking it from the ruin it'd been and breathing a new life into it.

I took just as much pride in the cars I had restored at a local shop, Roke's restorations, a garage I'd invested some money into when it had been threatened with going under.

Hell, I'd invested in a few failing businesses around Gingham Lakes, wanting to see something good rise out of the dust.

But the cars . . .

I loved watching them going from completely rotted to immaculate.

From a heap of junk to a priceless treasure.

Guessed it was a whole lot easier to fall for material things than things made up of flesh and blood and spirit.

Safer.

But sometimes not falling proved itself impossible.

Which was precisely the reason I was there today, driving this specific truck when I had five others to choose from in my garage.

Because . . . Evan.

The first time Kale had brought him to my place, the little boy had run through that garage like he'd gotten a lifetime pass to Disneyland and couldn't wait to visit it every day.

His big ol' bug eyes had been nothing but excitement behind his thick-rimmed glasses as he'd gone from car to car. His fingertips had traced the metal, and he'd sat behind the steering wheel of each car, pretending like he was flying down a racetrack.

Kale hadn't even protested when I'd let Evan climb onto one of my motorcycles.

But this truck?

It was his favorite.

He'd claimed it as his on that big spiral-bound notebook he always carried around, jumping up and down as he'd shoved it toward my face to tell me just how much he loved it.

Then he'd gone and left that ripped-out piece of paper on my coffee table so I wouldn't forget.

A light chuckle rippled out as I thought back to that day, to the way the kid had gotten right under my skin like he'd belonged there all along.

The same way Frankie Leigh and Ryland had done.

So, there I was, locking the door of that truck and reaching into the bed to snag the football I'd tossed back there for my little adventure to the park that sat smack-dab in the middle of our small city.

Meeting up for a motherfucking play date.

Talk about being a third wheel.

Out of place.

A damned fish out of water when this was the very pond I grew up in.

Kale, Rex, and I had spent many an afternoon running the fields as kids, kicking up dirt, causing trouble the way we'd always liked to do.

A couple of hours ago, I'd gotten a text from Rex to meet them there. I hadn't even hesitated. I needed to get the hell out of my loft.

Nikki's scent had been stalking me like a fucking drug since the second I'd woken up.

I could feel the fractures and splinters getting deeper and deeper. Cracking me open wide.

My thoughts dangerous.

My need dark.

The last four days, we'd basically avoided each other, me grunting hellos and her offering timid, unsure smiles as she hightailed it out the door as quickly as she could, spending as little time within the walls of my apartment as possible.

She'd be gone before I even woke in the morning and already fast asleep by the time I made it back upstairs after closing the bar.

You'd think with the little amount I actually saw her, it wouldn't be all that bad.

Not true.

I was constantly on edge. Need gliding across my flesh like the sharp edge of a knife.

Lust and regret a bottomless pit in the well of my stomach.

Worry this constant thud that banged inside of me.

Seth still had no word on who might have broken into her apartment, and until he did? I wasn't about to let her leave.

Guessed a little fresh air would do me some good.

I rounded the front of the truck and headed for the park.

Fields and playgrounds went on for what had to be a mile, all closed in by massive, ancient trees.

The second she saw me, Frankie Leigh came running in my direction. Long, brown hair flew behind her like a cape, wild and uncontained.

Grinning, I moved a little faster to meet her.

Like I said.

Sometimes it was impossible not to fall.

I dropped the football just in time to use her momentum to grab her under the arms and spin her around and around.

She howled with laughter, shouting, "Come on, Uncle, can't you go any higher?"

She was a wild one, that was for sure, so damned happy and full of life there was no way you could be around her and not smile.

She reminded me a little of Nikki in that way, the way Nikki had been at her age, so eager to experience life; though, Nikki had done it with a tiny bit more fear.

Doses of hesitation coming on.

Careful.

It had always been Sydney who'd spur her on. Telling her to run. Jump. That she could do it.

I wondered when Nikki had decided to get so reckless.

Brave.

Which fucking sucked because the last thing I wanted was for her to be brave, constantly having to worry about the position she might be putting herself in. Stepping up when she thought it might right a wrong.

Make someone's life better.

Even if it was just a conversation with a lonely old guy living on the street.

I beat back the direction my thoughts were going and instead focused on Frankie, who I was still spinning.

Her squeals of joy hit the air, and it didn't take too long before I decided she had to have had enough and slowed to set her on her feet. Wasn't surprised in the least when she went stumbling back toward the rest of the group, veering to the right, totally dizzy and off-kilter.

Had to admit, I felt a bit of that spin, too.

"She starts puking, and that's on you. Hope you have a rag or two in your truck," Rex shot in my direction as a smug grin tugged on his mouth.

He stood behind his tiny son, Ryland, who was facing out, both of the one-year-old boy's hands in Rex's as Rex helped him balance.

The little thing was doing his best to kick a soccer ball with his foot. Not moving it more than an inch but having a grand time doing it.

That shit was cute, that was for sure, the kid like a tiny version of his dad.

Sometimes it still fucked with my head to see Rex this way. Guy'd been one of my closest friends for pretty much all of my life.

He'd taken it about as hard as I had after Sydney had disappeared. Angry at the whole damned world because ours had been rocked, none of us able to make sense of something so brutal actually taking place.

Shocked.

Traumatized.

It'd taken that sweet little girl being born for his hardened pieces to start chipping away, meeting Rynna stripping the rest to the ground.

Disquiet tumbled through me. A rumble in that dark space. Sometimes it was hard to watch. Time moving on. People moving on. Sometimes, I wished that I could, too.

Didn't matter if I wished for it or not. Knew I'd forever be a captive of that day.

I shoved the thoughts down and snatched up the ball where I'd dropped it and pointed it his direction. "You wish, man. Puke duty is not a part of my repertoire."

Kale, who had been kneeling in front of Evan, pushed to standing and threw me a grin as he jumped into the conversation. "This from the guy who owns a bar and his sole purpose in life is to get people tanked. I'm pretty sure Olive's has played host to a hurl or two."

Kale was our opposite. All clean-cut lines and cleaner jaw, his title of pediatrician fitting him to a tee.

"Not a chance, man. Olive's is the classiest of establishments. Assholes get trashed, and they're out on their asses. Now you want to talk about what goes down on the front sidewalk in the middle of the night? That's an entirely different story."

"Language, man," Rex said, angling his head to the side. Knew the look on his face. If we'd been fifteen, that would have been delivered with a punch.

"Sorry."

Kale laughed. "Leave it to the bachelor not to be able to figure out how to act around kids."

He glanced down when Evan reached up and tugged him by the hand to get his attention.

Evan's hands flew through the air, quickly signing something I couldn't read.

Kale smiled like a damned fool and signed back.

My chest tightened like the yank of a belt.

Evan's adoption had just gone through. I wasn't sure I'd ever seen the guy happier than that day.

Not that he needed the paper. Pretty sure the guy felt that way from moment one.

Loved seeing my crew happy. Finding love after all the bullshit that'd been tossed our way through the years.

Brutal blow after fucking brutal blow.

Two of them had always had my back, stood beside me during the toughest time of my life.

Both of them had handled it differently.

Rex had fallen into that anger and grief right along with me. Like he'd wanted to take some of it on, shoulder some of the burden like he might be able to grant me some relief, ridden with a dark empathy when I didn't think he really had the first clue what I was going through.

Sydney hadn't been his responsibility. Hadn't been the one who was supposed to watch after her. Keep her safe.

Kale had stood up and become the rock and had been the one to eventually encourage me to move on. To find the bright side when my entire life had gone dark.

I waved back, moving Evan's direction and leaning down in front of him. I ruffled a hand through his red hair.

"Hey, little man," I told him, knowing he'd be able to read my lips. "Did you see what I brought?"

He dropped to his knees with that pad he used for communication, scribbled something quick. He turned it for me to see what he'd written, excitement streaking across the mass of freckles that dotted his pale face.

You brought my truck? I'm saving all my money from my chores so I can buy it when I get my license. I've got twenty dollars. Is that almost enough?

I chuckled under my breath when I read what he'd written.

"You're gettin' close, buddy. Real close. What do you say for now, we play for a bit and then we take it for a drive?"

His eyes went wide, and he mouthed, *Really?*

"Really," I told him, touching his chin.

Yep.

Impossible not to fall.

I stood and gave the football a small toss into the air. "Who's the next Gingham Lakes High wide receiver? Is his name Evan Bryant?"

His eyes lit up behind his thick-rimmed glasses, and he gave me an emphatic nod of his head.

I gave it a soft pitch in his direction, and he fumbled along for the ball.

Kale watched him like a goddamned hawk.

Always wary of the kid's heart.

Couldn't imagine having to carry that weight. But neither he nor Hope would let their own fears get in the way of the kid living a full life. Just because he was born with a genetic defect that had almost taken his young life, his parents weren't going to hold him back.

And man, did the kid live a full life. He was so full of it he shined.

He caught the ball against his chest, and Frankie went flying his way. Arms stretched out like she was soaring.

"Here, Evan. Throw it to me! I wanna catch it!"

Kinda made me sad that her adorable lisp had all but disappeared.

Guess time didn't stop spinning, no matter how badly I might want it to.

Didn't think it was possible, but Evan's face lit up even more when he looked at Frankie, and he threw it with all his might, sending it soaring.

You know, about ten feet in the air.

Fucking cute.

"You've got a visitor, man, three o'clock," Rex warned, and I turned in time to find Ryland toddling my way.

His arms were thrown up over his head, and he was giggling as he tottered over, anticipating that I was going to scoop him up.

I did.

It sent a tremor rolling through me.

Truth was, kids terrified me.

Terrified me in a way that wasn't healthy.

Didn't mean these three hadn't melted through the hard places at the center of me. Worked their way in, my care fierce.

Would do absolutely everything in my power to keep them safe.

Ryland yanked at my beard with his chubby fingers, his grin so wide as he flashed me a row of four teeth on the top and two on the bottom.

He grunted hard like he was talking to me.

"Ouch, dude," I chuckled, trying to unwind his death grip. "That hurts."

Kid laughed like it was the funniest thing in the world.

So did his dad.

Like I said, his dad's mini-me.

I scowled in Rex's direction. "And this is funny, why?"

"Uh, how about because you're holding my one-year-old like a backpack that might contain a bomb."

It was just then I was realizing I had him under the arms, holding him out and away from me. My beard was just out of reach of his flailing arms. "Self-preservation, man. Kid's about to tear me limb from limb."

Such a pussy, Rex mouthed, smirk on his face as he came to collect his kid.

Such an asshole, I mouthed back.

Evan was all of a sudden in my line of sight, his hand going over his mouth like he was trying to shield himself from my corruption.

Awesome.

Turns out, Kale was totally right. I had no idea how to act around kids.

"Such a bad influence. You're hopeless," Kale taunted from behind, picking up the football and hurling it my direction.

Just like the old days.

I ran back, caught it with an *oomph*, and sent it sailing right back.

"Not sure what you expect. Don't run into a lot of kids in my line of work. Sorry I'm not a kiddie doc who always knows the right thing to say."

Catching it, he lifted his arms out to the side. "Has nothing to do with my profession. It's just the natural charm."

I shook my head with a laugh. "Charm? More like constant flow of BS. People just pretend like they tolerate you."

"Which is why you show up to the *park* to hang out with me."

Kale threw the football to Rex.

"Pretty pathetic, if you ask me." Rex. Giving me shit just like the fucker always did.

Without a whole lot of effort, he reached out and caught the spiraling ball.

The look I shot him would have seared a lesser man in two. "Says the guy who said he would come drag my ass here if I didn't show. Now tell me who the pathetic one is? Just felt sorry for you suckers, that's all."

Rex grinned as he stepped back to hurl the ball. "You're just jealous our lives are filled with parks and diaper bags and spit-up rags. Super glamorous, right?"

"Jealous?" I tossed out, spinning on my heel to run, because Rex had an arm, that was for damned sure. The ball flew high and far.

Finally got out in front of it, and I caught it in both hands.

"Totally jealous," Kale piped in. "Dude doesn't have it in him to admit we have it right, and he's the one missing out."

"Right for you, man, right for you."

Truth was, I knew they had it *right*. Saw it on their faces. They were living for the good in life. But that was the kind of good there was no chance I could stomach.

Because I couldn't be trusted with the *good* things in life.

It's your fault.

I trusted you.

You were supposed to take care of her.

You promised, you'd take care of her.

An echo of those words assaulted me, and I could almost feel the fists beating against my chest as my mother screamed in agony, her anguish its own phantom that would haunt me the rest of my life.

I threw the ball with everything I had, like it might take the sorrow with it. Peel it from my skin. Or maybe take me back to that time. Where I could change it. Make it right.

Kale grunted when he caught the blistering spiral. His eyes narrowed in awareness. The guy knew me well enough to latch on to exactly where my mind had gone.

"Seriously, Ollie. Joking aside. You belong here, man. With our kids. Our families. Don't ever question that."

That was what they'd become. Didn't mean I didn't continually feel like an outsider. The leech who had nothing but was desperate for something, latching on, the whole time praying I didn't bleed them dry.

My voice went hoarse. "Love them like my family," I forced out, my gaze moving to the kids, who were playing so free.

"That's because they are your family. Think we all know well enough blood isn't necessary to make that bond." Rex's words were low.

Emphatic.

Like he needed me to know.

Like he was reminding me of the way it'd been when we were kids. And truthfully, the way we were then. Could trust both of them with anything.

Rex began moving my way, angling his head at Kale to follow.

We met in the middle, moving away from the kids a bit. Clearly moving out of earshot.

"So, what's this bullshit about Nikki's place getting broken into? Any idea who it might have been?"

My head shook, unease tying up my guts. "No. She's being tight-lipped about it."

"Stubborn," Kale said, almost offering a smile.

I huffed out a frustrated sound. "Tell me about it. Pretty sure it has something to do with that meeting she's helping to run. She goes quiet the second I bring it up. Think she's protecting someone."

A fresh round of fury pulsed through my veins.

The acute need to protect Nikki.

The urge to hunt.

Problem was, I wasn't sure what I'd do if I found the fucker who thought it'd be a good idea to mess with her.

"I called Seth this morning, and he said they still don't have any leads."

Couldn't stand the thought that he was still out there.

"I don't like this whole situation. Something just doesn't sit right."

That feeling continued to grow. Coming on stronger. An itchy awareness of an approaching storm. Something wicked wound with the wind.

"She's still staying at your place?" Kale asked.

"Yeah."

As much as it was driving me straight out of my mind, I wasn't letting her go anywhere.

Rex dipped his head quickly, happy with that answer. "Rynna is seriously messed up over it. Keeps bringing it up every night, worried about Nikki and what she's going to do. You know Nikki . . . she tried to play it off like it wasn't a big deal, but Rynna didn't buy it. She suggested we find a house to flip and have Nikki rent it so she's in a safer neighborhood."

In contemplation, he looked away before bringing his attention back to me. "There was a building that went up for sale by the river. One of the deserted warehouses down on Row."

Kale whistled. "Took a drive down that dirt road a few weeks back after we had a picnic at the lake. It's like a fucking ghost town out there."

Rex nodded. "Yup. Place is just about as dilapidated as they come . . . junkies using it as a drug house and God knows what else . . . but the location is mint. And you know Broderick, he's always thinking big. He wants in. Luxury condos right on the river. He's envisioning developing the area into a destination spot with stores and restaurants and maybe another hotel in the future. Think I'm gonna keep a couple units for investment, make it affordable for Nikki. She can stay there as long as she wants until she decides on a permanent place."

With me.

The thought struck me from out of nowhere.

Fuck.

No.

Not from out of nowhere.

I knew exactly which direction it hit me from. Where it lived. In that deep, deep space that would always fucking belong to that girl. The piece of me she would always hold in the palm of her hand.

The only girl I'd ever loved. The one I wanted but couldn't keep.

Throat lined with razors, I swallowed hard. "Sounds like a solid plan."

"Thought so, too. Stand to make a lot of money, so it isn't gonna hurt us a bit to keep one of the units for Nik, even though I know she's gonna be all up in arms about it. We're going to have to ease her into the idea."

"I agree."

He eyed me. "Not sure what she's going to do in the meantime. It's going to take us at least a year to get the first condos ready, but I don't like the idea of her staying at that apartment."

I rubbed my hand over my mouth, my small laugh incredulous. "Think it's safe to say that makes two of us." I sucked in a breath. "She's just going to have to stay with me until then."

Kale's brows shot to the sky. "And you think Nikki is going to go for that?"

"Hell, no," I said. "I'll just have to convince her."

Kale grinned. "Really?"

"Yup."

Rex laughed low, rubbing a hand on his chin. "That sounds like . . ."

Torture?

Torment?

I'd be ruined by then. Didn't matter.

"Fun," Rex finished with a smirk.

I wanted to smack the smirk off his face. "Fun?"

"What?" He was all wide-eyed innocence. "Nikki is all kinds of fun."

Asshole.

I punched at him.

Laughing, he jumped back, blocking himself. "Hey, don't get mad at me because she's . . . fun."

Kale chuckled. "Oh yeah, I bet she's all kinds of fun. Now you get to have *fun* with Nikki for a whole year."

"She's a pain in my ass, is what she is."

"Right . . ." Rex drew out. "You just keep telling yourself that. But if you do, make sure you don't break her heart while you do it."

Suddenly agitated, I scraped a hand through my beard. "Not gonna break her heart."

Not again.

Rex sobered. "That girl's been in love with you for as long as I can remember. Followed you around like a puppy all through school. You've got to be careful with that, man."

Wondered if he really had no clue that it'd been more than Nikki following me around. That it'd grown into something it shouldn't have before it became responsible for the single greatest regret of my life.

How even after I'd shut it down, cut her loose, it'd still festered and grown until it'd consumed me, and I'd found myself a pathetic beggar at her door.

Unable to stop myself from going to her.

Needing her.

Knowing I was just going to hurt her all over in the end.

"Just . . . get that building done. I'll take care of Nikki until it's finished. Barely see her, anyway, since we have opposite schedules."

"All right, then. It's a plan."

I nodded.

It was a plan.

A plan that left me completely screwed and somehow satisfied.

Needing a distraction, I pulled away from the guys and shifted to holler toward the kids, "Who wants to get ice cream with Uncle Ollie?"

Frankie Leigh tapped Evan's shoulder, the little girl signing to her best friend.

In a second flat, both of them were beelining toward me. "Me! Me! Me!" Frankie shouted as she and Evan raced my direction. "I want to ride with you, too!"

Rex laughed under his breath and scratched at the scruff on his chin. "Apparently, I'm going to need to have a talk with Frankie Leigh about ditching her little brother. Literally left my little man in the dust."

I chuckled under my breath. "Don't give her too hard of a time. She knows you never take your eye off him."

Frankie grabbed me by a hand, and Evan slipped his hand into the other, both of them grinning up at me like I was maybe the coolest person in the world.

I gulped down any unease and tightened my hold on their hands, leading them over to my truck parked on the curb.

I unlocked the passenger door and both of them clambered onto the seat, Evan first considering the truck was so his thing. He was running his palms over the leather dash, the steering wheel, checking out every detail.

I shut the door behind them and rounded the front, climbed inside, turning my face toward him so he could see. "Still your favorite, buddy?"

He gave me a thumbs-up and a smile that was nothing but bright shiny teeth. I ruffled a hand through his hair. "You have good taste, that I can tell you."

He nodded like crazy as he buckled in before he was grabbing Frankie's hand and weaving his fingers through hers.

I chuckled under my breath.

Oh, so that was how it was.

Little player.

He didn't even blush when he realized I'd caught him, my eyebrows lifting in question. He just gave me a look that told me she was his to watch over.

She missed the whole exchange, too busy vigorously rolling down the window.

"Start her up, Uncle Ollie," she shouted, and I did, the two of them laughing as I quickly flipped a U and headed in the direction of the ice cream parlor that wasn't even up the road a block.

Kale and Rex would walk, but I'd promised Evan a ride, and he was gonna get his ride.

I glanced over at the two of them sitting on the bench seat, so fucking cute, so sweet, so perfect.

Frankie Leigh's hair blown by the whipping wind, her little hand out the window, gliding up and down like she was riding a wave.

Evan's attention was wrapped up in the truck, the dials and gauges and the gear stick I shifted that climbed from the floor and basically stuck up right between his knobby knees.

Their hands?

Still linked together.

I needed to downshift to pull to the curb in front of the parlor, so I grabbed his free hand and wrapped it around the knob, guiding him through the motion.

He made this thrilled, scuffing sound that twisted my spirit like it'd been wrung up by a tornado. Seemed it was the simplest of things that made this kid insanely happy, and damn it, if that didn't make me happy, too.

I let him help me take it out of gear and put on the brake as we parallel parked on the street, and I told them to wait as I jumped out and headed around to the passenger side that butted the sidewalk.

By the time I was helping them out, Rex and Kale were already approaching, little Ryland taking a ride on his daddy's shoulders.

"You finally made it," I tossed out wryly.

"Whatever. I can walk faster than that old truck," Rex badgered.

Frankie hopped out and bounced over to him. "That was so much fun!"

Rex shook his head. "Why doesn't she go on about my truck?"

Frankie Leigh's mouth twisted with distaste. "Daddy, your truck is a work truck and stinky and dirty. Look how pretty Uncle Ollie's is."

She waved her hand out like she was one of those *The Price is Right* models.

Rex latched on to that real quick. "Ah . . . it is pretty, isn't it? Just like Uncle Ollie. Pretty Boy," he taunted.

If his kid hadn't been standing there nodding and agreeing like it was the truest thing he'd ever said, I would have given him a finger.

Pretty Boy, my ass.

"Come on, you two." I stretched out my hands for Evan and Frankie. "I promised you ice cream, let's get you some ice cream."

"Yay!" Frankie yelled, skipping along at my side.

Evan and Frankie went right for the display, pushing up onto their toes so they could see the different flavors displayed behind the glass.

They ordered sundaes, and Rex ordered a cone for Ryland. We found a place in the corner where the kids dug right in.

Conversation easy, Rex, Ollie, and I chatted, catching up since we didn't get to chill like this nearly enough anymore.

I froze when I felt the hairs at the base of my neck lift. A prickle of awareness. Not in fear.

Or hell.

Maybe that was exactly what it was.

Fear.

Because the weight of her presence was beginning to become terrifying. Affecting me more and more.

I slowly shifted in the hard booth so I could glance over my shoulder, wondering if my mind was just making shit up.

But no.

She was there.

Nikki.

Honeyed locks cascading down her back in a wild, erratic stream. Not curly in the least, but still all over the place.

Her back was to me, but she was sitting at a table sharing ice cream with this young girl who couldn't be more than seventeen or eighteen. At the girl's side, covered in chocolate ice cream, was a little boy who probably wasn't much older than Ryland.

Shoveling the ice cream in like he'd just discovered the Holy Grail.

By the look on his face, he had.

That wasn't what had my insides curling with a crazy sort of worry. Wasn't what had disquiet sinking slow and sure in to that vat at the bowels of my spirit where all the bad shit lived.

Compounding and sharpening.

It was the way the girl's expression held nothing but beaten-down fear.

Debased and degraded and disparaged.

Like she couldn't take a single thing more or she would crack.

Nikki held her hand in the middle of the table, her head dropped low and tipped to the side. Even though she was facing away from me, I could tell just by her posture that she was speaking to her.

Her words low but fast.

Desperate encouragement.

Awareness seeped through me like a parched desert sucking up a summer rain.

The suspicion that whatever was going on with Nikki had everything to do with this girl.

With that little kid.

Like my spirit just got that Nikki was desperate to stand up and protect both of them the way I would protect her.

Fully.

Wholly.

Without question or fear or any consideration to the consequence.

Because that's what it came down to.

I wanted to protect Nikki. Keep her safe. Not because I wanted a second chance at saving someone.

But because it was the only thing I had left to offer.

An eye and an ear and a ruthless heart that wouldn't think twice about striking down anyone who thought to fuck with her.

And whatever was happening at that table?

That unease climbed my spirit. Clawed and expanded.

Fury flamed. Licks of agitation. Stirs of anxiety.

"Uncle Ollie, Uncle Ollie!" Frankie tugged at my shirt. "Isn't that right?"

Damn it. I didn't have a clue what she'd even said.

"That's right, sweetheart," I mumbled under my breath.

Rex cocked a brow. Gave me a look that said *really?*

Who knew what I'd agreed to. Probably had told her the world was made of cotton candy. For her? I'd give anything to make that statement true. Sunshine and rainbows and everything sweet.

I rocked in the hard booth, rubbed my fingertips over my lips, trying to sit still.

Nope.

Couldn't do it.

"Give me a minute," I told the guys.

No one really even responded when I pushed out of the booth and stalked across the small parlor.

Coming to a stop at the edge of their table, I glowered, hands in fists as I stared at Nikki, who still clutched the girl's hand as she frantically whispered something to her.

My guts that were screaming cried out.

Nikki, what are you doing? What exactly have you gotten yourself into?

Reckless girl.

Because the girl across from her, who was little more than a child, all out shook when she jerked her attention my way and saw me standing there.

Fear.

So much fear.

I recognized it, written all over her.

When Nikki followed the girl's attention and her eyes landed on me, it was horror I saw all over that perfect face. "Ollie," she whispered through her shock.

Those indigo eyes went round, and her teeth clamped down on her lower lip. Behind her, the sun streaked through the window, glowing around her head, circling her like one of those rainbows I'd just been talking about.

Motherfucking sunshine.

"Nikki," I said, voice so hard it basically had to be pried off my tongue.

Energy lashed, something alive and painful between us.

"Give me a minute," she asked me, repeating the exact thing I'd just told my crew.

Both of us asking for time.

But time was something we'd never had.

None of it. Too much of it.

Forever lost.

I glanced at the girl and the little boy, who was still shoveling ice cream into his mouth, and scrubbed a hand over my face. "Yeah. Of course."

I stepped back.

But I refused to walk away.

thirteen

Nikki

I remained locked in a stare with Ollie, my hand still clutching Brenna's while I begged him with my eyes to give us space.

Questions billowed from him as if they were written in the rough, choppy air, concern and this knowing kind of anger that twisted my belly with a rush of anxiety.

My worry wasn't for him or what he would think.

It was fully for Brenna, the girl who was so completely terrified she was shaking and cowering in her seat as she wrapped a protective arm around her son's waist.

Ollie towered there. Appearing hard and intimidating.

Menacing.

A beast ready to charge.

What she didn't know was that, even though the man didn't know her, he would go down in a blaze to protect her. He'd never lift a vicious hand toward her. Not ever.

Or me.

It was his gentle hand that put me in danger.

Reluctantly, Ollie backed away. For a beat, my gaze followed him, my heart leaping into my throat when I spotted who he was there with, with those precious kids.

This was the problem of living in a small city. Their idea of a fun outing for kids was basically mine, too, thinking this would be a great place to keep Kyle entertained while I talked with Brenna.

I swiveled my attention back to her. "I'm sorry about that."

Her eyes warily followed the hulking man as he moved back through the little ice cream shop. "Who was that?" Her voice trembled.

"One of my oldest friends. I grew up with him." I gave her hand a squeeze. "He's a good guy. A great guy, actually. You don't need to be nervous."

Funny how it was too easy to sing Ollie's praises because they were true. The man just came with all kinds of other warnings.

"I'm sorry," she whispered, disgrace clouding her expression. She fiddled with a napkin on the table, looking away when she said, "God, I'm such a mess. I'm so sorry. I can't believe I reacted that way. I think I'm losing my mind."

"You aren't."

It was the vile asshole trying to make her think she was insane. Filling her head with lies, making her believe she was responsible for the way he treated her.

She'd called me this morning, telling me Caleb had been bothering her again. Sending her texts. Demanding to see Kyle.

I'd suggested we meet.

I just needed to see her face-to-face.

Needing the validation that she was really okay.

I was sure Caleb was unstable.

I hadn't told her the information I'd shared with Seth, my suspicion that it was Caleb who'd broken into my apartment and had left the two notes.

He'd advised I not. That I allow him to investigate a bit so we could find some proof to pin him to.

And . . . he'd told me to stay close to Ollie.

That was probably the hardest part of what he'd asked me to do.

"I promise you're not," I told her. "You have absolutely nothing to be sorry about. Nothing to be ashamed about. Heck, I'm pretty sure grown men cower when they see Ollie coming their way." I let the lightness weave into my tone, hoping it would allow her to relax.

"He's . . . big."

Light laughter filtered free. "Yeah, the man is a bear. A big ol' teddy bear."

So maybe that was a tiny white lie.

The man would tear someone to pieces with his teeth, but that side of him was not something she needed to worry about.

"Is he . . ." I heard the suggestion in her question, the pink that touched her cheeks.

Is he yours?

I was sure there was no way she hadn't sensed that intensity that blazed and burned between us. Heavy and fierce.

Combustible.

Ours was not a pretty sort of chemistry.

I forced a smile. "No. We're just friends."

She frowned as if she didn't believe me. "Doesn't seem that way to me, Miss Nikki."

Was that a tease?

Her attention darted to the man I could still feel from behind me as if he was offering up proof.

His presence overwhelming.

A rush of heat thrashing at my back.

No doubt, he was looking this way.

I cleared my throat. "We've just known each other a long, long time. That's all."

"I should probably head back to my momma's." She grabbed a wipe from the baby bag and began to wipe off Kyle's face and hands.

"No, Mommy. I eat ice cweam." He grinned a chocolate smile.

A soft jolt of affection escaped me. "Was it yummy?" I asked him.

"Yummy, yummy, to my tummy."

"Do you have a happy tummy?"

"Uh-huh."

"Good, then my job is done here."

"You just invited me over to fill my boy with sugar, huh? Seems to me like maybe you should have to watch him run wild for the rest of the day."

I loved it when this side of Brenna came out. When she didn't shrink behind her walls and the girl who wanted to be free peeked out from behind.

"I'll gladly watch him. Any time."

She sobered. "Thank you so much, Nikki. For everything."

Standing, she picked up Kyle and settled him on her hip. I slid out of the booth.

"For being here for Kyle and me," she mumbled as I stood with her.

"You're welcome."

I tickled Kyle's neck, and he giggled, burying his face in the fall of her hair while still peeking out.

Affection swelled in my chest.

The little thing was so adorable.

So sweet and innocent that it expanded that place inside me that somehow kept feeling more and more hollow. I wanted to take him into my arms, feel his weight, breathe him in.

God.

What was wrong with me?

"See you soon, sweet thing," I said, trying to keep my craziness in check.

He wrapped his little arms around his mom's neck and grinned.

I shifted my attention to Brenna before leaning closer to her, my words a hushed whisper, "Remember . . . you *are* strong. You have control of your life. You have control of your body. You have the right."

Her head bobbed along, her lips barely moving as she repeated the support group's mantra.

I moved in and hugged her tight, my mouth at her ear. "Believe it."

Stepping back, she swiped a tear from her cheek. "I do. Thank you."

For a beat, she looked over my shoulder at the people I could feel staring at me. Giving me space while invading it all at the same time.

I could hear Frankie Leigh jabbering the way she loved to do, and Rex and Kale added little things in. But it was Ollie's silence that was most notable.

"I'll see you Tuesday night?" It was an affirmation and encouragement all in one.

She had to make the commitment even if Caleb was making it hard for her.

"I will . . . I promise."

"Okay, then. I'll see you Tuesday, but if you need anything in the meantime, you know to call me. Don't hesitate."

"I won't."

A desperate sort of a plea wound its way into my tone. "Please . . . Be careful."

She blinked at me as if she were searching for the things I couldn't say. "I will. I promise."

For a moment, we both stared at each other before I gave her an encouraging nod toward the door. "I'll see you soon."

With a timid smile, she turned and made her way through the shop and out into the summer heat.

I just stood there, hoping beyond hope that she would stay strong as she ducked her head and headed down the sidewalk.

The whole time, I was contending with the shivers racing across my flesh.

The awareness that slipped and sped.

I ran my hands up my arms, trying to chase the overwhelming feeling away.

Pinning on a smile, I shifted around and headed in the direction of my friends.

Ollie had remained standing, leaning against the wall with his arms crossed over his massive chest, watching me as if I'd committed some sort of mortal sin.

I did my best to ignore it, the tumble of nerves that worked through my body just at the sight of him standing there.

So wickedly gorgeous.

Jeans and a fitted tee.

The man a wall of muscle.

I turned toward the table. "What are you guys doing here?"

Frankie Leigh squealed just as she was digging a big spoon into the ridiculous concoction she had in her sundae glass.

"We're eatin' ice cream!"

"Is that so?" A warm giggle slipped free.

Frankie started to ramble, staring up at me while she spooned ice cream into her mouth, "I've been missin' you, Auntie Nik! Where you been? Workin' at Pepper's Pies? Did you know my mommy made a brand-new kind of pie? Blueberry. I helped. I think I wanna name it Blueberry Blast. Will you write it on the chalkboard for me?"

"Of course, I will," I told her. "First thing Monday morning when I get back to work."

She grinned. "Did you know my daddy's going to build you a big, big house? Do you think it's going to be bigger than ours? Because my new house is so big . . . so high. But it's not a skyscraper. Nope. It's just two stories, but I have two stairs, one in the kitchen and one in the living room. My momma used to live there with Gramma Corinne. Did you know that?"

Frankie rambled on as if what she'd just let on was no big thing. As if she didn't have my entire being jarring back from the shock.

My attention whipped to Rex. A guilty expression rode on his too-handsome face. "Excuse me, but what did your daughter just say?"

Frankie sighed and lifted her voice. "I SAID, my daddy is gonna build you a new house."

A frown pulled across my brow, one I tipped in Rex's direction. "That's what I thought she said."

Rex scrubbed a hand over his face. "Not like that . . . was gonna talk to you about it once I had some more details."

My frown lifted. "More details? Sounds like there were plenty of details to me."

Kale laughed. "Don't get those knickers all up in a twist, Nik Nik. Haven't you ever heard not to look a gift horse in the mouth?"

"You mean, punch a gift horse in the mouth?"

He busted up laughing. "Feisty."

Not feisty.

Angry.

They didn't get to go making decisions for me.

I should have known Rynna was gonna say something to him. I knew she meant well, but that didn't mean it didn't make me feel as if they all thought I was helpless.

I turned back to Rex. "We're going to talk about this."

"I figured we would."

"Nothing to talk about." The husky voice hit me from behind.

Shivers raced, and I bit back the irritation that wanted to fly from my tongue. The rest of my friends were just worried about me, even if they were sticking their noses in my business where it didn't belong.

But Ollie . . .

I knew Ollie would be a whole different issue.

I tucked the conversation away for later and pasted on a grin, doing my best to change the subject, the direction of their thoughts so I could figure out a way to get out of there with the least bit of attention aimed at me.

"So, what's with all the hotties at the ice-cream shop with their kids? Breaking a million hearts just by being here. You guys are nothing but a danger to society."

Kale laughed. "Danger to society?"

"Um, yes." I gestured with my chin across the shop to the three women sitting together with their kids.

"The only thing left of those poor women over there is a puddle of drool and a mess of wet panties. It's a sad, sad state of affairs."

"Panties?" Frankie's nose was all scrunched up in confusion.

She was getting way too clever for her own good. I was going to have to watch that.

"Oh, I was just joking," I told her. "Your daddy and your uncles are just so good-looking, they break hearts without having to say a single word. Good thing your daddy only has eyes for your mommy."

Evan grabbed the notepad sitting in front of his dad and scribbled across it.

My chest squeezed.

Painful, perfect affection.

My daddy doesn't break hearts. He fixes them.

This kid.

"Of course, your daddy fixes hearts," I told him, wishing I could sign it because it meant so much, Evan's heart now beating strong because Kale had saved him almost two years ago. I could never quite imagine what kind of bond that might forge.

Unshakeable.

At least that I knew.

"Because your daddy is the best."

A rumble of something echoed from Kale's chest. "All right, all right, no need to get carried away. We already know I'm awesome."

"Ish," I told him.

Couldn't let it all go to his head.

He winked at me.

I took a step away, ready to bolt, to get away from the energy that crawled over me from behind. "Well, it was so nice to see you all. Hopefully we can get together soon. I've been missing my little pumpkins. I need some Auntie Nik time."

"Yeah." Chills flashed with the single word. With the rough caress of Ollie's voice. "I was just heading out, too. I'll follow you back to my place."

"I walked," shot from my mouth. If Caleb was keeping tabs on my car? The last thing I wanted was it sitting out front for him to see when I was inside with Brenna.

"Then I'll give you a lift."

My head whipped that way. "I don't think that's necessary."

He stuffed his big hands in his pockets. "Well, I think it is."

I could argue with him right there in front of everyone. What good would it do? It would just prolong the inevitable. But at least that would have bought me some time to figure out what to say.

I said my goodbyes, and Ollie said his. Frankie jumped into his arms and gave him a big hug, peppering his bearded face with little girl kisses that he didn't seem to know how to take yet reveled in at the same time.

The man a twisted dichotomy.

Ollie headed toward the door, and I followed.

Chained to him in some profound, inexplicable way.

Because honestly, I owed him no explanation. But there I was, following right behind him as if I didn't have a choice.

Bound by these zaps of awareness.

Electricity tapped.

Both of us feeding off the other until it became so big we were consumed by it.

We ducked out into the blazing heat. Instantly, we were washed in the overpowering scent of honeysuckle and blazing stars, the air so thick it was almost sweet as it slicked our skin in humidity.

The burly, overbearing man strode for his truck, which was parked at the curb. He opened the passenger door and held it open for me.

"Thank you," I muttered.

Ollie only answered with a tight dip of his head. His entire demeanor was rigid as he climbed into the driver's side and started the old, rambling engine.

I swore, that old truck only shook us up more as we traveled the short distance back to his building.

My lungs squeezed almost painfully when I attempted to draw in a breath.

Everything sharp and too tight.

He pressed the button to open the sliding door that led to his garage. Slowly, we entered into its darkened depths.

The garage door dropped behind us, and it felt as if it closed off the rest of the world.

We disappeared into it.

Into a place that was only Ollie and me.

Anger and attraction and regret.

God. It was so hard sitting at his side and feeling like that was exactly where I was supposed to be and knowing those thoughts were nothing but foolish.

I couldn't allow him to affect me like this.

He parked in the mess of all his metal, his collection of cars and motorcycles just as powerfully beautiful as the man.

He came around and helped me down.

I said nothing, just headed for the old warehouse elevator that had been restored with the rest of the place.

I felt as if I was stepping into a cage as Ollie slid the restored metal gate closed.

Prisoned.

Oh God.

His brutal energy hammered through the confined space, radiating from the walls, slamming back into me. Fed by the flashes of light that blipped through the bars as the elevator clanged and churned and rose.

The elevator jerked as it came to a jolting stop at the top floor, and I stumbled. Ollie's hand darted out to steady me.

Burning on my hip.

Fire flashed.

I sucked in a breath, pinned by that sapphire gaze.

His exhale was close to pained as he opened the gate where it dropped us right at his door. We moved out into the enclosed hall, and he unlocked the door to his loft, stepping in behind me.

Sunlight streaked through the big windows and poured into the rambling space, stretching for all the darkened, shadowy corners.

Anxiety clawed across my chest.

I wasn't ready to answer his questions about Brenna, even though I could feel the weight of them from the harsh pants he exhaled through his nose.

Dropping my head, I started for the hallway that led to the bedrooms.

Needing to escape.

"You gonna tell me who you were sitting with?"

His voice came from right behind me.

Heated chills streaked across my skin. As hot as the sun.

"A friend," I told him.

"A friend?" It was all a challenge, and I whirled on him, ready to put him in his place. Because I didn't owe him a damned thing and he sure as heck didn't have any right to question every single person I spoke to.

Ollie was right there, dipping to get in my face. I swallowed around his blistering potency.

"That girl was terrified of me, Nikki, and I'm pretty sure I know your friends, considering all your friends are mine."

"I don't owe you an explanation."

"Bullshit," he spat. The force of the word pinned my back against the wall. He only backed me further into it by taking another step forward.

Towering over me, his teeth ground as he issued the words a breadth from my lips. "Tell me what the fuck is going on. I know whoever that girl was is linked to what happened at your apartment."

I tipped my head up so I could meet his stare.

Black sapphire. Hard as steel.

"I already told you, there are some things you can't know, Ollie."

He tugged at his hair, agitation thick, eyes pinching before he loosed an uncontained growl as he flew around as if he couldn't stop himself.

A punch landed against the opposite wall.

I shrieked and flinched.

Fear tumbled down my spine.

Not for my physical safety. Just for the sheer ferocity of the man.

Ollie unhinged.

Losing it.

Hanging on by a thread.

He roared and whirled back around before his words dropped so low they seeped from between clenched teeth. "I know you're hiding something from me. I know it because *I know you.*"

He slammed that same fist into his chest, right over his heart. "And I can't protect you if you don't let me in."

I shoved at him, unwilling to allow him to do this. Unwilling to let him look at me as if I was the center of his world.

His gravity.

The only thing that kept him anchored when he continually kept me adrift.

"You don't get every part of me, Ollie. Not anymore." Hurt bled with the words.

I stormed for the bedroom I'd so stupidly begun to think of as my own. I had to get the hell out of there. I couldn't stay a second longer.

Seth had told me to stick close, but I didn't know how to do that, not with Ollie affecting me this way. I had no clue what I was going to do or where I was going to go.

All I knew was I had to leave.

I banged into the door.

The breath jerked from my lungs in another shriek when one of those big hands snatched my wrist and tugged until I was spinning around.

Before I could make sense of it—before I could process it—he had me pressed against the dresser that sat against the wall.

Both of those big hands had me by the face.

A war flashed through his expression. A battle that raged.

It only lasted a second before his mouth crashed against mine.

Crushing.

Devouring.

Overpowering.

And oh God, did it ever feel good.

I whimpered, and my lips parted.

He took it as an invitation.

Or maybe he was just breaking in.

His hot tongue slid against mine, and a ball of want so huge I could barely breathe around it built in my center.

Desire and need.

Old, old love.

If only it wasn't encased in a shell of bitterness. Gelled by jagged, broken hurt.

My hands flew to his wide, wide shoulders, and my fingernails sank in.

I didn't know if I was holding on or pushing him away.

A needy moan escaped my throat, and I clung to him in a way I knew I shouldn't. In a way I couldn't. Yet, there I was, wanting to crawl right inside him. Wanting to stay there forever. Where everything felt perfectly right and there weren't a million things wrong around us.

I felt so small against him, every massive inch of his body covering mine.

Eclipsing everything.

He kissed me as if he'd gone mad.

The man finally undone.

Lost but searching for a way to break out of the labyrinth that held him hostage.

Those big hands spread across my shoulders and rode down my sides until he was palming my bottom and tugging me against his hips. It elicited a pant, and my heart thundered in my chest.

As frantic as his.

I felt the world tremble around me when he rubbed himself between my thighs. His cock so big and hard where it pressed against his jeans. As daunting as the man.

Heat spiraled. A vortex of dark greed. A need I couldn't afford to feel.

But it was there.

I sucked in a desperate breath of desire.

Ollie struggled to get me closer. He rocked and rocked. Creating this friction I could feel sparking between us.

A match and gasoline.

"Nikki . . . sweet girl . . . God. Why do you feel so good? So fucking good."

I could feel his torment slide out with every word. With every wayward thrust of his hips.

I meant to push him away, but my fingers moved to the longer pieces of hair at the top of his head. I fisted two handfuls of it and held on while he consumed my mouth and my knees buckled out from under me.

Hiking me up, he wrapped my legs around his waist, holding me while his lips danced in a delicious push and pull.

Tongue exploring.

Teeth nipping and tugging.

Delirium.

I ripped my mouth from his and prayed it would afford me some good sense, gasping for air as I panted toward the ceiling.

It only made things worse.

Ollie kissed along my chin and across the exposed skin of my throat. He lapped up and down the sensitive flesh, nipping and biting as he continued to grind himself against my center, which throbbed almost painfully.

God.

I wanted him.

I wanted him so badly, but sometimes it was the things we wanted the most that would destroy us in the end.

"Nikki," he rumbled again.

A guttural groan of pleasure all mixed up with agony.

So dark and needy.

"Ollie."

It was a whimper.

Hope and love and everything I'd ever wanted.

He palmed my breast, and he brushed his thumb over my nipple that pebbled with his touch.

I ached.

I glowed.

I pressed deeper into his hold, and he practically growled. "These tits. Fuck, Nikki, you drive me out of my mind. What the fuck am I doin'? What the fuck am I doin'?"

Every fear I had came out with his own reservations that he rumbled across the skin of my neck.

Sliding over me like a slow warning.

Because I knew better. *I knew better.*

I knew this was only going to end with my heart splattered all over the floor, and no one would be there to pick up the pieces because he was the one who'd made the mess in the first place.

Even though it was weak, I nudged at his shoulders.

"Ollie," I cried. Softly. A prayer for him to stop doing this to me.

Pushing and pulling.

Taunting and ruining.

"Nik," he grated, moving back to my mouth. His lips were so plush and soft and smooth, the perfect contrast to the scruff of his beard that scratched at my chin.

The promise of so much pleasure.

Every rush of his hand across my body was fueled by rage.

Softened by affection.

God, this man would be my complete undoing.

My beautiful beast.

He worked his mouth against mine.

Coaxing and demanding.

His presence filled me.

Heart and spirit and lungs.

Toasted vanilla.

Barrels of oak soaked in liquor.

Just his presence was enough to get me drunk. His touch enough to desolate. But this kind of pleasure would only bring pain, and I was so not into that sort of thing.

I pushed again and squeezed my eyes shut when I whispered, "Stop."

It was so low I wasn't sure he could even hear it, but I knew he felt it.

A harsh exhale ripped from his lungs as he set me on my shaky feet. His chest heaved as he reached out and gripped the top of the dresser behind me, locking me in while he pressed his body away.

An earthquake shook, the man a rigid fortress that towered and loomed. Beneath him, my entire being trembled, the quivers starting somewhere in my spirit and rattling out.

Uncontrollable.

Both of us shaking and shaking.

Trying to catch up with what we'd just let happen.

Another mistake tossed in that mounting pile.

I swallowed around the love and need and the hurt. "You don't get to do this to me, Ollie. Not again. I refuse to let you do this to me."

I could feel the erratic boom of his heart, contending with rage and all the things he wouldn't allow me to see.

"Fuck . . . I'm sorry. I'm so goddamned sorry."

He eased back a fraction and shocked me again when he shackled me by the wrists. My hands locked between us, he dropped his forehead to mine. "You can't leave, Nikki. I know what you were getting ready to do, and I can't let you leave."

His voice was grief.

A plea.

He edged back and those blue eyes tangled with mine.

"And I can't let you keep taking pieces of me and discarding the rest. Not again, Ollie. My heart can't take it."

And God, he just kept turning everything upside down because he reached out and cupped one side of my face.

So soft.

So sweet.

His thumb moved across the moisture I didn't even know had seeped onto my cheeks.

"You can hate me all you want. I deserve it. I'm a bastard, and I know it. But I can't stand the thought of you out there by yourself. Can't stand not knowing who broke into your place. Can't stand the thought of knowing you're in trouble and not being able to do anything about it. Please. Don't leave."

"I don't know how to stay here with you. Not when things are like this between us. It hurts too much."

He flinched before all that rippling muscle tightened. Every inch of him hard.

"I need to take care of you. Tell me what's happening with that girl at the ice cream shop."

I started to form the excuse, but he cut me off. "No more bullshit. I know you're in trouble."

"I can't tell you that." It was the truth. I refused to break Brenna's confidence.

His voice somehow softened, and his head tipped to the side as he looked at me. "What have you gotten yourself into, Nikki?"

For a beat, I hesitated, and then I gave him a little of my truth. "I just want to make the world a better place."

Minutely, his head shook. Anger was clear in the clench of his jaw. "World is nothing but corruption and evil and greed."

Like a fool, I pressed his hand closer to my face, savoring the warmth.

For one more moment, I relished in this brute of a man I had no business taking comfort in.

But he'd always, always been my safe place.

"If I can help one person—just one, Ollie—then I made that ugly world better for them."

I wondered how long it'd been since I'd been that honest with him.

Pain struck on his features. Worry and adoration.

The last was always what nearly dropped me to my knees, but there was too much of that corruption piled between us for the last to count.

His soul soiled and brittle and hard.

There was no longer any place for me.

When he looked at me like that, though, it made me want to believe I was wrong.

He blew out a resigned breath. "I need to keep you safe."

I searched his face, my voice quiet but strong. Because for once, I wanted him to be honest with me, too. "You want more than that."

"No. What just happened was a mistake."

He might as well have punched me. That was what his denial felt like.

How many more of them could I take?

A smile wobbled on my face. It was so fake I thought maybe my face might crack. "Then you have to let me go."

"You know that's impossible. I would kill for you, Nikki. Die for you."

Then why wouldn't he live for me?

Devastation crawled across my chest like a disease. Oliver Preston the infection and the cure.

He took a lumbering step back. An agitated, tattooed hand roughed through his hair, which was sticking up everywhere from my desperate hands tugging at it.

"You aren't leaving, Nikki. Someone broke into your place, busted the door, trashed your stuff. You and I both know it wasn't some stupid kids."

My brow pinched in disbelief. "What? Am I your prisoner now?"

"If that's what it comes to."

Tears pricked at my eyes. "You're such an asshole."

He started for the door, mumbling under his breath, "Tell me something I don't know."

A second before he stepped out, he paused and shifted to look back at me.

The severity of it pinned me to the spot. "I'm just asking that you do this one thing for me, Nikki. One thing. All I'm asking is for you to stay."

Without saying another word, he turned and strode out of the room, shutting the door when he went.

How was that fair when the one thing I wanted was the one thing he would never give me?

Not when the only thing I wanted was for him to stop breaking my heart.

fourteen

Nikki
Fourteen Years Old

Nikki's stomach tightened. So tight she wondered how it was possible to breathe.

Grating laughter rolled across the stagnant blaze of summer heat.

She pressed her lips together and focused on plucking at the grasses beneath her that grew thick along the riverbank and not the girl Ollie had his arms around.

They were hanging out under the big shade tree where Ollie, Sydney, and Nikki had played for all their lives along the winding river about a half mile up from the lake.

Sure, Kale and Rex were there, too. They'd become a part of their group a long time ago. They belonged.

But it felt like Meredith was invading it.

Why would Ollie bring her there?

And why did the fact that he had make her feel this way?

It was stupid.

Dumb.

But she couldn't stop the way her insides felt sticky and gross when Ollie picked Meredith up and fell backward with her into the water.

His arms all around her as her screech of surprise ripped through the air.

The two of them were splashing and laughing as they resurfaced before he was kissing her again.

Nausea ran the length of Nikki's throat.

Ugh.

Nikki was gonna throw up.

Boys were so stupid.

Fingers snapped in front of her face, and Sydney's voice broke through the delirium. "Hello? Did you hear a thing I said?"

Nikki's head jerked up. "Yeah, I heard you."

Okay. Not at all. But she wasn't about to admit that.

Sydney's eyes grew round. "So . . ." she drew out.

"So, what?"

Her voice became a hiss beneath her breath. "Did Billie kiss you? I saw you walking with him behind the locker rooms at the park."

Redness flushed to Nikki's cheeks, and her face twisted in disgust. She hugged her knees to her chest a little tighter. "Eww. No way, Sydney. Don't even put that vision in my head. I'm liable to puke right here."

The thought of Billie putting his mouth on her made her want to gag.

Mix that with Ollie kissing Meredith?

She was gonna lose her lunch.

Sydney looked at her as if she was crazy. "Then why'd you go and tell him you'd be his girlfriend? You could have said no, you know? You know you don't have to say yes, right?"

Nikki bounced her leg. "Of course, I know that. Maybe I said yes because he's the only one who's ever asked me."

Everyone else had a boyfriend. Could anyone blame her for wanting to know what that was like?

"Who asked you what?"

Nikki jumped when the voice hit her from the side. She whipped her head that way. The tiny flush of embarrassment she'd been feeling at confessing it to Sydney bloomed like the red roses in her grandma's garden when she saw Ollie standing there holding Meredith's hand.

He had on no shirt and was dripping wet. Muscles on his arms that hadn't been there before. And his stomach . . .

She had to duck her head when she realized she was staring, her mouth going dry and her stomach that was already in knots making this fluttery feeling that had her thinking she might take flight.

No chance of that when her belly was filled with a pile of boulders that made her feel small and weak.

It was the same thing it kept doing whenever Ollie was around. It made her skin feel hot and her palms get sweaty. Anxious and excited at the same time.

She knew everything she was feeling was just plain stupid.

This was Ollie, she was talking about. Her best friend. The third corner of their triangle, even though that triangle had taken a few new angles since Kale and Rex were always hanging around.

"Ollie . . . don't you know when to mind your own business? We're having an important conversation over here. It's private," Sydney said. She angled her head at Meredith. "Besides, it looks like you have more important things to do."

She said it as if she actually thought it'd make him tuck tail and walk away.

They used to all tell each other everything. Their secrets belonged to the other.

The three of them had since Nikki could remember. Her heart lit in a flurry, wanting to cling to it, for it to always remain.

But she wasn't delusional.

Things had changed.

Ollie, Rex, and Kale had started high school last year, and this fall, she and Sydney would be starting there, too.

They'd all grown.

Changed.

They used to be together constantly, sharing all of their time, but their time together was coming less and less.

Plus . . . Ollie had Meredith.

Nikki would be a liar if she said that didn't bother her the most, her chest so heavy when she saw them together she thought it might cave in.

Ollie released Meredith's hand and set both of his on his hips, taking that overbearing stance.

He'd watched them like a hawk for all their days.

Their constant protector.

"No one?" he all but demanded. "I just heard Nikki saying, '*He was the only one who asked her.*' Now I want to know who *he* is and exactly what he asked her."

Embarrassment ripped through Nikki when Meredith giggled at Ollie's side while looking at Nikki as if she was a pitiful little girl.

That's exactly what it felt like.

It didn't help that water dripped from Ollie's hair and down his wide, tanned chest.

Heat blistered across Nikki's face, but she was having the hardest time looking away. Not when he was glowering at her like that.

Sydney made a tsking sound and brushed back her long, sandy-blonde hair. The color almost exactly matched her brother's, the same as their eyes.

Though that was where their similarities ended.

He was a grumbly bear, and she was a curious kitten.

He was brash, and she was delicate.

"We respect your privacy, so you need to respect ours," she said, calm and poised.

While Nikki thought she just might melt into a puddle.

Ollie's brows shot to the sky. "Your privacy? You're my responsibility, Syd. Dad put me in charge, so anything you do is my business. I've got to take care of you. You two get yourselves in trouble, and it's my ass on the line."

His penetrating gaze moved to Nikki. "Now tell me who you're talking about."

A shiver ran the length of Nikki's spine.

"I said it's girl talk," Sydney interrupted the stare down with a rebellious jut of her chin. As if it was gonna put a lid on the topic rather than ripping one off.

"Private," she reiterated.

Meredith laughed. "Aww . . . I think they're talkin' about a boy. Leave 'em alone, Ollie."

Nikki cringed.

"Yep. Private. Clearly code for boy talk," Kale said, shaking his hair out as he climbed from the glistening ripples of water. "Sounds to me like someone's got a crush."

Rex was hoisting himself out right behind him, trudging up the steep embankment. "Who's talking about me? Tell me she's hot."

"Hardly, asshole." Ollie waved an annoyed hand his direction. "You think everyone's talking about you."

"That's because *I'm* hot. Why wouldn't they be talking about me?" Rex grinned as he peeked over at Sydney.

Nikki swore that boy was in love with her, but Sydney swore harder, *not a chance.*

Sydney scowled and crossed her arms over her chest. "You wish, Rex."

Ollie turned back to his sister. "Tell me what you two are whispering about."

"It's none of your business what boy we're talkin' about," she shot back.

Ollie's eyes bugged out of his head.

Sydney had just given him all the confirmation he'd needed.

"Like hell it's not. You're my little sister, and Nikki might as well be. It's my job to watch over you both."

Sister.

Why'd him saying that hurt?

Sydney's pretty face twisted in a scowl.

"Not a chance, Ollie." Defiance blazed from her. "You've been bossin' us forever. You aren't gonna decide who gets to be our boyfriends, too."

"Don't need to pick because no one gets to be your boyfriend." Ollie's attention swept between the two of them. "Not either of you."

A huff dropped Sydney's mouth open while Nikki shifted in discomfort, biting her bottom lip as her attention darted back and forth with the exchange.

"Excuse me? You have a girlfriend standing right beside you, and you think you get to tell us if we get to have a boyfriend or not?" Sydney challenged.

"Uh, yeah, I do. You know Dad said you can't date until you're eighteen, and it's my job to watch out for you. Always has been. Always gonna be. So that means I'm the one who says, and I say no to whoever it is you both are talking about. How's that?"

"That's stupid, that's what it is. Just because I'm a girl, the rules are different? No way."

"Not joking, Syd. You aren't allowed to have a boyfriend. And if I find out you do? Someone's gonna get their ass kicked."

Rex laughed from behind him. "You'd better cover up her boobs if you're gonna make that work."

If Nikki didn't love Sydney so much, she might have been jealous of her. Sydney's boobs were already bigger than her mom's, and Nikki barely needed a bra.

There Sydney was, wearing a pink bikini top and shorts while Nikki was wearing her same white one-piece from two years ago with a pair of cut off shorts to cover up her bottom. Even though they were the same age, Nikki always felt as if she was struggling to keep up.

Nikki peeked at Meredith who was only wearing a bikini, so perfect and pretty and mature. Nikki didn't want to dislike her just because of it, but she couldn't help it.

"It is a stupid rule," Meredith agreed.

"It's not stupid when she has a body like that," Rex shot out.

As soon as Rex said it, Ollie flew around and pushed him hard, right back into the river.

Nikki sucked in a worried breath, and Sydney scrambled to her knees when Rex tumbled backward into the water with a splash. But they should have known Rex would only come up laughing, climbing back to the shore, shoving the flop of hair back that'd fallen in his face.

It wasn't like the three of those boys weren't constantly at each other, always tussling but never mad.

"Temper, temper," Rex said.

"That's my sister you're talkin' about."

"Just sayin' . . . she doesn't look much like a little girl anymore. Just like Nikki doesn't."

She didn't?

She hugged her knees closer.

"Watch it, or the next time I push you into that river, you won't be coming back up," Ollie warned; though, there was laughter running underneath the threat.

"That's right," Ollie started to shout, his voice carrying on the wind as he spun around and shouted, "Let it be known, anyone even thinks of messing with my little sister, and I'll be the one personally taking him down."

Rex shrugged and flicked some of the water from his hair. "It's Nikki with the boyfriend, anyway."

"Stupid boys," Nikki muttered under her breath, wanting to crawl into a hole and disappear.

"Aww, so cute," Meredith sang. Nikki knew she was trying to be nice, but it felt like a dig.

He wasn't looking in Nikki's direction, but she saw it. The way Ollie stiffened and the roll of something angry that shivered along his strong back.

Nikki felt that itchy feeling again. It tingled across her skin—something that felt good and bad and right and wrong. As if she didn't know herself anymore.

Kale ignored the whole exchange and tugged his shirt over his head. "Come on, let's go check out Stillhouse. Haven't been in there since last summer."

"Lucky if it'll still be standing," Rex said.

Nikki chewed her bottom lip. "You know it's not safe to go sneaking around in there."

Rex grinned. "Always so scared, Nik Nik."

"I'm not scared. I'm just not dumb. It's not my fault I hang around with bunch of stupid boys."

"I want to go," Meredith agreed, looking at Ollie with eyes that were begging him to take her along.

Nikki looked at Sydney, praying that she'd get it. That Nikki needed to get away. She didn't think she could handle watching Ollie with Meredith for a second more. "It's a bad idea."

And still, she was climbing to her feet, the same way Sydney was doing, because that was just what they always did, always following the guys around.

Sydney held out her hand to Nikki to help her stand. Excitement blazed in her eyes when she squeezed Nikki's hand and whispered just so she could hear. "Fly, fly, dragonfly."

Nikki sucked in a breath and gave her a nod, following her up the slope to where they'd left their bikes. Kale had already climbed onto his and was taking off down the trail, Rex right behind him, Sydney scrambling to catch up.

Nikki watched them. Rex looked over his shoulder at Sydney like he was challenging her to catch up. Beckoning her to his side. Something special moved through the air between them.

Nikki would bet that something special was something Ollie wouldn't like.

Warily, she moved to pick up her bike, but all her movements felt slowed. Sluggish.

As if she were trudging through a muddied bog. Held back by that same feeling Ollie radiated like his own special glow.

A brand the boy wore that only she could feel.

She peeked over her shoulder, and he was still there with Meredith, but looking all hard and pissed.

She shook it off. Her private life wasn't any of his concern, and what he did with Meredith was definitely none of hers.

She focused on peddling up the trail, through the weeds that had grown high, the long, floral spines of the purple blazing stars poking up through the spikes of the tall grasses.

As soon as Ollie was out of sight, she peddled harder, faster, thinking she might finally break away. She topped the hill and wound back around the trail toward the abandoned buildings down on Row.

What used to be a dirt road was now an overgrown path that was barely discernable, just like the earth that had grown up around the crumbling, deserted buildings.

They weren't supposed to go in, but they'd been doing it for years. It'd always felt like an adventure.

Thrilling.

A little scary.

A little wrong.

Nikki guessed that was what made it so much fun. What made her stomach still twist with the thought of sneaking inside.

She dropped her bike in front of the three stories of splintered wood and rusted steel.

Inside were old, vacant offices, metal filing cabinets tipped open with the drawers emptied and gaping. Canning facilities with battered, broken-down machines.

When they were younger, it had been a hide-and-seek heaven.

Right then, the only thing Nikki felt like doing was hiding. Because she knew she was stupid for even having these thoughts about Ollie. These feelings that welled so big inside her it made her start to think she was losing her mind.

And she just couldn't stomach the way Ollie had looked at her when she'd taken off.

As if he was angry.

Disappointed.

Just a dumb little girl who couldn't think for herself or decide what she really wanted.

Maybe she really, really was dumb, because what she wanted was him.

Her breaths came short, and her heart raced as she slowly inched toward the hole in the wall they'd always snuck through.

"What, are you scared?" She heard Rex shouting at Kale from inside. A reverberation that left a long echo through the vast stillness.

"Not even, dude. You're the only pussy around here."

Nikki angled to the side and slithered through. Inside the building, it was dark, the dusky space only illuminated by the murky rays of light. They stole through the cracks and the hazed-over windows situated up near the high ceiling that was caved-in on one side.

The urge to escape hit her, and Nikki fumbled for the stairway off to the right, her hands gliding over the splintered walls so she could find her way. Slowly, she edged up the stairs as quietly as she could. No matter how light her footfalls, the aged wood creaked with each movement.

Laughter rang through the cavernous space.

Echoes and joy.

Sydney.

Always so free and brave. Living life the way Nikki had always wanted to.

Nikki made it to the second floor, not even sure where she was going. The only thing she knew was she needed to get there.

The wood moaned when she stepped onto the second-floor landing, and she weaved deeper into the old halls where she'd hidden so many times as a child.

She shrieked when a hand latched on her wrist, and she was suddenly pulled into one of the rooms.

Ollie.

He was there, backing her into a wall, that same look on his face that he was wearing when she'd left him standing down by the river.

"What are you doing?" she demanded.

A glittering beam of light lashed across Ollie's face, one part aglow and the other a shadow. He grinned in that way that made her spirit sing a million songs.

"What does it look like I'm doing," he whispered. "Finding you."

He'd always had an uncanny way of sniffing out her hiding places.

"We're not playing," she managed. She swallowed the big lump that had grown in her throat. Trying to pretend she didn't have that feeling again. "We haven't played that game in years."

Two only.

But that summer felt like a lifetime ago. Before everything got strange and different and better and worse.

She could almost hear the tinkle of Sydney's laughter. *That's what growing up is. It hurts and it's amazing at the very same time. That's called living, Nik. Don't ever be afraid to live."*

"No? With the way you went running, I sure thought we were." Ollie's voice was a rumble, so much deeper than it'd been.

She shook her head. "I was just looking for everyone."

She tried to shake out of his hold, duck away. The funniest thing about that was he wasn't even touching her.

"Where's Meredith?" she asked, her voice feeling too fragile.

His lips pressed into a thin line that looked like frustration. "Downstairs. She decided she didn't want to come up."

"You should be down there with her."

Nikki didn't know a whole lot about relationships, but at least she knew that. Ditching your girlfriend in a deserted warehouse was not cool.

She could see the shift. As if the lightness he'd found her with had only been a mask, and she stood there watching it be peeled away. Beneath it was confusion. A kind of disorder and anger she hadn't seen him wear before.

Something about it made her shake.

He suddenly reached out and took her by the chin. "Is it true?"

She jarred back a fraction. "What?"

"That you have a boyfriend?"

Her gaze dropped to the side.

"Look at me," he demanded, and her eyes fluttered open, just like the flutter in her belly.

He stared at her, eyes drawing together, teeth gritted. "I don't like it."

A sound scraped from her throat. "You have a girlfriend, but you're telling me you don't like it?"

His jaw clenched, and lines pinched his forehead as if he were trying to make sense of something. "I don't like it. The way it feels. The way it makes me feel."

His eyes moved over her. Nikki felt as if he was looking at her for the first time.

He hesitated, and his tone twisted in confusion. "You make me feel different."

"What's that mean?"

He fiddled with a piece of her hair.

Softly, watching the movement as if he was in awe.

Her knees wobbled. "Ollie." His name was close to a whimper, and if she hadn't been tied to him in this unseen way, she would have floated through the ceiling.

"It means I want to take care of you."

She tried to clear her head. "You have a girlfriend. Right downstairs. Remember? And I'm not a little girl anymore."

He looked at her in that strange way again. "No. You're not. But that doesn't mean you won't always be mine to protect."

Footsteps clattered up the steps and came their direction. "Hey, assholes," Rex shouted, "We're coming for you."

Ollie jumped back, putting a couple of feet of space between them, looking away from her as if standing that close to her was a sin.

Kale's voice carried, getting closer and closer. "Come on, shit sticks! We're heading to the lake. Cliffs are calling my name. It's hotter than the devil's backside in here. Think we walked right into the pits of hell."

"Alabama is hell. Thought you would have figured that out by now," Ollie shouted back.

"Ollie! Come on. It's hot in here, and this place is super creepy. I want to leave." Meredith's voice echoed through the worn walls, a bit of frustration behind them.

Nikki stumbled away. Confused and somehow hurt. "Just go. I need to go check on my sister, anyway. I promised her I'd take her to the movies today."

Ollie wavered, unsure before they heard Sydney's shouted words filter through with a laugh. "We are three. Forever and ever. You and me."

"Hey, what about me?" Rex's voice echoed.

Sydney laughed. So carefree. "No way."

Ollie gave a last fleeting glance at where Nikki stood trembling against the wall before he relented and headed for the door. "Comin'. Nikki is headin' home."

He was leaving her.

Was it stupid that hurt her, too?

"What?" This from Sydney. Nikki could hear her friend's footsteps growing closer while the guys clanged down the steps.

"Where are you?" Sydney called.

Nikki eased out of the room. Trying to play off whatever had just happened between her and Ollie. It felt so different. So wrong and so right, and Nikki was sure she'd never been so unsure of anything in her whole life.

"Come with us?" Sydney asked, stretching out her hand, head angling, knowing something wasn't right.

"I think I'd better go check on my sister."

"I'll go with you."

"No."

She squeezed Nikki's hand. "We are three. Forever and ever, you and me."

Swallowing hard, she let Sydney guide her out through the motes that floated in the dusky air. The steps creaked and groaned beneath them as they headed down the flight of stairs.

Nikki could feel it, though there was nothing she could do.

The wood giving, splintering beneath her foot.

Nikki screamed as the plank busted, and her leg wedged through the hole.

Sharp arrows of wood cut into her skin. Pain and fear turned her stomach again.

"Oh my God, Nikki!" Sydney cried, and footsteps were bounding again, and Ollie was right there.

His face was twisted in shock and concern.

She didn't want to find comfort in it.

She didn't want to feel as if he made her feel everything would be all right. But she did.

His touch was gentle as he eased her leg from the hole, careful to wind her ankle and foot free so she wouldn't get any new gouges.

She definitely didn't want the tears that broke free when Ollie pulled her into his arms, but a sob of relief broke free when he held her close and whispered, "I've got you. I won't ever let anything bad happen to you. I promise."

She wound her arms around his neck and buried her face under his jaw. His scent was all around her as she clung tight.

She couldn't make out all the words people were shouting around her.

Because Ollie had her.

And that meant everything in her world was right.

Ollie

My phone buzzed in my pocket. I wasn't sure why my damned heart went haywire because of it. Maybe it was because I was praying it was Nikki. Hoping she'd just text to shoot the shit, tell me how her day was going, or maybe ask me about mine.

Hell, I'd settle for a text just to remind me I was an asshole again.

Anything would be better than the two of us acting like the other didn't exist.

Two days of tiptoeing around my house.

We'd been walking on eggshells since I'd brought her there in the first place, just waiting for something to crack.

Come loose.

But now . . . now it was different. A boundary had been crossed. A dam busted. It left me walking through a fucking flood of need.

I was up to my goddamned eyes with it.

Twice, I'd passed her in the hall, and it'd taken every fucking thing I had not to grab her and press her delicate, delicious body up against the wall.

Needing to devour that mouth.

Desperate to take it further.

To slide my hands up her skirt and slip my fingers into her heat.

I'd felt it. How fucking bad she'd wanted me. It was almost as potent as the anger she felt for me.

The fear.

At least she hadn't taken off.

Sucking in a breath, I pulled out my phone and squinted at the text on the screen.

Sage: Got a call. Think I have something you might be interested in.

Sage was one of the guys at the shop I'd invested in where I had all my cars restored.

Disappointment was probably not the reaction he was going for, but I deflated with a heavy exhale as I tapped out a response.

Me: What you got?

Sage: '55 Bel Air. Seller is bringing it by in about 15. Thought you might want dibs.

His offering almost brought on a smile.

Me: Yup. I'll be there.

Sage: Cool.

Tucking my phone into my back pocket, I grabbed my keys and headed out the door, going straight for the elevator and riding it down into the basement. I hopped onto one of my bikes, figuring the fresh air would do me some good. Rid me of some of the anxiety and need bottled in my limbs.

Kicking it over, the engine roared to life. Metal vibrated beneath my hands. I took it to the road. Heavy on the throttle. Weaving through cars as I let the heat blast at my face and beat some of the bullshit away.

Could almost feel it scatter like fall leaves blowing away to reveal what they concealed.

Damp earth.

Darkness.

Blood.

Bones.

Dirt.

That date loomed. Right around the corner. A reminder that Sydney was what I was fighting for.

Ten minutes later, I took a left and then a right, winding down into the industrial section of Gingham Lakes. I passed by warehouses and shops and dingy offices.

Slowing, I made the last right through the big metal gate into Roke's Restorations. I was itching to get my fingers on something good. Something that could be brought back. Something that was safe.

The massive rolling doors of the shop had been lifted. Gliding to a stop, I set my boots out to balance the bike and kicked the stand. I swung off and rushed a hand through my windblown hair as I ducked through the door and into the shop.

Place was in its usual state.

Disarray with the promise of something good. Cars and bikes and parts sitting everywhere in varying states of repair.

When he heard the thud of my boots echoing on the concrete, Sage eased out from under a hood of a classic Pontiac. He lifted his chin, grabbed a rag. "Hey, man, you made it."

"And miss the chance at getting my hands on a Bel Air? Think you know me better than that."

He turned up one of his confident grins. "Which is exactly why I got with you first. Guy said he'd picked it up local and wants to turn it quick."

We both turned when we heard a car rolling into the lot.

"Ready to check this out?"

"Hell yeah."

Side by side, we headed out the garage doors.

Rolling into the lot was a four-door sedan that had to be ten or fifteen years old, beat to shit, and seen better days. But it didn't come anywhere close to looking like the hunk of rusted-out metal being towed in behind it.

How the fuck he even towed it out of whatever dump he'd found it in was beyond me. The tires were flat and rotted, and every inch he moved forward was met with the shrill sound of metal grinding.

Taking a look at the kid behind the wheel of the car, my first thought was desperate times called for desperate measures.

He put it in park and cut the engine. A dude that couldn't have been older than twenty came springing out of the driver's side, scrawny as fuck with ratted out clothes. Cheap ass, second rate, hacked out tattoos littered his arms.

"You Sage?" he asked.

"Nope." I shoved my hands into the pockets of my jeans and rocked back on my heels.

My gut instinct made itself known.

Standing there was something seedy.

I angled my head at Sage, who had to be thinking the same shit. "This is Sage."

The kid nodded at him. "Caleb. We talked on the phone."

Sage extended his hand. "Nice to meet you."

Nervously, the kid looked back at the car. "Well, this is it."

I wandered over to the rusted-out Bel Air. Windshield smashed to oblivion and all the rest of the windows gone, upholstery cracked and ripped with some of the rods and springs poking through.

Resting my hands on the windowsill, I ducked my head inside and peered around at the old gauges and dials in the dash, old style stereo still in its place.

It was gonna need a full overhaul, that was for damned sure.

It was exactly what I'd been looking for. Exactly like I remembered. I pulled my head back and looked his direction.

"Where'd you find her?"

Twitching, he gestured south with his head. "Down on Roddum. A guy is getting rid of some of his mom's old things. He said he needed to sell it quick because he needed the cash."

I stood, crossed my arms over my chest, and stared at the guy, trying to get a read.

Intuition.

My glare promised him I knew something wasn't quite right.

The punk shifted, about three seconds from pissing his pants.

Knew his type.

Badass until there was someone standing there who was bigger than him.

I ran my fingertips over the hood of the car.

There was something about it that was way too familiar.

Too close.

"What's the guy's name?"

Caleb shrugged. "Todd. Said it wasn't worth anything, and I might as well dump it in the lake."

Awareness pressed down on my chest. Todd. Nikki's uncle.

Maybe I should have recognized the car the second the kid had pulled up. Wasn't like there were all that many of these cars sitting around, which was why I'd been searching for one in the first place.

I'd fallen in love with this very one a long damned time ago.

Summers spent traipsing in and out of her grandma's house. Playing. Running wild.

We'd sit in this car where it was parked at the back of the lot, turning the wheel and yanking at the gear shift like it might take us to another place.

Fairyland.

Any place we wanted to go.

Todd used to live in a trailer that sat at the very back of Nikki's grandma's land. He had always been out working in the yard and the shed, fixing shit up.

Couldn't even say how long ago it'd been since he'd moved out of town.

Hit with the onslaught of memories, I pressed my palms to the side panel and dropped my head.

Honestly, I wasn't exactly sure of what Nikki would think of me buying this car.

If she'd be pissed or pleased.

Thing was, it was a part of who we were.

On top of that, Nikki's grandma was sick.

Loss was a motherfucking bitch.

What made it worse was I didn't know things were so bad they were needing to sell stuff off.

I looked over at the twitcher who'd probably swindled the car right out from under them. "You said Todd sold you this car?"

"Yeah, dude . . . pretty sure that was his name. Looking to get rid of it fast. I didn't do nothin' wrong, so if you're not interested, let me know and I'm out of here. No big thing."

I roughed a hand through my hair and turned my face up to the strikingly blue sky.

Blowing out a sigh, I looked back at him. "Need to make a call, and I'll let you know. Give me a minute."

Asshole itched, eyes darting around, desperation flooding his tone. "Man, if you're not interested, I'll find someone who is. Don't have time for this bullshit."

I flew at him, getting right in his face.

Off to the side, Sage chuckled, low and dark. Hell, the guy was probably more intimidating than me.

Punk staggered back, and I just backed him closer and closer into the wall until the only way out was through me. "Listen, asshole. I know the owner of that car."

I pointed at it as I said it. "Now give me one fucking minute to figure out if this is legit. Otherwise, I'm gonna take matters into my own hands and make that decision for myself. If you want to leave, be my guest. But you won't be leaving with this car. You got me?"

He shrugged me off, lifting his chin like he thought he was a badass who was going to take me out.

Bring it on.

I'd lay him out in a second flat.

He shook himself out. "Whatever. You have five."

Punk asshole twat. Little fucker needed someone to teach him a lesson.

I gave Sage a warning look.

And he gave me one back.

This shit didn't sit right with either of us.

I pulled out my phone and tapped out a message to Nikki. Hated that she was probably going to cringe when she saw my name come up on the screen.

But this was my job.

To protect her the best way I could.

Me: Hey, is your grandma selling some of her things from her place?

Three of us sat there in silence, waiting for a response. Five minutes passed, then ten.

The asshole smacked his hands out in front of him. "So, are we gonna do this deal or what?"

I groaned out a frustrated sigh. "What are you asking for it?"

"Ten."

I laughed out loud and gave a harsh shake of my head.

With the way he flinched, I was pretty sure it sounded like nothing but a threat.

"I'll give you four."

"What the fuck, man, that's bullshit."

Hands curling into fists, I edged closer to him, not quite sure why I felt like taking the stain out.

Got the feeling he'd been doing plenty of shady shit on his own.

This guy radiated sleaze.

Wasn't about to let him make out on this car. On Nikki's family's pain.

No fucking way.

"You're free to leave here, deal or not. But you're not leaving here with this car."

sixteen

Nikki

"All right, everyone. Have a seat, and we'll get started," I called to the group of women who had congregated along the back wall of the secluded basement room, pouring themselves coffee and chatting before the meeting.

Everyone moved to their seats.

I glanced around at their faces. Some familiar, regulars who were there week after week, but there were a few new faces, all of which looked unsure of themselves and what they were doing there.

Their expressions ranged from hopeful to sad.

Their ages, heritage, and economic statuses didn't matter. Each of them was so very different, yet in this setting, they were all the same.

Recovering from one trauma or another.

Abuse.

Loss.

Whatever it may be, it united them in solidarity.

Nerves strained tight across my chest at the anxiety I felt each time I sat in this position. The weight and the burden I was gladly taking on.

Their counselor.

Their encourager.

The chatter quieted as everyone settled into their seats, and Dr. Kathy gave me a nod, giving me the go ahead.

I was leading group tonight.

My stomach dipped as those nerves soared.

My gaze met Brenna's, and she gave me a timid smile.

I smiled back and cleared my throat, letting my attention bounce around the group. "Good evening, everyone. Thank you for being here. It's great to see your faces."

"It's good to be here," echoed back.

"For those of you who may not know me, my name is Nikki Walters, and I'll be leading group tonight. Before we start, I'd like to reiterate that this is our safe place. Everything said within these walls is confidential and won't leave this circle. We won't judge each other, but rather we will hold each other up."

Agreement rippled around the circle.

"Let's start this off with our group mantra. Our prayer. We'll remember it with everything that is shared tonight."

I strengthened my voice and began to recite, "I am strong. I have control of my life. I have control of my body. I have the right."

Some of the women chanted it loudly, claiming it, while others merely mumbled it under their breaths.

That was okay.

The only thing that mattered was that each of them would hear it again and again until they believed it.

"Okay . . . tonight I would like us to talk about some of the emotions you experienced when you decided it was time to make a change. No doubt, standing up for what we deserve when we might be in a bad situation is met with a gamut of emotions. Fear and joy and conviction and doubt, just to name a few. Let's look at those and how they impacted your decisions to make a change. Who would like to start?"

Lynetta raised her hand. She was good about sharing first. Getting the words flowing, instilling trust and comfort in the rest of the women who might be nervous and on edge. Exuding her own kind of peace in the way she shared the memories of her abuse as a child.

She wasn't ashamed to admit she still dealt with the scars every day. But that didn't mean she hadn't overcome it and found joy in her life.

"I remember the very moment I'd had enough, and I couldn't take any—"

She stopped speaking when timid footsteps echoed from the stairwell as someone made their way down.

It was very typical for a new member.

Many times, they came in late as if they weren't sure they should be there at all, needing to convince themselves to take that step.

I put a welcoming smile on my face and shifted to look over my shoulder toward the stairwell.

My heart froze in my chest when my eyes landed on the figure standing on the last step.

Ice slicked down my spine.

Horror.

Dread.

Worry.

They twined through me like the roots of a tree breaking through the foundation of a home.

Destructive.

Unseen until the damage was already done.

That was what it felt like, sitting there staring at my little sister and having no idea why she could be there.

Her face was so much like mine.

It felt as if I was looking into a mirror.

Only her eyes widened in shame and disgrace and mine widened with questions.

Why are you here?

What happened?

Why didn't you tell me?

I didn't know. I'm so sorry. I didn't know.

My lips parted on a soft cry while dread pumped through me with so much force I could feel the thunder of it in my ears. The hardest part was the impact I felt in my spirit.

As if a hammer had cracked me wide open, and everything I'd held true spilled out.

Knees shaking, I climbed to my feet. Metal screeched as the chair slid when I reached out to hold on to the back for support.

I slowly turned all the way around to face my little sister.

That was all it took for her to spin around and bolt.

Footsteps echoed on the concrete as she pounded upstairs. The sound of her escape was what finally shot me into action.

"Nikki." Kathy hissed the warning, trying to stop whatever line she thought I was crossing.

I ignored her and shoved the chair out of my way. It toppled over. The reverberation of it hitting the ground echoed against the walls.

The sound only seemed to gather strength.

Distraught, I stumbled around it.

Everything felt as if it had been set to slow motion, my own steps slackened as I tried to process what was happening.

Because this felt like a nightmare. Like I'd wake up and realize it'd only been brought on by worry. By the reminder that the anniversary of Sydney's disappearance was approaching so fast.

Too fast.

It always made everything raw and new.

But my eyes were wide open.

Too wide.

My spirit screamed that I'd been blind all along.

"Sammie," I cried, chasing her up the stairs. I gathered the hem of my dress with one hand and clung to the railing with the other so I could make it up faster. "Sammie. Sammie, please. Wait."

Tears stung my eyes. A knot grew in my throat, so big that I choked over it.

I couldn't breathe.

"Sammie!" I shouted, her name strangled as it ripped free.

She was already shoving open the glass doors by the time I made it to the first level.

I raced after her and caught the door just before it closed, clamoring after her.

Her brown ponytail swished madly at her back as she rushed for her car that was parked on the street.

"Sammie," I begged, scrambling that way, pleading with her to stop.

To look at me.

To tell me what was happening.

My fingers brushed down her back. She flew around as if she was terrified of me.

Tears soaked her face, but it didn't do anything to conceal the grief.

"No," she rasped. She put out her hand to stop me from coming any closer. "No. This . . . this was supposed to be confidential. Private."

Angrily, she swatted at her tears. "Why are you here? You aren't supposed to be here."

Guilt blazed a path through me.

Clearly, she felt trapped.

Ambushed.

More tears streaked free, and she choked around the words, "It was supposed to be confidential. You . . . you aren't finished with school yet. Why are you here?"

"Sammie," I attempted again, my voice cracking. "I'm sorry. I'm interning here."

I guessed when I'd told her I was almost finished, she hadn't realized that I was actually overseeing a group. That I'd stepped out beyond the online classes to learn the things I could only learn by interacting with people.

I struggled to find the words to give her comfort when I felt so lost.

Bewildered and crushed.

Clearly, my baby sister had kept me in the dark about something awful.

I could feel it, radiating from her in waves of shame.

"Whatever is going on, whatever reason you're here, I'm here for you. It isn't your fault."

She blinked and backed away. "You don't know anything."

Steadily, she kept inching toward her car. She opened the door. "Please . . . just . . . forget you saw me here."

Then she turned, jumped inside, and drove away.

I stood there on the sidewalk as the streetlamps slowly blinked to life.

Stricken.

Broken and not having the answer as to why but knowing there was no chance I could ever forget.

Drained, I snapped open the door and was met by the silence of Ollie's loft radiating back at me.

I didn't really want to be alone, but I didn't have anywhere else to go. No one to turn to. No one to talk to.

Maybe this load really was too heavy. All I'd wanted was to make a difference. Pour goodness into a cruel world. In some small way, make it better.

Now, everything felt so wrong.

It'd taken every single ounce of willpower I had not to jump in my car and chase after Sammie.

She needed time, and my pressing her for answers wouldn't be doing her any favors.

I had to give her space.

It left me feeling mashed up inside. As if I'd been beaten and left for dead.

Wounds bleeding out when I didn't have the first clue how they'd been inflicted.

The vibration of the band playing downstairs at Olive's seeped through the floors and trembled the walls with revelry.

Voices carrying.

Laughter riding.

I'd never felt so brutally alone.

Heavy, sluggish beats drummed in my aching chest as I stepped into the space and let my purse drop to the middle of the floor. Not even caring where it landed.

I felt . . . stunned.

Dazed.

As if another piece of my world had broken loose.

I was happy, wasn't I?

So was my sister. We were close.

I'd always believed it.

Where had things gone wrong?

My gaze was drawn to the bank of windows that overlooked the city below.

My sluggish heart drummed a wayward beat, a thrum of adrenaline through my veins.

It had nothing to do with the view and everything to do with the man sitting on one of the oversized loungers on the balcony.

He faced out, just his head and the expanse of his massive, bare shoulders in my view.

A shiver rolled, and I felt as if my spirit crawled right out of me to make its way to him.

There was nothing I could do. It didn't matter what had happened on Saturday. How much I wanted to protect my heart.

I moved.

Drawn.

The way I'd always been.

Toward him had always felt like the only direction I could go.

And tonight, that feeling was overpowering.

Helplessness streamed through me like an out-of-control current that was getting ready to go right over the edge.

A free fall into nothingness.

I kept my footsteps subdued as I inched across the floor, my motions measured as I slowly opened the glass-plate slider.

Ollie stiffened in the cushioned chair, but he didn't say anything as I stepped out onto the balcony.

Distorted music floated through the muggy air, and that chill scattered. Binding deeper as I eased over to the ornate wrought-iron railing. I wrapped my hands around it and held on tight.

As if it might keep everything from splintering away.

His presence slammed into me from behind. Beat after beat.

Fierce.

Intense.

"Shouldn't you be downstairs working?"

"Was worried about you," he finally grated, blowing out a long breath toward the sky.

"I told you, you don't need to worry about me."

"Tell me how the fuck I'm supposed to do that when the only thing on my mind is you."

His words were delivered quietly, though his voice somehow boomed in the dense, thickened air.

"Texted you earlier. Never heard a thing. Then when I came up to talk to you, you never showed. Went as far as calling Lillith to find out if she'd talked to you after your meeting tonight."

He inhaled a deep breath. "Your meeting ended two hours ago, Nikki. No one's heard from you since, some asshole broke into your apartment during last week's meeting, and you want me *not* to worry about you? Think you know me better than that. I was about five seconds from starting a door-to-door search."

There was a confession to his words. The depth of his worry and the lengths he would go.

I lifted my face to the mild breeze that blew through.

Cars accelerated below with small bleeps of their horns, and cicadas buzzed in the towering trees that reached to our level.

I wanted to dip my fingertips into it. To find the peace it seemed to offer.

But I felt as if I'd completely lost ground. Everything I'd been fighting for somehow felt like a sham.

Warily, I peeked back at him. The man sat in the chair, looking like the king of his own city sprawled out below him.

A conqueror.

A warrior.

Chest bare and abdomen rippling.

Eyes keen.

The longer pieces of his hair whipped around him like a flaming crown, the sides cropped, making the man look every bit the beast that he was.

Yet, there was something about him that remained so unbearably lost.

Sapphire eyes so soft I could fall right inside.

It took about everything I had not to drop at his feet.

I wanted to remain strong. Push him away. Remember how being this close to him only hurt me time and again.

But right then, the only thing I felt was weak.

A tremor rolled through my being.

Or maybe it wasn't weakness.

Maybe I really just needed the one person who could fully understand.

My hands cinched tighter around the metal. "Do you ever wonder where our lives went wrong? Where we changed course or if we were just heading this direction all along?" I hedged, trying to find the best way to invite him into my heart.

Into my grief.

He huffed out a strained breath. "Every day, Nikki. I think about this shit every day. I think we both know exactly where it went wrong."

I glimpsed him from the corner of my eye. He lifted a tumbler to his mouth, a half-empty bottle of amber fluid sitting on the table next to him. He took a long drink.

"It only gets worse when the date gets nearer," he reluctantly added.

Yet, to me, it felt like a gift. His words, his *heart*, something he had refused to offer me over all these years.

"Fourteen years," I agreed. "I can't believe that much time has passed. I can't believe it's been so long since our foundation was ripped out from under us. It shaped us into different people," I offered, praying he'd get it.

That I needed him to listen.

That I needed him to be there.

For me.

His grating words filled the distance that separated us. "It doesn't matter how many years go by, it feels like it was yesterday. Feels like I'm stuck there, and I'm never gonna get out."

His confession was hardened with regret.

Muted in sorrow.

"I was there with you. But you wouldn't let me be there for you. You wouldn't let me stay." My voice was a whisper that got swept up in the wind. It felt as if Sydney was caught in it, a ghost howling as she blew through.

I felt him flinch. The man hit by the weight of the reality, even when I knew he never wanted to face it.

"Couldn't let you stay there because you didn't need to be in the middle of my mess."

I looked at him from over my shoulder. My breath hitched.

My beautiful beast, who was so angry at the world, angry at himself, sitting there with his chin lifted and his nostrils flaring.

I knew he would charge into the distance and change it all if he was given the chance.

I knew he would be willing to sacrifice everything.

"If it was your fault, then it was my fault, too."

"Don't ever say that," he spat, jumping to his feet.

Fire and rage.

They lit like a fury inside him.

My head slowly shook. "You know it's true, Ollie. You can't erase the fact that I was there with you. That we were together. That I'm every bit as responsible as you."

"No. I was responsible for her. Just the same as I am for you."

Those eyes blazed as he took a step forward, and he fisted his hand over his heart. "I was the one who fucked it up. I was the one who pushed things between us when I knew I was crossing lines I wasn't allowed to cross. I was the one who sent her away."

Grief lined his voice.

Emotion tingled my throat, and my eyes stung.

Part of me wanted to stop it.

Walk away and pretend all of this wasn't crashing over me, threatening to bury me alive. The other part wanted to hang on to every second.

It was the first time in years Ollie had opened up to me. A door opened when it'd forever been closed.

"She would have understood," I told him, knowing with all of me that she would have.

He turned his head, looking to the far corner of the balcony. "We had a pact."

The memory it shivered around us. A reel playing in sync in our minds. The vow we'd made before we'd understood that one day we would grow and change and things would no longer look the same.

If I focused hard enough, I could still feel the cut Ollie had made on my palm.

"We were eight years old, Ollie. You were nine. Kids," I told him. "We grew up. All of us changed."

Slowly, he swiveled his attention back. Every muscle in his body was held in restraint. "And you know exactly what happened when we did."

Grief pulsed through the silence that raged between us. So many things left unsaid for so many years. It tickled our ears and hammered our hearts as we finally brought our truths out into the light.

Tears stung my eyes, and I swallowed Ollie's intensity and forced myself to speak. "Fourteen years ago, did I leave everyone else behind, too?" I whispered, the words a tremor.

A plea.

A confession.

"Was I so consumed by that grief, by that loss, that I let everything and everyone else fade into the background?"

Ollie's face pinched, and he was moving closer. "What are you talking about?"

"I missed it. I failed to see what was right in front of my eyes, Ollie."

He was at my side. The magnitude of his presence nearly knocked me from my feet.

"What are you saying?"

"My sister." The words broke on my tongue.

In that moment, I felt something crack.

Chip away.

Secrets slayed.

And all I wanted was this man to hold all of them.

seventeen

Ollie

"My sister." Her confession carried on the wind.

Like a never-ending echo of horror that would ride on the soundwaves forever.

Regret.

The kind I knew all too well.

Grief clustered in my chest as I looked down at her.

Tears streaking down her defined cheeks.

Nikki. Fucking. Walters.

The bane of my existence.

The one who drove me right out of my mind. Left me clinging to the edge of sanity. Made me weak in the damned knees and hard everywhere else.

She was a carrot dangled in front of me like a tease. Always right there, always just out of reach. A connection I couldn't keep but wanted more than my next breath.

Because that was what she was.

Breath.

Life.

The goodness and light in the middle of my dark, dark world.

I wanted to lean in, press my nose to her delicate neck, and suck her down like a sweet, satisfying drink.

Sunshine and lemonade.

In the breeze, locks of that honeyed hair whipped around her head. A few errant pieces stuck to her face, those eyes so wide and innocent, and that mouth so goddamned deliciously pink.

It made her look like the girl I'd fallen so hard for.

She'd driven me crazy then, just like she was driving me crazy now.

Swore to God, the burn of that kiss from the other day was still flames on my lips.

"What do you mean, your sister?" My words were guarded. Careful.

Fuck. Maybe I didn't want to know.

Because a sob tore from Nikki's throat.

"I think someone hurt her."

Rage. It was instant. The fury that banged through my being. It struck in the air.

As deadly as a thunderbolt.

I grabbed her and pulled her all the way around so I could fully see her. "Who?"

She stared up at me. Indigo eyes flashing in the night. Agony wheezed out on her words when she reached up and pressed both her hands to my chest. "I don't know. She . . . she came into the meeting tonight. Neither of us were expecting the other. She saw me . . ."

She choked.

In a flash, I had both my arms around her waist, pulling her up tight against me as I tried to process what that meant. "What was she there for?"

"She ran off before I could get any answers. I . . . I chased after her. Called her name. And she ran, Ollie. She ran from me as if she was scared of me. Like . . . like she didn't trust me."

That description all wrong.

That role was one reserved for me.

My mind spun with a shit-ton of horrible possibilities. There was nothing I could do but gather this girl closer, rocking her slowly, knowing I'd give absolutely anything to take this away. "She didn't know you would be there?"

Burying her face against my chest, she shook her head. "No. I don't think she realized that my internship meant I would be working in the field."

I kissed her crown and ran my fingers through her hair, praying it would soothe her. "You know it wasn't because she was scared of you or didn't trust you, Nik. You know better than that. She just didn't know what to do with exposing her own secret. You took her by surprise."

Hot tears landed on my bare chest, and the girl's lips moved across the flesh. "I don't know what I'm supposed to do."

I was such a twisted fuck.

Depraved.

Because just that touch had my mind going where it couldn't go.

Laying this girl out.

Taking her.

At the same time, I wanted to wrap her up.

Protect her and take every drop of her despair away. Shield her from all the bad shit that ran rampant in this vile world.

I tried to rein in the stampeding need.

"You'll figure it out, sweet girl. Sammie knows you. She's just got to deal with whatever she's going through before she's ready to confide in you."

"I can't stand the thought of someone hurting her. Of her being in pain."

A shudder raked down my spine, spreading out beneath the surface of my skin.

Rage and grief.

I hugged her closer at the same time as she pressed tighter against me, those sweet arms bent and pinned between us as I wrapped her whole. "I know. I'm so fucking sorry. So fucking sorry."

There'd never been truer words.

She pulled back. Just a fraction. Enough that those mesmerizing eyes were gazing up at me.

Casting their spell.

Sucking me under.

"I need you," she whispered, ducking down and placing gentle kisses all over my chest as her fingertips ran down my abdomen.

My muscles tensed beneath the assault.

Her perfect, perfect assault.

I grabbed her by the wrists, voice a warning. "Nikki."

"Please," she whimpered. "I need you. I need you. Take it away."

My mind flashed to a year ago. I could almost hear my own words echo through my spirit. My pleas when I'd needed her in a way no one else could offer.

Like she needed me now.

The two of us knew each other better than anyone else.

Trusted in a way we shouldn't.

"Nikki," I said again, another warning that only sounded like giving in.

"Please." She pressed the word right against my heart that thundered and roared and sent an earthquake through me.

Protection and greed.

"You are so much better than what I've got to offer. I'm messed up."

"What if I want to be messed up with you?"

A low chuckle rumbled out, and my fingertips were tracing across her lips.

Everything coming closer.

Closer and closer.

"It's my job to protect you, remember? Even if that means protecting you from me."

The smallest smile pulled across her sexy mouth, a tease barely winding into the words. "I guess I like your brand of pain, don't I?"

Lust flickered low. Right where it'd always burned for her.

Embers and ash.

An aching, smoldering glow. "Don't want to hurt you, Nikki, and I'm pretty damned sure you don't want me to hurt you, either."

She blinked up at me. No reservations when she should be running for her life. "Then don't."

"Not sure I know anything else."

Need flickered through those bewitching features, and I brushed my fingers through the wild pieces of her hair, holding her by the side of the head.

"If I could, I'd do anything for you. Give you anything."

Her nails scratched over the cross etched right at the center of my chest.

Right over the boom of my heart. It pulsed my blood harder and harder, every thrum winding me higher.

Lust bottled in the air. Wobbling. Teetering as everything threatened to spill.

Stark vulnerability seeped into her words, a line pulling into a scowl across her brow. "Please, Ollie. Touch me."

Need tied my guts into a thousand knots, and I gripped her as we swayed. To the beat of the music that filtered up from below.

The bar alive.

Nikki and I elevated above it.

Removed.

Two strangers who knew each other better than anyone else who'd landed in a realm where they shouldn't be.

My thumb traced along her cheek. Right over those freckles that made her appear so sweet and a little untamed.

She was.

But she was more. So much more.

She was beauty and belief and the sun.

Made up of her own mistakes and her own regrets.

She was fear and challenge and perseverance.

She was the girl I'd thought I would spend my life with until I'd lost it the day I'd lost Sydney. "I will ruin you, Nik. We both know it."

Nails scratched across my skin, searching for a place to sink in. "You ruined me a long time ago."

My nose brushed across hers. "Nikki." Her name was a moan. A plea. It was giving in. "What do you need?"

"You."

A groan rumbled deep in my chest, and I swept her off her feet, one arm under her back and the other under her knees. That was right as my mouth was slanting over hers.

Possessively.

Protectively.

My tongue plundered that smart, delicious mouth.

Deprived of the taste of her for far too long. For too many fucking years.

After the tease I'd gotten the other day, I was desperate for more.

Damn the consequences.

A whimper pulled from her, and she murmured, "Ollie," on a needy breath of surrender.

For a moment, both of us were giving in.

Her arms wound around my neck as I moved across the balcony. I owned that mouth the whole way, Nikki clinging to me the entire time.

Kissing me back.

Just as hungry.

Desperate and needy.

Needy for me.

Heaviness stretched my chest taut, everything I'd ever held for this girl swelling.

Getting bigger.

Consuming in a way that I knew would never let me go.

Angling to the side, I slid open the door with my elbow.

Shadows played across the floor and walls of my loft, and I carried her across the dusky, dimly-lit room. When I laid her on the couch, a surprised breath gushed from between her lips.

I swallowed it.

Made it my own.

Wanting more. So much more. Wanting it all.

Fuck.

I had to focus. Focus on this girl, who was squirming on the dark leather, wearing this ridiculous short floral dress and boots.

Those legs bent as her hips bucked from the couch, begging for me. That dress slinked up to reveal the silky skin of her thighs. It gave me a peek of the black lace covering her underneath.

Desire clutched every cell.

Heart and mind and body.

There was nothing I could do. All I wanted was to take her away from there. To a reality where it was us and nothing else.

I stood, staring down at her through the darkness.

Eyes tracing every slender curve of her mouthwatering body.

"You are so fucking gorgeous."

She tucked her bottom lip between her teeth, and her chin lifted as her back arched. She pressed her hands to her belly and squirmed.

Unable to sit still.

So needy.

Hot.

Her flames licked out. A spark against my body.

My cock twitched and strained against my jeans. I was blasted by thoughts of how easy it would be to rip all of our clothing away and sink inside.

Get lost in her heat and her sighs and her support.

Forever.

Use her up the way I'd done before and didn't even have the decency to remember.

Motherfucker.

I wasn't about to go there.

This was about her.

Nikki.

I reached out and trailed a single finger down her arm, running from her shoulder to her wrist. "Just have to look at you and another piece of me falls. Breaks away. You were every fantasy I ever had. Teenaged kid dying to get inside you. Knew it'd be heaven."

"Ollie," she whispered, spreading her hands across her dress that had ridden all the way up to her waist, her hands running the length of her thighs of her bent legs. "You were always more than a fantasy to me. You were everything that was real."

God damn it.

She was going to wreck me.

Destroy every ounce of self-control I had. I'd done it once. Lost it. Let her wreck me. Didn't think she could afford for me to lose it again.

So, I kept myself in check, careful as I let my index finger explore, running over the fabric of that dress and riding up her thigh. I palmed the inside of it and dipped down to kiss across her knee.

Shivers rolled through her, running her spine and crashing into me.

Those hypnotic eyes watched me through the pale, muted light, knowing me too well. Seeing too much.

Each movement measured, I slowly crawled over her, bracing, keeping some distance between us while she fought to get closer.

God only knew what would happen if I plastered myself against the shape of her.

A sigh filtered from between her pink lips that were swollen and plump and damp from the force of my kiss.

So damned sexy.

I planted my hands on either side of her head, gaze moving over that unforgettable face. "You are real, Nikki. Don't ever mistake that. You were the most real thing I ever had."

Her fingertips brushed down my chest. "I'm still yours," she whispered.

I slammed my eyes shut and jerked my head to the side like it might protect me from the impact of her confession.

Inhaling deeply, I let my forehead drop to hers, our breaths mingling and our noses grazing.

Both of us hanging at a precipice.

A breath. A pant. A heated second.

Bated, suspended.
Then the band holding me back snapped.
Our lips met in a collision of greed.
Taking and giving.
My lips closed over hers.
Top.
Bottom.
Sucking.
Releasing.
Tugging.
Again and again.
A perfected dance that wasn't close to being slow.
I pressed up higher on my hands, and my head dipped down as I swept my tongue into the wet welcome of her mouth.
Thought I might die right there.
It was met with a whimper at the back of her throat and a tangle of her tongue with mine.
Her fingers scruffed through my beard, and then her hands were fisting in my hair.
Begging for more.
Her body lifting to meet mine as our tongues coiled in a desperate play to get closer to the other.
I took her by the inside of her thigh, making myself room, rocking my cock against her pussy.
Her cry was quiet and needy. A plea lighting in the combustible air. "Ollie. I need you. I need you."
A groan rambled through my spirit, and I tore my mouth from hers. This was not about me.
I'd taken enough.
I plucked at her bottom lip with both of mine before I was kissing a path down her chin, her jaw.
Fingernails scraped my shoulders.
I sucked and licked along the delicate column of her slender throat and to those fucking collarbones that drove me straight out of my mind.
Delirium.
My head spun, and I was kissing across her chest, down over her heart that drummed violently.
Pound, pound, pound.
I felt it beating.
Desperate in its bid to meet with mine.
As if it could catch up to the bolting thunder that raged within the confines of my ribs. Thrashing at my insides.
Seeking a way out.

I sucked in a breath and fought back that feeling. That feeling that she was mine and she was always gonna be.

I kissed across the neckline of her dress, right over the fabric to the swell of those tiny tits.

Fuck.

Why was that so sexy?

So damned sexy that I was yanking the neckline down, exposing her dark, peaked nipple. My tongued licked across the tip before I sucked it into my mouth. One hand came up, palming the bit of flesh, bringing it deeper into my mouth.

Nikki bucked, rubbing her center against my dick that begged at my jeans. She moaned, and her hands were everywhere.

My hair, my face, my shoulders.

Raking down my back, eliciting the most tortuous, pleasured kind of pain. "Ollie. Oh God. That feels so good. You feel so good. I need you. I need you so much."

Her panted words lifted into the dense air, and I sat back on my knees. I grabbed her by the waist, cinching my hands around her. "You want me to make you feel good, sweet girl?"

Her head rocked back on the pillow. I swore, the girl was so damned pretty it hurt to look at her. A punch right to the center of my chest.

"Yes," she drew out, tongue darting out to swipe across her lips. "Please. I need you. I never stopped needing you."

I beat back the guilt. I had no clue about the way I'd treated her last year. But I knew full well the way I'd left her when she was sixteen.

My hands slid up the top of her thighs.

Shivers raced beneath my palms, the girl quivering and shaking like she was seconds from falling apart, and I hadn't even touched her.

I let my hands glide around to her back, lifting her a little as I palmed her ass, her knees dropping open wide when I did. "This ass, baby."

And I was wondering if anyone had been in it. Who'd been in her, taking this sweet body.

Aggression I didn't have any fucking right to feel curled through my being. A dark, violent sickness.

I wanted to possess her.

Every part.

Every inch.

She was supposed to be mine.

I kneaded her cheeks and let my fingers run down her cleft.

"Ollie. What are you doing to me?" Those indigo eyes met with mine as she sucked frantic breaths into her lungs. "You make me crazy."

A low chuckle of warning escaped my mouth. "Safe to say it's the other way around, Sunshine. You make me insane. That mouth, and this body. I want to fuck you wild, Nikki. Mark you. Keep you."

I was saying things I shouldn't be saying. But I couldn't stop the words from scraping from my mouth.

Her dress was bunched all the way up to below her tits, the one I'd been sucking on peeking out the top, nipple still hard and wet from my licks.

Her hands spread out across her flat, naked belly. "Please."

And I knew she'd let me. Knew that she'd let me use her. Maybe . . . maybe she'd use me, too.

The passion roiling in her eyes was untamed. Fierce and savage.

She wanted to get reckless with me.

I snagged my fingers in the edges of her underwear and began to peel them down.

"Shit," I hissed. The ground quaked beneath me as I revealed what was waiting underneath.

Totally un-fucking-prepared for seeing her this way.

Spread out for me.

Pussy wet and glistening.

Lifting her legs between us, I unwound the lace from her ankles and dropped her underwear to the floor, setting one of her ankles on my shoulder as I barely dragged just the tips of my fingers through her slit.

I almost went off right then.

I'd been wanting this girl for far, far too long.

Just that little touch had her hips hiking up, pressing from the couch.

"You want me to touch you, sweet girl? Is that what you want?" The words rumbled from me as I shifted, planting a single hand next to her head.

Caging her in.

She nodded, hair swishing across my couch. "Don't tease me, Ollie. My heart can't take it tonight."

My chest tightened, and I had the wayward thought that there'd be plenty of time for that later.

Teasing and playing.

I knew better than to let my thoughts go wandering that direction. I forced myself back to her in this moment.

To the girl who was shaking on my couch. Desperate for relief.

I slicked my fingers through her pussy, watching the way her lips parted, tasting the sigh that slipped from her tongue when I tucked a single finger into the tight clutch of her body.

Her hands flew to my shoulders and held on. "Ollie."

I drew back, added another. I drove them in slowly.

"Like that?" I murmured at her mouth, teasing her a little.

She swallowed hard, searching for air. "More."

"That's what I thought," I rumbled, nipping at her chin. "I'm gonna take care of you. Sweetness. Sunshine," I rumbled, lips moving across her cheek.

A little moan jetted from her mouth, and I edged back, pulling my fingers free.

Protest had her loosing a tiny groan, and I gave her a lopsided grin. "I've got you. Trust me . . . I've got you."

Those words were out before I could stop them.

Trust.

I deserved none of that.

But she could count on me to give her this.

I spread my hands wide and slipped them up the insides of her thighs, spreading her wide. Hands going back to her bottom, I lifted her from the couch when I leaned down and licked.

She yelped, and those needy little hands flew into my hair.

I turned, kissed the inside of her thigh, whispering against the flesh. "Is this okay, sweet girl?"

Sweet, fucking, delicious girl.

"If you stop, I will stab you, Oliver Preston."

There she was. My smart-mouthed Nikki.

A smile pulled free, one I hid against her skin before I buried my face back in her heat.

Kissing her cunt like I had kissed her mouth.

Laps and licks against her lips, tongue driving between. I licked back to the tight pucker of her ass before I moved to lave at her clit.

Swollen and red.

I rolled my tongue around it.

Sucked.

Licked.

I pressed my hand to her belly, pushing down as I pressed two fingers into her pussy.

Her walls clenched around me, and she gasped, arching and begging and rubbing herself on my face.

Going a little wild the way I knew she would.

My dick pressed painfully at my jeans, so goddamned hard I was pretty sure I was gonna lose my mind if I didn't get inside her. That was all right because this girl had always driven me insane.

After tonight, I feared I would never come back down.

Feared I was never going to be the same.

Guessed I hadn't been since the first time I'd kissed her.

It was Nikki who'd marked me. Written herself on me. Hers when I could never belong.

I fucked her with my fingers, slow and hard while I ate her frantically.

Matching the frenzied beat that hammered my heart.

Driving her mad the way I knew I could. Wishing I could say screw it all and fuck her right.

"Ollie . . ."

She started chanting my name. Lifting her hips and begging me for more.

I could feel it coming.

Pleasure winding her tight.

So tight she was gonna take me with her.

I sucked and licked and drove my fingers into her tight body.

Everything lifted.

Her body.

My spirit.

She cried out as her entire body arched and bowed. Her stomach flexed, rippled with her sexy little six-pack, and her head rocked back, pressing into the pillow.

Bliss streaked through her and slammed into me.

Swells of pleasure.

A full-body glow.

So fucking gorgeous.

I wanted to sink inside her so bad I couldn't see.

Wanted to disappear in her.

Get lost.

Or maybe find my way back.

Because I didn't think I'd ever felt so close to home than I did while I was holding her like this.

As I led her through her orgasm, I climbed back over her and swallowed every one of her pants like they might be able to sustain me. The girl my breath.

"Ollie," she whimpered as she came down, her hands going back to my bare chest, sliding down my quivering stomach.

She went for my fly.

Quickly, I reached between us and snatched her by the wrists. I pinned both of them over her head. "Told you I was gonna take care of you, Nikki. I meant it."

Hurt washed across her face, and I leaned down and kissed it away.

She sighed into my mouth.

I eased back, grabbed her underwear from the floor, and helped her back into them before I resituated her dress.

Something about it felt so damned intimate.

Like I hadn't been closer to her than right then.

Her eyes tenderly watched me.

"Now, you rest," I told her.

I scooped her up the same way as I'd carried her inside.

Though this time, I carried her to my bed.

I laid her in the middle of it and stood at the side staring at her through the faint light that filtered in from the hall.

It left her nothing but a silhouette.

Still, laid out across my bed, that spellbinding girl was the most gorgeous thing I'd ever seen.

Magic.

Doing something crazy in me.

"So beautiful," I murmured, my damned hand shaking when I reached out and ran my knuckle from her temple to her chin.

She lifted to it, relishing in the touch, her voice a whisper in the night. "You, Ollie. It's you who's beautiful. You just don't see yourself the same way as I do."

I didn't say anything, I just moved to my dresser and pulled out a tee, helped her from her dress, and tugged my shirt over her head.

It swallowed her, and I couldn't help but grin.

I shrugged out of my jeans, leaving myself just in my underwear.

Could feel the fever in her gaze.

A smirk pulled to my mouth. "Told you, one look and you wouldn't be able to think straight."

"I can't see you that well . . . why don't you turn on the light?" The tease spun through the air, and I chuckled, climbed into my bed, and tucked her back against my chest.

So maybe it was stupid, but I pressed my hard cock to her ass. "Then we'd really be in trouble."

She snuggled deeper into my hold. "Don't pretend like we haven't always been."

Somberness moved between us, that awareness that had always been ours. Magnetic.

I wrapped an arm around her waist and pulled her closer, all distance erased, my mouth at her ear. "I've resisted you for so long."

She danced her fingertips over the mourning blazing stars on my forearm. "Until last year."

My eyes closed, and I pulled in a deep breath.

It was like inhaling life.

"I can't tell you how fucking sorry I am that I did that, Nikki. I . . . lost myself that night. Instead of getting easier, it seems to get more difficult every year. I needed you."

Even though my mind didn't process it, remember it, my soul had sought her out.

"And tonight?" she quietly asked, a million questions in the two tiny words.

What did we just do?

What does this mean?

How long until you hurt me again?

I nuzzled my nose into the locks of her honeyed hair, comfort gliding through me like a balm. "And tonight, you needed me."

I paused for a second, gathering my thoughts, my words. They trembled with the quiet truth. "Stayin' away from you is getting harder to do."

She weaved her fingers through mine and pulled our entwined hands to the thunder of her heart, so loud it ricocheted through my room. "Things are changing, Ollie. I can feel it."

What terrified me most was that I felt them changing, too.

eighteen

Ollie

Sixteen Years Old

The sound of water crashing below them filled their ears, the spray of the falls cooling their skin as they stood at the edge of the cliffs with the sun beating down above them.

"Hey, pussies, are you coming, or what?" Rex hollered from the lake below, his head bobbing as he treaded water, moving out of the way so the three of them could jump.

Kale was already swimming back toward the beach so he could climb back up to jump again.

"Don't be an asshole, Rex," Sydney shouted.

He laughed, swiping his hand across the top of the water to make a wave. Like it could possibly fly all the way up to splash her.

Ollie chuckled under his breath. Sydney was right. Rex was an asshole. Constantly throwing jabs and gibes, Kale and Ollie throwing them right back.

Didn't mean Ollie liked him any less.

They'd just gotten back from football camp. Third year they'd gone. All of them would be starters on the varsity team this year. It'd been . . . exhilarating. Pushing himself, testing his limits.

But fuck.

He'd missed home.

He'd missed this.

He glanced to the girl, to her trembling hand wound in his.

He'd missed *her*.

Nikki Walters.

The girl who was supposed to be his best friend.

His second sister.

In that second, it slammed him.

The admission no longer something he could deny.

He'd missed her.

More than that, he wanted her.

Wanted her in a way he wasn't supposed to, but with the way he'd been feeling at night in the dark—hell . . . with the way he'd been feeling in the light of day—it was getting harder and harder to ignore.

She'd had a boyfriend all last year, even though he'd told her he didn't like it.

Not *liking* it was a damned disrespect to the way he actually felt.

He hated it. Abhorred it. It made his insides feel like they were shriveling up and disintegrating.

Not that he could say a whole lot since he'd gone through at least ten different girls in that time. But not one of them made him feel like Nikki.

Sweet, timid Nikki who was shaking in her floral bikini that showed off her rail-thin body, the girl nothing but skin and bone.

Didn't matter. His body reacted no matter how fucking bad he begged it not to. There was just . . . something about her that twisted him all up inside.

"Come on," Sydney urged, angling her head. "You can do it."

He could feel his sister squeezing Nikki's opposite hand.

There they were. Teenagers. Close to grown. Three of them holding hands the same way as they'd done since they were little kids.

Best friends never leaving the others' sides.

Call it lame.

Hell, Rex constantly razzed him about it, giving him shit that he liked the girls better than him.

He did.

His crew was cool. His friends the type of guys he could count on for anything. Guys who would always have his back and he'd have theirs. No matter the circumstances.

But not like this. He didn't care that the rest of them didn't understand. Ollie's entire world was watching over these two. Protecting them.

Problem was, that protectiveness for Nikki had grown into something new.

Nikki nervously peeked over the edge. She sucked in a staggered breath and started backing away, shaking her head as she tugged her hands from theirs. "You guys go ahead. I'll take the trail back down."

Sydney turned to face her, wearing her own bikini. That made him angry, too.

He'd kill whoever looked at her the wrong way.

The last year, he'd gotten into trouble twice for fighting some dipshit who thought he could mess with his sister.

One he'd overheard talking about her in the locker room, saying how easily he could get in her pants. The other had the audacity to think Ollie would actually turn a blind eye when he'd found them making out in the back of the senior's car at a party.

Fuck no.

"No way, Nik Nik," Sydney said. "We aren't going without you."

"Really. It's fine."

Sydney perched a hand on her hip. "No, it's not fine. It's fun. I promise. You don't want to miss this."

Nikki shook her head, timid the way she'd always been. "I've never done it before."

A giggle lifted from Sydney, and she bounced forward, taking Nikki by the hand. "That's the whole point. It's the experience. About living. You know this. Every day counts, every moment matters. Don't ever forget it."

Ollie reached out and gathered back up Nikki's hand. "Yeah."

Every moment mattered.

"Come on, you can do it," Sydney reassured again. "You don't have anything to be scared of. Ollie and I are right here. We'll be with you the whole time."

All three of them squeezed hands and inched up to the edge of the cliff.

The roar of the waterfalls pouring into the lake a few yards away filled their ears, loud and stirring. Nikki drew in a deep breath, and Sydney peeked around her, his sister's gaze bouncing between the two of them in her soft kind of encouragement.

Then she whispered it, the words no longer a shout but just as loud. "Fly, fly, dragonfly."

They jumped.

Hand in hand.

Nikki screamed, and Sydney shrieked through her laughter.

Joy.

Always joy.

Ollie shouted as they plunged downward.

Loving it.

The feel of just . . . falling.

Falling.

He was falling.

He knew it then.

They hit the water. It split, swallowing them whole, sucking them down deep.

The three of them floated beneath the surface, surrounded by gushing bubbles and the streaks of light that penetrated the cool blue waters. Sound was distorted against his ears, and his heart beat harder in his chest as he used up all his air.

Or maybe it was Nikki who was doing it.

Stealing his breath.

She started to kick her legs through the water, and her foot scraped his upper leg as she propelled herself upward.

Just that graze rushed through him as if she'd raked her nails down his back.

The three of them broke the surface, laughing and gasping for air.

Nikki giggled the way she always did when she overcame a fear. After she'd tried something new that she wouldn't have done without the two of them.

The roar of the waterfall was almost deafening as he looked across at Nikki with her head kicked back toward the sun.

Everything was so loud and silent at the same time as he stared.

Freckles and olive skin and honey hair.

He wanted to put his mouth on her so badly it hurt.

Sydney was already swimming for the shore, splashing with Rex as they drifted off in the distance, the two of them throwing barbs the way they did.

Ollie ducked under the water. He came up right in front of Nikki.

She gasped in surprise, then her mouth dropped open with more when he wrapped an arm around her waist and started to paddle them toward a cove in the cliffs.

"What are you doing, Ollie, you brute?" she asked, but it was a whisper.

All breathy from exertion.

Or maybe she felt the same way touching him as he did when touching her.

Like it meant something.

Like it meant everything.

Because she wrapped her arms around his neck and clung to him. Her scent was all around him, his thoughts going haywire with having her like this.

"If you dunk me under that waterfall, you're gonna pay for it," she warned, trying to put lightness in her tone.

But there was no missing the way it came raspy from her throat.

Ollie tugged her into one of the secluded recesses carved out in the cliffs. A small vein of the waterfall dumped water into the lake from the rock protruding above their heads, making the cove completely secluded from the shore.

His feet barely touched, and she floated where he still held her around the waist.

"Ollie, what's going on?" she whispered again, so low it was swallowed by the thunder of the waterfall.

He only wavered for a second before he threaded his fingers through her hair and murmured, "This."

He dipped in and brushed his lips against hers.

Softly.

Barely there.

It didn't matter. It was the most powerful thing he'd ever felt.

Intense and overwhelming.

Nikki gasped, but her hands went to the back of his head to pull him closer.

His tongue swept across her lips, prodding, praying she'd want to kiss him back.

Thank God. She did.

Her lips parted, and she plastered her body against his, her tiny boobs pressed against his bare chest.

Ollie grunted, overcome.

Was this really happening?

Their tongues danced.

Carefully.

Cautiously.

Her breaths soft, and his pants hard.

She pulled back, something like awe and confusion in her features. Exactly what he felt.

Confused.

Awed.

He ran the pad of his thumb across her bottom lip. "I've been wanting to do that for the longest time."

A shy smile pulled across her mouth. "I've been wanting you to do that for the longest time, too."

"Yeah?"

She bit at her lip. "Yeah."

Her gaze traveled over his shoulder. Worry climbed to her face. He knew where her mind had gone.

"This is just between us, Nikki. You and me. It's not anyone else's business."

"What about Sydney?" Guilt and more of that worry filled her words.

"Don't think we should tell her." He brushed back her hair, needing to touch her. He didn't ever want to stop. "Not yet. One day . . . just . . . not yet. I don't want her to get upset."

We are three. Forever and ever, you and me.

Their pact swam through his mind. He shoved it down. For right then, he didn't want to contemplate they might be doing something wrong. Leaving his sister when she'd been the one who'd brought them together in the first place.

Warily, Nikki looked back at him like she'd just thought all the same thoughts. "Okay. You and me."

Then Ollie . . . he kissed her again.

And he knew he didn't ever want to stop.

nineteen

Nikki

I snuggled deeper into the massive arms locked around me, and contentment left me on a sigh as I relished in the steady thrum of his heart at my back.

I couldn't believe I was lying there with Ollie wrapped around me like a blanket.

A big, gorgeous, burly blanket.

Heaven.

That's what it was. Even when so much felt unstable and wrong, this felt . . . right.

In the dark recesses of the night, I let my eyes drift back closed, only for them to fly open again when I heard what must have pulled me from sleep in the first place.

Ringing.

Ringing from down the hall.

Shit.

I'd left my phone in my purse where I'd dumped it when I'd come through the door.

Trying not to disturb Ollie, I carefully peeled his arm from me and slid out from his hold, keeping my footsteps quieted as I tiptoed across the floor and out the door.

Once I clicked the door shut behind me, I quickened my pace, rushing for my phone that was ringing again. Both praying and terrified that it would be my sister.

Dropping to my knees, I fumbled through my purse, hands shaking when I grabbed it and spun it around to find the number on the screen.

Not Sammie.

Brenna.

"Shit, shit, shit," I muttered, quick to accept the call and press it to my ear. "Brenna, what's happening?"

My attention darted to the kitchen so I could look at the time on the microwave.

Three twenty-seven a.m.

Not good.

Panicked cries echoed from the other end of the line, and she rambled something I couldn't make out.

"Brenna, calm down. Tell me what's happening."

Staggered breaths ripped from her. She tried to suck them down. Keep them contained. "Caleb . . . he keeps texting me. Telling me he's going to take Kyle from me if I don't go back to his place."

That little asshole.

"I think he might be outside," she all but whispered, as if he could hear her.

I pushed down the anger that surged and gave it my all to remain professional, searching inside myself for the right advice. "You need to hang up and call 9-1-1. Right now. I'll be over as fast as I can. Don't go outside."

There I was. Crossing more lines that weren't supposed to be crossed. But what was I supposed to do?

"Okay," she agreed, and the line went dead.

I started to push back to my feet when I felt the surge of energy blast me from behind.

Potent.

Intense.

That power alone was enough to shift me around to face him.

A magnet.

"Ollie."

"Who was that?" he grated.

I'd realized earlier I wanted this man to hold all of me. Have all of me. My body and my secrets and my heart.

Even if it was foolish. Filled with risk and danger and peril.

But I refused to be the girl who was too scared to live her life.

I needed him.

Wanted him.

And I was taking this chance.

"That was Brenna. The girl you saw me with at the ice-cream shop the other day. Her ex-boyfriend keeps texting her and threatening to take their little boy if she doesn't cave to him."

Ollie's hands clenched. "Piece of shit."

Ollie had it spot on.

For a moment, I wavered before I lowered my voice. "I think he might be the one who broke into my apartment. I was with her the first time she called the cops on him. He was angry. Called me a bitch. There were two notes left on the windshield of my car over the last week that basically said the same thing."

Rage blistered across his handsome face. "What? Someone's been following you? Fuck, Nikki. Why didn't you tell me?"

"I didn't have proof, and I didn't know what you would do."

His jaw clenched, and those sapphire eyes flashed. "I think you knew exactly what I would do."

It was true.

It was exactly why I was afraid to tell him.

I nodded, then started toward him so I could move down the hall. "You're right. I was afraid of what you might do and what that might mean. We can talk about that later. But right now, Brenna needs me, and I need to get over there."

I let my fingertips brush across his bare abdomen as I passed.

He shuddered.

Fire rippled and danced.

I'd almost made it to the guest bedroom when his voice boomed in the enclosed hall, and I froze in the doorway. "I'm coming with you."

Of course, he was. I wasn't even going to argue it. I glanced at him from over my shoulder and gave him a nod before I rushed inside and pulled on some jeans and a tee and slipped my feet into some shoes.

Five minutes later, we were flying down the road in Ollie's Mustang, taking the corners fast.

Intensity bound the air. Worry and fear and fury.

I felt it radiating from Ollie's flesh. Dripping from his pores.

His protection of me. Maybe the protection of a girl he didn't even know.

"Take a right here," I told him.

The tires squealed as he took a sharp turn.

Two seconds later, Brenna's mother's house came into view.

My stomach dropped to the floorboards.

Caleb was in the driveway, shouting at Brenna, who was cowering against the back of her car.

Dread spiraled through my senses. "Oh my God, I told her to stay inside."

Quick to release the seatbelt, I sat forward, hand already on the doorlatch as Ollie screeched to a stop.

"What the fuck?" Ollie growled. "It's that little fucker who sold me the car." His arm flew out in front of my chest, his body ridged in hard lines, muscles bristling as he took in the scene. "Don't move out of that seat, Nikki."

His door flew open, voice low. "I mean it."

I didn't pause.

Didn't listen.

I jumped out of the car.

Caleb whirled around when he felt me approaching him. "You bitch. You're responsible for all of this. Telling her not to be with me."

No, Caleb. You're responsible. You twat.

I didn't say it.

Not wanting to incite him more.

It didn't matter because he started for me as if this time he was going to take his anger out on me.

His warnings never so glaring than right then.

A tremble of fear rocked through me as I prepared for him to hit me.

A blur of movements had me taking a shocked step back.

Before I could process it, Ollie had an arm hooked around Caleb's neck from behind, his hold cinched tight.

No fear.

No reservation.

Brenna shrieked, and Ollie wrangled Caleb, who clawed at his arm, flailed and kicked and shouted as if he might wrestle out of his hold.

I doubted it took a whole lot of exertion on Ollie's part to keep Caleb restrained. Ollie had the scrawny kid in a lock that there was no chance he could break free of.

Once he knew he had him contained, Ollie sent me an angry glare. "Told you to stay in the car."

"Since when do you get to tell me what to do?" I shot at him.

He scoffed and pretty much rolled his eyes while he kept a tight hold on Caleb who continued to flail and kick. "And you say I'm impossible," he said.

"You, asshole. Let me go, you piece of shit. You're gonna regret it," Caleb ranted.

Ollie tightened his hold. "Pretty sure it's not gonna be me who's feelin' the regret, fucker. You really think I was gonna let you play us all? Is that what you thought? You thought wrong."

Confusion wound through my mind, Ollie's words making absolutely no sense. But my only concern right then was Brenna. Brenna who started sobbing when I pulled her into my arms.

She clutched me and buried her face in my shirt. "Nikki . . . you're here."

"I've got you. I'm right here."

Sirens rode on the night, a quiet toll that grew closer and closer with every second that passed. "The police are on their way. You're safe. You're safe."

Her fingers curled in my shirt. "I'm so sorry. I'm so sorry. But he was trying to get inside to take Kyle. I couldn't let him take him. I won't let him take him."

"Shh . . . I know. I know. It's okay."

Kyle's cries lifted on the dense air, fearful and distraught, and I peeked over to where Brenna's mother was holding him, her wary attention darting between all of us.

"That's my son," Caleb shouted. "My girlfriend. You can't keep them from me. They're my family."

He thrashed against Ollie's restraint, and Ollie was hauling him farther back, out into the street.

Away.

But I could hear him. The low warning he uttered at Caleb's ear. "Shut the fuck up, asshole. You don't get to claim someone as your family when you threaten them. When you hurt them. That's not what family is. You think you can mess with her? Take advantage of her? I'll end you if you even look at her again. You hear me, asshole?"

Two cruisers rounded the corner, lights reflecting off the darkened sky. I knew neighbors were peering out, could feel the eyes of morbid curiosity, but the only thing I cared about was Brenna.

That she was safe.

Four officers slipped out of their cruisers, their guns drawn. Thank God, one was Seth.

"Don't move," one of them shouted.

"Stand down," Seth ordered, pushing a hand out at the officers as he moved toward Ollie and Caleb, cuffs out.

"On the ground," he told Caleb.

Ollie released him, and Caleb dove to the pavement.

"Motherfucker," he gritted, face in the ground.

"Motherfucker is right," Ollie spat, backing away and letting Seth read Caleb his rights as he cuffed him and patted him down.

Seth hauled him to his feet, looking between Ollie and me. "This him?" he asked me.

I nodded. "That's him."

Ollie roughed an agitated hand through his hair that flashed with the colors of the lights that spun through the night, his face lit up.

So bold and striking I lost more of my breath.

My beast.

"Asshole came into Roke's this afternoon with an old car that used to belong to Nikki's grandparents. Nikki told me about the notes. He has to have been stalking her. Finding out who her family was and trying to get close."

Caleb flailed and tried to jerk free from Seth, the guy so clearly high he looked deranged. "What the fuck are you talking about? That's bullshit, man. I haven't been stalking that stupid bitch. I don't want anything to do with her. That car was on the straight."

"Save it. You can make your statement at the station." Seth led him to the back of one of the cruisers and placed him in the backseat.

Brenna breathed out another cry, but this one was made of relief.

I looked over at Ollie and mouthed, *Thank you.*

He just stared back as if he were promising he wouldn't be anywhere else.

Inside, Seth took both Brenna and her mother's statements. First and foremost, Caleb had violated his restraining order. More charges might be coming. Ones related to me and my apartment.

They were still waiting for prints to come back.

Seth was going to put a rush on them, hoping we got something to substantiate our suspicions.

Seth left promising he'd be calling soon.

"Thank you so much," Brenna told him as she showed him to the door.

"Take care of yourself," he told her. "Unfortunately, he'll probably make bail in the morning since he didn't cause any bodily harm. It'd be good for you to have someone with you at all times."

Slipping out, he let his eyes move to Ollie and me in some kind of warning before he disappeared down the walk.

From behind, we watched as Brenna tremored with a fresh round of fear.

Ollie stood.

Gruff and rugged but his voice was soft. "Think it'd be good for you to come to my place tonight until we get this sorted out?"

Brenna turned around, her fingertips pressed to her mouth. "You'd do that for me?"

Ollie rocked in discomfort. I saw it for what it was. The way he wanted to protect the world from horrible people. From the type of man we were sure had stolen Sydney from us.

He dropped his gaze when he finally said, "Don't have a lot to offer people, Brenna . . . but if I can offer this? Take care of you and your son for a little bit?" He looked up. "There's nothing I'd want more."

"I can't tell you how much I appreciate what you did tonight." Brenna spread her hand over the comforter in the guest bedroom, clearly needing something to busy herself.

"You keep telling me that," I told her with a soft smile where I sat next to her with my knees hugged to my chest.

"But I really mean it." Carefully, she peeked up at me. "You know when he started texting me, the first person I thought to call was you. You have a way of making me feel safe."

"I want you to both feel it and live it, Brenna. You don't have to live in fear. We'll make sure of that."

Silence moved through the space, and I could feel her reservations, a new kind of heaviness moving through her heart. "You really think he did that to your apartment?”

I studied her face. “You don’t?” I asked carefully.

She lifted a shoulder. “The drugs changed him. He was so sweet to me when we first started dating.”

Her voice had turned wistful. Filled with longing of that time. She shook her head. “He’s just fine when he’s not using, but when he does? He becomes rash and impulsive, and a lot of times it translates to aggression.”

She blinked at me. “It’s hard for me to imagine him thinking to go to your place to scare you that way. Leaving those notes.”

I set my hand on her knee. “People do crazy things when they’re desperate, Brenna. It’s part of the problem. The spiral. They dig themselves deeper and deeper until they can’t see a way out, and then they’re doing everything they can to fight it—change it—all the while they’re making the worst choices all over again.”

“I just wish he’d go back to bein’ the person he was when he asked me to the dance in ninth grade.” Her bottom lip trembled. “I know you think it’s stupid. That we’re young. But there was a time when he really loved me and I loved him. We messed up. Did things too young. It got away from us. But we did love each other.”

I took her hand and squeezed it. “I don’t think it’s stupid. Not at all. Don’t ever let someone tell you young love isn’t real. But sometimes things change. Things we can’t control. All we can control is the here and now—and right now—you and that little boy deserve so much more than what Caleb has been giving you.”

“I know that.”

“Good.” I blew out the strain that weighed heavily and stood. “What do you say I go get your little cutie so you two can get some rest?”

“Tell me that man of yours didn’t feed him sugar,” she said, voice turning wry.

“Man of mine?” I challenged, lifting my brow with a smirk. “I already told you he was a friend.”

“Oh, come on, Miss Nikki. You pretty much have drool dripping from the corner of your mouth every time you look his way.”

“Is that so?”

“Uh-huh. And every time he looks at you, I’m pretty sure he’s picturing ripping off your clothes with his teeth.” She grinned and wiggled her brows. “I have to say, with a man who looks like that? I wouldn’t mind all that much having him fantasizing about me, either.”

My mouth dropped open. “Hey, don’t go making any moves on my man.”

She laughed. “See, told you so.”

A giggle slipped out. It should have been impossible with everything that’d happened tonight.

But I thought maybe . . . maybe some *good* things were finally coming together.

"I'll be right back," I told her before I eased out the door and down the hall.

Ollie had insisted he would get Kyle a snack while I helped Brenna get settled in the guest room. I'd left them with Kyle sitting on one of the high-backed stools, babbling something Ollie was clearly pretending he understood.

Now I slowed, inching forward when I noticed all the lights had been doused, the open living space only illuminated by the lights that poured in from the windows.

I peeked my head out at the end of the hall.

My chest squeezed and my heart expanded.

Oh God.

This man.

He was absolutely undoing me.

He was sitting on the couch, Kyle fast asleep in his arms. The little boy's thumb was in his mouth and his cheek was pressed to Ollie's chest as Ollie softly patted his back, tattooed arms wrapped so protectively around Kyle's tiny body.

Tears pricked at the back of my eyes, and that old, old love burst free.

No longer held.

No longer bottled.

"Hey," I whispered as I inched out, keeping quiet so as not to startle Kyle.

Ollie's eyes popped open.

And he smiled.

He smiled the softest smile and it moved right through the center of me.

"Hey," he said. "He started to get fussy, so I walked him a bit before he fell asleep."

I nodded at him, unable to speak around the lump that formed in my throat. I moved that way and carefully pulled Kyle from his arms.

Ollie stood behind me, and I walked down the hall, my knock quiet before I pushed open the door and brought Kyle to Brenna who was fixing a spot for him to sleep.

I passed him to her. She gazed down at him, adoration on her face.

And I felt it all around me.

Adoration.

Love.

"Sleep well," I told her.

She just nodded, and I moved back out, Ollie waiting for me right on the other side of the door.

He took my hand, and I followed him back to his room.

He flipped on the bedside lamp, and I went directly into his bathroom. I washed my face, peeled off my jeans, and moved back out to where he lay on the bed.

Wearing only his underwear.

His big body sculpted of muscle. Covered in ink.

But those eyes. They pierced me from across the room.

I started for him, only to falter a step when my attention caught on what was on the other side of his room.

A wall covered in pictures.

Not just any pictures.

It was pictures and newspaper articles and prints tacked everywhere.

Layer upon layer.

Sucking in a ragged breath, my eyes narrowed as I inched that way.

Horrified.

And somehow in awe.

Sydney's smiling face beamed from all of the pictures, her expression so free and full of belief.

The way she'd always lived. What she'd always been so patient to instill in me when I'd always been the timid one itching to shed my sticky skin.

There were a ton of pictures of the three of us. Playing. Laughing. Arms hooked over each other's shoulders.

Inseparable.

But it was the newspaper articles that gutted me.

So many of them were about her from the time when she'd gone missing.

More of other girls.

Cold cases.

Kidnappings.

Rapes.

Murders.

Strings were attached between some of them and notes jotted across others.

Clues.

Questions.

A chill slicked down my spine and spread across my skin.

Warily, I looked back at him. He'd sat up on the edge of the bed, his legs flung over the side, raking a nervous hand through his hair.

"You've been looking for her this whole time?"

He looked up at me, his voice quieted so Brenna wouldn't hear. "What else could I possibly do? Forget? Give up like the detectives? Looking for her is the only thing I've ever had, Nikki. I can't give up the hope that maybe, just maybe, one day I might find her."

My stomach twisted.

A coil of misery and desire and affection.

I looked back to the things that he had tacked to the wall. My fingertips reached out to flutter over the red woven bracelet with the charm inscribed with '*fly*'.

It exactly matched the one I still wore around my ankle.

Ollie's piece.

The third one would be forever missing.

They say heartbreak isn't physical.

I believed it was a lie.

Because I could feel it. Could feel his. Just as I could feel the same crack running right down the center of me. Everything adding up and becoming this weight I didn't know how to bear.

It was a rending of my chest.

A splintering of my soul.

Cautiously, I moved toward him.

The space between us coming alive.

Shimmering.

Streaks of color.

Flashes of light.

Chemistry.

Ours had been ugly for so long. Like a shadow hanging over us.

Now, I waded through it like the gift it always should have been. I got down on my knees in front of him and pressed my hand to the side of his face.

"Ollie," I whispered.

Like praise.

Did he know? Could he possibly understand what I felt for him? What I always had? Part of me hated him for not seeing it. Or maybe it was just that I knew he saw it, felt it, and he'd rejected it anyway.

Most of me understood it fully. The guilt he bore. His own bitter cross. The one marked over his heart that would forever bleed for his sister.

In the dim light, those sapphire eyes captured mine.

Emotion brimming over.

So many questions. All the reservations and walls that were still there.

The hurt laid out between us, and the love that had been the base of it all.

He weaved his fingers through my hair. "Nikki."

My name was a breath.

I smoothed my hands up his strong thighs.

A ripple of need trembled through him. "Nikki."

This time it was a warning.

I edged up and pressed a bunch of kisses across his wide, wide chest.

"What are you doing?" It was a low grumble.

"Taking care of you the way you took care of me."

His fingers sank into my hair, taking fistfuls as he tugged me back. "Don't think that's a good idea."

"And why's that?" I whispered, letting my kisses glide down his abdomen.

Cut and carved.

Perfection.

His muscles twitched beneath my touch, and I felt him grow hard in his briefs.

Earlier on the couch, I'd wanted him to take me. Desperate to feel him inside me again. That greedy place within lighting up with his touch.

Wanting more.

Wanting it all.

But this?

This was for him.

"Because I don't get this. I don't get you," he said, holding on tighter as if he wanted to push me away but couldn't let me go.

I edged up on my knees and pressed my mouth under his jaw. His short beard tickled my face, and there was nothing I could do but inhale, fill myself with this man.

His pulse boomed, a thunder against my lips. I kissed down his throat and across his pecs, the massive muscles straining as he arched.

Yearning to get closer, to receive it, while his broken spirit believed the only thing he deserved was to suffer this alone.

"You already have me, Ollie. You always did. Did you feel me all that time?" I murmured across his hot flesh, my tongue licking out to taste. "I was right there. All along."

He grunted, and his hands fisted tighter in my hair, words grating as they hit the air. "I fucked it all up. I'm fucked up, Nikki. You deserve much more than what I've got to offer you."

"No, Ollie. You're wrong. You don't see yourself clearly. You don't realize how amazing you are. You don't realize the guy I see when I look at you. The guy I saw tonight."

The man who would have given it all for any of us.

He was a masterpiece. Sculpted and carved and chiseled. Massive. Bigger than life.

I wanted him to see he belonged in my life. The way he always had.

Desire twisted my insides, and I caressed my mouth lower, over the fabric of his underwear where the head of his dick begged for me.

"Nikki." This time it was confusion. My name hanging like a precipice.

So close to letting go.

"It's me, Ollie. Me. Lose yourself in me. I want to take care of you." I peeked up at him and let a small smirk work to my face. "I think it's only fair since I let you take care of me, don't you?"

A dark chuckle resonated in his chest, filled with restraint and lust. He brushed his fingers down the side of my face. "Think the only thing unfair right now is the way you're looking at me."

My tongue darted out to wet my lips. "And how am I looking at you?"

"Like I mean something."

I kissed across the definition of his hip, burying my nose in his skin as I muttered the words, "You mean everything."

He groaned, and he reached down and took me by the sides of the head, lifting me to look at him.

Gently.

So gently it shouldn't have been possible for a hulking man like him.

Beast.

Old memories spun, and a wistful smile swam on my mouth when I took one of his hands and urged him to standing.

The power of his need shook the walls. I could feel it radiating and crashing.

I looked up at him, and he cupped my cheek. "Sweet girl," he murmured, tracing his thumb under my eye. "I don't want to hurt you."

He kept looping back to that. Didn't he know the only way he could hurt me was by letting me go?

"I know, Ollie, I know."

I dipped my fingers in the waistband of his tight black briefs and began to peel them down. My heart raced, and my skin caught fire.

Because his cock jumped free, bouncing in front of me. Every bit as intimidatingly beautiful as the man.

Every previous encounter with Ollie had been a fumble in the dark. Teens sneaking around and the disaster at my apartment last year.

This . . . this was Ollie and me. Both of us here. Present. No one to tell us we were doing anything wrong except for the guilt we both wore like a shroud.

I saw when he flipped. When he stopped trying to resist *this.* Or maybe he just couldn't any longer.

Blue eyes blazed down at me with a lusty, harsh sort of desire.

He gave a demanding tug at the back of my hair, voice muted, meant only for me. "You gonna let me have that mouth, Sunshine?"

My heart beat frantically. Madly. Every cell in my body was swept up in the intensity.

Stomach trembling, my tongue darted out and licked across his engorged head.

He jerked, gritting his teeth as he tightened his hold in my hair. "Little Tease. Been teasing me all these years. Coming in my bar acting like we didn't know each other. Talking to your friends like I might just be another conquest."

"It was the only thing I could do not to fall at your feet."

"Wanted to kill every guy I ever saw you with."

Hands running up his hips, I whispered, "You managed to chase them all away anyway."

He ran a thumb over my lip. "Couldn't stand the thought of another man with you."

I didn't think he understood the way I felt every time I saw him with another girl. As fleeting as they were, every time, it was the stab of a knife. Bleeding me dry.

I took him in my hand. The velvet flesh was smooth on my palm, such a contradiction to the heavy, hard length that begged for release underneath. "I never wanted anyone else."

A shudder rocked him as I stroked him once. "Fuck."

I wrapped my other hand around him. Both hands running his rigid length as I pumped him, lightly at first, gathering the glistening bead at his throbbing head before I tightened and began to stroke him.

"Nikki . . . you're gonna kill me. Shit . . ."

I peeked up at him as I wound him higher.

Magnificent.

His jaw clenched as he stared down at me, his chest wide, beard full on his immaculate face.

All man.

The man I held in my hands.

Stroking him greedily, my breaths became pants. Need welled in me like the swill of the rising river.

Higher and higher.

Threatening to overflow.

I squeezed my thighs together while his shook.

Splintering control.

"Feels so good," he grunted. "Those sweet hands, Nik . . . they've always been so sweet. You always hid it with that smart mouth . . . but I knew. I knew."

His words were grit. Lined with a tenderness I felt brushing across my flesh like a lover's caress.

I leaned in and pressed a gentle kiss to the tip of his cock. I tasted the salty manliness of him. The intensity of who he was.

My oldest friend.

My first love.

My only love.

His fists were a petition where they wound in my hair. "Please, Nikki. Sweet girl. Take me. Suck me. Need to feel you."

Desperation spun, riding that tether that kept us tied. Binding.

I pressed my tongue to his engorged, fattened tip before I sucked the crown into my mouth.

"Yes," he rumbled, jutting forward, urging me to take him. I laved at the purpled flesh, squeezing his fat base with my hands before I began to take him deeper.

A course groan pressed between his lips. "I have always loved that mouth."

My heart squeezed.

Love.

It was so strong.

So strong it made it hard to see.

Deeper and deeper, I took him, my hands working the base, the feel of him overwhelming.

Moans ripped from his mouth, low and guttural.

Needy in a way I'd never heard this man be. "Yes, baby. Fuck. You feel so good. So damned good."

His hips began to snap, and I was nothing but an offering on my knees in front of him.

Lost.

Lost in him where he was lost in me.

His hands moved to my cheeks, and I relished the feel of them as he started to rock and jut. Harder and deeper.

Slow and measured before he picked up a rigorous pace.

His grunts struck the air, and that energy crackled, licked at my skin, stirred the need into something potent.

Compulsive and seductive.

Inescapable.

"Can you take it?" A question and a warning spoken in a low growl. I answered by moving my hands to his ass and hanging on.

At his mercy.

"Yes," he groaned, fingers spread out wide, holding all of me he could.

Then he fucked my mouth.

Mercilessly.

Wildly.

Madly.

Every thrust raw.

Every rock needy.

Possessive.

Consuming me in a way I'd never before been consumed.

I opened to him and took him as far as I could, my lips stretched thin around his hard, imposing length, jaw burning and my spirit soaring.

"You . . . Nikki . . . You."

The words tumbled from him, jumbled and rushed and as clear as I'd ever heard him.

My eyes welled with tears as I swallowed around him, taking him to the back of my throat.

"Fuck . . . yes," he hissed, and his hips snapped savagely.

Frenzied.

Succumbing.

Just like me.

Energy flashed.

Colors painting the room.

A river of emotion.

A stream of lust.

His teeth ground to hold back a roar when he came, pouring into my mouth, his gorgeous body bowed as he shivered and jerked.

My beautiful, beautiful beast.

I swallowed, wanting to drown in him, reveling in the sheer bliss etched in his expression.

Streaks of pleasure tore through every tremoring muscle of his body.

The man a mountain.

A rock who'd just crumbled in my hands.

Slowly, he pulled back, still holding my face, and he tenderly ran the pad of his thumb across my bottom lip.

I was almost nervous, having no idea what direction we were going, terrified he would send me crashing into another brick wall until a smirk took hold of one side of his mouth.

"Guess you really are the orgasm fairy," he murmured, lifting me from under my arms and scooping me back into the safety of his hold.

I tried to hold back the shock of surprised laughter. "I told all of you I was. No one believes me. I know a good match when I see one."

Chemistry.

Ours pulsed through the air. Fierce and unrelenting.

He climbed onto his bed and pulled me onto his chest.

Oh God. And he thought I was going to ruin him?

He gentled his fingers through my hair. "Hmm . . . guess I shouldn't complain about getting on the receiving end of that, now, should I?"

My teeth raked over my bottom lip, warmth heating my cheeks, loving that this lost boy wanted to play. "Definitely not. There are some gifts that should never be shoved in a closet or returned."

I began to casually tick them off. "Heirloom jewelry. A child's handprint set in plaster. Orgasms. Orgasms should never, ever be considered anything less than the gift they are," I said, the quiet tease playing from my tongue.

A thrill of shock vibrated through me. It felt like a dream that I was with him like this. Closer than we'd been in so many years.

My fingertips trailed over his chest. "Well, unless you give one to yourself," I ribbed. "No orgasm fairy required. My services are rendered totally useless."

That was like buying yourself a fake engagement ring.

He grabbed my hand and brought it to his lips. "Don't doubt that you caused a few of those, too, Nikki. All these years, thinking about you . . .

wishing it was you."

Chills.

They flashed across my skin. My voice quieted, and I scratched at the beard on the side of his face, "I wanted it to be you, too."

He pushed his fingers into my hair, somberness stealing into his expression as he stared up at me. "What if I hurt you?"

My tongue swept across my bottom lip. In hesitation or need, I wasn't sure. "You keep sayin' that, Ollie, and I'm just gonna keep tellin' you not to. Treating someone the way they deserve to be treated is as simple as making the choice to."

His head minimally shook on his pillow, and he tightened his hold on me.

I didn't want him to ever let go.

"Sometimes life doesn't give us the choice. Sometimes it takes from us. We have no control over that. No say no matter what we give up to change it."

My voice softened, close to a plea. "And sometimes it's as simple as how you handle what life gives you. How you treat the people around you. How you treat *yourself*."

"You deserve better than me, sweet girl. Don't you see that yet?"

Scooting up, I pressed both my hands to either side of his head and stared down at him, hoping he could see. Hoping he could feel what I'd always felt for him.

"You're right, Ollie. I deserve to be loved. To be held and cherished. To have the family I've always wanted. I deserve everything this life has to offer. To make the most of each day. And you . . ."

The words became a wisp from my lips. "You just have to see that you deserve all that, too. That you deserve to be loved and held and cherished. To live life for all it's worth. Every single day. Whether that's with me or not."

Silence swam between us. As heavy as when we'd lay by the lake at night and stare at the sky. When we'd felt so small and still so incredibly brave. Stars strewn out across the black canvas, promising there was more out there than a vast expanse of nothingness.

He trailed his fingers down my cheek. "I want to be that guy, Nikki. Just not sure who you see is real. Think he went missing the day his sister did."

Old grief whipped through my spirit. "I know, Ollie," I said, affection thick. "That guy got lost. But I know he's real. That he's right here."

I reached down and set my palm flat against his hammering heart. "You just have to find him."

He pressed my hand tighter. "We need to stop doing this until I do. Until I know I won't hurt you again. Because I do *cherish* you, Nikki. Don't ever doubt that. I cherish you, but I'm still not sure I deserve to keep you."

His words slashed and cut and healed.

A searing hurt and the sweetest solace.

I gently pressed my lips to his.

Tenderly.

With all I had to give. "Let me help you discover him."

He shocked me with his slight nod, our lips gently brushing. "I need you to be patient with me because I refuse to be the guy who hurts you again."

Then he pulled back, eyes going hard as he gripped me by both sides of the face. "Need you to stop keeping secrets from me. I have to figure out how to be the guy you really deserve, but more than that, I need to know you're safe. Keep you safe. And I can't do that if you don't let me in."

"I told you where I was going tonight for a reason, Ollie. Because I trust you. Because I want you in my life."

He grimaced but didn't reject it before he continued, "How did that punk get your grandpa's old car?"

A sad, slow sickness rolled through me. My grandma was sick, and I wasn't sure how to deal with that.

My mama was worn out.

And my sister . . .

I tucked the thoughts down and focused on what Ollie was saying. "I don't know."

Contemplation rode heavily on the exhale from his nose. "He said your uncle was selling off some stuff . . . they needed money quick."

Unease slithered through my consciousness.

Ollie's voice hardened. "Tried to get in touch with you to make sure it was legit. Needed to know this kid wasn't trying to pull some shit over on us. Bought it either way. Too many memories in that heap for it to go anywhere else."

Heat bloomed at the center of me, a welling of memories. "I'm glad you did."

He caressed his thumb beneath the hollow of my eye. "Yeah . . . me, too."

My head shook. "I'm not sure exactly what's goin' on over at my grandma's. What I know is things . . . aren't good. They could very well be selling stuff off, although I'm not sure how Caleb got involved."

Sorrow took over that confession.

"I'm so sorry. I had no idea."

"I know . . . it's really hard." I paused for a beat before I continued, "I'll go over there this week and find out the details of what they're planning. All's I know is after my grandpa passed, Grandma went through what was left of their savings pretty fast. Wouldn't surprise me if they're needing to get rid of a few of her things to pay for some of the expenses. Mama said it's been a struggle. But I'll find out. You don't need to worry about that. I doubt it's a big deal."

"Everything's a big deal when it comes to you, Nikki. I'm sorry if I ever made it seem like it wasn't. Like I didn't care."

I forced a grin onto my mouth. "Oh, I knew you cared. No mistaking it when a big, overbearing brute constantly puts his nose in your business."

He grunted like he was exactly that.

A beast.

"That's because you are my business."

I traced my fingertips along the swishes of color written across his chest. "Thank you so much for being there tonight. For being there for Brenna and Kyle. Being there for me."

"I promised you that I'd always take care of you. Right?"

I nodded. "Yeah."

I was okay with that.

He tugged me all the way on top of him.

On all things holy, he was not helping things. A tiny moan escaped my throat at the feel of his bare body beneath mine. Strength bristling as our hearts mended.

Going back to not being able to touch him was just plain cruel.

Pretending again.

But this man was worth the wait.

He *deserved* patience.

Understanding.

He *deserved* me.

And God, every part of me knew I deserved him.

twenty

Ollie

I woke with a start.

Un-fucking-prepared to find the girl nestled in my arms.

Unprepared for the way my heart took off racing, drumming with satisfaction.

Unprepared for that voice inside me that shouted that this was the way it was supposed to be.

Hell, only a moron would think waking up next to Nikki Walters was anything less than paradise.

Didn't mean I wasn't assaulted with a ton of images flying through my brain.

Sydney.

Sydney.

Sydney.

The weight of my debt.

The truth of what we'd done.

I blew it out on a harsh breath and strained to listen to the voices that filtered through the walls.

Brenna was quietly talking to her son, who was blabbering back.

So damned cute.

My insides twisted with a swell of protection.

I jerked with the shrill sound of my phone ringing from my nightstand. Reaching behind me, I swatted for it, trying to silence it before it woke up Nikki, considering we'd gotten all of three hours' sleep.

The second I saw who it was, I peeled myself away from Nikki's body and sat up on the edge of the bed. "Seth."

"Hey, man, I've got good news."

Relief gusted from me. "Yeah?"

"Caleb was in front of the judge this morning for his intake hearing. He willingly accepted the offer to go to inhouse rehab for ninety days, plus anger management and parenting classes. In exchange, the restraining order violation charges will be dropped. We still don't have proof of the break-in, so none of that was taken into consideration."

My guts curled.

That little fucker was getting off.

Still couldn't stomach the idea that he'd been in Nikki's apartment. Trashing it. Following her and putting notes on her car.

That he might hurt Brenna and Kyle again.

"Is that supposed to be good news?" It was close to a growl.

Seth chuckled like he was fully expecting what I was going to say. "A whole ton better than him hitting the streets this morning, don't you think?"

I scrubbed a palm over my face, glancing back at Nikki, who'd rolled over in my bed, looking like the fucking best thing when her eyes fluttered open.

She smiled at me.

Sunshine.

"Yeah, man. You're right. Just hope it makes a difference."

twenty-one

Nikki

I pulled up in front of the small house. Even though I felt a huge amount of relief that Brenna and Kyle were safe, anxiety still held me captive.

My hands clammy.

Heart racing.

Stomach twisting with the kind of nausea I felt all the way into my soul.

Twilight held fast to the sky, a purpled gray that hugged the earth. The hurricane lamp hanging on the wall at the side of the front door welcomed the approaching night with a soft glow.

A single, mammoth tree stood proud in the yard. Broad branches stretched out as if they were arms of protection. Leaves green and dense and full.

Sucking in a deep breath, I cut the engine and stepped out onto the walkway, trying to keep my feet steady underneath me. Still, I wobbled as I headed up the sidewalk and climbed the steps leading to the porch.

Through the walls of the small house, I could hear the distorted sound of Penelope crying, the echo of movement around the house.

Quietly, I rapped at the door. Praying the gentle sound would let my sister know I wasn't there to hurt her, but there was no chance I could respect her petition for me to turn a blind eye.

To pretend as if I hadn't seen her at that meeting.

For the moment, it might have made it easier on her.

But in the end, I knew it'd be nothing less than a disservice.

Shuffling resonated from the other side of the door, the little cries getting louder the closer the footsteps came. A sheer drape covering the long, vertical window that ran the side of her door rustled. I could feel the way she froze.

Hesitated.

Debated.

The longest second passed. I knew that was all it was. But in it, all my sister's reservations and fears pummeled me.

Stone after stone.

I was gasping by the time metal slid, the lock gave, and my sister peeked out the crack in the door.

She didn't ask what I was doing there. She already knew.

"Sammie," I whispered.

A tear leaked from her eye, and I could see that she was bouncing Penelope, holding her tight while the little thing fussed.

"I asked you not to come here like this. I can't do this with you."

A lump grew thick at the base of my throat. I tried to swallow around it, but still, the words stuck. "How could I ignore it? Ignore you?"

Old wounds lashed across her face. She seemed almost frantic as she dipped down and pressed a bunch of kisses to Penelope's forehead, the tiny girl's fussing increasing to an-all out squall, obviously hungry, little fists reaching for her mama.

Sammie bounced her a little more. "I'm not ready yet, Nikki. I'm not ready. Not yet."

"But you went to that meeting looking for help. The last thing I want is to get in the way of that."

A tremble ran through her, and my chest ached. God, I wanted to reach out and take it away. Hunt someone down. The hardest part was not knowing who or what I would be looking for.

I dug out the business card I'd tucked into the back pocket of my jeans and held it out for her. "Take this. Her name is Kathy. She's been my mentor. She's amazing. You can trust her, and I promise you that she won't tell me a thing. Just . . . call her."

With a shaky hand, Sammie reached out and took it, and then she wrapped her arm right back around her baby, card still in her hand.

Relief surged.

I took a step back. "I'm sorry . . . for whatever is going on. For whatever happened. But I want you to know whatever it is? I'm here for you whenever you're ready to talk about it. You don't ever have to be ashamed. And that is not the counselor talking . . . that is your sister, who will always, always be here for you. No matter what."

Tears soaked her face. "Thank you."

I nodded quickly and took a step back, letting her know I was giving her space, but that she wasn't alone. "I'm . . . I'm just gonna go check on Mama and Grandma. It's been too long since I stopped by there."

Sammie blanched, but nodded.

I started for the steps before I paused to look at her over my shoulder.

"Call her, Sammie. Please."

"Soon," she murmured, hugging her daughter close, eyes meeting mine intensely before she stepped back and snapped the door shut.

Leaving me standing there wanting to break through that wall of wood to find her. Fight for her. Hold her up.

All I could do was pray the little nudge I'd given her would be enough.

Headlights cast a dingy illumination on the secluded area as I wound down the bumpy dirt road. It was only a half-mile outside of town, but it felt like a million miles and another world away.

Trees lined the path on both sides and reached for the heavens where they had been planted along the barbed-wire fences that marked the property boundaries. It isolated the entire ten-acres from the country road that ran along the river and closed it off from the neighbors that sat on either side of the land that had been in my family for as long as anyone could remember.

Oh, my grandma could tell some stories about that. I never knew what was true or exaggerated or plain made up. What I did know was I'd spent what felt like half my childhood listening to her go on about them while my little sister and I baked and sewed and ran the property.

So many of our summers had been spent here.

Sydney and Ollie always in the midst.

How many times had we raced our bikes down this lane, shouting that the last one there was a rotten egg?

Apparently, I stunk, considering I always came up short.

Funny how I'd always had a smile on my face while doing it.

Nostalgia rippled around me like the small waves that lapped at the shore of the lake as I made it to the clearing and pulled up in front of the old house.

The historic structure oozed a vintage charm, even though it was rundown and needed a whole ton of TLC.

The porch planks were warped and worn and the paint peeling, not to mention all the junk that sat around the property—broken-down cars and machines and sheds filled with who knew what.

No wonder they were wanting to unload some of this crap.

Turning off the ignition, the headlights cut and the interior light glowed as I snapped open my car door. I climbed out and was smacked in the face with the overwhelming scent of honeysuckle and the river and decaying earth.

The dirt was rich and heavy, as heavy as the air and the overhead canopy of the darkened sky that was smattered with twinkling stars.

In the distance, a dog barked and bugs trilled in the trees.

Inhaling deeply, I held the warm familiarity of it all in my lungs and ambled up the creaking steps and onto the porch.

I didn't knock at the door, I just turned the knob and poked my head inside. "Hello, anyone home?"

My mother appeared at the top of the stairs. "Nikki. What on earth are you doin' here?"

"Thought I'd stop by and check in."

"Well, it's about time. Think it's been an age since the last time I saw you. I don't even recognize you."

Light laughter filtered free.

This was exactly the reason I'd come here.

For the warmth.

After everything that had been happening, I just needed to see my mama and grandma. The two women who had been there for me through thick and thin.

There had been so much upheaval in my life.

I started for the wide set of stairs. I slid my hand along the railing as I climbed. "Now, don't go exaggerating. It's been a whole two weeks since you've seen me. Not all that much has changed."

That was a lie.

It felt like everything had changed. Ollie and my sister and my world. I was struggling to make sense of it.

She sent a playful smile my way. "Two weeks is like an eternity when it comes to your kids."

"So, you're saying you missed me?" I teased as I mounted the last step. "Guess people really just can't get enough of me. I am kind of amazing, aren't I? My being around just makes everything better."

I leaned in and dropped a kiss to her cheek.

She reached out and cupped mine. "Totally amazing." Then she hitched up a grin. "You are my daughter, after all."

I laughed. "My, my. Someone is full of herself."

She swatted at me. "Just tellin' it like it is, just like you. No reason to be coy when everyone knows it anyway."

My heart squeezed. Love overflowing.

The truth was, my mama was *amazing*.

Through and through.

And she was a load of fun, too, always laughing and joking and teasing.

Taking life by the reins and leading it where she wanted it to go.

But Ollie was right about some things.

Sometimes, life didn't give us the choice, and tonight, there was no missing the strain that lined my mother's face.

"How's Grandma?" I whispered.

Mama smiled. "Ornery as ever. Why don't you go see for yourself?"

Buoyed, I grinned and moved down the narrow passageway for the master bedroom at the end of the hall. The door was open, and the television blared as it blipped and threw colors across the room.

Affection pulled tight across my chest, thick with nostalgia. Pausing in the doorway, I tapped at the wood. "Hey, Grandma," I called.

She snapped her head my direction. She was sitting propped against a bunch of pillows in her bed. Frailer than she'd once been, but all that vigor still glinted in her eyes. She grabbed the remote and lowered the television volume. "Well, there's my knockout of a granddaughter."

I made a scoffing sound. "Which granddaughter is that you're talkin' about?"

A wide grin pulled across her wrinkled face. "What? You think I'm senile and blind like the rest of this bunch does? Don't go writing this old lady off just yet."

I crossed the room and sat on the edge of the bed. I kissed her forehead. "Never."

She wrapped her hand around mine. "As if I wouldn't recognize you. Tell me you've been tearing up the town and bringing all those boys to their knees."

A soft giggle slipped out. "Oh, you know that I am. None of them know what hit them."

Her eyes narrowed. "And how's *the* boy?"

A quiver rolled down my spine, belly tipping and my pulse giving an extra kick. "I have no idea what boy you're talking about," I said, just as innocently as I could.

Probably about as innocently as the day Ollie'd brought over a bunch of firecrackers and we'd accidentally set the back lot on fire.

"I think you know exactly what boy I'm talkin' about. *Your* boy, trouble maker that he is." She reached up and cupped my cheek. "Tell me he hasn't been causing trouble in your world."

Well, hell.

Was it written all over me?

Guessed it must have been because heat went rushing across my flesh and rising to meet with the hand she held on my face.

"Who, Ollie? No," I defended a little too quickly.

Amusement danced across her face. "Think he's always been the one causing all your troubles, hasn't he?"

I attempted to suck down the emotion that followed the blush and painted a big smile on my face. "No, Grandma. He's just a friend. That's all he's ever been."

She patted my cheek. "It's always the one who causes the biggest commotion inside us who leaves the biggest mark. Isn't that right, Megs?" She turned to look at my mom, who was watching us just inside the room.

She started our way. "Sure is. And that boy has been nothing but a commotion since the day Nikki met him."

I waved them off. "You two are ridiculous. He wasn't anything of the sort."

"Ha," Mama said, starting to clear up Grandma's dinner things that were on a tray. "You were the shyest thing in the world and then those Preston's came in and shook you up."

I frowned, and she continued, "Now don't go looking at me like I said that was a bad thing. Those two had you soaring. Not a lot of us get to say we had friendships like that."

"That they did," Grandma agreed before she lowered her voice conspiratorially, "Bet that boy sends you soaring now."

She winked.

I swatted at her. "Grandma."

Mischief sparkled in her eyes. "What?" she defended as if I was crazy. "Have you seen him lately? Whoo-ee. Now that's one fine-looking boy."

On all things holy.

How did I stumble down this rabbit hole?

"Grandma," I scolded again. "That's my friend you're talking about like he's a piece of meat."

As if I hadn't ogled him like he was every time I watched him slinging drinks behind his bar.

So sexy.

Powerful.

Beautiful.

Hell, I'd straight told Lillith I wanted to eat him up at least ten-thousand times.

But this was my grandma we were talking about.

"Besides, he's not a boy."

Memories from last night flashed behind my eyes. Hitting me hard and fast and hot. Heat gathered in my belly, pulsing low.

I inhaled a sharp breath.

He was all man.

Grandma grinned like she'd just won the lottery. "That's what I thought. And the fact he's no longer a boy just means it's time to make him your man."

"I don't need a man to make me happy, Grandma."

I just . . . wanted this one.

To fall into his safety and care because I knew I'd always belonged there.

She waved me off as if I was silly. "I know, I know, you modern women livin' it up by yourselves. Bet that gets lonely after a bit," she said, eyeing me from the corner of her eye, knowing she was hitting it just right.

Dishes clinked as my mama picked up the tray and set it on the desk by the window. "Now, now, Mama, think our Nikki here knows what she needs. Don't give her too hard of a time."

A huff left Grandma's mouth. "Is it too much to ask for another great grandbaby before this old girl rides off into the sunset? That sweet Penelope could use a cousin to run around and get in trouble with. Nothing would make me happier than seeing a new generation taking over before this one blinks out."

I brushed my fingers through her hair. "Don't talk like that."

"You know it's true . . . not gonna be around forever."

Somberness moved through the room, and Grandma patted my hand. Not the teasing way she'd done my cheek. But with such tenderness is brought moisture to my eyes.

"I'm just playin' with you, girl. Not about to pressure you into something you don't want. But I sure would be happy to kick your tail in the direction that you actually want to go."

Sydney's voice moved through my mind like the softest breeze.

"I think it's the things that hurt the worst that mean the most, don't you? Good or bad. That's what's gonna shape us. Make us into who we are. Guide us on the path to what we want the most. I think we'll know it when there's no other direction we can go. And I'm not going to be afraid of walking it anymore."

"Some things are just worth the wait, Grandma."

I felt compelled to at least give her that.

She smiled. "Mm-hmm . . . just don't let him drag his feet too long."

I wondered if she could possibly know how complicated our lives had been. What the tragedy of losing Sydney had done to both of us.

She sighed and settled deeper into the pillows, and I adjusted the blanket higher on her chest. "So, Grandma, I wanted to ask you . . . did you sell Grandpa's old Bel Air?

A small smile lit at the corner of her mouth. "Yeah. Todd came back to take care of me the way your mama has been doing. He's cleaning up this place, getting it back into shape. Lord knows, I've let it go to rot these last few years. Gave him the go ahead to sell whatever he wanted since he dropped his job to come out here and fix up the house."

I smiled at her. "It's good he's here. How long's he gonna be staying?"

Her lids drifted closed. "Probably as long as I last. As long as it takes him and your mom to get rid of this place."

Grief.

Stark and quiet and resounding.

It echoed through the room, from the clench of my heart to the flinch of my mama where she fiddled with something across the room, her back to us as if she was giving us privacy.

"Did you go through that box with your sister yet?" Grandma asked, her words starting to jumble, her pain medicine surely kicking in. "Wasn't ever rich, but everything I've ever had worth anything I put in there where I kept it in the attic."

I cringed, unable to confess someone had taken it. I didn't know what would be worse. Admitting that or the fact my apartment had been broken into in the first place.

I smiled softly. "Not yet. We will soon."

The lie fell so easily.

I just didn't know what else to say.

"Want you and your sister to do it soon. See what you might like."

She peeked an eye open at me. "As long as it doesn't lead to the two of you getting in one of those fist fights like you used to have over those dolls. No hair pullin', now."

A light chuckle rippled free. "Nah, I'm pretty sure we can handle ourselves. Unless you have something extra awesome in there."

I winked at her, and she laughed, the sound hitching when she began to cough.

"You two . . . find the important stuff. Keep it. That would make me happier than you know."

I couldn't bring myself to respond. Instead, I eased forward and kissed her cheek. I pulled back a fraction. "I'll let you rest."

She gave a small nod before she was already drifting off.

Reluctantly, I stood, watching over her as she got swept away into a deep sleep. I turned to face my mama who was watching me. Slowly, I approached her and wrapped my arms around her.

She stuttered through a deep breath, doing her best to quiet a sob that clawed at her throat. I just . . . held her while she cried, knowing there were no words that would make it better.

"I'm sorry," she whispered in my ear after a minute.

My head shook. "Nothing to be sorry for, Mama."

She nodded, and I held her out by the arms, voice serious. "If you need to rest, call me. I'll be happy to sit with her."

Regretfully, she looked at her mother before turning back to me. "I think I'll take all the minutes I have. They'll be plenty of time for rest later."

Quiet sorrow moved between us. "Okay," I said, wiping the tear that escaped my eye. "Just . . . promise you'll call if you need me."

"I will."

"I'll be back soon."

My worry for my sister was right there, hovering in my spirit, wanting to be released.

No matter how heavily it weighed, I wouldn't break my sister's trust that way. I had to let her come to me—to us—on her own time.

"I love you, Sunshine," she said, and I almost blushed at the way Ollie's nickname for me had spilled over and clung to the rest of my family.

"I love you more," I told her, backing away.

"Not a chance."

We smiled at each other as I edged across the groaning planks before I turned in the doorway and bounded back downstairs.

I shrieked when the door suddenly burst open just as I was reaching for the latch, my hand flying up to cover the thunder that was suddenly pounding my heart. I stepped back, still rattled. "Uncle Todd," I said, trying to force down the nerves that spiked in my body.

I hated that I was still on edge after everything that had happened.

"Well, if it isn't Nikki Lou."

He stood there, years older than I remembered, looking so much different. Lines creased his face, and a few more pounds were around his middle.

But the oil and grease staining his hands wasn't new.

"It's nice to see you," I said.

"Good to see you, too. It's been way too long."

"It has."

Awkwardness spun around us, and I hesitated before I said, "I just wanted you to know my friend bought that old Bel Air. I'm glad it's going to someone we know."

A frown pulled across his brow. "The Bel Air?"

I smiled at him. "It's fine. Grandma told me she is having you sell off some stuff since you left your job to come here and help out. It's good you're here for her."

Unease moved around him, and he nodded, as if he wasn't sure he wanted to take the praise. "It's not a problem."

I gestured for the door. "Well, I was just leaving. We'll have to catch up more soon."

I sidestepped around him.

From behind, I could feel him swivel around to look at me. "Which friend was that?" he asked.

I peeked back at him. "Ollie."

He grimaced and then gave a tight nod. Without another word, I ducked out into the night, wondering why it was that I felt so off-kilter.

twenty-two

Ollie
Seventeen Years Old

A pebble pinged against the window. When it got no response, he picked up another and did it again, feeling impatient and antsy as he stood outside of Nikki's grandma's house in the middle of the night.

Heart in his throat, he picked up another and did it again. This time the pebble he picked up was a whole lot closer to being a rock. He cringed when it clanged against the glass, then breathed out in relief when Nikki's face appeared in front of the drape.

There was confusion in her expression before a smile pulled to her face when she saw him standing beneath a big tree. She ducked away, and he was sure it was his pulse that would wake the entire house with the way it boomed, excitement and want filling him so full he thought he just might burst.

Not pretty.

But it was the truth.

This girl drove him right out of his mind.

He was already moving her direction by the time she slipped out the front door and silently snapped it shut behind her. She padded across the porch and down the stairs as he jogged her way.

They met in the middle, and he lifted her a couple of inches from the ground so he could feel her weight, spinning her around as he buried his face in the sweetness of her skin.

Honey and light.

She giggled and clung to him, her voice quieted to a whisper. "What are you doing here?"

"I needed to see you."

"And what if it had been your sister you woke up instead of me?"

He shrugged a little and settled Nikki back on her feet. "Then I'd tell her I was here to check on you two. Pretty much the truth, anyway."

Nikki stepped back and bit her bottom lip. She took his hand in hers, swaying lightly, spinning around, peeking back at him as she danced them off into the secluded cover of the towering trees. "Is that all you're here for, Oliver Preston? To check on us?"

There was a tease to her voice, and every inch of his body reacted.

He followed.

Where else was he going to go?

He was enraptured.

Enchanted.

This girl magic.

He rushed her, scooping her up from behind. Her feet kicked into the air as she squealed quietly, her back to his chest and his mouth at her ear. "You know why I'm here."

"And why's that?" she played along when he set her back down. She swung back around to face him.

He rushed his fingers through the softness of her hair. "For you."

"And now that you're here, what are you going to do with me?"

In a second flat, he had her pressed against the old car her grandpa still drove where it was parked behind a shed at least a hundred yards from the house. Where no one could see them. "First off, I'm going to kiss you."

He did. He took her face in his hands and he kissed her. Slow and long. He felt like he was standing in the middle of the river, taken by the current, unable to stand.

She sighed, and he hummed as he dropped his forehead to hers. "I was going nuts not getting to do that all day."

Rex and Sydney were around the whole time, and he hadn't gotten to sneak a second alone with Nikki.

Hiding this was getting harder and harder, but somehow, finally telling everyone after all this time felt harder to do, too. They'd been doing it for so long, it was beginning to feel like a lie.

A sin.

"You're driving me crazy, Nik," he whispered at her mouth. "Don't know what I'm supposed to do. The second I'm away from you, all I can think about is the next time I get to be with you. You've got me so spun up inside."

Her hands fisted in his shirt. "And the second you walk away, I feel a piece of myself go missing."

A breath left him, and he ran his lips up her cheek and whispered at her temple, "Sunshine."

"Beast," she teased quietly.

He fumbled with the door latch behind her, and Nikki was giggling as he angled her around to open the door. He fell into the seat and took her with him. She was quick to straddle his lap, hands on his shoulders, rocking against him.

If he didn't get to feel all of her soon, he might die.

He was sure of it.

Because her rubbing on him like that was nothing but torture.

The best kind of torture.

He just didn't know how much more of it he could take.

His hands went to her waist. "What if we stole the keys to this car and just drove away?"

She was kissing him, murmuring at his mouth, "Where would we go?"

"Anywhere . . . everywhere . . ." he rumbled. "Just so long as we're together. Can't wait until it's just us. You and me . . . my girl riding at my side in my badass car."

She giggled. The sound of it vibrated right through the center of him. "Mmm . . . you want an old car like this?"

Their hands were everywhere. Touching and exploring.

He groaned. "Hell, yes."

"Hot rod, huh?" she whispered.

"You know it. Nothing cooler than that. Gonna have one by the time I'm eighteen. Just wait. Then it's just you and me. No more hiding."

"Are you going to wait that long to take me?"

He stilled at her question. Because her voice had gone different. Something needy. No longer a tease.

He pulled back and looked at her through the milky light of the moon. Trusting eyes and freckled skin and heated body. "You want that?"

Didn't matter it was dark, he could feel the warmth rise to her cheeks. "Yes."

He swallowed around the lump that almost strangled him.

Nerves and excitement and lust.

He stared up at her, watching her expression when he said, "Next weekend . . . there's a big bonfire at the lake. Supposed to camp with a bunch of people from school. Tell your mom you're spending the night with Sydney."

Her head angled to the side, that same worry they had over his sister taking over her features. "And what am I supposed to tell Sydney?"

A sigh pilfered free. He didn't want to be annoyed. Irritated that they were sneaking around because they were afraid they might offend her or hurt her.

"We'll . . . figure it out, okay? We'll make it work. I just want to be with you."

She wound her arms around his neck. "I just want to be with you, too."

twenty-three

Ollie

Traditions.

It was hard to pinpoint exactly how they were formed. How they came into existence. It was like a slow slide of habits that gathered and merged until they stuck. Most people viewed them as a good thing.

Holidays and family and celebration.

Cherished memories repeated again and again.

This tradition?

It was nothing less than masochistic.

Hot blades cutting into my skin.

Needlessly, considering the scars were already there. Etched in me so deeply they could never be erased.

Kale and Rex both inclined back on different pieces of furniture in the back office at Olive's, Rex with the bottle this year, pouring it into the shooters. "Seems crazy this date has come up again. Years going by faster than I can make sense of them."

A sorrowful, wistful sound filtered from Kale. "Yeah. Time just keeps rolling, things changing so quickly, and still I can close my eyes, and I swear, I'm back there at the lake that night."

Shivers scraped across the surface of my skin.

Agony.

Rex peered over at me. "You sure you want to do this again?"

"What's changed?" My voice was grit, even though the words were feeling more and more like a lie.

The first time we'd gathered on the anniversary of this night? We'd been eighteen. They'd found me at the lake.

Alone.

Looking at the water like it might conjure her existence on the glassy, darkened surface.

They'd climbed down on either side of me.

Kale with all his quiet understanding and support. Rex wearing some sort of unfathomable grief on his face.

He'd pulled out this massive bottle of cheap whiskey, twisted the cap, and handed it to me.

I'd chugged what had to have been half of it until I'd choked on the burning liquid that'd pooled in my empty gut, then the three of us had sat there for hours, passing it back and forth until it was empty and the sun was coming up.

Two of them swimming in my loss. Keeping me from drowning.

I'd pushed Nikki away. Hadn't seen more of her that unbearable year than stolen glances which had damned near destroyed the last bit of me.

Cutting her out of my life had hurt like a fucking bitch. But how could I have her when the cost of wanting her was my sister?

I couldn't.

And I'd hated and hated and hated, and that feeling had built for so many years until it suffocated me. Until I could no longer see straight, which was how I'd ended up at Nikki's door a year ago tonight.

Nothing but a selfish bastard.

Taking her.

Of course, I couldn't even remember how I'd gotten there since I'd been so messed up that my rational mind could no longer convince my spirit that I wasn't allowed to have her.

It was like finding peace in the darkest night.

Then, like a piece of shit, I'd slipped from her bed before dawn, fucking wrecked, leaving her lying there naked where I'd been tangled with her.

The whole time wanting to climb right back into her arms.

To wrap her up and never let her go.

But I'd left her there because I'd had to.

What other choice did I have?

Didn't think I'd ever been so torn about anything.

I had been wrong.

Tonight, I felt like I was being shredded in two. Never so caught up in right and wrong. The girl once again a secret.

My best secret.

One I wanted to keep.

Just didn't know what kind of person that made me if I did.

Rex handed Kale a shot glass and then gave one to me. The three of us met in the middle of the small office. We lifted the shots above our heads. "To Sydney. We'll never forget."

Glasses clinked, and we tossed back the shots. I swallowed it down. Heat blistered my stomach and crawled through my senses. This date would haunt me forever—but I could feel something . . . something changing.

Kale clapped me on the back. "You okay, man?"

A huff left my nose, and I scrubbed a palm over my face. "Not sure that's the right description. Okay would mean forgetting."

He looked at me seriously. "Not sure there's any chance of that. Don't think you're ever going to forget. And I don't think you'd want to."

He started to move around me to head for the door. All the girls and Broderick would be waiting, probably wondering where the hell we'd slipped off to.

He paused when he was right at my side, both of us facing opposite directions. He reached out and squeezed my shoulder, his attention cast to the ground. "But it's been fourteen years, Ollie. If I knew Sydney at all? She's looking down on you, wishing you'd finally let her go. Wishing that you'd finally let yourself live."

I didn't say anything, and he opened the door and stepped out into the bar, the muted thrum of the band playing tonight growing loud as he did. Without looking back, he snapped it shut, closing Rex and me in, the beat once again distorted, faint and vibrating through the walls.

Warily, I looked up to meet Rex's piercing gaze. Something about it was unsettling. Remorseful but strong. "He's right, man." The words caught in his throat. "It's time."

I looked to the floor, hand running down my beard. "Not sure that's possible. Not until I find her."

He winced, eyes slamming closed and hands curling into fists. "You're hung up on an impossibility, Ollie. It's time you admitted that."

Part of me wanted to lash out at him. Tell him to fuck off because he couldn't understand. This was my sister we were talking about. They'd barely even been friends, only knowing each other because he and I hung out.

The other part knew he was right.

Fourteen years, I'd been searching. Cutting out every fucking news article about her that had ever been written, comparing it against other cases, sure that, if I was patient enough, I would notice something. Piece together a clue that had been missed.

Hell, that'd been part of the reason I'd opened this bar in the first place. Figuring one day, someone would slip, say something they shouldn't. Or maybe someone would say something they didn't know was important in the first place.

I felt that hope slipping away.

What scared me most was I didn't know where that left me.

Rex hesitated, the words almost a groan when he released them. "I miss her, too, man. You think if I could go back, I wouldn't do things differently?"

I looked up, trying to gauge where he was coming from, what he was trying to get at.

He sighed, shook whatever thoughts he was having off. "Everyone's out there. Together. The people who care about you most. Don't neglect that. You're gonna regret it if you do. Time goes by so fast, Ollie. So damned fast. You've got to treasure the days you're given."

An echo of my mother's screams filled my ear, the impact of them thrashing in my spirit, her fists a phantom pain on my chest.

It's your fault.

I trusted you.

You were supposed to take care of her.

You promised, you'd take care of her.

"Not sure I even deserve to be out there with them."

Rex strode for the door, pausing with it open as he turned, his words pointed. "Don't you?"

For twenty minutes, I sat alone with only my thoughts and the sounds of the bar seeping through the walls to keep me company.

Processing.

Sifting through my thoughts and my worries.

The deep-seated need to cling to this day—to the memory of Sydney—to give her the devotion that she'd deserved.

The other part was all fucked up over Nikki.

Nikki. Fucking. Walters.

Invading my life when I didn't know how to keep her there.

How to make her fit.

The girl so fucking wrong. So fucking right.

Like I said, I'd never been so torn.

Finally, I forced myself to get it together, got behind my bar, and went to work.

Seemed impossible, but the smile tacked to my face wasn't all that hard to find, considering I was surrounded by the group of people who had gathered directly across from me.

Laughing and treasuring and *cherishing*.

Most of all . . . Nikki was right there.

Safe.

I poured Lillith a glass of chilled white wine, whipped up a pitcher of margaritas for Rynna, Hope, and Jenna. After that, I handed a beer to Rex, filled a tumbler of whiskey for Kale, and passed a glass of red wine to Broderick.

I went to work on Nikki's drink, listening to my friends carrying on, having a great time.

Their laughter rang free, blending with the beat of the band where they'd taken up residence at the bar like they owned the place.

Their voices were loud and their mood a little bit rowdy.

From across the bar, Nikki met my eyes.

Tentatively.

Tenderly.

The girl sending me her soft encouragement. Aware and sweet and filled with all that light I'd taken for granted for all these years.

I sent her a covert smile back as I slid her pink cosmo across the gleaming wood in her direction.

Telling her I saw her. That I felt her. That I knew this day wasn't easy on her either.

That she had just as much on her mind as me.

Maybe more.

I was grateful there was a smile on her face, too.

That she was acting like her normal self.

Her old self.

Laughing and teasing and playing with her friends.

Jenna, who was Hope's best friend, squealed, jerking my attention away from Nikki's hypnotizing stare. "I knew there was a reason I loved you."

She wrapped both hands around the margarita glass rimmed with salt, bringing it to her nose and inhaling like it was some kind of rose or some shit.

My brows pitched high. "That's the reason you love me? My bar?" I razzed, shaking my head like I was completely outraged.

Jenna's brown hair swished around her face. "You've got to admit that having a friend who owns a bar is filled with all kinds of perks. I wish I would have known you earlier. A girl could use a guy like you right about the time she turns twenty-one. I have major catching up to do."

"I take offense to that."

Rex waved his beer in the air. "Why do you think I still put up with your sorry ass?"

I lifted my arms out to the sides. "Uh . . . because I'm awesome. That's why."

This was always just our way, going from heavy to light in a second flat, giving each other shit as if they hadn't just been right there, coming beside me when they always knew I needed them most.

Kale laughed. "Sure, sure, man, you just go on thinking that."

Hope swatted at his chest. "Leave Ollie alone." She turned her attention to me, her eyes wide with playful sympathy. "I know you're awesome. Ignore these monsters."

Incredulous, Kale snorted. "Monsters?"

"Monsters," I agreed, giving Hope a smile.

Kale pointed at me with his index finger, the rest of his hand still wrapped around the glass. "If anyone looks like a monster around here, it's you. Seriously, I've seen grown men shudder in their damned boots at the sight of you. Little do they know, you're nothing but a pansy under all that muscle. What a damned waste."

A smile threatened at the edge of my mouth.

Assholes.

All of them.

"Keep dreaming. Nothing wasted here." I flexed like one of those fuckers showing off on Venice Beach. "Guys piss their pants when they see me because they know I'm not to be fucked with. Unlike you." Was doing my best to keep a straight face and not bust out laughing as I played along.

Kale puffed out his chest. "Oh, come on, Ollie. You know I could take you."

I laughed under my breath.

"You think so, huh?"

"Yup. Remember that time in fourth grade behind the swing sets? Totally whooped your ass, my friend."

My brow lifted. "That's because I let you win."

Nikki widened playful eyes, her attention bouncing around the group, that mesmerizing color so pretty where they glinted under the lights.

"I can now attest to the fact that Ollie is, in fact, a monster. A bear. Or maybe an ogre. I'm concerned for my safety. The man actually growls in his sleep."

The last week had been nothing but cruel.

Being with her and not being able to touch her.

Trying to keep that promise that I needed to figure my shit out before I hurt her again.

She draped an arm around Jenna's shoulders. Swore, two of them might have been twins separated at birth.

Lillith's hawk eyes darted between us. Swore she could spot a rat from a hundred miles away. "So, how is the whole roommate thing going? Should I thank you for not killing my best friend yet?"

I glanced at Nikki for a flash before I set my palms on the bar and leaned toward Lillith. "*Yet* being the operative word."

Rynna giggled. "Tell me she's not as messy at your place as she is at Pepper's Pies. I swear to goodness, that whirlwind leaves a trail of crumbs everywhere she goes like she's leaving behind a distress call."

Nikki's mouth dropped open. "What in the world are you talkin' about, Rynna? I bus those tables faster than all those kids you hired combined. I run circles around them."

"Oh, so that explains the crop circles of bread crumbs scattered around the floor."

"That's it, I quit."

Nikki was fighting a grin behind her overexaggerated pout. But there was no missing the way her sexy mouth twisted with affection.

"I'm just playing!" Rynna cried, rushing her friend and taking up her other side. "Don't leave me yet. I might up and die. Don't know what I'm going to do without you. Crumbs and all."

"We'll find someone awesome to take my place, don't worry. I mean, hello, *not* as awesome, because we all know that would be totally impossible, but someone who will make do."

Rynna pouted. "But I love you best."

"I'm feeling totally left out here." Hope pursed her lips where she was tucked against Kale.

Nikki reached out and waved her in. "Well, get in here then . . . we aren't complete without you and Lillith."

Hope didn't even hesitate. She rushed into the circle.

Lillith rolled her eyes. "Are we seriously group-hugging in the middle of the bar?"

Nikki's brows shot to the ceiling. "You know what they say, how are your friends going to know you love them if you're not drunk at two a.m. on a Saturday night?"

Lillith glanced at the glittering diamond watch wrapped around her wrist, a gift from Broderick for her birthday. "Its nine, Nikki. Nine."

"Semantics. Get your ass over here."

From behind, Broderick gave her a tiny shove, his grin wolfish when she looked back at him. "Go on, baby. Get a little of that group love. That's enough fantasies for an entire week."

Nikki pointed at him. "Eww, Brody. Just no. Don't you dare go there."

Yeah. Don't go there. And here I'd thought I liked the guy.

But Rex was shaking his head, Kale was chuckling, and the girls were standing and hugging and jumping and laughing as they swayed in this big huddle, and there was nothing I could do but grin right the hell along.

My chest tightened.

Sweet agony.

Because a piece was missing, and I'd give fucking anything for Sydney to be there. My mind flashed with what she might look like now.

Fourteen years gone.

Where she'd be in her life. If she'd be married. Have kids.

Or if she'd be living in some faraway city, chasing down a dream.

"Hey, boss," Cece called from the other end of the bar, breaking into the thoughts that cut me down at the knees.

I jerked my attention that way.

So maybe Nikki had a few things right about Cece.

My head bartender was nothing short of a tattooed sex goddess.

Long, jet-black hair, the scraps she wore screaming seduction, almost as loud as the red painted on her lips.

Maybe it wasn't so strange for Nikki to make assumptions about us.

People would probably take one look at Cece and think her my perfect match.

Two of us cut from the same cloth.

Or maybe chipped from the same stone.

Truth was, I had never even had the urge.

Didn't mean it didn't bug the hell out of me that Nikki had brought it up. I hated the idea that she had ever felt an ounce of what I'd felt when I'd had to stomach looking at her with another man.

Wanted to dig my nails into my mind and claw all those images from my consciousness.

"What's up?" I hollered, grateful for the distraction.

She cocked a wry grin, and the poor asshole sitting at the bar across from her was nothing but a puddle at her feet.

"Could use backup. Pack of f-boys, eleven o'clock."

I laughed under my breath.

Only Cece.

Fuckboy.

Fratboy.

As far as she was concerned, that title was as interchangeable as the guy's that held it were abhorrent. She slapped them with a "douche" label across their pretty-boy foreheads before they even had a chance to make it through rush week.

I rapped my fist on the counter, pointed at my friends. "Be right back."

I moved to the opposite end of the bar, sliding in beside Cece to help her fill the beers for the rowdy table that was up close to the band.

Did my best not to cringe when I saw the guy who walked through the door.

Talk about a douche.

Matt Walker.

Asshole we'd all known since high school. Something about him festered right below my skin.

Oh, that was right.

Fucker had wanted to get his grimy hands on Nikki for just as long as I had known him.

Didn't matter that he was all fitted, posh business suits and shiny fucking shoes to match his shiny fucking smile.

Asshole was slimy as fuck.

A weasel.

"You good?" I asked Cece when I'd finished helping her fill the huge order. Could feel the tether pulling me back that way. Toward Nikki who I knew would be the prick's target.

Time and again.

She'd left with him once, a few years ago, and I'd about damned lost my mind.

Thought of it happening again had panic laying siege to my veins.

"Yep. Think we have it under control now. Let's just hope they don't eff up the rest of my night."

The girl smirked, hip tossed out to the side.

My laugh was wry.

Wouldn't want to tangle with that one.

I booked it back to my post.

Lillith had already spotted Matt, and she bumped her hip into Nikki's to get her attention. "Oh, look who just walked in. It's Make-Out Matt," she sang like she didn't know she was basically crushing me beneath her red-soled shoe.

Nikki's gaze flashed to me.

Remorse and awareness and a lifetime of unanswered questions.

Where do we go from here?

Who are we?

Do I belong to you?

Most importantly, do you belong to me?

I gulped under the force of them, wanting nothing more than to reach out, touch her face. Maybe climb right the hell over this bar, take her in my arms, and kiss her in front of all our friends.

Claim her as mine.

She'd been a secret for so damned long. Problem was, I still didn't know if I deserved to stand in her light.

Possession tearing through my senses, I watched as the prick made his way through the crowd like he had no real destination, no care in the world.

Still, it was obvious as hell he knew exactly what direction he was heading.

Lillith nudged Nikki with her elbow. "You should totally give him a chance, Nikki. That poor man has been salivating over you since the day he joined the track team your senior year just so he could watch your tits bounce when you ran."

Nikki visibly pushed back the discomfort that surged between us and pinned one of those faked smiles on her mouth.

"Pssh . . ." Nikki stepped back and gestured at her chest.

I wiped my brow.

Why the fuck wasn't the air conditioner on? Was dying in there.

"What tits? I'm as flat as Kansas," she said, laughing and joking the way she'd done for all these years.

Images rushed. The girl on my couch. Her tit in my mouth. My hands on her body.

Need spun and licked and teased.

She had no fucking clue just how perfect they were, peaking below that satiny material. Nikki's own personal form of harassment.

"Matt seems to be just fine with that." Rynna nodded emphatically.

Great. That was all I needed.

Nikki had yet another meddler urging her along, not that Rynna could have a clue.

I glared between Rex and Kale.

Where was my crew when I needed them most?

Did they not see this bullshit?

I mean, I know I'd taken responsibility for Nikki's well-being. But there were times when good friends should step in.

Like when a douche tried to make his way into territory he didn't belong.

Fuck that.

Rex met my eyes, narrowing his, studying me as he took a swig of his beer.

Did he have any idea? All that time Nikki and I had been sneaking around, hiding away, hoping Rex and Kale would be enough of a distraction that Sydney wouldn't notice. Guess I hadn't given it all that much thought as to if they had.

Hope landed a bunch of excited smacks against Nikki's arm, her eyes wide and her lips barely moving, like she thought she was telling a secret that she was actually issuing to the world. "Oh, oh, don't look behind you . . . but he's coming this way. Oh, wow, he really is good-looking."

"Hey," Kale defended.

Now the asshole has something to say.

She looked up at her husband, her red hair moving over her shoulders. "Oh, Cowboy . . . I was talking about for Nikki. Don't get your britches in a twist."

He leaned down, rubbing his nose against hers. "Cowboy? I'm your king, baby."

Had to resist from balling up a dish rag and throwing it against the side of his face.

Yeah, this was not gonna end well.

Because my guts were churning when Matt, the fucker, came up to the bar just behind where Nikki stood.

He grinned at me like we were the oldest of mates. "Hey, man." Still standing, he leaned his forearms on the bar. "How's it going?"

Fan-fucking-tastic, that's how.

"Good," I rumbled. I tossed a napkin down in front of him. "What can I get you?"

How about the door?

"Whatever's on tap."

Everything's on tap, asshole.

But I didn't say anything, I just filled up a chilled mug with a light.

Figured that was all the pussy could handle.

I smiled at him when I slid it across the bar.

All teeth.

"Thanks, brother," he said like he didn't even notice I was five seconds from ripping him to shreds.

He lifted it in the air before he took a big swallow.

"Sure thing."

He was grinning when he moved into the circle, going right for her. "Hey, Nikki. It's good to see you."

She peeked my way.

A flash of indigo.

A glimpse of the freckles on her defined cheeks.

My chest tightened.

She offered him a small smile. "Hi, Matt. How have you been?"

"Good, good," he said. "Work's busy, but other than that, I can't complain. You?"

"Same here."

Seemed like so many lies fell from her mouth with that simple statement.

Like all this bullshit wasn't going down in her life.

This was brutal, watching them chat like every word wasn't killing me.

I was a hot second from losing my cool. Turned out it was Nikki who was getting ready to do all the shredding, and the girl didn't even have to lift a finger.

Our friends had turned to each other, talking quietly, giving them space, while I scrubbed at the bar with a rag and tried to pretend like it wasn't any of my business.

Didn't matter.

The turn in Nikki and Matt's conversation hit me like a loudspeaker screaming in my ear.

"Band's good tonight. You want to dance?" Matt asked.

Of course, that was when Lillith found it fit to pipe in. She all but shoved Nikki his direction. "Sure, she does."

There was no missing the resistance that lined Nikki's posture when Lily pushed her that way, the way her shoulders went up and her shoes slid across the floor.

An inch, and then two.

Enough to make my mind tip to the side. Axis creaking. Threatening to crack.

Nikki peeked back at me.

Was that an apology or her own anger and frustration, her spirit screaming out that I was responsible for this?

I'd known all along that one day . . . one day she'd move on.

Find joy.

A husband and a family and a load of kids, exactly what she deserved.

The way she'd dreamed about growing up.

How many kids are we gonna have?" she'd whispered when she was just fifteen, laying on a bed of blazing stars, nestled on my chest as we'd looked up at the night sky.

"Three. One little girl with your eyes and two boys just like me."

She giggled. "I don't think I could handle three of you."

It was what I'd wanted for her even though the thought destroyed something inside of me.

Of her finding that with someone other than me.

Then I'd gone and ruined every chance she'd had. Chased off every guy. Certain they weren't good enough for her.

Amusement was suddenly in her smile, wry as her gaze moved across all the girls, then she turned back to Matt. "Actually, all my friends would like to dance."

Another warning in her expression when she looked back at them. "Wouldn't they?"

She spun around, facing them as she backed away and waved for them to follow. The girl was wearing this short, frilly skirt and a silky tank, heels on her feet making her legs look like they were a mile long.

Everything about her was exotic and still as comfortable and down to earth as a home-cooked meal.

Yeah.

I wanted to fucking eat her.

Devour every inch.

Jenna clapped in excitement, while Hope passed her drink off to Kale, pecking him on the lips before she rushed to join them.

Lillith? Lillith hit me with a smirk as she let go of Broderick's hand and then followed Hope.

Swore to God, the world was against me.

Cursed.

They edged into the thick, pushing through the raving throng. Bodies surged and swayed and pulsed. They all made their way to the dance floor at the base of the elevated stage.

Nearly choked when Matt edged up to Nikki from behind and tugged her against his chest.

In the roiling crowd, she was facing me when he splayed his hand across her belly.

From across the space, those mesmerizing eyes, so odd of a color you could vanish in the depths, tangled with mine.

Hypnotizing.

A motherfucking spell.

Black fucking magic.

That was what she was.

Rage blew in like a bleak, black storm.

Rex looked that way before he turned back to me with a grumbled laugh. "You're so fucked, dude."

I wiped at the bar, so hard I was pretty sure it was rubbing off the glossy stain.

Stripping it down to bare bones.

That was exactly what I felt like.

Bare bones.

"What's that supposed to mean?" I gritted.

He shared a look with Kale before he turned back to me. "If you saw your face right now, you'd know exactly what that means."

"Don't know what you're talking about."

"You still gonna stand there and deny it after all this time?"

Unease rippled through me. Maybe he really had had a clue. "Deny what?"

Disappointment came out with the shake of his head before he tipped back his beer and drained the bottle. He stood and slammed the empty on the bar. "Think I'm gonna go claim my girl before some poor, unknowing bastard has to die trying. Someone else here might want to do the same."

And he wasn't looking at Kale or Broderick when he said it.

twenty-four

Nikki

Chaos drummed through the air. I felt caught up in it.

Elevated and lost.

My feet not quite touching the ground. Held by the sapphire gaze that ravaged me from across the space.

Intense, fierce, and blistering.

Torment and need and possession.

Crash after crash.

Matt slipped his hand around my waist and pulled me flush against his body.

A shudder ripped free of my lungs. It wasn't even close to being elicited by Matt's touch. It was because the only thing I could feel was Ollie covering me.

I didn't even have to close my eyes to imagine the man was touching me everywhere, the sensation of his hands from last weekend still alive and vibrant.

Sizzling across my flesh.

Turmoil played across Ollie's striking face.

It was possessive and wild, and still, incredibly sad.

Unable to remain upright under the severity of it, I tore myself out of Matt's hold and whirled around to face him, turning my back to Ollie because I no longer knew how to stand beneath it all.

The sorrow and the regret and the need.

In the throbbing crush, I struggled to maintain balance where my friends danced around me as if they couldn't feel the quake of the earth that rocked beneath my feet.

Dim lights were at one with the smoky fog that twisted and twined in the air, the bar nothing but a dizzying haze.

Bodies pulsed, a mass that toiled in the hypnotic beat.

Matt slanted me a smile, what he thought was seduction carved out on his face, and my stomach turned.

I didn't want this.

Not tonight.

Not when I wanted to turn around, go to Ollie, and tell him I wasn't going anywhere.

Promise him I'd stay.

Matt edged forward again. This time, he placed both his hands to my hips in a bid to bring us closer.

I set my hands on his chest, intending to tell him I was sorry but I couldn't do this. Even if it was just a dance, it felt wrong.

But my mouth went dry, and my tongue got stuck on the roof of my mouth when I felt the energy surge over me from behind. At the same time, the waters parting as the air rushed and whirled.

I didn't even have time to process it before Ollie was there.

Towering next to where Matt attempted to bring us together.

The man so big.

Savage and fierce.

Hands fisted at his sides and something like anger in his expression.

There was no chance I could breathe through the impact.

He turned all that intimidation on Matt. "Sorry, *brother*, but I'm gonna have to cut in."

His tone was a low threat.

Irritated, Matt's attention flicked to Ollie.

For a second, I thought he was going to refuse. Maybe he hadn't known who it was before he'd looked, or maybe it hadn't been until then that he'd caught on to the possessive indignation that radiated from Ollie's flesh.

But Matt jolted and started to slowly back away. Eyes darting between us for a beat, annoyed and off-put before he seemed to give and disappeared into the fray.

Then Ollie looped a massive arm around my waist as he wound the other hand into my hair.

A gasp burst from my lungs.

Never, ever had Ollie touched me in public. Not like this.

He pulled me flush against his heat and strength and battering heart.

His forehead dropped to mine, and our bodies began to sway, to move in time to the beat, our hips rocking as we fell into the dance.

People throbbed around us, and he held me tighter. He bent down, wedging his knee between my thighs.

One hand gripped me by the waist, that thumb running dizzying circles on my hipbone.

"Nikki," he murmured. My name sounded fragile and unsure where he released it an inch from my mouth. "I'm going to lose my mind, looking at you on this floor, another man touching you."

My hands fisted in his shirt, desperate to get him closer.

"Ollie," I whispered, close to begging.

What is this?

I can't handle being this close to you, and you push me away again.

His nose brushed mine, and his expression verged on pained as he drew in a ragged breath.

Trembling with need.

We rocked in hesitation, and his mouth was in my hair, at my temple, running tenderly down my cheek.

Fire on my skin.

Then he brushed his lips across mine.

Once.

Twice.

So sweet.

Lightheadedness swept through me like a slow dream.

Then he crushed his mouth to mine.

Indecision erased. The man consuming me in a way he'd never done.

Openly.

It felt like a claiming.

His hand moved to the back of my head as he angled me just right. His tongue demanding all of me right out in the middle of the dance floor.

My heart took off at a sprint, racing for his that hammered in the air.

And we spun.

Kissing.

Kissing and kissing and kissing.

Desire flashed.

Ollie groaned.

I burned—every cell in my body coming alive under his touch.

He suddenly pulled away, and I was blinking, trying to find my senses. But the only thing I could see was this man.

Peering down at me, something so different in his gaze.

Powerful and unending.

My knees shook, and he took me by the hand, and that was when I noticed that all of our friends were frozen in the middle of the floor.

Shocked, every single one of them stared back at us.

Rex cracked a grin in Ollie's direction, and Ollie just gave him a finger as he began to haul me back through the crowd.

Heat flushed my body, my cheeks.

Not because I was embarrassed or ashamed but because, for the first time ever, it felt like I was finally right, and I had no idea how long this feeling would remain.

I struggled to keep up on my heels as Ollie wound through the groups packed around the high-top tables, the man on a mission as he beelined for the darkened hall.

The second we were in it, he had me pinned, my back against the wall and my legs around his waist. He ground himself against my center.

Pleasure sparked.

He groaned, the man plundering my mouth as he did.

"Nikki," he muttered, hands running the outside of my bare thighs. "Nikki."

Without setting me on my feet, he jerked me from the wall, never ceasing that frenzied kiss as he carried me the rest of the way down the hall and started up the zigzagging stairwell.

We banged up the steps, the man spinning and pressing and clamoring, his hands everywhere.

Needy.

As needy as his mouth that consumed mine.

As needy as my pleas that whispered from my soul.

My hands threaded in his hair, and my body rocked against his.

Every brush spurred me higher.

"Ollie. Ollie," I whimpered, swept away in his madness. Willing to float away forever if it meant getting to be with him.

He stumbled up the three flights of stairs. The music from downstairs became a dull, vibrating hum, our hearts becoming louder as he made it through the door to his loft.

He didn't stop before he pinned me to the wall right outside his bedroom door. He pulled back, his cock straining against his jeans, pressed hot against my panties.

The man panted as he stared down at me with crazed, hungry eyes.

I searched for air. The only thing it accomplished was inhaling him. Taking on more.

Reaching out a trembling hand, I ran it slowly—tenderly—through the longer pieces of his hair. My head angled with the plea that cracked at the back of my throat. "I want this, Ollie. I want you. But I need to know this is what you want. I can't allow you to trample my heart all over again. If you take me in that room, there's no going back for me."

twenty-five

Ollie

Her words blasted through my consciousness. A reminder of all the mistakes I'd made. The continuous hurt I'd inflicted.

Forcing myself to slow down, I spread my hand out across the side of her face. Wishing I could hold all of her.

Wishing I could tell her I'd love her forever.

Instead, a confession was falling from my mouth. "This date . . . it nearly ruins me every time it comes around. But this . . . this isn't about Sydney. This is about you. This is about us. This is about finding what we lost."

My words grew low and fast. "You make everything feel different. Always have, Nikki. Like I'm someone else when I get near you. Like I'm someone better."

Those indigo eyes moved over my face. Searching and memorizing. Drinking me in. Remembering this moment for what it always should have been.

"When I went to you last year . . . I was so fucked up. But I know now, I couldn't go anywhere else. Because you made everything right when it was so fucking wrong."

"Ollie . . ."

I pulled her from the wall, the girl still in my arms, my face buried in her hair. "I need you. I need you in a way I never thought possible," I muttered, praying she'd get it.

That it was different from when I went to her a year before telling her the same thing.

This was a promise.

This time, when I moved, it wasn't frenzied or panicked like it'd been when I'd carried her upstairs. It was cautious and slow. Holding her the way she'd always deserved to be.

Tenderly.

The girl precious.

I'd always wanted to wrap her up.

Protect her.

All these years, it'd made me crazy, and I'd wished for a way to scrape it from my psyche, from who I was. It'd taken until tonight to realize she'd only driven me mad because I refused to allow her where she was always meant to be.

With me.

Mine.

I laid her out across my bed. Slowly, I crawled over her. Hovering. Staring down at her through the milky glow of the moon that spread over the room and set her aglow.

Light.

"No more, Nikki. Can't go on pretending that I don't want you. That I don't need you. I want to try to be the kind of guy you deserve."

Grief fisted my heart.

Thoughts of my sister running rampant.

If I was gonna be with Nikki, it was time I ripped myself open wide. My eyes squeezed closed, and my teeth ground together as I forced out the words. "I'm so lost, and I don't know if that vacant feeling is ever going to go away. Only thing I know is when I'm with you, it doesn't feel so vast."

Hands caressed both sides of my face, and my eyes eased open to see the girl staring up at me. Her breaths short, so much evident in her adoring gaze. Words I wasn't ready to hear. Really didn't matter if she said them aloud, anyway, because I felt them when I dipped down and kissed her.

Slow and tender, the softest kind of adoration on her tongue.

Her fingertips slipped through my beard and found their way into our kiss, running over my lips. "I'm right here, Ollie. I've always been. Waiting for you. I can't take it away, but we can hold each other through the middle of it."

I edged back, sitting up on my knees and bringing her with me. She straddled me where I knelt on the bed, this gorgeous girl wrapped around my lap.

My dick strained, and my muscles ticked.

I wanted to devour her.

Inch by inch.

I held her by the side of the neck, her pulse going wild against my palm. "Want to be right for you. Good for you."

The hint of a smile played across her lips. The girl so sexy.

Olive skin and honeyed hair and freckled cheeks.

Sunshine.

She slipped down my body until she was resting on her knees. Our bodies swayed. A breadth apart.

Her fingertips fluttered out, running down my shirt.

Need raced my veins.

She gathered the hem and began to drag it up, peeking at my face as she did. "You've always been right for me. You just need to accept that you are. That none of us are perfect. That the world is cruel, but it's also given us the greatest gift."

She dragged the shirt over my head and dropped it at her side.

A shudder ripped through me.

Lashes of fire.

That feeling again.

Energy.

"It gave us this," she murmured so softly, hands tender as they pressed to the thunder at my chest. "*Us.*"

A moan climbed my throat, and that was all I could take, and I was pulling that silky tank over her head.

No bra.

Those tiny tits perky. Nipples pebbled and hard.

God. She would be my undoing.

That moan turned to a growl, and I pushed her onto her back.

She bounced on the bed and a giggle slipped from between her lips.

"Beast," she teased.

My entire chest squeezed.

Warmth and fire and need.

My mouth went for the flat planes of her belly, kissing across the satiny skin, my hands winding in the hem of her skirt. "Don't even know if I can bring myself to get you out of this skirt. Do you have any clue what you were doing to me all night? Looking like this?" I grumbled at her stomach.

Vibrations of low laughter shook beneath my lips, and her fingers were winding into my hair. "I thought you told me the way I dressed was ridiculous."

"It is ridiculous. It's ridiculous how hard it makes me. Ridiculous how much it makes me want you. Ridiculous how much time I've spent fantasizing about peeling you out of those clothes."

Her laughter turned into a needy gasp as I started dragging off her skirt. I took her underwear with it.

Sliding the fabric down those long, slender legs until every inch of her was laid bare.

"Shit . . . ridiculous," I hissed, letting a smirk climb to my mouth. "Ridiculous how gorgeous you are."

She trembled, and her hips arched just from the heat of my stare. "Ollie, I need you."

And I knew . . . I knew that I needed her more than she could ever need me, and that was kind of fucked up, but I couldn't go on for one more second without her.

She was everything. *Everything.*

"So gorgeous," I told her, the tip of my index finger running the center of her chest, riding down, across her trembling belly.

I eased off the bed, standing beside it, watching her in the night as I shrugged out of my boots and jeans and underwear.

Her lips parted and her gaze swept over me. Want darkened those indigo eyes.

Lust and desire and something that was so much bigger than that.

"You are what's beautiful, Ollie. So beautiful. All these years, it's been hard to look at you because I missed you so much."

Sadness tinted the words, and I knew it came from that hurt I'd inflicted. Years of rejecting us both.

I reached in the drawer, quick to cover my cock, which was pointing for the sky, begging for her, before I was crawling back over her, between her thighs.

Desire brimmed and boiled, threatening to blow.

I cradled one side of her face in my hand.

"Sunshine," I whispered.

Emotion thick, her face pinched, and her chest heaved with each shallow breath.

I wanted to swallow every single one of them down. Keep them tucked away as a reminder of the way I felt at this moment. So I'd never forget.

"Are you mine, Ollie?" whispered from her swollen, damp lips.

My mouth brushed hers, tasting the words. "I've always been."

"Then take me." She wound her arms around my neck. "Keep me."

A thunder lit up my heart, pulse raging as it careened through my veins, our bodies catching as I nestled deeper between her thighs.

Her pussy slick and wet, my cock hard and ready.

That beast she was always all too pleased to remind me I was wanted to devour her. Take her fast and wild and hard.

There'd be plenty of time for that later.

Tonight, I wrapped her up and nuzzled my face in her hair. My murmur climbed into the dense air. "You owned me from the first day that I met you."

She hooked her arm around my head, her perfect tits pressed to my chest, her body arching, begging for mine. "I had no idea that day that you'd become the focus of my life. The one I longed for. My whole life, all it took was a glance from you, and I knew I was exactly where I was supposed to be."

Emotion clutched and clenched. I eased back a fraction, rubbing against the slick heat that burned between her thighs.

The tip of my cock caught.

Our breaths hitched, and our gazes tangled.

For the flash of a second, it was like I felt everything snapping into place.

Worlds aligning and spirits syncing.

Us.

She was right.

Exactly the way it was supposed to be.

She stared at me through the shadows, her lips parting as I pressed just the tip of my dick in to the silky welcome of her body.

"Tell me this is what you want," I grunted, holding back.

"I want you more than you could ever know." Her words struck me like arrows, and that was all I needed.

I nudged deeper into her warmth.

The girl so damned tiny that she was gasping and my jaw was clenching as I slowly spread her.

Felt so much like the first time I'd taken her, when she'd cried out from the pain and begged me for more, and I'd held her and whispered that I'd love her forever.

Didn't matter that I'd only been a kid. Seventeen. I knew I'd never be given a greater gift than that.

And somehow, this felt just as big.

Because the girl?

The girl was giving her trust.

Even when I knew I didn't deserve it. That I hadn't *earned* it. But fuck . . . I was gonna try.

"Shit, Nikki," I wheezed as I took her by the caps of her delicate shoulders, trying to hold myself in check when this girl had always made me lose all control.

She panted, her legs dropping wide, jagged gasps from her mouth as she adjusted to me again. Nails sank into my shoulders, and we both held tight until I fully buried myself in her body.

Nothing had ever felt so right.

"Are you okay?" I managed, propping myself up on an elbow so I could look down at her.

Need prowled my spine, begging me to move.

To take her right.

Those eyes met mine, so intense, that feeling gripping, sinking all the way inside.

She looked up at me like maybe I might be her sun, the way she was mine, her voice scratchy when she said, "You always take my breath away."

My forehead dropped to hers. "Fuck . . . Nikki . . . Sunshine."

She splayed her hands out wide across my back, and I was gathering her in my arms, getting her as close as I could get her. I began to move, measured rocks of my hips as I took her.

Stroke after stroke.

Friction and gravity.

Her whimpers struck the air, and I held her, took her slow and deep while I kissed her like the treasure she was.

While I cherished and adored.

Because Rex was right.

We never knew how many days we'd be given, and I'd already wasted too many.

Her breaths came harder. "Please." It was a prayer from her mouth.

I shifted back to kneeling, taking her with me, and the girl began to ride me like that was what she'd been made to do.

Motherfucker, if it wasn't the most magical thing.

Her body stretched out like a sensuous band, head tipped back, her tits in my face.

Desperate hands yanked at my hair. I licked at one of those dark nipples, swirling it with my tongue and sucking it into my mouth.

I pressed my thumb to her clit, winding her up.

She whimpered, "Yes."

It was like the girl cast a single-word spell.

Yes.

She went off, an orgasm streaking through every cell of her body. Energy and light.

She writhed on me, walls clutching my dick so damned perfectly.

Taking every inch of me hostage.

Held by this girl.

The way I'd always been.

Yes.

Bliss.

It exploded, splintering out.

Blinding my eyes and battering my senses.

I came with a shout that I released right at the center of that giving heart.

She sagged her sweat-slicked body against mine, and I burrowed my face in the sweet essence that radiated from her neck.

Nikki sighed, my name her breath.

Couldn't believe that I was holding her like this. I tightened my arms around her waist and held her as we drifted on that energy that swam around us.

Soft, lulling waves.

Comfort and all things right.

Light.

Yes.

Yes.
I'd give this girl my life.

Ollie

"Someone has some explaining to do."

Couldn't stop the roll of my eyes as I climbed into Rex's huge-ass work truck.

"You think I could at least get in before you start riding my ass? Might be just as easy to roll down your window and shout it at me where I'm standing on the sidewalk."

Drive-by style.

When I'd gotten his texts at the ass crack of dawn, claiming that he needed my help with a project, I knew I was in trouble. Wasn't like I wasn't asking for it, mauling Nikki on the dance floor right in front of our friends before I'd dragged her off like some kind of madman.

I just couldn't hold it back a second longer.

That band had stretched too thin before it had finally snapped.

Rex kicked up a smirk that he punted my direction. "Pretty sure it's not me doing the whole ass riding."

Punk had the nerve to waggle his brows.

I shook my head, but there was no stopping my grin as I hopped inside his truck and snapped the seat belt into place.

Rex pulled away from Olive's, the diesel engine loud as he accelerated down the road.

From the side, I looked at him. "So, did you actually need help this morning or did you just need to say I told you so to my face, sooner rather than later?"

Low laughter escaped him. Totally at my expense. "Little of both, man, a little of both."

We headed out of town toward the old buildings on Row that he and Broderick would be turning into luxury condos and God knew what else.

It still impressed the hell out of me that my best friend, who had been little more than a handyman, had taken the small construction company and built it into a massive enterprise.

Each project got bigger and more complicated. Dude was leaving his stamp all over this small city.

"You don't have a crew for this shit? It's barely nine in the morning, on a Sunday, mind you."

He kneaded the steering wheel as he made a right, hitting the two-lane road that led out of the north end of town. Taking another right up about half a mile would lead to the lower lake where we'd spent all our time as kids, and the old warehouses that lined the river up on Row were about a mile up from that.

"Yeah, yeah. I know, your lazy ass always wants to sleep half the day away."

That was not the case this morning.

This morning, the only thing I'd wanted to do was stay wrapped up in Nikki instead of leaving her naked and twisted in my sheets. The girl so damned gorgeous, all lit up in the emerging morning light.

Rex leered over at me like the punk he was, pure suggestion bleeding from his words. "You do look a little tired this morning. Didn't get a whole lot of sleep last night?"

I chuckled under my breath.

Asshole.

"Nah . . . didn't get a whole lot of sleep last night," I admitted, fingers scraping at the seam of my jeans, needing to do something with my hands. Agitation and residual need clamored through me, leaving my insides scrambled.

My mind was still trying to catch up with what had gone down last night.

Thing was, my heart was already there.

The girl inevitable.

Should have known it all along.

After we'd finally given in?

It was on.

Nikki and I had gone at it again and again. Hard and rough and tender and soft and every-fucking-thing between.

We'd collapse in each other's arms, drifting off for a half hour or so before one of us would, once again, be seeking the other in the night.

Had taken all I had to peel myself away from her sleeping form when my phone had lit up with a string of texts, Rex prodding me out of that place that had become a sanctuary.

"About time, man," he said with a harsh shake of his head.

Didn't even know if I should deny it or play dumb.

He was right.

It was about time.

"So, what changed?" he attempted, stealing a glimpse at me before he looked back out through the windshield.

Trees hugged the narrow road, whooshing by as he wound deeper into the area where the woods became dense, giving way to the tall, thin, spindly trees that made up the forest that surrounded the lake and river.

"Not sure what you mean."

Deflecting.

Sometimes that was all I had because I didn't think I had an answer for that.

"Are you kidding me?" Rex laughed an incredulous sound and gave a harsh shake of his head. "You've been tiptoeing around this thing with Nikki for years. Don't act like you haven't wanted her all this time. Second she'd walked into the room, your spine would go stiff. Willing to put down bets your dick did, too."

I rubbed my hand down my beard, taunting him. "Looking at my dick now?"

"You wish, asshole. They don't make glasses that thick."

"Now who's wishing?" I tossed back.

Both of us laughed for a second before we fell into silence.

"Seriously," he prodded, "what changed?"

Could feel him pushing, edging me a direction I wasn't sure I was ready to go.

I blinked through the protective anger that wound back through me when I really evaluated it.

Yeah.

I'd felt something coming.

Something wicked and dark.

But there'd been a tipping point.

"Finding her apartment that way . . . knowing she could have been in danger . . . that someone might have hurt her?"

My teeth ground so hard I could hear my jaw popping in my ears. "It . . . brought everything crashing down. Turns out the punk had been leaving notes on her car, too. Just the idea of someone hurting her made me want to hunt down any fucker who even looked at her wrong and silence that threat forever. I guess that was the moment I realized I could no longer stand the thought of her being anywhere else than with me."

He blew out a strained breath. "So, this wasn't you pulling any of that one-night bullshit? You know Nikki doesn't deserve that, and you know she wants more than that."

He slowed and took a right onto the bumpy dirt road that wound down the hill.

The glittering river stretched out below us, trees reaching for the sky like they were offering up prayers to the sun.

In the distance, the roofs of the old buildings jutted up through the cover of the branches, a reminder that this area had once not been so desolate.

My chest clutched when we wound around a corner that opened to a field of purple blazing stars that swayed in the breeze. A million memories slammed me. One after one.

"This way."

"Follow me."

"We'll be together forever."

Sydney's sweet voice as she'd run and explored and looked at the world with so much wonder in her eyes. Nikki and I in tow.

I pushed out a sigh. "Why do you think I've been ignoring it for so long? Last thing I want to do is hurt her. Makes me insane to hold something so precious and know that, chances are, in the end, I'm going to crush it in my hands."

"And why would you do that?" Wasn't so much of a question as a challenge.

I looked out over the landscape. "Men are prone to destroying beautiful things."

He swallowed hard. "Maybe. Unless they finally open their damned eyes and see that beauty for what it's worth. Make the choice to build it up. Protect it and keep it."

Unease wound through me, and I swore my throat was closing tight.

Didn't want to go there.

But Nikki deserved for me to.

To stop fucking hiding.

"What happens when you want to protect it and fail anyway?" It was a wheeze I forced out. My inadequacy a glaring defeat.

Rex came to a stop in a small clearing that had been made.

Equipment and machinery had already been delivered and was set up within a temporary chain-link fence as they prepared for construction.

He hesitated for a moment, squeezing the wheel, staring out the windshield to the splintered wood and crumbling stone of the weathered building. "We do our best, Ollie. We live and we love. We cherish and we hold."

He killed the engine, set his hand on the latch, and looked over at me. "We fight with everything we have, even when we know we might lose."

He clicked open the door. "We do it because we can't do anything else. Because we love so hard, loving is the only thing we can do. Rynna and my kids? I love them so damned much, Ollie. With every single thing I have. Never thought I'd get that chance, and I'd be nothing but a bastard and a fool not to recognize it."

His message slammed me on all sides. Pointed and demanding. Forcing me to evaluate the way I'd been living.

He climbed out and moved toward the bank of the river, staring out over it. I got out and followed.

"Do you remember playing here? Growing up? Running wild?" There was something somber in his tone.

"Of course, I remember."

Pretty much had spent the last fourteen years living in the past.

"We were all close."

I glanced at him, no clue what had climbed into the tone of his voice.

"Yeah. Not many people get lucky enough to grow up the way we did. Remain friends the way we have."

Saw the way the muscles in his arms twitched and bunched, apprehension in his stance. "I need you to know you aren't alone in the regrets, either, man. That you don't shoulder that alone."

A gust of doubt rustled through, my nerve endings zapping with unease.

"You're wrong, Rex. She was my sister. My responsibility."

Wasn't trying to be a dick. It was just the cold, bitter truth.

His eyes flashed in a kind of grief I didn't quite understand. "It was my fault, too. I was there that night. Remember? You think I don't wish I could go back and change everything? I'd give anything to. But I can't. And neither can you. Both of us have to accept that."

"I was responsible for her." My words were a low, harsh rasp.

He dropped his head, his hands landing on his hips as he struggled with what to say as he stared at the ground. "Ollie—"

"Just don't, Rex." Shooting my hand out between us, I cut him off before he could get whatever bullshit he was going to say out of his mouth. Didn't need another person to tell me it wasn't my fault when I knew full well that it was. "I don't need a therapist. I need a friend. That's it."

Something moved through his eyes.

Regret and . . . guilt.

Glaring guilt.

I tried to process it.

He blew out a breath toward his boots. "Fine. Just forget it."

Good damned idea.

Yesterday was hard enough without Rex trying to make it more difficult. The worry about Nikki had only compounded it.

Since the threat was gone, I just wanted to forget it all.

Push it into the past where it all belonged.

Question was if I was capable of that.

I forced some lightness into my words. "Ready to tell me why you had to go and drag me out of my bed when I'd finally gotten Nikki into it?"

He laughed a little, shooting me a grin. "Sorry about that."

"Not cool, man. You owe me big."

"Maybe this will suffice."

"What's that?"

With his chin, he gestured toward the row of run-down buildings. They'd been near falling down when we'd played in them, and time sure hadn't improved them. They were covered in graffiti, there was garbage everywhere, and the frames were sagging toward the ground like they didn't have the will to stand for much longer.

"Back building will become upscale condos, one of which will go to Nikki. First two will be what becomes the hotel and shops."

He looked down the riverbank before he eyed me carefully. "Plan to put in a couple of restaurants and a bar. Broderick and I want you to open a second Olive's here."

Stunned, I stared at him, minutes or an hour passing, waiting for the punch line. "You're serious," I finally managed when he didn't say anything.

"Hell, yeah, I'm serious. You know Olive's is the best bar in Gingham Lakes. Brody plans to make this a destination. Only the best. So, of course, it only makes sense to add the best bar to the list of attractions. He's funding the upfront costs, but you'll have shares in the entire development."

"You want me to partner with you and Brody?" Still wasn't making sense of it, shock lurching through my senses.

"It's not like we weren't partnered on Olive's to begin with."

"Yeah . . . but I hired RG Construction to redo the building."

No risk on his end.

He looked over at me. "You act like you haven't been investing in this city. Taking failing businesses and breathing new life in to them."

"But it's always been my money on the line."

If I failed, it was on me.

It's your fault.

I trusted you.

You were supposed to take care of her.

You promised, you'd take care of her.

It should have been me. It should have been me.

In silence, we both stood there while I contemplated. Warred with all the reasons I shouldn't do this.

I inhaled sharply, filling my lungs with the scent of the river and damp earth and possibility. "You guys really trust me to be a partner?"

"Wouldn't ask you if we didn't." Rex started back for the truck before he paused to look at me from over his shoulder. "Think maybe the only person you need to prove to that you can be trusted is yourself."

I stood there, staring at him as he hopped back into the truck.

Business done.

My attention darted between him and the old buildings, imagining what this place would look like one day, while Rex just sat in the truck, giving me time.

Finally, I hefted out a breath and strode back for the truck. I hopped inside, slamming the door shut as I said, "I'm in."

He started the engine. "Good."

I scrubbed a sweaty palm on the thigh of my jeans. "And don't count on Nikki needing that condo."

Rex laughed, loud and with a grin. "Had a feeling you might say that."

twenty-seven

Ollie

The low grumble of my bike filled my ears as I eased into one of the parking spaces in front of Pepper's Pies. The damned grin plastered on my face was so big that there was no chance I could wipe it off.

Inside, heads turned at the sound of my rumbling bike, but the only one that mattered was the girl who stood in front of one of the booths right by the window, her head jerking up and those eyes meeting with mine through the glass.

My chest tightened.

That feeling hitting me hard.

So intense that I could feel it riding through my veins. Itching through me. Same way as I was itching to get my girl on the back of my bike and those long legs wrapped around my waist.

Kicking the stand and killing the engine, I swung my leg over the side just as Nikki was peeking her head outside.

A smile danced on her pretty face. "What are you doing here?"

I glanced at my watch. "You get off at two."

"And?" It was a playful challenge.

"And I missed you. You have a problem with that?" I all but growled, stalking her way, looping an arm around her waist and tugging her against me as she stepped all the way out onto the sidewalk.

Hands clutching my shoulders, she bent back, swaying as she smiled up at me. "No, Beast. I definitely don't have a problem with that."

"Good," I told her. "Go get your stuff."

"Bossy," she tossed back as she started toward the door.

I swatted her sweet ass. "You have no idea."

She yelped and then giggled. "Why do I get the feeling you're going to take all kinds of pleasure in educating me on that fact?"

A smirk caught on one side of my mouth. "Maybe you do have an idea."

Her laugh was low.

Sexy.

"Oh, Ollie. We're gonna have so much fun."

My smile went soft.

Yeah.

We were. And we'd wasted too much time, and I was so over that. "Hurry up and get that sweet body back to me."

"I need to change," she said as she was stepping back inside.

"I'll wait."

Those pink lips twisted in a teasing pout. "You'd better."

Like I was going anywhere.

Not without her.

Five minutes later, she was bursting back out the door, pretty much skipping her way over to me where I was waiting by my bike.

She looked so young when she was like this.

Free and excited.

"Come here," I told her, taking her hand and guiding her to stand between my knees. I situated the helmet I'd brought for her on her head, tucking some of those warm, honeyed locks back away from her face.

The girl's breaths came shorter just from that simple touch.

And that's what this felt like.

Simple.

Simple and complicated and perfect.

Like it'd been coming all along.

Or maybe it'd just been set to pause, and we had to pick up where we'd left off, even though I knew it couldn't be as *simple* as forgetting all those hurtful years stuck in the middle of us.

Only thing I could do now was make up for them.

"Where are we going?" she asked, eyes glinting with a thrill.

"You'll see," I told her, moving to straddle my bike and taking her with me.

"Ah, come on, Ollie. That's totally not fair. I want to know." Her voice was filled with laughter.

She slid in behind me, the insides of her thighs pressing to the outsides of mine.

Electricity.

It zinged and shook.

A chuckle rumbled free as she wrapped those arms around me. I patted her hands that locked to my stomach. "Don't you trust me?"

I could feel the draw of her breath, the way she snuggled as close as she could get, holding on tight.

Her words dropped so low I could barely hear them. "Yes, Ollie. I trust you. I trust you more than anyone else."

Trust.

It was the first time I wanted her to give me hers.

Swallowing any heaviness down, I kicked over the engine, rolled my bike back, my feet guiding us, before I hit the street.

I kept our speed low.

Controlled.

Careful of my girl who was hugging me from behind. Her heart beating into my back. Hard and wild and drumming with passion.

Washing me in that warmth.

We headed through town, taking a couple of turns, before I hit the road that led out toward the river and lakes. The air shifted as we left the traffic behind, full, lush trees growing up at the sides of the two-lane road and closing us in.

It felt like an embrace.

A welcome back to the place where we always should have been. I passed by the turn-off to the lake.

We'd go there one day. To our sacred place. But this felt too raw and new to dive so deeply into the past.

I'd give us time. Time to adjust.

My bike glided around a swooping curve in the road.

Swore, it felt like we were flying.

Nothing but the feel of the wind and the sound of my bike and the aura of us to fill our senses.

Suspended.

Taken.

Funny because I'd never felt so close to home.

I slowed when the dirt road approached, and I could feel her shiver of excitement that zipped through her body when I began to wind down toward the river.

We curved and wound, rounding a corner, and that same endless expanse of purple blazing stars came into view where they grew along the riverbank.

Instead of continuing on to the old buildings were Rex and Broderick would be developing—where I'd be opening up a second bar, which still blew my mind—I took a right on what was nothing more than an overgrown, bumpy trail down toward the river. It rippled a glittering blue.

I eased to a stop beneath the big tree where we used to play.

Its thick branches were stretched out like protection.

A canopy of security.

The old rope swing we'd swung from a thousand times as kids was now frayed where it hung from one of the branches that reached over the river, swaying in the light breeze, in time with the spikey blazing stars that poked up through the high grasses.

I cut the engine.

Peace covered us.

The only sounds were the gurgling river and the thunder of our hearts.

For a few minutes, we just sat there. Taking it in.

Finally, I took her hand, and a shiver of nervous anticipation rolled through her. Like she wasn't quite sure why we were there or what my intentions were.

I started to walk backward, tugging her along. "Come here, I want to show you something."

A giggle slipped from between those flirty lips.

So easy and sweet.

Carrying on the wind. "You do, huh?" she teased. "What exactly do you want to show me? I know your style of show and tell, Oliver Preston."

Laughter rumbled in my chest. "I'll show you plenty of that later, sweet girl, but right now, I had something else in mind."

Her brows rose. "Really? You have something else in mind? Tell me why I don't believe you. I don't even know how I'm walkin' right now. You might as well keep me tied to your bed."

Lust twisted through me.

Hard.

Fast.

Couldn't even come close to stopping the visions that assaulted me with just the thought of getting inside this girl again.

Over the last week, I'd taken her over and over. Every second I could get her.

"That sounds like a great idea. I knew you were a smart one."

Another giggle. "Smart? I call it needy."

"I like you needy and begging my name."

"Is that so?" She was stumbling along as I hauled her toward the tree, a smile written on every inch of her face.

Hell.

I could see it written all over her body.

That rail-thin body I'd had to pretend wasn't close to my taste so I could try to rid her from my mind for all those years. Going after girls who were exactly her opposite. Praying when I closed my eyes, I wouldn't see her face.

Impossible.

She was the only thing I'd ever seen.

"That's so. I promise to make you beg it a little bit later, but right now, I want you to sit right here."

I took her by the outside of her shoulders and led her to the exact spot, urging her to sit down.

"What are you doing?" she laughed through the words, shaking her head by following along.

She settled on the small incline under the shade of the tree.

I took a step back, my attention rapt.

"Perfect," I said.

She rocked her knees that were bent, tucking her bottom lip between her teeth like she was both shy and relishing the way I was looking at her.

Without a doubt, I looked like a starving man. All I wanted was to eat her all over again.

Consume and devour.

I backed up a few more steps so I could better take her in.

"What are you looking at?" she finally asked, her voice breathy from that connection that sizzled through the heated air.

Two of us alive in the other.

How the hell had I lived without this?

Without her?

"You."

"I know you're *looking* at me, but why?"

A grin pulled at one side of my mouth.

"That's exactly where you were. Right there."

I could never forget it.

She frowned. "Ollie, what in the world are you talking about?"

I pointed at her. "That's where you were the day I finally admitted it."

Her brows drew closer, and she minimally shook her head in question.

I took a slow step back her direction. "When I admitted to myself that you were something more than my best friend. When I realized you made me feel different."

I turned my gaze away, lifting it toward the wind as I let some of the memories pummel me. Hit me and slam me.

Instead of hating them, I welcomed them.

Finally, I looked back at her. "You were whispering with Sydney. She said something about a guy, and I just knew it. Knew it. That you had a boyfriend or someone had kissed you."

I took another step forward, and she sucked in a shivered breath.

Energy pulsed.

"I'll never forget the way that felt, Nikki. The way my stomach balled up in a fist and it felt like my heart was gonna bust right out of my chest. I played it off that I was just looking out for you, but it was more."

One step closer, and I dropped to my knees in front of her, my hands going to her knees. I palmed them, dipped my head in closer, my mouth an inch from hers "You were more."

She reached out and cupped the side of my face, tenderness moving through her expression as she studied me. Her thumb traced along the hollow of my eye, and her head tipped in emphasis. "I think you were always more. I just didn't know what that meant yet."

I lunged at her, tackling her to the soft earth. She gasped and yelped and then laughed.

That sweet, sweet sound floated on the wind.

Twisted through me.

I pushed up onto my hands and stared down at her. The girl who'd always been my forever.

There she was, all laid out on a bed of blazing stars.

Purple a halo around her head.

I reached out and plucked one, twirled the stem between my thumb and index finger. I brushed the tip down her cheek.

Softly.

Her lips parted on a sigh.

"Did you know the first time I saw you, what I noticed was your eyes? I thought they were the exact same color as these flowers, but like they were floatin' through the air. Transparent. Like I could see right inside of you. I won't ever forget that moment, either."

Her fingertips scratched through my beard. "I don't think I could ever forget a moment with you, Oliver Preston."

I kissed at the tips of her fingers, wanting to take in every bit of her.

The movement was almost playful, but my words were somber. "We've got a lot of bad memories, Nikki."

She nodded slow. "Yeah. But we have a lot of good ones, too. That's what makes up life. The good and the bad. We couldn't have one without the other. We couldn't share a life without experiencing both sides of it."

"That what you want? To share a life with me?" My voice was gruff.

"I always wanted that."

"Good," I said, making her squeal when I suddenly reached around her and flipped our positions. She straddled me at the waist, her hands on my chest, all that hair blowing around her, whipped by the wind.

Stirring our spirits.

I tightened my hold. "Don't think you could get rid of me if you tried."

She grinned. "And why would I want to go and do something like that? Not when all my matchmaking skills have finally started to work in my favor."

"Oh, you think you're responsible for this, too, huh?"

She widened her eyes. "Um, hello, I am the Orgasm Fairy."

"And who's the one giving them?" I teased. "Guess I'll have to stop handing them out like they're candy and then we can decide who's really responsible."

Nikki dipped down, pressing her mouth to mine.

All kinds of possessive.

Just the way I wanted her.

Then I could feel the weight of her grin. "Don't you dare. You owe me all the orgasms. All. Of. Them. Forever."

"Greedy girl."

"Accept it. You created a monster."

"I thought you said I was the monster. Ogre, to be correct."

"I told you . . . you're my beast. Get used to it."

I laughed.

A laugh that came from my belly, but I was pretty sure it originated in the depths of me. In that dark place that was somehow feeling a fraction lighter.

Like maybe I was finally letting a little of me go.

Didn't mean I wouldn't still battle demons.

But what Nikki and I had going?

Maybe it was stronger.

That's what I wanted to be.

Strong for her.

Right for her.

I brushed my knuckles down the defined curve of her face, and she leaned into my touch. "Everything I have, I want to give to you. I belong to you, Nikki."

And I wasn't going to let anything get in the way of that.

An hour later, I weaved back into town, Nikki clinging to me where she sat on the back of my bike.

Wasn't sure anything had ever felt so right.

I rumbled to a stop in front of the old market that we used to come to all the time as kids, saving up coins so we could go in to buy ice cream or candy or sodas.

The second I stopped, Nikki was climbing off and going through the buckle of the helmet, grinning back at me as she headed for the entrance since she'd said she would just run in really quick to grab something to make for us for dinner tonight.

I hopped off, stalking right behind her.

She'd barely made it onto the sidewalk when I snagged her wrist, spun her around, and pinned her to the wall.

Plastered myself against that sweet body.

I kissed her hard.

Tongue gliding against hers.

My hands wrapped up in that honeyed hair.

She released a tiny moan, and I rubbed myself against her, and she was moaning again before she was laughing and pushing me back. "What are you doing, Ollie? You're gonna get us arrested for indecency."

"The only thing indecent around here is how hot you look."

"Ollie," she admonished, a flush lighting up those cheeks.

Sunshine.

"What? My girlfriend is smoking hot."

Her eyes went wide.

So yeah, it was the first time I'd said it in what felt like a hundred years.

I'd said it before.

But I'd never gotten to claim it.

I grabbed her hand and started leading her toward the entrance, my voice lifting a little louder than it probably needed to be.

Strike that.

It was completely, one hundred percent necessary.

"My girlfriend is hot!" I shouted.

"Ollie."

Nikki's head whipped around, wondering what attention we'd gathered, but she was giggling under her breath. She struggled to keep up as I hauled her inside and grabbed a cart.

I started pushing it down the first aisle.

"I thought I was just running in by myself?" she asked.

"What, I just wanted to be near my girlfriend."

Yep, the words were elevated again.

A woman who was probably only a handful of years older than us cut us a glance.

I totally ignored it. "What are we having for dinner? I'm going to need to hang down in the bar for a few hours to make sure things are running smoothly, but I won't stay too long."

"Chicken and potatoes. And you don't have to take off more time, Ollie. You've barely been down there all week."

"What? I just want to be with my girlfriend." The last I all but shouted.

An old lady blushed, peeking our way, her husband grinning wide.

"My girlfriend is gorgeous, isn't she?" I asked them as they ambled by. I swept an arm at Nikki like she was a prize.

That's exactly what she was.

"Sure is," the old guy agreed, "almost as pretty as mine."

His wife shushed him with a blush, and I was grinning so fucking hard I thought I was gonna break my face.

Nikki's smile was just about as big, but she was shaking her head, tugging at my hand like she needed to get me out of there before I caused any more of a scene. "Are you insane? You're going to get us kicked out of here."

"Wouldn't be the first time," I told her.

"Uh, yeah, and the last time I had to have my mama come pick me up at the station because you and Rex had knocked that whole display over playing chase. Whole wall of glass mayonnaise jars smashed on the ground. It wasn't pretty."

"But you're pretty," I shot at her.

"Ollie." She was smiling as she searched my eyes, clearly wondering what had gotten into me.

She had.

She so absolutely had.

I yanked her close to me. "I want everyone to know it, Nikki. That you're mine. No more hiding."

She set both of those hands on my face and hiked up on her tiptoes. She pressed the gentlest kiss to my lips. "No more hiding."

"C'mere," I told her, voice going soft as I wound her in front of me, wrapping my arms around her and taking the cart again.

She giggled and sank against my chest, my mouth planting kisses along the side of her jaw as we wandered down the aisle. "Mine," I whispered against her temple.

"Nikki?"

The voice stopped both of us in our tracks, and our attention jerked to the source.

There was Sammie coming the other direction, a baby sleeping in her arms and her husband pushing a cart beside her.

Bottled rage rumbled in that ugly, dark space inside me. I knew it wasn't gone. There were some things that didn't just go away.

Like the fury I felt that some asshole had hurt her in some way.

Nikki had confessed to me a few days ago that she was having trouble sleeping because she was so worried about her sister. That her sister hadn't called her or come to her, and Nikki was fearing she wouldn't be able to sit idle for much longer.

Worried her sister might be in trouble.

Surprise streaked across Sammie's face as she took in the two of us.

Nikki was still caged between the cart and me, my head barely angling toward them, two of us about as close as we could get in a public place.

I could feel the strain return to Nikki, and she unwound herself from my hold and cleared her throat.

Sammie actually grinned.

Wry and knowing.

Eyes so close to the same as Nikki's were locked on me for a beat before she turned her attention to Nikki. "Looks like we have some catching up to do."

A nervous giggle escaped from Nikki, and she fidgeted with her hair, trying to straighten it which was impossible after the ride on the bike. She peeked back at me. "Yeah, we definitely have some catching up to do."

Nikki seemed to shake the surprise off and stepped toward her sister, lowering her voice. "How have you been?"

Awareness moved through Sammie's expression, and my eyes were locked on her husband.

Studying.

Searching.

Watching for any sort of reaction that might be off.

Sammie glanced over at her husband.

There was no warning for her to keep quiet. No hardness. Just a soft understanding in his eyes.

The anger that threatened to boil inside me eased back into a simmer. I was pretty sure this guy wasn't the one responsible for whatever Sammie was going through.

Sammie turned back to Nikki. "I've been good."

Swore, a thousand unsaid words were offered between the two of them.

Nikki suddenly reached out. "Gimme that baby."

Light laughter filtered from Sammie. "Bossy."

"I'm your big sister. It's your job to listen to me."

"You wish," Sammie tossed back at her, but she was passing a sleeping bundle off to Nikki.

Nikki took the baby, a soft sound leaving her mouth as she shifted the tiny thing and set her against her chest. The little girl's head turned to the side, still sleeping, face scrunched up as she snuggled against Nikki's warmth.

Nikki bounced her.

Sometimes it was a little too much when your connection to someone was so intense.

Because I could feel her spirit doing some crazy thing. Making the air seem too thin.

She looked up at me with those indigo eyes.

Adoring.

Hugging the baby to her chest, she whispered up at me. "Ollie . . . this is my niece, Penelope. Isn't she incredible?"

Her smile was so soft I felt it cut right through the center of me.

Tentatively, I reached out and ran my knuckle down the baby's soft, plump cheek. "She's beautiful."

Nikki looked back down, her voice not intended for me. "She's the most beautiful thing I've ever seen."

I stepped back, watching her as she rocked and cooed and pressed kisses to the crown of Penelope's head before she reluctantly passed her back to Sammie.

The sisters embraced with the baby between them, the two of them whispering words, ones I knew were of encouragement.

Because that was Nikki.

Spreading her light.

Giving.
Doing her best to pour a little good into this wicked world.

twenty-eight

Nikki

I stood at the wall of windows that looked out on the city spread out below me. It was nothing but a maze of twinkling lights—streets and neighborhoods and cars.

Behind me, the door creaked open.

At the sound, my spirit jumped into a frenzy, instant and eager as it stretched out for him.

Slowly, I shifted to look at Ollie, who had frozen in the doorway.

My breath hitched.

Caught up in his potency.

He stood stock still. I thought maybe he couldn't believe I was standing there any more than I could, unable to fathom he was coming home.

And he was coming home to me.

"Are you already finished?" I asked, flashing him a smile as I turned the rest of the way around and moved into the kitchen. "I thought you decided you needed to stay a little longer tonight?"

He stepped into the loft and clicked the door shut behind him. "Think I was missin' someone."

"Is that so?" I went to the stove where I was making a lemon garlic chicken and roasted potatoes. I peeked over at him, lifting a shoulder as I did. "And just who was it you were missin'?"

So what if I put a little flirt into it? This was my man we were talking about.

He stalked across the space, coming right up behind me.

Towering.

Eclipsing.

He was all too quick to tug me against that wall of muscle. The man was so big, I could wear him like a blanket.

He gathered up my hair in one hand so he could run his mouth along the sensitive flesh of my neck. "You," he murmured.

Chills flashed. Streaking across my skin. That feeling took a dive directly in that pool of desire that had taken up permanent residence low in my belly.

"Mmm, that's good," I whispered, bringing the wooden spoon to my mouth to test the sauce. "Because I was thinking about you."

"You'd better be." I could feel his smile at the side of my neck.

"Like I ever stop. How was it downstairs?" I asked.

"Busy."

"And you're here?"

"It's where you are, isn't it?"

Butterflies.

They should have been impossible after all this time. After everything we'd been through. Yet, there I stood, feeling like that fifteen-year-old girl who'd been kissed for the first time under a waterfall.

"Besides, I was pretty sure I could smell you making dinner all the way down there. Stomach was growling."

He kissed up and down my neck. "Among other things."

"Insatiable."

"I thought you told me earlier that you wanted all the orgasms?"

It plucked a laugh free. "You have me there."

"See, we're completely on the same page. Think we totally have what it takes to make this work."

I could feel the tease tinting every single one of his words.

Today had been bliss.

It just kept getting better and better.

"Want a taste?" I asked, spooning some sauce onto a spoon and lifting it to his mouth.

He groaned when it touched those full, full lips, framed by that beard that turned me on more than should be possible.

Everything about him was sexy.

That monstrous body and those knowing eyes and those demanding hands.

And God . . . that sound he was making at the back of his throat when he tasted the sauce.

"That's it, you're tryin' to ruin me, aren't you? Knowing my girl is up here, waiting on me while I'm downstairs working. Then I show up, and you're wearing *this*."

He flattened his palms on the short slip of a nightgown I was wearing. Silky and trimmed in lace, slits up the sides that were entirely unnecessary considering it barely covered my bottom in the first place.

I knew Ollie would love it.

His teeth nipped at my earlobe. Catching and releasing.

Didn't mean I wasn't completely ensnared.

I peeked back at him, unable to stop the grin that pulled to one side of my mouth. "Someone once told me the way to a man's heart was through his stomach. Well . . . that and rough, sweaty, amazing sex."

I bumped back into him and had to stifle a groan.

He was already hard and needy for me.

Was it wrong that I loved it?

That I reveled in the fact that one brush of a hand, one look, and we were both laid bare?

A rumble rolled from his chest and slid through me like a caress. "I like this someone. Tell them I approve."

I giggled. "You can thank my grandma."

Easy laughter rippled from his lips. "Oh God . . . your grandma is really gonna want to kick my ass now, isn't she? God knows she always wanted to back in the day. She'd see me coming down the road, and the first thing I would hear was her shouting from the porch that she was watching me."

"That's because you were nothin' but trouble."

Those massive arms tightened around my waist, and he nuzzled his face under my jaw. "Gave her plenty of ammunition to hate me."

I tsked quietly, loving the feel of his mouth where he was kissing on the cap of my shoulder. "She loved you."

Obviously, she still did.

"Hardly."

I stilled a little, hoping he'd hear the truth of my words. "You have it all wrong again, Ollie. You're impossible not to love."

His hands slipped down to the fronts of my thighs, riding up. "Could use a little of that lovin' right now."

I shivered and tried not to moan. "Think we better start on the stomach part before we get too distracted."

He ran his nose through my hair.

Chills scattered.

"This kind of distraction is worth it, don't you think, Sunshine?"

My knees went weak when he spread his hands out across my belly, the feel of him and the silky fabric gliding through the center of me.

"I think you're gonna need your strength," I breathed.

Another growl.

"You're in so much trouble, Nikki Walters. So much trouble."

"I can't wait," I told him.

Peeling himself away, he pulled two plates from the cabinet and poured a glass of wine for me and a scotch for himself. We plated our food and moved to the long high-top table that took up most of his kitchen space.

The view breathtaking.

The city and the night and the man sitting angled right next to me.

We ate and laughed.

We drank and reminisced.

Old bonds strengthening and new ones forming.

We tiptoed around the mention of Sydney, ignoring how it seemed as if she was right there in the middle of us. I couldn't help but feel she kept coming closer and closer. Filling up the space between us and forcing us to look at the things that might be a true threat.

The things that would rip us apart.

I'd never been so sure of it than when Ollie suddenly palmed my knee under the table.

Though this time, it was different than the flirty, playful touches. A current of severity moved through it, and his voice went hoarse. "I missed you, Nikki."

"You said that," I teased, going back to what he'd said when he'd come upstairs.

He shook his head, refusing the lightness, and I knew he was stepping into the rough terrain we'd avoided.

Both of us knowing it was there.

Underfoot.

Unsure if we could navigate it.

"No, Nikki. I *missed* you. All these years, I *missed* you. So bad that I could physically feel another piece of myself missing."

His words shivered through me like the warmest breeze, and he reached over and cupped the side of my face in one of his big, protective hands.

"I think that's what missing someone means. They're missing from you, not just from your life, but from your heart. And nothing, no matter how hard you try, really works or fully functions because you're missing that piece."

Moisture gathered in my eyes, and emotion rushed to thicken at the base of my throat. I covered his hand with mine and pressed him closer.

Wanting to erase everything between us.

Space and time and questions.

"I know, Ollie. I know exactly what you're saying. Because I was missing that piece, too."

He swallowed hard, his throat bobbing beneath his beard. I could feel the switch. The way every muscle in his body tightened.

Edged in grief and radiating with hope. "And Sydney . . ."

Her name struck the air like a sword. A whirring slice right down the middle, cutting us in two.

"She's always gonna be missing from me, Nikki. There's always gonna be that piece that isn't entirely whole. I've got to accept that I'm never going to know what happened to her. Accept that part and try to let it go the best that I can. Because I want to be whole for you."

Trembling, I set my hand on his face. "I would never ask you to let her go. All I can ask you to do is love me in the middle of it. Forgive yourself. Forgive me. Forgive *us*. Because I know Sydney would have forgiven us for falling in love. All she wanted was to experience life. All of us. She would never ask you to give that up."

His entire body flinched, and his eyes slammed closed. "I'm trying, Nikki. I'm trying to believe that."

"I don't want to be your sin."

Draining the rest of his third scotch, he looked away from me and out over the city.

Turmoil rolled through him.

A blackout.

He turned that sapphire gaze back on me. "I saw the look on your face today."

I blinked, unsure of what he was getting at.

His tongue darted out to wet his lips. "When you were holding Penelope."

My spirit thrashed in its confines.

"You still want that? A family? Three kids and a husband and a little house?" His voice cracked when he said it.

Pain breaking free.

My eyes could no longer hold back. A tear slipped down my cheek. "I do. Someday, if I get lucky enough, I want that."

I wouldn't lie.

Not to him.

His forehead dropped to mine, and I reached out and held him by both sides of the face, my voice a quiet whisper, "But I would never push that on you."

His breaths came shorter, panted into my mouth. "I . . . don't know if I can give you that, Nikki. I don't know what kind of father I would be. If I could be trusted to be the kind of man that a kid would deserve."

My heart broke a little more, overflowing from the crack.

This man.

I pressed my lips to his.

Gently.

"You are the best man I know."

His head shook against my forehead. "Not even close, but I'm going to try. I'm going to try to be right. To protect you and take care of you. I want to be enough."

"All I want is for you to love me."

He didn't tell me that he did.

I knew he wasn't ready for that.

All of this would take time.

I wasn't fool enough to think that gulf that had roiled between us for years would suddenly evaporate.

He needed to learn to trust himself before he could fully give himself to me.

He pulled me to straddle his lap.

Energy flashed.

A bright light through the swimming darkness.

My heart raced, a thudding drum, drum, drum, a match to his.

He watched me in the shadows, as if I might disappear. He pulled the bottle of scotch from the table and chugged from it, that stare never leaving mine.

His gaze hot.

Feral.

Verging on wild.

So different from when he'd been so carefree earlier today. As if him seeing me with Penelope had unlocked something inside him.

Slammed him directly into our reality.

I guess I'd felt a little of that shift, too.

Holding my niece with him looking at me, my sister there with her secret that had brimmed so fiercely between us I could taste it.

Riding on her tongue.

Desperate to be set free and held back by her shame.

I could only pray she would open up to me so she could heal.

The way I wanted Ollie to heal.

Not to forget.

But to live whole and free in the middle of it.

Right then, he seemed compelled to live in this moment.

Those sapphire eyes intense. Staring at me as if he were racing through time to meet with me.

A shiver rolled through my body.

He tipped the bottle up to me, and I drank from it.

The amber fluid lit a path down my throat and landed directly in that pit of desire that lapped in my belly.

A few droplets trickled out the side of my lips.

Ollie leaned in and licked them clean.

"Ollie," I moaned, the man my seduction.

"What do you need, Sunshine?"

"You . . . I always need you."

Hot hands landed on my bottom, and he squeezed and tucked me against his hard cock.

He nipped at my bottom lip, dragging it between his teeth in a pleasured sort of pain. From the look that took over his expression, I knew he was gonna make good on his warning.

Tonight, I was in so much trouble.

I knew it the second his tongue stroked into my mouth, deep and demanding and desperate.

I fell in, consumed by his presence.

My senses filled with him, the man washing me through, claiming every crevice.

Toasted almonds.

Barrels of oak.

Liquor kisses.

They were dizzying.

Drugging.

Maddening as the intensity increased.

Our energy flared.

Licking out to touch me everywhere.

His fingers sank into my sides as he pushed to his feet, taking me with him. He didn't go far. He settled me on my feet behind the couch that overlooked the city.

I gasped when he planted my hands on the back of the couch.

"Hold on, Sunshine." It was a whisper of warning in my ear, and my knees went weak when those hands were gliding up my thighs, dragging the silky material up and over my bottom.

"Little Tease," he muttered.

Words grit.

He squeezed my bottom in both hands.

"Do you have any idea what you did to me when I came through the door and saw you dressed in this?"

I pressed back into his hold. "I want you to look at me and never forget it."

He groaned a needy sound. "You think that's even possible? Forgetting you?"

His hands swept up my sides, taking the material with them, making me shiver as he ripped it over my head.

He left me bare, save for the scrap of my underwear.

"One look, and I was yours." He curved himself over my body, pushing my chest to the couch.

His mouth was at my ear, heat across my skin. "One touch, and you owned my soul."

I gripped at the cushions, trying to stay standing, to maintain sanity.

But it was far too late.

I'd already completely lost myself in this man.

I could feel him taking pieces of me.

Bit by bit.

Until he held every part of me in the palm of his hand.

Magnetic.

Gravity.

"Don't move," he demanded.

I shook.

I could feel him undressing behind me while I stood there chained by his potency.

A breath ripped from my lungs when he was suddenly on his knees, his nose pressing against the fabric that covered my center.

"You have the sweetest cunt. Pure fucking honey."

My knees knocked, and he held them apart, tongue teasing at the fabric.

"Ollie."

He ripped my underwear free, his hands and fingers spreading my cheeks, his tongue licking up my center.

I gasped, taken by the sensation that assaulted me before I pressed back.

Begging for more.

With Ollie, I wanted it all.

He licked and stroked with his tongue, his hands moving all over my body.

My stomach.

My breasts.

Running down my thighs.

As if he needed all of me, too.

He sucked at my clit, dragging back, his big fingers finding me.

Pressing deep.

It felt like a claiming.

Like something had changed.

Like Ollie was dropping another brick from the walls he'd built around his hardened heart.

He kissed my bottom, teeth raking the skin.

Chills scattered while his fingers drove me higher.

Right up to the edge.

"Ollie," I pled.

"What is it, sweet girl"

"I'm so close." My fingers curled into the cushion. "I need you."

"You have me."

You have me. You have me.

His words tumbled through my spirit.

He was suddenly right there, plastered to my back, his cock nudging at my folds.

"And I want all of you," he said.

I cried out when he took me in a possessive stroke.

He gave me no warning.

No time to adjust.

One hand was wound up in a knot in my hair and his other hand was pressed flat to my lower belly as he began to fuck me.

Fuck me hard and fast and deep.

Our pants filled the dense air.

Needy rasps.

"You . . . you feel so good . . . nothing is better than this . . . you are mine. Mine, Nikki. I'm not ever letting you go."

Ollie's words spun and lifted, floating out as our bodies slapped, the sound matching his grunts.

He filled me.

Again and again.

Touching me everywhere.

Heart. Spirit. Soul.

I met his fierce gaze through the reflection of the window. The man behind me. Taking me. Owning me.

While I offered him everything.

All of me.

Nothing left to hide.

He tugged at my hair, pulling my head against his shoulder, his cheek on mine.

"Look at you," he demanded.

My body was stretched out against his, bowed back, my breasts pointed, tingling with the flickers of pleasure that grew more intense.

Every nerve ending alive. Zaps and pulses and zings.

It gathered fast as Ollie took me deeper and harder and higher.

He spread me with his fingers, stroking my clit.

A match tossed on kindling and gasoline.

Incinerated.

I'd never felt anything like it.

The fire that engulfed me.

Burning and singeing and scarring.

My body arched with the orgasm, and Ollie held me tighter, an arm around my waist as he drove deep.

So full I couldn't see.

His hips snapped.

Frenzied.

His groan guttural.

Teeth sank into my shoulder when he came, his body going rigid as he grunted through his release.

My beast.

My mind tilted, the floor going missing from under me as we both struggled to come back down.

"Fuck," he muttered as we both gasped for the nonexistent air.

"Fuck," he whispered again, almost frantically.

Fuck.

Another shiver rolled, and he held me up. Keeping me from falling.

His mouth was at my ear. "I just want to be the one to give you everything."

I wanted to believe that he was ready to take that leap. But there was no missing the desperation that bled through his words.

Fueled by an urgent desire to tighten the tether he feared might break.

I stood right there, at that edge, ready to jump.

I just prayed Ollie wouldn't let me fall alone.

twenty-nine

Ollie

I pressed my cell to my ear. "Sage, man, what's up. How's it coming?"

I hadn't heard from him in a couple of weeks, which wasn't uncommon for restorations. It took a shit-ton of time to get anything accomplished. The search for replacement parts could take months, not to mention the actual work that needed to be done.

He hesitated on the other end of the line.

"What's going on?"

He blew out a sigh. "Not sure, man. There's just some weird shit with this car."

Only thing I heard was Sage shouting dollar signs.

"That car's special to me. Doesn't matter what it costs."

He inhaled, stalled, and an odd sensation gathered in my chest while I waited for him to fill me in.

"No. This isn't about money. There's some . . . shit in the trunk that doesn't sit right."

"What's that mean?"

I could hear him pacing on the concrete floors. "There's some rope. A torn shirt that looks like it's splattered with blood."

Unease moved through me, silence falling over us as Sage let me catch up to what he was implying.

I sucked for a breath, teeth gritting as I spoke through the anger that lit inside me. "That kid Caleb . . . he . . . who knows what the fuck he was mixed up in. Knew he was trouble the second I saw him."

"That's what I was worried about. And it might not be anything. Someone could have just as easily cut themselves and tossed the shirt in there. Just have to verify it before we gut this thing and start on the actual work."

I was always quick to jump to conclusions.

Sage was just taking the steps needed to get things done.

I shoved down the swelling rage.

"Of course."

"Honestly, the more I think about it, I'm sure it's nothing, but it's gonna nag if I don't call it in."

"Do what you've got to do, man. Can't blame you for that. Just let me know when you get started."

He was right. It was probably nothing, and if that punk had been up to something shadier than we'd thought, at least he was in rehab. If he did try to leave, he'd land his scrawny ass in a jail cell.

I couldn't worry about it right then.

Because my girl was peeling off her panties and grinning at me as she climbed into my bed.

And no matter how awesome that old car turned out, it wouldn't ever come as close to looking as good as that.

Nikki

$\mathcal{M}$y phone buzzed in my hand, and I was already grinning when I slid my finger across the plate.

Then my heart . . . it pattered when I saw the text that had come through. Was that normal? I was thirty, for God's sake.

But it did.

My eyes traced across the screen.

Ollie: Pretty please.

It probably wasn't the words that got me so much as the picture that he had sent along with it that had my pulse skipping a beat. My teeth tucked my bottom lip between them as I was hit with a rush of giddiness.

Because there was an up-close selfie of Ollie.

He was leaning against the bar downstairs at Olive's. An arm was crossed over his chest, and one of those tatted hands held onto his opposite shoulder.

The man was grinning at the camera, at me. And his eyes? They glinted. Glinted with happiness, and there was no description for how happy that made me.

Walking down the busy sidewalk, I tapped out a response.

Me: Not a chance, playboy.

I hadn't made it two steps before my phone buzzed again.

Ollie: Come on, gorgeous. Show me that face and just a little bit of

that body. I'll make it worth your while 😉

There was that patter again.

Six weeks had passed since that fateful night on the dance floor when everything had changed. When the anniversary of Sydney's disappearance had changed us again. Although this time, it had pushed us together.

Closer and closer each day.

Our lives knitting together, so tightly we'd become one.

Easy.

The way it was always supposed to be.

Things had settled.

Caleb was still in the long-term rehab center, hopefully making a real effort to piece his life back together and become the type of man Brenna and Kyle deserved.

I tried not to be skeptical.

Sometimes that was hard because it turned out I was protective, too.

Sammie still hadn't confided in me, but she'd been calling more, asking me over, and I got the feeling she was working herself up to the place where she felt comfortable enough to do it.

I would never push her, even though sometimes I had the itch to beg her to tell me, that part of myself that wanted to make everything better screaming out to do something.

I had to accept I didn't have that kind of control.

All I could do was love and support and be there for her when she was ready.

Two weeks ago, Hope and Kale had announced that they were expecting, which filled me up with an intense joy for them and also lit a few sparks of jealousy.

I'd pushed those feelings down.

Of course, I ignored all of Lily's ribbing when Ollie and I stepped out as a couple. We'd had a heart to heart, and I'd finally confessed to her that I'd loved him all along.

That it'd always been so much more than a crush.

That it was everything.

That Ollie was everything.

Which was exactly why I was grinning like a fool as I hurried the last few steps down the sidewalk and swung open the door to the old building.

Instead of going right for the basement stairs to set up like I typically would have done, I slipped into a deserted hallway to the left and tucked myself into an alcove where I'd be out of view.

I lifted my phone and snapped a picture, giving the barest hint of the pretty much nonexistent cleavage revealed by my pretty blouse.

Ollie definitely didn't seem to mind.

Me: That's going to have to tide you over until later.

Ollie: Dying.

Ollie: So gorgeous.

Ollie: You're ruining me, baby.

Redness flushed across my skin as I read the words that kept blipping through.

Me: I think you have it all backward. It's you who's ruining me.

Ollie: Hurry up and get that sexy ass home. I'll see you at ten.

Ollie: I miss you.

Me: I miss you, too.

I felt as if I was riding on a cloud, floating down the stairs that led to the basement. I was halfway through setting up the circle of chairs when Ms. Kathy came in, started a pot of coffee, and arranged the donuts she'd picked up on a tray.

"I hear congratulations are in order."

I beamed. I couldn't help it. "I can't believe I'm really finished."

Yesterday, I'd gotten my certificate in the mail from the online college.

I officially had my bachelor's degree. All I needed to do was take the state test and I would be certified.

"This is when the fun part begins." She winked at me.

"Uh-oh. Tell me that wasn't a warnin'," I said, laughing a little.

She made a humming sound. "Some days will make you feel like a champion and others will drop you right to your knees. But what you can count on is it will never be dull."

I hesitated for a second, peeking over at her. "Is it worth it?"

She reached out and squeezed my shoulder. "Always."

Fifteen minutes later, the secluded basement was a rumble of voices and screeching chairs as we all gathered around the circle.

I opened the session with our mantra. "I am strong. I have control of my life. I have control of my body. I have the right."

I looked around the group of faces. Even though so many were full of sorrow, it filled me with extreme hope. I did my normal introduction, telling them this was their safe place and completely confidential.

"Tonight, I would like us to talk through how you might look at situations differently since you've been attending this group. How has this changed the way you've reacted? How has it changed the way you handle the hurdles you face? Would anyone like to start?"

I was surprised when Brenna raised her hand. "I'd like to start, Miss Nikki. There's something that's been bothering me, and I want to make sure I'm handling it right."

Over the last few weeks, she'd really come out of her shell, exuding a confidence that had been lacking before.

"Okay, tell us what's happening."

Almost nervously, her attention darted around the group before she began, "Well, Caleb has been in rehab for six weeks now. He's now allowed to make calls. He's called a couple of times and is promising me he is changing. That he's making a real effort. I don't want to walk through life with a chip on my shoulder, but I also don't want to be naïve."

Pride welled inside me, and I started to speak, but I stilled when tentative footsteps echoed down the stairs.

I paused to look over my shoulder, and like all those weeks ago, my sister appeared in the doorway.

Her eyes met mine.

There was something so broken there that my heart froze in the middle of my chest.

I tried to swallow around the apprehension that climbed to my throat as my little sister moved around the circle and tentatively took an empty seat.

I should have been relieved.

I should have taken solace in the fact she was there.

But I swore, I felt the air go cold.

thirty-one

Ollie

"You want another?"

"You know I do," the old guy said as he drained his fourth beer of the evening.

I filled a chilled glass, foam overflowing down the sides as I cocked him a look. "You better watch yourself, or I'm gonna have to cut you off."

He laughed and waved a flippant hand over his head. "You think this old-timer can't handle his liquor? Couple of cold ones sure aren't gonna hurt me. Why do you think I'm still alive and kickin'?"

Laughing, I slid him the pint glass. I'd been chatting with him all afternoon. He was either telling some tall, tall tales or the old bastard had lived quite the life.

Olive's had been quiet during the dead hours between the lunch rush and the after-work crowd. Evening was setting in, and the place was beginning to fill up.

For so long, my bar had basically been my entire life. Now, I couldn't wait for the night to pass so I could get back upstairs.

Fact I kept looking at my phone was proof enough.

"Who ya got on that phone? You got yourself one of them sassy modern girls? Bet you do."

I chuckled under my breath, setting my phone aside. I had to have looked at Nikki's picture at least a thousand times since she'd sent it an hour ago.

"That I do."

Still blew my mind that I did. That Nikki was mine.

My body rumbled with possession.

Every inch.

"She pretty? Let me see."

Old pervert.

Amusement swimming through me, I started wiping down the bar. "Hell no. Do I look like the kind of guy who shares my girl?"

His laughter was some kind of ridiculous guffaw and he smacked his hand on the wood. "Don't reckon you do. Look like you'd tear a poor sucker limb from limb."

"Sounds about right," I said, grinning when I felt the presence standing across the bar from me.

I looked up.

Seth.

My smile started to widen until I caught the expression on his face.

I straightened. "Seth, man, what are you doing here?"

His voice was quiet, lined with a tremor. "Need to talk to you. In private."

I tossed the rag onto the bar and hollered at Cece, who was manning the opposite end. "Watch things for a bit. I've got to step outside."

"Sure thing, boss."

I wound around the end of the bar and followed Seth. He headed straight down the back hall, passing by the sign that read: Employees Only.

Could feel the disturbance radiating from him, riding on the air that suddenly felt too fucking thick.

My breaths grew hard, and my heart fisted in an unknown sort of pain when he blew out the big metal door and into the vacant back lot.

Only thing back there were the employees' cars and the dumpster the kitchen used.

Humidity slapped me in the face, but it was Rex standing with his back pressed to the brick exterior wall, his head rocking up and down and his fists shoved deep in his pockets, that felt like a punch to the gut.

My attention swung back to Seth. "What's going on?"

His eyes squeezed shut. "I'm breaking a thousand rules by doing this, but I needed to tell you before you heard it somewhere else."

Tension stretched across my chest.

Pulling and pulling.

Any harder and it would rip me right in half.

"What?" I had to force out the word.

Seth hesitated, looking to the ground, inhaling deep. Sympathy shaded his eyes when he looked back up at me. "You know they started excavation down on Row."

I glanced over at Rex, confusion so thick I was having a hard time seeing through it, before I swung my gaze back to Seth. "Yeah, of course, I know. Rex said everything was given the go and the permits had been approved."

Seth blew out a strained breath, a bluster of hesitation coming off him.

Overwhelming waves.

"Ollie." There was nothing but pity in the word.

Could feel Rex flinch from the side.

Foreboding ridged like ice skating down my spine.

"What the fuck is goin' on, man?

Seth blinked, and the words came from his mouth like a slow purge. "A body was unearthed at the work site."

My knees gave with the blow, and my hand shot out, catching on the wall. I shoved it down and gritted my teeth. "What's that got to do with me?"

The words might as well have been darts.

Sharp as arrows.

Denial and defense.

Seth's brow twisted, lines distorting his face, and his words were a choked breath. "They're speculating they're Sydney's remains."

"No." My head shook, and my lips pursed as I rejected the idea. "No."

Seth reached out and set his hand on my shoulder. "I'm sorry, Ollie. I know you always hoped for a miracle."

Hoped for a miracle.

Hoped that my sister was still alive.

That someone hadn't buried her like she was trash.

Blood.

Dirt.

Bones.

I gasped for nothing. My lungs no longer functioning.

Seth edged back, and his attention jumped between Rex and me. "God, I'm sorry. This is the last kind of news I want to deliver. I'll give you guys some privacy. If I find out anything, I promise, you'll be the first to know."

He turned, and I stood stock still, watching him jog away.

Frozen.

Brittle.

It only sent a crack running down the middle of me that I knew would shatter me in a million unrecognizable pieces.

Rex groaned a devastated sound. "Fuck, Ollie . . . I—"

I flew around to face him. "It's not her."

Grief blistered across his face, through his red-rimmed eyes. Etched and carved and wrecked. He pushed from the wall, approaching me carefully.

"It was her, man. The foreman . . ." He blinked a bunch of times. Like he couldn't see through the horror wracking my mind. "He called me away from the architect when they uncovered something."

My head shook.

Rejection.

I didn't want to hear it.

I just couldn't make the words from on my tongue.

"I ran over there . . . thinking it was gonna be an old sewer system or something like that and they needed my direction."

He pressed both his hands over his face. His voice cracked on a cry. "The necklace, the one your mom gave her for her sixteenth birthday, it was there with the remains."

"No . . . she must have dropped it there sometime."

His hands dropped, and he took a step forward, getting in my line of sight, misery etched across his face. "She was wearing it that night."

My head shook. "No. She couldn't have been. You don't know that."

A groan ripped from him. "She was wearing it, Ollie. She was."

I pointed at him, trying to put some space between us. Refusing what was trying to suck me under.

Darkness.

Terror.

Hate.

"You don't fucking know that," I grated.

He stared at me, something so raw on his face that my heart slammed against my ribs.

"I do know, Ollie."

"How the fuck would you know that?" I spat, unable to keep the anger out of my words.

"I was with her." It was a raked gasp. Words barely formed.

My brow pinched. "We all were with her."

His hands fisted in front of him. Regret and frustration and something that look too much like guilt. "Fuck. Listen to me, Ollie. I was *with* her."

I blinked. "What?"

"I was with her." It was a shamed whisper.

There was nothing I could do.

The rage that poured free, leaching into my veins.

I shoved him.

Hard.

He flew back against the brick wall.

"What did you say?" I demanded.

"We were together. I told you it wasn't just your fault."

Red blurred my vision, and everything spun.

The sky and the earth and my spirit.

A jumbled chaos that took over inside of me. "You fucked my sister?" The accusation was full of disbelief.

Of disgust.

No words came from his mouth.

But guilt was written all over his face.

Anger burst in my blood. "You fucked my sister?"

Disgust met the roar as I lunged for him. My fist flew. Connected with flesh and bone.

Pain burst in my hand, and Rex just . . . took it. Face pinched up in pain as a trickle of blood dripped from his nose. "I'm sorry," he whispered.

He slid down the wall, hitting the ground with a thud. His head rocked back and he buried his face in his hands. "So fucking sorry."

I backed away.

Gripped by sorrow.

Grief swooping in.

Clouding my mind.

Shutting down my spirit.

My lip curled, and I backed further away. "Sorry's not good enough."

I turned and left him there, unable to see as I stumbled up the three flights of steps in the darkened stairwell.

Everything was blurred.

My eyes and mind.

An altered state of consciousness.

It couldn't be her.

It couldn't.

I had to keep searching. Keep watching. Keep hunting.

I would find her.

She would be safe.

Fly, fly, dragonfly.

Her voice danced all around me, and I choked, a cry ripping free.

It echoed on the enclosed walls.

Bouncing back.

Grief.

Grief.

Grief.

I couldn't stand.

I dropped to my knees, crawled the rest of the way up the last flight.

At the top, I forced myself to standing as I staggered out into the short hall, hands pressed to the wall to keep myself from falling.

Falling.

I'd thought I could live.

That I could see through this.

Past it.

That I could let go.

But this?

It was all I could feel.

All I could feel.

Pain.

Excruciating.

"We are three. Forever and ever, you and me."

I fumbled through the door and into my loft.

Nikki's scent hit me like a blow.

It blasted me back, and a sob ripped free from deep within my chest.

What did we do?

What did we do?

I stumbled to the cupboard, pulled out a brand new bottle, twisted off the cap.

Anything to dull the feeling of my skin being sheered from my bones.

Flaying me open.

I tipped it up and gulped half of it down, drenching my stomach in morbid heat. Praying for reprieve.

I moved to the couch, and like a fool, I grabbed the remote and flipped on the television.

I slugged back another huge gulp.

Another and another.

Time passed.

A minute. An hour. A day.

I didn't know.

It didn't matter.

My head lolled against the back of the couch as I drifted through the haze.

Darkness spun.

Color blipped and flashed from the television. A slur of voices landed on my ears. Too loud. Too much.

A woman in a purple dress stood in front of the yellow tape that blocked off the old building where investigators swarmed, delivering her news.

A body had been discovered.

Forensics was on the scene.

Speculation.

Speculation.

"Sydney Preston was sixteen years old when she went missing fourteen years ago."

That storm rumbled from the depths of me.

Rising and lifting and consuming.

For months, I'd had the gut-deep intuition that something was coming.

Something wicked.

Ruthless and cruel.

A warning before it'd been overhead.

I'd known it was coming.

I'd known.

Like a fool, I hadn't realized what that'd meant.

It's your fault.

I trusted you.

You were supposed to take care of her.

You promised, you'd take care of her.

It should have been me.
It should have been me.
I'd done this.
Agony sliced through the center of me.
Excruciating, blinding pain.
Gutting and destroying.
My body wept. Bleeding out.
I could feel her spirit whip through the room.
An earthquake.
It spurred a tidal wave that decimated the coastline.
I saw it.
Felt it.
I welcomed it when it crashed over me.
A gulf overhead.
Taking me under.
Suffocating.
Drowning.
Me.
It should have been me.

thirty-two

Ollie
Seventeen Years Old

Flames from the bonfire licked and lapped, jumping toward the canopy of night that covered overhead.

Embers popped and snapped before they broke away like golden ash that floated for the heavens.

A ton of their friends were out there tonight.

More than Ollie had planned. Half the town had caught wind of the lake party, and people had kept showing up.

Wouldn't have been that big of a deal had a bunch of chicks from their class not climbed in the bed of Rex's truck to share the case of beer Rex's older cousin had scored.

Clearly, they thought they were gonna nab a piece of the star quarterback and defensive end as well.

What made it worse was Ollie's sister was there, sitting on the tailgate of the truck with her legs swinging over the edge.

Tonight, she looked pissed and bored and annoyed, and Ollie tried not to be annoyed right back.

He'd given it his best to convince her not to come tonight. He and Nikki had even concocted a story that Nikki wasn't feeling well so she was staying home.

He'd planned to pick her up on the way so Sydney wouldn't know. Guys wouldn't question it since Nikki was always with him, anyway.

Plan was solid.

No harm. No foul.

That was until Sydney had shoved a bunch of stuff into a tote bag and jumped into his car, saying he wasn't leaving without her.

Nikki had *magically* started feeling better.

Now, Nikki sat all the way on the other side of the fire, sitting on the same whitewashed log they'd dragged up from the lake when they'd all first started camping out here in middle school.

Those sweet freckles glimmered like glitter on her face as she watched him through the flames.

Her eyes dropped closed for a second, lashes casting a shadow on her cheeks.

God.

She was pretty.

So damned pretty he was sure he was going to lose his mind.

His insides twisted in a need that was close to painful, and he swore that the condom he'd brought was burning a hole in his back pocket that was as hot as the sparks that flickered from the pit.

Giggles rolled from beside him, and Ollie had to stop himself from rolling his eyes when he glanced that way and saw Jessica straddling Rex's lap.

Sydney's mouth pursed in a prissy way.

God, what was her problem?

She'd gotten so weird lately. She had to be catching on about him and Nikki. It wasn't like she was an idiot.

But he couldn't worry about that tonight.

They were going to tell her soon. This weekend.

After they were together.

All they wanted was this night.

Something special.

Rex laughed, and he set his hands awkwardly on Jessica's waist.

Dude was such a pansy, acting like he wasn't interested in getting laid. Hell, Ollie could hardly remember the last time Rex had a girlfriend.

He looked Rex's way, grinning wide and covertly blocking Kayla from climbing into a similar position on his lap. "Stop being a pussy, dude. It's about time you saw some action. Get that dick wet before it shrivels up and falls off."

Rex laughed. "The hell? I get plenty of action."

"Yeah. Complements of your hand."

Sydney hopped off the tail, spun around, and crossed her arms over her chest. "You guys are such assholes. Can you stop being pigs for five seconds?"

Anger pinged at his ribs. Sydney had always been right there. He'd never had a minute to himself. To figure out who he was outside of watching over her.

And she thought she could judge them? Call them assholes when he was the one to bring her out there?

The one who'd always taken her everywhere.

"Take me home." She was looking directly at Rex.

Jessica giggled and snuggled closer against his chest.

"Think he'd rather be spending his time kissing Jessica than running you around. Wouldn't you, Rex?"

Ollie lifted his chin at Rex and Jessica. Prodding him.

Rex laughed before he kissed Jessica, so damned clumsily you'd think he'd never kissed a girl before.

But, hell, Ollie wasn't joking.

It was about time his best friend saw some action.

Kale was already off with his new girlfriend, and damn, it would be nice if Rex had a distraction, too.

All he needed was to finally get Nikki alone.

"Told you not to come," Ollie told her.

Hurt twisted up Sydney's face, and crap, that was all it took for regret to start tugging at Ollie's conscience. At that place carved out that would forever give up anything for his sister.

She was supposed to be his priority.

His best friend.

It tugged and it tugged.

Only it wasn't as strong as his need for Nikki that pulled at the inside of him.

Two of them tethered and hooked.

Just one night. All he wanted was one night.

He looked at his sister, whose expression was so pinched with betrayal he almost apologized.

He swallowed it back, his voice a little rough when he said, "Go home, Sydney. Told you tonight wasn't for you. Call Mom to come pick you up at the dock."

Wounded disbelief glistened in her eyes as she looked at Ollie then turned her attention to Rex.

A beat passed.

Then two with no one saying anything.

Like she was waiting for someone to change their mind.

To tell her to stay.

Guilt clawed through Ollie, but he forced it down.

One night.

On a choked cry, she finally turned and started to walk away.

Nikki scrambled to her feet to go after her, and Ollie sent her a pleading glance.

Stay.

She blinked between them, torn, before she settled back onto the log.

All of them watched Sydney walk down the dirt road, her receding silhouette getting dimmer and dimmer before she disappeared around a bend.

Ollie breathed out, a loaded sound of frustration and relief. This was so messed up.

He watched as Nikki got up, clearly upset. She headed toward her things she'd left behind in one of the tents.

Pushing to standing, Ollie hopped over the side of the truck, feet landing hard on the dirt. "Got to take a piss."

He skirted around the camp, going around the long way until he found Nikki standing with her head dropped. Without saying anything, he grabbed her hand and the rolled-up pallet he'd made.

Silently, he clutched her hand, guiding her through the maze of spindly trees.

The voices and laughter grew more distant the farther they went, the sound of the waterfalls growing more distinct.

Nikki finally tugged at his hand, and he spun around to face her.

His breath hitched.

Air gone.

It was the exact same thing it did whenever he looked at her.

That feeling sweeping through him with the strength of the falls that crashed into the lake below.

But her voice, it was pained and whispered. "I think we should go after her. This isn't right."

He dropped the pallet to the ground and gathered her face in his hands. "Just tonight, Nikki. I want it to be us. For one night. That's all I'm asking for. Tomorrow, we'll apologize to her. Confess everything. We'll make it right."

Those mesmerizing eyes searched his face. "Why can't we do that right now?"

"Because you know it's going to be a thing. She's going to be upset. It would ruin tonight. It would ruin everything we have planned."

Her gaze drifted, worry written in her expression. "I just hate the idea of her going home angry. Feeling like we don't care."

Nikki fiddled with the red woven bracelet she wore on her wrist. The one that matched Sydney and Ollie's. Like if she touched it, she might be able to touch Sydney through the distance.

"She'll understand. It might take her some time, but she'll understand."

Nikki looked out over the streams that ran over the smooth rocks and tumbled over the cliffs. "I just . . . don't want her to be mad at me. When this comes out, I don't want it to change things between her and me."

He gathered her closer. "Is that what you're so worried about?"

Nikki nodded, eyes dropping when she confessed, "I've been worried all week. So worried, Ollie. She's been my best friend my whole life. I don't want to ruin that."

Ollie brushed his fingertips across the moisture on her cheek.

Moonlight poured from above, caressing her olive skin, spinning it into silk.

"You don't need to worry. We'll make this right. I promise. But for tonight, it's just you and me." He brushed his nose against hers. "And me and you."

She set her delicate hands on his trembling stomach. "Us."

"Us," he murmured, so softly, a promise that came from his spirit and fell from his lips.

He took her hand again, picked up the pack, and silently wound her the rest of the way to the meadow secreted by a break in the trees.

It was the spot where he'd found her every single time they'd played hide and seek there at the lake.

Where they'd grown and learned and changed.

Where she'd run and hide and wait for him to come for her.

To find her.

He spread out the cushion and blankets, and they both knelt on their knees as he silently, slowly undressed her and she timidly undressed him.

A blush on her skin as she peeked up at him.

Energy roiled between them.

Soft surges.

Gentle prods.

She was shaking when she laid down beneath the covers, but it didn't come close to the quakes that rolled through Ollie as he fumbled to cover himself.

He'd had sex with two other girls.

It hadn't come close to feeling like this.

He was overwhelmed that Nikki trusted him with it.

With her.

He crawled under the covers with her, and he gathered her closer, holding her in a way he never had.

Their noses touched. Their breaths mingled. Their hearts joined.

And Ollie . . . he found her again, in their hidden spot, though this time, they would never be the same.

He knew as they moved beneath the moonlight that he was going to keep her.

That he'd give up anything for her.

Anything.

Anyone.

Protect her with all he had.

If she was lost, he would always find her.

That was what loving someone was all about.

Giving all of yourself.

Completely.
And Nikki Walters owned every part of him.

thirty-three

Nikki

I sucked in a shattered breath as I stumbled to stand, catching myself on the back of the chair.

"What did you just say?"

I'd still been staring at my sister.

Caught up in the fact she was there.

But there was no missing what Maggie had whispered to Nina after she'd looked at something on her phone.

"I'm sorry, Miss Nikki, I wasn't trying to disrupt the group. My mama just texted me three times in a row, and I figured I'd better check to make sure my kids weren't tearing her house down."

I blinked, frantically shook my head, and tried to swallow around the sticky dread that had wrapped me in chains so quickly I was sure I was being strangled. "No . . . tell me what you just said. What you just whispered."

She frowned. "They found a body out by the river near those old, abandoned buildings. News report said they think it's that poor girl Sydney Preston who went missing all those years ago. So sad."

No.

Oh . . . God . . . no.

My hand went to my stomach as my body bent in half, and I tried to draw air in to my lungs. Through that haze of disbelief and sorrow.

I only managed to draw in more.

Shock.

Anguish.

A chatter of uneasy, confused voices sounded, each one hitting me so hard they had to be boxing my ears.

I shoved my chair back, stumbling as I broke out of the circle that was suffocating me. My head spun, faster than the walls that canted and tipped.

At the same time, every evil force in the world pressed down.

I could feel it crush my heart right in the center of my chest.

I didn't know how I made it across the floor, but my hand shot out to keep myself from dropping to my knees when I reached the stairwell, my feet failing beneath me.

Like everything else. My heart and my spirit and my belief.

From behind, an arm looped around my middle, holding me up. My sister's voice was so soft as it moved through the daze. "I've got you, Nik. Oh, God, I'm so sorry. I'm so sorry. I'm right here. I've got you."

She helped me to stand. Eyes the same color as mine searched my face as I sagged against the wall. "I need . . . I need to get to Ollie."

She nodded. "Okay . . . I'll drive you."

I didn't even process the ride over. The grief was too overwhelming. Every single beat of my splintered heart was excruciating.

Rynna had texted me a hundred times, my phone blipping incessantly when I'd fumbled to turn it on where I sat in Sammie's car.

Rynna: Are you okay?

Rynna: Call me.

Rynna: I'm here if you need me.

Texts from Lily had started up right after, a bunch of calls that I couldn't bring myself to answer.

I had to get to Ollie.

My sister kept glancing over at me, kneading the wheel, so much concern and care on her face. "I can't imagine what you're feeling right now."

My head shook, voice barely breaking the air. "I . . . I always knew she was gone. But it'd always felt like her spirit had just been swept away. In my mind, I'd imagined she'd ridden off on the wind to find some new adventure. This . . ."

A gasp pulled from my spirit, and sickness bubbled and churned in that well of grief. That place deep inside that had been shored up and protected. A vat of misery and despair and questions.

That dam had been broken, and every ounce of it surged through me. A devastating flood.

She glanced at me before turning her attention back to the road. "They aren't even sure it's her."

She cringed when she said it.

Because we both knew it was her.

It was Sydney.

Her name begged from the depths of me.

Sammie pulled to the curb in front of Olive's. I jumped out and bolted for the door, flinging it open, gasping as my attention jumped around the space.

Ollie wasn't behind the bar, and Cece lifted one of her defined brows and gave a shrug, but there was concern behind it.

And I knew.

I knew, I knew, I knew.

Ollie had already heard.

Dread balled in the pit of my stomach.

I didn't slow as I raced down the hall and up the three flights of stairs to his loft.

My feet had finally found their purpose.

Ollie.

Ollie.

I burst through the door.

Then I skidded to a stop.

Dense darkness echoed back.

So dark it coated my eyes.

Coated my spirit.

Only the blips coming from the television that played illuminated what was stricken on his face.

Torment.

Agony.

Slowly, his gaze lifted to mine, as if he couldn't process that I was there.

Vacant.

I could feel the distance grow so immense between us I had no idea how I would reach him.

Rushing for him, I dropped to my knees in front of him where he sat on the couch.

Unmoving.

"Ollie," I whispered, desperation on my tongue. I lifted onto my knees so I could hold his face.

His beautiful, tortured face.

His eyes dropped closed, and there was nothing but pain on his lips. "Please, don't touch me."

I clung to him tighter. "Ollie . . . I'm so sorry."

As if my words had snapped him out of the daze, he flew to his feet, writhing as if he were being burned alive.

Misery in his eyes and alcohol on his breath. "This can't be happening, Nikki. Tell me it's not happening."

I fumbled to standing, my arms across my middle as I tried to keep myself upright, as if I could physically hold myself together. "I'm so sorry"

What else was I going to say. That it was okay? Because this was most definitely not okay.

"Tell me what I can do," I begged instead.

His brow pinched. "What can you do? You can't *do* anything, Nikki. It's already done. My sister is gone."

Him saying it sent shards of glass blasting through me.

He whirled away, gripping fistfuls of his hair as a groan erupted from his soul.

His entire body clenched, and he harshly shook his head, voice gravel. "I was supposed to save her. I spent my whole life looking for her. Searching for her. Thinking someday, I would make this right. That I'd fix what I'd done. And I can't fix it."

A sob raked from him, and he dropped to his knees and buried his face in his hands.

"My sister is gone. Oh, God. She's dead. She's dead."

Whimpers echoed from him.

A shattered, broken cry.

The man was falling apart in front of my eyes.

I wanted to hold him.

Fix him.

But neither of us were capable of fixing this.

He was right.

It was already done.

The only thing we could do was be there for each other in the middle of it.

Slowly, I inched toward him, kneeling as I set a hand on his arm.

He flinched.

"I'm right here, Ollie."

Under my touch, I could feel the tremor roll through him.

Crushed, he finally turned his potent gaze on me. "I have no idea who the fuck I'm supposed to be."

My mouth quivered, and I searched his face. "You're supposed to be mine."

Sorrow swam.

So thick.

So deep.

Quicksand.

"I don't know how to do that when all I see when I look at you is Sydney standing at your side."

Pain squashed my lungs.

Obliterating air.

I blinked. Wanting to negate it. To tell him we could overcome it.

"Ollie?" I begged quietly.

Praying he'd refute it.

Say what he'd implied wasn't true.
But his expression shifted.
Hardened.
The walls coming up.
They swore there was no way for us to overcome *this*.
My nod was slow surrender as I pushed back to standing.
"I have to go."
I turned and fumbled for the door.
Barely able to stand.
A new kind of grief cut through me.
Overpowering.
Overbearing.
Too much.
How was I supposed to stand under it all?
"Nik," he suddenly begged. His voice gruff. "Don't just take off."
It only propelled me faster.
I needed to get away.
Run from this grief.
I clamored back out into the hall.
I could feel his presence from behind, a shockwave that banged against the walls.
"Nikki."
His voice sounded like heartbreak.
Like an apology.
Like a goodbye.
I paused to look back at him, barely able to force out the words. "I will always love you, Ollie, but I can't be with you when you don't know how to love me back."
I'd known to guard my heart.
I'd known. I'd known all along.
Oliver Preston was armor and stone.
Bitterness and venom.
Broken fragments.
Shrapnel waiting to bust.
He was the bullet that pierced right through the center of me.
Barely able to see, I ran back down the hall and hit the door that led to the steps. Holding onto the railing, I bounded downstairs.
Sniffling, trying to hold back the sob that bottled in my throat.
At the bottom, I blew out the backdoor and the sob broke free.
It echoed on the night.
Resounding.
A boomerang.
It bounced back, slamming into me, adding to the turmoil that sieged

every cell in my body.

Hands shaking, I fumbled into my purse and pulled out my phone, barely able to make the call.

Sammie answered on the first ring. "Are you okay?"

I could hardly speak. "No. I'm not okay."

"Where are you?"

"At the back of Olive's," I begged through another cry.

"Stay right there. I'll be there to get you in five minutes."

"Okay."

I ended the call and hugged my arms across my chest, tears streaking free.

There was no way to stop them.

Solid ground had finally been ripped from beneath our feet.

My heart shattered, pieces scattered.

Verification that we'd lost Sydney in this horrible, horrible way crumbled the last of our foundation.

I guessed it'd been flimsy and unstable, anyway.

But now it was Ollie who was lost beneath the rubble.

Unable to see his way out of it.

Unable to see past what he thought was a failure.

And he'd broken my heart all over again while mine broke *for* him.

I wanted to hold him and make promises I couldn't keep.

That one day it wouldn't hurt so bad.

But I knew that would only be a lie.

Headlights cut into the back-alley road, and Sammie's car came to a stop in front of me.

The front passenger door flew open, and Sammie jumped out, her husband Lyle in the driver's seat.

I collapsed in her arms and wept.

"I've got you, Nikki. It's going to be okay."

I nodded against her, even though I couldn't bring myself to believe it was true.

Finally, I pried myself away and climbed into the backseat with Penelope, took the little girl's hand, clinging to the comfort she brought.

Looking at her had always made me feel as if the world could be a better place.

I just wished I could still believe that as the truth.

They swung by where I'd left my car outside the building, and Lyle took my keys and said he'd meet us back at the house, doing what he could to lighten some of the load.

As if I'd give my car a second thought.

But he'd always been a doer, and I understood the feeling of being helpless, desperate to find something to do.

Sammie moved into the driver's seat.

I stayed stagnant in the backseat, silent tears running down my face.

They didn't stop or slow when we went inside.

Choked sobs erupted at unexpected times, as if the sorrow would bottle and pressurize and then burst to do it all over again.

Sammie made me a spot on the couch to sleep, and I hugged the blankets around my body as it if might offer comfort.

"Do you want me to sit with you?" Sammie finally asked, fidgeting, her house quiet in the dark hours of the night.

"No, you go on to bed and get some rest. There's nothing you can do."

I needed to be alone.

To process.

To grieve.

She wavered as if she was going to stay anyway. "I want to be here for you, too," she whispered, as if she were trying to cross a bridge.

My eyes blinked open to her.

Bleary and blurry.

Burning from the tears.

Something passed through her expression.

"I know that. Thank you."

She nodded quickly and then ducked her head down the hall, shutting off the last light and casting the entire house in a dreary darkness.

I didn't toss.

I just laid there.

Frozen in the silence.

Tied by sorrow.

Cutting, blinding grief.

I'd felt as if I'd lost both of them all over again.

As if I was taken back to the day when my world went dim.

Because Ollie . . .

He'd always been my great big world.

Finally, I drifted on it, exhaustion taking hold of my consciousness. Horrible dreams just raced in to take its place.

My eyes popped open, a fresh sob on my breath, night still all around me. Disoriented, I blinked through it. I jerked my head when I felt the presence at my side.

"Sammie," I gasped, my eyes going wide when I found my sister sitting on the floor next to me, her knees tucked to her chest as she rocked.

Even in the darkness, I could see the shimmer of tears that stained her cheeks.

"What's wrong?" I whispered fiercely, shooting up to sitting, the worry for her chasing away the weight that wanted to pin me down. "What happened?"

Shivers of pain radiated from her.

"I went to that meetin' last night, thinking I was going to be able to talk to you.”

Oh God.

My heart raced.

Banged at my ribs.

“And I’m so sorry this is comin’ now . . . when you’re going through so much. I just don’t think I can keep it inside anymore. Everything feels wrong.”

I knew this was her way of opening a door.

Breaching a divide.

Inviting me inside.

I wanted to be there. For her.

Even though I was terrified I might not be strong enough to handle anything else. If my emotions might get the better of me.

“I’m *always* here for you, Sammie. No matter what is happening in my life, I will always be here for you.”

“I know that,” she mumbled, hugging her knees tighter, her attention darting all over the living room as if she was searching for ghosts among the shadows.

Finally, she turned her tortured gaze back on me, the words forced from her mouth. “He’s back.”

Confused, I sat forward more as I tried to decipher what she was trying to say. “Who?”

She swiped the back of her hand under her nose. “Uncle Todd.”

“What?”

The name rocked me back.

Shocked.

Stunned.

Horrified by the look on Sammie’s face.

Sickness turned in my guts, and I was sure I was gonna throw up.

She blinked a bunch of times, as if she were seeing things she didn’t want to see. “I . . . I thought I was okay, Nikki. For all these years, I’d convinced myself it was okay because he was gone. All my prayers had been answered because he’d just . . . moved. Was gone. So, I shoved it down and pretended like it didn’t exist, and then he came back to help Grandma and . . . and . . . it was all right back there again.”

Dread.

It chained and bound.

Everything felt too heavy.

Crushing.

I tried to breathe around it. To convince my heart it was okay to still beat.

I needed to be strong for my sister.

She needed me. She *needed* me, and I needed to be there for her.

“What exactly are you sayin’?” I tried to keep the question soft. Frame it like I would to anyone who came to me for help.

But it felt impossible when my baby sister was the one sitting there looking at me.

"Didn't you think Uncle Todd was a creep?" she almost begged.

Leading me. Trying to get me to a point without her having to say it.

I swallowed hard, my mind reeling through a million memories.

Had I missed it?

Because it hit me.

The way he'd been too attentive.

Too interested in what we were doing.

Always asking me questions.

Where I was going and who I was with.

But at the time, it'd barely blipped on my radar.

"He was . . . odd."

More tears streaked from her eyes, soaking her face. "He wasn't odd, Nikki. He was a monster."

Horror locked up my throat, and my hands went to my chest as if it might shield me from her words.

"He was a creep and a monster, Nikki. Of the worst kind. A vile, disgusting creep who stole my childhood. My innocence. He made me believe I could never trust a man until Lyle came into my life. And . . . and . . . and I just have this sick feeling . . ."

Her grief spun through the room. Hanging on the dense air. Clinging to the walls.

I swore I could feel it crawling across the floor and climbing into me.

My spirit shook, so heavy I could feel the weight of it sagging in the middle of me.

Regret and confusion and anger.

Who knew hate could be such an instant thing?

But I did.

I hated him.

Hated that he could hurt my sister.

"Sammie." Tears flooded down my face. "I'm so sorry I didn't know."

She swiped at the wetness on her face and released a brittle, frustrated sound. "How could you know when I kept it a secret? It was my darkest secret, Nikki, because I couldn't stand the thought of someone knowing. Of someone knowing what he'd done to me."

My eyes squeezed, and I forced out the words, praying she hadn't gone through this alone her whole life. "But Lyle knows?"

She barely nodded. "He knows what happened to me. He doesn't know who. He thinks it was a stranger. I didn't know how to tell him if I didn't want my family to know. God knows what he'd do."

Oh, that made two of us.

Fury bristled through my being, and I thought maybe I could relate to the things Ollie had said. To the way he'd wanted to hunt down whoever had hurt his sister.

The overwhelming need to make something right when you had absolutely no control over it.

But at least in this circumstance, we could still do something.

Sammie suddenly gasped for a breath. "I didn't . . . I didn't want to burden you with this when you were dealing with so much, but I couldn't keep it in any longer. Not with him out there. Not with my baby girl in her room . . . not with other little girls out there. Not after all these years of hiding it. I . . . I—"

A shadow of grief clouded her face. "What if he's hurt someone else? What if I never told anyone, and he did it to someone else? I'm responsible for that."

Dropping onto my knees on the carpeted floor, I inched her direction, took her by both of the wrists, and lifted her arms in between us.

They'd been hanging so helplessly at her sides.

I needed her to know she wasn't weak. That she had strength.

"No. You can't blame yourself. You were just a little girl."

Conflict pinched her face. "It was still happening when I was fifteen." Her voice clogged with a ragged cry.

"Fifteen, Nikki," she begged, as if it changed things, and she was all of a sudden somehow responsible.

But that's what predators did. They made their victims believe they were somehow to blame. That they should be the one's ashamed, manipulating and filling them with fear.

A panicked disgust clotted in my chest, and I was sure my heart was no longer working. "It's not your fault. It's his. But . . ."

My voice shifted to a quiet plea, praying my sister would find comfort in me. That she would understand she no longer had to be afraid. "We have to report this to the police, Sammie. We can't let him get away with this."

"I know." The words cracked, and a cry ripped from her throat.

It was born of desperation. Of grief and sorrow and shame.

She began to ramble, "I just . . . you have to give me a little time. I've been trying so hard. So hard to get to the point where I could tell you, and I trust you more than anyone."

She squeezed her eyes shut and struggled for a breath. "They're gonna ask for details, Nikki. I know they are, and I don't think I'm ready yet."

I squeezed her hand. "How long was it going on?"

She dropped her attention to the floor, shuttering, her chest heaving with her breaths. "He always . . . made me uncomfortable. The way he used to look at me. The way he'd brush against me. I was twelve the first time he took me to one of those abandoned buildings by the river."

Shock blew me back, and the air sucked into my vacant lungs.

A cloying type of awareness shook through me.

"What did you say?"

She blinked. "The buildings. Down on Row."

Tremors rocked through me.

Full body.

Jolting.

"Oh, God. Oh God."

I couldn't breathe.

No.

No.

It couldn't be. I was making assumptions, anxiety and fear getting out ahead of me.

Dizziness swooped down, making my mind tilt and the room cant.

I tried to get to my feet, but the weakness that had taken hold of my knees nearly dropped me back to the ground. My hand darted out to the couch as I forced myself to stand.

Nausea churned, twisting my stomach in painful knots. I tried to swallow around the bile I could feel crawling up my throat.

"Oh God," I whispered again, looking around as if I were searching for an answer when there wasn't one there.

Sammie pushed to standing, her hand on my arm, worry moving all over her face. "What if it was him?"

My eyes shifted to her.

I knew they poured with sorrow. With speculation.

The same as hers.

It hit me light a freight train.

What she'd been implying all along.

Why she felt compelled to tell me now.

I stumbled back, hand scrubbing over my face in hopes that it might break up the confusion. "I need to go. I need to think."

I stumbled back into the kitchen and grappled for my purse, which I'd left on the little breakfast nook table last night.

I jerked open the door.

A tease of daylight danced on the horizon, cool morning air splashing my face.

It didn't matter.

I felt sticky.

Clammy.

I stumbled down the two steps, unable to move any farther when I lurched forward and puked in the shrubs.

My spirit revolting.

Purging the instinct that had kicked up at the back of my mind.

Sammie was behind me. "Nikki, what are you going to do?"

"I just . . . I need to think. Figure this out."

I didn't even want to contemplate it. Didn't want it to be true.

"He was a monster."

Sammie's confession whipped through my spirit.

"Where are you going?" she begged, clinging to the railing on the steps.

"I don't know. I just . . . I need to go."

I had to make sense of this before I made accusations I couldn't take back. Even though my gut screamed they were real.

"Please, don't do something stupid."

I ran to her and pulled her into my arms, squeezing her so tight I could feel her heart battering against mine. "I'm so sorry, my sweet sister."

Then I turned and rushed away.

thirty-four

Ollie

*F*ootsteps pounded on the damp earth.

Desperate.
Frantic.
Trees rose on all sides, sentries and witnesses, and branches tore into my skin as I ran through the oppressive night.
Searching.
My eyes blurred in the darkness. Muddied by despair. I stumbled through the forest. Gnarled roots twisted, like spindly fingers that had clawed out of hell to hold me back.
Tears burned my cheeks as the wind blasted my face.
Cruel like the laughter I swore I heard before it was swallowed by a gust of air.
I screamed in the middle of it. "Sydney!"
Voice hoarse, throat bleeding with the pain. "Sydney!"
Sydney. Sydney. Sydney.
I dropped to my knees.
Sydney.

I roared, trying to break free of the sheets that were twisted around me like ropes and chains. Sweat slicked my skin, and my heart was busting right through the confines of my ribs.

Panted cries clawed at my raw throat.

Panic and desperation.

I kicked off the sheets and sat up on the edge of my bed.

I blinked through the dusky shadows that leapt through my room, trying to ignore what had pulled me from sleep.

Banging.

A constant pound, pound, pound at my front door.

The room spun like a bitch, that bottle I'd drained sitting in my stomach like a lethal dose of poison.

Or maybe it was just the poison of what I'd done.

Sydney.

Sydney.

I could still hear my screams echoing back from the forest. I'd hunted for days, which had turned to weeks . . . months . . . years.

Listening and waiting, and for all these years, the tiniest spark of hope had remained.

The hope that she was out there somewhere, safe and happy but trying to get home.

A fool's dream. A dream that had kept me going.

Moving.

Breathing.

Pain attacked me from all sides.

Knives stabbing deep, driving all the way through.

Piercing. Cutting.

My guts spilled out onto the floor.

I'd wanted to be a better man. Fuck, I'd wanted to be a better man.

"All I want is for you to love me."

Nikki's voice danced through the void of my room.

Taunting. Coaxing. Prodding.

Little Tease.

Little Tease.

I wanted to cling to it. Hold it. Cherish it.

But it hurt too bad.

More pounding echoed from the front door.

"Go away," I shouted, knowing there wasn't a chance in hell they could hear me from my room.

Whoever it was just kept on. Becoming more and more demanding. Harder and harsher with each boom.

Someone wanted to get their ass kicked.

Scrubbing a palm down my face, I glanced at the clock.

Four in the afternoon.

Fuck.

I should have gotten up.

Gone to the station.

Demanded answers.

Hunted more.

Hopelessness wrapped around me.

Chained to bricks and stones that dragged me down into the blackest abyss.

What the fuck good would it do?

I had nothing left to find.

Nothing left to give.

I hadn't checked in downstairs. Had no clue if the shifts were manned. If the bar was running smoothly or if everything had gone to hell.

Thing was, that bar could burn to the ground with me in it, and I wouldn't even blink.

Because I was already in hell.

A brutal, unrelenting hell.

Another round of pounding.

I did my best to keep the rush of fury in check, but my blood was already boiling.

At myself. At the world. At whoever had done this to my sister.

Pain clutched my stomach when I let the idea slink into my mind. Swore that it physically shredded my insides.

Still couldn't process it. Didn't want to.

Couldn't stop it.

It was the only thing I could see.

Blood.

Dirt.

Bones.

A cry raked from my lungs.

More pounding.

I staggered out that way, careening across the floor, ready to tear into any poor fucker who was waiting on the other side.

I peered through the peephole.

Rex.

Motherfucker.

That was a whole new layer I couldn't process.

Couldn't stomach.

A fresh round of hatred went skating through my veins. Boiling over.

"Not sure you want me to let you in here."

"Need to talk to you," rumbled through the wood.

"Not exactly up for chit chat."

Because what the fuck was he going to say?

"Not going anywhere until you open this door, so you might as well open up."

"Then you're going to be there all night."

"God damn it, Ollie, this isn't a fucking game. Open the door. I need to talk to you."

Rage had me twisting the lock and flinging the door open.

"You got something to say?"

Bitterness bled out.

Hurt right behind it.

Rex stood in my doorway.

Dark bags under his eyes. Hair a complete mess.

Like he hadn't slept for a second last night.

Ridden with guilt.

Good.

Warily, he glanced up at me. "Deserve for you to hate me, Ollie. I should have told you a long time ago."

Sharp laughter bounced from the walls. "You should have told me? Told me what? That you were fucking my little sister? That the two of you had something going on that night? That you knew where she went?"

I moved to get in his face, words flying, razors on my tongue. "Is that what you've got to tell me?"

He shoved me.

It was enough to knock me back a foot.

He jabbed his finger against my chest. "You want to blame me, Ollie? Blame me. Fine. If you think I haven't been blaming myself for all these years, you're a fool."

My teeth ground as I got back in his face. "Yeah, you made me a fool. Keeping this from me? Are you kiddin' me, Rex? You were supposed to be my best friend. I trusted you with her, and you were the one I should have been protecting her from."

Rex stalked deeper into my loft, hands ripping at his hair, growls coming from him like he was the one who was about to lose all control instead of me.

He whirled back around. "I fucking loved her, okay?"

He gasped, like saying it was met with gutting relief.

"I loved her, and you made it plenty clear that I couldn't. That any guy who even looked at your sister was getting his ass kicked. Tell me how the fuck we could contend with that?"

His face contorted in anger.

In rage and grief.

"So, we snuck around. Kept it a secret so we wouldn't hurt you. Because your sister didn't want you to be angry with her. Didn't want you to be angry with me. She was keeping the peace the exact same way as you did with Nikki."

I jarred back.

He scoffed. "Don't act like we didn't know. All this time, and you think we didn't know? That she didn't know?"

Shock beat through my blood. "Sydney knew?"

Rex huffed a breath. "Of course, she knew. She was pissed you wouldn't tell her. That you thought you had to keep her out. That you wouldn't let her in."

More regret.

Could I shoulder any more of it? I didn't fucking know how. I could feel it piling on me.

Rubble and rocks and debris.

A fucking bomb.

It'd destroyed any semblance of peace.

Old grief curled through Rex's hard expression, something sour seeping through.

"And I was too big of a pussy to stand up and say something. I should have said something. Instead I—" His words broke off, and Rex gave a harsh shake of his head.

Heartbreak.

I knew exactly what it looked like.

It clutched and clung and tortured.

Slamming him from all sides.

"If I'd have just stood up that day and made a claim, Ollie."

He choked, trying to bite back a sob.

Like it'd come from out of nowhere.

Balled up grief that had simmered for too many years.

His eyes filled with moisture, and my heart was beating out of my fucking chest.

Regret. Confusion. Sympathy.

For a beat, I covered my face with both my hands.

What the fuck was I supposed to think? What was I supposed to feel? Because right then, I was feeling too damned much.

Rex stood up straight. Stretching his arms out wide. "It was my fault. Be pissed off at me, man. Hate me. Blame me. Because it was my fault. She was there that night because that was where I was gonna be. She was pissed *because* of me. She left *because* of me."

With every line of confession, he hit his fist against his chest.

Harder each time.

"Because I kissed that chick because that was what I thought you expected me to do. You were right that night. I *was* a pussy. I was a pussy because I didn't have the guts to tell my best friend I loved his sister." He slammed his fist against his heart again.

"My fault." It was a rasped cry that boomed against my walls.

I blinked at him, trying to see through the daze. To process and add and make sense of what he was saying.

His mouth twisted in agony. "We loved each other. We did. Just like you loved Nikki, and you're a fucking fool if you think that it was any different."

He sucked in a choppy breath. "We're all responsible. All of us . . . a bunch of stupid, ignorant kids who didn't know any better. We made mistakes. Mistakes we didn't have any clue would lead to what they did."

My back hit the wall, and I was searching for air, lungs squeezed tight.

Regret shook Rex's head. "The next morning when we found out she hadn't made it home . . ." He stumbled like he couldn't handle the memory, his voice hoarse and raw when he finally spoke. "I wanted to die. I wanted to curl up and die, Ollie."

Hurt blistered through me.

His.

Mine.

My body rocked.

I didn't know how to stand under it.

"Rex," I attempted. Needing to shut him down. Because I wasn't sure how much more of this I could take.

Torment rushed from him on a torrent.

The guy beaten up and mangled.

In a way I'd never seen him before.

Like maybe there was a chance he felt an ounce of what I was feeling right then.

He held his hand out like he was the one stopping me. "Just fucking listen, man. I've kept this in for so long. For so long, and I can't bear it anymore."

A harsh breath wheezed into his lungs. "I didn't say anything because I didn't know how to admit it. I didn't know how to tell you I was the one to blame. I was fucking terrified and heartbroken, and all I wanted was for it to end."

An exact echo of me.

Rex took another step back in my direction. "We fucked up. We fucked up so bad. But I see it clearly now. I get it in a way I couldn't then. Those mistakes weren't malicious. They weren't cruel or intended to hurt. They were mistakes we made as we tried to figure out who we were."

His brow twisted in emphasis. "Figure out how to live and who we were supposed to be. How we'd all fit because every single one of us knew things had changed. No longer kids but not grown, either. All of us were fumbling through."

His entire face pinched.

Agony and grief.

Lifting an arm, he drove his finger toward the door as he chucked the words. "But there is someone out there who *is* cruel. Someone who *is* malicious. Someone out there who did this to her. Someone who hurt her. He's the one to blame, Ollie."

Stumbling back, he bent in two, his hands on his knees as he tried to catch his breath like he'd just been struck in the stomach with a bat. "He *did* this. Not you. Not me."

I could barely form the words, the weight of them so heavy on my tongue. "We sent her out into the night. By herself."

"I know." He angled his face up to look at me. "I know. I've carried that for so many years, just like you have. And God, it hurts so bad, thinking about what she might have gone through. But I *knew* Sydney, and so did you."

He seemed to have to force himself to straighten. "And I know you know she wouldn't want this. You know she'd want you to live. To experience and to love and to take this life for all it's worth."

My hands curled into fists, my mind and my heart and my spirit at war.

For a minute, we got lost in it, both of us trying to catch up, before Rex took a step forward, his head angling as he started to speak.

"Rynna? My family? They are *that* life. I didn't think I could love again after Sydney. It took me so many years of hating myself, thinking I deserved to be alone, that I didn't get to find joy because of it. Thinking I deserved to suffer."

Tremors raked down my spine, his words like claws sinking into my skin.

"I know better now. I know that's not what Sydney would have wanted. I got that chance to live, Ollie. I was given it, and I'm not going to reject that gift. I won't waste it. I love Rynna with all of me. Wholly. I was the fool who thought I didn't have anything left to give when really I had everything. Right there. Waiting for me."

Emotion curled and crushed.

Overwhelming.

Too much.

He shifted away, his hands on his hips, speaking the words toward the wall. "Don't waste your life blaming yourself, Ollie. I've stood aside and watched you in misery for too long. I was a fucking coward who couldn't tell you the truth because I was afraid you'd hate me. I'd convinced myself it'd only hurt you more, knowing about us. But I know better now."

He looked back at me. "It's time for us to both stop making those mistakes. It's time for us to live. To embrace life the way Sydney would have wanted us to. Don't waste that. Don't waste what you and Nikki have. I haven't seen you happy in so goddamned long . . . and these last weeks? That's what you've been. Happy."

Could feel my heart clattering in my chest. My voice shook. "I don't know how to do that . . . how to live knowing she didn't. I've spent my whole life searching for her. I don't know how to accept that she's . . . gone."

Saying it was a blade.

Cutting deep.

Tears blurred my eyes.

Sydney was gone.

He looked back at me, his mouth wobbling with the truth. "You remember who she was."

Fly, fly dragonfly.

We both jerked when the door leading to the outside stairs banged open. I moved to peer out into the hall.

I had to blink to clear my eyes, my spirit soaring at the sight before I realized it wasn't Nikki.

It was Sammie.

Wringing her fingers nervously, attention darting all over the place like she thought she was doing something wrong.

"Sammie," I said, stepping out into the hall. "What are you doing here?"

She gulped and tentatively looked up at me. "I'm worried about Nikki. She left early this morning, and I can't get in touch with her. I was hoping she was here."

It was instant.

The worry that blasted through me. "She's not here. I haven't talked to her. What do you mean, she left early?"

Sammie's face fell. "I think she's in trouble."

Felt the world crashing down on me when Sammie nervously told me her suspicion of her uncle, and I grabbed my keys, rushing for the door.

Rex told me to go, promising that he would get Sammie home safely.

No one needed to be alone until we were sure.

Sammie didn't want to speculate.

Terrified she was pointing a finger that shouldn't be pointed.

But my guts screamed, my spirit sure.

I didn't wait for the elevator. I took the three flights of stairs faster than I ever had, busting into the garage after I'd punched in the code.

Dread leeched through every inch of me when my sight landed on my turquoise truck.

The windshield was smashed in.

Fury rumbled like a storm.

Coming closer and closer.

My garage was a fucking fortress.

A place not a soul who wasn't welcome should be able to get in to.

I inched forward.

Fear leeched into my flesh when I reached out and plucked the tiny folded note out from under the wiper.

Heart in my throat, I unfolded it, horror eating me up when I found what was written inside.

She can't hide. She's always been mine.

Nikki

It was funny how different it felt being out there alone. When there were no voices to cloud the calm beauty of the scene spread out like a painting in front of me.

The gurgle of the streams and the rush of the water as it gathered strength, rolling over the side of the jagged cliffs and tumbling to the lake far, far below.

I needed it.

Peace.

For hours, I'd driven in search of an answer, and I'd ended up here, seeking a place to process what had become a muddled, chaotic disaster inside me.

One made of sorrow and hurt and an onslaught of overwhelmingly devastating questions.

I lifted my face to the blazing sun that pounded from above, falling through the Alabama sky that was the purest blue.

The sweeping stretch of beauty laid out below was almost a mirror, the blue, expansive lake and the twist of the river that wound around the mountain in the distance.

My spirit throbbed and pulsed, and the prayer silently spilled out into the vast expanse of land below.

Sydney, I'm so sorry. I'm so sorry this happened to you.

I hate it.

I wish I could go back to that day and change it.

Take it back.

Let you know that we loved you. So much. It was the fear of it that had held our tongues. We'd never, ever wanted to sever those bonds.

Yet, those bonds had been severed in the worst, worst way.

And my sister . . .

Hugging my knees to my chest, I rocked where I sat on a dry patch on a smooth stone that had been carved out by the flow of the waters.

Sadness cut through the center of me. I had no idea how to piece it together.

If I was attempting to draw lines that didn't connect or if I was just praying that they didn't.

A gentle breeze rippled through, swishing through the tops of the trees. I hugged my knees tighter.

I swore, I could feel her brushing across me, a whisper in my ear.

Fly, fly, dragonfly.

A wistful smile tugged at one side of my mouth, and I let my eyes drop closed and relished in her memory.

In her hope and her beauty and the way she had looked at life.

I was almost too lost in the moment to hear the movement behind me. It took me a second before I froze just as the hairs at the nape of my neck prickled in awareness, standing on end.

"They'll be coming for me soon."

The voice swallowed me from behind.

Low and menacing.

Disgust swam with the fear. Lighting my nerves and jumping into my veins.

Todd. He was there.

And I suddenly got the sensation of something I should have known all along.

The way he'd watched.

The comments he'd made.

Always right there, gaze directed at me in ways it shouldn't have been.

Tremors rolled, and I tried to hold them back when I slowly pushed to standing and cautiously swiveled around to face him.

He stood at the edge of the woods that grew up the side of the mountain behind him.

The same mountain where I'd played as a child. Ran and laughed and believed.

"Uncle Todd." I attempted to send him a surprised, welcoming smile as if this were all one big coincidence when all I wanted to do was throw up again.

This was the man who'd hurt my sister.

Inflicted a kind of pain I couldn't comprehend.

My mind flipped back through everything that had happened over the last few months.

My apartment getting broken into.

My grandma's box stolen.

The notes on my windshield.

Caleb shouting at Ollie that he had no clue what he had been talking about.

It wasn't until that second I realized he hadn't been lying.

It wasn't Caleb who had done all those things.

Todd cracked a smile that sent a cold chill skating over me. "Well . . . if it isn't Nikki Lou."

I tried to smile again. All I managed was a grimace with the way he was looking at me. "What are you doing all the way out here?" I asked, going for coy.

As if I were clueless.

A naïve little girl.

That's what he'd always wanted, right?

"Looking for you."

My knees knocked.

Oh, God.

I had to stay strong.

I frowned at him in an innocuous way. "Well, you could have just called. I would have been happy to come out to Grandma's for a visit."

"Think we both know it's too late for that."

My mouth went dry. "I don't know what you're talking about."

It was a lie.

I knew it would be so much better to play dumb with a desperate man.

He laughed. Biting and hard. "Come now, Nikki. You think I don't recognize it in your eyes? You think I don't see the way you're looking at me?"

So badly, I wanted to refute it. To stand my ground. To continue to pretend. But the denial of his claim won out. "You don't know anything about me."

An ominous chuckle rode on the dense, dense air. "I know everything about you, Nikki."

My blood froze.

My heart stuttered.

I tried to remain steady. To draw out time. Studying the best way to beat him.

Fight or flight.

I still wasn't sure.

All I knew was I wouldn't let him win.

His nose curled in some kind of unknown disgust. "I should have known better than to trust someone to do what they're told. Should have known that punk kid would get greedy and not follow directions."

Confusion had me shaking my head. "I honestly have no idea what you're talking about."

It was true.

He was talking in circles.

Unbalanced.

I guessed I'd just missed out on the fact he was deranged.

He made a low sound. Disbelief and outrage. "He was supposed to dump that old car. Should have done it myself, but I figured the farther away I kept myself from it, the better. Hell, should have done it all those years ago, but I figured I'd better get gone."

A disorder shifted through the breeze. Branches lashing as if they felt the tumult.

He took a step forward, coming out of the shade of the trees and into the light.

Depraved darkness standing in the rays.

Brown hair greasy and unkempt, the same way as it'd always been. Clothes a little ratty. Those few extra pounds prominent around his middle. None of those things mattered.

It was the evil in his eyes that made him ugly.

"Never imagined that tweeker would run straight to that asshole who was always watching you like he thought you belonged to him."

Uncertainty moved through me, a niggle at the back of my mind that was quickly adding up.

He was talking about the Bel Air.

Ollie had bought the Bel Air.

"You know Caleb?" I asked.

Keep him talking.

Keep him talking.

"Of course, I know who Caleb is considering you do. Wasn't sure if I should run out and protect you from him that night a couple months back when I followed you to his and that girl's apartment. Had to stay back when the cops showed up a few minutes later."

Dread spiraled.

He'd been following me all this time.

Since the first time Brenna had called me for help.

"About a week later, I found him downtown, all itchy and antsy, and I knew it wouldn't take all that much to convince him to haul it away." Todd smiled as if his thought process was genius.

"He was supposed to dump it in the river or the lake. Should have known, even with all the rust, he'd be seeing dollar signs. Didn't want to get close to it, touch it, dirty it up more."

"Dirty?" Fear blazed. So hot I could feel the bead of sweat slide down my spine.

I took a step back, trying to keep as much distance between us as possible.

"What do you mean by that?"

His voice was nonchalant. "I was watching. Figured it wasn't such a bad thing when they were gonna take it into that garage and fix her up. That might even be better than dumping it in the lake. But the second I saw that pig show up and the police take it away, I knew I had to speed things up. That you and I didn't have that much more time."

He was moving closer, rounding to the side. For every step of his, I took one in the opposite direction.

"And my apartment?" I asked, hating that I had to, but knowing my only chance of getting away from him was understanding his depravity.

"Sorry about that, but I had to get that box. Put some stuff in there for safe keeping 'fore I left. When I heard my ma was starting to sell stuff off, that she was failing, I knew it was time I came back. Been planning it for a while, needing to get back to you. It was a sign when your mama told me on the phone she'd been clearing out the attic. That was my collection, you know?"

Nausea surged and my heart hurt.

God only knew what was in that box.

"Didn't help matters that you had to go and run those classes for women in that basement. Bunch of hens cackling and gossiping and saying things they have no business saying. Your head all filled up with that nonsense."

"How do you know that?" I shouldn't have said anything, shouldn't have bitten, but the scraping words pulled free of my throat.

His chuckle could have been construed as affectionate—soft and warm— if it hadn't skated through me like ice. "Told you, I know everything about you. Been watching you for your whole life. Knew the second I saw you that you were mine. 'Course, I had to stop watching you for a bit when things got messy, and I had to go away."

Messy.

Sydney.

Sydney.

I'm so sorry. I'm so sorry.

Bile prowled my throat, stomach twisting in sickness.

Vomit threatened at my mouth, and I struggled to keep it down. To stay strong.

But I was so close to falling to my knees and weeping.

For my sister.

For my best friend.

For me.

We'd begun to circle. Our footsteps crunched beneath us, his forward, mine back.

I was trying to figure out the best direction to run, the quickest route to help, when the wicked words strummed from his tongue.

"Didn't mean to kill her."

A stifled gasp jerked into my lungs.

The air stifling.

Suffocating.

"Why?" It was a plea. "Why would you hurt her? Hurt my sister?"

Why if he'd always been after me?

He shrugged as if it didn't matter. "Some things you just have to test out."

I choked.

"I had to protect us, Nikki. Everything I've ever done, I've done for you. So we can be together."

My knees wobbled.

"They weren't supposed to find her . . . and that damned car . . . should have burned it." He said it all as if I should feel sorry for him.

As if the world was against him when he was the monster prowling in the midst.

"Now everyone's gonna know. Means we don't have much time.

thirty-six

Sydney
Sixteen Years Old

Tears stung her eyes, and her heart physically hurt. She hugged herself around her middle as she trudged along the side of the curving country road.

She should have called her mama like Ollie had suggested, but she needed to think. Clear her head before she went and said something she would regret.

She tightened her arms around her as a hot wind blew through, her skin sticky from the exertion and her face hot from the tears.

She was so over this. It was as if all four of them were playing a stupid game and none of them were gonna win.

She almost rolled her eyes.

As if she didn't know about Ollie and Nikki.

She'd known for years that there was something extra special about the two of them. That they were more. Their spirits seemed tangled in a way that'd been intended before time existed.

Made for each other.

Did they really think she would consider that a bad thing?

Did they even know her at all?

She just wanted them to embrace it.

Live free.

The same as she wanted for herself and Rex.

And the only thing it felt like was they were clipping her wings.

Cutting little bits of her away as they pushed her further to the outside.

There was no reason for them to be hiding, just like there was no reason for her and Rex to be hiding.

Rex.

At the thought of his name, her chest pulled tight.

Stretched and yearned.

She loved him so much. She didn't think she really knew how much until she'd had to watch him kiss that girl.

And she was the one who got to stay.

The one who was with him.

New tears pricked at her eyes.

He hadn't come after her. Hadn't stood up for her. Instead, he'd just driven a knife into her heart.

No more.

She stumbled to a stop.

No more.

Maybe Rex didn't know what she wanted. That she wanted him to stand up for her. Make a claim.

Fight for her.

She'd just have to do it herself.

She touched the red, woven bracelet that she always wore around her left wrist. The other two matching pieces belonging to Ollie and Nikki.

Her best friends.

But they had to realize her life was changing, too.

All of them had to make room for something new.

She came to a stop.

Realization struck.

She was gonna turn around, go back to that camp, and demand Rex say it.

Tell Ollie.

She was his and he was hers and no one would have anything bad to say about it.

Because *it* was good.

They were good.

Ollie and Nikki were good.

She started to cross the road but froze when headlights cut into the night and a loud car roared around the corner.

She took a step back away from the road as it flew by before the red brake lights flashed, splashing the color all over the night as the old car skidded to a stop.

Her heart trembled with a dose of anxiety.

She squinted her eyes, relief leaving her on a breath when she realized she recognized that car.

Nikki's grandpa.

He could give her a ride back to the lake.

She jogged that way with a smile on her face, and she saw his silhouette as he leaned over to fling open the passenger door as she approached. She started to duck her head inside to say hello when her knees wobbled beneath her.

Not Nikki's grandpa.

It was Nikki's uncle.

Todd.

He grinned, his teeth stained yellow from cigarettes, his hands still greasy from always working on cars.

There was something about him Sydney had never liked. The way he looked at Nikki. Watched her too close.

"Well, look who it is. Sydney Sue. Where's my Nikki Lou?"

Unease rippled through her consciousness, a cringe rolling through her at the stupid, creepy nicknames he'd give them, as if it was actually their middle names.

"She's at home," Sydney lied. Not sure why.

He frowned. "That so?"

His eyes moved over her, and a cold shiver rippled down her back.

"What are you doin' out here all alone?"

"I'm just heading home," she said, angling back.

"I'll give you a ride."

She backed away. "No, that's okay. My brother should be coming this way in a second, anyway."

She pinned on a smile and hoped he'd fall for the lie.

He wasn't exactly the smartest guy she knew.

His eyes flicked from her face and down to her chest. "You look different than her."

He said it as if she should be ashamed of it. As if it were disappointing.

Then he shrugged. "Guess for tonight, you'll have to do."

thirty-seven

Ollie

"Don't do anything until I get there, Ollie. I'm right behind you."

"No promises, man."

Not when it came to Nikki.

My Nikki.

My girl who'd been desperate to be there through this with me, and I'd been too much of a fool to see it for what it was.

Thinking I forever owed a debt, the girl nothing but a tease, a torment of what I couldn't have.

When in reality?

She'd been a gift, always right there, waiting for me to accept it.

I tossed my cell to the seat beside me and made a sharp right onto the drive that was close to being hidden under a thicket of trees that ran the land.

Engine roaring, I gunned the accelerator. My Mustang bounced on the dirt road, wheels kicking up a cloud of dust as I flew down the narrow lane.

The heart I thought I no longer had thrashed at my chest, my teeth clenched just about as tight as my hands were clenched on the steering wheel.

I barreled around the corner, and the old house came into view.

There were a million memories here. I could get lost in them. Stuck like I'd been.

But I realized when Sammie had stood there in the hall, I couldn't change the past, no matter how fucking badly I wanted to.

I had nothing but this moment and the future.

Nothing but Nikki.

Swinging into the rounded drive at the front of the house, I rammed the brakes and jumped out, not bothering to shut the door when I thundered up the rickety porch steps that had seen far better days.

I pounded on the door and then began to pace, roughing a hand over the top of my head as I waited.

As seconds ticked.

As I felt myself going insane.

I couldn't let this happen.

I couldn't let someone hurt her.

I promised I'd protect her.

That I wasn't ever gonna let anyone hurt her.

I could hear the car coming up the road, and Seth's cruiser rolled into view right when Nikki's mom swung open the door with a smile on her face.

A smile that slid off the second she saw me.

"Oliver Preston." She looked around, spotting the approaching patrol car. Worry took hold of her expression.

"What are you doing here? What's going on? Is Nikki okay?" Each word came faster than the last, panted pleas winding into her tone when she stepped outside.

Anxiety fisted my throat, and I pushed the gritted words through it. "I was hoping you could tell me that. You haven't seen her?"

She shook her head, and there was no missing the glimmers of fear that streaked through her expression when Seth stepped from his car.

Her brow pinched with confusion. "No . . . I haven't seen her for a couple of days. Sammie called a few hours ago, wondering if she'd come by, but she didn't say anything else."

Apprehension trembled her voice, and she reached out and grabbed my arm. "Tell me what's going on."

"I need to find her."

"What's happening?"

"Where's that piece of shit Todd?"

The question knocked her back a step, and her brows twisted into a knot. "I . . . I don't know. Heard him leaving late last night. I don't think he's been back."

Fuck. Fuck. Fuck.

I fisted my hands in my hair, searching for the air. Desperation climbing.

"Does he still stay in the trailer in the back lot?"

Warily, she nodded.

I spun around.

Seth caught me by the arm as he came up to the door. "Where are you going?"

I ripped my arm away. "To find Nikki."

I bounded down the steps and ran for the trailer that sat a little more than a quarter mile back from the house.

"Ollie," Seth shouted from behind me. "Wait, man. We need to let the warrant come through."

I didn't even stop to ponder it. I pounded the heel of my fist on the door.

Nothing.

No movement.

Holding on to the railing, I leaned back and lifted my leg.

"Fuck, Ollie, you can't just bust in there."

"Watch me."

There was no way I was sitting idle.

Waiting.

Not when waiting meant we could be running out of time.

I slammed the sole of my boot into the door at the side of the flimsy knob. The old wood splintered and gave. Nothing holding it together.

I wrenched open the door, flying inside.

The place was a disgusting mess. Dishes piled in the sink, garbage everywhere.

Decay and rot.

Silence hung in the air.

Vacant.

Ominous.

A stark emptiness echoing back.

Still, I couldn't stop myself from pushing deeper into the rat hole, rushing down the short hall and throwing open the door to the only bedroom.

The sight bent me in two.

Pictures.

Everywhere.

All of them were of Nikki.

Baby pictures.

Ones of her as a little girl.

A few with Sydney as a teenager.

But it was the current ones that sent panic sloshing through my system.

There were a bunch of Nikki at the diner.

Some outside of Olive's.

One of her walking up the steps to her apartment.

Motherfucker.

Her apartment.

It was him. It was him.

My eyes darted around for anything else, and I started to push out of the room, when my sight snagged on something in the closet.

The sliding door had barely been left open a sliver.

A floral box.

A box.

Anxiety gripped me everywhere, and my movements slowed as I edged forward. Slowly, I slid the closet door open farther. The lock had been broken, the lid ripped off, the contents tossed aside as if someone had frantically dug through it to find what was hidden underneath.

A groan climbed out from my soul.

Agony.

Sydney's bracelet.

It was there in the middle of it as if the asshole had needed to hold it.

Sick and deranged and twisted.

"Oh God," I whimpered, unable to stomach it.

Sickness clawed, and I was clutching my head, trying to see through the web of darkness that spun through me.

Cruelty.

Cruelty.

My sister.

Fuck, my sister.

It hurt. It hurt so damned bad.

The reality.

I'd hunted for so long.

And the proof was right there.

It was like the idiot wanted everyone to know. Or maybe he'd just realized once they'd found Sydney, there was no place left to hide.

I'd die before I let it happen again.

"Shit," Seth whispered in shock from behind me, pulling me back. "Get out of here, Ollie. Don't touch anything. This is evidence."

I blinked at him, seeing nothing but red.

He didn't have to ask me twice.

I was busting back out the door and running for my Mustang.

"What do you think you're doing?" he shouted.

I jumped inside. "I'm going to find Nikki. You go to her apartment . . . he's been there. Call me if you find anything."

"Where are you going?"

"Up the river."

"I can't just let you take off like some kind of vigilante. I'm calling it in, everyone will be looking for them."

"And you can't expect me to stand aside and wait for that to happen. I'll call you if I see anything. Swear, man. I'll call. But you can't expect me to sit here. Go. Find her," I begged him.

He gave me a reluctant nod before he jogged back to his cruiser.

I was throwing my car into first when I met Nikki's mom's stare through the windshield. Her hands were pressed against her chin and tears blanketed her face.

I made her a silent promise.

I'll fight for her.

I'll die for her.

Most of all, I'll live for her.

Twenty minutes later, I'd made it through town. Dusk sat heavily as I wound down the twisty, country road.

My nerves were speeding while I drove like a motherfucking snail, foot itching to hit the gas. But I was looking for a hint of . . . anything. Anything that felt off.

I passed the turn that lead to the lake and wound around a bend, heading for Row. There were at least a hundred little offshoots of deserted roads, no more than trails carved out between the trees.

Anxiety clawed, the sharpest talons in my flesh.

Flickers of awareness.

Realization and a tease.

Little Tease.

I jammed on the brakes in the middle of the road as a sticky feeling came over me.

Drawn.

Compelled.

Row would still be crawling with investigators.

And Nikki . . . she wouldn't go there.

I knew it.

I knew it all the way into my soul.

Heart taking off at a sprint, I flipped a U-turn in the middle of the road, tires sliding off into the shrubs and dirt. The tail end whipped behind me when I forced the accelerator to the floor, and I righted the car when it skidded.

Two seconds later, I was cutting across the road to make the left.

Praying the whole way that she was there.

That she was alone.

That she was just seeking the solace this place had always given us.

Needing that peace when I'd done the exact thing I promised her I wouldn't.

I'd hurt her.

Shunned her.

Left her.

When she was dealing with the same damned thing.

I was so finished with being this selfish prick. The guy who thought it was his duty to suffer. Only thing that stupidity accomplished was taking the ones he loved down with him.

Again, I was gonna be the beggar. Pleading for forgiveness when I didn't deserve it. Couldn't change that.

All I could do was fucking fight.

Fight for her.

This time, I would make it right.

The lake shone a vibrant pink as the sun sank at the far end of the sky.

Off to the left was the public beach.

I knew that wouldn't be where Nikki would go.

I barreled on to where the road curved at its end, and I took the same worn-out path we'd used for all our lives.

It wound up through the trees and back down again.

My pulse thudded when I caught sight of the glint of metal in the dusky haze. I edged forward until it fully came into view.

Nikki's car.

But it was the beater truck sitting next to it that punched the air from my lungs.

Sent a quiver of stakes through my spirit.

An earthquake.

Hate and fury and devastation.

I wouldn't let this happen.

Hands shaking like a bitch, I dialed Seth.

He answered on the first ring. "You got anything?"

"They're here. At the secluded cove at the far end of the lake. Both of them. I'm parked behind both their cars."

"Fuck," he shouted. I could hear the siren blip on the other end before it became a full, shrill cry, the sound of his cruiser quickly accelerating. "Do not approach them, Ollie. I'll be there in ten minutes."

"Send help," I told him before tossing my phone back to the seat without taking the time to end the call.

I reached for the glove box and pulled out the handgun I'd taken from the safe before I'd headed for Nikki's grandparents' land.

I jerked open the door, blood pumping so hard I could feel it as it slogged through my body.

Taste it on my tongue.

Rage and desperation.

Fear and hope.

As silently as I could, I edged up the path, terrified of what I was going to find.

If I was too late, I wasn't sure I would survive it this time.

My guts clenched in both relief and misery when I heard the whimper. The rumble of a low voice came out behind it, but the words were indistinguishable.

The threat of night hugged the earth, the day slipping away and stealing the light. Twilight swam through the trees in a dreamlike haze.

Footsteps quieted, I inched all the way up to the spot where we used to jump from the cliffs.

I pressed against a tree, trying not to shout out when they came into view.

In pain.

In vengeance.

In the violence that twisted through me like the blackest storm.

Ravaging.

Annihilating.

Destroying.

Nikki was on her knees, arms twisted behind her back as he stood behind her and shackled her wrists and ankles with a thin twine.

The sick fuck had her gagged, the same twine running across the rag he'd stuffed into her mouth and tied behind her head to keep it in place.

But the hardest part was the terror that blazed in her eyes.

I nearly dropped to my knees when I was slammed with the gutting relief that overwhelmed her when she saw me at the line of trees.

Tears spilled out, and she released a gurgled cry as she sagged forward.

And that energy.

It surged.

So intense.

The greatest thing I'd ever felt.

Wave after wave.

Blast after blast.

This girl was everything.

All of me.

"None of that," the vile piece of shit seethed, yanking her back up, and I had no reservations left.

My feet were moving, the gun lifted in the air, boots crunched beneath me.

His head whipped up. "You little fuck. Always hanging around her. Thinking she belonged to you. I never should have waited so long. It needed to be perfect. It needed to be perfect."

The last spiraled in derangement.

I almost laughed, an unhinged sound I felt bubble at the back of my throat. "Let her go. Let her go. Don't think I will hesitate to kill you."

He killed my sister.

He killed my sister.

Oh God.

Bile swam, and every muscle in my body bristled. Flexed with aggression.

With this possessive protection that seethed from the depths of me.

I took another powerful step forward, promising him I wasn't playing games.

He yanked Nikki to standing, and her gaze was on me, mine on her.

Trust me.

Trust me.

It was a silent plea, praying she would feel me. That I wouldn't allow anything bad to happen to her.

That I was there.

I wouldn't ever leave her again.

I choked, stumbling to a stop when I saw the glint of the knife he had pressed to her side.

"I'd rethink that." His voice was all sneer as he dragged her back against his chest.

They were teetering right at the edge of the cliff. The asshole had backed himself right into a corner, nowhere for him to run.

"Let her go," I demanded, trying to keep the tremble from my voice.

I wasn't backing down.

Like I'd let him take her.

"There's nowhere for you to go. Nothing left. The police are already on their way, and they know what you did to my sister. The game is up. Let her go."

He cracked a demented grin. "She and I have a little time, don't we, Nikki?" he whispered in her ear.

She cried out.

Disgust and revulsion rolled through me. Sickness and that hate.

Hate. So much hate.

For so long, I'd pinned it on myself. No more. This was all on him.

He'd hurt my sister. Sammie. Nikki. God knew who else.

No more.

No more.

My head shook, and the bitterness quivered my lips, but my hand was steady. "Wrong, asshole. Time's up."

Somewhere in the distance, sirens blared, riding on the encroaching night. Coming closer and closer.

As soon as he heard it, deranged panic lit in the sick fuck's eyes. Like he actually thought he was going to make it out of there with Nikki.

Saw it the second he let desperation take him over. He jerked Nikki closer and started to run to the side.

Nikki flailed, swinging her shoulders, kicking her feet.

She broke free, stumbling back and away from him.

He whirled back to look at her. Stunned. Like he couldn't believe she would fight him.

Like he was witnessing his own kind of horror.

That was my chance.

I was taking it.

I rushed that way, intent on tackling the fucker to the ground.

His eyes met mine, and I saw the shift. When he realized he had no choice left.

Madness filled his eyes, his vile gaze darting all over, searching for escape.

The piece of shit started running my direction, charging me with the knife drawn.

Thinking I was going to let him get through me.

Disappear in to the forest.

"Stop," I shouted.

He just kept coming, the knife raised above his head.

"Stop," I roared.

He made a sound to match as he rushed me.

Insane.

Crazed.

Unwilling to stop.

Squeezing my eyes shut, I pulled the trigger.

The sound was deafening.

Ricocheting on the cliffs and rocks and moving through me.

He crumpled into a pile at my feet.

My lungs squeezed, and I panted through the haze, everything set to slow as my mind tried to catch up.

Ears ringing, my attention swooped across the space for Nikki.

She teetered at the edge of the cliffs.

Bound feet sliding out from beneath her. Hands tied behind her and setting her off-balance on the slick, wet surface.

I was running that way as she struggled to regain balance on the slipping rocks.

Those indigo eyes went wide as her feet gave.

Falling backward.

A shout of agony tore from me as I watched her tip over the side.

My pulse thundered, and my heart screamed as loud as the screams that tore from my mouth.

"Nikki! Nikki. God, no, Nikki!"

I raced for the edge.

I skidded right before I hit the crumbling ledge.

Sucking in a staggered breath.

Blinking as I swore I saw Sydney standing at the cliff, her flowy dress billowing around her, hair soft as it whispered across her face.

Her voice lilted on the breeze. *"You were my protector. My savior. My hero. It's okay, Ollie. It's okay to be hers."*

"Forgive me," I begged, the words so small.

She smiled. The softest smile. *"There was never anything to forgive. Just promise me one thing."*

"Anything." It was my own plea.

"Never stop going after what makes your heart feel right."

She angled her head toward the edge and lifted her chin.

"Fly, fly, dragonfly."

I blinked, and she was gone.

And I dove over the side.

Falling.

I'd been all along.

I hit the water. It split, swallowing me in a pit of darkness.

I couldn't see anything, and I started flailing, searching the water, my chest burning from the exertion and the loss of oxygen.

And I felt my sister. All around. And I wondered if she'd always been.

I pushed myself harder, a little deeper.

My fingertips just brushed against something.

Didn't matter.

I saw it.

Could feel it.

The flash.

A spark.

Energy.

Light.

The meaning of life.

A half second later, I had an arm around Nikki's waist, and I propelled us up. We broke the surface, and I was gasping for breath, frantic as I freed her of the bonds.

But Nikki.

She wasn't breathing.

And I was crying out, floating on my back as I turned her so her face was out of the water, swimming back toward the shore with one arm.

The sound of the sirens traveled across the water, and swirling lights came into view from the shore, hitting the lake and blinking across the sky like an endless mirror.

"Nikki," I cried, my feet finally hitting the bottom of the lake. I gathered her in my arms and staggered up the rocky beach as officers came rushing down the incline.

I screamed with everything I had. "Help!"

thirty-eight

Ollie

The monitor blipped quietly in the still of the room, the lights muted and her soft, soft breaths filling the air.

Swore, they breathed right back into me.

The sound of her where she slept on the hospital bed.

Olive skin and honeyed hair and freckled cheeks.

Sunshine.

She still hadn't gained consciousness, but they thought she was going to be okay.

Her saturations and pulse ox had been good, but they would be taking her for scans to make sure her lungs were clear.

I leaned forward, taking her hand in mine, bringing it to my lips.

I was swept by an undercurrent of that energy. A sated fire that streamed between us. Our connection quieted but so goddamned bold.

Overwhelming.

I inhaled, and I swore, it felt like I was inhaling the breaking day.

Something fresh and new.

I stared at her, eyes tracing every unforgettable line of her face.

She was so pretty.

So pretty my guts clenched and my heart was drumming its song, the way it did whenever Nikki stepped into a room.

When she took up my space.

"You're going to be just fine," I whispered at her knuckles, praying she could feel my promise. That it was touching that bright, bright spirit.

That she'd know she wasn't alone.

Her mom had been here.

Her sister.

Lillith and Rynna and Hope.

This girl surrounded by love.

Because that's what she was.

Love.

The lightest tap sounded at the door, and I shifted to see Kale popping his head inside.

Thank God for Kale.

Kale, who'd come running when I'd sent out the distress call that we needed him. Even though he was no longer a physician at the ER, there wasn't anyone I trusted more than him to be there, acting as Nikki's intercessor, making sure no stone was left unturned.

"Hey," I said, voice so low it barely broke the air. "Is it time for her to get the scans?"

He grimaced a little as he stepped inside. "Not quite," he told me.

Unease wound through my being, and I couldn't keep the quiver of distress out of my voice. "Did the tests come back?"

"Yeah. Everything looks good. CBC is good, and her O2 sats have been normal."

Relief blew out on the heaviest sigh, and I was nodding, rubbing my face as this feeling came over me. This stunning gratitude that had taken the place of the weight that had been on my shoulders.

Was close to outweighing the amount of the love that pressed through me.

Filling me full.

He studied the readout on one of the monitors. "Has she opened her eyes yet?"

"No . . . but . . . I can feel it. She's gonna be okay. I think she's just sleeping off the trauma."

It wasn't like I was some kind of medical guru.

It was just like I'd said.

I could *feel* it.

He came to stand beside me, looking at Nikki.

"That's what she needs the most. Rest." He angled his attention to me. "And support. Someone to be there for her when she wakes up so she knows she isn't alone."

I shifted in the seat, tightening my hold on her hand. "I'm not going anywhere."

"Are you finished running, Ollie?" he asked, staring at me like he was searching for the truth of my answer. Something hard in his expression.

My gaze traveled back to Nikki.

Nikki. Fucking. Walters.

The girl I'd thought the bane of my existence.

The girl nothing but a tease and a taunt of what I couldn't have.

I'd just been too blind to recognize that she was my *very* existence.

"Yeah, I'm done running," I murmured, more to her than to him.

He cracked a smile. "Good." He gave a pat to my shoulder before he moved for the door. "Oh, and she won't be getting those x-rays."

I shifted in the chair so I could see him. "Why's that?"

He paused to look back at me. "Because she's pregnant."

thirty-nine

Nikki

My eyes fluttered open, the sound of a constant, low *beep, beep, beep* filling my ears. But my sight, it was filled with Ollie.

Beautiful Ollie who was staring over at me.

The man who had wrecked me.

The one who had saved me.

He'd always been an enigma.

The hardest jaw and the quickest smile.

"Nikki," he murmured as he watched me studying him, and he reached out and set a big hand on the side of my head.

Energy flashed.

The connection so intense that I felt my insides clutch.

"Ollie."

"You're okay. You're okay."

I flinched as all the memories came flooding back.

My sister.

Sydney.

The cliffs.

"What happened?" I rasped, my throat achy and raw and my lungs too tight, but there was no stopping the panic that seized my heart. "What happened to Todd?"

So many things moved through his expression.

Hate.

Worry.

Regret.

Relief.

"He can't hurt you anymore."

"Oh." It was a breath. A strike of realization. The sound of a gunshot ricocheting in my mind.

Ollie brushed his thumb over my cheek. "I'm sorry I didn't get there sooner."

My lips pursed, and I fought the tears that worked in my eyes. "You saved me."

"I told you I would never let anyone hurt you again. Protecting you is my duty."

I could feel the twist of my brow. The sorrow on my heart, and it hurt so much to say the words.

But it was time.

I couldn't do this anymore.

Not after everything.

"I don't want to be your duty, Ollie. I can't be a sin you're trying to make amends for."

Regret streaked across Ollie's handsome face.

Sapphire eyes flashed with intensity as he sat forward, his hold on the side of my head tightening.

Hand spread out as if he wanted to touch me everywhere.

"I've spent my life living in the past, Nikki."

His voice was gruff. Strained as he seemed to struggle with the words. "I spent years searching for something that wasn't there. It'd felt like hope. But I know now I was trying to pay a debt. That I thought I didn't deserve to live because Sydney hadn't."

Grief billowed from him.

"My mom . . ." His voice broke, and my heart fisted because never in all these years had he mentioned her.

Their relationship severed.

I'd never been privy to the details.

"She blamed me," he whispered as if it hurt too much to say it aloud. He gave a harsh shake of his head. "I'll never forget when the police left after taking my statement, she . . . lost it."

He gulped. "She just . . . started hammering on my chest. I'd barely been able to hear what she was saying, she was crying so hard. But I did, Nikki. She was saying that she'd trusted me . . . that it was my fault . . . that I'd promised I would take care of her. She said I failed her. Failed Sydney."

Sympathy stretched so tight I couldn't breathe.

"Oh, God. Ollie. I didn't know."

He looked at me. Laid bare. "In some way, I did fail, Nikki. We all did. We made mistakes, but none of us meant to hurt her."

He blinked through the dim lights of the room. "I thought . . . I thought for all these years that I couldn't be trusted. That I didn't deserve to be."

He gathered up my arm and pressed the underside of my wrist to his lips.

A sound hitched in his throat. A guttural cry that I felt move all the way through the center of me.

"I'm always gonna miss her, Nikki. I will miss her every day of my life. I thought that made me a lost soul. That I had no home. But you . . ."

He eased off the chair and moved so he was completely hovering over me, taking both sides of my face in his hands.

He squeezed me tightly. As if he were begging me to hear.

"You, Nikki . . . you are my home. You've been leading me there all along, calling me there, and I was too blind to see that was where I belonged. Too afraid to accept it. Too afraid to believe in it. Too afraid to *trust* in myself."

His throat bobbed when he swallowed, and he edged back to standing. He set one of those tattooed hands over his heart.

"I'm a simple, man, Nikki. If I were Kale, I'd have planned some big thing. Wooed you. Impressed the hell out of you," he said, mouth tweaking into something that resembled a grin before it fell flat again.

"But I'm not . . . I'm just here . . . this lost soul who finally found his home, begging her to open the door and let him in."

Tears rushed to my eyes, and a ball of emotion rolled through my chest.

Pressing and pulling and pleading.

"The door has always been open, Ollie. Always. You just had to make the choice to walk in."

"Only if you let me stay forever."

I hated the reservations that scrambled to be heard. That wall that wanted to rise up and protect my heart that he'd broken again and again. But they shouted at me not to be a fool.

"What about Sydney, Ollie? The fact that you can't look at me without seeing her? Without thinking of her? I don't want to be the girl standing in her shadow."

He was back to hovering over my hospital bed, this time his nose so close to brushing mine. "How could you stand in the shadows when you are the brightest thing in the room?"

His lips brushed against mine in the softest kiss.

"Sunshine," he murmured like praise. "You are light and life. My life. My everything. Let me be yours."

Tears streaked free, and I lifted my chin, our mouths meeting as I whispered, "I've always been yours."

Our foreheads met, and we shared our breaths.

That energy rippled and danced.

Climbing into the atmosphere.

Colors and light.

Chemistry.

He kissed me again as one of his hands slid down my face, cupping my jaw, my chin, gliding to my heart. "I've got something to tell you."

Nerves tumbled. "What's that?"

His hand kept moving, slipping over my hip until he moved it over my stomach. His hand resting between us. "We're gonna have a baby."

Ollie

"Ollie, I'm not crippled." She swatted at my shoulder.

Playfully.

I had her swept up in my arms, holding her as the elevator clanged for the third floor of my building.

I nuzzled my nose along her jaw, inhaling deep, my lips a soft brush against her cheek. "How about you just let me hold you for a while, yeah?"

Her arms were looped around my neck, and she buried her face in my beard. "If you insist, big boy."

I squeezed her as the elevator jostled to a stop at the top floor, cages sliding open to the hall. "Plan on holding you forever, sweet girl."

She giggled.

God.

Was it possible I got this? Her giggles and her smiles and all her days?

I wanted them. Fuck, I wanted them so bad that I held her a little tighter against me as I carried her down the hall.

"That might get awkward, you know?"

"What, you don't think people would approve of me carrying you to work?"

She was chewing on her bottom lip as she looked up at me, a flush on her cheeks that screamed of so much life. "People might get weird ideas about us."

Us.

I grinned. "Let them get all the ideas they want."

I angled to the side so I could fumble with the lock on the front door. I was still carrying her when we got inside.

It was late when she'd been discharged from the hospital this evening.

Her attending doctor had told her the exact thing Kale had told me.

The most important thing she needed was rest. To give her body time to recuperate from the trauma. I took her straight to my bedroom.

Strike that.

Our room.

I laid her on the bed, and she giggled again, just as I was crawling right up with her, unable to leave any distance between us.

Needing her near.

I propped myself on my elbow, making sure to keep my weight off her, and ran my fingers through her hair. "How are you able to keep smiling after everything you just went through?"

It wasn't an accusation.

It was awe.

Pure. Fucking. Awe.

This girl.

Goodness and light.

With a shaky hand, she reached out and ran her fingers through my beard before she let them drift up, moving across my cheeks, my eyebrows, my nose.

Closing my eyes, I sighed and relished the sensation.

Her touching me.

So freely.

"How could I not be?" she whispered.

That aura she wore rolled through the room.

Thunder.

Colors and strobes.

I eased back so I could look at her.

She caressed along the line of my hair, head tilting as she spoke softly. "My sister is home. Safe with Penelope and her husband."

She stroked across the shell of my ear.

So tender.

So sweet.

It sent a chill trembling through the middle of me. "My mama is safe. My grandma is safe."

Her brow pinched as she moved to trace down my jaw. "I'm here, with you."

Her fingertips plucked at my bottom lip, her words turning to wonder. "And we're gonna have a baby."

One side of my mouth pulled up, twisting into a smile. "I can't believe it."

She searched my face. "I know you question it, Ollie. But I want you to know I *trust* that you are going to be the best daddy this baby could have."

Overcome, I kissed her, long and deep.

Who could blame me?

I was just a man loving on his girl.

I threaded my fingers through her hair, our gazes locked.

I was entranced by that energy.

The girl a spell.

The best kind of magic.

Caging her in, I pushed onto my hands and knees. I dove in to kiss across her bright, bright heart, and then I worked all the way down until I made it to her stomach.

"Thank you, Nikki, for trusting in me," I mumbled at her flat belly.

I sucked in a deep breath and made a promise that I would never, ever break. "This baby will always know that her daddy will be there for her. No matter what. No matter what mistakes she might make. No matter what life throws our way. For all my days."

Nikki's fingers were in my hair, and she was nudging me up. Eyes glistening with adoration in the muted, dancing light. "You want this? With me?"

I finally settled my weight between her thighs.

Carefully.

I wrapped her up.

Held her close.

Because I was never going to let her go.

"There's nothing more I want than to get to have a family with you, Nikki Walters. Nothing I want more than to spend all my days loving you. Nothing that makes me happier than you loving me back. You are my home."

Because I finally got that life was worth living.

It was worth cherishing.

And I had everything to live for.

Nikki stared up at me, her words so soft. "You have it all wrong, Ollie. I always trusted you. You just had to figure out how to trust yourself."

I pulled back and gazed down at her, running my thumb across her temple. "Forever and ever, you and me."

I felt it.

The spirit that fluttered through the air.

And I knew that Sydney would always be there, too.

Free.

Watching over us.

A smile forever on her face.

epilogue

I peeked out into the hall, frantically waving Hope and Jenna in where they had parked in the back lot. "Do you have it?"

Giggling, they both bustled inside, slinking through the big metal door.

"No, Nikki, we totally don't have it," Jenna said with all kinds of sarcasm dripping from her smart mouth as she lifted the huge pink cake box a few inches higher, waving it in my face.

"Stop that," I swatted at her. "I just want this to be perfect. Goodness, I'm nervous."

"You're bein' ridiculous, Nikki. Ollie is gonna love it," Hope told me in her sweet way. She was two months further along than I was.

Excitement blistered through my veins, and my hand was caressing over the tiny mound growing in my stomach, my skinny jeans still fitting but just barely.

Goodness, I couldn't wait to be a mommy. The proof that the world really could be a better place. That good things were still granted.

Blessings and joy.

Jenna let go of a loud laugh. "That, or he's going to go all savage ogre on our asses and kick us to the curb for throwing him a surprise birthday party. I'm not sure which one to put my money on."

"I'm putting all my money on my man," I told her, lifting my brow as they passed by.

"Oh, someone has it bad," Jenna sang as she started down the hall toward the main area of the bar.

"Well, if thinking about someone twenty-four seven and missing him like crazy all day while he's gone is having it bad, then so be it."

I might have it bad.

A damned fever when it came to Oliver Preston.

Rex and Kale were supposed to be keeping him busy today. A guy's fishing trip for his birthday.

It really was just to give me the time to set up.

Streamers and balloons and twinkle lights had been strewn across the entire space, and one big area had been sectioned off just for our friends and family.

The Italian caterer was already setting up at the back of the roped off area.

We rounded the corner, and Cece was setting up the private bar next to the caterer. "Made sure to stock you two some ginger ale," she said with a wink as she tossed a few bottles of it into the big ice bucket.

Turned out, she wasn't so bad after all.

I laughed. "Oh man, I do miss my wine." Tenderly, I ran my hand over my belly. "But she is definitely worth it."

Yep.

She.

Just like Ollie had insisted since the day we found out.

He may have been a bear before, brash and protective and nothing but a brute, but he'd taken it to all kinds of new levels. Watching over us so carefully, love shining so bright in his blue eyes.

Sometimes I still woke wrapped in his arms and thought I was dreaming, having wanted this for so long, tied to a man in such an intrinsic way, that it didn't seem real.

Then he'd tuck me close, and it'd all come rushing back.

He was mine, and I was his.

"Is there a cool place we can put the cake?" Hope asked Cece.

Cece grinned. "Tell me that cake is complements of A Drop of Hope."

Hope laughed a light sound. "Well, of course it is. As if I'd trust anyone else to make the cake for Ollie's big day. I mean, unless he wanted a pie," she teased.

Sometimes I wondered how there wasn't a baking war going on between Rynna and Hope.

"And it doesn't even have sticks with pictures of Ollie on it." Sadly, Jenna shook her head. "What a shame."

"Don't even remind me of you going and pulling that with Kale. Putting pictures of my man on cupcakes for all the girls to devour. That's sacrilege."

"Um, those cupcakes were delicious," I told her. "Everyone needs a little sex on a stick."

She shooed me. "You've got your own man, Nikki. Don't be licking on mine."

"But I don't have one," Jenna whined.

"Me, neither," Cece called.

"Y'all are ridiculous." Hope was laughing when she took the cake from Jenna as if she no longer trusted her with it. "Where to?"

Cece lifted her chin. "Go through the swinging door there. Cleared a spot in the refrigerator."

"Thank you."

Hope waddled her way back there just as the band was striking up.

Ollie's favorite.

Carolina George.

One of his oldest friends was the guitarist, and it only made sense for me to invite them.

I rubbed my palms together. "Am I missing anything?"

Cece squeezed my shoulder as she strutted by. "You're good, Nik. Ollie's gonna love it. Relax."

"Thank you."

Didn't mean I wasn't totally nervous. This was his first birthday that we'd really been together, and I wanted him to remember it forever.

What life was like when it really started.

Guests started showing up at a quarter to six. My mama and then my grandma in her wheelchair, which just made my heart sing.

Sammie and her husband were next, Penelope at home with a sitter. Even though we *were* in Alabama, we definitely didn't need any babies hanging out in the bar.

Lily and Broderick waked through the door with Rynna.

Some of Ollie's friends, guys from the bar and the shop that he had a partnership with came as well.

My heart stammered when I saw who warily came through the door, nervous as her gaze jumped around the bar.

Ollie's mama.

I eased that way. "Margaret, I'm so glad you're here." I gripped both of her hands between mine.

"Thank you for inviting me."

"Of course."

Their relationship had a long way to go, but when Ollie had started counseling to work through his lingering guilt over Sydney, his therapist had urged him to make peace with his mother.

Even if she didn't accept it, he had to seek it.

Come to terms with it.

Forgive himself.

She'd broken down when he'd reached out, also haunted by their separation.

Sometimes forgiveness took time, but they were well on their way.

Ten more minutes passed, and we all gathered together when Hope got a text from Kale that they were almost there.

I held on to Lily and Hope's hands when we saw the guys walking up the sidewalk, laughing and joking, Ollie thinking they were coming in to share a beer before they went on their own way.

They opened the door and stepped inside, and everyone yelled surprise.

But they weren't looking at Ollie.

They had all of a sudden all turned to look at me.

They made a circle around me, a gap at the front as Ollie slowly approached me.

He tipped me up a cocky, gorgeous smile. His beard was a little shorter, hair neat, definitely not wearing the jeans he'd been wearing when he left this morning.

Instead, he wore a fitted button-up with the sleeves rolled up his forearms, flashing the ink that danced above his muscle like the beat of the song that was quietly playing.

A tremble of something rippled through the air.

Something so big.

And I didn't know why, but a tear slipped from my eye.

"Ollie," I whispered, looking around at everyone who was grinning.

"Nikki."

He started moving my direction, a grin on his striking face but the world in his eyes.

That's what he was.

My great big world.

"It's your birthday," I whispered like I was issuing some kind of plea, trying to catch up to what was happening.

"You're right, Nikki, today is my birthday. Call me selfish, but I had a certain present in mind."

All the voices had gone quiet, and Carolina George eased out of a song in the middle and struck up another.

The lyrics filtered through the mic.

Richard's voice was so rough when he started playing the cover from Train. It was a song about how forever could never be enough.

My fingertips went to my lips.

Ollie took another step forward. "Nikki . . . you were my first love. My only love. The one who was always supposed to be at my side."

He inched forward and set those big hands on my swelling belly. "You're the mother of my baby girl. You're my life."

He dropped to both of his knees, pulling the silver box with a black ribbon from his pocket. A present in the palm of his hand. "So, for my birthday, I want you to tell me you'll be my wife. Tell me that forever you'll be my home."

I dropped to my knees with him, tears streaming free, blurring my eyes, but I was sure I'd never seen so clearly.

I saw the future.

I saw joy.

I saw love.

I saw my life.

"Yes. Oh, Ollie . . . yes."

He cocked a smirk. "You haven't even seen the ring yet."

A soggy laugh pilfered free. "Give me that ring, you bear."

"You sure you want it?" Mischief danced around his face.

Happiness. The pure, innocent kind we used to share.

"Yes, Ollie. I am sure. Let me see it."

"Someone's eager."

I swiped under my eyes with the back of my hand.

Yes, yes, someone was eager.

He tugged at the little bow and pulled off the lid.

A gift.

For me.

For us.

The ring appeared antique.

Vintage.

Unique.

Encrusted in diamonds, a purple solitaire in the middle.

I breathed out between the tears that kept streaming down my face, eyes flicking between him and the ring. "It's gorgeous, Ollie."

"It's different, I know. But I saw it, and it reminded me of you. Not close to being traditional, and still so beautiful it stole my breath."

My spirit rumbled, a whisper from the deepest part of me. Where I'd always held this man. Ollie took the ring out of the box. "Marry me, Nikki."

"Yes."

I just caught a glimpse of it. What was etched on the inside of the ring at the base.

A dragonfly.

Everything soared.

Flapped in a flurry of emotion and memories.

And I swore I could hear Sydney's voice echo through the bar.

Whisper in my ear.

"Fly, fly, dragonfly."

Ollie slid the ring onto my finger. It fit so perfectly.

He pulled me into his arms, kissing me wildly, both of us on our knees while our friends and family shouted and cheered.

Carolina George continued to play "Marry Me." The song so profound.

As if it it'd been written for us.

We finally climbed to standing, and Ollie was holding my hand as everyone came up individually to give us congratulations.

Hope was there, the lid off her cake, congratulations written in curvy letters, a field of purple blazing stars as the decoration.

I choked over a laugh. "You sneak."

"Hey, you were trying to sneak the party in on Ollie. Don't blame me that he one-upped you."

He turned to me before he started backing away, dragging me along with him, right up to that gleaming, carved bar.

He hopped on top of it, staring at me. He lifted his arms up and shouted toward the high ceilings. "Nikki Walters is gonna be my wife!"

Like he needed the world to know.

That he was proclaiming it to the heavens.

My attraction to him was so intense I wondered how he didn't taste it in the air.

Well, I guessed he did. Because he was watching me as if he was lost in it, too.

Bristling and brimming and begging.

Chemistry.

Bigger than life.

Somehow even bigger than the man that was this hulking tower of muscle and brawn and intricately drawn ink.

Every inch of him was rugged and rough and commanding, all dressed up in black fitted pants and a button-up, his body dripping sex.

An enigma.

A veiled mystery.

A cliffhanger waiting to be written.

And we were getting ready to write the rest of our story.

He hopped down and picked me up and spun me around as if I didn't weigh anything at all.

"I love you, Nikki Walters."

"I love you, Oliver Preston."

I love you.

My beautiful beast.

the end

Thank you for reading *Fight for Me*! Did you love getting to know all the men of Gingham Lakes?

I invite you to sign up for mobile updates to receive short, but sweet updates on all my latest releases.
Text "aljackson" to 33222
(US Only)
or
Sign up for my newsletter
http://smarturl.it./NewsFromALJackson

Need more? See Evan and Frankie Leigh all grown up in
Hold on to Hope!

More From A.L. Jackson

<u>Fight for Me</u>
Show Me the Way
Hunt Me Down
Lead Me Home

Hold on to Hope – A Fight for Me Spin-Off

<u>Bleeding Stars</u>
A Stone in the Sea
Drowning to Breathe
Where Lightning Strikes
Wait
Stay
Stand

<u>The Regret Series</u>
Lost to You
Take This Regret
If Forever Comes

<u>The Closer to You Series</u>
Come to Me Quietly
Come to Me Softly
Come to Me Recklessly

<u>Stand-Alone Novels</u>
Pulled
When We Collide

Hollywood Chronicles
A collaboration with USA Today Bestselling Author, Rebecca Shea

One Wild Night
One Wild Ride

ABOUT THE AUTHOR

A.L. Jackson is the New York Times & USA Today Bestselling author of contemporary romance. She writes emotional, sexy, heart-filled stories about boys who usually like to be a little bit bad.

Her bestselling series include THE REGRET SERIES, CLOSER TO YOU, BLEEDING STARS, FIGHT FOR ME, and CONFESSIONS OF THE HEART.

If she's not writing, you can find her hanging out by the pool with her family, sipping cocktails with her friends, or of course with her nose buried in a book.

Be sure not to miss new releases and sales from A.L. Jackson - Sign up to receive her newsletter http://smarturl.it/NewsFromALJackson or text "aljackson" to 33222 to receive short but sweet updates on all the important news.

Connect with A.L. Jackson online:

Page **http://smarturl.it/ALJacksonPage**
Newsletter **http://smarturl.it/NewsFromALJackson**
Angels **http://smarturl.it/AmysAngelsRock**
Amazon **http://smarturl.it/ALJacksonAmzn**
Book Bub **http://smarturl.it/ALJacksonBookbub**
Text "aljackson" to 33222 to receive short but sweet updates on all the important news.